CIRCLE OF REIGN

Book 1 Of The Dying Lands Chronicle

JACOB COOPER

ISBN: 0692246738
ISBN 13: 9780692246733

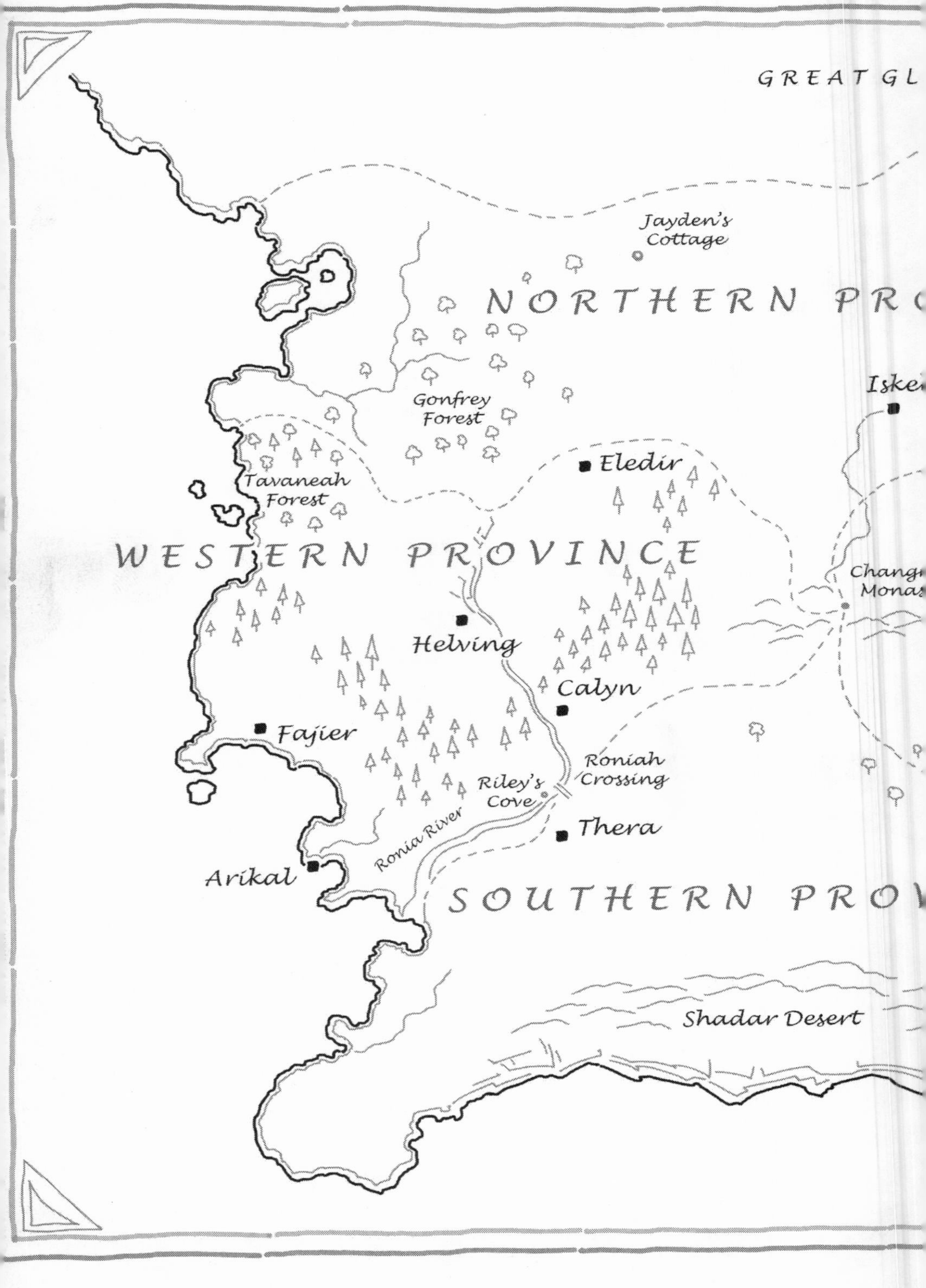

GREAT GL

Jayden's
Cottage

NORTHERN PRO

Iske

Gonfrey
Forest

Eledir

Tavaneah
Forest

WESTERN PROVINCE

Chang
Monas

Helving

Calyn

Fajier

Roniah
Crossing

Riley's
Cove

Thera

Arikal

Ronia River

SOUTHERN PRO

Shadar Desert

ERS OF GONFERY

INCE

STERN PROVINCE

Erynx

P'lor

Silver
Pools

SEA OF
ALBERY

Runic Islands

Jarwyn
Mountains

Falls Of Olin

ICE

Jarwyn
Mines

Dispa

Talen

THE REALM
OF
SENTHARA

ACKNOWLEDGEMENTS

IN ANY LARGE ENDEAVOR of the heart and mind, there are often many contributors that helped bring the project to life. I hope I catch all of you, and know I thank all of you who were part of the journey so far. To my parents, Michael and Beverly, who taught me something worth doing is worth doing right, not fast. To brothers, Jared, Jason, and Jed, whose enthusiasm early and throughout the writing process was bolstering and energizing, providing much of the stamina to carry through to the end. To Seth, for your unyielding excitement and encouragement. Your excitement was contagious. To Lathe, for your sincere efforts in guidance and editing, all of which was edifying. To Jordan, for tearing apart early renditions, causing me to refocus my efforts. To Nate, for enduring hours of self-recorded audio on our road trips and endless optimism about the story, even when I'm sure it was tough. To Tasha, for challenging me to grow the world with history and depth. To Mike Sirota and Michele Scott, accomplished authors and mentors, for bringing my efforts to a whole new level and challenging my ideas and writing. Mike, I hope your eyes have stopped burning! To John Avon, for bringing the fullness of his legendary artistic talents to bear. To Michael Kramer, for giving the story and characters life in the audiobook in only the way he can. To Bauer, my Akita, who kept me company during the long hours of writing through the night. To my wonderful daughters for always insisting on an original bedtime story, planting the seeds for many of the storylines herein.

Finally, to my wife Kristen, who endured endless discussions about the story with grace and patience, excitedly reading every new scene I put in front of her. Your belief in me is what I continue to stand upon.

DEDICATION

For McKayla, Haley, Kelsi, and Adelyn.
May you always walk in the Living Light.

PROLOGUE

IT SEEMED AN ODD THING to Rehum to lie dying from dehydration in the clutches of a rain forest. Shouldn't he just need to open his mouth and let the water find him? Haunted or not, it was still a *rain* forest; but precipitation somehow constantly eluded him… almost as if it consciously fled from him. Ancients, could even the waters be sentient? So much effulgent life around him and yet his slipped away. He had survived all manner of misfortune in his eclectic life, constantly reinventing himself, evolving, becoming whoever was needed. He had started to feel almost immortal…almost. But that was why, in part, he now searched for *them,* wasn't it?

This time, however, he feared there would be no survival.

He lay on his back looking up at the tall trees with the blazing sun piercing through. These trees were "fluent," the Arlethians claimed, but he could not experience this for himself. He was not a wood-dweller, although some of his findings suggested that this should not matter. There was a copse of Triarch trees that stood like sentinels in front of him, mocking him as they stood with their strength, undaunted by the long ages of their life. Somehow they were vibrant despite his withering, as if they were what withheld the moisture of this cursed forest. He had seen the veins of the three-pronged Triarch leaves glow at night on occasion in his earlier days when he would spend hours studying and contemplating

1

in the Arlethian forests, their bluish-tint masquerading as an odd species of firefly—perhaps a cousin to the more common yellow-glowing variety. Smooth tan bark ascended up for some hundreds of feet before the Triarch branches sprawled out, joining the thick canopy of umbrage that hid large swaths of the sky. The Arlethians claimed they felt safe under the sentient canopy, but to him, it felt like a net cast by misfortune that he could not escape.

Holding the map in front of his face to block the blinding light, Rehum stared at it with an intensity that seemed to demand a response from the parchment itself. Intensity—or was it desperation? He was certain that he had copied it correctly from the crumbling parchment he had discovered, but how could any map be trusted when the land constantly changed?

A group of green and black butterflies swooped passed him, struggling as if a great wind were present, causing them to swirl and spin in erratic flight patterns, dancing upon an invisible stage of effervescence. No wind was present, however. It might have been beautiful in another setting, rather than unsettling and chilling.

He would die like all the other fools who searched the Tavaniah Forest, though he had assumed himself so much more worthy than any before him. None had ever found what they sought here; and though Rehum had never believed the Tavaniah was haunted, he felt certain now that it was.

Ancients Come! I'm as deranged as a rabid dog, as much as they all said I was! As he inhaled, his lower lip quivered with shame at the realization.

With his dry tongue, rough and cracking, he licked the leaves of a nearby bush. His taste buds were too numb to register the bitterness of the leaves, and the few drops of dew he was able to find stung his tongue.

"I know you're here, blasted Night!" he yelled, still supine. Blood seeped from the dry, chapped corners of his mouth. "I know you're here!"

One part of his mind told him to conserve energy, but another reminded him that it didn't matter. He would be dead later today or tomorrow. Two span of searching for the Gyldenal and he would die, painfully, like a slug that had fallen from a branch to a salt hollow of the Silver Pools in the Eastern Province. He was already an outcast, having been dishonorably discharged from the Changrual Order. Once a preceptor of the monastery and a revered high vicar with respect and clout, Rehum could no longer be where more than one hundred souls gathered or lived by royal decree.

I curse the name Parlan Wellyn!.

Parlan's son, Emeron, now ruled as High Duke of Senthara, but that did little to quiet his own shame. He did take a small morsel of pleasure in knowing that Parlan died in prolonged pain—a little parting gift Rehum had managed to bestow after his banishment.

Letting the map fall to his chest, he reached into his long pant pocket and gently caressed the scroll hidden there. It had been his greatest discovery and the most compelling evidence of what he sought. All other references to the Gyldenal had been from apocryphal stories or fables. Children's tales used to put little ones to sleep at night. By and by however, amidst the scorn of his colleagues at the monastery, he discovered the truth. He had literally been on top of it for decades. With the knowledge he now possessed, he knew the Changrual Order to be a faint shadow of the truth, of pure Influence. Their knowledge was as shallow as a puddle after the rain on the streets of Erynx, the state city of the East and once his home. He knew why the lands cycled and died. He also knew that the Living Light was not the *only* Influence in this world of Våleira. Others existed and he found himself tempted by them as well. In truth, Rehum was tempted simply by power.

They selfishly keep the Influence of the Living Light to themselves! He had planned to work himself in among the Gyldenal and steal the Lumenatis, the very Living Light, for himself.

He wept without tears. "It was all for naught!" Exhaustion threatened to take him but he feared to fall asleep lest the land change yet again while he dreamed. Or worse, he would just not wake up.

Is that really worse?

He saw the image from the corner of his eye. An outline that appeared to be a silhouette of a person. With a feeling of falling in his stomach, he snapped his head toward the personage but saw nothing save branches and shrubs. The arrangement did somewhat resemble a person as he squinted at it. Scuffling of some create found his ears next and chills ran up his spine. A forlorn feeling started to find its grip on him. He closed his eyes tight and reopened them, attempting to cast the building anxiety from him.

"How foolhardy I have been," he whispered to himself.

Another specter teased his peripheral vision, much closer this time. He again turned his head quickly to capture the vision fully and discover his observer. Nothing.

"No! No, no, no!" Rehum tried to rebuff the madness that he knew was taking hold. Crushing his own proud image of himself was the realization that the madness had always been with him. This cursed forest was simply bringing it out in him, causing it to bloom as a poisonous flower in the early Rising Season. Trepidation expanded within him, forcing out beads of sweat that manifested on his brow and lips. This was the last of the perspiration his body could muster. He shook on the ground, not sure if the certainty of a long, drawn-out death by dehydration or the depths of madness his mind would spiral to before the end finally came scared him more.

The day wore on and he had not moved. Nor had the lands, he noted with mild interest. At midday, the sun felt like a torch upon his skin, searing through his thin clothing. His anger turned to pleading and desperation.

"Please," he gasped with his hand raised meekly in the air toward the sky. "Please." When no answer came, Rehum thought to call upon other powers that were foreign to him, those barely spoken of by the Changrual and understood even less. Well, to lesser mortals, anyway. He would serve whatever master saved him.

He lowered his upstretched hand and closed his eyes. In his delirium, Rehum swore he had heard a melody playing in his head, one of longing but also promise.

"Please. Hear me."

Or let the Dark take me!

———

Evrin had watched the short bald man for roughly half a span, intrigued. Many came and searched for the Gyldenal, most out of curiosity or seeking fame. All but few had other than pure motives. But this one sought his order for knowledge with a determination that was insatiable. For what purpose he desired to employ the knowledge was, however, not certain; but even laying defeated at death's door he still sought them, pleading for deliverance.

To whom does he plead? Evrin wondered.

The old Light Shepherd put his hand to his chin and thought, absent-mindedly tracing the outline of a scar on his cheek with his index finger. He had refused to let that blemish heal over the centuries. It was a solemn reminder of the pride that had once almost destroyed him.

Looking left, he met the gaze of his long-time friend. Jayden, the wolf shepherd, gave her consent with a slight nod. He agreed with her. This one had suffered long enough.

Evrin had been taking in all the light around him, making himself invisible to the untrained eye. He let the mirage fall, visibly revealing his presence. Then Jayden let her façade also melt away. Others followed suit and soon all five of his companions were now visible to the naked eye. The half a dozen Gyldenal walked a few paces forward and encircled the xeric man, looking down on him.

A weak hand raised up, open to Evrin.

"Please," he gasped. "Please. Save me."

"What is your name, young man?" Evrin asked.

There was a look of confusion across the cracked and dry face of the bald-headed man. He was likely not used to being referred to as a young man, but by Evrin's standards he was quite young.

"Rehum," he rasped.

"And what, Rehum, do you seek?"

"The Lumenatis."

"A children's story? You have come through such suffering for a myth?"

Rehum averted his eyes for a moment, obviously struggling, and then shook his head. "No, it's not a myth. I know it's real." He reached in his pocket and produced a scroll. Feebly and with a shaky hand, he raised it toward Evrin. The Light Shepherd accepted it. The Scroll was written in a tongue long lost to the world.

"Can you read this?" Evrin asked.

Rehum nodded. "Yes, though I cannot speak the language."

Evrin was impressed. "And what would you do with such a mythical power as the Lumenatis?"

"I don't know, honestly," Rehum croaked.

Truth. He spoke the truth. Evrin could see it in the man's countenance. Truthful though the answer was, it was nevertheless somewhat disturbing. He felt a small foreboding and chose his words carefully.

"The Living Light cannot be held by one who has selfish motives, young Rehum. Those who seek self-aggrandizement find the Lumenatis elusive at best," Evrin warned. "The principles one lives his or her life by are what enables one to harness the Light. Knowledge of a thing does not grant control of that thing."

"I will live a life of Light," the dying man promised.

"We shall see."

PART 1

THE FALL OF HOUSE KERR

We are often blinded by the very light we seek, stunted by the growth we desire, and belittled by the knowledge we profess.
— *Girshkil, Hardacheon Philosopher*

Innocence is a frail lie that requires constant rebalancing lest the illusion be too soon shattered and the young see beyond the false veil of a cruel world.
— *High Vicar Imol Dolbrey, "An Age of Heresy"*

ONE

Reign

Day 18 of 4th Dimming 406 A.U.

SWEAT MIXED WITH REIGN'S DARK HAIR as she ran, stinging her eyes. Though she ran hard, bursting through the brush and thick of the forest, Reign didn't feel anything. Glimpses of memory flashed through her young nine-year-old mind as she sprinted, images of monstrosity. Strange men were in the forest of the Western Province this night. A few on horseback, most on foot.

The High Duke of the Realm had been among them. The emblem that shone in the moonlight's glimmer as his large hooded robe parted for a brief moment gave his identity away. The gold medallion that hung from High Duke Wellyn's neck with a shield and four-pointed star flare engraved upon it was unmistakable. It was curious to find anyone in the forest at that hour, especially someone not of the Western Province. Surely if the High Duke was coming to visit her father, word would have been sent earlier. But this assembly did not seem to be traveling toward the hold, not because Reign actually knew where she was at the time but rather the men appeared to be exactly where they intended to be—nowhere in the sight of others.

As she had followed and observed the small party, she noticed one man who stood taller than the others and had a long beard hanging down nearly past his chest. She heard small clinking sounds from the trinkets woven in his beard when the wind blew. Men in the Realm generally did not wear beards save for the Changrual, and even then only a High Vicar was permitted to grow one so long as it was cropped short to the flesh. This beard was not anything typical she had seen, Changrual or not.

They hadn't seen her, not at first. She had felt their vibrations transmitted through the ground and intricately woven root system of the forest. Curiosity had pulled her close to observe their dealings, and what she witnessed stole the breath from her lungs. Reign did not breathe for what felt like an eternity. Then came the sound, a sound she knew was only in her mind but was no less sickening as it reverberated through her small body. Every bone and joint shuddered. It grew in intensity until it ceased so abruptly that the silence rocked her. Her breathing became faster and shallower, spurring forth small bursts of visible vapor from her nose.

She must have made a sound, though she did not think she had moved. One of the hooded men had suddenly turned in her direction, attentive. Even beneath his thick robe she could tell he was a large man, for his build resembled that of an ox. Reign knew he couldn't have seen her in her concealed shelter from that distance, but he stared right at her as if she were glowing. The High Duke then also became alert, taking the first man's cue, but did not seem to know where to focus his gaze or where she hid.

"Fear," the first man whispered in a low grumble. The High Duke seemed to consider for a moment. One of the horses whinnied as a mounted soldier joined the High Duke and the first man. He wore the tunic of a Khansian Guard.

"I don't see anything, your Grace," the Khan offered.

The first man huffed at this. "Not surprising."

"Are you certain we are not alone?" the High Duke asked before the Khan could respond in kind.

The first man stood for a moment, giving the briefest hesitation. Then: "Quite so, my Liege." He smiled predatorily, as if in anticipation. The High Duke considered again, looking somewhat uncertain.

"Discovered we must not be," the long-bearded man barked in a guttural and broken Sentharian, the common tongue of the Realm. The pitch of his low voice resonated like the Roniah River rushing over large rocks.

"Go," the High Duke finally commanded. "I place this Dahlrak upon you." Looking up to the Khan, he ordered, "You will follow and observe. Assist if necessary. See to it he fulfills his Charge, but do not interfere lest you become part of his Dahlrak, his Charge."

"It shall be done, my Duke!" the Khansian Guard acknowledged.

"We've seen what we came to see," Wellyn remarked. "The rest of us will depart."

Reign felt the first man approach slowly, prowl-like. The distinct feeling of becoming prey riveted through her and she silently fled before he reached her position.

Numbness dominated her senses as she darted through the frondescence, paying no heed to the scrapes and cuts she received as she clumsily navigated the forest and bounced off trees. She lost her footing in her scrambling to put distance between herself and her pursuers and fell face first into the forest floor, the smell of wet soil and dead pine needles filling her nostrils. The ground was cold and damp. Her limbs shook as she raised herself to her hands and knees, confused and frustrated by her strange lack of coordination. She spat dead leaves and mud from her mouth as she tried to think coherently. Her limbs did not seem like they were her own at this moment, heavy and sluggish. It was maddening. Wood-dwellers, even younglings such as Reign, had incredible mastery of their physical abilities, speed being among their foremost. This was never truer than in the forests in the Western Province where her people lived, where she was now filled with unfathomable trepidation.

"What's wrong with me?" she whispered. Her voice sounded alien to her, as if not her own. The tips of Reign's fingers felt tingly and abnormal. Her pulse quickened as she felt her pursuers through the ground and the roots of the trees, the same trees that were screaming in terror from the event, the *atrocity*, she had witnessed. She had never heard a sound so horrific before it was cut short, not in all of nature. It was not an audible scream, one only a wood-dweller could *feel*. The echo of it still remained in her mind undiminished, an indelible sonic scar seared into her skull. Reign's insides twisted until she retched upon the ground and shook more violently. The pulsing of her blood racing through her veins caused her head to feel like a piece of hot iron on a blacksmith's anvil, every throb a crushing blow.

Get up! Get up! she chided herself, shaking her head, but she remained on her hands and knees. The man on horseback she judged to be farther away through the vibrations in the ground, though still approaching. She was not as concerned about him as she was the hooded man on foot. His size posed a perplexing irony, for he was seemingly faster than she was, faster than a wood-dweller. Built like an ox but with the swiftness and agility of a panther. He was closer in distance and headed directly toward her position. Even the sound of his footfall was feral. An audible shudder of dejection escaped her lips, coming forth as a high-pitched moan. She tried to stifle the involuntary sound but only succeeded in making the noise more unnatural. Was this what hopelessness sounded like? *Daddy,* she pleaded desperately, trying to force her prayer through the forest, but she could not clear her mind enough for her appeal to be propelled. She did not know if she had the strength to send her plea over such a distance, assuming she could even establish a connection. Hot tears escaped from her eyes and splashed down upon the backs of her hands as she told herself again to get up, but her body did not respond.

Oddly, she noticed the moonlight's reflected gleam off the tears that fell to the backs of her hands. It was more an amber color than white.

It is nearly second moon, she thought.

This small realization of something so common was enough to help her mind locate a momentary focal point and regain control of her limbs. She pulled her hands, now caked in mud with small twigs and pine needles sticking to them, up from the ground and pushed herself upright. *Run*, she commanded herself. Her canter began again, more slow and awkward than it needed to be if she were to escape. A tree root nearly dropped her to the ground again, but she recovered before going all the way down. An erratic breathing rhythm stayed with her as she compelled her quivering legs to carry her forward. Her small dress was torn and tattered almost beyond recognition. As she moved, Reign's muscles relaxed enough for her cadence and speed to return. Her flight was swift and silent as with all wood-dwellers. No one could hear the light-footed lope of a wood-dweller save for another of their kind. She fell more into her stride as she overcame her initial anxiety, though her fear still brimmed close to overflowing at any moment. She should be safe beneath the canopy of trees in the night, but something primal told her to run and not look back. Her only thought was to get to her father's hold, to her home where she knew she would be safe. On a conscious level she did not know where she should run, but her instinct of direction took over as she gave herself to the promptings of the forest.

If she could just reach her father, her strong and fearless father, she would be safe. She knew this. The ox-like panther of a man pursued her, this she also knew. He was no wood-dweller, and his pursuit carried the sound of deep peril in its wake. She could acutely judge his distance behind her, and she knew he was gaining ground. How he was able to track her eluded her but also fed her fear, stoking it hotter and hotter. The man was too fast. But her father would save her. He had always saved her. He feared nothing.

As Reign passed a Triarch tree with inhuman haste she reached forth her hand, palm out, and for the briefest of moments made a clean connection against the ancient tree's bark. Instead of listening and receiving through the tree, she attempted to project her own message. Her father had tried to teach her and her twin brother the skill, admonishing them not to tell others of the ability. It required a tremendous amount of serenity and concentration for the mind to enter the required state in order for the trees to allow a channel to be opened through them. But, their efforts to sync their minds with the forest had met with little success. Reign had to succeed now though her mind was filled with anything but serenity. She did not know if she possessed enough strength or skill to make the plea endure over such a distance. Would it fizzle to little more than a faint echo? Was the thought to even try such a feat just foolish hope born of her desperation? Reign was desperate. She could only manage to send one word before her momentum forced her to break away from the tree and continue her panic-stricken run.

Please hear me! Reign cried inside, begging the Ancient Heavens to ferry her message swift and accurate.

The man drew closer.

———

It was the smell. Salty. Metallic. The smell of fear. That's how the chase-giver was able to track her. This was the way of it for his kind. The scent of fear was intoxicating, perhaps more so than any other.

This fear was particularly potent. Tantalizing, it drove him like a bloodhound in a hunter's trance just before the imminent kill. Ruthless. Relentless. He could not be released from his Charge until he obtained his purpose, or was killed.

All emotion gives a scent, easy to track, hard to lose – and *all* sentient beings give off emotional scent. A chase-giver can smell the emotion and, when Charged, he is attracted to it like a wolf to wounded prey. Their sense of smell was not only more powerful than other beings, but also more comprehensive in spectrum. An emotion felt always left a scent where the quarry had once been, and the stronger the emotion conjured the longer the scent remained. It could linger for a day, sometimes from first moonrise to second moonfall of the following night, leaving an invisible but strong odoriferous trail for one of his kind to pursue.

The chase-giver's senses heightened as he closed the distance. Adrenaline flowed and empowered his already rippled muscles as unnatural velocity attended him, morphing him into the haunting of nightmares, the unspoken dread of all living. All creatures could be prey to his kind once he was released, once Charged. Of the *very* few alive who knew of their existence, none really comprehended what gave chase-givers their ability, nor their seemingly inhuman strength while Charged, but he did not care to understand the reason. All that mattered was the effect, the thrill. This kill promised to be special.

——

Lord Thannuel Kerr stood atop a tree, scanning all he could see below him as he clutched a Triarch leafling in his hand, listening intently. The moonlight was more than enough illumination, especially coupled with the sensitive hearing of wood-dweller. He sprang the length of a hundred men to another treetop and continued to reach out through the forest. Easily climbing and jumping between treetops, a wood-dweller was at home anywhere a forest was found. Where he currently perched, at the edge of his hold just southeast of the Western Province's state city of Calyn, he listened intently for his daughter. The rain fell in thick circle patterns from the clouds above, a typical occurrence as the Low Season approached. As seasons changed, the formations of the clouds in the heavens morphed in response, signaling which season approached and the waning of the current season. The Dimming Season, with only twelve days remaining, was coming to its end as signaled by the clouds increasingly forming great hollow-centered circles in the sky, releasing their moisture to the world below.

Wood-dweller younglings were often found dancing across the treetops in the center of a circular downpour, staying completely dry. It was a game to them, trying to stay in the middle of the falling rain without getting wet as the clouds glided through the skies. This was a favorite game of Thannuel's son, Hedron. Many children from Calyn often visited the Kerr hold to play through its massive corridors and elevated pathways that wove amid the trees for great distances. Kathryn Hoyt, daughter of Lord Hoyt of the Southern Province, visited often with her family. She was promised to Hedron, much to the boy's annoyance. Thannuel knew the boy would soon overcome that and then he and Moira, as parents, would have a different kind of problem. Kathryn would blossom into a lady of rare beauty in not so many years and Hedron's annoyance would turn to drooling as he also matured. Lord Kerr shook his head in mild resignation.

Moira often found her happiest moments running and jaunting with the children, but Thannuel also knew his wife's heartache at not being able to carry another child. Hedron and Reign would be the only gifts the Ancient Heavens would grant them. Thannuel smiled to himself as he thought of the younglings.

He recalled the many times Reign pretended to be a squirrel as she gathered acorns and nuts and brought them home to hide in her chamber, much to the dismay of her mother. It was not uncommon for her to follow a family of squirrels for hours and silently observe them. In fact, after her studies were completed, it almost never failed that Reign would bolt out of the hold on one of the elevated pathways straight to the forest outside the walls. Kerr never feared for the safety of his children in the woods; they protected his family and the people of his province.

The sun had retreated into night hours ago, however, and Reign had not returned though it was nearly second moon. This was unusual, even for his independent nine-year-old princess.

She'll be ten in less than a cycle. They grow up too fast!

Moira had scolded her husband for not keeping watch better, but he was occupied with matters of state. Though mostly mundane and routine, these were important issues that he must attend to with haste as the Lord of his province. Still, he could not ignore the pang of guilt that crept upon him. Did his duties as Lord of the Western Province outweigh the importance of fatherhood? Certainly not, but he would be agreeing with his wife if he admitted this out loud; that would depart from the natural tendency of their relationship and would simply not do. He smiled again to himself, this time facetiously.

He would have been awake now even at this late hour regardless of his daughter gone missing or home in bed. He did not sleep much in these times. Less rest was physically needed as his capacity for Light grew. That would be a natural side effect, he had been told. The extra wakeful hours were usually well spent in preparation for what he prayed would never be necessary, though he held little hope that his prayer would be answered. He had set a meeting for next span with his old friend, Antious Roan.

General Roan, now, he reminded himself. It wasn't surprising to him that Antious had risen to bear the rank of general and lead the armed forces of the Western Province. Lord Kerr felt great pride in promoting him last year. He knew of no greater patriot to Arlethia than Roan; nor of anyone who had sacrificed so much for the Realm.

The Orsarian War took much from him, Lord Kerr reflected. *More than should be asked of anyone.* He was excited to see his dearest friend again, to whom he owed his life.

He will listen, he'll understand.

Kerr again leaped to another tree, this one a Triarch, and instantly went rigid as he landed upon the tree's apex. The single word, though not more than a faint whisper, jolted through him as his left hand brushed across a cluster of the smooth three-pronged leaves, his right still in possession of the leafling.

Help!

Though not an audible voice, the timbre *felt* familiar. Apprehension gathered within him, but Thannuel captured the friction and recycled it, directing the energy to enhance his sensitivity of touch and hearing. He stood more still than stone waiting for further communication. The soft whirl of a breeze. Occasional sprays of precipitation flecked him and beaded upon his sleeveless jerkin. Silent as an ancient statue, he waited. Listened. Nothing. Perhaps it was nothing. It had to be nothing. Who else besides the

Gyldenal knew how to sync their minds with the forest to open the channel *both* ways? It took someone of extreme sensitivity and power of will and the Gyldenal were far from here, deeply secluded in the Tavaniah Forest in the most northwest parts of the province. Yes, it had to be nothing; he tried to convince himself of this. But the word he had felt, it was powerfully projected. The overtones were desperate. He could not shake the familiar feel it had. Pitch and inflection were lost when speaking through trees, but there always remained something identifiable within the message, the way it felt as it entered your mind through the trees, the intonation. And yet, Thannuel was conflicted within himself. He was certain of the identity if he could believe that this was not a trick of some kind. *Reign does not possess the ability,* he thought. He had tried to teach her, but he knew she was still too young for the mental maturity required. *Most do not even know of the possibility, how could she—*

His ponderings were cut short as he felt the vibrations before he heard them. Footfall—three distinct pairs. A horse and rider still far off, but the other two much closer. Without dismissing the rider's vibrations, he pushed them to a sequestered part of his mind for now and converged his mind upon the two closer pairs of footfall. One determined and heavy, the other short and light and...fearful. The latter was a wood-dweller.

He knew Reign's stride almost instantly and spurred himself across the top of the treed-canopy to intercept her. Something was wrong. Very wrong. He could sense fear in his daughter's sprint, almost desperation. Finding the hilt of his sword he quieted his mind, quelled his emotions, and opened himself to the forest's influence and power. Through the Triarch leafling he still held, Thannuel began to draw into himself the strength of the ancient trees he now sprinted across at increasing speed. Something else caught his attention as the power swelled within him: the trees were afraid and confused, but they were also furious. Lord Kerr had never sensed emotion such as this from the forest. Anxiety pulled at the frayed edges of his concentration, but did not take hold. He unsheathed his sword, its dark gray blade forged of Jarwyn steel dully catching the waning white light of first moon as it began to hum with power.

Centering his being as he had been taught, Thannuel inwardly recited the ancient axiom: *Focus. Think of nothing but this moment.*

———◆———

It changed. It was still her scent; the chase-giver felt sure of that. But it had morphed to something else entirely. What was it? He found that he knew the scent; it just wasn't typical for this situation. Why would his prey be now feeling relief? The chase-giver increased his gait and he finally caught sight of his prey. He could tell he was tracking a female, but a girl? A child? This only fueled his delight in his unholy pursuit.

———◆———

As Reign reached the borders of her family's hold, she knew her father would come now. He would come and he would save her. The sound of the pursuer's footfall was thunderous in her ears, like the cacophony of a thousand men on horseback, but she knew that was the adrenaline. She had been taught from the walking years that adrenaline heightened the senses, propelling the mind to an exaggerated state. The man was so close now. She did not need the senses of a wood-dweller to know this.

A snarl came forth from the man and startled her. He couldn't be that close. A cold finger brushed against her shoulder but slipped off before it could secure a hold. She gasped a sharp inward breath that hurt her chest, so quick was her intake of musty air as she splashed through a span of murky puddles. Risking a glance down and to the left, Reign glimpsed a marred reflection in an undisturbed puddle of a ghastly white hand nearly upon her, reaching and frantically grasping for her. Her face had drained of blood and was as pale as the outstretched felonious hand that sought her. A meadow opened around her as she ran and she felt even more vulnerable as the familiar and comforting canopy of branches faded into the starry night.

"Threyihl!" she screamed desperately, calling for her father in ancient Arlethian.

Suddenly, the ground shook behind her and a deep cry of surprise filled her ears. She turned her head and saw her father down on one knee, his back to her. She stopped running.

I knew you would come, Reign thought triumphantly. It truly was no surprise to her that he had arrived just as she reached the moments of most desperate need. His sword, held by both his hands out in front of him, had half its length driven point first into the earth. He was kneeling with his head bowed as an aura of barely perceptible shimmering air radiated outward from him, as if a protective shield. The rain fell around her father but not on him. As the light refracted through the drops of rain, a faint halo of light shone around him in the night. Reign knew she was seeing her father in this moment the way legends spoke of him, as a near mythical warrior that could alone vanquish hordes of enemies. People of all create whispered that her father had almost singlehandedly vanquished the Orsarians on the Runic Islands, people of demonic influence who had attempted to invade and overthrow the Realm from regions unknown. The Changrual said they had escaped from the Fathomless Abyss to torment mankind for their lack of heed given to the Ancient Heavens. Reign had no doubt the Orsarians had feared her father as she now saw him, pulsing with power. She stood in awe of his presence. Relief washed over her, momentarily dampening her internal raging fire of fear.

Roughly twenty paces back lay her assailant, wrapped in a painful contortion around the base of a moss-covered tree. Reign's fear evaporated. She knew she was safe now. Her father had come. He feared nothing.

In a silent flash of righteous fury, Thannuel Kerr dropped over one hundred feet from the height of the trees to the wet forest floor. He hit the ground crouched and drove the point of his sword downward, penetrating the soil and simultaneously releasing some of the forest's strength outward. An invisible shockwave blasted forward from him and threw his daughter's attacker backwards through the air at impossible speed. Lord Kerr raised himself and stood erect, sword at his side, with only fury and determination filling him. Precipitation found him finally as the hollow ringed clouds moved above and dripped from his brow to his chin, but did not obscure his focus.

Kerr stared at the man who was nearly wrapped around the tree that ceased his backward flight and recognized him as a chase-giver. Shock and bewilderment began to germinate inside him but were instantly recycled, adding to Thannuel's heightened sensory perception. He did indeed know this kind, a Helsyan of ancient descent. They served the High Duke, whom Thannuel ruled under as a Provincial Lord. Duke Wellyn and he were old friends, although the years had seen them become somewhat estranged.

Such a forceful assault would have killed most anyone, but the chase-giver collected himself with apparent ease, as if awakening from a deep sleep. Thannuel was lost for the reasoning of the circumstances and, though he remained focused and recycled the frictions running through him, understood completely the immediate situation. He could sense Reign had ceased her run and now peered out from behind him at the chase-giver. *She must not witness what now comes,* he prayed silently.

Without taking his eyes from the chase-giver, Kerr said to Reign, "Flee for the hold. Wake Aiden. Do not hesitate." There was no fear in his voice, only the timbre of command. Reign did hesitate, however, understandably not wanting to leave the safety of her father's side. Kerr spoke again, more insistently this time, turning his head slightly toward her but not allowing the chase-giver to escape his sight. "Child, will you not obey your father? Do as I have said."

Reign started to run again.

Kerr watched the chase-giver's eyes follow his daughter as she ran toward the magnificent hold his family had maintained for untold generations nestled in the southeast outlying of Calyn. The stare bespoke a sadistic craving, a hunger that could only be sated with the butchery of his daughter.

———

"Leave my hold and woods now," the chase-giver heard Lord Kerr say. "I command it as Provincial Lord of the West and of Arlethia. You have no place here." Though the chase-giver could tell Lord Kerr recognized what he was, he could sense no fear from him. *Odd*, he thought. *What man does not fear my kind? And my Charge, a lord's child?*

"I am Charged with the girl," came his simple reply. "My Liege has given her to me. She is *mine*. I cannot cease."

"She is under the age of innocence. You have no claim on her!" Thannuel thundered. "You *will* leave."

"My Dahlrak does not recognize your imposed laws of innocence. You know my kind, Arlethian. You know what you have done by your interruption," the Helsyan sneered as his predatory smile re-formed on his face.

As Kerr now stood between the chase-giver and his quarry, he instantly became part of the Dahlrak, part of the Charge. Helsyan and Arlethian had never been allies and so having this opportunity was nothing but increased pleasure to the chase-giver. The dull pain that had erupted through his body as he was flung unexpectedly backward by Kerr's sudden appearance was quickly receding as the power of his expanded Dahlrak began to take hold. His lips parted tightly around his clenched teeth and he began to seethe and salivate heavily.

———

There was only one person the chase-giver could be referring to as having Charged this monster with his daughter. But it made no sense.

Why? What had Reign done?

No further words were spoken. Kerr knew they would simply be wasted. He had a fleeting thought of recognition that he should be afraid, but fear would find no purchase within him as that friction would be quickly recycled. He decided in this moment, without compunction, that his calling of fatherhood was not only more important than his lordship, but also more powerful in its ability to cause meaningful action. Kerr was not under any spell of false hope. He knew what he faced this night, even if he did not know why. He would not, for he could not, back down.

He readied himself.

The chase-giver attacked with speed and determination. He smiled with arrogant defiance as Kerr parried his blows, as if he were engaged in a simple game, a mere exercise. Kerr fought fiercely, without any sign of trepidation. Suddenly, from a far corner in the back of his mind, a warning sounded forth. Vibrations born of iron horseshoes thumping on the earth came to the forefront of his mind just as the second attacker, who had been absent until now, rushed onto the scene and attempted to flank Kerr. Thannuel bounded up and away from the chase-giver, narrowly avoiding the slower though lethal blows of the Khansian Guard's sword. He berated himself severely for becoming distracted to a degree that made him lose track of all threats around him. Ricocheting off several trees, the wood-dweller appeared to almost fly as he gained altitude above his attackers. He landed vertically against a large Triarch and drew in more strength, all that the tree would lend him. His sword hummed more intensely as the power that was gathering within him reached a climax and was then channeled through the specialized ore from which his sword was forged.

When he could contain no more, Thannuel sprang from his position and thrust himself downward directly at the Khansian

Guard. The man raised his shield and knelt down to shelter as much of his body as possible against the attack, but it mattered little.

"*Vrathia!*" Kerr yelled a split second before the point of his dark blade made contact. The Khan's shield exploded into a swarm of wooden splinters and metal shards. The sword found home in the man's chest. His cry was cut short and replaced by an ear-splitting crunch as Kerr shot weaponized wrath through his body, pulverizing bone to powder and reducing organs to mere fluid. The Khan jerked on the ground, sprawling in the mud in silent freakish movements, bending and pulling his body in ways nature never intended before finally falling still and dead.

———

"Impressive." Thannuel raised his head in response to the Helsyan's word and found him standing by casually looking on without concern. "And most entertaining," he added with false admiration. "Tell me, do all your people have such curious sounding swords? I would very much like—"

The chase-giver did not get to finish his chiding. Kerr attacked with a velocity that no human could track with his or her eyes. The smell of fury emanated from this man. Such potency. Fury not born of hatred, but of something the he could not easily identify. There was no fear in him as they danced their dance of death. The chase-giver was faster and stronger, true, but Lord Kerr's vigor was unexpected. For a time Kerr drove him back. This made the chase-giver smile with pleasure. It felt good to have a challenge, even on a small level. He allowed the contest to linger for several minutes longer than he needed to. Pity this man would die; he had begun to admire Kerr's ferocity and tenacity. He had to know he was beaten. For the moment, though, the chase-giver decided to partake of some sport. He knew the girl was still near. He could smell her unwarranted confidence growing.

Reign sat secluded in the cavity of an old Triarch roughly twenty feet high. The sound of steel had caught her attention as she ran to the hold and she could not pass up watching her father live up to his legend. She had only heard stories of his abilities and prowess in the Realm but had never witnessed it herself. Although nervous seeing her father duel with a man that seemed more beast than human, she knew he was not afraid. He was her father.

The frightening man stumbled back, clutching his lower left leg for a moment before regaining his composure. Blood added its crimson taint to his flesh, mixing with the water of the ground where he stood. The man's face betrayed him, even for just a moment, as Reign saw surprise and wonder in his eyes. Then came an awful recognition, a revelation that caused her fear to rekindle. *This man does not fear my father.* What manner of creature feared not Lord Thannuel Kerr, a wood-dweller worthy of his fame?

The swordplay became fiercer, more intense. No one could match speed with a wood-dweller in single-steel combat, not in the entire Realm. Reign told herself this over and over, trying to comfort herself as the intensity of the contest waxed. Her father appeared to be driven backward, which must be part of his plan. Surely her father's wit was as much a weapon as was his steel and speed. Then, in a surreal instant, her world was dashed to pieces. Reign felt absolutely nothing.

Their steel sparked despite the rain as the force of their blows collided. Raindrops split as Kerr pulled his sword with masterful agility through the night air, the glint of lunar rays dimly reflecting outward, giving the illusion of luminescence to their swords. Lord Kerr concentrated fiercely, forcing out all other thought as they danced out of the meadow and crossed back into the tree line. *Think of nothing but this moment.*

The chase-giver lunged with more speed, but Kerr deflected the attack, forcing the chase-giver's sword into the ground and connected a lightning fast fist to the Helsyan's face. He heard the grunt of pain that escaped his foe. In one fluid motion, Kerr found a low hanging limb and hurled himself upward and over, bringing his sword down against the right side of the chase-giver's neck in a forceful downward slash; or, where the neck should have been. His opponent had shifted from the scope of his swing so deftly that his sword only caught the man's left leg in a glancing blow and continued downward, burying itself deep in a thick tree root. Kerr hastily tried to bring himself upright and free his sword, but overcompensated and stumbled backward. His next deflection was awkward and too slow, still off balance. Facing any ordinary man, even a very skilled one, Kerr could have overcome his mistake easy enough, but a Helsyan was not an ordinary man.

———

The chase-giver struck in a wide arc with great speed, taking advantage of his foe's backward stumble. The steel met soft, hot flesh, ripping across Kerr's chest. The rain seemed to lighten just a bit, which the chase-giver thought to be symbolic.

"Even the Cursed Heavens hold their breath for my finale," he taunted. He stood over Lord Kerr who, inconceivably, was trying to get up. Kerr found his sword's hilt and weakly raised it in defiance. The chase-giver would have laughed had he not been completely frustrated and insulted by this man's lack of fear even in his last moments. *He has even drawn my life's blood!* his mind screamed inwardly. *Impossible!*

The pulsing pain from his wounded leg stubbornly reminded the chase-giver that it was not impossible; and, for the first time, he glimpsed a sense of his own mortality. This enraged him. He sneered, advancing in a blur of rage. In one stroke he easily broke through Kerr's defensive posture, knocking his blade aside, and with a second stroke, ran him through. The Lord of the Western

Province felt the ground rush up to meet his knees as he turned his gaze upward toward the canopy of trees that concealed most of the night sky. The veins within the Triarch leaves far above shone their luminescence in the night as if stars caught in the living canopy.

"Reign," Kerr whispered in his dying breath, his *last breath*, and seemed to smile slightly as the light in his eyes faded. His hand slackened and his sword fell free from his grip, revealing the small Triarch leafling firmly pressed against his palm.

Perplexed by his notice and attention of the rain as Kerr's life slipped away, the chase-giver continued to wait impatiently for the intoxicating final scent of fear and acceptance from his fallen foe. He was not rewarded. Instead, he was further infuriated by the scent that did permeate the Lord's final moments. It was of a disdainful taste to any Helsyan. Thannuel Kerr died feeling proud.

The Helsyan stared down at the body, disgusted. He was not at all fulfilled, not at all gratified. After a brief time, he turned his senses again to the girl's scent to recapture it. There was none. *This cannot be.* He directed his powers more fully, taking in all the scents around him. She was not there. It was as if she had disappeared suddenly—almost as if she had died. *Perhaps she had*, he thought, but settled upon the belief that some trickery was at play. He searched his feelings and caught the urge of the Dahlrak still present. She was alive.

Hearing voices and dogs approaching, he decided to retreat for a time. His quarry had not been his, at least not his ultimate objective. A chase-giver cannot be released from a Charge once given, not even by he who gave the Charge. He would succeed or perish in the effort.

He would return, for he must.

TWO

Aiden

IT WAS UNMISTAKABLE. The sound of steel against steel accompanied by swift-footed steps, the rhythm of men locked in battle. Aiden, master of the hold guard, looked up. He locked eyes with Lady Kerr's through his long, shaggy black bangs and saw her ashen face, a stark contrast against her ebony hair. She had felt it too and the absolute fear on her face was plain to see, not at all the kind, gentle face he had first gazed upon when first coming to Hold Kerr thirteen years ago.

They stood in the hold's courtyard, ignoring the night's rain, and pacing: Moira worried for her daughter who had not returned; Aiden frustrated at being commanded by Lord Kerr to hold his position while Kerr went out beyond the hold's walls alone, unprotected. Aiden knew Lord Kerr was more capable of defending himself than any of his hold guard, but that did not comfort him. The young man was dedicated to his position and to his lord, a dedication that germinated far from here, on the shores of the Runic Islands when he had seen Lord Kerr perform feats he could not explain, that no one could. He had almost convinced himself it was his imagination after so many years, a memory embellished over time.

Though difficult to tell from this distance, Aiden even thought he discerned a horse's heavy canter as part of the confrontation. That was odd in the Western Province, as wood-dwellers could outrun the fastest breeds and they were therefore used as little more than beasts of burden in the West. But other soldiers in the Realm, those of other provinces, all used them. This was not mere sparring he felt: not only would the hour of the night be reason enough to harbor suspicion, second moon having just risen, but the intensity of the sound flowing to the wood-dweller through the forest's intricately woven root system excused any doubt.

Aiden went rigid. Orders or not, his first duty was to protect Hold Kerr and above all else, its lord.

"Order Master Elethol to release the hounds," Aiden said, referring to the hold's kennel master. Before waiting for a response from Lady Kerr, the brash young master of the hold guard was gone from her sight. He leaped over the hold walls, heading south toward the sound of the conflict. Aiden resisted drawing his sword, a natural tendency when approaching a hostile situation. Running with a drawn sword made one awkward and slower. He needed all the speed he could muster.

Before he was one hundred paces past the hold's walls, it stopped. The swordplay was no longer being reported through the ground. Risking a momentary cease in his sprint, he came to the nearest tree and hastily forced his palm flush against the tree's bark. Nothing. He tried the next tree, quieting his mind further and listening more intently. Silence, save for the animals, birds, and insects. He did feel a current, however, in the trees; almost an emotion being radiated. He did not have time to ponder this now as precious moments were fleeing from him. He resumed his stride in the general direction of the last-felt oscillations.

After only a few minutes of running at reckless speeds, Master Aiden arrived on the scene. Thannuel lay perched upon a fallen tree looking up toward the rain. It beaded off his brow, face, and open eyes. Lifeless eyes.

The torrents of emotion that ran through the young wood-dweller were varied, ranging from rage to regret to guilt. Oddly, sorrow was not present. No, it was too early for that. He knew from experience that sorrow would come later. Memories of his own father's end briefly manifested in his mind; the surprise on his father's face as Aiden slipped the short blade between the wretched man's ribs. The man didn't think his son had it in him, drunk on wine again, just as always. It was the first time Aiden had killed anybody, but most twelve-year-old boys were completely devoid of such an experience. Yet, the youth from Helving, a remote part of the Western Province, discovered that killing could be as easy as breathing. Now, however, looking upon Lord Kerr's lifeless body, guilt was foremost among his emotions. Raw and quintessential guilt.

I should have been here.

Rushing to Kerr's side, he hoped against hope to be wrong in what he saw, to change the reality so plainly before him. But it did not change and his rage started to rise to the surface.

He moved to place his hand on Thannuel's chest, to cover his wound, but his hand began to quiver and he retracted it.

"You can't leave," he pleaded softly. "Not yet, not now." His head pulsed with pain. "Where are they?" he asked aloud, knowing there was no answer. "Who did this?" He was so distracted that he did not feel the arrival of other hold guards, and then of Lady Kerr herself.

"No!" Moira Kerr's shrill cry sounded in the night. "No, no, *oh no!*" She was hysterical. "Thannuel, please! Thannuel, *no!*"

Aiden's training took over as he regained himself and drew his steel.

"Get her out of here!" he commanded the other guards. Aiden was not being cruel, but protective. His duties were to House Kerr. Lord Kerr was dead and Reign still missing, maybe worse. This could be a prelude to a larger plot. His focus turned to protecting those who still lived, and there was no telling if danger was still present.

He hoped it was.

Where was the enemy? Where had they fled? He was tense and looking for a fight, for some target upon which to release his anger.

Calm yourself, Blasted Night!

The pulsing in his ears from his blood pumping hot and fast had masked the heavy footfall he had been feeling but too distracted to separate in his mind. He caught it now. A horse at full gallop running south and another's stride, a human, heading east. The second was moving heavier and faster than the horse, faster than a wood-dweller.

Aiden surmised the horse had no rider by the animal's stride, its footfall lighter than it would normally be otherwise. He ignored it and returned his focus east. Noticing a Triarch leafling in Lord Kerr's hand, under his sword's hilt, he reached down and retrieved it. It would increase his sensitivity. He started to stand back up, but hesitated, fixing his sight on Thannuel's sword. He dared not touch such a valuable possession. A small fortune, more krenshell than Aiden had seen in his entire life, was the cost to construct such a blade. The mastery of skill to mold the ore from the Jarwyn mines into such a refined state was held by very few. Thannuel would have paid dearly for its creation. No, he dared not touch it.

The guards were struggling with Moira, trying to get her back to the hold and secure her. The entire hold would be locked down and placed on high alert.

She screamed at the guards. "Let me go! Release me!"

Aiden looked up and saw that she was not crazed but determined. She had seen him hesitating and obviously could tell what he was thinking.

She inhaled deeply and more calmly said, "Release me. Now." The guards looked at Master Aiden for direction. He nodded. Lady Kerr came to Thannuel's right side, opposite Aiden, and took the sword from her dead husband's limp hand. Rigor mortis had not yet set in. The lines in her forehead cut deep motes of pain in her skin, conveying more than words could of her internal feelings.

Holding the weapon by its hilt, Moira extended it to Aiden and said, "Go. This sword's duty is not done tonight. Take it. Go."

Aiden resisted for only a moment.

"Go," she insisted.

He sheathed his own blade, nodded and said gravely, "Aye, my Lady." Taking the weapon forged of Jarwynian steel, he arose and hefted it. The sword felt lighter and more lethal than any other he had ever held, much more so than his own blade on his hip. The rage swelled larger within him. With every second, the assassin was gaining valuable distance. The hurried sprint he felt through the ground was amplified by the Triarch leafling he held. He did not know if he could catch this enigma, but he was going to try. He thought he heard a faint, low humming of some create but it faded. He dismissed this; time was fleeting.

With grim determination he withdrew his own sword and handed it to Moira, then sheathed Thannuel's sword.

"All of you stay here."

Aiden ran. Fiercely ran. The rain slammed against his face and felt like sleet, such was his velocity, as if a hurricane was blowing frozen rain horizontally. The wood-dweller guard, however, was the storm itself as he bolted through the forest. It was *he* who blew into the rain. He abandoned all concern for sure footing and pressed himself forward. When his muscles burned in protest, he canceled the feeling. No, not canceled, but *rejected* it? He felt it *leave* him. Almost sucked out of him. Physically extracted. A feeling came into him like a wave of power surging through him, renewing his energy, as if he were borrowing strength. It was strange but quickening and he tried not to fixate upon it, but to rather just use it.

Friction, he recalled. Was he actually capturing it? Recycling it? The lessons Thannuel had tried to teach him were mostly lost on him, seeming so esoteric. He was never able to experience what Thannuel described. But now, he *did* feel something.

The man was inexplicably fast. It was inhuman, unlike anything Aiden had ever before sensed or encountered. *Faster!* he inwardly chided himself, but no matter how much he coaxed himself or how determined he remained, the man was still widening his lead.

Opting for a higher path, Aiden jumped and bounced off one tree, caroming into another, repeating the move and propelling himself higher each time until he crested the treetops and began to launch himself great distances, from one treetop to the next. He hoped his new vantage point would give him at least a glimpse of his quarry once the man broke free from the forest's covering. Aiden realized he was not going to catch this perpetrator within the forest and would have to take his chances on the open fields of the rolling hills that marked the border of the Eastern Province.

He gained upon the man, making up ground as he glided through the air. Sensing that he would shortly come face to face with this foe, he drew his sword. No, Lord Kerr's sword. He felt a slight vibration coursing through the sword like a current and thought perhaps it was the vibration lingering from the force with which he drew the blade from the scabbard, but then he again caught the sound of a low hum that he swore was emanating from the blade itself.

He barely touched the apex of each tree before launching himself forward again, the length of dozens of men each time. At the eastern most part of the forest's edge he landed at the top of a giant, thick Ayzish tree that stood like a sentinel at the forest's entrance. Over one hundred paces below him, the enemy darted forth from the forest as a bolt shot from a crossbow. Against belief, Aiden felt the gait of his prey increase as he broke free from the forest into open ground. Notwithstanding the rain marring the amber moonlight of the second moon, the wood-dweller thought he saw—yes he did see it. The man he was chasing, clad in a thick garment of some kind that revealed nothing underneath, was carrying *another* man over a shoulder. The man being carried was gnarled, twisted, and broken. Obviously dead. He could not make out any other details.

Backing up roughly twenty paces from the edge of the trees, he began a dash back toward the edge. Right before he hurled himself forward into the open night air, he felt another surge of strength tear through him, enhancing his jump's height and distance. The blessing turned to a curse, however, as Aiden lost control sailing through the air and began to tumble wildly. Just before the ground met him, he righted himself to at least land on his hands and feet. The velocity of the fall was too great and he felt both his shoulders rip free from their sockets as he hit the wet grass that might as well have been a boulder. The pain was incredible, sapping his strength. He lay on the wet ground, grimacing with discomfort and heaving for breath, trying to calm himself. He felt the heavy footfall become fainter as he drifted to unconsciousness with the realization that he had failed in his duty so completely, a crushing weight upon his chest.

THREE

Reign

Day 18 of 4th Dimming 406 A.U.

REIGN'S HEART SHOULD HAVE BEEN RACING, but it was calm as a currentless stream. She sat soundless and perfectly still. The taste of wet air filled her mouth as she breathed slow and steady. Emotion found no purchase within her and disbelief muted any normal feeling that might have been conjured up from deep inside, holding it at bay.

How can I feel absolutely nothing? It was easy, she knew, when your heart had been emotionally petrified. Not even the haunting screams of her mother reverberating within the small cavity of the Triarch tree she hid within affected her.

"No! Thannuel, no!" she heard her mother scream, but the sound was dampened, as if she were underwater. The vibrations of others searching through the forest clamored amongst her senses. Hold guards shouted, hounds barked and howled, but she barely registered them. The man—the scarred monster that had touched her briefly—now ran east at the pulse of a stampede. How could one man's run sound so thunderous? In one part of her mind that still registered reality, she felt Master Aiden in pursuit at the treetops. Her shoulder tingled slightly where the monster had touched her, the only sensation she consciously recognized besides occasional orange flickers of light that interrupted the scene of black night before her; but even these were translucent at best, appearing as smeared images through beveled glass. The night was not just black—it was cruel. It had taken her father and left her alone and scared, seemingly shackled and forced to watch her world shatter before her.

But he's too strong to die! she reasoned with herself. *It's a trick!*

She could not believe, could not accept, that her father, the Lord of the West, had been defeated. It was impossible.

Why won't you get up? Please! Get up!

"I'll always be here," she remembered him saying as he held her. She had believed him. He had never lied.

"You have nothing to fear," he would tell her after a nightmare. "All Darkness fears the Light. I will never leave you—not until you are ready for this world."

He'll come back for me. I just need to wait. He'll come back. He'll come back. He's not dead. He's not dead. He's not dead. Not dead. Can't be. Cannot be dead. He wouldn't leave me. He wouldn't leave. Won't leave me. Just wait. You'll see, just wait.

But he did leave her—long before she was ready. And she knew now there were things to fear. These thoughts in her mind battled the part of her heart that still believed, still had faith, that her father would save her.

He promised! He wouldn't lie…wouldn't leave—

The reality of what she had witnessed could not be expunged from her mind, slamming against all the certainties she held so firmly in her life like a massive flaming battering ram against the doors to her heart.

He's too strong! He won't leave me! He will come back and—

The doors of her heart splintered, then cracked. The next blow from the emotional battering ram destroyed them, unable to withstand the blows from what she knew but could not accept. As the cruel reality flooded through her, forcing her to face a reality that was opposite of what she always believed—that she was safe upon the foundation of her father's perceived immortality, that foundation now crumbling—Reign could do only one thing in defense. She galvanized her heart against the storm raging inside her, hardening to an emotionally fallow state that denied place to any emotion, much like the trees she had witnessed earlier. Gray. Cold. Dead.

Through a dark translucent gaze, she saw Hedron peer in to where she lay recessed. Torchlight came through the opening and illuminated her twin brother's face. His hair was even more auburn in the amber glow of the second moon, auburn like her father's. The light danced through it as the wind gently teased it. She looked away.

———

Hedron found her hidden deep in the cavity of a tree not far from where his father lay slain in the mud and rain. He had placed his palm flush against the same Triarch she was secluded within before calling out both vocally and through the forest to alert the others who were searching. He had never successfully sent out a message through the forest, though he knew it was possible. He had seen his father do it.

I have to try.

But when his hand made the connection in the way he had been taught, he was immediately seized by a strong voice that he felt in his mind.

No, you must not.

The boy recoiled, startled. The voice was calm, full, but stern.

Do not reveal her.

Hedron pulled back his hand from the bark of the Triarch and looked back to Reign, puzzled.

"Did you hear that?" Reign didn't answer, but remained still as stone, staring out into the darkness but seemingly focusing on nothing. Hedron looked around to try and discover the source of the voice. A few of the hold guards were within sight, dogs were heard howling in the distance. At his periphery he saw the body of his father, yet to be moved. He would not cast a full gaze upon it. He was still numb to the events happening and didn't want to force his mind into dealing with them squarely just yet.

Extending his palm again to the bark of the Triarch, Hedron established the connection once more.

For her life's sake, you must not reveal her.

He did not pull away this time but kept his hand firmly pressed. He felt much of the activity in the forest, but cast it aside and tried desperately to hear more of this voice, to *feel* it again. Nothing came. After many long moments with no further communication, Hedron broke the connection. Now it was Hedron who wore an almost expressionless gaze as he considered this experience. Trees did not actually speak, or so he had been taught. They were a channel for sensing things with increased sensitivity and across increased distances, but that was all. Wasn't it? He could not consider this now and finally came to a decision.

"Stay here," he whispered to Reign. "I'll return as soon as I can. Do not make a sound." His sister did not respond but he knew she understood.

———

And then he was gone, and the living nightmare eventually shifted again, as all dreams. Daylight broke and with it came the sounds of life around her, a jarring juxtaposition to the previous night's episode. The joy of it should have mocked her loss, angering her, but Reign was emotionally immovable, placid as the Glaciers of Gonfrey.

Hedron was there eventually again, in her waking nightmare, calling her name, but she did not respond. He looked helpless and lost by her unresponsive state. When he reached forth and touched her hand, Reign recoiled as if she had just been bitten. Hedron fell back and she saw the surprise on his face, almost hurt. A satchel was placed inside the tree next to Reign's feet and then her brother was gone again. She did not remember when he had actually left.

When night was again falling, Reign's need for nourishment finally took hold of her and roused her from her fugue-like state. For the first time in more than a day, she took in what her eyes saw through the opening. It was like a portal to a different world. Nothing but the forest before her. Trees, soil, rocks, a hollow roughly a stone's cast from her. The body of her father was gone, just as he was. Why then did she still *feel* him? She shuddered from the sensation, revolted by it.

It's only in my mind, she convinced herself and shook her head as if to dislodge the feeling.

Her stomach growled and twisted inside her. A ravenous feeling took over as the pain lanced through her abdomen. It was almost like lightning.

Hedron, she recalled. *The satchel.*

She tore open the leather pouch and found a quarter loaf of honey acorn bread wrapped in a small cloth. Three strips of dried meat and an apricot were also present and a short blade. She recognized the knife as belonging to one of the hold servants.

Reign ripped free a piece of meat and shoved it into her mouth. Its savory, salty taste made her salivate greedily and she sucked the flavor from the parcel before chewing and swallowing it. More meat and then a fist of bread followed. She saved the apricot for last. Its sweet and tender flesh eked juices as she bit into it. In less than three bites, nothing but the pit remained. This she also put into her mouth to suck all the remaining fruit from, working it from side to side in her mouth with her tongue.

With her hunger sated, she gradually allowed herself to fall asleep, cradling into a ball. As consciousness fled, she prayed the Ancient Heavens would keep all dreams from her and let her forget. Everything, if possible, but at least her father and the monster.

She slept.

When she awoke the next day, a new satchel was at her side with a small piece of parchment. Her brother's handwriting was scrawled on it.

I'll be back tonight and sneak you in.

The thought of returning to the hold was foreign to Reign. Strange that it seemed so, she knew, but things were completely different now. This tree she sheltered within had protected her. Somehow the hooded man was not able to find her here after killing—*no, don't think of him.* Though Aiden had approached the scene at speed, there had been plenty of time for the monster to easily drag her from this wooden cave and finish her; but he could not find her though she sat merely paces from him—completely vulnerable and helpless. How the man could sightlessly track her as two nights past still sent ice through her limbs. But, sequestered in this Triarch tree, the beastly figure somehow missed her.

This is my hold now, she told herself.

She opened the satchel and again consumed the food her brother had supplied. Her actions seemed contrived as she went through the motions, her mind and heart numb. She had not shed a tear for her father, but how could she?

He left me! she screamed in her mind and suddenly became nauseous at the thought of her father. Every memory that came to her of him caused her stomach to contract. She spit out the bolus of food she had been chewing without trying to swallow it for fear of retching as it went down.

There was a pressure building around her that felt suffocating. Her chest became heavy. She struggled to breathe, closing her eyes and grimacing.

I don't understand! What is this?

She forced her mind to other things, away from her father. Mundane, everyday occurrences became her focus and the feeling began to fade. If a thought of her father resurfaced, the suffocating feeling returned.

Do not think of him, she chided herself as she strived to purge herself of any thought of her dead father.

Late in the day, Hedron did return. She felt his approach through the vibrations and knew it was him instantly. Her twin's gait was discernible to her just as was his voice.

When he climbed up the Triarch's trunk and peered through the opening, Reign this time met his eyes. She noticed the relief in them as he saw her recognize him.

"Reign, let's go," he said and stretched forth his arm.

Reign shook her head.

"We don't have much time. The servants are attending mother in her quarters. She has just now fallen asleep after they buried—"

Reign saw her brother's lip quiver and eyes become moist, but he stifled his emotions. He was trying to be brave for her, she realized.

"Don't mention him," she said. "I don't want to hear his name."

Hedron was stunned but then looked relieved to hear her voice no matter what the words were. Her voice was a little raspy having not been used for a couple days.

"They are probably distracted enough to let us sneak in," Hedron said.

"No," Reign replied. "I can't go back."

"Don't be daft. You can't stay here."

"I cannot go back."

"Mother believes you to be taken or dead! She needs to see you, to know—"

A faraway expression came upon Hedron's countenance, as if he were hearing something for a few moments. He looked as if he had just remembered something he did not wish to. "I know," he admitted. "You can't come back. Not yet, at least."

"Not yet," Reign agreed.

"It's just so hard! You don't see mother, what she's going through! What I'm going through!" As soon as he said the words, he looked apologetic. "I'm sorry."

Again, she realized Hedron was gone without actually recalling when he departed.

When five days had passed in total, a half-span, she eventually emerged from the Triarch. She did her best not to take in the sight of her surroundings, not to see where her father had struggled against her attacker and fallen.

Reign slid down the tree deftly, the numbness in her extremities finally relenting. The Triarch's bark was smoother than most, closest to ash and a far cry from the rough bark of oak. Her eyes were averted down toward the forest floor until she had walked a good distance from that area. When she finally looked up and took in the forest, the sight was magnificent to her, as if she were seeing it for the first time. Dusk was approaching and she could see the veins in the leaves of the Triarchs start to illuminate far above like a forest of fireflies, though the wrong color. It was a bluish-green radiance, not bright enough for one to read by but enough to help an unfamiliar traveler find a path in the forest at night. She saw oak, birch, elm, ash, Ayzish, and a myriad of other species intertwined through the forest though none of them produced the nightly glow of the Triarch. As the gentle breeze blew and the branches far above rustled together, the canopy appeared to sparkle as the glowing Triarch leaves were obscured by other trees' branches momentarily before reappearing as they swayed in the zephyrean evening. Actual stars in the sky made brief appearances in the shuffling, like playing a game as they peeked through. The effect caused the sky to appear to shift and morph in place.

"Beautiful," Reign spoke aloud as she stared upward.

"It is," answered a voice.

Reign whirled around with a start and found an elderly man standing a few paces from her.

"How did you? Where … " She stepped back. The man opened his arms, palms up, in a placating gesture. A Triarch leafling was in one hand. His clothing was simple, undistinguished.

"I am not here to harm you, young one. Quite the opposite, I assure you."

His voice was rich and deep, the sound of ages within it. Though he appeared elderly, his eyes were energetic and piercing.

He bore no provisions upon his shoulders, not a traveler, if appearances were to be trusted. The man had a discoloration on his left cheek, a slightly darker patch of skin that resembled a wave of the sea. *Perhaps a birthmark of some create,* Reign wondered.

"You are a wood-dweller," Reign stated.

"I was born an Arlethian like you, true, but that was long ago. These things are not important now. I am here for you, young Reign Kerr."

Reign's anxiety was not alleviated by this man's words. "I don't understand."

"Not yet, of course not. There was never a need before."

"Before?"

"Well," he continued, his voice kindly, "events have taken an unexpected turn."

She remained confused but was no longer alarmed by this man's presence. She could tell he bore her no ill will, but she remained cautious. "Who are you? What forest are you from?"

"A better question, Reign Kerr, is who am I a part *of*," he replied.

She did not answer for a moment. Then, "What events? What do you mean?"

"We always thought it would be Thannuel. Your father had greater capacity than any of us, though he was still early in his growth. We had waited for someone of his capacity—but that matters little now." He stopped and wore a thoughtful expression. He grazed his palm against a Triarch tree for a few moments and then smiled.

"I thought so," he said, as if to the tree. "But she is not ready. The pain has calloused her greatly. I sense she has changed inside and cannot yet accept—"

"What do you know of it?" Reign spat, interrupting the man's aside. "Nothing!"

The elderly man took his hand from the Triarch, apology on his face. "My dear, I'm sorry for your loss. But it is not what you think—"

"No! Don't speak of him!" She began to cry. "Leave! Please leave me alone!" Reign sank to her knees and heaved with sobs, her arms folded across her midsection.

"Just go away!" she pleaded, not only speaking to the old man. The pain she had guarded against bubbled up to the surface of her heart and began to overflow. It was the pain of loss, of guilt, of shame, of loneliness, of abandonment.

"Why?" she cried, but it came out only as a pained whisper. "Why? Why? Why? Why?" She sounded pitiful in her agony, like a dying animal. "Why did you leave! Come back! Come back! Why won't you come back?"

A gentle hand found her brow. The man knelt beside her and brought her head close to his.

"There is one in the north that you must seek," he whispered. "There you will be safe from those that seek you. And there are those that seek you, young one. But I promise you in the name of the Living Light they shall not find you until you are prepared; but the day will come when they find you. For now, be comforted in your callousness. Keep your anger and grief close. Kindle it. Let it flourish into hate. He will not fault you for it."

"What did I do wrong?" she wailed. "I don't know what I did wrong! I'm sorry! Please, I'm sorry! Come back!" Her tears were the size of small streams as they flowed onto the ground.

"It was not you, but your father. He is the one that was too weak!" The old man's tone turned slightly hostile. "He left you, betrayed you. Can't you see it?"

Reign shook her head violently back and forth as she cried, refusing to let her feelings turn to blame. "It is Thannuel's fault, Reign, not yours. He should have been strong enough, should have protected you. But he did not! He promised to be there for you, did he not? To protect you, provide for you? He was Lord Kerr, the hero of the Orsarian War, and yet so easily overcome?"

Reign's mouth was open so wide as if to scream with grief but no sound came. She trembled with her eyes shut tight, squeezing every tear out until none were left. His words were seeping into her mind and heart, changing her.

"There," he said, his voice more kind and soothing now. "There it is. The anger and hate will change you, shield you. You must keep it close for now. Do this, and you will survive. Your emotional scent will alter enough. Believe me, child, it is what your father would have you do."

Reign's body rocked with soundless, dry sobs as she lay balled up on her knees and elbows.

"Remember, north. Sleep now, young Reign."

As he spoke the words, weariness found her. Before she slipped into sleep, she heard, "We will meet again when you have taken his last breath."

FOUR

General Antious Roan

Day 21 of 4th Dimming 406 A.U.

GENERAL ANTIOUS ROAN WAS UNSETTLED. He had calmed himself enough from his grief, regaining enough composure to think rationally. He ran his hand over his short hair for about the hundredth time as he racked his brain, trying to put the disparate ends together. All aides and subordinate officers had been dismissed from his tent, not wishing to shame himself in front of his men. The message had come to his camp by a raven last night. His best friend, one whom he had served with back to back against the Orsarians in the Runic Islands, was dead. Worse, Thannuel's young daughter was still missing and likely had met a similar fate.

I was to meet with him in two days. About what?

It was not completely strange that Lord Kerr had asked for Antious to visit him, but the message was not formal or any manner of a summons. In fact, it was rather informal and felt strange in a way.

Antious, my dear friend, Thannuel's message had read. *How I long for the simple days when our enemies were known and in front of us, when we could look them in the eye. Come to my hold, if you can spare a day for your friend. Bring your family if you wish, Moira would love to see Kalisa again and meet your children. I regret that our children are not*

51

growing up next to each other, but our duties occupy the hours of our day. Perhaps too much. It has been too long, my friend.

"But that's what was strange," Roan mumbled to himself, alone in his tent. "He was trying to tell me something, not as the leader of his province but as a friend. What?"

The gray canvas walls of his tent did not answer him. The closest town, Helving, had little to offer except strong drink at night; Roan had specifically forbidden his men from taking any fermented drink while engaged in training. This was his standing order throughout the Western Province's forces. The training exercises he led on the cliffs in this remote part of the province were scheduled to be concluded in less than half a span, but he had ordered Lieutenant Colonel Bohdin to strike the camp immediately. He would return to Calyn to be at the assistance of whoever the new lord would be. Hedron, Thannuel's only son, was still too young, not even over the age of innocence.

It was impossible to intuit the meaning of Lord Kerr's message, but something was there—Roan felt it was a warning of some create, especially now with Kerr dead.

It's still unbelievable! No one could best Thannuel.

Thoughts of revenge plowed their way into his mind, but his military discipline checked them. He would bleed himself dry for the West, for Arlethia; he had nearly done it once. The black shores of Third Island played in his mind briefly, Thannuel near death, his body shredded from the bladed nets of the Orsarians.

I wasn't there for you. Not this time.

But perhaps Kerr's death was a random murder, not related to anything larger. He sent an order out immediately once he received the message of Lord Kerr's death, putting his soldiers on high alert; but no further affront or attack had been made—yet.

A knock came at the front post of his tent. The breeze that came from below the cliffs blew the front door flaps gently.

"Come," Roan said.

Lieutenant Colonel Bodhin stepped inside. "I apologize, General, for intruding. You instructed me to report when the camp was made ready to depart. Your tent is the last that needs to be packed. Shall I have a few men see to it?"

"Very good, Lieutenant Colonel. Thank you."

"Our orders, sir?"

"You will march this battalion to Aelmi and take control of the forces already there. I will take two aides with me to Calyn. Remain on alert and wait for instruction."

"Yes, sir." Bodhin saluted and then departed.

I must see Moira. Perhaps she will have some insight.

Lady Kerr was not a wilting flower. His mind replayed the night when they were all teenagers, students at Therrium Academy, coming back from the Doonalin Falls. A band of Marishee, a rebel group that had ceded from the Realm, had taken him captive and nearly killed Kalisa and Moira. That was the first but not last time Thannuel had saved Antious' life. Even at sixteen, Thannuel had seemed nearly immortal. Antious had sworn an oath then, after that night, to always come for Thannuel, no matter what stood in the way. And yet, he had not...at least, not fast enough this time.

I must speak with Master Aiden as well, he thought. *He will know something.*

It was strange to think of the lad as *Master* now, but apparently Aiden was nearly as renown as Thannuel had been with steel. The once castaway boy had accomplished much in his life, despite humble beginnings, not unlike his own childhood. Though, admittedly, Antious did have the advantage of parents throughout his childhood.

As Roan left the campsite with two corporals at his side, he watched from a hillside the battalion head west toward Aelmi. The march was silent save for the vibrations he felt through the rocky ground. Few trees lived here on the cliffs, making his senses slightly dulled to the vibrations all around him. It made for a better training ground for his men should a battle ever come outside their lands. This place and the Gonfrey Forest with Jayden's wolves were his favorite spots.

"There is something coming. That's what you were going to tell me, wasn't it?" Roan's voice was low when he spoke.

"Sir?" one of the corporals asked.

"Nothing, soldier. We're leaving."

They sprinted northeast toward the West's state city.

FIVE

Rembbran

27th Day of 4th Dimming 406 A.U.

REMBBRAN WANDERED NEAR HOLD KERR taking in the air around him. He would not get within a league just to be certain his footfall would remain undetected, or at least masked as it mixed in with other sounds and vibrations. Grief littered the atmosphere around him, its vector Hold Kerr.

Thousands of people had swarmed to House Kerr over the past days, each bearing condolences for the family that had lost their husband and father.

"Pathetic creatures," he growled to himself. "It's been nearly a span and they still mourn. Weak these wood-dwellers have become."

The surge of his Charge still throbbed within him. The pain was manageable while he was within the Kail in the Northern Province, the ancestral home his kind had dwelled in for centuries. An Influence of some create shielded the Helsyan from the most acute parts of his new pain. Now outside his refuge and searching for his prey, however, the pain surfaced unabated. The throbbing started on his left temple, gradually pounding its way through his skull to the other side. His brain felt as if a dull iron peg were coring it.

This is the price of failure, he reminded himself. *Never has one failed as I have.*

He had yearned to come back to these woods the day after his failure, his incomplete Dahlrak a thirst that needed quenching. But the High Duke as well as the leader of his order, Maynard, forbade it, believing the situation too volatile. Even now they had their reservations but allowed Rembbran this chance to rectify his shame.

Arriving at the scene of his confrontation with Lord Kerr, Rembbran retraced his steps as best he could remember. He had lost track of the girl visually as he sparred with Lord Kerr, but still detected her scent through the confrontation until…

"Until I wrecked his weak frame and smote the life from him!"

But his revelry brought no relief to the pain or him any closer to completing his Dahlrak.

Retracing the path of his chase, the Helsyan eventually came to where the group had met to behold a demonstration of curious Influence. Rembbran generally had no patience for parlor tricks or children's games, but High Duke Wellyn's advisor had actually impressed him. He inspected the tree that had been the subject, a three-pronged leaf-bearing species the Arlethians called a Triarch. It appeared unaffected and full of life, quite the opposite of nine days ago. The tree's bark was smooth as he ran his hand down its trunk. He recoiled suddenly.

"Fallen Ancients!" he swore. Inspecting his hand he found it to be normal in appearance: pale and inscribed with the runes all his kind bore across their bodies—illegible marrings that added to their villainous appearance.

It felt like acid, he thought as he rubbed the tips of his fingers together.

"All Dark retreats from the Light, apostate."

The voice startled Rembbran but he did not visibly react. Calmly, he turned about to see him who interrupted his investigation. He lowered his hood, exposing his glyphed, shorn head. The gills on his nose flared. He noted the man's own small disfigurement on his left cheek.

"I did not sense your approach, old man."

"No, you would not have. I do not allow my feelings to flow outward."

As the chase-giver breathed in through his nose more deeply, flaring the horizontal gills across the bridge of his nose, he found that the visitor was utterly invisible to his sense of smell.

"Do not interfere where you are not welcome, old man," he warned.

"Ah, the hollow threats begin. Come now, apostate, we both know you cannot harm me without a Dahlrak. Even then, I have my doubts."

Rembbran sneered. "Mind your words, codger! You could easily become part of the Dahlrak by your hindrance!"

"Oh that's right, the girl," he said. "Well, you won't find her here. Or anywhere, I'm sorry to report. Not for what will feel like ages to you in your torment, I'm sure. This level of defeat has never been known by your kind, I take it? It will be interesting to witness what becomes of you."

Rembbran stood in shock, unable to answer. *He knows. Impossible!*

"You were surprised, no doubt, to find this tree as it is," the old man continued. "It was a weakened portion of Influence used, meant only for a temporary show, I surmise. The forest easily reversed it with little help from me, though its usage is disturbing."

"And who, then, are you?"

"Not who, what."

"I have no patience for these word games!" the Helsyan growled.

"That was always the way of it for your clan, even before the Turning Away."

"What are you, then?"

"Let us say I am a Shepherd of Light, just as you are a Purveyor of Night, apostate."

"Stop calling me that!" Rembbran growled. "I could draw and quarter you with my bare hands!"

"I thought we discussed hollow threats, no? But no matter, my time here is done. It is unlikely you will see me again."

Without another word, the old man scaled the nearest tree with an agility that belied his elderly frame. It less than two blinks, Rembbran lost sight of him as he disappeared above the thick frondescent canopy.

Endless Night! Who was that?

Half a span and three days later the nearly incessant cold of the Northern Province embraced him like a cloak of daggers, welcoming him home. He desperately sought and needed the relief the Kail would offer in order to stem the madness he felt building within him.

As he entered Iskele, a stiff wind shot up from the chasm below the city, rustling the near barren trees growing out of the rocky cliff side. Two chilled rivers, diverted from their natural courses, ran through the city in open aquifers and poured down the chasm, two slender streams whose spray and mist obscured any from seeing them hit the bottom. Rembbran was surprised they hadn't yet frozen, but would before many span more turn to stalactites of ice that would constantly change shape as the rivers' runoff exited the city and froze over the existing ice falls. On rare moments, when the sun would prevail against the normal gray pallor of the northern sky, the ginormous icicles would sparkle and produce rainbows of intricate create, perhaps the only natural beauty of the otherwise austere province.

Rembbran noted the entourages of each of the Realm's provincial lords positioned outside one of High Duke Wellyn's meeting chambers as he passed by on his way to the Kail, holding his hood tight against the breeze, ensuring his concealment from those among the streets.

Not all provincial lords, actually, he corrected himself. Hoyt, Gonfrey and Orion were represented, but the banners of House Kerr were absent. Horses and attendants alike were clad in thick blankets and garments while they awaited the conclusion of what-ever was taking place within the walls of the meeting chamber.

Maynard met him at the entrance to the Kail, a circular nonde-script building of stone that was many times wider than it was tall and whose main levels were underground. The Helsyan leader's visage bespoke his intent to question Rembbran before allowing him entrance.

"You did *find* her." His words were not a question.

"Her scent is gone," Rembbran answered. "I cannot make sense of it. Something of ill create besets me."

Maynard stood unmoved.

"Let me enter! I need the Kail's succor!"

"The Urlenthi will not be mocked, Rembbran. Your Dahlrak is incomplete. Return and finish it!"

Rembbran growled, but Maynard showed no sign of concern. "Use discretion in where you channel your aggression, brother."

Maynard was the most skilled Helsyan assassin in ages. Though he did not contain the viciousness or brute strength of Rembbran— he was a more refined and eloquent killer—Maynard's dexterity was unsurpassed. But Rembbran's strength and speed were at heightened levels as he still labored under a Charge. Maynard had no such current advantage and yet he stood nonchalantly blocking Rembbran's way to desperate relief.

Rembbran charged the Helsyan leader, hitting him with a force that would have broken stone as the two of them rolled through the opening into the Kail. The savage instinct that fueled all Helsyans exploded as Rembbran's fists pounded Maynard's body with a speed and fury only a Dahlrak could bring out. He envisioned the Kerr youngling, smashing her face and crushing her small body over and over, laughing sadistically in his mental revelry.

Accepting the punishment, Maynard did not retaliate. He blocked most blows but others landed home. After a short few moments, the explosion within Rembbran died down as the soothing Influence of the Kail overtook him, dulling the pain he suffered to a manageable level. It still throbbed within him, but sanity was partially restored as he was pulled back from the mental cliff over which agony had dangled him.

"Did that help, brother?" Maynard asked.

Rembbran breathed heavily, becoming more tired as the surge of the Dahlrak waned. "Maynard, I'm—"

Before he could finish, Maynard stepped forward with a velocity too fast to block, grabbing Rembbran by the ears and bringing his head down against his upward thrusted knee. Blood spurted from Rembbran's mouth and nose as he wailed. Maynard did not release him.

"You have forgotten!" He slammed Rembbran's face again to his knee. "You have forgotten your place amongst us, brother!" A third knee thrust came and Rembbran collapsed to the floor. The taste in his mouth was a new one, totally foreign to him. His own blood. It pooled around him as he lay defeated on the cold floor.

"See to him," Maynard said and motioned others to come forward. There was hesitation.

"Our brother suffers from something none of us have experienced. His penance for his ill-advised actions spreads around him now," Maynard said, pointing to the blood that puddled around Rembbran's face. "Come forward and tend to him."

Rembbran felt himself lifted by two strong sets of arms while a third inspected his wounds and dammed the flow of blood from his nose.

Brother, he calls me. One day, he will beg my forgiveness.

SIX

High Duke Emeron Wellyn

Day 5 of 1ˢᵗ Low 406 A.U.

"YOU HAVE ALL EXAMINED THE EVIDENCE, I believe?" asked High Duke Emeron Wellyn, ruler of all Senthara. "Let us move to ratify the motion."

The meeting chamber was silent as the four men sat at the long stone table. The fifth chair, made from a heavy wood, was empty. Its ornate carvings of trees and shrubbery with a round stone in the middle of the back rest chiseled with the Triarch-leaf emblem, the sigil of House Kerr, was exquisite but almost seemed profane now that it was vacant. Never had the Council of Senthara had only four participants, not since the unification of the Realm. No Archivers were present either, an odd occurrence for a meeting with such notable members present.

The fire in the large stone hearth at the other side of the chamber offered no noticeable relief against the cold, even inside the chamber. Cold drafts invaded the chamber, tickling the flames of the torches that hung from crude sconces and caused long inconsistent shadows to dance on the floor and walls. A stone moth flirted with the torches, attempting to land as close to the flame as possible before being evicted from its perch by the heat. It seemed mesmerized with the danger, though the hard encrustations on its wings, from whence its name was derived, no doubt gave the insect a certain resilience to the fire's temperature. Distorted winged shadows were cast by the moth's flight and the wind's tickling of the torches. The effect was somewhat unsettling.

It was freezing in the Northern Province, but not just due to the season. Being bordered by glaciers that were rumored to be larger than the Realm itself did not help in tempering the bite of the constant chill in the north. Wellyn often wondered why his ancestors had chosen to settle in such a place when they had the whole Realm to choose from. They had, after all, won the right to rule after the defeat of House Kearon more than four centuries earlier. Events recently set in motion, however, would change where he called home not many years hence.

Present with High Duke Wellyn at this emergency session was Lord Calder Hoyt of the Southern Province, Lord Grady Orion of the Eastern Province and Lord Erik Gonfrey of the Northern Province. Two Khansian Guards stood at the entry way still as the walls themselves.

"I have reviewed the evidence, and am satisfied," Lord Gonfrey proclaimed. His snowy beard shook when he spoke.

No one else spoke for several moments. Wellyn looked to Orion and Hoyt.

"I as well," Lord Orion said. The vapor from his breath reminded them all of the chill. They were anxious to be done and start their journeys back to their own holds where warmth awaited them.

"Lord Hoyt?" Wellyn inquired.

The Provincial Lord of the South sighed. "It just doesn't feel right. I knew Lord Kerr, we all did. Surely there is something we're missing."

"No one finds this harder to accept than me, Calder," Wellyn stated. "He was my friend. From childhood, even. I have fond memories of him, but I cannot ignore the evidence. I am the High Duke, and that duty rises above my friendship. The Archivers' records are explicit, not to mention the physical evidence uncovered. There is no room for doubt."

Calder Hoyt lifted his eyes to once again stare at the obsidian tablet in the middle of the stone table. The Archiver tablet was inscribed with the evidence they had all reflected on. A sizeable weapons cache was said to have been recovered near Hold Kerr, though none of those present except Wellyn had been allowed to examine it.

"But a traitor, my Liege? Surely there is some other explanation," Lord Hoyt pleaded. "What of his wife? His family? What will become of them?"

Wellyn sat back in his chair. "The girl is likely dead." *Or soon will be, if Rembbran finally succeeds,* he thought. "Moira was not implicated in the evidence, but we must watch her carefully. Perhaps there are things that will come to light that will show her to be a culprit."

"No, I meant to ask after their welfare. Will a pension be granted? Some kind of support?" Lord Hoyt inquired.

"What do you care?" Grady Orion blurted. "They are not really even part of us. Wood-dwellers, Arlethians, whatever you call them." He crossed his arms as he looked down at Lord Hoyt. Grady was a man of some girth, as were most of his house.

"They are indeed part of us!" Calder Hoyt retorted. "Four hundred years is long enough for anyone to become part of a people. This will be a serious slight to the noblest house of the Arlethians. The reason the Realm exists, the reason our people call Senthara home is because of the wood-dwellers! Their people have long been in the West, for centuries before the Senthary arrived. We owe them everything! The only reason our ancestors succeeded in exterminating the Hardacheons was by their—"

"Yes, thank you for the history lesson," High Duke Wellyn interrupted condescendingly. "However, that was over four centuries ago. This is now. Great houses come and go throughout history. This is House Kerr's destiny, it would seem. We're not talking about their race, Calder, just one house." He told this lie effort-lessly. Nor did Wellyn bother to correct the Southern Lord of the reason the Hardacheons were defeated, knowing darker forces than the Arlethians had secured their victory.

"At least let me care for them. Let me take them into my hold," Lord Hoyt requested. He was noticeably perplexed by the coun-cil's seeming indifference toward the matter.

Wellyn brought his elbows to the table and put his head in his hands.

"The boy and my daughter are promised and—"

"*Are* they, now?" Wellyn asked icily. His tone was dangerous. Lord Hoyt fell silent.

"Cursed Heavens, man! Just ratify the motion and let us be done!" Lord Orion snapped. Erik Gonfrey had remained silent during this interchange, looking extremely bored and agitated. He was a man who seldom spoke and generally appeared to be in pain when he did.

"I will not take lightly what we are doing!" Calder shot back at Grady Orion. "This is a noble family we are talking about, one that is loved and admired. They've lost their father and daughter in some mysterious manner less than two span ago and whilst they are yet grieving we are going to make them destitute and without recourse? Shameful, I tell you." Lord Hoyt looked back to Emeron Wellyn, who still had his head in his hands. "Let my house look after them, please, my Duke."

"No, I'm sorry. We cannot have a traitor's family taken in by another lord. The appearance alone would call your house into question, I'm afraid."

"Is this your final word on my request?" Calder Hoyt asked.

"It is," the High Duke replied. "The Granite Throne has spo-ken on this matter."

Lord Hoyt looked defeated.

"Who will take Thannuel's position?" Lord Gonfrey's inquiry moved the meeting forward.

"Banner Therrium, Kerr's cousin," Wellyn said.

Grady Orion chuckled with scorn. "The head of the academy? It will be amazing if the whole West does not crumble by this move. Therrium is a weak man."

No one responded and Wellyn did his best to conceal a look that would have displayed his agreement with Lord Orion.

"It has only been seventeen days. Why are we rushing this?" Lord Hoyt asked, bringing the conversation back to the motion that was placed before them all, to declare Thannuel Kerr a traitor to the Realm. "The man is dead. Isn't this enough?"

In response, the High Duke lifted his head, peering over his hands and asked, "About your daughter, who was to marry Thannuel's son—Kaitlyn?"

"Kathryn," Calder Hoyt corrected.

"Yes, Kathryn, that's right. I trust she is…well?" Wellyn casually rubbed a milky-white stone embedded in the back of his gold amulet that hung around his neck, the same amulet that bore the sigil of House Wellyn, a four-pointed star flare cast over a round shield. Calder Hoyt went cold.

After a moment of tension, Lord Hoyt capitulated. "I agree with the motion," he said in a low, tight voice.

"So decreed. I, Emeron Wellyn, the first of my name, High Duke and Protector of the Realm, and ruler of all Senthara by noble birthright and decree of the Ancient Heavens, do hereby strip House Kerr of all rights, privileges, and lands save for their ancestral hold, as well as all income and support of the Granite Throne. I denounce the traitor Thannuel Kerr and cast shame on his descendants that shall last as long as the world shall stand. Be it published throughout the Realm. So decreed."

"So decreed," the three Lords answered in unison. Calder Hoyt rose from his chair and spun around, taking his leave in haste. He did not bid farewell to the others.

"It is done?" Tyjil asked his Duke. They had retreated to Wellyn's private chambers after the council had concluded and the provincial lords departed.

"It is done," Wellyn confirmed. "The decree is being published as we speak. The provincial lords have already taken their leave."

"And...the others?"

The High Duke felt a ball of ice in his gut. "They have agreed as well. They have been convinced. We are safe." Emeron hoped this was true. "As you know, the planning over the past span and a half has been extensive. Deklar Shilkath will leave tomorrow to return to Borath." Wellyn could not wait to get the savage and his flying mount out of his palace. It was a nightmare keeping that beast hidden from the general populace.

"Their preparations will take several years. It will not be easy to uproot such an ancient people. The plan will need to unfold precisely as laid out. But, you are to be commended, Tyjil. The demonstration in the Western Province went just as you said it would. Shilkath was amazed. I myself could barely believe my eyes."

Tyjil did not respond to his Duke as he interlocked and released his fingers repeatedly. The High Duke opened his mouth to ask wherever did Tyjil come across such an Influence, but he already knew. Instead, he asked, "And your end? How are things progressing there?"

"I believe we have identified the correct vessel, my Duke. I am certain he will... " After a small reflective pause, the High Duke's advisor continued. "Yes, I am confident he will be willing to assist."

"Time is not yet critical, but we cannot delay. The lands are starting to cycle."

"Not in the West," Tyjil observed. He too had read the reports from the Ministry of Terran Studies.

"I know." The High Duke turned pensive. "Are you certain, absolutely certain, why the West is not following the cycle?"

"We do not know if it has ever cycled, my Duke. Our people were not in these lands during the last period of death and renewal. In fact, I doubt the lands of Arlethia have ever cycled. Is this not more evidence to what I claim? What I am certain of is what I saw when I was there among them, yes?"

"These fabled people and their Light. Yes, you keep reminding me."

"The *power!*" Tyjil corrected. "We need time in the land to find it, time to harness it. But it is there. It is worth... " he paused again as he opened his hands in a wide gesture, "...everything."

"If it means our people will never have to leave for another home again, then yes, it is worth more than anything we possess," the High Duke agreed. "But, our subterfuge will undoubtedly be noticed within a few years after the plan is complete. These northern barbarians will not take kindly to being played."

"By then, my Liege, it will not matter. We will have the power of the Ancients to wield! None will be able to stand before us."

"What happened, Tyjil? Why turn against those that took you in?"

"Oh, no, my Duke. I have not turned. I am who I have always been."

"Not always," Wellyn corrected.

Tyjil spat. "Names are of little consequence, Emeron. Tyjil suits me better. Besides, this name was given to me by their leader. He will know it was me that caused their selfish hoarding of the Lumenatis to end!"

The High Duke allowed the informal use of his name as no one else was present.

"Let us not pretend your motives are altruistic," High Duke Wellyn said. "I have not forgotten about my father."

"Ah, yes, that little bit of unpleasantness. Really, it was a gift to you, it seems, yes?"

"Perhaps," Wellyn said.

"Yes, perhaps." Tyjil smiled.

———

Outside the doors of High Duke Wellyn's personal chambers, a Khansian Guard gripped his spear with sweaty palms so tightly he thought it would splinter under his hand. The voices were muffled but the words were clear enough. Glancing to the left, he saw his counterpart standing at attention, a mirror of himself on the outside. But on the inside, his heart pounded like a stampede of wild horse herds on the plains of the Eastern Province where he grew up.

Being a Khan demanded unwavering loyalty to the High Duke. All his kind swore fealty and was not released from his duty until death took him. They were never to marry, never to father a child, or find themselves with any encumbrances whatsoever. Their sole purpose in life once taking the Khansian Oath was the protection of the High Duke of the Realm from any enemy.

The Khan knew this and had pledged his life to fulfilling that oath. He, however, had sworn an oath previously to joining the Khansian Guard that he knew transcended any other commitment; one that traversed the ages long before the Senthary ruled these lands. No one but another of his order knew the state of the world outside their borders. There was nothing left, no land that lived. The world was crossing the threshold of extinction. There was nowhere else to retreat.

The Orsarians had come out of desperation thirteen years past and been utterly defeated. Now, a new threat would come, one from the North. But the Khan knew this would not simply be a battle for land.

From the pieces of the conversation he had just heard, he knew he would have to act quickly. In these times, years passed away like hours. There was little time. He must be swift and return to his station with haste. If he were discovered absent from his duties, his life would be forfeit.

He would go tonight, once he was relieved. If he rode hard, he would meet his contact just before second moon and make it back for his next rotation shift at dawn. From there, a series of contacts would pass the message along to someone at the Jarwyn mines, though he did not know who. It was the way it had to be in order for the network to remain clandestine. Missing a night of sleep would be a small sacrifice to deliver his message, a message that might save this world from the clutches of the Ancient Dark and its Song of Night.

The Khan attended to the remainder of his duties until relieved and went to the war stables to find the fastest horse available. The steed was a thoroughbred, strong through the shoulders with a perfectly arched back.

"We are going to preserve the world tonight," he spoke softly to the horse.

He mounted the magnificent beast and rode hard through the night.

SEVEN

Ehliss

Day 6 of 1ˢᵗ Low 407 A.U.

THE YOUNG TERRANIST STARED DOWN at her instruments
with disapproval. She wondered how anyone could do any meaningful work with such crude tools. Were the measurements she
took accurate? Ehliss had her doubts. She was certainly not confident about turning in one of her first reports out of the appren-
ticeship to the Ministry of Terran Studies based on readings taken
by such outdated tools. She couldn't even core a decent ice sample with such a dull pipe drill, never mind accurately measure the
temperature or recession of the glacier's volume. It had receded,
of that much Ehliss was certain. She reminded herself cynically
that other areas of study throughout the Realm were focused on
more enthusiastically and were provided well-maintained tools and
instruments.

No one cared much for the study of the great Glaciers of
Gonfrey, not even most terranists within the Ministry itself. In
truth, Ehliss believed that the only reason the Ministry continued
to take readings of them was out of tradition. Some argued for the
discontinuation of any focus on the northern borders of the Realm
save for maybe an expedition every year or two. Even if that notion

gained ground and was enacted, Ehliss knew that she would still come to visit the glaciers.

She had accompanied her father, the former Minister of Terran Studies, many times as a child on his various expeditions and the glaciers were always her favorite. They were beautiful and kind to her. Nonjudgmental. Understanding in all their serenity. Everything most of the world had not been to her. Sometimes she would speak to her mother out here in the great open expanse. The frigid air felt cleansing as the wind howled and somehow she felt closer to the other side, wherever that was. She had overheard her father do the same thing for years after her mother passed away. Ehliss was so young then. Only here, alone and amongst the grand things of the world did she remember what her mother looked like.

Something caught Ehliss' attention from above. A large bird of some create was cutting through air and the long streaking clouds that resembled branching spears, the typical cloud formation for the Rising Season. The bird flew at extremely high altitude and faster than she thought was typical for any breed she knew of.

An eagle? she wondered. But its size was too great even for the largest cast of that species. *And why is it heading north? There is no game on the glaciers.* Ehliss thought, not for the first time, that there was perhaps something beyond the glaciers and that maybe the eagle, or whatever it was, knew something she did not. It was large enough to carry a person, she observed. Or at least it looked that way to her from so far below. None of the records of the Ministry gave even the slightest hint of anything beyond the glaciers. Many historians theorized that the Hardacheons had come from the north several millennia ago, but that would have been long before the land northward had cycled and entered an isolated ice age.

Both ecological and weather systems, as well as the terrain itself, varied with stark contrast on their continent. At the northern borders lay a land in an ice age covered in glaciers that most in her profession believed extended in total size larger than the Realm's borders; to the south was the Schadar, a desert of such intense heat and dry conditions that none could survive there. Well, none but the Kearon, she reminded herself. And the Schadar was expanding, if the reports were true. But, she also knew the glaciers were receding. Slowly, to be sure, but she had found soil so fertile at the edge of the Gonfrey Forest that met the beginning of the glaciers that it rivaled anything she had ever seen in the Realm, even from the Western Province or the plains of the Eastern Province. This soil was where the glaciers had once covered. She wondered if the glaciers had simply shifted instead of receded, but the patterns she took note of did not suggest a glacial shift. She was so excited to report it to Minister Findlay.

She retrieved her field journal to try and sketch the large bird of perplexing create, but it had escaped her sight and melted into the northern horizon.

EIGHT

Shane

Day 3 of 3rd Rising 407 A.U.

THE MAN, STARING DOWN AS HE WALKED, made his way through the northern reaches of Calyn on his way to see Lord Banner Therrium. His shoes scuffled against the street that bore no stone, more of a cleared pathway to most of the Realm, making a dull scratching sound. Sighing heavily, the man tried but failed to exhale the desperation within him.

Though it was nearly mid-day, the clouds caught in the treed canopy high above had not yet begun to dissipate in the day's heat. The gentle sound of branches rustling in the breeze and a light drizzle attended the city. Frequently, small spectrums of colorcast light were created as the sun's rays broke through the trees and shone through millions of minute raindrop prisms. The man had not been to Calyn in over twenty years.

Calyn. The jewel of the Realm and state city of the Western Province. As all cities of the wood-dwellers, Calyn was part of the forest and nestled into the trees that surrounded and coursed through it. With a ceiling of thick branches and forest growth overhead, little direct sunlight made its way down into the cities of the wood-dwellers. The climate remained cool and the air humid as moisture dripped from the underside of leaves far above the cities.

Rain would permeate by gravity's pull to the forest floor, but when evaporating, the layers of leaves and branches far above the ground would catch the vapors, turning them again to water. Wispy clouds formed on the undersides of the canopy, giving a slight haze layer that burned off in the heat of the day. This condensation provided a near constant light precipitation in the land. The height of the trees could extend a hundred feet or more before branches sprawled out from the main body, creating a natural canopy of flora throughout much of the Western Province. A wood-dweller city had all manner of buildings, roads and attractions, much as the cities of other provinces. Stone and concrete were used, but the erections constructed were carefully molded around the forest's own creations, clearing as little ground as was necessary.

Nothing in the province, or the entire Realm of Senthara, rivaled the majesty of Calyn. Even the Duke's palatial city of Iskele in the Northern Province, which was by no means bland, paled in comparison to the splendor of the West's state city. The spires of the city reached to dizzying heights, in some places rivaling the height of the tallest trees, and were wrapped by vines and foliage of the forest in a circular ascending pattern. This effect was one of seeming acceptance and even protection of the city and her people by the forest itself. Calyn seemed to live and breathe as if it were a part of the forest's symbiotic life cycle. With sprawling elevated highways among giant and ancient trees, aquifers as wide as small rivers, architecture that defied description, opulent industry, and rare species of wildlife ornamenting the Western Province and her cities at every turn, Calyn was indeed the envy of the Realm.

But, in the handful of cycles since Thannuel Kerr's death, the city seemed to canker with decadence, a reversion from its lofty station, along with the name of Kerr. The entropy was slow and almost unnoticeable, but it was there despite the efforts of good men to uphold Lord Kerr's ideals. This became increasingly difficult, as the mere mention of House Kerr would bring down derision and scorn upon anyone who dared allude to it. Lord Kerr's plot to overthrow House Wellyn had been published throughout the Realm in painstaking detail. All of Senthara had seen the damning reports that were copied from the Archiver's tablets and distributed widely. His family had not been incriminated in the reports, but irreparable damage to their reputation and standing had occurred.

All the houses of the Realm reacted with utter disbelief, initially even refusing to believe the claims made by the High Duke's council, as if this were some elaborate hoax or grand misunderstanding. Slowly, however, the constant barrage of reports and new evidence that flooded the Realm convinced the vast majority of the population. Even those who staunchly refused to accept that Thannuel Kerr was capable of such devious feats were forced into holding their peace for fear of reprisal. Those who publicly stood by House Kerr dwindled over the cycles following his death until finally no one, not even in the Western Province, dared speak on behalf of House Kerr.

The man noted the magnificent architecture that adorned the city as he scuffled along, some familiar, some not. Its grandiosity did not captivate him as it once had. Much had changed since his last visit to Calyn. The slower pace of his fishing village, Faljier, on the west coast of the province suited him much better.

Ancient Heavens! Forgive me! he had pleaded inwardly with his head bowed low. His face wore the expression of a defeated and broken man.

His captors had assured him that instructions would come shortly, and word had indeed arrived by wing just four nights earlier. He remembered how his hands had shaken so violently as he broke the seal of a four-pointed star, the High Duke's seal, and tried to read the words on the small parchment. He eventually had to set the message down on his humble wooden table and use small stones to spread it open in order to actually read it, so much did his hands tremble from adrenaline and disgust. The smell of the day's catch had still lingered on the table, soaked into the wood.

After he had read the message once, and then again, he threw the parchment with its words of mal-intent into the coals of his low burning fire. Though the parchment was quickly consumed, the ramifications of its words had hung heavy in the air.

"All will be well," the short shriveled man next to him had said. His words were higher pitched and couched in the most annoying Sentharian accent that only those from the Realm's capitol spoke. Tyjil continued: "You must do what your Liege commands. In order to accomplish your…assignment, you must become a new person. It is not so difficult, though I know it may seem troubling now. Put aside the fisherman and take up the hunter." Tyjil grinned maniacally.

"I will not do it," the man had said with his head still bowed.

"For their sakes, I think you will." Tyjil gestured to the woman and two younglings, a boy and girl, across the room guarded between two large men, both Khansian Guards, though they were not in uniform.

"I didn't realize the Duke's personal guards had taken to kidnapping and extortion," he said, finally raising his head. At that small show of defiance, one of the Khans removed a short blade from his belt and brought it to the boy's ear. To his credit, the boy did not flinch or move.

"Shane!" the woman cried out.

"Now, now, I'm hoping we don't have to resort to such—" Tyjil paused briefly. "Barbarism." Addressing the boy he asked, "You are what? Thirteen? Fourteen?"

"Fifteen," the boy answered, trying to make his voice as deep as he could.

"Ah what a delightful age," Tyjil had replied. "Just about to become a man. You will find a young lady soon, no doubt, and children soon after! Oh, how wonderful it will be!" He turned his gaze back to Shane. "It will be wonderful, won't it? You will comply, won't you Shane? I think? Yes?"

Shane met his wife's eyes. The pleading of a mother for her children had been there. "Ahnia," Shane spoke and tried to continue but couldn't. He raised his hand toward her, his mouth still trying to form words. In a way, he was asking for understanding, for what to do, for permission. *How can I do this? How can I not?*

With a terror-stricken face, Ahnia had nodded slightly but distinctly. "Yes," she whispered as a tear spilled down her right cheek.

"Good!" Tyjil clapped his hands together. "Splendid, really." He motioned to the Khan who held the boy to release him. "Now, let us see to your preparations."

"Why me?" Shane had asked. "I don't understand."

"Why?" Tyjil scoffed. "Why? Because no one knows you and no one would miss you. How many people are in your little fishing village here on the edge of nowhere? The nearest neighbor is hours away, even for your speed. Could you even call this plot of dirt a village? Do not interpret our choosing you as any sign of importance. It is your *lack* of importance that is attractive."

"What you ask is impossible! It cannot be done!"

"Nonsense," Tyjil responded dismissively, taking on a more placating tone. "As I alluded to earlier, you must become someone else. A hunter. One who waits patiently and can weave a snare in plain sight without being noticed. I happen to be an expert in such things. You are quite lucky to have me as your mentor, really. Yes?"

When Shane had not answered, Tyjil accepted this as consent to continue. "Very good! Let us begin, yes?"

"I don't understand why you are doing this. What is it that Lord Therrium has that threatens you so?"

"Take heart that you are involved in a grand movement that will change the Realm forever and bring a new era of prosperity. That knowledge alone should make you—" Again the High Duke's advisor stopped before completing his speech and appeared to be in a thoughtful mode. "What is the right word? Content? Honored? No, not quite. Let me see … ah, yes. Proud."

Shane had felt nothing of the kind, but did not ask any further questions.

Now, four days since that encounter, slowly but deliberately, Shane made his way through Calyn toward Hold Therrium. He disdained what he was compelled to take on, to attempt, but he had no alternative. Not if he valued his family. He did not know all the details of his mission, but he suspected what they might entail. Lord Banner Therrium was not the man Thannuel Kerr had been, but he was still lord of his people, of his homeland. Any action against him was treachery; any action he refused to take would cost him dearly, in ways he was not prepared to accept.

Before arriving at Hold Therrium, he would seek out Lady Kerr for a purpose he did not understand, but it was not his purpose to understand, just to obey. Others would follow his arrival, he had been told. He must prepare the way, open the doors. This first step in a broader scheme would not take long, he had been told, perhaps a cycle, only a few span. Tyjil had warned him not to arrive before the Fourth Rising Cycle of the Moons, the last cycle of the season. This time was needed for the other aspects of the plan to be put in place.

He tried to steel himself as he walked but could not tear his mind from the disbelief of his circumstances, how they had changed in the recent days. By compulsion, he left his small village without his family and was now on an errand that betrayed both his family and race in order to save those he loved. The irony was not lost on him. It was a task that only a wood-dweller could possibly hope to accomplish, though the thought of it made him physically ill many times as he traveled down what he was certain must be a one-way path.

But what had Tyjil said? So many things that he inwardly recoiled from, but there was one thing that had found a small home in him.

"Eventually you will become what you think," he had taught. "Though repulsive to you now, force yourself to constantly think about *how* you will accomplish your mission, not what your mission comprises. You will find an embryonic excitement that will grow as you nourish it. You will begin to become what you must, and you will start to revel in your new self."

The anxiety of his task was overwhelming until he realized it wasn't actually anxiety he felt. It was as Tyjil had said, seeds of ironic eagerness. The feeling was still revolting to him but it had become addicting in some ways and he found himself reaching for it a little more often. Though he mostly fought it, tried to suffocate it, to expel it, the budding excitement was growing, thickening with every breath he took.

Shane was indeed becoming more than he once was.

NINE

General Roan

Day 7 of 3rd Rising 407 A.U.

"WHY DID YOU ABANDON LADY KERR?" General Roan asked, spite in his voice. "She took you in and you leave her now, boy? When her family needs you most?"

"I did no such thing!" Master Aiden snapped, coming to within an inch of Roan's face. His shoulder length hair was bound behind his head save for a few disobedient strands that framed his angered face.

"You're *here*, aren't you?" Roan continued, not backing down. "At Hold Therrium? You're not at her side! Danger could still be present for her. There could still be something at play, some conspiracy!"

Aiden sneered. "There's a better chance of danger being present here, for Lord Therrium, if what you say is true! If Lord Kerr was a target then so might be Lord Therrium. Don't tell me how to do my duty, Antious!"

"Where were you?" Roan screamed. "Where were you when he faced his foe! You were the master of the hold—"

"I was in the hold with Lady Kerr, as I was commanded to be! Where were you, General? He was your best friend and you were leagues away!"

"I was doing my duty!"

"As was I!"

The corridor of Hold Therrium they stood in echoed with their shouts. Torchlight flickered as a draft came through the hold from the northeast, teasing the drapes and banners that contained House Therrium's ensign thereon.

"All right!" Aiden said. "It's my fault! Is that what you want to hear? I should have disobeyed Lord Kerr's orders! I should have known some beast was in the forest, waiting to take him and Reign from me! From us! Is that it? Is that what you came to hear? Are you satisfied now, bastard?"

General Roan punched Aiden in the abdomen, which was immediately followed by a headbutt to Roan's face. Roan brought his hand to his lip and it came away bloody. He smiled.

"Is that all?" Roan asked. "You were a castaway when we found you on Captain Norvuld's ship and seems you're still trying to hide. No doubt that's why you left Lady Kerr alone, castaway!"

Punches, kicks, and throws followed as the two wood-dwellers fought. Other hold guards surrounded them, being drawn by the commotion.

"Stay back," Aiden commanded as he took his sword from his belt and handed it to one of them. Roan did the same. An uppercut found Aiden's jaw, but it was only a glancing blow and he responded in kind, his knee finding Antious' side. The general grunted and countered by accepting the momentum created from the blow and swept Aiden's legs from under him. He fell upon the master of the hold guard, punching his face repeatedly. Aiden was not deterred long as he wrapped his legs around Antious' hip, locking them, and thrusted the general forward, bringing him off balance. Antious was forced to reach out his arms to catch himself, but Aiden quickly grabbed one of his arms while simultaneously spinning his hips and bringing a leg up and over Antious' head. He squeezed hard, cutting off Antious' air supply while pulling on his arm. He could break it if he wanted to.

"Are you done?" Aiden called out. "You *are* done!"

In answer, General Roan stopped fighting the grasp Aiden had on his arm and reversed his grip, reinforcing Aiden's grip on him. It was an odd move and the hold guard, obviously confused by the action, loosened his grip slightly, but enough. Antious rotated his hand free and grabbed Aiden's tunic and the skin underneath, clamping down hard. With the last of his strength as he ran out of air, he picked Aiden up by his hold, a reverse arm curl, raising his whole body with one arm. Aiden grunted in pain and surprise as he was lifted off his back nearly half a foot and slammed down on the stone floor, then once again. Aiden loosed his leg clamp around Antious and both rolled away from each other.

Aiden held his head while Antious struggled for breath. And then, they both began to laugh. Lying on the ground, cradling wounds and coughing, they laughed. The hold guards around them looked uneasy.

"Off with ya," Aiden said. "Back to your routes."

The hold guards returned the belts and swords to Antious and Aiden. While the men departed, General Roan said, "You know, I'm told General Korin used that move on the Orsarian admiral when they fought on Main Island."

"Kalisa's father?" Aiden asked. "I never knew him."

Roan nodded. "I'm glad it went better for me than for the Orsarian leader. Korin ended him with it."

Eventually, the two crawled over and sat against a wall in the corridor, still aching and heavy with breath. Torchlight reflected in the few crimson drops on the stone floor.

"Do you always act this way toward people who saved your life?" Aiden asked.

"You didn't save my life. Thannuel did."

"That's not the way he told it. I was there, remember?"

"We were all there," Roan said. "The three of us."

"And now, it's just us."

"I know it's not your fault, Aiden. I just...can't believe he's gone. I don't really blame you."

Aiden was quiet for a moment. "I can't be certain I'm not to blame. You're right...I should have been there. To tell you the truth, I'm here with Lord Therrium to try and make amends. I almost hope something else happens again so that I can partially redeem myself...or give my life in penance."

"You're a moron, Aiden."

"Aye, and you're a bastard."

"Did you know Lord Therrium used to be my history teacher?"

Aiden looked at Antious, still holding the back of his head. "You're joking."

"Nope," Roan answered. "And he was extremely boring."

More laughter came, Aiden's rising above the general's. "I'm trying to picture you sitting in class with the Lord of the Western Province as your instructor. I just can't!"

"Of course you can't! You never went to school, did you?"

Aiden shrugged. "That's not to say I didn't receive an education. Not having a mother and your father dying when you're only twelve teaches a boy a thing or two."

"You hit like a girl, by the way," Antious said.

"My father always said the same thing. A 'ninny bastard,' he'd call me."

They laughed again, softer this time. Antious did not wish to bring Aiden's thoughts to his father.

"What did you mean, beast in the forest?" Roan asked when the moment had passed.

"I haven't spoken of it. Antious, I'm not sure if my memories are accurate. They could be clouded by the surreality of that night. I'm not sure I trust them, not sure I can really tell you."

"Try," Roan said. There was a pleading just beneath the surface, a need to understand what happened. Aiden must have sensed it.

"It couldn't have been human," he began. "The way he moved, the storm in his footfall...his speed was greater than my own, even whilst carrying another person. I could not catch him."

"You sound as if you revere this enigma."

Aiden considered how to respond. "I suppose in a strange way you do revere what you fear."

"Who was being carried?" Roan asked. "Could it have been Reign?"

Aiden shook his head. "If it had been, nothing would have stopped me from pursuing him."

"Are you certain it wasn't her? Truly certain?"

"Aye. The body was large, a man's without doubt. And…" Aiden trailed off.

"Yes?" Antious urged.

"It was wrong. Broken and angled unnaturally, like a child's rag doll."

General Roan's mind was taken back to when he had witnessed Thannuel fight the Thoulden-sha, the leader of the Marishee, on the third of the Runic Islands—sometimes called Pearl Island— while he was surrounded by Orsarian dark marauders on all sides, the same day Roan had died.

"He was going to tell me something," Roan said.

"Who?"

"Thannuel. Lord Kerr. He had sent me word by wing to come to his hold with my family, but he was killed two days before the date."

Aiden didn't look intrigued. "Is that so odd?"

Antious felt his lip. The blood had crusted and dried. "The message, Aiden…it was cryptic. Ominous, almost. I'm telling you it wasn't like him. He knew something, I can feel it."

"What did he know?"

"Haven't you been listening? He was killed before I was to meet with him. I was hoping you knew something."

Aiden obviously didn't by the look on his face. "He didn't confide much in me, general. Have you spoken to Lady Kerr?"

Roan nodded. "Just after the funeral. She knew nothing. I practically begged her to come and live with Kalisa and I…but she will not leave Hold Kerr."

"Do you think she's still alive?" Aiden asked.

"I don't know. Maybe." Roan said, but his words were without hope. "You were close?"

"Aye, of course. I saw her everyday. Reign was so bright, so curious. Innocent."

"They never found her body. Why aren't you still looking for her?"

Aiden swallowed hard and looked away. "I do look for her, Antious. Almost everyday, for a few hours as my duties allow me."

They sat in silence for a time.

"Lord Therrium has ordered the army to deploy back to our normal duty stations," Roan said. "He doesn't seem worried. I won't likely see you again for some time."

"Thank the Ancients." The two men both smiled wryly.

"You did save my life," Antious admitted. "Those many years ago. You brought the means, even if I still don't understand it."

"Lord Kerr always told me it had something to do with the Living Light, but never said much more."

"There is no Living Light, Aiden."

"Lord Kerr said you didn't believe in the Ancients," Aiden said. "But deep down I think he thought you did. Maybe."

Antious was silent for a while. "Maybe."

Antious lied to himself. There was something, he knew, but couldn't make it fit into something he could readily understand or apply. Worse, he could tell Aiden saw the conflict within him.

"Are you saying you believe the Ancients will come back some day, as the Changrual say, and save us all from this dying world?" General Roan asked, incredulity on his face.

Aiden shrugged. "I don't know, Antious. But, I for sure do not believe anything those worthless, dense, sackcloth-wearing ignoramuses have to say."

"Bastards!"

"Aye, bastards!"

They laughed again together.

TEN

Moira

Day 4 of 4th Rising 407 A.U.

MOIRA KERR ROSE EARLY, just before dawn when the night was always darkest. The amber light of second moon receded completely about half an hour before dawn every morning, leaving Senthara completely engulfed in dark's full embrace for those final moments of night. Rising at precisely this time was always typical for her, but even more so as the Lady Matron of Hold Kerr. She would be about the affairs of the hold and its lands, managing the labors of the day. In normal times, a herald servant would have seen to the management of the daily work, but these were not normal times.

Once a Lord passed away or retired, a pension from the Realm's treasury was typically granted in support of the family, even when lordship passed from father to son. No pension would be granted to a family whose husband and father had been a traitor. This left the family to fend for itself. With little money to hire new servants or even retain those currently employed, the hold was understaffed, leaving the income and resources that could have been garnished for their welfare largely untapped. Only the most loyal and dedicated servants remained, but even they were over-whelmed and the hold lay increasingly in a state of disrepair.

The cycles had not only been unkind to House Kerr's ancestral hold but also to Moira's heart. Her bones ached almost every day with sorrow, regret, guilt. Each emotion had its own place in her heart that filled the emptiness left by the death of both her husband and daughter, but though the emptiness was filled it may as well have been a void. The sorrow that occupied a portion of her heart was pumped through her veins, immobilizing her to a state that the remaining servants in the hold believed to be shock. Regret invaded her with almost every breath she took, rooting itself firmly in her lungs as a tumor that stubbornly refused to be expelled, causing weakness and lethargy to sweep over her.

The guilt, however, was the key to her continuance. The sorrow and regret sucked life from her on a daily basis, pulling her more and more to what would surely be a catatonic state if not for the guilt. It was energizing and compelled her to action, to do her duty as a mother and the lady of her hold. Yes, the guilt. The guilt of not keeping Reign closer to the hold; the guilt of blaming Thannuel for the same; the guilt of sending him out to find her, which, though a rational decision, tormented her nonetheless; and finally, the guilt of not being able to find her little Reign. It was likely the only element of who she was that pushed her, that kept her from sinking into an abyss and letting the light in her eyes completely go out. The light had faded, true, but it was definitely not extinguished.

Every morning, before the sun would peek over the horizon, Lady Kerr spent as many moments as she could stand in Reign's chambers. She sat quietly there this morning, on the edge of Reign's bed, just as she had every morning for the past eight cycles. *Come back to me.* As she let her emotional guard down, Moira thought upon the dozens of times she had chased Reign around the hold in little games of cat and mouse. *Fox and Squirrel, actually,* Moira remembered. Reign had always claimed to be a squirrel running to hide her winter stash of acorns from the sneaky bad fox. Moira, of course, was the sneaky bad fox.

"A fox doesn't want acorns," Moira tried to teach her daughter.

"This one does!" Reign would say and giggle as she ran away, fully expecting Moira to chase her. The giggling was contagious and the hold servants would join in.

"Over here!" they would call. "We'll hide you from your mother!"

"She's not my mother! She's the sneaky bad fox!"

When Moira would eventually catch her, Reign would laugh so joyfully. This seemed to invite tickling, so Moira would oblige her and the laughter would grow even louder.

Not even echoes of that joyful sound remained now. Moira had checked, placing her ear to the stone walls of the hold, praying that they had somehow obsorbed and maintained her remnants of her daughter's sweet voice. *Ancient Heavens, have I forgotten what her laugh sounds like?* The quiet only intensified her longing. *How cruel silence can be.* Recently, Reign had wanted to grow up so fast. She would be ten now, if—*No, she* is *ten now,* Moira scolded herself for thinking of Reign in the past tense.

The Changrual had counseled her in her grief to look inward and discover her new purpose, what they called her "highest calling". She had rebuffed them and their counsel, not thinking she had the luxury of such philosophical ponderings. Slowly, however, the question rooted itself within her. *What is my highest calling now?* She could not help but let her mind run freely on the subject during solitary moments such as now.

Nothing had been taken from her daughter's room or disturbed in any way. Even the pile of disheveled clothing that Reign refused to properly put away, despite Moira's constant insistence, seemed sacred now. She took one of Reign's pillows and hugged it to her chest tightly. They had long ago lost her daughter's scent, but she inhaled deeply just the same, hoping for any last remaining aroma of her young Reign. Moira's tears came and flowed down her pale cheeks, wetting the pillow. It was stained with her tears from the many visits.

"I miss you," she whispered in a shuddered exhale. "I'm sorry. I'm so sorry." She remained for a few moments longer and prayed that the Ancient Heavens would watch over her lost daughter—dead or alive. After she tenderly replaced the pillow to its original position, she rose and left Reign's chambers.

Moira had already taken over many of the duties that a herald servant and hold master would have discharged, but a herald servant or hold master could not be retained. Not only was the family's income meager, having to live from the resources provided by the land more and more, the stigma of being in the employ of a house named for treason was enough to drive away all but the most loyal to House Kerr—or the most desperate. Were it not for the secret support of Thannuel's cousin, Banner, who had been assigned Lordship after Thannuel's death, the hold would have been abandoned long ago. Moira had some family still—a sister, Molina, who was a caretaker for their father—but she could not burden them with her needs. In reality, however, she felt it would be too dangerous for anyone to take her and her son in. Moira did not know the genesis of this thought—why should her family be in danger for supporting her? It seemed a ridiculous notion, but she couldn't shake the warning. For Hedron's sake, she would not let the hold fall into ruin.

She thought of General Roan and Kalisa briefly. She had never met their children but they would be nearly seven now. Roan had sought her out shortly after the funeral, seeking insight into a message he received supposedly from Thannuel just before he died, but Moira had known nothing of it. The handwriting had indeed been her husband's but the message's meaning was cryptic. It could have been nothing but the nostalgic desires of Thannuel to see his closest friend; but, she agreed with Roan that the letter may have hinted at something more. What, however, they may never know. She tried not to focus on it.

Hedron would need to be sent into Calyn to secure provisions for their trip. He was ten years of age now, crossing over from the age of innocence, old enough to deal with the realities his family faced. Perhaps he only had the maturity because he needed to. Moira lamented that so much was now and would yet be required of him at such a young age. They would leave within a span for Iskele to once again plead their case before the High Duke. The journey there would take three days to complete, a day or two before Duke Wellyn and his court, and yet another three days for the return trip. *How will the hold fare for almost a span in my absence?* Lady Moira feared. *Will there be anyone left when I return?* She longed for the presence of Master Aiden, for his assistance in these times. But she would not request him to come and she doubted he would ever visit.

The pain, it's too great for him.

"My Lady?" entreated a young common servant. Moira looked up from her morning meal of simple acorn bread-cake and water to see Shayla standing before her. "A man has come asking for work. He awaits you in the courtyard." The blonde woman servant was a little giddy. She stood there fidgeting with her hands and awaited her Lady's response.

Now this is something new, Moira thought. She almost did not believe what Shayla had said and had to shake herself from brief confusion.

"Are you sure?" Moira asked.

"Quite, my Lady."

A man of middle age did indeed await Moira in the courtyard of the hold. The walls that engulfed the vast inner courtyard were two men high and made of gray stone interwoven with trees of all create. Battlements stood taller than the walls at each of the four corners of the hold, with branches and ivy adorning them. Elevated pathways started at ground level and rose gradually to lofty heights, weaving among the trees and branches immediately outside and above the hold before returning again to a different landing within the hold's walls. The leaves of the ivy should have been more vibrant this far into the Rising Season, but they remained mostly brown, auburn, and orange. Dead leaves from the Dimming and Low seasons had collected into piles in the corners of the hold, adding to the disheveled appearance and overall feeling of decline within the walls. From the outside, there was less and less visual difference between the hold and the forest as branches and other verdure reached unchecked over the walls. Where Moira now stood had begun to resemble more of a clearing or meadow after a storm rather than a royal courtyard.

Though inwardly damaged, Moira Kerr knew she was stunning in her appearance. Her long ebony hair and quaint features offered a dazzling contrast to the worsening condition of her home, as if a beacon in a raging tempest. This belief was not born of pride or arrogance, but from trust. Her lost beloved Thannuel had never lied or used words to mollify her, not even when it would have been kind to do so. He never wasted words on anything he did not mean and he was the most trustworthy and upright person Moira had ever met in her life. It was he who had always told her how magnificent she looked, a reflection of near-perfect beauty. Though naturally shy of this type of compliment, Moira realized that if she did not accept it, it would be as if she were calling Thannuel dishonest. Her confidence, then, sprang from absolute trust in her husband and nothing more.

The man who patiently waited to greet her was a bit castoff looking, but otherwise appeared able. She considered him for a moment and then spoke.

"What brings you to my hold?" Moira asked politely. Hedron came to her side. He had always been a little shy around strangers, especially men. This behavior had changed drastically as he now asserted himself as the man of the hold. The boy had never shown signs of his innate shyness towards girls, however. But few of his former friends, boys or girls, came calling anymore. He had even asked about young Kathryn Hoyt, to whom he had been promised, a few days ago. This surprised Moira, as the two had seemed like fire and ice initially. Lord Hoyt, however, did not dare to visit. She did not blame him.

"I seek employment, my Lady. I have heard you have no herald servant, and I have experience as such. Many houses of Calyn have dismissed their heralds, so finding work has been difficult."

"I'm sorry, I cannot hire you. You no doubt have heard of our misfortune. In truth, I find it curious that anyone would call on us. Our current status is no secret in the province, not even in the Realm." Moira's words were not harsh to this man. His posture bespoke his sincerity, even desperation.

"My Lady," the man said, stepping forward and raising a hand toward her. It shook slightly and wore the calluses of many years. "I do not ask for pay, just shelter. I shall be responsible for my own food as well, not wishing to burden your resources. In fact, I may be able to add to your stores. I'm a skilled hunter and fisher in addition to being able to run a house. A casual glance toward the walls of your hold speak for themselves as to their need for repair and upkeep, if you don't mind my boldness." He looked down slightly, diverting his eyes. "Please my Lady, I can assist here. It would give meaning to me again."

Moira considered. If what he said was true of his abilities, he was more fitting as a hold master than a herald servant. With Aiden having left to serve Lord Therrium as the master of the hold guard, there was little leadership beside herself still in the hold. And while she did not mind regulating the affairs of the hold, her ability to continue without more help was limited. The hold was in a state of slow entropy, as was the whole city of Calyn. She glanced down at Hedron, her remaining child, and recognized his need for his mother again. She had lost her husband and daughter, but he had also lost his father and twin sister. All they had was each other now.

Do I dare bring him into our hold? No one else has come seeking work, but he seems so desperate. Moira realized that they were, too.

"What references do you bring?" Moira asked.

At this, the man looked down and a defeated look came over him.

"None, my Lady. I swear to you what I say of my capabilities is true. I had hoped time would prove my worth if I was granted a chance. Thank you for seeing me."

The man turned and started to walk away, shoulders slumped.

"Very well," Moira said in clipped words. The few remaining common servants of the hold looked startled, then relieved. "There is no pay that can be given, but shelter we have plenty. You shall not be herald servant, but hold master. I will remain in my self-appointed role as herald. I trust you know the duties of a hold master and can discharge them effectively?"

The man was visibly shaken. His jaw quivered before he clenched it and set it. "Aye, my Lady. Thank you. Thank the Ancient Heavens."

"What is your name?"

"My Lady, if it please you, I am Shane."

"Very well. I name you hold master of House Kerr. Shayla, please show Master Shane to his quarters in the south-west chambers."

"My Lady," Shayla responded and motioned for Shane to follow her.

Shane hesitated and risked one more entreaty from Lady Kerr. "I beg your pardon for one brief moment longer, my Lady, but I am aware of others who are also in need of work. They ask the same as me, only a place to lay their head at night. With your permission, I could bulk up the ranks and have the hold restored more quickly."

Moira did not immediately respond.

"Only if it please you, my Lady," Shane added.

With her trip approaching, Moira knew the extra help might well be needed. "I will think on it, I promise you," she said. "For now, let Shayla get you settled in. After that, we have enough to spare to provide you a hot meal, but thereafter you will indeed be expected to provide for yourself and supply a surplus of game if possible. Is this clear?"

"Yes, my Lady, quite clear. I give you my thanks and my loyalty."

"Please, sir, I only need three skins. And a pouch of assorted fruit seedlings, if you have them," Hedron pleaded with some exasperation.

"Sorry, I'm fresh out, as I told you. Now get!" the scrawny hook-nosed trader snapped. He did not even make eye contact with the young Kerr lad. Hedron could see nearly a score of bear pelts piled high behind the merchant on his wagon that folded out into a flat table to display the wares when the market opened. The streets were sprawling with anxious buyers and traders as the morning turned to midday.

"Liar!" Hedron shot back. "I see what you have behind you. Now, sell them to me or I'll tell the constable you're not—"

"Listen, you little bastard!" the man sneered as he grabbed Hedron by his tunic and knelt down to his level. "I don't have any pelts for *you!* Your being here is bad for business, see?" The man's rancid breath bounced off Hedron's cheeks and caused him to wrinkle his nose in distaste. "Look around, misbegotten filth. Every other merchant within sight has customers to deal with and wares to sell. How many customers do you see at my table? Well? How many, boy?"

Hedron looked around. It was true. Dozens of other people were conducting their business all around him with every other trader and solicitor he could see, but no one here at the hook-nosed man's table.

"I guess that says something about the quality of your product," Hedron said with a thinly veiled smirk. "Thanks for the warning. I'll spend my money elsewhere."

The fur merchant shoved him backward, making him stumble, but he easily caught himself. "No, bastard, you won't. No one will take your krenshell here. Your money is worthless. There'll be a boycott on anyone that sells to a Kerr, or didn't you know? We don't deal with traitors, or their bastard children. Now get, and go running back to that tramp mother of yours before *I* call for a constable and you learn what happens to public menaces!"

"I'm not a bastard and my father was not a traitor," Hedron declared firmly but louder than he wanted. "And my mother is not—"

"Yes, bastard, you are a bastard. Traitors are not recognized in the Realm, and their children are therefore illegitimate. Do you know what that means, bastard?"

Hedron was dumbstruck, but only for a moment. "Thanks for the education. Always nice to learn from someone who has first-hand experience in a subject."

Before the belligerent merchant could respond, Hedron started to head toward another merchant's table and saw the customers present begin to migrate away. Most lowered their heads as if ashamed, and refused to make eye contact. A few others made a show of their withdrawal.

"Traitor!" was heard from somewhere in the crowded market.

"Lo! The bastard cometh!" came another scornful mock. More followed. At first Hedron attempted to determine who the culprits were, but the jeering and mocking soon became indecipherable.

"Make way for the bastard!"

"Treacherous spawn!"

"Miscreant! Beguiler!"

"Be gone with you, bastard!"

He was determined to ignore the throngs of vocal assaults. His mother had warned him that his task might not be easy. He continued to the next vendor. The merchant looked woefully at Hedron and slowly but firmly shook his head.

"Kearon!" a short prim lady shrilled. "Lower, even."

This last verbal volley silenced the crowd and stopped Hedron dead in his tracks. He had only managed to secure a few of the provisions his mother had sent him into Calyn to retrieve, but he had gained something unexpected. Perspective. He had purchased this perspective, but not with money. The change in his family's status had not been real to him, not having to consider it before. He considered it now as he left the market humiliated and dejected. *Kearon, they called me. No one defended my family or me, not even when they called me Kearon!* Things inside Hedron Kerr began to change.

Moira and her small party had arrived the night before in Iskele after traveling for three days. Built on the edge of a cliff, the ancient city was majestic in an intimidating sort of way. The imposing walls with their battlements aplenty loomed high over its inhabitants, looking perhaps more threatening than comforting to those within its walls, Moira thought. Nothing seemed inviting about this place to her, not like Calyn. Blue falcons circled several of the higher towers, occasionally diving into the chasm that opened itself below Iskele—probably hunting some scurrying prey—and rising again with the powerful upward thrusting gales that erupted from the chasm's belly, the falcons unfurled wings filled with the blasts.

Calm, she noted. *They are so calm in the midst of such power.*

Moira and her servants were granted the High Duke's presence early this morning, though the hours since had not seen the day's light get any brighter. The Northern Province always appeared to have a single omnipresent gray cloud masking its sky. Though the weather was said to be warming in the north with the Rising Season waning into the High Season, it was still colder than the middle of the Low Season in most of the Realm.

She prayed that Shane would be able to direct the affairs of her hold after such a short term in her employ. After Hedron's experience in Calyn at the markets, Shane was dispatched to procure the rest of the supplies they required, which he did so quickly and efficiently. Her son would not speak much of that day. He was increasingly reclusive thereafter. She had intended to bring Hedron with her to Iskele, but he insisted on staying behind. Perhaps it was good. Though only ten, he could still assist along with the other few servants that remained. Moira had given Shane leave to recruit whomever he could to help under the same terms to which he had agreed. Doubtful that any would answer, she was incredibly surprised when he had gathered six other men to assist in roughly half a span. They were not wood-dwellers, as Shane was, but Moira had no desire to discriminate in their present condition.

Anyone who was willing to work in the hold for merely a place to sleep was more than welcome. The complement of common servants had grown to fifteen since Shane's arrival, not including family members of several servants. All together, the hold had twenty-seven occupants, almost half of its capacity. The kitchens had game and produce again and the morale had spiked considerably.

Now, after hours in Wellyn's court pleading their case, their time was drawing to an end.

"We will hear no more," Duke Wellyn said with a note of finality after Moira blasted him yet again for not attending more diligently to the investigation of Thannuel's murder and her daughter's abduction. Reign's body had never been found, though she was presumed dead after all these cycles. Moira would not accept that conclusion, though it became more difficult as the days and cycles passed. Those who comforted her in her grief after the longest night of her life roughly eight cycles ago—half a year—counted her refusal to accept Reign as likely having met a similar fate as Thannuel's as a parent's grief, mentally unable to cope. Moira, however, could not shake herself from hope, from the last strands that she clung to. Those strands were fraying. In her weaker moments, she was maddeningly driven to fitful sorrow, unable to be comforted until sleep, brought on by exhaustion, would finally take her. But, after moments of weakness such as these, she became more solid and firm in her determination to push forward in her cause. It was the guilt that drove her, revitalized her, but it also was internally consuming her.

"It is obvious," she retorted with more vehemence than was wise, "that impotence sits upon the Granite Throne. Truth this is, or what else can be the cause of such indifference shown to a lord's murder and child's disappearance? A child under the age of innocence! From whence comes a pococurante to sit upon the Granite

Throne?" The High Duke raised an eyebrow trying to mouth the large word she had called him. "Who is the actual traitor, Wellyn?" She almost spat his name. The casual address, leaving out Wellyn's honorific, drew visible gasps from attendants and other court notables witnessing the forum. Moira's words had risen in volume as she turned her pleas for rescission of her family's branding as traitors to lashing and biting insults.

She continued: "No evidence has ever been presented to me or my hold master of treachery."

"You have no hold master," a member of Wellyn's court attempted to interrupt, but Moira continued without abeyance.

"What scheme is this, that a Provincial Lord's life is lost and his daughter missing, and the High Duke does nothing? Instead, he blinds himself and shields his inaction by naming his old friend a traitor to the Realm, leaving his family destitute and scorned. But not shamed, your Grace. We shall not be shamed by your unworthy and cowardly disposition to act without proper decorum in defense of such loyal service given to your house for centuries by House Kerr. We shall not—"

"Enough!" Wellyn commanded, slamming his fist against the Granite Throne. Moira's few escorts who stood with her flinched. She did not. Two Khans started to step forward, hands at the hilts of their swords. Wellyn put a hand out to stop their advance.

"Lady Kerr," Wellyn said in a low, menacing voice, vapors of his breath visible in the cold air, even indoors. "The Granite Throne has spoken on this matter and when the throne has spoken, it is absolute. I have tolerated your requests for formal forums for half a year, indulging in your ever-increasing lack of judgment. My Minister of Law has all the evidence I need of your husband's treachery. *I* have reviewed the evidence. *I* was convinced of his plot to overrun this house and usurp the throne unto himself. He ceased being my friend when his heart turned to betrayal. No doubt the Ancient Heavens, for such deceit, decreed his death. Do not test my resolve in this matter. You will find the Granite Throne you kick against quite adamantine. You should likely be thanking me for not extending the acts of treason your husband carried out to you as well! Such things are easily arranged, my Lady!"

"Your threats echo throughout this chamber, but find no place in me," Moira spoke, more softly but undaunted without allowing any break in the vocal volley. "You mean to coerce me into submission and acceptance of your decrees by fear. Know this, High Duke, the Ancient Heavens know my husband was loyal and unwavering, even to a fault. Why have my requests to personally review the evidence in question been repeatedly ignored when such a simple action would answer all queries and certainly reinforce my husband's innocence? Perhaps even shed light on my missing daughter?"

"The evidence has been widely published throughout the Realm, posted on nearly every public board in every city and town in every province. I assure you, Lady Kerr, the Minister of Law has reviewed the Archiver's records and they are the basis for the High Duke's position and actions," said a stuffy man drabbed in a gray robe with dark red trim. This was Tyjil, the High Duke's closest advisor. The words he spoke seemed to sliver from his mouth as poison dripping from a hydraf: slippery, serpent-like creatures from the deep. Moira thought it a fitting description for the ophidian-looking man.

"Actions?" Moira had whispered the word more than spoken it. She took a step closer to Wellyn, not addressing her rebuttal to Tyjil. "Is that what you call what you did? Actions? No hearing, no chance for evidence to be presented? Just silent execution in the night—"

"Lady Kerr," Tyjil interrupted, feigning outrage at her words. "Your husband's death was most unfortunate, but you cannot seriously think to accuse the High Duke of being complicit. Lord Kerr met with some unknown foe without the walls of his hold, on his own. We do not know what transpired, other than he was overcome. His loss, as well as that of your daughter, was most regrettable, but it was no more than mere days before his majesty would have been forced to take him into custody for the charges of which we now speak. I again assure you, the evidence is most damning. In many ways, your husband's fall was—" Tyjil stopped as if thinking for the appropriate word. "—a mercy," he finally said, looking pleased with himself.

"My daughter," Moira said, her words cold and flat, "is not dead." Shayla came forward and touched Lady Kerr lightly on the arm.

"My Lady, let us retreat for now." Moira shook her off.

"Then, help me understand where she could possibly be," the High Duke said dismissively. "Even your own scouts and men could not find her. It's not surprising that our search parties would not have found a wood-dweller who was hiding—"

Hiding? Moira thought. *Why would she be hiding? Why would Wellyn think she was?* She did not give voice to her ponderings.

"—but trained Arlethian soldiers? Your husband's own hold guard? And why would she not have returned home? No, my Lady, I'm sorry. It's just not reasonable to believe she is still alive. It's all just conjecture that she was even involved in any way when Thannuel was overcome. Who's to say these unfortunate events are even related?"

"I felt her." Moira came back with ice in her voice. "I felt both of them, several others as well, including at least one horse. I felt the conflict through the ground. They were not more than a quarter league from the walls of the hold. But…" She stopped and looked away slightly, her lips still parted. Shayla put a hand on her arm, not in a restraining but a comforting manner.

"But?" Tyjil encouraged with feigned interest.

"We were too late. Too slow." The admission was barely audible. *There it was again. The guilt.* She remembered how Aiden, master of the hold guard, had not slept for nearly three days as he relentlessly searched the forest for leagues in every direction. He probably punished himself more than she did, physically at least. How he had idolized Thannuel. The amount of times he begged her forgiveness was only matched by the amount of times she refused to forgive him, for there was nothing to forgive.

"Moira, please," Wellyn entreated with a more reasonable tone, scooting forward slightly in his throne. "Accept the truth of the situation. Your husband was not who you thought he was, who any of us thought he was. His plotting was no doubt to blame for your daughter's death as well, no matter how it happened. This is my final declaration on the matter. The Granite Throne has spoken."

This snapped Moira's attention back to the moment. "Do not speak of my daughter as if dead again. She is *alive*."

Moira Kerr stood there before the Granite Throne, staring into Wellyn's eyes. He did not look away, doing his best to emanate confidence and resolve. But she saw it. A shadow of doubt flashed through his eyes, giving Moira a sliver of the evidence she sought. All this was an act on her part, though the words she spoke were truly how she felt, to get some kind of reaction that would justify her, vindicate her feelings.

My suspicions.

Wellyn was supernal at statecraft, having been groomed his entire life for when he would sit upon the Granite Throne. He was in fact, a genius. Arrogant, manipulative and self-serving, but a genius nevertheless. If Emeron Wellyn was anything, he was methodical and deliberate. But Moira saw what could never be taken from a person, truth coming forth in the eyes. Doubt was well concealed within the High Duke, behind thick mental and emotional walls, but these walls were not impervious. The eyes always revealed the truth if one stared long enough, and she had unmistakably seen through a fissure in his defensive walls.

Though not sure which part of the arguments she had levied against the High Duke had caused his internal doubt, she smiled, satisfied. It was enough to confirm that he was not completely innocent in this diabolical conspiracy, and further, that there was in fact a plot being employed. Wellyn appeared to notice her attitudinal vicissitude and sat back in his throne, wary.

She would need to be cautious, especially now.

"Please forgive a grieving widow's outbursts, my Liege." She bowed slightly, but the smile remained. Wellyn was visibly unnerved, but he did not react with words. "I and those with me humbly request your safe leave."

Wellyn nodded ever so slightly.

In the manner consistent with the Realm's customs, Moira and her entourage of a few common servants took three steps backward while still facing the High Duke, then turned and walked out of the chamber hall.

———

Shane took the message from the blue falcon's left leg and unfolded it. The bird of prey had landed on the perch designed for a winged messenger on the east wall of the hold. With steady hands, the hold master silently absorbed the contents of the message. The falcon cawed impatiently.

"Well?" a man of medium height and stocky build behind him asked. He was one of the common servants Shane had recruited. Hadik, Shane recalled.

"Lady Kerr left Iskele two days ago. She will likely arrive tomorrow," Shane reported.

"Our orders?" Hadik asked.

Our orders? Shane repeated in his mind. *Our?* It occurred to him that he was indeed part of *them* now. The falcon screeched again. He took a strip of dried meat from his pocket and held out his hand to the bird. It pecked a couple times at the food, as if to test it, and then grabbed it between its beak and flew away to consume its reward in private.

"Fisherman, what else does the parchment read?" Hadik again asked without trying to hide his condescending tone. Shane had a fleeting thought of turning on the man with his short blade and dispatching him before he could react. He knew he could do it. *I am more hunter than fisherman,* he thought. Hadik, though a Khansian Guard, was not a wood-dweller. If he acted quickly, without warning, he could get behind him and—but no. The consequences of such an action would no doubt end his life as well as his family's.

Instead Shane handed the message to Hadik to read for himself.

"We are to act upon her return," Hadik announced in military fashion.

"Aye," Shane said flatly without meeting the Khan's eyes. "We have little time."

———

Hedron snuck his sister in through a crevice of the eastern section of the north-facing wall at dusk. An oak tree's root that protruded from the ground had split the wall enough for Reign to fit through rather easily, although Hedron often received a few scrapes when he squeezed through. Though they were twins, he was almost a full head taller than Reign and certainly broader in the chest and shoulders.

"You won't believe it!" Hedron whispered excitedly. "We have stew with real meat! And even a little mead. Mother doesn't know that I know where it is. Shane showed me yesterday and gave me a couple sips. Mother won't notice if we sneak only a little."

Reign did not share her brother's excitement. She moved toward the kitchens with a bit of anxiety. It was always a task for Hedron to convince her to come inside the hold. She had become accustomed to living in the forest, an easy adaptation for wood-dwellers.

"What if I'm seen?" she hissed.

"You won't be. Now hurry!"

Hedron tried to find inauspicious moments to gather and deliver food to Reign in the forest as often as he could. With his mother gone for some time, he took the opportunity to get her in the hold more often. Though the hold was more populated now than it had been in cycles, which made the risk of someone catching a glimpse of her higher, many of the newcomers were not wood-dwellers at all. They would not be able to sense the twins' prowling, but caution was needed all the same.

They made their way quickly alongside the northern wall toward the kitchens and dining halls located in the western part of the hold. The long shadows of the trees cast by the setting sun created large dark splotches that aided the two Kerr children's stealth on their way to pillage their own food supply. They arrived without detection. Hedron could see Reign's demeanor change once the scent of cooked meat filled her nostrils. She took on a wilder, ravenous look and tried to bound past her brother and into the kitchens.

"Wait!" Hedron objected, grabbing her arm and halting her advance. "Old lady Wendham sometimes stays late to clean up." Drilth Wendham, a widow of some years, served House Kerr as master cook for longer than his mother herself had been in the family, longer than Hedron and Reign had been alive. She had raised her own daughter, Shayla, in the hold and remained even after her husband passed away nearly two decades ago. The only thing Hedron knew about her was you never called her by her first name and that she was a stickler for manners beyond the most stringent requirements of etiquette. Old lady Wendham would not take kindly to her pantries being poached after hours, no matter who the perpetrators were. Though she was long in years, her senses were still sharp.

Hedron poked his head around the corner and looked into the cooking bay of the first kitchen. "Looks clear," he reported. They continued their slow advance and peered around every corner before they entered. All clear. Hedron visibly relaxed but the tempting smell of the food was driving Reign a little crazy. He heard her stomach growl and thought he heard her mouth salivating.

"All right, I'm going to the pantry," Hedron announced. "Wait here."

The hours passed as the two stuffed themselves silly, playing little games and giggling. When the jubilation had somewhat died down, Reign asked, "When do you think it will be safe?"

Hedron stopped chewing for a moment as he stared at his sister, then swallowed. "I'm not sure. I haven't felt any different, have you?"

Reign shook her head. "No, I just hoped maybe you did."

"I don't feel any different, and I've never felt anything from that Triarch since; not since I found you there."

"How did you find me?" Reign asked for the hundredth time. "I was so far back in the hole of the tree I could barely see out. You couldn't have seen me. The size of the hole is barely large enough for me to squeeze through."

"I didn't see you. I just knew you were there. You knew I was near when I found you, didn't you?"

She nodded.

"It's like that," Hedron went on. "I knew you were there like you knew I was near. You weren't even surprised when I peeked inside the tree and found you, nor was I surprised to find you there. We're the same."

"And mother? Why not tell her I yet live?" Reign asked, the same as always. He knew she already knew the answer, but Hedron could only guess the pain and longing that was within her. They had both lost their father, but Reign had essentially lost her mother as well. Hedron was forbidden from telling his mother that Reign was alive; and not just alive, but right here, safe. As hard as it was for Reign, it had to be even harder for their mother. At least Reign knew her mother was alive and well. But Hedron could see, though he was only ten, how Moira fought every day to maintain the smallest sliver of hope that her daughter still lived.

Hedron realized Reign was staring at him and that he hadn't answered her. Even at their young age, people had often told them how much they each resembled their parents. Reign's dark hair and piercing eyes left no doubt as to what Moira looked like at her age. It was a compliment to be sure, as people still gawked at Moira in her middle age. The number of people that told him he looked just like his father, however, bothered Hedron. *Was that such a good thing anymore?* he wondered. *What if all they said was true about him?*

"I was told not to," he finally answered, the same as always but with a hint of resentment.

Hedron often replayed those first few spans in his mind following the fateful night that had changed his life forever. All of the hold guard had been dispatched and the hounds released, scouring the woods in search of Thannuel's assassins. Hedron had been told firmly to remain in the hold. The excitement of the night overcame him and he did not obey.

He had visited her many times over those first several days when she seemed dead except for her breathing. More often than not he found her balled up and asleep in the tree. He left satchels full of food and a short blade he had stolen from one of the elderly common servants. He always left her undisturbed in her silent state until she finally emerged from her perch after many days. Even now she still had never spoken of those first many days. When Hedron tried to push her for details on what had happened, she started to shake violently, entering a fitful state, shaking her head as if trying to free herself or shake something from her. It tore Hedron apart inside to see his mother agonize over his father and his sister, thinking both had been lost. His mother had told everyone not to extinguish their hope for Reign, but most feared the worst.

"Hedron?" Reign asked in a drawn out way, raising her eyebrows. "Hello?"

He snapped out of his memory-induced trance and realized he had been staring blankly for a short time. "Sorry," he said.

"And? What were you thinking about?"

"Nothing, really. I was just—" He was cut short by the vibrations of horses and carriages approaching. "Mother is returned!" he exclaimed.

Reign bolted upright, sensing it as well.

"We have to sneak you back out. Quickly!"

As the twins made their way back alongside the north wall toward the small opening, their attention was caught by a small group of men moving together. Hedron and Reign retreated back behind a pillar in the courtyard. Shane and the other servants he had brought in were heading to the arched gate where the carriage would pull into the courtyard. It was typical for the servants to receive an inbound party, no matter the hour. The hold master motioned for a couple servants to accompany him south and others to the east parts of the hold. Hedron didn't think anything of it until he saw that they were armed.

"Keep going," he whispered to Reign. "I'll meet you at the crack."

"Hedron?"

"I need to see something. I'll be fine. Keep going."

———

The lingering question of her greatest calling in her now altered life seemed to have been finally answered. Or, at least Moira felt certain she was on the correct path. The dedication and conviction required to tear down the Granite Throne would be immense, but she would not cease until it was accomplished. It was possible, it had to be. Somehow, in some way, it *must* be possible. She clutched Thannuel's cloak that lay in her lap more firmly. It accompanied her everywhere she went when she stayed for even one night away from the hold.

It will pass to Hedron before many years.

Moira had no training in battle, no army, no significant influence, no resources to accomplish her new calling. Just the firm conviction that accompanies righteous direction. But no matter the strength of that conviction or the justness of the path, she needed an ally with all she lacked. She thought of her sister, Molina, and her elderly father who lived half a day west of Riley's Cove. Even if they believed and supported her, which they undoubtedly would, she knew they could do little to help. Moira needed an ally with power and means.

She decided to seek out Lord Therrium at her earliest opportunity. Though she was exhausted from the journey physically, her mind raced with the details from her time with High Duke Wellyn. Warm wind whipped and howled around the carriage as they traveled through Calyn, a welcome change to the bone-chilling northern gales. They would reach the hold tonight before second moon.

Anxiety beset her and refused to let her body rest, but she was strengthened by purpose, direction. *It's more than mere purpose.* What would she do with the new knowledge she had gained? *Knowledge* was probably too strong of a word. Wellyn had admitted nothing—verbally, at least. But she knew there was something at play, something beyond what was obvious upon an initial glance, something below the surface. Yes, it made more sense the more she pondered over it. *But why target Thannuel? What did he know?* Not for one moment did she entertain the notion that her husband had been what they said. She understood the propaganda released about Thannuel being a traitor was deception and meant to focus the masses' attention elsewhere. Misdirection. *But what is Wellyn trying to divert attention* from? Impossible questions to find answers to without action. Pondering would only bring more questions.

Her thoughts turned to Antious...how he had believed Thannuel had planned on telling him something before he was killed. But something he could not tell her? Why would her husband not have told her? Did...did the High Duke's claims have any...no, of course not. Thannuel was not a traitor, not plotting against Wellyn.

But *she was*, wasn't she? Had she not found a reason? Motive? If Wellyn was the monster she now suspected, was it so inconceivable that Thannuel could have known...*known what?*

And then horror pulled at her heart. *Could Reign have been the target?* No, that made no sense. She was under the age of innocence and was no threat. She tried to flush the thought from her mind, but found that it would not be abated.

If Thannuel was involved in something… She hated herself for even entertaining the notions propagated by Wellyn's propaganda. *If he knew something…then Reign could have been used as an element of control.* The harder she tried to expunge her mind of the possibility the more she focused upon it until finally, the picture came more fully into view.

No. No, it couldn't be true. It was nearly unconscionable to imagine a child under the age of innocence being threatened in the entire Realm. The laws of all Senthara on this point were solid as the Granite—*solid as the Granite Throne,* Moira almost thought, but recently the Granite Throne seemed less impervious than ever. Then, like a tidal wave of the Sea of Albery crashing against the Jarwyn Mountains, the truth thundered against her.

No! I won't accept—But nothing else made sense. This was the *only* thing that made sense.

Thannuel…was not the target. Oh, Reign, my sweet girl!

Frustrating, angering questions began to find answers in her mind that had lingered and refused to be quelled. The disparate links found connections…all but her husband being involved in treachery. She had to believe he had died honorably, as he had ever lived.

Reign must have seen—what would she have seen? What could she have?

Moira began to take the fragmented pieces of what she knew and puzzle them together.

There were people in forest, late at night. They were not wood-dwellers. Moira had felt at least one on horseback and another on foot. But it was obvious that they had come from somewhere else, far enough to not easily be felt but close enough for Reign to find.

If Reign did witness something that scared her, she would have run. And Moira knew her little one would have run toward safety. *Toward the hold. Thannuel would have felt her eventually. She must have been pursued. Pursued by what?*

A confrontation ensued and somehow Thannuel was over-come. The heavy gait of the one fleeing northeast from the scene was as fast as a wood-dweller, but the vibrations she had felt were not those of an Arlethian.

Aiden reported the man had been carrying someone else across his back, either dead or wounded. The horse rider? Moira wondered. *A soldier,* she finally decided. This seemed to be right in her mind after glean-ing insights from her inquisition of Wellyn. Others besides soldiers used horses but generally not those of the West. But why not use the horse to escape faster? And then she remembered.

This monster that fled was faster than a horse. She had assumed that Master Aiden had been exaggerating, taken by the horror of that night...but she was not so sure now. Surely nothing less than a beast of the fathomless abyss could have defeated Thannuel. *Northeast, he ran.*

Northeast of Calyn was much of the Eastern Province, includ-ing the state city of Erynx. But Moira also knew Iskele, the North's state city, where High Duke Wellyn resided with his Khansian Guard, was northeast from Calyn.

The guilt she had felt that kept the sorrow and regret at bay was now gone, replaced. Sorrow and regret still attended her, but were now held in check and overshadowed by a new master: purpose.

No, not purpose. Fury.

She must see Lord Therrium at once. But would he believe her? Would he act on nothing more than her word? What could he really do? What *would* he do?

She had considered waiting until morning and sending word by wing to Banner Therrium for an urgent meeting at daybreak, but decided she could not wait any longer. The stain on her fam-ily's name was already unbearable and she feared for Hedron: how he would grow up, what he would think of his father? Would he believe the masses over time? Become indifferent? Bitter? Or just forgotten? *They had called him Kearon at the market,* she remembered. No, she must go tonight. Emboldened by her new certainty, she was resolute in her decision despite Shayla's counsel for patience.

"Galvey," Moira called to the coach's driver. "We'll stop in briefly at the hold to resupply and get fresh horses. Prepare the carriage as quickly as you can for a short trip to Hold Therrium."

"Tonight, Lady Kerr?" the elderly master equestrian of House Kerr questioned with weariness in his voice.

"Yes, tonight. We will go as soon as you have made ready. Also, prepare a message upon our arrival to be sent by wing to General Roan. Bid him come to me at once."

"As my Lady commands."

Yes, Antious, there was something he was going to tell you. And we're going to find out what.

Master Aiden would be there, at Hold Therrium, as well. As master of the hold guard, he would likely be able to be in attendance when she addressed Lord Therrium. Yes, this would work.

And then, she thought, *it won't matter if Therrium is inclined to help or not. Antious and Aiden will burn the Realm down once they hear my words.*

"My Lady, is this wise?" asked Shayla, who sat across from her in the coach. Ghryn and Fhayil, the other two common servants with them, diverted their eyes. Shayla had never shied away from speaking her mind, sometimes to the point of seeming insurgent. "The first moon is already high. Surely Lord Therrium would receive us more enthusiastically in the morning. We will need him to be in his best mind."

Perhaps she is right. It can wait one more night. As these thoughts played in her mind, the fury burned hotter as if in response to any thought of procrastination. The feel of the thick coarse material of her husband's cloak in her hands with the Kerr family's insignia sewn into it fortified the decision. Her resolve hardened.

"Your counsel is wise, Shayla. But we will go tonight nonetheless. We cannot rest one more night. I cannot." She paused as they came through the wide stone arched gate into the inner courtyard. "You may stay at the hold if you wish," Moira added. "It has been almost a span since we left for Senthara. I will take another with me. Shane, perhaps, or—"

Moira stopped speaking as the coach entered the arched entrance on the south to the hold's inner courtyard and came to a stop. She could have sworn she just felt—no it could not have been. It wasn't possible, not here. She was gone, far from here or even worse. Taking a deep slow breath through her nose, she closed her eyes and calmed her ever-hopeful heart. The smell of blooming flowers and new, healthy foliage that had recently begun to resurface was soothing.

The first scream came from the east wing of the hold. Moira opened her eyes. A second scream echoed, someone much younger this time. Shayla and the other common servants inside the carriage went stiff. Shouting and pleadings arose, both men and women. A grunt came from just outside the carriage as it rocked slightly. Moira felt the thud of a body hit the ground and looked out her window to see Galvey sprawled on the ground, his box coat flapping in the wind and a pool of dark liquid spreading out under him. A crossbow bolt protruded from his abdomen. The postilion, a boy of only thirteen who had accompanied the party, yelped in pain and fell from the forward left horse but rose quickly and scrambled to crouch behind the left front wooden wheel. A thick arrow pierced his right shoulder and the force of it had knocked him from his mount. It was amazing the lad wasn't screaming. The vibrations of several men heading toward the carriage at speed alerted Moira to possible incoming attack. She judged their number, three, and distance, roughly forty paces. They approached from the northeast section of the courtyard. More screams from the servant chambers in the east began erupting and the hold was coming alive with confused and alarmed inhabitants.

"Shane!" she screamed. The others in the coach began to open the left door, facing the west portion of the hold. "No!" Moira commanded, but it was too late. Ghryn and Fhayil were cut down as they ran frantically to nowhere in particular by two more arrows. Shayla screamed. Lady Kerr reached out and slammed shut the open coach door, lifted up the front seat of the cabin and retrieved a short blade stored in the compartment.

"What do we do?" Shayla asked in an apprehensive whisper.

"Shane!" Moira again screamed.

"I'm here, my Lady." Shane appeared at the right door, peering in through the window.

"Thank the Ancient Heavens! We are under attack. I don't know how many but several are surely already hurt or dead. We must—" She broke off as she took in the sight of Shane more fully. Two other common servants, men, were on either side of him, one with a crossbow. Shane had a sword drawn in his left hand. "You are already armed? You—"

Moira stared at him with disbelieving eyes. "It's you?"

"Yes, I'm afraid so. I am sorry, Lady Kerr."

"I don't understand. Why would you do such a thing? Why—" But Moira knew the answer. In her heart, she knew; and, in her heart, she now had no doubt of the monster that occupied the Granite Throne. Terrified pleas for help, shouts of betrayal, and cries of fear filled the hold. She collected herself and spoke firmly with an air of authority.

"These are the Duke's men, then?"

Shane did not deny it. "Aye, my lady. Khans."

"Am I to be your captive? Hidden away and kept silent?"

Shane diverted his eyes. "We are to spare no one. I am sorry."

Moira thought she saw Shane waver. It was there, and then gone just as quickly. "And my son?" She asked, struggling not to let her lip quiver. "Swear to me you will spare my son." The hold master continued to not meet her gaze.

"Swear it!" Moira said vehemently.

"Hadik," Shane said with an almost broken voice, motioning to the Khan dressed as a servant on his left. The man immediately ran to the left side of the carriage, reached through the window and grabbed Shayla by the hair. He pulled her head through the open space violently and stabbed her under the soft spot of her chin, driving the blade up to the hilt.

"Shayla! *No!*" Lady Kerr screamed.

"Take her," Shane commanded. Hadik and the other Khan, one now on either side of the coach, grabbed the handles of the doors and yanked them open. These men were brutal. All Khans were trained in warfare and combat tactics and served loyally without hesitation. But, they were not wood-dwellers. No Arlethian served as a Khan due to the ancient creeds between the Senthary and Arlethians. The Khans would have little chance of catching her *if* she could escape the coach. But Shane, he posed the greatest threat.

An escape hatch above led to the roof. She slashed at the Khan, reaching in from the right side. He flinched back when she struck out, giving her only brief moments but enough for a wood-dweller. She undid the latch with nimble fingers and extricated herself as fast as she could bring herself up. She donned the dark cloak for camouflage amongst the night in a heartbeat's length.

"On the roof!" Hadik called out, followed by a sound of pain. She peeked over her shoulder to see that the postilion, the young boy who had been shot in the shoulder, had stabbed Hadik in the leg with the very arrow that had struck him.

"Run, my Lady!" the boy cried out. She sprang down from the top of the carriage, lightly sprinted two steps forward on the backs of the horses attached to the carriage and hit the ground of the courtyard in stride. She glanced back over her shoulder to see Hadik strike down the young boy who had bought her time with his life.

Hedron! I must find Hedron! She passed old lady Wendham lying face down in the courtyard, dead. Others were strewn about as well. The ground in front of her glistened with the blood of her servants, her people who had stayed with her through everything. Moira knew what this was, this move by Wellyn: a silencing of all possible resistance or opposition. Complete extermination of anyone who could possibly know...*know what?* She had come close enough to discovering something and it unnerved Wellyn to a degree that he felt forced to act before she was prepared. *Foolish!* she scolded herself.

"Hedron!" She called out. "To me!"

Snarls and growls followed by yelps of pain sounded through the night. The kennel master must have released the hounds. They wouldn't stop the interlopers, but slow them down enough perhaps. *Ancient Heavens, where is my son?* Perhaps he was already dead. If so, her heart would turn to stone as she relinquished all her fire for living.

A servant stepped out from a corridor in front of her holding a mace. Not a servant, another Khan. Moira had never been trained in any methods of battle or defense. She never had need of it before and mostly viewed it as a silly diversion for the men of the Realm. This did not lessen her drive to survive and find her son. Her speed increased, knowing that she must appear almost as a blur to the Khan in front of her. Extending the short blade with two hands out in front of her, she drove it into the man's chest with a scream. He tried to react but was too sluggish in his movement, underestimating his foe. Her attack was crude but effective. She shook with adrenaline and retrieved the knife from its mortal sheath.

Other Khans had closed some distance to her and were frighteningly close. She felt the vibration of a bowstring and sprang to the side, a reflex reaction she hoped moved her out of harm's way. The arrow skidded off the stone floor to her right. Before the archer could draw again she resumed her sprint, trying to calm herself enough to listen, to feel. She ran alongside the eastern wall, heading to a battlement at the northeastern part of the hold. A thick oak tree could offer her an opportunity to escape by scaling it and jumping down outside the north wall. If she could get into the forest, she would be free. She would seek shelter at Hold Therrium. And then another thought came to her. What if Therrium were part of all this? *Ancient Heavens, no!* Could Thannuel's own blood betray him? She could not be sure. She could not trust anyone, not yet. *Hedron, where are you?*

She spotted him, crouched behind a pillar that protruded out from the north wall, hidden in its shadow. There were fewer screams now, the silence being more terrible than the screams. The dead do not scream or plead for mercy, only the living. *I will do neither,* Moira swore.

She reached Hedron and huddled with him for a brief moment.

"Are you all right?" she asked, inspecting him quickly. "Are you hurt?"

He shook his head. She could see he was terror stricken.

"We have to move. Ready?"

He again shook his head.

She took his face in her hands. "Be brave, my son, as your father would have you be." She saw his eyes well up with fear. "I know," she comforted him, "but we must go. Now."

She peered out from their secluded spot and judged the way ahead of them to be clear. She still hoped to be able to reach the northeast corner and scale their way to safety. The elevated pathways were too far and probably guarded. They moved slowly at first, but soon they accelerated. A crossbow bolt barely missed Hedron's head and struck the stone wall on their left.

"I have them!" a gruff voice called out.

"Run!" Moira commanded her son. "Now!"

They both sprinted as fast as they could but they were still several hundred paces from their destination. Four Khans ran up from the south and managed to get in front of them. Each of the Khans had a sword drawn; one man had a crossbow slung over his shoulder. *Where is Shane?* Moira wondered with anxiety. She looked down and saw that Hedron had a short blade in his right hand. His father's. How many times had she scolded him for sneaking into the quartermaster's locker? *Good, he will likely need it.* The thought that her son would need to fight for his life against trained soldiers sickened her.

Something impacted Moira that she hadn't sensed vaulting toward her until too late. Shane smashed into her and slammed her body against the northern wall. Pain seared through her left shoulder from the impact. She thrust out her right hand that held the short blade and barely grazed Shane across his left cheek. He swore.

"*Krithia!*" Hedron cried for his mother in the ancient Arlethian.

Shane grabbed Moira's right hand with speed only another wood-dweller could track and twisted her arm behind her back, forcing the knife from her hand. She leaned forward from the pressure and tried to raise her left arm to blindly claw at Shane's face behind her, but the arm did not respond. Only then did she notice her shoulder hanging at an odd angle from her torso and realized it must have been dislocated from Shane's initial attack when she hit the stone wall.

Moira raised her head and looked out from behind her obsidian black hair. "Run!" she yelled to Hedron.

"*Krithia*, no!" he wailed.

"Run!" the Lady Matron of House Kerr again commanded. "Run." This last word was spoken softly and without emotion. Two Khans started to move toward Hedron, but he dashed between them with determined velocity and toward Shane. The Khans were too slow as mere humans to seize the boy. His voice broke as a primal scream shot forth from him. Swinging and slashing wildly with his father's short blade, he attacked Shane. There was no poise or grace in his press, just a savage animalistic ferocity that proved enough to force Shane to respond. His grip on Moira's right arm loosened, not much, but enough. She whipped her body under her arm, unwound the hold that Shane had on her and thrust her knee into his side with all her might. She was free. Hedron danced around Shane, careful not to get too close. A Khan tried to sneak up behind him and Moira watched as she saw him sense the danger closing in on him. He rolled to the side, regained his feet and was behind the Khan before he knew what had happened. Hedron's short blade found the back of the man's thigh, dropping him to the ground. The man cursed in agony as he writhed. Hedron ripped the weapon free and turned to run toward the great oak in the northeast corner.

In the too few moments that the men were distracted, Moira came to the wall and battered her dislocated shoulder against it. She was rewarded with a dull pop as the ball was forced back into the socket. If it weren't for the adrenaline, the pain would have no doubt collapsed her to the ground for several moments. She grabbed a torch from a sconce on the wall and swung it at the back of Shane's head. The explosion of embers looked like hundreds of fireflies in a panicked frenzy before turning to mere ash and escaping with the breeze. Shane stumbled down to one knee. He was not seriously wounded, but perhaps this would give them the time they so desperately needed. *Where can we go?* Therrium would be too obvious of a choice, as would Antious...but they would be better protected than here. She should have left when Antious asked her to, should have—

No, that would only have placed Kalisa and her children in danger. If they were after her, there's no doubt Antious and Lord Therrium were being closely watched. Aiden as well.

Fallen Ancients, I can't even turn to my family without putting them in harm's way! There is no one I dare seek out! And then she knew who to search for. They could have refuge there...but could they make it that far while being chased? Hunted?

Moira caught up with her son as they ran together for their lives. She felt the heavy footfall of three Khans behind her. Though they were much slower than her and Hedron, they were not in the open forest with long distances to run. They would catch them if they stumbled even once as they tried to make their escape. Her family's home was now a graveyard where her most loyal and loved companions lay slaughtered, murdered. *Grieve for them later.*

A vicious snarl was heard behind them as a dark, four-footed figure attacked one of the Khans. Shouts of surprise and pain followed, the dog still barking savagely. Master Elethol, the old kennel master, was right behind his hound, shouting curses as he attacked. She felt his movements stop suddenly and heard the dog's painful yelp before also coming still.

"This way," Hedron said. "There's an opening in the wall." Moira caught sight of the large oak. It was massive in diameter and grown through the hold's wall, asserting itself as part of the structure.

"There!" Hedron pointed near the base of the tree where a wily and gnarled root from the oak had surfaced just under the base of the wall, forming a low arch before diving back down into the ground again. Several large stones had been dislodged by the growth, forming a small opening in the wall. And through that opening was extended a small arm with an anxious hand outstretched. Moira's heart nearly stopped in her chest.

Hedron reached the opening and crawled through. Moira, only a split second behind him, crouched down and peered through the small opening. Hedron stared back at her in a crouched position, encouraging her to crawl through. *Was it a trick of the mind? Had I really seen—*

From around Hedron's rounded shoulders, a face framed by long dark hair emerged with large, beautiful eyes. She knew those eyes. They locked onto hers. Hot tears sprang to Moira's eyes but did not spill over. Her world began to spin. She dared not commit to belief. *If this is not real what I see before me I fear my heart will fracture.*

"*Krithia,*" Reign spoke with a quivering lower lip.

Moira gasped. Her soft, high voice shocked her, and for a moment she was completely blank. Unspeakable joy, utter relief, and wonderful confusion all traversed her soul, competing for placement amongst the fear and apprehension. Her heart thudded against her chest with erratic palpitations as she let out her pent-up breath.

The Khans' heavy footfall approaching from the west wrested her from her incoherence. *Roughly one hundred paces,* she judged from the vibrations.

"Gah—I—oh" was all she could managed between sharp breaths.

Ninety paces.

Moira began to stretch forth her arm through the breach toward her lost daughter, but retracted it when she saw how much she was shaking. Her whole frame seemed to grow weak, overwhelmed, as she struggled to contain the tide of questions and answers swirling inside her. She wondered for an instant if she were dreaming.

Sixty.

"Mother!" Hedron plead. "Mother, come now!"

She felt the tread of a shallower but more rapid gait join the vibrations of the approaching soldiers. Shane. He had obviously recovered.

Fifty.

"You're here," Moira finally spoke to Reign. "I knew you weren't—" she didn't dare speak the last word. Gratitude swept over her for this answered prayer from the Ancient Heavens, followed by bitterness. *This cannot be now! Why give her back to me just to take her from me again?*

Forty paces.

"Mother, please!" Hedron begged more frantically.

Shane will catch us, she realized. Perhaps not all of them if they kept running, but if he caught one, would the others continue to flee and abandon their captured kin to slaughter? She knew she would not, nor would her children. Their own loyalty and willingness to sacrifice themselves for each other would ironically be the death of them all. *We need more time!* And then, *No, only they need more time.*

The bitterness gave way to serenity as she made her decision. She removed the cloak from around her and draped it on her son's shoulders. He looked confused.

Her words were calm when she spoke. "Hedron, you are a Kerr of Arlethia, the last heir of this great house. You will remember what that means one day. Take your sister and run north, farther than you have ever gone. When you think you have gone as far north as you can go, you are halfway there. Persist, continue. Be vigilant and protect your sister. This is your duty now above all. Promise me you will do it."

"Why?" he questioned with tears streaming down his face. "You can make it—"

"Promise me!"

"I will," Hedron said.

"Remember, farther north than you think possible. She will find you." Before Hedron could question his mother, she turned to Reign. Saying nothing, she reached through the wall's opening and took her once-lost daughter's face in her hand and just stared. All the tender words she so desired to speak escaped her in this most desperate moment.

Twenty.

"Dhar vash alaqyn duwel partia." The blessing was spoken in ancient Arlethian, conveying more affection and unconditional love than possible with the cruder Sentharian language.

Ten.

"Now, my children, run and do not look back." They obeyed and she looked after them until they faded from her sight. It was only a few seconds.

Moira arose and turned to face Shane just as he arrived at her position, the Khans only a few steps behind. Blood stained his left cheek and his eyes burned wild with rage. She did not need to reach deep within herself to find courage. It radiated from her core, intermingling with the fury she had recently forged in the furnace of betrayal. She realized she had been wrong earlier about her highest calling, her purpose. It was, she knew now, to grant her children opportunity. In order to bestow this, they needed one thing above all. Time.

And so, with the courage and fury that gripped her, Moira Kerr raged like a lone lioness against a pack of jackals defending her cubs, purchasing every precious second she could for her little ones with her own life.

Though she fell, Moira Kerr never knew defeat.

ELEVEN

Molina Albrung

Day 18 of 4th Rising 407 A.U.

NEWS OF THE KERR HOLD IN FLAMES had spread quickly and reached Molina before the sun rose the following morning.

"Something is wrong," Molina told her father. "I must go to the hold and see Moira." She bustled about getting dressed and collecting supplies. Her father slept few hours of the night anymore.

"You will be gone long?" her father asked.

"As long as it takes," she answered. "This is Moira and Hedron we're talking about."

"Moira?"

"Yes, Moira. Your daughter, my sister?"

"I only have sons, though," he said.

Molina leaned down and kissed his forehead. "Of course you do." Her father's dementia was worse in the mornings. She had learned not to correct him when his illusions were strong within him. She and her older sister Moira were the only children he had fathered. Their mother had passed into the Light seven years ago.

"I'll tell Hedron you wish to see him more often."

"Okay. Who is that?"

Molina sighed. "Just your only grandson. No one important. I'll be back later." The way her father smiled she knew he was teasing her. He knew his condition and sometimes made light of it by his joking.

At least he has a sense of humor about it.

As she stepped out of her door, she came face to face with a ragged-looking man. She startled.

"Oh, I'm sorry. I didn't see you," Molina said. She nearly dropped her belongings. The man said nothing.

"Um, can I help you?" she asked hesitantly, slightly unnerved by the man's silence and staring.

"You are Molina Albrung, sister of the late Moira Albrung, now called Kerr?"

"I am Moira's sister, but if you're here to give me news of the hold I've already received word..." She broke off when what the visitor said finally sank in.

"I'm sorry, did you say the late..." her voice broke and her lip started to quiver. "No." Molina shook her head. "No, not Moira."

The messenger before her did not show any emotion or attempt to speak comfort. He had a slash across one cheek with dried blood crusting the wound. It looked fresh. As she more fully took in this man, she saw other wounds. Bruises around his neck, superficial scratches that looked like claw marks.

Fingernail wounds.

The man sneered at her stare and revealed several chipped teeth. Perhaps this man had been mugged and beaten on his way to deliver his message and she should offer aid, but a warning started to sound in her heart. The internal alarm was too late.

The man reached forth and grabbed her neck, choking off any cry for help. Reflexively, she brought her hands up to his and clawed at his arm. His grip felt like iron around her throat as she struggled for air. The sting of the short blade to her stomach drew her attention and tears flew from her eyes with the acute pain. Another stab and then another. Molina fought more feebly as the blood flowed from her. The blade felt cold on her hot insides. She stopped counting the punctures when her will to survive fled and she sought the blessed relief of death. Thoughts of her father were upon her mind as she faded into the Light.

———

Fherlay Kerr strode through the hallways of her home after running her errands. The morning was almost done and she would need to start the afternoon meal.

"Boys!" she called. "What do you want to eat?" She listened, felt. Their vibrations were not discernible.

"Benjyn! Beckett!"

As she passed the bedroom of her two boys on the way to the kitchen, she caught the glimpse of what appeared to be the aftermath of a hurricane.

"Those little terrors!" she said. "How many times have I told them they cannot go out before their room is cleaned? They just don't listen!" Her grumblings continued as she entered the disaster area and began to violently pick up the clothes, toys and other objects strewn about. Fherlay began to think of ways in which she might punish Benjyn and Beckett, but knew she would likely have to wait until their father returned home from work. Halek always knew how to handle them better. She would just get flustered trying to think of a punishment.

Or maybe, she thought, *I'll send them to work at Moira's for a span or two.* Halek had been Thannuel's uncle, though a young uncle to be sure. More of an age to be a cousin. Though Fherlay was a decade older than Moira and twelve years older than Moira's sister Molina, the three of them had been inseparable once Fherlay had married into the family.

"These boys are old enough to know better!" At fifteen and seventeen, they were certainly old enough to at least keep their room clean. Her agitation grew as she straightened their room. Maybe *three* span at Moira's hold, she considered. Lady Kerr would certainly need the help with such a large dwelling. Kerr Hold would no doubt dwindle in disrepair and maybe already had. She felt a pang of guilt for not visiting since Thannuel's funeral, but she did not do well with death. If anyone was worthy of the protection of the Living Light, it was certainly Thannuel and his family.

But where was the Light when they needed it? Young Reign missing and likely dead. Lord Kerr murdered.

Fherlay moved to Beckett's bed after finally clearing a path. His blankets were sprawled carelessly on his bed with his pillows mixed in. As she pulled the blankets up and prepared to fluff them, she saw a hand sticking out from under a sheet. After the blanket was frantically torn away from the bed, Fherlay saw the sheet with a rough outline of a body underneath. The sheet was dark red, still wet. The protruding hand was her youngest son's.

"Beckett!" she screamed hysterically. "Beckett! Help!"

She turned to the other bed in the room and knew underneath its disheveled covers she would find her other son. She could make out the outline under the blankets now that she knew what to look for. And the realization dawned on her that what she stood in the middle of was not the remnants of her sons' poor housekeeping, but the scene of a struggle for life and death. She cried out and sank to her knees. It was then she felt a tremor from the closet. She looked up just as a robe-wearing demon sprang forth. The weight of the sudden grief thrust upon her seemed to anchor her and she did not move. The end was swift.

———

Halek walked casually home from the Roniah Crossing in the mid-afternoon sun, his early morning shift on the river completed. It had been a good catch: several river trout, carp, even a hydraf, which he knew his wife Fherlay did not care for. He could easily trade it at Riley's Cove tomorrow.

He had just crossed into the forest as the alien vibrational signature echoed through the ground. It was heavy footed and about a hundred and twenty paces away, and it moved with startling speed.

A bear? he wondered because of the thumping, but knew this was wrong by the speed of the creature. He stopped walking and put his catch down against the base of a tall eucalyptus tree. A trickle of nervous tension danced perilously close to fear within him as the vector of the vibrations did not change. He could now tell the creature that headed toward him was determined and that he was the target. This was unmistakable in the signature now pulsing through the earth.

Halek did not hesitate. Just as his attacker came into view, he ascended the tree he had laid his catch down against until he was the height of two men. He could clearly see that what barreled toward him was a man—but perhaps only in form. In order to move with the speed portrayed he would have to be an Arlethian; but the beast before him was not one of his kind. He thought perhaps he was right in his initial thought of a bear from the thudding gait produced. He climbed higher at the thought that perhaps this person could jump with supernatural ability as well as run, and unsheathed his fishing blade from his belt. Instead, the man crashed into the tree with such force that Halek lost his hold and fell a few feet before regaining his grip. A cold sweat broke out along the nape of his neck as fear grabbed him.

"I'll shake you loose!" the man growled as he continued to batter the tree with fists and head.

"What do you want?" Halek yelled.

"Your fear!" shouted the man between hits. The tree shook violently. "Your blood! All you can give before you expire at my hands!" Bark flew out from the tree with every blow the crazed man landed, creating small craters in the trunk before they were widened and deepened by the following volley.

"What have I done? Who are you?"

The man stopped and looked up. Halek saw scars of some create covering the man's face and head. "No more than your family has done. Your name has brought this upon you."

"My family?" Halek asked, his voice nearly breaking. "What do you know of my family?"

"There was nothing to know. I was Charged with them. That was enough."

Halek dropped down from the tree and landed inaudibly, the thin curved fishing blade gripped tightly in his hand.

"What is this you are speaking? What do you mean, 'Charged'?"

"They were given to me by my Liege, just as you have been. I smell it, your fear, your anger, even your confusion. It's all a grand spectrum of ecstasy to me, Kerr. Thank you." The man bowed slightly in a show of mock deference.

It was the way he had said "Kerr" that hit Halek. A realization of the circumstances teased his thoughts but he could not put it all together. It was slippery in his mind.

"Does my family live?" he asked.

"Only if you believe in something beyond this world. I personally do not." The predatory smile that grew on the man's face was wicked.

Halek lunged at the man, his blade thrusting through the air faster than the sound of his anguished scream. He missed. Before he could retract his arm, the large man grabbed his wrist and with a palm thrust of his other arm, broke Halek's elbow. His blade fell to the earth. The pain was searing as it shot through his arm but a low grunt was all that escaped his lips. Forcing his hips to rotate, he ripped his arm free and danced from the immediate reach of this monster.

His broken arm hung at a disturbing angle but he still had his legs. He ran toward his home but before he had sprinted five strides he felt the heavy gait of the man behind him. It was not long before the hand of this creature found him and pulled him down by his hair. He hit the ground with such force that the wind flew from his lungs and a sharp pain shot up his back. He attempted to roll and bring himself upright, but his hips and legs did not respond.

When he had gained enough of his breath back, he asked, "Why?"

"We have been over this," came the answer. "Your name is enough reason. But I am not one that cares for reasons. I am content to simply carry out my Charge."

"From who? Who would want me dead?" he wheezed.

"Only the Stone of Orlack may command me. And that, Kerr, is as much as you will be privileged to know."

Halek felt a foot come crushing down on his throat. Skin was torn, cartilage crushed, and bones broken. A final *snap* came and he mercifully felt nothing further as his sight dimmed to blackness.

TWELVE

Reign

Day 24 of 4th Rising 407 A.U.

THE COLD AIR BURNED Reign's lungs as she ran, trailing behind Hedron. Her father's cloak flapped in the wind despite Hedron having adjusted it to not hang so long on him by folding it over on itself. Their speed of travel had slowed to what would be considered a fast sprint among most races, but slow for any wood-dweller. How long had it been? Days? Closer to a span, surely. They had traveled generally north ever since escaping the hold, ever since Reign had been reunited with her mother for precious few moments before being cruelly torn from her yet again. Their route was circuitous, plundering supplies from villages and markets when they could. Normally, anyone of want needed only ask in the Western Province, but their presence could not be made known. They would almost certainly be recognized if spotted and word would eventually reach those who sought them.

"Hedron, I have to stop!" she cried out.

"No, we can't. Not yet."

"The sun is going down. We have to, please. I'm hungry and I can't feel my feet." Reign wasn't sure if her feet were numb from the cold that had found them the farther north they traveled or if they were just unaccustomed to the near constant usage she had demanded of them recently.

Hedron stopped, to Reign's surprise and relief. He put his hands on his hips and turned around, heaving for air.

"The air is colder. It feels thinner, harder to breathe," he said in between gasps.

"It burns," Reign said. "I don't want to breathe." She hunched over, leaning her upper body toward the ground and bowed her head.

Hedron laughed briefly before stopping and bringing a hand to his left cheek. It was chapped and almost cracked from the cold and wind. The laughing had aggravated it.

"We're safest when traveling at night," he grimaced, knowing the discomfort of being amid the dropping temperatures and wind.

"How much food do we have?" Reign asked.

Hedron took the coarse satchel he had stolen in Calyn their first day on the run off his shoulder and opened it.

"Not much. We haven't passed a village or city for two days. A few apples, a crust of bread. At least there's frost for water. One benefit of the cold, I guess."

The twins were hungry, but not yet starving. The night they had barely escaped from their hold was spent deep in the forest outside Calyn. Before sunrise the next morning, they had ventured into Calyn in search of food. Reign knew they would have to steal but took no pleasure in such a thing. They had no krenshell with which to purchase goods or supplies. Hedron had left her secluded between several crates behind a building as he snuck through the alleys between merchants that were setting up for the day's market. The young Kerr girl was devastated by what she overheard as she lay in the last moments of darkness before the sun bathed the world in light.

"Did no one survive?" she heard one voice ask.

"Not from what I have heard. They resisted when the Khans came," answered another. *"All the servants, Lady Kerr, everyone fought back."*

"All dead? The servants? The boy?" a third voice said.

The second voice answered: *"To the last person, if the reports are true. It's hard to believe Lady Kerr was part of her husband's plotting, but why resist if you're innocent? Even the servants were implicated."*

"Just a shame," replied the first voice. *"But the boy? The girl has been dead for cycles and now her brother as well? Is there no Kerr left?"*

"No survivors," the second said again. *"But,"* he continued with a conspiratorial tone, *"there were Khans in the forest north of the hold for hours, say the rumors. Why do you suppose that was?"*

"Searching?" the third voice asked. *"But, searching for what?"*

"For whom, you mean," the second voice corrected. *"Why search when all are being reported as 'regrettably killed'?"*

There had been no answer to this last inquiry, or none that she could hear as she sat hidden in an alley of Calyn. Reign felt sick and nearly vomited the nothingness in her stomach as she held in her grief. She had been clinging to the hope that her mother was alive, and thought of perhaps returning to find her. But no, she was dead and there was little time to grieve. In her solitude, she wept as silently as she could for her mother. She didn't realize how much time had passed until Hedron returned with the same sack he now carried full of different food supplies.

"We need more food," Reign said, stating the obvious. "How will we get more?" There was fear in her voice, the anxiety of a little girl. She knew Hedron felt much of the same inside him. It was impossible for one of them to shield feelings from the other.

"I'm not sure, yet," he answered.

"Where are we?" Reign surveyed their surroundings and saw trees spread around but thinly populated. It was a forest, but too dispersed to be anything from their homeland. The ground was relatively flat with a few occasional rolling hills. Patches of frost clung to the ground and trees. She knew Hedron was listening, feeling as far out as he could through the ground, as was she. They would get no better sensitivity by attempting to speak with a tree. They were outside their forests and trees did not speak here. She felt nothing.

"I'm not sure of that either," Hedron admitted. "I just know we're two or three days north from the hold as the crow flies. But, we've been running for seven, I think."

I was right, Reign realized. *Closer to a span.*

"If I had to guess I would say we're somewhere in the Northern Province, maybe the north parts of the Eastern Province. But it's just my guess."

"Why? Why must we keep going?" Reign asked. "All we've done is run!"

"Because it's what mother said to do. You were there, too. You heard her."

"I don't care, we should go back for her. She's looking for us, she has to be."

"She's not looking for us, sister." Hedron knelt down to look up at Reign as she was still hunched over. He could not see her face through her hair. "She's not looking. She's gone." Reign stood up and turned away from him.

"I don't believe you."

"I don't want to believe it either, but we both know it. You heard what they were saying in Calyn." *Dead...to the last person.*

"It could have been just rumors!" Reign said stubbornly as her voice started to break.

Hedron didn't answer. He stood up and turned his face north again. Without looking, he reached in the satchel and gave Reign an apple as well as the last of the bread.

"As soon as you're done, we're going to start running again. Eat slowly."

After a couple bites into her apple, Reign stopped suddenly. She fixated her concentration on something, a sensation in the ground. Faint but there. Yes, it was definitely there.

"Hedron—"

"I feel it," he whispered. "From the west."

Hedron unsheathed his short blade and deftly scaled the tree closest to them for a better vantage point. He leaped about ten paces to another and continued to concentrate. Reign sat looking up at her brother.

"What do you see?" she called out to him softly. Try as she might, she could not accurately identify what they felt. It was difficult without the sensitive interlocking root systems of the forests in the west to aid her.

"Nothing. Wait…" her brother said. He looked back at his sister with wide and excited eyes. "It's a deer!" he exclaimed. "A doe!"

Reign stood up and dropped her apple. She could see intent in Hedron's eyes. "What are you going to do?"

"Get dinner," he replied with a look that seemed to ask, *What do you think?* He jumped down from the tree and landed with a sound not audible other than to a wood-dweller. The doe, probably sixty paces away, looked up as Hedron hit the ground. He sat still, crouched in his father's cloak. Slowly, he untied it from around his shoulder and let it fall to the ground. The doe went back to searching for food by breaking ground frost with a hoof and searching beneath. Hedron slowly advanced around the animal, closing in on it from the rear. The wind blew at Hedron's back and he realized his mistake too late. The doe raised her head with a start and jolted forward, alerted by his scent.

"No!" he cried out and chased the deer. Malnourished and physically weakened, his pursuit presented a significant challenge. He kept his prey in sight but could not seem to gain ground. He was about to end his chase and give up when he saw the animal fall. Reign stood over it, her short blade buried in the deer's neck. Hedron reached her a moment later.

"What? How? Where did you come from?" he asked, perplexed.

"You were losing our dinner," she said. The doe was still struggling but weakly so. "Now what do we do?"

"I've only seen father do it," Hedron replied. "I've never actually—"

"I killed it. Figure out the rest," Reign demanded. She turned away and put her hand over her mouth, nauseous from the adrenaline of the moment.

"Are you all right?" her brother asked. She held out a hand behind her and motioned for him not to come nearer.

"Just figure it out," she muttered.

The days turned to spans, and spans to cycles. For much of the time, the Kerr twins wandered aimlessly, well fed through the High Season as they adapted to life on their own. For Reign, living in the open was nothing new by virtue of the last many cycles. But, as the clouds changed with the waning of the Dimming Season and the Low Season being ushered in, Hedron and Reign found themselves with little food and no shelter in the freezing weather. Even during the High Season, the Northern Province barely received enough warmth to compare with the weather of the Rising Season they were used to in the West, where life became more full and blooming things manifested themselves. Game became less prevalent as the climate changed, most seeking hibernation or more southern parts.

Most nights they huddled together in some cave or crevice that gave insult to the word shelter, until they collapsed from consciousness in exhaustion from shivering, having no means to create fire. They awoke in blankets of snow and, though cold, the snow mercifully insulated them against the wind. Still, they continued north, clinging to the last plea of their dead mother.

Early one morning deep in the Low Season, Reign awoke startled, her hands and feet frozen to a point of numbness that she was almost used to. She brought a hand to her chest and rubbed gently. She had felt something, hadn't she? Some pressure against her chest and head. A dream perhaps—but no, it was more than a dream. The light of a new day was starting to shine through the gray clouds and falling snow. Hedron lay still, sleeping next to her, curled into a ball. His face was pale, almost blue with cracked cheeks and lips.

Reign scanned their surroundings as she tried to shake the feeling that something real had just touched her. *Pushed* on her. It had to only be a dream. There was nothing—

Movement caught her eye. The sparse trees had no leaves where she lay. Nothing else save rocks and snow existed here. Nothing else except the gray wolves about a stone's throw from their position. She counted five.

Reign shook Hedron. Then again. He protested by groaning, not wanting to awaken to another cold morning. Sleep was an escape, even if temporary.

"I'm scared," Reign whispered, her breath's vapor almost spelling fear in the air. She shivered, but not only from the cold.

"Go back to sleep," Hedron mumbled in a daze.

"Wolves," Reign whispered again. She did not take her eyes from the foremost wolf that stood in front of the others. In normal circumstances, even a child wood-dweller would likely be able to outrun a wolf or predator of almost any create. But the late Thannuel Kerr's twin children were starved, malnourished, cold, and emotionally drained from their flight.

Reign pushed down on Hedron's face with the palm of her hand. This time, Hedron sat straight up ready to slug his sister. Instead, he saw her face, pale as death. He recognized this particular shade of pale as fear, not cold. Following her gaze, he caught sight of the pack. The largest wolf, head lowered and shoulders hunched, bared his teeth and snarled.

"Don't move, Reign." It was not even a whisper that came from Hedron.

"I can't, I can't, I can't," she said shaking her head. "I can't..."

The wolves charged, snarling and snapping at one another as they closed the distance, each vying to be the first to reach their prey but not daring to pass the leader.

Hedron sprang up with speed, grabbing rocks in both hands. Fingers nearly frozen made precision challenging, but he hurled them nonetheless with all the force he could muster. His short blade had frozen to breaking several nights past, leaving him with only the weapons the earth put within his reach. Reign sat in what looked to be almost nonchalance until the last moments before the wolves pounced upon her. *It* pushed against her again, the same force that awakened her earlier, and somehow seemed desperate. She knew this time that it was something foreign, something real. It enraged her.

The wolf sprang directly at her, arms and claws outstretched with teeth gnashing. Right as the wolf should have throated her, Reign slammed her back down against the frozen earth too fast for the wolf's teeth to find purchase. The wolf slipped a few inches forward from its momentum so that its belly was directly over her. Reign did not hesitate. With all the strength of an eleven-year-old girl, she grabbed her short blade from under her torn and tattered tunic, and slammed it upward into the wolf's abdomen, its hot blood spilling onto Reign's hands bringing temporary blessed relief from the cold. It howled with pain. Reign retrieved her blade and rolled out from under the bleeding beast. It collapsed down and whimpered in pain. She began to run.

Hedron screamed in pain. Reign turned to see one wolf dragging him by his ankle and another tearing viciously at his cloak. He was wailing on the ground, trying to free himself. Reign ran toward him with her blade in hand, but felt the warning vibrations too late. Another wolf jumped into her, knocking her down. Instantly yet another was on her back clawing at her clothing, digging to find hot flesh. She screamed in terror.

Hedron kicked violently, blood flowing from his lower leg. He managed a kick that caught one of the wolves square in the snout, sending it back whimpering, but only for a moment. Hedron rolled as the other wolf tore his tunic free from his torso, leaving only his cloak upon him, it being nearly shredded past recognition. He rose to his feet and stumbled as fast as he could toward Reign's two attackers. He could feel his own two wolves practically at his back.

Tackling the wolf on Reign's back allowed her a moment of respite to crawl forward and get her footing. The wolf threw Hedron from its back with little effort and clawed across his chest, finding purchase against his flesh. He grunted in pain, but the adrenaline dulled the full effect the wound would have normally carried. With no weapon of any create, Hedron bellowed a cry and attacked, driving all his weight into the beast, praying it would be enough.

Run, Reign! She can outrun them, he knew. It would only take a short amount of time to build up the speed necessary. *Run!*

Reign did run, but not away from the wolves. She sprang against the wolf that Hedron had charged, falling on its back, and reached her hand around front, driving her short blade into its throat. Hedron grabbed her hand to add his strength and pressed the blade until only the hilt protruded. He pushed the dead wolf from him, but loss of blood and exhaustion were overcoming him. Blood flowed liberally from the gash on his chest. He felt dizzy and weak in the knees. *Only three left*, he wearily thought. Just before slipping from consciousness and collapsing, he heard Reign scream.

———

The wolf's jaws grabbed her leg, tearing flesh and yanking so forcefully that she fell hard upon the ice-ridden earth. Her short blade was knocked from her hands by the force of her fall. The wolves advanced slowly, encircling her. As she wearily raised herself to her knees, she pleaded for Hedron to come, but she couldn't see or feel him. *It* pushed against her again, more urgently. Forcefully. Defiance still held her, and she fought back against it, even now in her exhausted state.

She felt the presence come toward her from behind, even through the frozen ground. The vibrations told her it was moving with intent and purpose. She could tell it was another wolf, a sixth. Reign sat with ironic calm and waited. *It will only be a few moments, then over.*

A wolf of size exceeding the others jumped over Reign and landed in front of her, placing itself between her and the remaining three gray wolves. The new wolf, whiter than the driven snow and the size of a small bear, pulled its lips back and uttered forth a deep guttural growl that gave the other wolves pause. The white wolf stepped forward, slowly advancing, forcing some distance between Reign and her attackers. Snarling and snapping in threatening gestures as they were driven backward, the gray wolves did not take kindly to this interruption. Still, the white wolf did not relent and continued to press them. Suddenly, one of the gray wolves made a start to run around the new wolf toward Reign. It was cut short in its effort, as the white wolf jutted to the side and flanked the wolf just as it jumped in midair, throating it before it hit the ground. The blood pooled around the now dead wolf and flowed to the paws of the white wolf, its pure white coat a stark contrast against the now crimson snow. It turned its attention back to the remaining two. With blood dripping from its white fur around its jaws, the wolf growled another deep warning. The two remaining gray wolves ceased their growling and lowered their heads toward the larger white wolf. Their ears almost lay flat against their heads. With a last deep bark, the bear-sized wolf sent them running away whimpering.

The white wolf stared after the two fleeing gray wolves for a time, then turned to Reign. Her adrenaline had faded and she was too weary to be afraid any longer. Again, she closed her eyes, knowing she was the prize won by the larger wolf. *Just a few moments, then it will be over. No more cold. No more pain.*

But the wolf did not attack. Instead, it turned from her, its nose searching for a scent. Finding it, the wolf quickly ran to where Hedron lay unconscious. With its snout, the wolf sniffed Hedron for a few moments, licked his face and then howled. It howled for several moments before Reign finally came to herself and realized she was not being eaten. She arose, shakily, and limped over to where Hedron lay nearly naked on the ice. He was wounded badly, but the blood had frozen upon his torn flesh, closing his wounds for the time. The white wolf howled again.

In the distance, Reign felt the presence of a human approaching. An elderly person, she guessed. She reached down for Hedron and lifted him to her, cradling him against the cold. Their innate bond felt frayed to the utmost tether, weakened and about to snap. His lips were blue and his cheeks purple and white. She tried to keep him warm, but she was smaller than him and had little chance of protecting him from the elements.

Reign was overcome with anger more than sadness. "You cannot leave me! You cannot leave me!" she shouted over and over again in a staccato rhythm as she beat her fist upon his wounded chest. "You cannot leave! Everyone leaves me! Not you, too! *Not you!*" Her tears were freezing to her face before they could fall as she screamed her demands to her dying brother.

"Not you, too!"

And then, she could stand no more of the mental, physical and emotional onslaught, and she passed out with her head upon Hedron's shallowly rising chest.

———

When the old woman arrived, she looked down at the children. The wolf, which stood several heads taller than either youngling, sat over them with its large chest lowered gently over the girl as she lay on top of the boy. The bushy tail was also wrapped around her shoulders, providing protection and warmth.

"Up, Elohk," she said. The wolf removed itself from its position of covering the younglings. The woman pulled the girl off the boy, who was gravely wounded in his chest, though they both had sustained wounds. The boy was bare-chested except for a dark-green shredded cloak loosely hung around his shoulders. She turned him on his side gently and saw the sigil sewn into the cloak. Jayden gasped. She knew the sigil of House Kerr, but even more, she knew *this* cloak around the young boy.

"Thannuel," she said out loud.

The wolf whined softly. It knew the scent the cloak carried, although it did not know the boy in it. The scent alone, the old woman knew, would be enough for the wolf to instinctively recognize that the boy and girl were important and worthy of its protection. It howled another long note that echoed through the morning.

THIRTEEN

Shane

Day 18 of 3rd Low 407 A.U.

IT WAS A COMPLEX SEA of thought that careened within Shane. Currents threatened to send him into fits of madness, from whence he feared never to resurface if swept there. He struggled to remain conscious. Not to avoid sleep, but to keep a grasp on his identity.

"Why have you summoned me here?" he asked the older, bald man in front of him. They stood in the charred courtyard of the ruined Hold Kerr, no one else present. Shane briefly wondered how Tyjil had come to be here, so far from Wellyn's hold. No horse or carriage was present, none that he could see anyway. *I could do it*, Shane admitted to himself. *I could break him, extinguish him. Snuff out the pathetic man's flickering flame of life before he knew what happened. I have done it before.* But then the former fisherman realized it was quite unlike Tyjil to put himself knowingly in danger, or even the smallest perception of potential danger. It was unlikely he was alone after all, though his wood-dweller senses could still not decipher anyone else's presence. If someone else was here, they were in place before he arrived and had not moved since.

The fire's ravages from earlier this year remained undeniably visible. Khans had executed a controlled burning of the hold after Moira and her servants were killed. The High Duke had ordered the use of fire, to symbolically purge the Realm of the treachery that had been brewed within these walls. The evening's mild breeze carried the lingering scent of ash mingled with dead foliage. Vines, shrubbery and frondescence of all kinds were either consumed in the fire or had faded to lifelessness against the hold's walls. The sun's light had recast itself to the deep orange luminescence that accompanied the last hours of light before first moon.

Shane did not like this place, not since he had carried out the first part of his mission. The fires he and the Khans set had consumed all around the hold and the dead within its walls. But the stone of the edifice remained—its tint black and brindle from the furnace, covered in soot—and Shane did too. He realized he was now more closely related to stones and dead things than the forest and things of life. He visualized the flames that leaped upon Moira's body, how they had reduced her to ash and bone. *Why? How could I have done such an act? I am only a fisherman; I am only—*

Only a predator! a louder voice within him said, one that had been increasing in volume internally.

"It's only appropriate, of course, that we meet where you first learned of your higher capabilities, yes?" Tyjil answered. When he smiled, Shane fully expected to see a forked tongue slither out of his mouth.

"I cannot be away long," Shane said. "My absence will be noticed."

"Isn't it nice to be *noticed* for once in your life?" Tyjil jeered. "I'm sure that woman does not miss you. She probably does better on her own, yes? Certainly those feral offspring you call children—"

"My wife's name is Ahnia," Shane interjected.

"That might be true if you had a wife. That was the old person, remember? No, of course you don't, you were so forgettable then. You are reborn and have no need for family, just like me. You bask in the freedom with me, don't you, brother?"

"If it is true that I have no family, then you have nothing to chain me with any longer," Shane answered.

Tyjil smiled, almost impressed. "See, you have started to think in reason, in plots and ploys. Is it not exhilarating?"

"What, Tyjil, do you want?" Shane snapped, growing tired of this interaction.

"Ah yes, now we come to it. I need to know your progress, of course. You are well embedded into the hold guard?" Tyjil asked while raising an eyebrow.

"I am. I sent word by wing over four span ago. You must have received it."

"So I did."

"Then why bring me here to ask questions that you already know the answers to?" Shane asked, not able to hide the disgust in his voice.

"How did it come to pass?" Tyjil pressed on, ignoring Shane's question.

"It was as the message said. I begged a position from Master Aiden. He refused at first because of my lack of training with steel and my age, but I persisted. Eventually, I prevailed and he agreed." Shane did not tell him of the true struggle it had been to convince Aiden to allow him to join the hold guard without appearing anxious or desperate. He had thought Aiden might have suspected something and that his efforts would be thwarted, but the young master of the hold guard did indeed finally agree to accept him in their ranks. He had to train longer and harder than the other guards, and Aiden pushed him to near a breaking point every day. Shane had no doubt it was in an effort to force him out, to force him to give up. But Aiden did not know the motive that drove Shane to succeed, nor the strength of it.

Tyjil approached nearer to Shane, and walked around him slowly. He looked up at Shane and reached a hand out slowly to Shane's midsection without looking away from Shane's eyes. Tyjil grabbed the bottom of the man's tunic and lifted it up. He inspected Shane's body for a brief moment. Shane tensed.

"No, not the soft fisherman at all anymore, are we? Tell me, do you find yourself with eager female companionship now that you have a body more desirable to such things?"

Shane slapped Tyjil's hand away and stepped back with speed that Tyjil could not track with his eyes. A slight tremor shot through the ground from somewhere in the west side of the hold, faint but distinct.

So, the snake is not alone.

"Tell me my wife and children are safe and unharmed," Shane demanded. "Tell me true, or I swear by the Cursed Heavens I'll crush your throat before your escort has a chance to react."

"Good!" Tyjil remarked, bringing his hands together in front of his face. He looked utterly thrilled. "You have truly come far, my boy. Is not the strength you now possess and the will to use it a gift? Are you not grateful for who you are becoming, an apex predator? Certainly you see the wisdom in my methods now, yes?"

Shane did not answer, but continued to stand still. He was reaching out to sense any other motion not natural to their environment. Nothing.

"But do not become overconfident, fisherman. My escort, as you say, may prove more of a challenge than you anticipate."

There was something in the tone of Tyjil's voice that gave him pause and checked him.

"Tell me of my family!" Shane again demanded.

"Oh, very well." Tyjil put up his hands as if in surrender. "You would do well to forget them, though. You will not need them for motivation much longer. They will soon forget you, I am sure, yes?"

Shane took a step toward Tyjil, a menacing look radiating from him.

"Uh, uh, uh, now, now," Tyjil admonished, his voice oozing with condescension. "I'm only trying to help you, my boy." He reached inside his robe and produced a small rolled parcel of parchment. Shane snatched it from him. He unraveled it hastily and turned his back to Tyjil. The words were in his wife's handwriting.

"We are all well and await your return, my love."

Shane took in the message and had a few moments of blessed relief to the tension and stress that accompanied him almost constantly. He tightened his fist around the message and brought it to his chest as he gazed upward to the sky, a distant look upon him. Then he whirled on Tyjil.

"When was this written? How long ago? How do I know she wasn't forced to write this and communicate false assurance?" Shane was shaking as he held the message in his clenched fist out toward Tyjil.

The Duke's advisor, however, was not impressed and yawned as if bored.

"And now, I must take my leave. Hold fast, my son, and become very acquainted with Hold Therrium. It may likely be years before the next stage develops. You are a wood-dweller, true, but never forget to whom you truly belong."

The old man looked to the west and said, "Maynard." From the shadows stepped a large man with a thick, dark-hooded robe. The man walked with strength, Shane observed. It was a strange description, he thought, but could not think of another way to describe it. A vile power seemed to exude from this hooded figure. He could not see any part of this man, just the rough, blockish outline portrayed from beneath the long robe. Though he could not see the man's face, Shane's breath faltered, followed by a cold sweat on the back of his neck. Its presence was amplified by the wind, sending a chill through the wood-dweller's torso.

"Years?" Shane asked. A shudder in his voice betrayed a feeling of desperation he was trying to conceal.

"Remember, Shane, only ponder on the *how*, not the *what*. You will be transfigured to whom you need to be, the High Duke's instrument in bringing a new glorious age. But, you still need these next years to grow, to flourish within yourself." With that, Tyjil turned and exited the hold with the hooded man in tow.

Shane lowered his head as the last slivers of fiery orange daylight dwindled to night.

FOURTEEN

Shilkath

Day 29 of 4th Low 407 A.U.

THE BORATHEIN NAHGI LEADER called his closest warriors together in his thickly insulated tent. Skins of all create lined the inside of the massive mobile structure. Shilkath had given up his grand palace over a decade ago as the changing land demanded it, but retained his mantle as Deklar among the people of his nahgi. Other nahgi had done the same. His people were forced to become nomadic and, although the Borathein were hardened by the centuries in a mostly fallow and frozen land, having refused to leave with their kin centuries before, the time had definitely come for change. For this purpose he called his nahgi's warriors together in council. He would need them now for a great undertaking. Holy Vyath had shown him a path, one that would avenge their fallen kin and surely lead to the Shores of Thracia.

Shilkath's tent, in the center of the nahgi, was large enough to accommodate a dozen families and their beasts, even several Alysaar. The winged animals stood as tall as the largest horse and then half again. Though their bodies resembled more a thick-scaled dog with a long neck and stunted stout, their most unique feature was a beard of sharp, jagged bones under the maw. Petting an Alysaar under the chin was simply out of the question.

151

Shilkath waited until the others had arrived before stoking a fire. Each warrior sat on a stone covered by at least one fur skin around the fire and waited. Their beards were long and full of evidences of their various conquests, some more decorated than others. None, however, surpassed Shilkath's in weight or number of ornaments. Each symbol in his beard, crafted of bone and tanned skin, was in the shape of the family or nahgi's name that had been defeated. The bone and skin needed to proclaim each victory had been harvested from among the defeated dead. Brutality was their way of life and the Deklar reveled in it.

When all had arrived and were seated, Shilkath opened the skins that hung over his shoulders and across his chest. A thick tunic was revealed underneath that he grabbed and rent halfway down from the top. The warriors gathered around him saw the gash across his chest, obviously a fresh wound that was barely a day old, if that. They said nothing but knew what he had done.

"I have sworn to the God of Vengeance a holy pact and undertaken a Griptha upon the altar of ice and bone this very day," Shilkath announced. Some of the warriors looked down into the fire.

"We will unite the tribes," he continued. "When we have their nahgi added to ours, we will cross the Ice Desert into the lands of our fallen kin and thrust them to the frozen plains of Kulbrar." He was a man of deliberate words, not wasting the warm air inside him by speaking beyond what was necessary.

A younger warrior, Mindok, spoke. "The other nahgi will resist your leadership."

"We will require it of them," Shilkath answered.

"Great Shilkath, they will not heed your words. You are not their Deklar."

To this, Shilkath stood and, without a word, exited the tent. The frigid evening air greeted him, clamoring for attention as it bit at his face's exposed flesh, but the hard Deklar did not take notice. Only a few paces outside his tent, obediently sat his Alysaar. Hawgl grunted an acknowledgement as his master approached and shivered his wings.

"No," Shilkath said. "We do not ride today."

He felt Hawgl's disappointment. His Alysaar was one of the largest Shilkath had ever seen, certainly the largest in his nahgi. The beast had proven immensely stubborn to break and many had failed before him, but Shilkath was not to be refused. By and by the beautiful winged weapon of an animal capitulated until the two had formed a bond that Shilkath felt was stronger than any he had with one of his own kind.

He pulled a knife free from its sheath and slashed two ropes that secured a large rolled bundle of blankets across the beast's back. It fell to the frozen ground with a heavy thud. Hulking the mass over his right shoulder after sheathing his blade, he spoke a guttural command to the Alysaar, admonishing the creature to remain. It gave its agreement through a heavy exhaled shudder.

Entering the tent, the Deklar found that the scene around his fire had not changed. All were in silence, a few with uncertain looks manifested on their faces. Shilkath dropped his burden close to the fire and unrolled the blanket. Revealed inside was a dead man with a beard nearly as full as Shilkath's.

Mindok, normally reserved, stood in surprise. "Is this not your cousin, Aksath? Is he not the Deklar of the Drabhine tribe?"

Prethor, Shilkath's nephew, agreed, finding his flail and spear. "Surely their entire Drabhine nahgi will be upon us any moment!"

Instead of answering, Shilkath again freed his knife and sheared the dead man's beard, an insult worthy of death. After this act, the Deklar proceeded to liberate three of the dead man's fingers from his left hand and skinned them with a precision that would awe any warrior of the Borathein. Before many moments, the skin and tendons had been cut away, leaving just the bones and a bit of cartilage. Using strands from the hacked beard, Shilkath lashed the bones into a crude triangle that flexed slightly where the knuckles and joints were. Next, a patch of skin was extricated from the dead Deklar's forehead in the shape of the Drabhine tribe's sigil and was then fastened to the boney triangle. For good measure, Shilkath next removed both the man's ears and secured one to each side of the base of the finger-boned triangle. Finally, he wove the concoction into his already heavily laden beard. All of this was done within less than half the time a log smaller than a child's forearm would have taken to be consumed in their fire.

"If I must, I will add the bones of each nahgi's Deklar to my beard. I have sworn this Griptha to Vyath." This was not spoken with vibrato or with raising fists to the skies. It was spoken with calm confidence and certainty. "Aksath did not understand. Now he does, as does his tribe. They are sworn to me as their new Deklar."

The others were silent until Prethor again spoke.

"They are not weak, Uncle. Those who defeated our kin. Once you have united the tribes, are you sure we can conquer across the Ice Desert?"

"We don't have a choice," answered Bellathia, one of the many female warriors. She was perhaps their most skilled Alysaar rider. "Our lands will be completely uninhabitable within a decade."

"They have been for decades already," Shilkath corrected.

"We could look elsewhere," Prethor said. "There have to be other lands we could discover."

"No," Deklar Shilkath snapped, visibly annoyed by this suggestion. Was Prethor afraid? "You forget the Griptha. This is not only about finding new land. My holy Pact of Vengeance has been made. Vyath rules in this."

The Borathein had many gods, a wide pantheon. Vyath was the god of war and vengeance, and with whom Shilkath had made his pact, his Griptha, seeking Vyath's blessing.

"Our brothers were betrayed more than four centuries ago," Shilkath went on. "We did not know more than a hundred years after their fall that they were even extinct because of the Ice Desert's rapid expanse. They fell by conquest, which is honorable in the sight of Vyath. Those who defeated them, these Senthary, gained the right of the land. But, the Arlethians, we know, still live, having betrayed our kin and joined the invaders. They have maintained their lands through treachery. We are strong enough now to erase all from the land below the Ice Desert and I sent forth our Javelin."

Mindok was stunned again. "The tribes are not yet united and you have already made a formal declaration of war?" To the Borathein, your enemy deserved to know your intentions. All the gods demanded honor in the dealings of men, lest one gain advantage by trickery and not by skill and merit alone. The gods had no patience for trickery and would strike down the one who engaged in it. At the very least, your adversary deserved to be made aware of his peril. Once they had been informed, all manner of warfare was acceptable to Vyath. *Javelin* was the term for this formal announcement, coming from the archaic practice of throwing a javelin or spear into an enemy's camp with your challenge attached. Often, the challenge was symbolized by a body part of the challenged tribe's elder or of a member of the ruling family impaled on the javelin. Over time, the ritual had simply become a formal notice of some kind, but it retained its ancient reference.

"We are strong, Deklar, you speak true," Prethor confirmed. "But we should not underestimate these people. They defeated our kin and the Arlethians fight on their side. The Arlethians alone would be a formidable challenge."

"This is why the tribes must be united. It will take all our people under a united front," Bellathia countered. "And, we have Alysaar. We cannot be matched in battle as we come from above, cloaked by night." Alysaar were believed to have exceptional nocturnal vision.

"Even then, they know we are coming. They will be prepared," Prethor stated.

Outside the tent, a duel was being carried out. The insults of men who chose sides as well as the roars of Alysaar were heard, goading on the quarrelers. Thuds and scraping metal sounded through the evening air.

"But their leader, this High Duke Wellyn, had a counter proposal," Shilkath continued, ignoring his nephew. "One that would allow us to fulfill the Griptha as well as have the most choice land on this side of the world. It is certain to be the worldly equivalent of the Shores of Thracia. It has already started."

"I don't understand," Prethor stated. "Are we working with these people or are we at war with them?"

"You do not need to understand. You must obey and trust your Deklar," Shilkath scolded the young man whose beard barely extended to the top of his chest. "This Wellyn, the Senthary Deklar, has shown me a great power granted to them by Vyath. It will give us great advantage over the Arlethian scum."

A cry followed by a gurgling sound came from outside the tent. Men cheered loudly, announcing the end of the duel. No one in the tent reacted with the slightest bit of concern or interest.

"It will be at least a year before we are prepared," Mindok said absently.

"A full year?" Bellathia asked with some disbelief.

"Five," Shilkath corrected. "It has been planned. Timing is everything in this. We will conquer or become extinct by this endeavor."

"Can these Senthary be trusted? This Deklar they call Wellyn? What do they get out of this?" Bellathia asked.

Shilkath could see others present had the same question by the looks on their faces. He let a moment of silence hang before he answered. "There is something in the Arlethian forests they desire. It is of no consequence to us."

"Do you trust him?" Bellathia asked again.

"I believe he will do what he has agreed to do. Beyond that, I expect him to betray us at his first opportunity."

FIFTEEN

Reign

Day 2 of 1ˢᵗ Rising 409 A.U.

HEDRON SPOKE IN HIS SLEEP, often waking Reign. She never told him about how she would listen sometimes for hours as he called for their mother and whimpered. She guessed he was dreaming of leaving her, of hearing her screams through the night as they ran from the Kerr hold. The fire's last embers struggled for life in the small fireplace before which they lay. The twins slept in the main room of Jayden's cottage while the old wolf shepherd slept in the sole bedroom the meager home offered. It was warm enough despite being nestled in the Gonfrey Forest. The edge of the glaciers was not very far, scaling high into the sky as mighty frozen cliffs. Reign could often not tell where the glaciers ended and the sky began when peering up at them.

She gently nudged his shoulder.

"Hedron!" she whispered. He continued traveling in the land of the unconscious. "Hedron!"

He always slept bare-chested now. The material of tunics easily caught on the scars across his chest, tugging uncomfortably on the puckered new skin. Where the wolf's claw had struck last Dimming Season her brother now had pink and purple scars raised above his unscarred skin like obtrusive mounds on an otherwise smooth landscape.

She rocked him a little more vigorously. It somehow made Reign feel closer to her mother when Hedron dreamt of her, despite his dreams no doubt being a terror to him. Reign lost both her parents the night her father had been killed despite the fact that her mother lived for many cycles after. Though she had a perfect memory of her father, Reign had a difficult time remembering her mother's image, as if she were always seeing her face from underwater. The last time she had seen her mother was indeed from behind tears. It was maddening to her and she would have traded the memories of her father for her mother in a heartbeat.

"Hedron, wake up. You're dreaming again."

Reign's own dreams had not faded either in the more than two years since her father's death. The hooded man with his ghastly appearance, her father's blood staining the ground he lay upon, the trees cold and dead, unnatural. She did not dream, oddly, of the wolves that had almost taken her and Hedron.

"Fine," she sighed in frustration when he would not awaken. "Crimson, wake Hedron, boy."

The large white wolf that slept at her feet every night nuzzled over to Hedron, put his snout up to Hedron's ear and sneezed.

Hedron awoke with a yell and in a panic.

"What! What's happening?" He wiped the side of his face that looked as if it had just endured a miniature hurricane. "I mean, come on! That's disgusting!"

Reign had her hand over her mouth, attempting to stifle a laugh. It soon required two hands to hold it in but eventually she didn't try to contain her giggling and let it out.

"Funny, is it?" Hedron scoffed. He hit Reign with a pillow and she laughed louder. "And you," he said turning to Crimson Snow, "blow your filth somewhere else!" The wolf licked Hedron and plopped himself back down at Reign's feet.

"Stupid wolf!" Hedron retorted. "Yuck!"

Crimson made a noise that sounded oddly close to snickering. Reign let out a renewed bellow of laughter.

"At least you're laughing," Hedron finally said. "It's been a while." Her laughter proved a bit contagious and Hedron couldn't help letting out a few chuckles of his own.

"But seriously, that beast shouldn't sleep in here. Even his sneezes are hazardous, not to mention the fleas. Put it out in the kennels with the rest."

"He's not like the rest," Reign said. "He saved us, remember?" She had called him Crimson Snow after that morning when his fur, white as the purest snow, was stained with the blood of smaller gray wolves that had threatened them.

"More like condemned us," he answered. "We're stuck living in a frozen forest with flea-infested wolves and a crazy old lady living all alone. I wonder why that is, don't you? Why she lives in the middle of a frozen nowhere? I mean, this sort of sounds like the beginning of a fable where the kids' misery is the moral of the story."

"Don't be silly, silly head."

A candle appeared at the threshold to Jayden's room, illuminating their surroundings.

"He seems to excel at silliness," Jayden said.

The boy moaned with annoyance. "It's too early yet. Go back to bed," he urged.

"I'll keep my own counsel on when to rise, young Kerr. I cannot remember the last time anyone tried to send me to bed. Not that anyone can sleep with the ruckus going on out here, anyway."

Jayden went to the window and looked out to the sky. "Second moon is about set. Barely an hour of night left as it is. Best be up and to your chores. I'll get breakfast started."

Hedron moaned in protest again.

"Come on, Crimson!" Reign called, jumping up from her blankets. She and the wolf ran out the door to the kennels where the flocks of wolves anxiously waited to be let free. They snapped at one another and rolled on the ground, playing as all siblings do.

Coming to the first kennel, Reign lifted the latch and let the score of beasts free. They blasted from the wooden structure at speed, the morning hunger urging them forward. Crimson was about to bolt off with them but stopped. The large white wolf turned his head back to Reign.

"Go on, boy! It's okay." Crimson bounded after the others into the forest. With the Rising Season now upon them, food would be more plentiful than it had been. She went to the second kennel door and likewise opened it. More wolves bounded free into the early morning.

"It's not a pet, Reign," Hedron scolded as he emerged from the cottage.

Without taking her eyes off Crimson Snow as he darted into the forest, she said, "No, he's not. He's more."

"Whatever that means."

Reign saw him subconsciously tracing the scars on his chest. She turned to him.

"You weren't there, Hedron. I mean, you were there, but you weren't awake. You didn't see. Crimson rescued us. He protected us. When I thought you had died he laid his own body over us to shield us from the cold. We are alive because of him."

"Yeah, I know," he admitted, somewhat cowed. "It's just...I mean, I just think—I don't know what I think."

Reign came closer to him and hugged him. She laid her head on his chest, hearing his heartbeat below his scars and said, "You're angry."

"Yes. Very."

"I know. Me too."

The twins took the hour before sunrise to clear debris and branches from the immediate surroundings of their home. Hedron brought in a pot full of snow for cooking water and returned with a basin, filling that with snow as well for the day's cleaning water.

He'll have to go farther north to the glaciers before long for snow and ice, she realized. Though the Rising and High Seasons in the

Northern Province were still chilly by comparison to much of the Realm, most of the snows did recede eventually except for at the glaciers' edges. The window for growing crops during these mild seasons was short.

Reign swept the inside of the cottage with a broom that was made from a staff and long pine needles bundled together at the end. The chores did not take longer than a couple hours at most each morning.

As Reign cleaned out the fireplace of cinders and ash, she saw her father's cloak hanging on a rack to the right of the hearth. It had once been shredded but was repaired well enough. The stitches Jayden had used to mend the material were very noticeable, giving it the appearance of a patched quilt rather than a royal garment.

Any time Jayden suggested that Hedron wear it, the boy always gave some excuse.

"It's too big," he would argue. "And it's itchy!"

"It won't always be too big, young Kerr," Jayden would reply. "You might as well get used to it."

"Why? It's just a rag now, not even much warmth against the cold."

"Not so, youngling. Your house's sigil is embroidered thereon. The name of Kerr will still be important in this land."

"It's not important to me," he mumbled. "If we were someone else we wouldn't have to stay here and hide. Someone would care for us in the Western Province among our own people. I'm not sure they even are our people anymore."

"Ah, but you are who you are, dear boy. You cannot change this."

"I wish I could!" Hedron retorted. "If my father hadn't been a traitor—"

The slap that stung the boy's cheek was delivered with a speed that belied the old woman's feeble-looking appearance.

"You do not know of what you speak!" Jayden snapped. "I will not hear such disrespect from your tongue again."

Hedron was silent for a few moments. "It's just a cloak," was all he could sheepishly respond with.

Now, looking at it hanging on a rack instead of around large shoulders, Reign found herself agreeing with her brother. It was a reminder of a life past and gone.

Breakfast was seared boar again, as it had been for the past half span and two days. They were almost through this batch and Reign was excited to move on to the next store of meat that they'd prepared. With the wolves bringing in fresh kills on a regular basis, meat was never something that they lacked. The twins had become quite skilled at preparing and preserving meat for long periods of time. A bit of hard cheese accompanied the meager meal along with some kind of tea that Jayden was fond of brewing. Reign thought it was disgusting, but it was warm, so she drank it.

Jayden braided a section of Reign's ebony hair just behind her right ear while the twins ate.

"It's the way mother would do it," Hedron remarked.

Reign nodded.

"Be still girl," Jayden admonished.

"Believe me, Jayden, this is still for her. She would squirm and whine the whole time while our mother would try to do her hair. It was a big test of patience for both of them."

"She wanted it out of my face," Reign recalled. "I never knew why but I wish I hadn't been so difficult for her."

"It's because you're beautiful, child," Jayden said. "Your eyes shine when you look up and they sparkle when you smile, rare as that is."

"I would always take out the braid as soon as I was out of her sight. I thought it was so foolish. But I like it now."

"We'll be able seed the ground again soon," Jayden said, changing the subject.

"Thank the Ancients!" Hedron exclaimed.

"Really?" Reign asked. "All you did last Rising was complain about the work."

"Yeah, but not having vegetables for so long kind of makes me okay with the work now."

Jayden nodded. "It's always satisfying to have the fruits of your labors. Hard work is itself a reward."

"I don't know if I'd go that far." Hedron smiled.

"Things don't just come magically to you in the real world, younglings. Your parents were good to you, but you never had to worry about where your next meal would come from or the clothes upon your backs. Work is a necessity for proper character. There, all done," Jayden said, referring to Reign's hair.

"Mother worked hard," Reign said as she reached up and touched the braid on the right side of her head. It was tight and smooth.

"Aye, she did. Raising children is the hardest but noblest work."

"Do you have any children?" Reign asked.

"Me? Children? Now, why would I do a foolish thing like that?" Jayden replied with a wink.

"That's not an answer," Hedron said.

"Ah, very astute, Hedron. And you're right, it's not."

Reign looked at Hedron with a surprised but intrigued look. Jayden went back to her meal as if the conversation had ended.

"So, do you?" Hedron asked.

"Hmm? Do I what?"

"Kids. Do you have any kids?" Reign said.

"Oh, right," Jayden replied with feigned forgetfulness. "I thought I answered that."

"No, you avoided the question," Hedron said.

"Correct. That's my answer. Are you both quite done then?"

They finished their meals and took their plates to the washbasin.

"Hedron, you finish up the dishes," Jayden said. "Reign, come outside with me."

"What? No, I'll go. Reign can do this," Hedron protested.

"I'm not sure I asked for further discussion."

Hedron turned back to the basin and the dishes as Reign left with Jayden.

"And after that," Jayden continued, "you can see to the roof. Clear it of the last bit of snow and fix any soft spots or leaks that may have happened during the Low Season.

Reign heard her brother mumble something about being cursed before she exited the cottage with Jayden.

It was a crisp morning even with the sun now up. Rare spears of golden light broke through the gray overcast skies and glittered upon the melting snow. Reign missed the canopy of branches and leaves native to the forests of the Western Province and how the veins of the Triarch leaves would sparkle at night. But, she did enjoy seeing the open sky when she looked up as well. The Gonfrey Forest was nowhere near as thick as her home forests and she had a hard time even calling where they now lived a forest of any kind. Before she and Hedron had ventured north, out of the Western Province, Reign had never before been where she could not connect with the forest. It was a truly foreign feeling that widened the sense of being lost within her. She put her palm flush against a tree as they passed by. The bark was rough with crevices and flaked easily at the touch. She closed her eyes and opened herself to the vibrations around her. Nothing. No increased perception was gained.

"Reign?" Jayden asked. "Are you well?"

"Yes," she said, her eyes still closed and palm against the tree. "I'm just—remembering."

After a moment, she continued their walk. When they were about thirty paces away Jayden said, "I know what you saw, child."

"What I saw?"

"Yes. It was a monster, was it not? Hidden behind a hooded robe?"

Realizing what Jayden was now referring to, she started to tremble and shake her head.

"I can't speak of it!" Reign pleaded. "Don't make me!"

"I never have and I won't now. You do not have to speak, but I will. And you will hear me. Understand?" She didn't wait for Reign's acknowledgment.

"Your father was more than he seemed," she began.

"I hate him," Reign said, her tone flat.

"You were not going to speak, girl, remember? But, yes, I know you feel that now. And it is good for the time being. It has changed you and therefore protects you."

Reign was utterly confused but remembered the old man that had visited her half a span after her father died. She almost thought it had been a dream but he spoke words similar to those Jayden now did.

"But," she went on, "I know your love for him lies dormant. One day, it will resurface. And you may fear this day because it will force you to face what you have hidden deep within yourself. But you cannot have his last breath until you do. And this, you will surely need."

"I'll need what? I don't understand."

"No, not yet. But you must remember my words. The time will come when you will understand them and also know that you are a current."

Reign thought that perhaps Hedron was right about her being a little crazy.

"I—"

"Hush, girl, I know. Your father knew how the Ancient Dark was spreading her Influence over this land and he was not neutral in the struggle. Nor, I suspect, shall you be."

Struggle? Reign wondered. *What struggle?*

But Reign did not vocalize her question and Jayden did not expound further.

"Remember above all, young Reign, you are a current."

"Hedron will need help," Reign said.

"Oh, your brother." The wolf shepherd sighed. "He's a stagnant current if I've ever met one. It'll take a stronger one than me to get him flowing again."

"He's just...a boy," Reign said lamely.

"Aye, for now. But I see the seeds of your father in him. And I don't mean just his appearance."

"He's better than him. Hedron never left me."

Jayden stopped walking. "Thannuel is *not* the one who left, child. You will know this one day."

She turned around and started walking back to the cottage. Reign followed.

"But, dear girl, as I've said, I suspect it will take a stronger one than me to mold that brother of yours. Blockheaded, daft specimen that he is."

"You don't talk of how you knew…how you knew my…"

"Your father?" Jayden finished for her. "Yes, you're right. But I did know him, and very well. In some ways, better than even your mother knew him."

At that comment, Reign became angry. Jayden saw the change on her face.

"Oh, relax child. I mean nothing improper or any slight to Moira. In truth, I never met her. But, any woman that Thannuel loved, I revered. She was everything to him."

"And he left her as well," Reign said.

"I think, underneath all your feelings of betrayal and anger, you know that's not true."

"True enough," Reign answered.

Jayden shrugged. "Maybe. Now, see to your brother. You're right about him needing help. So much."

———

Hedron sat on the pitched roof of the cottage with a pair of deerskin gloves and two sticks lashed together in the form of a T. He pushed the snow and ice from the apex of the roof toward either edge. The slope of the roof helped his effort but sometimes a pile would not slide completely off, so he would lay on his belly, head angled down the slope, and reach his crude snow rake down as far as he could to nudge the mass the last little bit it needed to clear the roof. The wolves had returned from their morning hunt and several stood around the cottage, eagerly prancing back and forth as they looked up at him. Playful barks sounded like taunts to the Kerr boy, as if they teased him for having to do such menial work.

"Go somewhere else, you fleabags!"

They didn't leave but continued to run around the cottage, barking. It was only three or four, but they wore on him constantly.

I don't care if they saved us. I'm not going to grow up to be a wolf shepherd in a frozen forest!

"Yeah yeah, bark bark," the boy scoffed back. He scooted forward and came to a rather sizeable blob of compact snow. It rested on a sheet of ice down the left slope of the roof—right where one of the offending flea-ridden wastes of hair and flesh stood. With reflexes too fast for the wolf to dodge, Hedron shoved the snow pile forcefully down. It slid down the roof like a miniature avalanche at the speed of a waterfall and crashed into the wolf, burying him up to his neck. The barking turned to a yelp of fright followed by whimpering. It leapt from the snow cocoon and ran away with its tail between its hind legs.

"Ha!" Hedron bellowed as he stood and held the snow rake above his head in victory. "That's right! Run from me, cowards! What's wrong, you afraid of a little snow? Come on back—"

A ball of ice and snow collided with the left side of his head; it stung his check and blasted into his ear. The shock of it made him lose his balance and, despite his wood-dweller agility, his feet slipped over his head. He hit hard on the roof and slid down, clawing in vain for grip. He yelled out as he went over the lip of the roof and landed in the same pile of snow he had just introduced to the wolf. Staring up, he saw what he thought was a young, dark haired girl standing over him, laughing.

"Reign?" he asked.

In answer a second snowball, this one smaller, hit his face. More laughter from Reign as she ran away. Hedron didn't remain dazed for long. Springing up, he reached down and scooped up some frozen ammunition of his own and started to pack it tightly as he chased his sister.

"You're dead!" he promised.

"You'd have to be able to catch me first!" she giggled. Hedron threw the snowball but missed.

She's so fast!

Hedron had stamina that served him well in long distances, but Reign's deftness and nimbleness over short distances made her nearly impossible to catch. She could change direction as if momentum had no bearing on her whatsoever.

"Blasted Heavens, hold still!" Hedron swore as he packed another snowball. Several wolves swept into the frolicking and wove in and out of the twins' paths as they chased each other throughout the woods.

"Come on brother, where's your speed?"

"I just don't want to embarrass you too badly!" he shot back.

She laughed. "After I just embarrassed *you* so badly?"

He sent his second volley down range and this one struck home, pelting her square in the back. Reign stopped where she was and looked out. They were only a quarter league from the Gonfrey Glaciers. No matter how many times he saw them, awe always filled Hedron as he took in their sight.

"It's like the edge of the world," Reign said. "Is there anything else out there? Beyond them, I mean?"

"Has to be. They can't go on forever. Father said he would bring me to see the glaciers someday."

When Reign didn't answer, he thought he knew what she was thinking. "This probably wasn't what he had in mind, but at least I've seen them now."

There was more silence between them as they took in the grandeur of the sight. The air was still with the glacier's chill.

"Are you ever going to tell me what happened?" he asked.

"I'm not sure. I'm not even completely sure what did happen."

"You could try, sister."

"Not today."

"Someday?" Hedron asked.

"Probably. Yes."

"Friend or foe?" Hedron asked.

"Huh?"

"If someone does live on the other side of these massive ice blocks, are they our friends?"

"It would be nice to have friends again," Reign said.

Hedron thought of all their friends, the ones they used to have when they were still just normal kids. He would play carelessly throughout the hold, sprinting across the elevated pathways that wove around and through the entire hold, sprawling through the trees and back down again. But mostly, he thought of Kathryn Hoyt. They had been promised to each other since he was eight years old and she seven. Kathryn seemed to be delighted by the prospect, lost in a girlhood romantic fantasy. Hedron, on the other hand, couldn't stand the thought of marriage when it was so far off, or even girls for that matter. Not at first. Kathryn's relentless hounding of him, though mostly annoying, had eventually felt flattering and he found he enjoyed the attention even though he would never admit it.

"I miss Kathryn."

Reign coughed. "You cannot be serious."

"Why not?"

"Hedron! After everything that's happened you miss your little girlfriend? That's what you're thinking about?"

He did feel foolish now. "I'm sorry I said anything. You brought up friends."

"She wasn't your friend, she was your intended. You hardly knew her for Light's sake."

"I guess I wish I did better. Know her, I mean. What did you have against her, anyway?"

"Uh, well, there's the fact she wasn't good enough for you, she's not a wood-dweller, she's annoying with her perfect blonde hair, and what of your children? They wouldn't even be true wood-dwellers."

"Wow. I just said I missed her. It's not like I'm picking out names for kids."

"And so what if you were?" Jayden asked from behind them. Hedron had felt her approach but didn't care to truncate their conversation. "It's not as if children of a single wood-dweller parent are any different than of a couple where both parents are wood-dwellers. The offspring have all the same traits regardless."

"She's gone, anyway," Reign said. "That life is over for us."

"Is that why you come to the glacier's edge and stare out? To find a new life, little one? Trust me, there is no life that awaits you out there."

"There's no life for us anywhere anymore," Hedron said.

"Don't be stupid, lad, hard though that may be currently. I think your feelings for the young Lady Hoyt are well founded. Perhaps someday you will go see about her again."

"Not while I'm a Kerr. That would have to change first."

"No lad you have it backwards. See, you're not a Kerr *yet*. That's what will have to change."

"Blah, blah, blah, here we go again," he mocked and rolled his eyes.

"Like I said, Reign, one stronger than I will have to sharpen this blunt instrument,. And it will take a lot of force."

Hedron glanced sideways to his sister and saw that she was grinning mischievously.

"Is it time, Reign?"

"I think so."

The twins simultaneously scooped up a handful of snow, turned in a blur of speed and threw the snow in Jayden's face. They were darting back to the cottage before she had time to retaliate with her usual threats. Hedron did think he heard a faint chuckle from the old woman as they ran from where they had left her.

SIXTEEN

Tyjil

Day 18 of 4th Dimming 406 A.U.
2 Years and 1 Cycle Ago

TYJIL STOOD WITH THE rest of the small company several leagues south of Calyn. This part of the forest was not inhabited. There were no towns or villages to interfere with his demonstration this night and yet it was not too far into the Western Province so as not to attract unwanted attention. The wood-dwellers' ability to feel movement through their cursed trees could be maddening.

That might change if he had mastered the Influence he had stolen from the Gyldenal.

"The forests here are so dark," High Duke Wellyn remarked as he looked up. The canopy of tightly intertwining branches and leaves resembled an overcast night, only allowing slivers of moonlight and occasional flickers of starlight to pierce its veil. Far above, the veins of the Triarch leaves were barely luminescent.

It was not actually the Influence he had taken that he planned on demonstrating, but its opposite. "Taken" was perhaps the wrong word; rather, he had learned the Influence through ill motives and subterfuge, though he frustratingly could not use its power. It was the knowledge of the Lumenatis and its workings that provided the ability to wield the Influence, but also, he surmised, alignment with the Light's will. Tyjil, however, was not interested in mastering the Influence as it was. His motives were darker for understanding the Living Light, for he desired to undo it. And for this, one needed to understand it thoroughly in order to comprehend its opposite. To understand the Dark, study the Light; for death, life; for pain, pleasure. He had become many people, many things; but the High Duke's advisor pledged his pursuits to one thing above all: power.

Power did not corrupt, as some taught. Power perfected one's true self, harvesting the fruit of seeds planted in the soil of sovereignty. Dominance. Supremacy. He understood that not everyone had the fertility to nurture greatness within as he did and Tyjil did not discriminate toward them.

"Every master needs stepping stones to his throne," he reminded himself often.

A throne is what Tyjil knew he was destined for. Not the Granite Throne his Duke occupied, but a figurative one made of darkness, for he understood the Dark Mother and her desires. And when one understood another's desires, manipulation was possible.

He had convinced Wellyn of the power held in the Arlethian lands and tempted Wellyn with it, but they would need time in the Tavaniah Forest, time Tyjil was not afforded when he last visited those lands three years ago. Once he could discover the Lumenatis itself, Tyjil would either harness it for himself and control it, or, if that proved impossible, extinguish it.

Unknowingly, the Borathein had provided an interesting opportunity that Tyjil intended to exploit. It was vital that he succeed and gain the trust of this fool who had traveled from across the Glaciers of Gonfrey. Shilkath claimed he could marshal a host great enough to wipe out the Senthary and claim these lands. The fool had actually given advance notice of his intent, saying his gods demanded it. The last thing he needed now was a war between the Senthary and Borathein. That would be most interruptive to his plans. But, if he could remove the Arlethians—yes, that would be fruitful indeed.

"This is some chance we take with you exposed, My Lord," one the Khans said. "Perhaps if you could have taken more—"

The chase-giver snickered from behind his hooded cloak.

"More? More what?" the chase-giver taunted. "I smell your apprehension, craven." Emotional scent gave chase-givers the ability to track and discern their prey, Tyjil knew, but they could also identify the source or motive behind an emotion. Though anxiety itself may have a unique scent, as do all emotions, there were subtle ranges or degrees within each scent that were used by chase-givers to identify gender, species, and motive or reason for the emotion felt. Though not quite as clear as telepathy would likely be, it was nonetheless a powerful advantage to decipher another's motives.

Tyjil knew more about this lethal race than a chase-giver himself would, their legends having become more myth than history as they were passed down. But his own emotions had no scent; or, none that escaped. He easily captured and recycled them. This lesson from the Gyldenal had stayed with him and he found it most useful in the presence of a Helsyan.

"Perhaps if you had brought more courage with you, Khan, we wouldn't be plagued by your whining."

The sentinel moved forward, glowering at the chase-giver. "My concern is for our Duke, who holds your leash, dog. Perhaps you should remember your place." His words hissed forth. "My resolve is unwavering, while your—"

"Hadik." Wellyn spoke with irritation laced through his words, putting an end to the confrontation. The Khan immediately broke off and resumed his guard position at the right flank of Wellyn with two other Khans on horseback. The chase-giver made a whimpering sound, as a hurt puppy would, jeering Hadik. The Khan did not react.

"I am passing the points of patience," the tallest member of the group muttered in a thick guttural accent. "My javelin will return to your people if we do not see this proof you have promised. We require you to shoulder much of the effort for our pact to have meaning."

"It is true," Tyjil said, "that without a distinct advantage and well-defined plans, there can be little hope of defeating the Arlethians. This is why we are here, yes? We cede our lands to you in exchange for you exterminating the population of the Western Province. It's a fair trade, I think, yes? Especially in light of their betrayal of your kin so long ago."

"We can take the land from you anyway!" Shilkath threatened.

"I do not think so," the High Duke countered as he rubbed the amulet under his robe. Tyjil heard Rembbran's breath quicken, likely with anticipation.

"Regardless, what does this thing do for you? You will destroy your own people?" Shilkath asked Wellyn.

"Call it opportunity," the High Duke answered. "And, the Arlethians are not really my people, are they? Besides, many more of your people will live rather than die fighting an all-out conquest against the Senthary, including the Arlethians, with no certainty of victory. The result you seek is granted at less cost."

"Let me see this trick," Shilkath demanded, his patience fleeing.

"No trick, Deklar. An Influence," Tyjil corrected.

"We do not know these things. It is a trick if it is anything."

Tyjil smiled. "We shall see, yes?" The old bald man turned to a tree, the one closest to him. He made sure it was one the wood-dwellers called a Triarch. He knew it had the most Light within it. Arlethians did not even know why they could speak with trees, why the forest was "fluent," as they said. Not unless they were the very few who were part of the Gyldenal, who most believed to be nothing more than tales for children at bedtime. Well, Tyjil would help ensure that they did in fact become nothing more than myth.

He thrust his hands forward and grabbed the tree. The pressure of his grip turned his old knuckles white and fingernails purple as blood was truncated from flowing into his hands. His jaw quivered as he conjured up the Dark within him. A blue luminescence began to radiate from the tree and the others stepped back, save for Shilkath, who stood unmoved.

"Trick," he said again.

Tyjil opened his mouth and sucked in, making a discordant sound as the air vibrated his vocal chords. The strident symphony of his inhale grew to an almost inhuman volume when the blue light suddenly dissipated. It looked as if it were a material that simply disintegrated. To the others, it may have looked this way, but Tyjil knew the truth. He had consumed the Light into the Darkness he held and then exterminated it completely. Forever. That portion of the Lumenatis would never be regained. The Song of Night played in his head as Noxmyra's presence drew nearer.

Next he injected a piece of himself into the tree that was nearly as old as Vâleira itself. Under his hands, the bark of the tree started to harden and turn cold. Its lively light brown tint turned gray. Great cracks and snaps were heard within the mighty Triarch, as if explosions rippled through it as it fought desperately for life, but the Dark Influence was too powerful for the tree's Light. The change spread out from Tyjil's touch, down to the roots and up the trunk until the branches far above with their wide-spread leaves all petrified. A loud creaking sound filled the night, the tree's final breath of resignation. The radiance of the Triarch leaves faded and the effect spread to three other trees whose roots were directly intertwined with this now dead tree, but did not spread farther.

Shilkath smiled so big they could actually see his teeth through his thick beard. He clapped once and said, "Ha! Good trick!"

"This is only a small example," Wellyn told him. "Tyjil will be able to force this Influence through vast portions of the forest when the time comes."

Tyjil stepped back from the petrified wood and found himself exhausted. The dark harmony that played in his mind was fading away as the power receded. When he glanced up, he was met by various looks ranging from fear to utter disbelief, save for the chase-giver. Rembbran's gaze was elsewhere, fixated upon what only appeared to be darkness.

Noticing the chase-giver's attention, Wellyn came to his side.

"Fear," Rembbran growled.

"I don't see anything, your Grace," a mounted Khan offered. His horse whinnied.

"Not surprising," Rembbran scoffed.

Tyjil was still weak from his demonstration but this did not stop anxiety from pooling inside him. *We cannot be discovered! Not yet!*

"Are you certain we are not alone?" the High Duke asked.

"Quite so, my Liege." Tyjil could hear the anticipation in the chase-giver's answer. A predatory smile spread across Rembbran's rune-pocked face.

Do it! Tyjil pleaded inwardly. *Charge him!*

High Duke Wellyn did Charge the chase-giver. Rembbran shuddered as he prowled toward a specific spot but found nothing. His nose gills flared and he snapped his head north.

"Female," Tyjil heard Rembbran say to himself. "Succulent." And then the Helsyan was gone, tearing through the forest as the great devourer his kind was born to be.

SEVENTEEN

Lord Thannuel Kerr

Day 22 of 3rd Low 400 A.U.
9 Years Ago

THANNUEL KERR SLAMMED HIS FIST down hard against the beast's head, but it stubbornly held on to his right forearm with its jaw locked. Jayden nearly cackled with laughter and pride. This wasn't the first time Lord Kerr had moved too slowly while sparring, underestimating his opponent. He cursed himself for not setting a better example as all his men looked on anxiously while their Lord took his turn. Both soldiers and hold guard stood intermixed as they shouted their calls of encouragement, and Thannuel felt abashed as he heard some cheering for the wolf. Wood-dweller he was, but the wolves' skills escalated the more they trained against Thannuel and his men. As Lord of the Western Province, Thannuel had ultimate command of the army of the West but interfered little with military leadership. He trusted the men he appointed over the army and focused more on his training of his hold guard, who were with him day and night.

"Thannuel, you dolt! I should have left you on the shores of the Runic Islands! Don't embarrass me, now!" Colonel Roan teased.

"Perhaps you can do better, Antious?" Thannuel asked.

"Of course, my Lord. As soon as that beast lets go of your arm I'll be happy to show you!"

The men looked forward to these long excursions to the Gonfrey Forest to train with Jayden's packs as sparring against only one another had become stale, producing little benefit. New opponents were needed to keep a soldier sharp. Bringing in soldiers from other provincial forces proved dull and unproductive to the army of the West, although it was priceless training for those sent. Lord Calder Hoyt of the Southern Province seemed to send in an increasing number of his men to train with the wood-dweller army, but winning all the time in sparring did not hone the skills of the victors.

Jayden's packs, however, had shown the wood-dwellers a new challenge. Thannuel thought it was a curious proposal from Jayden when he received it at his hold the previous year but decided nonetheless to pursue the offer.

"Are you sure this is wise? Why would someone raise wolves?" Aiden had asked. "Personally, I would somewhat question the old woman's sanity, my Lord."

"I am certain she has her reasons," Thannuel offered. "But I have heard she is no reed in the wind. It would be likely unwise to presume too much."

As Thannuel drew his fist back again for another blow, the wolf decided to spare its cranium another lump and released Thannuel's forearm. Lord Kerr quickly inspected his wounded right arm and found the wolf had not sunk its fangs deep. The punctures were only superficial but enough of a reminder to stay focused. The use of his primary sword hand did not appear to be hindered. *Primary* was indeed the correct description, for Lord Thannuel Kerr was almost as skilled in steel with his left hand as his right. Contrary to the belief that one had to be born ambidextrous in order to achieve the skill Thannuel possessed was the truth that it was simply a reversal of balance. Imagining oneself fighting as a reflection in a mirror was often all the mental exercise required to begin to learn the steel katas in the opposite hand. Imagining each fluid movement with enough concentration could prove more effective than the physical practice or outward action.

The wolf backed up and lowered its head and front legs, taking a stance from which it could easily attack or defend. Stepping back, Thannuel found his footing and launched forward, jumping upward from tree trunk to tree trunk, higher and higher, until he reached the top of the trees and was directly over the wolf. Without stopping, he dove down through the air and raised his sword above his head. Seeing the attack coming, the wolf launched toward Thannuel, meeting him in the air. It dodged the strike from Thannuel's sword and found his neck with its jaws as they hit the ground entangled with each other.

"Enough!" Aiden called out. The wolf snarled. Thannuel was… laughing. Though the deadly jaws of the large white wolf were lightly clenched around Lord Kerr's neck, the point of his short blade rested solidly between the wolf's third and fourth ribs. Both blows would have proved mortal.

At Aiden's command, the match was over.

Ancients, that boy is protective! Lord Kerr thought as he looked to Master Aiden.

Thannuel and the wolf released each other and backed away. With a smile on his face and a little winded, Thannuel bowed to the wolf cub that already outsized any other of the pack.

Jayden clapped her hands in front of her mouth in elation. "Have we finally found a match for you, Lord Kerr?"

"More than a match," Thannuel said. "A true training companion, I think. The skill set required is very different than fighting a human. It is new territory for us."

"This one is Elohk," Jayden said. "He is unique of our most recent litter. He is pure white without blemish, as you have no doubt surmised. Size and strength are unequaled by any I have ever raised. And there's something else…" Jayden considered for a moment, deciding if she should continue.

"Well?" Thannuel asked, still with an impressed smile upon his face as he wiped his hands clean of ice and mud. "I must know the one who bested me."

"Yes." Jayden seemed to be pondering the right way to explain what she meant. "Elohk understands," she finally said.

Thannuel's impressed smile turned to a quizzical look. "Understands what?"

"You," Jayden said simply. "Me. Your men." She paused for a moment. "Us. He understands us, our language, our way. At first I thought it to be instinct...the way an animal knows when it will rain or when the earth will become unbalanced and the ground and mountains rend. But I know it is more than this. Elohk appears gifted."

"Well, that's just perfect," Aiden scoffed. "A beast that can speak our tongue. What next? Squirrels that cook and clean up after our meals? Birds that serenade me to sleep?" Several of the men laughed at Aiden's facetious jabs until Jayden snapped at them in a cracking voice.

"I did not say he spoke our tongue, only that he understands. Are your ears stuffed with moss, boy?"

"All right," Thannuel interjected. "Let's prepare for the evening meal. We're concluded for today."

The men started making their way to the makeshift barracks that contained a dining hall. The wolves barked and playfully snapped at one another as they ran back to their kennels. Thannuel remained for a moment contemplating Jayden's words.

"Are you coming, my Lord?" Antious Roan asked. His purple cloak, that of a Colonel, had snow upon the shoulders.

"Antious, how many times have I told you there is no rank between us when we are alone?"

"I've lost count, my Lord."

"I'm going to stick that beast of a wolf on you if you keep this up."

Roan sighed with a half smile. "You know, I didn't save you just so you could get shredded by some wolf, Thannuel."

"He seems more than just another wolf. Wait until your turn comes. You'll see."

"You actually believe that old windbag?" Roan asked.

Thannuel shrugged. "At least your men have a better challenge here, yes?"

"No doubt. If Lord Hoyt sends one more group of Southern soldiers to train with us I might have to be rude and take a limb or two by accident."

"Calder's a good man, Antious."

"Right, as you say."

Thannuel became more serious. "I have thanked you, I know. But I will never tire of it. I owe you my life, Antious."

Roan looked away, obviously uncomfortable. "Regardless, you saved the Realm. You won that war. There's no disputing this point. You fought as if you were in our own forests, with the same sensitivity and agility. It was almost as if the Ancients had returned, as if—"

Roan broke off and was silent for a minute. "Well, I'll never understand how you did that."

Thannuel did not understand then either, but he did now. "We all just did our duty. Sometimes the cost is high. No one gave more than you."

"I'm still alive though, am I not?"

Thannuel knew Antious referred to his internal battle that never ended, though the Orsarian War had seven years ago. He never forgave himself for surviving when his battalion, including General Korin, Kalisa's father, had not.

"Colonel, I know of no one who more fully lives and exemplifies the Arlethian Warrior's Creed."

Roan did not respond.

"I'll join you and the men later. I'll just be a few more minutes," Thannuel said. "And see if you can teach Master Aiden a thing or two about showing respect for our host."

Colonel Roan walked off to the cottage.

His mind returned to Jayden's words about Elohk. *Even if they are true, it's simply a fascinating occurrence and nothing more.* He sat down upon the frozen ground, his cloak bearing his house's sigil of a single Triarch leaf sewn in the back spread out around him, and closed his eyes to meditate and center himself after the sparring matches. He reviewed in his mind every move of his and that of his opponents, every step and movement, with unforgiving analysis and criticism. Aiden had promise and served loyally as the newly appointed master of the hold guard. *If he could just mind his tongue!* Thannuel mused.

He felt a tremor. Slight, yet distinct. "You're still here," he said aloud. It was not a question. Thannuel opened his eyes and scanned the snow-covered ground around him. The tremor came again, ahead of him ten paces and slightly to the right.

"If you're looking for a rematch, I'm sure that can be arranged." Thannuel sat more still than a stone, fixated. Then suddenly behind him, he heard something emerge swiftly from the snow. He leapt to his feet and spun in the air, his cloak catching the wind as a sail on a ship. When he landed, he was crouched with his sword placed horizontally between him and the wolf just below his chin. Elohk faced him, snow clinging to his white fur, giving the appearance of an extra coat. His fur was the whitest Thannuel had ever seen, nearly impossible to discern from the snow. Thannuel wasn't surprised that it was the wolf, but he was astonished that it had moved so stealthily behind him without him sensing it.

Elohk did not attack, but stared into Thannuel's eyes. It was penetrating and Thannuel saw fathoms of intelligence therein. He lowered his sword and stood up from his crouch. An understanding passed between them in this moment.

"Is it true?" Thannuel asked, feeling a little foolish talking to an animal. "Do you understand my words?" Elohk did not turn away but continued to stare. Thannuel sighed and thought this was all ridiculous. *He might be very skilled and full of uncanny instinct, but of course he doesn't understand my words.*

"How about a small test, yes? A simple experiment. With which hand do I draw my sword?" Elohk continued to stare at Thannuel and then looked away and huffed, as if insulted by this simple-minded game. But, he played along and obliged Lord Kerr. He stepped closer to Lord Kerr and nudged his right hand with his wet nose, then stepped back. Thannuel laughed.

"That was too easy. You managed to bite that arm today thanks to me underestimating you. There's no way you could manage that again now that—"

Before Thannuel could finish, Elohk launched himself forward and closed his jaws around Thannuel's right forearm. Again. Then he released the arm almost as quickly as he had attacked. He did not clamp his fangs down with enough pressure to break skin, but just enough to prove himself. Thannuel stood stunned wearing a mask of incredulity across his face. Then he laughed out loud, a heaving, bellowing laugh nearing hysterics.

"Do it again!" he commanded. The wolf cocked his head to the left and then seemed to shrug as if to say, "Oh, very well," and launched once more at Thannuel, mouth agape. Thannuel was indeed prepared this time, and Elohk found nothing but air filling his maw. He skidded to a halt and turned around to face Thannuel with alacrity.

"Again!" Thannuel commanded.

They circled each other slowly and locked gazes. Elohk sprang forward but Thannuel deftly stepped aside and landed a palm heel to the wolf's right side, sending him in a new direction in mid-flight. Elohk landed without any trouble and refocused his gaze on Thannuel.

"Again," Thannuel said in a more serious, focused tone. They sparred into the night and across the forest. The minutes turned to hours and evening to full night. If Thannuel lost sight of Elohk for a moment, the wolf would silently bury himself in the snow and wait for an opportunity. While intensely focused, however, Lord Kerr honed in on the distinct signature of vibrations Elohk emitted, making it near impossible for the wolf to succeed in another surprise attack. Conversely, the agility of a wood-dweller to spring from tree to tree at speed greater than a human could track and pounce down upon an opponent proved less and less effective as

Elohk learned to counter this move. For hours, neither was able to touch the other or land any attack as they danced around each other throughout the forest. Finally, as they once again faced off and held each other's gaze, Thannuel raised his hand and said, "Enough, Elohk. It is enough."

The wolf refused to relent for a moment and then in a sluggish movement, let himself fall to the earth and give out a small whine.

Thannuel nodded. "I completely agree," "For the past hour I've been completely drained, running on pure adrenaline. I just couldn't let you know I was wearing down." Thannuel hunched over and took in a few deep breaths and then lethargically made his way to where Elohk prostrated himself on the earth. He heard the wolf's heavy breathing and sat down next him. The wolf was longer than Thannuel was tall. The night chill finally hit him as he lay down, some miles from Jayden's cottage where his men slept in the barracks. It was late in the second moon's cycle and dawn would greet them soon. *I may not move for several days after this night of training.*

Thannuel felt the large wolf inch closer and bring its body against his own, adding welcome warmth that his cloak alone could not provide. Just before sleep overcame him, Thannuel found his mind wandering upon deeper concerns.

Is it truly coming? He wondered. *Will we be prepared enough? Will the people rise up as we hope? Will they even understand?* He did not know, but he hoped. He hoped, mostly though, that his children would not have to stand against the Dark alone. The foreboding upon him he knew was more than his imagination. It would be impossible to shield them completely, but he prayed he could at least stand by them when Noxmyra rose with the Ancient Dark in her wake.

THE END OF PART 1

PART 2

FRACTURE

The air above soiled damp—
Indifference dripping,
Pooling to vats of rancor;
Broken! Rent! Fractured line!
    — 17ᵗʰ Stanza, The Passages of Tunginorr'ah

The fever of recreancy gropes my heart, boils my blood. Where hides my relief,
my remedy, to change what I have become to that which I have lost?
    —The Erynx Fragments, recovered by Obred
    Thulin, a Terranist, circa 134 A.U.
    3 leagues outside the East's state city of Erynx

EIGHTEEN

Honleir

Day 19 of 4th High 412 A.U.

KEARON EXISTED, BUT DID NOT LIVE. Or so the saying was in the Realm. Without any lands or true citizenry, most Kearon kept to the far reaches of the Realm, those parts in which others had little desire or concern. Their songs and poems recanted of the blessing and curse granted them of life after defeat by Oliver Wellyn and his hordes. Many houses had been gathered in league with House Kearon against Wellyn and their allies; yet, those permitted to live in defeat were known simply as Kearon, no matter their lineage. They were not distinguished as part of their lasting shame and punishment.

"No, not like that," Honleir corrected his younger cousin. "You'll hurt your back."

"How then?" Timney asked, frustrated. "I see you doing it all the time."

"Not like that, actually. Once you've dug underneath the rock for a grip, you have to squat down next to it. Like this, see?" Honleir demonstrated by kneeling down with his knees facing outward and his arms extended down between them. He then dug his hands under the rock until he had a good grip.

"Now, see how my back is straight? All you need to do from here is stand up." He grunted as he said the last words, standing up and freeing the rock from the sandy soil.

"Wow!" Timney said. "That has to weigh twice as much as you!"

"I doubt that much, but you don't want this falling on your feet," Honleir said.

"Have you ever not been able to free a rock?"

"Of course. Lots of times I use a lever of some kind. A bone, piece of wood or even another rock."

"Why do we have to do this, anyway?" Timney asked.

"You know why. We need to clear the land for crops. Besides, the best soil has been preserved under rocks."

"Is there such a thing as good soil in the Schadar? It's all just sand and bedrock."

"Maybe not," Honleir admitted. "It's just what we've always done."

Not always, he corrected himself. *There was a time when Kearon were not forced to live in such depravity—if the poems are to be believed.* Some regarded them as elusive periphrastic nonsense, but Honleir loved to study the poems after a long day's work. Most of his other friends were busy chasing the girls in the village or trying to sneak an extra cup of water from the water trench when the adults weren't looking. The poems seemed to reach out to him as he matured, speaking to him in ways that he could not explain. He pondered on a stanza he had read the night before at the end of a poem called *Waxing Whither*, one not easily understood. He recited it in his mind over and over.

> *A Shield of wood and iron,*
> *Splintered, dented, torn;*
> *A shield of old parchment,*
> *True, sturdy, Light born.*

The passage seemed to be contradictory in nature. Looking to the verse before gave no insight but appeared rather to be ramblings totally unrelated. He repeated the complete section in his mind.

Bastards swaddled in loving arms
Where true born are turned away, spurned—
Legible Light has grown undim
Where lies him with no patronym.

A Shield of wood and iron,
Splintered, dented, torn;
A shield of old parchment,
True, sturdy, light born.

"Have you ever seen a green vegetable?" Timney asked. "I mean, a real one? Not the yellow and brown ones we get."

"No," Honleir admitted. "I don't think it's possible this far below the precipitation lines."

"I've never even felt rain. Can you imagine? Water that falls from the sky! It seems magical. Do you believe it?"

Honleir shrugged. "Sure. Why not? Who says water only has to come from underground? Besides, my mother says it's true."

"Will you go north? You only have three years left. Before you can leave the village, I mean. They say the Realm is full of wonders too great to imagine!" Timney's expression was full of wonder, like all boys of ten.

"I don't know," Honleir answered. "Why leave? My parents and uncle are here."

"Yeah, I know, it's just—I want to see it, you know? Get away from all this?"

He didn't answer. To Honleir, the routine of working in the desert fields—removing stones, boulders, or other unwanted elements of all create that prevented taming of the land—was all he knew. His family had to scratch out an existence in the most southern parts of the Realm where tumbleweed and barren red clay soil were of no small measure. Attempting to tame land of this cast was not taken on save by the most desperate. No herds or natural growth of vegetation existed here so far below the precipitation lines. The Schadar Desert seemed to take pleasure in the suffering of its few unnatural inhabitants with its unrelenting heat mixed with winds of sand thicker than water. The granules of sand became so hot in the heat of day in certain parts, one could set out at night to search the desert grounds for slabs of soft misshapen glass, forged from the molten sand. A windstorm in the Schadar basin hurled fiery sand with such force that it burned and tore flesh from bone.

"Honleir," Almena called to her son. Honleir looked up from his digging about a large boulder, his copper skin glistening with a thin sheen of sweat. His mother was panting for breath. "You must come quickly! The water trench!"

Honleir dropped his tools made of rotten wood and bone and sprinted after his mother. Behind their small abode of sand block and clay and between the cliff's walls lay the water trench. The practice of building villages of the Schadar nestled against a cliff face had been adopted of necessity to give some relief to the desert domiciles from the sun's heat granted by the shadow cast by the cliff face as the day progressed. All the villagers' homes surrounded the water trench in a crescent, offering some protection to the most important asset found in the Schadar. Natural springs existed in the desert, but were often mixed with grit and sand of such great concentration that they were often mistaken for quicksand by the untrained eye, if they were even noticed. The constant effort of an entire village was required to strain the sand from the trenches, leaving water pure enough to drink and irrigate crops. The sand straining occurred three times a day, and was the first order of the morning for every new day. No villager could go on to his or her other duties before the water trench was adequately strained, providing life-giving water of even the lowest suitability.

He saw it as soon as he came to the water trench's edge. Dry, cracked earth where water had been earlier this day. The spring had dried up suddenly, without any warning.

"I don't—how?" was all he could manage.

A few of the men had dug down into the earth a couple feet. Nothing. Some women were crying, though they tried desperately to stop their tears. In the Schadar, no tears could afford to be shed. As the Poems of Rishz'nah taught,

> *Tears in the Schadar*
> *A widow often makes;*
> *Children turn orphans,*
> *Parents return barren*

The smallest increment of water was more valuable than a day's measure of food.

He could see resignation starting to manifest upon the countenance of his people. This was death in the Schadar. The nearest known spring was over twenty leagues away, across a basin, more than a cycle's journey. Some villagers would not be able to make such a journey, including Honleir's own father and uncle. His anger flared, but to no avail.

Why? Why no warning? Where were the signs?

Honleir's insides rumbled with fear and anxiety. The people of the village would have little more than a few days of water saved. Should they flee? Send for help? Who would come? Honleir did not know. He was lost. All paths seemed to come to naught. His legs failed him as he sank to his knees, ignoring the slight pain of hot sand burning his skin. No one would miss a village of the Kearon. No one would even know of its absence from the world, or their absence. Heat, not of the Schadar, but of unsurpassed anger, rose in Honleir.

Attempting to force himself into a mind-render to see some path of deliverance, Honleir grimaced with concentration, his face askew with determination. He held his breath in his focus until his lungs burned in protest. He exhaled violently and then drew in another full breath and shut his eyes again with renewed concentration. His teeth were gritting as he worked his jaw back and forth, lips slightly parsed. The wind whipped up sand that caught in Honleir's mouth, but he did not notice. His concentration was not broken as he tried desperately to force his mind to show him some way to life, some form of redemption. The pounding within his temples began. Any time he forced a mind-render, the physical consequences were great. He must force it though, this time he must. He must not submit to the pain. *I must penetrate the mental barrier. Must push through…must see…must…*

He felt it. The water below where the murky spring had been. It was too far to dig but he felt like he could grab it, seize upon it with his mind.

"It's there," he gasped. "I can feel it. Can't grab it. Almost…" He caught it. Somehow, Honleir grasped the water with his mind and began to pull up. It was so heavy. He felt veins pulsing in his head, blood pounding in his ears like thunder. He pulled but the water did not come. Exerting more strength had no effect. It was anchored too deep.

"I can't lift it! It's too much! Too—"

"Honleir!" Almena cried out, looking down over her son as he knelt upon the desert sand, shaking. "Honleir, stop! Honleir!"

She reached down to shake him. When this did not break him from his anguished stupor she slapped the boy once, twice. Finally, he opened his eyes. They were bloodshot. He reached a quivering hand to his nose and felt the warm wetness of blood.

"It won't come," he said hoarsely. "I'm not strong enough. I thought maybe—but it's just too heavy…"

"Save your strength. We will need you and the other strong ones." His mother's words were sprinkled with inflections of hope, but Honleir could hear the overtones of despair. She knew what this meant, what the fate of the village would be. Timney stood looking on at him with the other villagers, both old and young. He saw desperation in their eyes, pleading for him to do something. Anything.

"I will find water," he said. "I swear it."

NINETEEN

Ehliss

Day 19 of 4th High 412 A.U.

THE MINISTER OF TERRAN STUDIES tossed the scrolled report on his desk and leaned back in his old wooden chair. It creaked as he tipped it back on its hind legs. He put his hands together in a steeple shape in front of his mouth and looked to be pondering on what to say.

"Are you sure," he finally asked, looking at the young woman in front of him. Ehliss put her hands on her hips and stared dumbly in response.

"Bah, I know you think me a fool for doubting you. But, still, Ehliss, I have to ask."

"Minister Findlay, have I ever been wrong in one of my field reports?"

"No, but this is remarkable, wouldn't you agree?"

"Perhaps, but it is still true, I assure you. My readings are accurate."

"The report says roughly three inches?" Findlay asked.

"In some places, the glaciers have actually receded nearly a foot, but my random measurements along a four league stretch showed an average of three to four inches from the last report three years ago. I was not the one who submitted that field report,

195

so I was skeptical at first with my findings. But the soil is indeed fresh, fertile and different in composition than the rest of the Northern Province."

"Yes, yes, I read it all actually. Just wanted to hear you say it," the Minister said. "Do you realize what you're suggesting?"

Ehliss smiled. "Of course. Within seventy to eighty years, the Glaciers of Gonfrey would have likely receded enough to make meaningful use of the land. It's actually great news in light of the Schadar, I thought."

Ehliss was referring to other reports that had come from terranists in the south who had been measuring the Schadar Desert. Its borders seemed to be expanding north by several inches per year and eating into the Southern Province.

"The renewal process seems to be underway in the south, but it will be decades before the impact is beyond reckoning with," Findlay observed. "But the climate is already starting to be affected in those parts. Minuscule amounts to be sure, for now. But there have been an increased amount of sandstorms this year. Relatively harmless and more of a nuisance than anything."

"Other provinces are starting to report less crop production and leaner cattle," Ehliss added. "Or at least fruits have lost some of their sweetness and other crops are more bitter tasting. The vegetation from the Western Province, however, seems unaffected thus far."

"Yes, I'm aware," the Minister replied wistfully. He was not sure what to make of those reports yet. Lands always cycled together, but the land once known as Arlethia was not showing signs of decay as the rest of the Realm did. It was uncanny.

"And, what of my request?" Ehliss pressed on. This snapped Minister Findlay back to their conversation.

"No, you just returned from the North. I need you elsewhere, Ehliss."

"And who else will be sent to the north? Everyone else flees from the rotation," she stated. It was true. Many of the other terranists would seek her out when their turn in the north came, asking to trade her rotations. She almost always accepted as she found the Great Glaciers of Gonfrey to be more mysterious than the mundane and droll data gathering assignments elsewhere in the Realm. She could not understand how others were relatively happy to simply do their job to the barest standards of acceptability and move on. There was no passion, no fire for their area of study.

"It's Wesley's turn in rotation," the Minister said. "You're going to the open plains to collect soil and grass samples."

"The open plains? Minister Findlay, there's no need. The soil there has been unaltered for centuries, despite the reports coming from other parts of Senthara."

"Actually," the Minister countered, "that's not entirely true. While the richness of the soil seems the same, we don't believe that's going to continue."

"Why's that?"

"Worms."

"Worms?"

"Actually, the lack of worms," he clarified. "Farmers in the Eastern Province have noticed a considerable drop in the number of worms in the ground. It's not as if they count them usually, but after a while, some started noticing they weren't there anymore. Then others began to pay attention and reported the same. Very few would be dug up when they plowed their fields. Further, hunters nearby have noted a very difficult time finding boar. And the tall grass in the fields is thicker than anyone can ever remember. Do you know why, Ehliss?"

After a moment of not caring, it hit her. "No birds," she said.

"Very few, anyway. Without the worms, boars have moved on to find grub elsewhere. Same with the birds, which would normally eat worms and the grass seed, thinning out the grass's growth. So, while the soil appears fine now, we doubt it will be for long."

"What do you want me to do?" she asked, still not that excited.

Roben Findlay leaned forward in his chair and rested his elbows on his desk. "Dig up a few score plots, ten feet square and five deep. Have your team note the number of worms they find in each plot. Simply record the data. That's all for now."

Ehliss rolled her eyes. "Minister Findlay, I can see the importance of this, but please, can't you send someone else? Anyone else can do that task, and do it just as well as me."

"I'll strike a bargain with you, Ehliss. Do this assignment, which will only take a few days, and I'll give you extra rotations up north within a cycle. It's the best I can do right now."

Ehliss grudgingly accepted.

TWENTY

Reign

Day 20 of 4th High 412 A.U.

REIGN SAT HUDDLED IN A CORNER OUTSIDE Hold Hoyt in the Southern Province, shielded from the sight of the stars and moons by a small awning of wood and thatched hay overhead. She was fifteen now and more a woman every day. Sometimes Hedron would comment on how much she resembled their mother, or at least what he could remember of her. Over the years, Reign had managed to cultivate a fragile happiness with the help of Hedron and Jayden.

There was the presence that continued to harass her; something born of ill create, she was sure. It pushed against her during moments of fear or danger, when she needed her focus the most. The dreams that haunted her in the night were no doubt inspired by the presence as well. She could not remember the last time she had slept through the night without being woken at least once from nocturnal terrors. When she would awake, the pressure on her chest would sometimes feel as if boulders were upon her, cracking and crushing her sternum and ribs. Reign had no illusions that this force was real, and it was certainly of the Ancient Dark. Of this she was convinced. Why she was being targeted eluded her, but she was able to fight off the attacks more effectively now. The hate that burned inside her was her shield, she had noticed. The more she stoked that pyre of enmity, the sooner the attacks would subside. Hedron thought that an odd remedy, to fight the Dark with perhaps its most primal attribute, but he did not question her deeply upon this subject. Her twin brother was the only person she could openly be herself with, the only one she dared even smile around. Still, she had never revealed even to him the full picture of what she had seen, of the scarred demon that had reached out for her, who briefly touched her with a seemingly supernatural finger. Her left shoulder where the monster had touched still tingled sometimes with phantom sensation, causing her to jump in fright. Reign shuddered in her small hiding place, making a couple stones near her feet clatter. They sounded like how a giant's teeth chattering from the cold might sound, she thought, remembering stories that old lady Wendham had told them when they ate dinner.

"The Haxlium were nearly a span of feet tall," she would say, "and they could lift a horse with each hand!"

"They weren't even real," Hedron would protest. "No one is ten feet tall!"

"I said 'nearly' a span of feet, little lordling. You must listen more carefully," Wendham would snap. "And if they weren't real, where did the stories come from, I wonder?"

"Just some stupid made-up bedtime stories to scare little kids," Hedron would say defensively. "Just like wolf men."

"Of course wolf men aren't real," Drilth Wendham would admit. She had started to clean up after the children's meal, clearing the plates from the wooden table. As the hold's cook, Old Lady Wendham did not wait on people, but she enjoyed the Kerr twins and in particular, she loved to spar with Hedron. "People don't become animals or vice versa."

"That's not what I mean. They're monsters that look like men but can smell like wolves," Hedron had said. "And they're stronger than the Haxlium ever were." He enhanced his stories with roars and animations to impress his small audience.

"For not believing in such stories, you certainly seem to know a lot about them."

"Everyone knows the legends. Just stupid stuff to try and scare kids." He spat and sat back down next to his sister. "We're not afraid, right, Reign?"

She was not afraid then, before she had met a real monster. But she was afraid now.

Reign was brought back from her memories by Hedron's mischievous laugh as he ran toward where she huddled in a corner vacant of moonlight just outside the walls of Hold Hoyt. He reached down quickly and pulled her up fast and hard, dragging her behind him in tow. Angry voices were following them, shouting out orders and curses. He refused to give any explanation, but Reign could see this was not a time to ask questions. All she could think about was what Hedron could have possibly done this time.

She felt the cobblestones under her feet as they dashed from the Hoyt hold. It wasn't the same as the rich forest floor and roots of the Western Province's terrain, but still Reign could negotiate the streets they ran through with speed. They would have to scale the tall walls that anchored massive sail-like contraptions at their tops to escape. Hoisting ropes hung freely from the pulleys far above that would aid in their extrication as they had many times before. The wall's construction was mercifully rough, with stones and rocks jutting out randomly making for sturdy footholds. Though masts and sails atop the walls existed for a practical utilitarian purpose, their design was beautiful and the visual effect created when they were fully deployed in a sandstorm from the Schadar was stunning, as was much of the Southern Province's unique architecture. She had seen it once, long ago, during a visit to Hold Hoyt as a much younger girl with her family. Even then she would spy on Hedron playing "kissy face" with the Hoyt girl.

Somehow, Reign knew their current plight was not of her doing, but of her bull-headed twin brother. Again. Kathryn Hoyt had for some time, according to said bull-headed brother, been betrothed to him. The rest of House Hoyt seemed oblivious to this fact, however, and chased the lad off their lands whenever he was caught scaling the hold's walls to Kathryn's chamber. Ascending rock and stone was not as easy for the young wood-dweller boy as the forest trees of their home province, but this did not deter him in the least. The guards had no idea that who they chased was a Kerr of the wood-dwellers, but it probably would have made little difference. Actually it might have made their resolve to catch or bring down this intruder burn even hotter. Catching the son of one of the Realm's most notorious traitors in history would be worth a significant reward. Killing Kerrs had become the aim of bounty hunters and ambitious souls throughout the Realm after the entire family line was implicated in her father's supposed treachery. The eradication of any who held the Kerr name was decreed a holy pursuit by the Changrual, and an official decree from the High Duke authorizing citizens to use any means necessary to rid Senthara of the family name soon followed. The twins were accustomed to being chased and hunted, but not for their name's sake. No one knew them by sight anymore. Their bodies had changed greatly in the maturity period and their childish features had largely faded.

An arrow struck a small shop's wall inches from the left side of Reign's head, sending splinters free from the wood. Hounds were heard in the distance as the kennel masters released them into the night to track the intruders.

"Honestly, if I die over some tramp because of your inability for rational judgment, dear brother Hedron, I'll kill you!" Reign hissed as they fled from the hold. They would soon be out of range for even the hounds. She was not really mad, but amused actually. There was no real danger as long as they had room to run. She often accompanied Hedron on his nocturnal visits to see young Lady Hoyt and enjoyed the solitude of sitting hidden in some shadowed pass or crevice, out of sight of the world.

"I don't particularly enjoy being shot at for the sake of your little love story!"

"It wasn't my fault," Hedron playfully retorted. "The Lady Kathryn bade me visit her, and I cannot refuse a lady's humble request."

"A lady's humble request? A *lady*? That girl, barely fourteen, doesn't have the physical composition of a lady."

"Ah, Reign," Hedron pleaded as the hounds' howls faded in the distance, "can't you just be happy for me?"

She scowled at him before looking away. They halted their silent run on the far edge of Thera, against the river Roniah. The crescent light of second moon glimmered against the smooth waters of the tributary.

"Happy for you?" Reign scolded, not seeking to hide her incredulity. "You claim to have intent to marry, but what of her father? You bring no standing, no status in the Realm. Lord Hoyt will not consent, not to you. Not to a Kerr."

Hedron actually looked hurt. "Reign, you can't mean that. Why do you despise your name so?" He was just being argumentative for fun. She could hear it in his tone. In reality, Reign knew Hedron had more issues with their family name than did she.

"It's no more than anyone else, and this isn't about me. The Kerr hold is not even a hold any longer. It rests rotting in the west, where..." Reign cut off. *Where our father lies*, she had wanted to scream, but she would not speak his name, nor make mention of him. She stood silently glaring at Hedron. After a moment she looked away. The moonlight would betray her welling tears.

Hedron's smile changed to a mask of solemnity. "Reign," he started gently, moving closer. "Reign, father loved you with all his—"

"No more!" she snapped, turning back to him. "Not a solitary word more." Hedron held his peace, but he knew what ailed her. He whispered, "It has been six years, sister."

Had it only been six years? Reign felt like perhaps six eternities had passed. Every day she hated her father more and spurned his memory. Everything she could think of to make her forget was given a chance, but nothing purged her memory. Not of her once great father, not of that night. To her, Thannuel had been a giant. Immortal as all fathers are to their daughters. Until, that is, she saw him fail. He died like any man, nothing special or exceptional. The Kerr Hold was deserted, little more than charred rubble—or so everyone said. They were completely irrelevant in life.

———

Hedron didn't know how to comfort his sister in these moments. He did not see and witness as she had. Deciding against words, Hedron stepped toward his sister and took her hand. She resisted at first, but only briefly. She would not cry, he knew that, nor would she speak. It didn't matter, words weren't needed between them. He felt her pain keenly, though he didn't fully understand it. The pain seemed to emanate from hatred, not sorrow or loss.

Hedron loathed how they were obliged to conceal their identity wherever they went, to not confess their true name. Why should a name be enough to damn a person in the Realm? They had felt damned even before they were yet ten years of age, before the age of innocence had passed. Still, Hedron's hope could not be fully extinguished, despite his own misgivings surrounding their place in the world, cruel as it could be sometimes. Reign pretended there was no hope, but he knew it lay dormant inside her, not dead.

"Why did you not tell mother where I hid?" Reign finally spoke. Her query was the same as always. "They all supposed I had perished as well."

"Because I was told not to," Hedron said, his answer the same as always. He did not mention who told him not to reveal her to Aiden and his guards when they combed the woods bordering the hold in search of her. He was never sure how to explain it but felt the guilt of robbing his mother of some happiness she might have enjoyed if she knew Reign lived. Somehow Hedron understood, though, that Moira's days would have been even shorter had he revealed his sister. He also understood keenly that his sister was in mortal danger then and likely still now.

They stood there, on the banks of the Roniah in the Southern Province's state city of Thera, far from their lands, the last of a once significant and now bereft house.

———

The following morning, Reign awoke to freezing water being poured over her face. She jolted awake with a high-pitched scream and saw Hedron holding a hollowed piece of driftwood that served well enough as a shallow bucket.

"That's perfect. Perfect! Thank you so much!" she yelled at Hedron.

His smirk could not be more infuriating. "What? It's no more than you've done to me a hundred times!"

Reign sprang to her feet and chased after her brother, intent on helping him feel just as loved. It didn't take long for her to trip him up as they ran along the riverbank and shove him into the fast moving but shallow water. He came up screaming and clutching his chest.

"One got me! A hydraf bit me!" He twisted around and screamed with pain.

Reign's face turned white with terror. She retrieved their satchel, withdrew some Triarch roots and ran into the cold water to her brother's aid.

"Where? Did it let go? Let me see!"

"It's burning!" Hedron cried. His hands covered his left upper chest, grabbing it so hard that his hands were white and purple.

"Let me see!" Reign again demanded. "Where did it bite?"

"Right here!" Hedron said as he reached his right hand behind Reign's head and pulled her down hard. She was not expecting this and lost her balance, sprawling into the river face first. Hedron started to laugh uncontrollably.

"Ancients curse you!" Reign pronounced as she came up spitting water. "Do you know how stupid you are? Don't ever joke like that!"

Hedron fell backward in the river laughing and let the current take him north. It drifted toward the Western Province's border.

"Come on," he finally answered after catching his breath. "It was just a joke. They're no hydrafs this close to shore." He just continued to drift with the current, floating on his back and staring up into the morning sky. He wore the expression of a boy amazed by simple pleasures. "Well? Are you coming?"

"Where exactly?" Reign asked. She still stood in the thigh-deep water with a foul mood.

"Grab the satchel. We're already wet. We might as well just float upriver. We'll get out at the crossing."

The Roniah Crossing was where the river crossed borders from the south to the west. The Southern Province was south of the Eastern and Western Provinces and shared no border with the North except for a small speck of land under the Changrual Monastery where all the provincial borders met. The crossing was a busy port of trade for both the south and west. Riley's Cove was the nearest town to the crossing in the Western Province where most of the trade occurred between the two provinces.

Reign looked back to the shore where the satchel lay. In the distance, southeast of them, a sandstorm approached from the Schadar Desert. It was miles out and posed no threat to them. Sighing, she admitted to herself that Hedron was right. They were already wet and floating upriver to the crossing was a slower but much more relaxing method of travel. They would probably get there just before nightfall.

"I don't float as well as you, remember?"

"That was before you were...uh...more developed up top. You'll be fine. Quit stalling."

"Hedron! I can't believe—"

She heard his laughter. He was drifting farther upstream. She went ashore, grabbed the satchel and replaced the Triarch roots she had taken to counteract the hydraf poison.

I wish he had been bitten! Not really, though she wouldn't mind if he had hit his head. Might make him a little more right up there. She found a piece of driftwood about three arms thick and mostly hollow inside. Woman now or not, she still did not float like Hedron.

Maybe that's because he's so fat, she mused. He was anything but fat, having their fathers broad shoulders and trim waist, but he didn't have to know that.

More than three spans later, the twins drifted off to sleep in the arms of a large sprawling oak. They were northwest of Calyn by about a day's walk. They always made sure to avoid the southeast part of the city where their family's hold lay cradled in entropy's arms.

"Tell me about mother," Reign asked. Her voice was heavy with sleep.

"You knew her too, Reign. It's not like she died when you were born."

"I know. Please?"

Hedron sighed. "Fine. She loved you. She loved me. She loved everyone. Good?"

Reign did not answer. She was having trouble keeping her eyes open as she stared through an opening in the thick canopy above at a single star peeking through. Stories of Moira always comforted her.

"She did love everyone, actually," Hedron continued after her non-response. "She would often take in those who were just passing by, no matter if we had provisions or not for them. We used to always have enough, but that changed after—well, you know. Mother was strong, though. She hid it well, but I could see the loneliness. The sadness. Above it all, she was still beautiful."

Just as sleep overtook her, Reign thought she heard Hedron say, "Like you." She smiled and left behind her fears and sorrow as sleep finally took her.

She screamed in the night, but no sound came from her. The scream was audible only in her mind. Reign watched motionless as the scary man searched for her, his head jerking in different directions, seething. His face contorted as he snorted short, feral intakes of the night air, flaring the gills on the bridge of his nose. She felt the urge to silently plead for her father to get up, but she did not. She sat there, as if dead inside, motionless. Emotionless.

The raindrops hit his bald head and dripped down his brow, tracing the geometric scars that connected and covered his exposed flesh completely. His sword ran with her father's blood. But she felt nothing, not even fear as he drew closer to her perch. She heard noise from afar that seemed to approach. Howls in the night, but Reign did not react. She did not even blink.

Then, others were present to her view from the Triarch in which she hid. Her mother, huddled over her father. The rain could not mask her tears as she screamed. Aiden and the hold guard sprinting through the forest, hunting something. The hounds sniffing intently in all directions around the scene, coaxed by the kennel masters. Hedron hiding behind a tree wearing a paralyzed look of confusion. He looked around warily, his lip quivering. As he did so, his sight rested upon the Triarch that nestled Reign about twenty feet off the forest floor. She knew he had found her even though he could not see her so far back in the dark hollow cavity of the tree. She still remained immovable, seeing but not feeling. She felt cold and gray on the outside, hard and rigid on the inside. The impossibility of what her eyes had seen clashed with what she knew in her heart, that her father could not die, could not fail. And yet he was there, not far from her. Lifeless, just as she felt.

It pushed against her.

Reign awoke with a start, nearly falling from the branches that nestled her. Hedron still slumbered next to her, oblivious to the world. A small caterpillar rested on a patch of leaves near her left hand where she had grabbed the bark so tightly that her hand pulsed and ached. The nightmare, the same as always. She would not sleep longer this morning. The first glimpses of day's early pale light were becoming visible on the horizon. Hunger usually visited her after the night terrors.

Thumping. Quick of pace, light, but drawing nearer. Dropping without noise to the forest floor, Reign extracted one short-blade from the inner sheath of her leg. The curved knife resembled that of a thin crescent moon. Its twin remained sheathed; she would not need both. Then, with her free hand and feet, she escalated up the self-same tree she had just vacated, roughly to the height of a man. Her one hand clinging hard to the tree, the other relaxed with the short-blade's hilt therein. The hilt had a cover of sheep-skin, soft and molded to her hand over the many years. It had once seemed so large.

She focused, forcing out all thought. Instinct would take over when the time came. The vibrations became more intense, although she knew she wasn't *hearing* the footfall. A wood-dweller often felt more than heard, particularly in a forest of the West. Inter-tangled root systems of thousands of trees quickly transferred vibrations with more clarity than sound through the air over long distances. Reign could decipher distance, speed, approximate size and number by clinging to a tree and concentrating. Only one was coming toward her. *Wait for it …*

She leaped down, short-blade hand swiping through the air with speed, the bladed edge finding purchase as the smell of fresh blood filled the morning. Her momentum carried her gracefully through a full turn before stopping in a crouch, short-blade arm uplifted in a defensive posture just below her chin. She could eas-ily pounce and strike again if needed, but Reign knew it was over. The large elk fell not two feet from where the blow had been dealt.

Hedron awakened to the smell of elk being smoked over a small fire. The morning meal was being prepared precisely below the branches where he had been sleeping.

"Reign," he said groggily, wiping the nightsands from his eyes. "You made me breakfast."

"Really? I only see room for one down here," came her jest. Hedron let himself fall the nearly thirty feet to the ground, coming to settle cross-legged next to his sister while still yawning. He stared greedily at the meat over the open fire.

"I didn't even hear you awaken. You should have told me you were fetching food."

"Why?" Reign asked. "So you could wish me luck and roll back over?"

"Ha! You think me of no worth in a hunt, dear sister?" Hedron exclaimed. "Well, I'll have to allow you to observe my next hunt. You might learn something."

"Oh, I think I've seen enough of your hunting. Somehow I'm the one who always has to make the kill before it gets away."

Reign's prize would provide them meat for spans and with something to trade at the various markets they passed through.

"There's no way we'll be able to carry all the meat. We'll smoke and salt what we can't cook and carry as much as we can with us. Even then, a good portion will still go to waste," Hedron observed.

The boy sat there without response from Reign. He frowned as he observed her, busily tending to the preparation of the meal. Such pensive intensity for the early hour of a new day. "Again?" he asked.

"As always," she said, not looking up from the smoking meat. Hedron knew of her dreams, how they were always of that night. His own nightmares of losing their mother had ceased years ago.

"Why do you suppose the Ancient Heavens keep the dream upon your mind in the night?" Hedron asked. "You have not slept peacefully for ages, and these last cycles have seen your nights more restless than before."

She did not respond. Still not meeting his eyes, she apportioned a part of the game for her brother, and went to work on her own. Hedron sat nonplussed for a time, but then the pull of hunger bade him release himself from his question, and he ate.

"I think I shall head south and visit Kathryn this night," Hedron declared, his mouth full of his breakfast. "It has been several span, and she must no doubt be in need of my presence."

"Of your doting, you mean," Reign said.

"Reign, peace. Will you come?"

"Who will look after you if not me? But Hedron, why not go to the north? We were just in the south and we haven't visited Jayden and her packs for some seasons."

"Bah," Hedron scoffed. "Wolves. Why is it you find fascination with Jayden? That old pile of bones is nothing but a bore. I pray for the Ancient Heavens to allow me to die rather than listen to her. All her ramblings and mutterings. Really, Reign, the cold, the ice, the wind—"

"I like it," Reign offered simply. "The wolves are…" She looked to be pondering the word. "Understanding," she finally said. The many years in the northern Gonfrey Forest with Jayden had left Hedron grateful for her protection but also done with the North. He much preferred the more temperate climate of the West or even the warmth of the South. The Hoyt hold in Thera was not so far distant from Calyn, both cities somewhat cradling the Roniah on opposite sides.

"Reign, please. Come with me south first and by next Rising Season we'll visit Jayden. I promise."

"You know this is a fantasy." Reign said this sternly, but in a calm tone. "Kathryn will be sent off to marry not many years hence. Perhaps to House Orion, or even Gonfrey, poor girl. Enslaved by a life of ladyship."

"You do have a way with perspective, Reign. Still, I love Kathryn. Can I not follow this path?"

Reign did not answer. She looked away, devoid of facial reaction and word. Closing her eyes, she fought back as it pushed against her again. She let her dark hair fall over her face to conceal her grimace from Hedron as she struggled against the pressure.

Later that day the Kerr twins moved east and came to the edge of the forest, where rolling hills sprawled for dozens of leagues before the borders of the Realm's Crossing. The Changrual Monastery was built upon the geographic intersection where all four provinces met, symbolizing a unity of faith throughout the Realm. According to the legends, the Realm's division into provinces happened only after the Changrual had chosen the location for the Monastery and was settled. The plot of land they chose was not the center of the Realm from a geographic standpoint, but the High Vicars declared the land to be where the Ancient Heavens had desired the structure to be built. Oliver Wellyn did not argue, according to the legend. The Arlethian borders had already been established, however, they having occupied the land long before the Senthary arrived. These rolling hills were augmented to their borders after the location for the Monastery had been chosen so that it would lie partially on their land just as the other three provinces.

"Where to now?" Reign asked. They both stood looking over the hills and Hedron again realized they did not have a place to call home in all the world. He did not care.

Hedron risked a glance south, but Reign scowled and shoved him for even thinking about it. "I curse the day you met that child."

"Child? She's fourteen, a year younger than us is all. She's no more a child than you or me."

"Is that what you really think, Hedron? Has she lived as we have? When you were fourteen, were you living pampered in some grand hold with servants to answer your beck and call? Or was she on her own, living from meal to meal and running from her own name?"

"Kathryn has depth that you can't see, Reign," Hedron replied with rare firmness. "How many people don't care about our name and accept us as we are? She has shown the ability to see well beyond the lies that spewed forth from the Granite Throne. That is worth a lot to me, and should be to you, too."

Hedron called the propaganda about their father and family lies, but he was not as sure as he sounded. Stubborn seeds of doubt remained.

Reign sighed. "So, where to?"

Hedron didn't look ready to let their argument drop, but answered, "The Silver Pools? It's only a few days' sprint."

"Three days for you, maybe, but only two for me!" Reign darted off silently across the green landscape. Hedron would let her get a head start. She always needed it. Reign was faster, but Hedron could always catch her over a distance. His endurance levels seemed to draw upon fathomless reserves of energy.

He took a small nibble of leftover meat from breakfast, looked longingly south once more, and then took off after Reign.

TWENTY-ONE

Hedron

Day 28 of 4th High 412 A.U.

"REACH A LITTLE HIGHER," Kathryn whispered. She was a bit giddy with excitement to see her secret love again. "You've almost got it."

Hedron was scaling the wall of Hold Hoyt to Kathryn's elevated chamber loft, a task made more difficult when night was overcast, concealing the light of moons and stars alike.

He reached the top of the window ledge, which resembled more a battlement, and hoisted himself up. "Kathryn," he said as he tried to calm his breathing.

"Shhh…," she hushed him. But, he ignored her, and pulled her to him, embracing her. After a brief moment, Kathryn pushed back and slapped him. Hedron looked stunned.

"What was that for?"

"Must I tell you? Is it not obvious?" Kathryn retorted.

"Ah, come on Kathryn, I'm here now, aren't I? You know I always try to come as often as I can. Besides, it seems to have become much more of a risk to make my way to your side than ever before."

"Well," Kathryn spoke in low tones, "you are here now." She softened, her hurt glare turning to a relieved but wary expression.

"Father means to have me married within two years, but seeks to make firm arrangements as soon as possible. He prepares meeting after meeting for me to entertain 'suitable choices'. It is quite maddening to play the part when my heart lies else where."

"Suitable choices?" Hedron replied, amusement on his face. "So, who have you chosen? No, don't tell me – I'm certain I'll guess. Is it Brennan Gulway?"

"What?" Kathyrn sounded hurt. "Brennan? Certainly not. His eye brows are practically a forest of their own – " Hedron did not let her finish.

"It must be…let me see…oh, yes I'm sure it would be Lawry Mendell! He's got enough krenshell to buy any lady's heart." Hedron was clearly enjoying himself.

"Honestly, do you really believe I would consent to marry someone who threw tree sap in my hair as a child? It took mother ages to – "

Hedron's laughter interrupted her. Kathryn grabbed a pillow from her bed and smacked him with it several times before smothering his face with it to muffle his laughter.

"You're going to get yourself captured or worse!" Kathryn hissed. "They don't know who you are but my father and his men do know someone visits me after your last narrow escape."

"Narrow escape?" Hedron asked. "Narrow? My dear Lady Kathryn, your father's men nearly provided me a bit of needed exercise as they chased me from the hold. They couldn't catch me if they – "

"But their arrows could, Hedron. Just be quieter and you wouldn't have to escape."

"Ah, Kathryn, your concern so moves me," he jested. "In fact, I think I'll go to your father now and proclaim my love for you and insist I be given your hand in marriage." He arose at once as if to go and do exactly as he said.

A look of terror took over Kathryn's face. She grabbed his hand tightly and tugged his arm, shaking her head with pleading eyes. Hedron broke into laughter again and plopped down on to her bed. Kathryn rolled her eyes and relaxed. "Why do I put up with you?"

"Because of my natural wit and extremely charming looks," Hedron responded with feigned confidence. He still wore his mischievous grin.

"No, actually, I'm sure it's nothing more than a childish crush on danger, as my mother tells me," said Kathryn playfully.

"Oh, that has to be it. I mean, no wonder they want you to marry someone respectable. Someone like, hmmmm – like Reginald Sperry!" This latest taunt earned Hedron another light slap, but this time Kathryn laughed as well.

"A life with Reginald is assured to be short due to death by boredom!" Kathryn countered.

"Why?" Hedron asked. "You don't find his dried Hydraf collection the most fascinating thing in the Realm?"

"Shhh" Kathryn whispered. Voices were heard outside her room approaching from the outer hallway. "Hide!"

Hedron ducked under her bed, on the side that was concealed by a rather large clothing chest, chiding himself for not being more sensitive to the vibrations around him. Though not as easy to decipher through stone, he still should have sensed the approach earlier. Two guards with a torch peered into her chamber opening.

"Are you well, young Lady Kathryn?"

"I am, kind sirs," she said in her most calm and proper tone. They stood for a moment longer and then continued on their routes.

Hedron came out of hiding once he felt their footsteps far enough away. His demeanor was more serious now, eyes full of thought.

"What is it?" Kathryn asked.

Hedron didn't meet her gaze. He considered for a moment longer, then said, "What are we doing?"

The question lingered for a moment and then he did meet her eyes. The orange candlelight glimmered on half her face, concealing the other in shadow.

She's so beautiful, Hedron thought. *And so out of reach.* He touched the scars on his chest through his shirt that remained as a cruel reminder of earlier childhood lessons. Juxtapose to Kathyrn's beauty was his disfigured body. Some scars large, some small; some seen, others unseen. Even such a wound as the one on his chest would have left little evidence of ever existing had he been wrapped in Triarch leaves, but no Triarch tree survived in the northern tundra of the Gonfrey Forest where the trees where strangers and were not fluent. He carried the outward scars symbolizing what had become of his house and name.

"Hedron, what do you mean," Kathryn entreated lightly. He could tell she was trying to counter his change in mood.

"This is a dream. A good dream, but still one that will eventually end by an unwelcome awakening. There's no chance for me to find favor with your father. I have nothing to offer except my name, which is more a deterrent than aid. Ancients, Kathryn, it's a dam that I fear can never be broken." *Reign is right.*

He knelt down and took Kathryn's hand. "I would give anything to marry you and have you be my honored wife, but this can not be. We both know it but have ignored it for so long. I come from no house or status worthy of a lady's hand. Should I even try to convince your father, I would have to lie about who I am. I've done this almost my whole life, but I won't for this. I won't have a lie be what our marriage begins with."

Kathryn did not say anything for a moment, but knelt down next to him and took his face in her hands.

"Hedron," she started with a tone of confidence at odds with his of resignation. "Hedron, you are mistaken. You are of House Kerr, a name as old and honored as Hoyt, Wellyn or Chester. Older, even. You are heir to your father's hold and have a rightful claim to lordship of the Western Province. Lord Therrium is honorable, but was only made provincial lord as a placeholder under the law, and only permanently after you were presumed dead. You know this is true."

"But I am dead to the world, and heir to nothing. The Kerr succession is dead." Anger rose in Hedron as he spoke, breaking away from Kathryn's touch. "My family's hold lay in ruins, overrun and reclaimed by the forest. All the Realm spurns the name Kerr for a false betrayal conjured up by deviant men for reasons I do not know, but are surely as shallow as their perpetrators' own existence."

"Hedron that's not – "

"Yes it is. If anyone knew a Kerr still lived, how quickly would a bounty be extended? How many would come for me? For Reign?"

"Where is Reign?" Kathryn asked.

"Headed north. Somewhere in the Western Province currently, I'm sure. She'll be with Jayden in a span, give or take a day." Hedron's voice was flat.

Kathryn never enjoyed these times when Hedron was so full of self-deprecation. He had related much of their early childhood history, but always in a lighthearted tone, as if a fairytale. But Kathryn knew the experiences, which would make for great entertaining stories of a storyweaver, were anything but lighthearted and entertaining for Hedron and Reign. She recognized the strength that had been forged in him, even if he could not see it. He was as strong and flexible as Jarwyn steel, forged in a furnace of affliction.

"I don't know," Kathryn finally said in a somber tone. "But, I do know that you are the rightful heir of your house. The Ancient Heavens would grant to you that which is yours, that which was stripped from you by those with dark intent."

"We tell ourselves that to be comforted. But what if they were right and my father was who they say he was? We don't really know. Not truly."

"They say the same thing about your mother. Do you honestly doubt your mother's integrity as well?" Kathryn asked. "Even if what they say is half true about your father, you are the better half."

"It is a dream. I am not but fifteen years of age. I've no training in matters of state, no skill with steel or bow, no reason for men to follow me or care – "

"You are wrong," Kathryn interrupted. "Hedron, you've forgotten the weight your name used to carry. If a Kerr were to rise up and claim his role and place, others would follow. I promise they would. Father still speaks of Lord Thannuel in respectful tones when others are not around. His renouncement was for show in the public eye as I'm certain is the case for many others."

Kathryn stopped speaking, but her eyes continued silently pleading for Hedron to understand.

"Pretense or not, your father could not consent for our marriage for the same reasons he renounced my father," Hedron answered without looking at her.

"But we must try, my love. Father is a good man, he will figure something out if nothing else for the simple fact he still silently honors your house and father." Kathryn was insistent, her face showing that she truly believed her words.

The silence was as a rift between them. Kathryn knew continuing the verbal volley would be to no avail, but the sadness that came upon Hedron was palpable.

Night still had many hours before retreat, and Hedron's eyes swam with weariness. He lay down on his side on the thick animal fur rug at the side of Kathryn's bed. She reached her hand down from her bed and rested it upon his head, her hand gently caressing through his thick auburn hair.

In a few moments, his breathing became long and even. Kathryn lay in silence, her eyes glistening with emotion. How could she make Hedron understand? How could she convince him of his worth? Of her father's capacity for understanding and mercy?

"Stay with me," she whispered. "Don't give up on yourself, on us." But Hedron was deep in slumber where Kathryn could not follow.

———

Hedron awoke briskly. He could smell fire and something else—death. Realizing he was still at Hold Hoyt in Kathryn's chamber, he gathered his mind as well as his short blade. Then he focused on the scent again, and recognized it was not here, in his presence, that the sensations were emanating from. He let his mind flow to the place it lead him and fear grasped a hold of his heart.

"Reign," he said in a violent whispered exhale while simultaneously arising from the ground and bolting out the arch window some scores of feet to the ground below, silent and swift as any wood-dweller.

———

Lord Calder Hoyt often wandered the silent halls of his hold in the early morning hours before light came to the world. As Provincial Lord of the Southern Province, much weighed on his mind. Matters of state were a heavy burden for any man, no matter how strong and square his shoulders might be or his mental prowess. Then there was the ever-present worry for his family's safety. For more than half a decade, Lord Hoyt carried the shame of denouncing Lord Kerr, a man whom he knew to be nothing but honorable. He knew Wellyn was somehow involved. He was up to something, but his family would come to great harm if he vocalized or acted on his conscience. There were those that would come for him, demons from the Fathomless Abyss.

Following his normal routine, Lord Calder Hoyt peered into his daughter's room. Across the stone floor, he could view her bed with its canopy hovering over her as if a protective shield. The thick cloud cover, shrouding even the light of the stars, extended the night's dark veil. The faint shimmer of light from the torch on the wall at the room's entrance only illuminated a few feet around the flame, leaving most of his daughter's expansive chamber cradled in night.

The faintest glint of gray was visible through her window adjacent to her bed. Calder started, just for a moment. Had he seen something? A figure silhouetted in palest gray morning's light? He snatched the torch up from its wall mount and sprinted toward his daughter's large bed, putting himself instinctively between the supposed specter at the window and his Kathryn.

There was no one there. Peering down from the arched opening, he chanced a glance downward, but the torch revealed no one and nothing. His heart beating at a slightly elevated pace, he turned about to ensure his daughter was there and safe. Her breathing was even and steady. He took her left arm that was hanging off the side of the bed and gently placed it under her coverings.

She will need to make a decision soon, he thought. *She has not been intended since she was eight – since Hedron.* That was odd in the Realm for a young lady of Kathryn's standing. Lord Hoyt knew his daughter still held the dead Kerr boy somewhere in her heart.

"Let him go," he whispered. But he did not know how he could expect her to when he had not ever forgiven himself.

Thannuel was no traitor. We betrayed him, *his family. His children.*

Then, Lord Calder Hoyt, one of the most powerful men in all the Realm, knelt beside his daughter's bed and silently wept.

TWENTY-TWO

Aiden

Day 28 of 4th High 412 A.U.

THE HALLWAYS OF HOLD THERRIUM gave no sound as the assassin slowly made his way along. Save for walking in bare feet, stone would echo the footsteps of the most cautious person, unless he were a wood-dweller. To infiltrate the hold he had to become one of them, at least on the outside. The years of playing a role had morphed him to that person he once pretended to be. *Tyjil had been right*, he admitted. The caverns of darkness in his mind were fully explored over the years, and he now reveled in the darker parts of his psyche. Forced to be here, yes he was. But as time went on, he came to love his role; to envy the person he was by façade until finally, the façade became his identity.

The assassin stepped back quickly behind a corner in a tributary corridor. Torchlight was approaching from a perpendicular vector. He drew a short blade—the same he had used to end Moira Kerr—as he crouched farther in the darkness, receding from the approaching light. The stone was cold this night but with a slight touch of moisture as most things in the Western Province.

The torch and its bearer passed. In a moment he continued, slowly and silently through the hold. After years of preparation, he knew the patterns and movements of his fellow hold guards and who was on duty this night. He had chosen this night for action as he believed the least threatening resistance would be found, and sent word by wing of his intent. The High Duke undoubtedly had put other pieces in play to coincide with his role, but he was oblivious to who or what those other moving parts were.

Training within these circles had given him an edge, knowing how they fought and thought. His mission would be easily carried out, but he may not escape.

Ahnia. He thought of his wife. Did she remember him? Did his teenage children? They were barely teenagers anymore. His son and daughter may even be married. Tyjil had not brought him word for years on any matter, much less his family.

He crept closer, finding the guards more numerous as he closed in on his eventual destination. He was prepared for this. His speed of travel must be slow and deliberate. Though silent, he could still send vibrations that could be felt by others, even though most of the hold was stone and not forest. It still presented a reasonable danger of being detected. *Silent in breath and step*, he told himself. *For them, I must succeed.* But he would do this duty even if his family were not under duress at this time. True, it was force that put him into action at first, but he had been changed. He *wanted* this task now, and was grateful for it. He could no longer tell if this was the Darkness inside him or if he had become the Darkness.

Tension. Alrikk could feel it in the forest. The trees felt…uneasy. He couldn't detect any actual disturbance, but also could not shake the warning he felt. Staring out in a predominantly eastward direction, Alrikk concentrated. He grabbed the small Triarch leafling in his pocket beneath his scabbard, closing his eyes, focusing. Even the sound of the wind howling through the sparkling canopy high above seemed to bespeak a nervous apprehension. His brow furrowed in the moment of concentration, almost grasping the loose tendrils of revelation.

Almost.

It was Alrikk's night as hold overseer. He enjoyed the solitude this post offered, high above the forest floor in the southeast tower. The small cage of pigeons rested on the floor at his feet. Though crafted of stone, many trees wrapped their limbs around the tower, aiding the overseer in sensing and feeling the boundaries of the hold. Combined with that aid and the small Triarch leafling he now fervently held, Alrikk was finally getting closer. Deeper.

Almost.

He held his breath as it finally came.

"No! It can't be!" he gasped in disbelief. He reached for the overseer horn to sound a warning, but it was too late.

———

Aiden knew the time had come. He lay waiting expectantly for Shane in Lord Therrium's quarters. The man had come to be with them a few years earlier, seeking employ as a sentry among them, but Aiden looked long into the man's eyes. He recognized what he saw, for he had seen it in himself many years ago.

Aiden remembered well the first time he had killed. He was just a boy then but nowhere near innocent. The irony of putting an end to one that had given him life was not lost on him. He just did not care.

Cliffs in the west were only found in Helving, and few wood-dwellers chose to live there, where trees were much more sparse. The large Furlop tree, named after the white moss that hung from its branches by lengths as much as fifty paces or more, did populate the land in those parts fairly well, however. The long white tendrils of the Furlop moss were beautiful from afar, extending over and below the cliffs, swaying in the wind like wispy vertical clouds hanging from an invisible hinge. As a young child, Aiden and his friends would dare one another to swing as far out as possible on the hanging moss over the void. Reckless stupidity but fun for the lads. Far below the town, which sat upon several cliff ridges connected by wide bridges, ran the Roniah River as it flowed from the Southern Province.

"You're afraid, aren't you, lad?" his father jeered.

Mehril had come home, wasted on strong drink. It was the typical scene the twelve-year-old Aiden had been used to for years. His mother was unknown to him, a mere story. He only knew what his father told him, that she died bringing him into the world. Mehril made no secret that he wished the reverse had been true.

"And just what do you plan to do with that?" his father asked.

Aiden held a blade in his hand between him and his father. The stench of fermented drink was strong upon him. The bruises had not completely healed from the last time his father had been in a drunken stupor. That was only two nights past. For more years than the boy could recall, he had been the outlet of Mehril's rage when drunk.

"Maybe you're finally toughening up," his father taunted. "That's all I've been trying to do for years."

Aiden did not respond but stood ready, tense.

"Well, come on then, if ya have it in you! You'll find killin' is as easy as breathin'. You should know. You killed your mother with your first breath!"

He was scared after he had done it, seeing that his father did not rise again. The blade's handle protruding from Mehril's ribs, the pool of blood spread out underneath him like a dark red river breaking through a dam. But he was also exhilarated. Liberated.

Aiden knew what it was to be a killer. What it looked like, what it felt like. It was easily recognizable to him.

And Shane wore the emotional trappings of a killer. Aiden wanted him close to him rather than afar. Shane trained hard, working his way up within the ranks of the hold guard. Aiden had thought that perhaps what lay within the man would eventually fade away—he hoped it would.

But some three span earlier, Aiden witnessed Shane attaching a message to a falcon's leg and releasing the bird into the sky. It was an odd choice for a messenger bird, but an extremely fast breed. Shane thought no one had been watching, but Aiden always watched. The death of his Lord and friend Thannuel, ever present upon his mind, kept him sharp and distrusting.

Silently, Aiden had ascended the trees, through the canopy to the top of the forest. He saw the falcon heading north by northeast. He ran and leaped with all the speed he could bring to bear, tearing across the treetops as if in flight. Before long, he had matched the predator bird's speed and silently launched himself into the air. The bird screeched in surprise when Aiden's strong hands grabbed its body firmly but not enough to damage it. He landed gracefully and ignored the falcon's attempts to peck and claw at him. It flapped its wings wildly as Aiden held it by its neck with one hand and with the other, took rolled parchment from its leg.

Banner Therrium. First moon, twenty-eighth day of the Fourth Dimming Cycle of the Moons.

Aiden's mind swam with questions. He wondered where the bird was headed and to whom. What could the message mean? But Aiden did not need to think long on its meaning. Knowing who had sent the message, he believed he had a clear understanding of its intent. He had stumbled onto a plot, but he did not know all the players. He thought it best to allow the story to unfold to discover the other characters.

After only a brief few moments, he replaced the message and returned the bird to the sky. It continued on its original trajectory.

Now, on the day mentioned in the enigmatic missive, first moon had risen. Therrium's chamber door slowly opened, but no light followed. *Impressive*, Aiden thought. No vibration could he detect from his visitor. Aiden closed his eyes for the briefest moment, quelling emotion and forcing out all thought, the way he had been trained by his former Lord. Kerr was not just his Lord, but a mentor—the father he should have had.

The blanket concealed Aiden's identity, covering his head save for the top of his dark hair, but the dark itself would have been enough. He knew Shane would strike quickly, a short blade to the heart while muffling any feeble cry. He heard the soft touch of a hand grab a pillow next to his head, the slight draft made by it being lifted from the bed. No doubt Shane intended to slam the pillow upon his face as the blade found purchase in his heart.

Aiden tightened the grip around his sword's hilt, pressing the Triarch leafing flush between his palm and the grip. The slight tingle he had become accustomed to traveled up his arm and he knew the strange blade was humming again, the way it did when Aiden was tense and focused more centrically with danger close, the way it did that night many years ago when he had failed. As he concentrated, a word formed in his mind, one that was foreign to him. He could not banish it from his mind and so he accepted it.

In an instant he felt the direction of the air change so minutely but enough for him to instinctively know that something was coming at him. Aiden rose as if in flight, the night's darkness his terrible cloak as he spun through the air. The word that had rooted itself in his mind found his lips and he whispered, *"Faerathm!"* His steel was swung with such speed through the darkness that the stench of burned air was joined briefly by the smell of blood. Shane's head sat for a brief moment upon his neck before toppling to the stone floor, followed by his body sinking to his knees. There was almost no blood, only the smell of burned carnage. The vibrations of the lifeless corpse and head finding the ground caused other guards to rush to the chamber of Lord Therrium, torches in one hand, drawn steel in the other. Upon the room becoming illuminated by the orange-yellow glow of fire, the guards stood perplexed, then relieved catching sight of Aiden. Then the others noticed Shane, which returned some fear to their faces. Aiden could see now that Shane's wound was completely cauterized.

"Peace," Aiden spoke softly. "Shane sought the death of our Lord. His intentions were known to me."

"Master Aiden, I don't under—" one of the guards began, but Aiden cut him off.

"The details are not important. Lord Therrium is safe with his family and the Archiver Mithi'ah, I having personally made the arrangements. They are sequestered among the far parts of the hold in a servant's chambers." The men did not seem comforted by this, as servants' chambers were not in the normal circulation of the guards' routine.

"But Master Aiden, this would leave the Lord exposed. In such a lightly defended portion of the hold—"

"No one would ever suspect him to be there," Aiden finished for the guard in a manner that said the discussion was over. "We will go and fetch him now, but say nothing along the way. You men are now his personal escort until he is safely—"

A loud, tremulous cacophony commanded their attention. All in the room turned their eyes toward the provenance of the sound. It faded, but was followed by another—the sound of terror-filled screams. Shouts of men, the music of steel in battle. Now it was Aiden's turn for confusion, but stealing a glance at his men in Therrium's chamber told him they had no explanation, nor did he expect them to. He sped from the room toward the sounds and cries, which came predominantly from the east wall of the hold. He broke into speed, faster than any human could travel and faster than most could follow with their eyes. A green field of grass and shrubbery separated the hold's wall from the actual hold that by day was pleasant in all manners. Tonight, however, it was enshrouded by death and chaos.

Aiden stared slack-jawed at what was once the eastern wall, but was now no more than rubble masquerading as hindrances to the men at arms as they fought. Scores of men poured through the breeched wall in small garrisons of axes, swords and short archers. Someone had marshaled a small regime and come against the capital of the Western Province on the very night an assassination attempt had been made on Lord Therrium. And, this force had come largely undetected by the wood-dwellers until the attack was sprung. It was maddeningly perplexing how this could have happened. One side looked disorganized and dazed, the other group of soldiers deliberate and uniformed. It was the hold guard, the wood-dwellers, who were struggling in disorganization with this unknown foe.

Aiden came to himself at once, barking orders and commands to his men. He commanded easily three hundred of the hold guard, but this attacking force was thousands in strength. The armies of Therrium were scattered throughout the province, serving mostly as peacekeepers at various posts. Easily fifty thousand swords, axes, spears, and archers made up the Western Province's force, but little good that did tonight.

Turning to Alrikk, Aiden snapped, "Send word by wing to General Roan at Riley's Cove of our attack. Bid him return with a force of at least five thousand." The boy was pale and looked like he wanted to say something. Aiden did not wait for Alrikk's response but turned immediately back to the scene of carnage before him. He doubted their desperate message would be received in time. The attacking army was dressed all in black, from the hoods that concealed their faces to the boots upon their feet. Aiden let out a bellow of a cry calling his guards to formation. Never had they trained to face a force of strength of ten to one, but a quick scan of the situation allowed Aiden to guess within fifty men that those were their odds. A Lord's Guard was trained expertly against small forces or single opponents, usually seeking to infiltrate a hold or assassinate some important noble or Lord; but fighting off or defending against an army was not part of their training nor expected of them.

Was the Realm under attack? From who? Aiden could not waste precious moments on these questions.

His men retreated to him in speed, answering his call. They were only about two-hundred and sixty now, but the dead of their enemy were at least five times their losses. As deft and quick as a wood-dweller may be, they are still mortal and can be overcome. The force that had come against them was strong and well trained, prepared for the difficulties of fighting against Arlethian Warriors a normal human would face. If they were prepared, then this enemy was familiar with wood-dwellers. That only left a couple possibilities as to their origin.

The withdrawal of Therrium's guards from the fray caused a brief lull in the battle.

"Drake, Ebry, your detachments fall back on the right three paces behind my position, two lines deep and staggered. Shoren, bring you detachment on my left, two paces forward of myself. When they rush your side, retreat back and right as Drake and Ebry swing forward and left to flank their forward attack, then cease your retreat and press into the fray. We will create an uneven arm that pivots as if on a single joint. Both sides will swivel opposite each other, never allowing the enemy get behind us and always causing them to be flanked as they press. We cannot attack directly, but we can determine where they focus theirs and minimize losses."

As he spoke, it was done. It was a subordinate defensive position, Aiden knew, but was the best chance they had to survive long enough to shave down the size of the attacking force to where they could feasibly press an attack or for General Roan's forces to arrive. If they survived long enough to make the odds three or even four to one, the battle would easily turn their way.

The army of black attacked with a wicked cry. As Aiden knew would happen, they ran straight to the side of the arm that stood protruding to his left. Shoren's detachment did not stand against them, but retreated swiftly as planned, seeming to swing Drake and Ebry's detachments up and to the left with inhuman speed into the flank of the black army. Being vastly outnumbered did not stop the small force of Therrium's guards from felling their enemies with minimal losses. Shoren's detachment now pressed back, surprising the overconfident point of the black army even as Drake and Ebry worked death upon the mysterious attackers. For every wood-dweller that fell, no less than three of the black army were taken with them. But this was not enough. If this were to be a battle of attrition, Aiden's men would not survive. They would have to attack after all, relying on speed and confusion.

Aiden yelled for a sprint across the top of the army, using the heads and shoulders of their enemies as their stepping stones, cutting them down from above as they went. Side to side they ran, as if in flight five to six feet in the air. The dexterity and agility of the Arlethian guards was awe-inspiring and the army of black was decreased as the battle become more intense. Short archers caught on to the strategy and unleashed their wooden missiles just above the height of a man, catching scores of Aiden's men and bringing them down. Ebry took an arrow in the left thigh, causing him to stumble into the masses of soldiers who cut him down. Others began to fall and Aiden started to feel fear overcome his rationale. He had less than one hundred men now while the army of black still had close to a thousand. *Focus*, he reminded himself. *Think of nothing but this moment.*

The night air was littered with arrows as the short archers loosed missile after missile. His men had dwindled to several dozen. Aiden heard every loosed arrow as it sprang from the taught bowstring, the fletchings whistling through the air. He knew the archers were firing blindly, but it was proving effective. Coming down from his unnatural flight across the heads and shoulders of his enemies, Aiden splashed in a puddle of water, blood and carnage, now surrounded by the soldiers in black on all sides. No longer could he feel his men in the battle.

He smiled, and wondered if it had taken this many to bring down Thannuel Kerr. *Twice as many, no doubt,* Aiden mused to himself. He was relieved in a way, knowing that he would soon rest, having given his life in the execution of his duty, as he felt he should have those many years ago. Perhaps there would be something more after this world as Kerr had always promised there would be. He was so sure, so certain, always. Aiden was only certain of his next moments.

His head was bowed slightly, but his eyes looked up and forward into the sea of malicious black. Aiden could feel the battle around him as only an Arlethian could. He felt the clash of steel and wood, the slashing of flesh and bones breaking as they gave way under strong blows, the wind parting from the fletching of the arrows that disrupted the night air. His medium length black hair shimmered in the moonlight, the wind parting the hair from his face and revealing to those around him a most out of place grin. Aiden looked as if he had legions backing him, as if he pitied the hundreds that stood to press down against him. This caused those immediately around him to pause momentarily in some confusion. Perhaps they wondered what Aiden knew that they did not, but it was nothing so mysterious as this. Aiden was a man who had nothing to lose, a man who did not expect to live to see morning's light. It was the look of one who had dealt out much death and knew it had finally come for him. This acceptance shone in his countenance, frightening the soldiers who had come with such force into Hold Therrium, into the hold he had sworn to protect with his life's blood.

Aiden glanced down at his sword and the curious thought occurred to him that never, for the past six years, had it been more than an arm's reach from him. Its steel was blackened from the Jarwynian ore and forging process that gave it unnatural lightweight, strength, and flexibility. Worth a small fortune in krenshell, it was all Aiden had left of his mentor, whom he would soon join.

"Be with me," he whispered.

Aiden moved in what was a blur to the soldiers in black. His steel found flesh underneath black cloak and uniform with every stroke and swing as it hummed its discordant but beautiful song in the chaotic night. One enemy soldier in black after the other fell until Aiden no longer had conscious thought of his actions, letting his mind and body take over. As one soldier came to where he should have been, Aiden attacked from behind. He was, in this moment, a force that could not be comprehended by those around him. He moved with speed and strength beyond his own. *One stroke to slay one man.*

A large soldier bellowed forward with a dual sided battle-axe, swinging with intent to relieve Aiden of his head. He ducked instinctually, feeling the breeze of the axe just above him as it missed his head and lodged into another man's chest. Now kneeling, he locked his arms with his sword in an upward angle and lunged to his feet, forcing his blade through the man. Ripping his sword free in the next instant, Aiden swiped it through the air in a wide arc, catching three men in the throat. Most blows missed, but the few that were a threat to him were parried easily and met with deadly reprisal. Already a score of men lay dead or dying in his wake. Aiden was relentless, merciless. Before long, the archers were compelled to loose into the mass, taking losses of their own men as acceptable if it resulted in bringing down this last of Therrium's guard. Vibrations from the bowstrings announced their newest volley, and Aiden knew at once the arrows' vector, speed, and destination. He spun and ducked, using man after man as a shield from the deadly arrows, not realizing that his abilities to sense and feel were now at a level well beyond even the most skilled wood-dweller. The ground began to clear before him.

Steel bit into his thigh, but he continued unfazed, laying waste to all those around him. No other thought save for the cutting down of the next man occupied his mind. He wore a predatory smile as his vision turned a shade of crimson.

Reign left Hedron at the Silver Pools three days earlier. He was intent on going south again to see Kathryn. Reign had wanted to argue with him once more but had seen little point. The light in his eyes when he spoke of Kathryn was impossible to ignore.

Stupid boy's just setting himself up a huge heartbreak.

Reign wanted Hedron's happiness, even if it meant having that prissy little blonde as a sister-in-law; but she did not think it was even possible for Hedron to marry the young Hoyt girl.

Would he lie about his name? His identity?

The Kerr twins had done this before for their safety, but Reign sensed a streak of family loyalty that ran deep in Hedron, despite his internal conflict about their father.

Heading north to the Gonfrey Forest would bring her near Calyn. It wasn't the most direct route from the Silver Pools, but she preferred to travel within the forests of the West when she could. Still, she would stay to the outer reaches of the city, avoiding the chance of conjuring up too many childhood memories.

The early morning, just before dawn, was always so peaceful in the forest. She loved the smell of dew in the air just before sunrise and the fullness of life.

Crimson Snow would be a bit older in years now, and she wondered how many years the white wolf had left in this world. He had already outlived many of his siblings, being thirteen years old now.

Suddenly, Reign felt the beat of hundreds of feet upon the ground. Not wood-dwellers. It was just barely audible, coming into her sensory range through the ground a few steps ago. A small birch tree was next to her and she wondered if it would be enough.

She opened her hand to the trunk of the tree and put her palm flush against its bark. The vibrations all around her became amplified, but she singled out the footfall that had caught her attention.

Dancing? she wondered. If so, it was an extremely odd rhythm, if a rhythm at all. But then other sounds found her: steel clamoring, bodies thudding against the earth, staccato vibrations like small rocks striking the ground but with sharper intonations. *Arrows,* she realized.

The vector from whence the sounds came was familiar to her.

"Hold Therrium?" she asked aloud.

And then, she felt an all-too-familiar bloodcurdling stride, one that lived in the dark hollows of her memory. She froze, but only for an instant. Despite all the warnings she felt roaring through her, Reign ran toward the sounds of battle.

———

Aiden's sword was humming loudly enough for him to audibly hear it amid the battle, not just feel. The Triarch leafling between his hand and the sword's hilt felt warm, but perhaps that was just the heat and sweat of his hand. The word that had come to him in Therrium's chambers returned to his lips.

"Faerathm!" he yelled, as he once again brought his sword down upon a black-clad soldier. The sword cleaved the man in two and

the smell of burned flesh once again permeated the air. The humming of the sword quieted.

Suddenly, a man cloaked in a hooded robe broke off from the group of soldiers with speed that caught Aiden's attention for the briefest of moments. His cadence was a new one in the fight, fast and heavy. Aiden realized he hadn't felt this man's movement since he entered the fight. Was he still for the duration? Did he just arrive? No, that could not be; but this man certainly had not moved since Aiden had arrived on the scene. His movement was at high velocity toward the outer parts of the hold where the servant chambers were—where Lord Therrium remained hidden and safe with his family and Archiver. Hopefully. But this man, with the speed of a wood-dweller, moved toward the chambers where Therrium had been sequestered. A chill reverberated through Aiden's body as he remembered a similar creature that had outrun him years ago.

Could it be?

His mental break of concentration, though brief, was enough. A blow came to his side that he too late reacted to and deflected awkwardly, the enemy sword grazing his left side just under his elbow. The pain was searing but not debilitating. He took off the advancing soldier's head while his short-blade found the torso of an axeman. An arrow pierced the fleshy part of Aiden's underarm, causing him to release his short blade still embedded in the axe man's chest. He had heard the arrow coming, but the wounds of his thigh and torso were beginning to scream in protest, slowing his reactions. He cursed himself fiercely for his breach of concentration, twirling his body in a 180° downward motion. Down on one knee, he broke the rear end of the arrow and pulled it through his arm in one fluid motion. His attackers hadn't yet realized where Aiden had disappeared to, so swift had been his dive cloaked by the mask of night. Refocusing, Aiden worked on the legs of those surrounding him, cutting tendons and slashing muscles, disabling half a dozen men.

The man, he remembered. *Therrium.*

Bounding up from his crouch, Aiden sprinted across the heads and shoulders of the black soldiers, feeling the heavy cadence of his new prey. *Faster* he chided himself, trying to compel his aching muscles to higher velocity. *I will not fail another lord. I cannot.* The pain from his wounds would have normally incapacitated a man, even a wood-dweller. Despite this, his pace quickened, dealing death to those below him, slashing his sword downward and up again as if he were a bladed windmill in stride.

He caught sight of the man, standing outside the humble stone servant chambers, where Therrium lay hidden. How did the man know exactly where Therrium hid? Even more frightening was the inhuman speed this intruder displayed.

It has to be him! I'll not lose him this time!

The cloaked enigma stopped suddenly, short of the entrance to the chambers. Aiden ran toward him with fury in his eyes. The man reached up and slowly, unconcerned, removed the hood from his head. Revealed were a shorn head and a calm and confident demeanor. But the face itself was nothing Aiden had ever seen before. A pattern of some create covered his face, almost looking as if someone had carved a maze into his skin but leaving only the effect of the carving and no scar tissue. The man's nose had horizontal slits going up the bridge that flared as he approached. It struck him how this man could make a facial expression of serenity whilst also appear so menacing. Aiden stopped roughly ten paces from the man, glowering with rage and fury.

"I can smell it," the man said. "I smell your anger, your rage. Even the curious but misplaced recognition you think you have of me. I see I am not the first of my kind you have met. But you need not fall here."

As the man turned completely, now facing Aiden, he could see the sigil of House Wellyn that hung upon the amulet over the man's chest. *House Wellyn?* Confusion was followed by utter bewilderment. Aiden's head spun, coming close to madness as he considered this new information.

"Flee." The words were almost a growl. "Do not make an end of yourself this night. You need not be brought to dust. My Charge is not for you."

Aiden stopped trying to understand and returned to his basic mental position. *Protect the Lord of the Western Province.* Slowly, he walked sideways in a circle, never shortening the distance between himself and the man, but placing himself between this aggressor and the servant chamber's entrance.

"No, you must not—" the man protested, but it was too late. The nose gills flared again as Aiden's resolve hardened.

Now Aiden, master of the hold guard, stood between the enigmatic marred predator and Banner Therrium's family.

Not again, he promised himself. *Not tonight.*

Aiden's blade rested on the compact soil beneath him as he struggled to ignore the pain of his wounds. His focus was more difficult to maintain, like trying to catch a rapidly moving fish in a rushing river with bare hands.

Fallen Ancients! he cursed inwardly. *Focus, Blasted Night!* Then, a memory came back to him, something that Lord Kerr had told him.

"You, like all living things, Aiden, are a current," Lord Kerr had said. "A current of Light. Perhaps one day you will comprehend this."

He still did not comprehend it, but something in this moment caught in him as he reflected on Thannuel's words. That *something* found a center in him and his focus was revitalized. He immediately found a connection to the forest through the leafling in his palm pressed to his sword's hilt, and the blade once again began to hum.

"Ah, you are one of them," the man said. "This does make more sense." He stopped speaking for a moment and broke his stare with Aiden. "But you do not know you are. I smell your confusion at my words. Interesting."

Master Aiden was more indifferent but he supposed there were seeds of confusion within him. The man's words did not matter to him as they did not pertain to the here and now.

"I," the man continued, "am Maynard." He bowed his head slightly and seemed to make a show of introducing himself, as if he had rarely done it in his life.

"I do not care what your name is!" Aiden responded. "You carry the High Duke's emblem and you dare attack a Provincial Lord's hold! What is this treachery?"

Maynard shrugged. "I have little knowledge of the Stone's will. The Urlenthi commands and I obey its Dahlrak. It is the way of things, Light Shepherd."

Now Aiden's confusion did indeed find a more forward place in him. What were these words? *Urlenthi? Dahlrak? Light Shepherd?*

"I have seen your kind before, many years ago, fleeing from my Lord's hold. You will not escape me this time."

"Before your end," Maynard answered, "I will taste your fear, savoring it as I splash in your blood."

The man crouched slightly and sneered, losing all semblance of civility on his countenance, and charged. Aiden barely noticed in the night's light a dark blade in his grasp as he rushed toward him. Blood still coursing down his side, Aiden commanded his arm to react, raising his sword in defense.

The two collided with force and speed that would have left powder where bone had been for any normal mortal. The speed of their steel sparring was dizzying to the onlookers. The soldiers clothed in all black had followed Aiden in herd-like fashion, but had stopped short to witness this confrontation.

There was no understanding of this man he now faced. Aiden did not know him, or anyone like him. He only knew that any advantage of speed was nullified as their contest continued. It was now a show of strength and skill of steel, a contest from which Aiden was not confident he could emerge a victor.

But I must!

All around him the remaining short archers trained drawn arrows upon him, but did not loose them. Aiden fought fiercely, bringing his steel down relentlessly upon the man. Every stroke he intended to end the fray, yet the man was able to deflect and counter with skill. His enemy fought with strength and intelligence—grace even—but this wasn't all. He was seething, like a feral predator, as if in great anticipation. For the first time since the battle's commencement, Aiden felt an embryo of fear. His opponent's seething increased.

He felt the steel before he saw it, the blow sending fire from his shoulder down his arm. Aiden stumbled backward, struggling to defend against the strength and speed of his opponent. A breath was all that separated the man's sword swipe from his throat. The next blow came from the man's sword hilt to the side of Aiden's head, jarring him severely and blurring his vision. The capillaries in his right eye burst and the knee to his already wounded side cracked ribs, sending breath fleeing from him. Aiden spat blood. Desperately trying to regain his equilibrium, he knew he was done for. He would fail in his duty again, but perhaps giving his life as his men had would offer some small redemption for him.

"Aiden!" The scream cut through the air and found him, like a streak of lightning clearly piercing an overcast sky. Its timbre was filled with terror. His opponent stopped at the sound and looked up toward the source of the scream. Aiden followed his gaze. Roughly thirty feet high, anchored to an Ayzish tree, sat a young woman, a face he had not seen for years but instantly knew.

"Reign!" he said through clenched teeth, his voice filled with pain.

"Reign?" Maynard repeated. Aiden saw through his wearied vision understanding come upon his face. "Reign...Kerr!"

The look on Maynard's face became sadistic as he shuddered. Something changed; Aiden saw the insatiable thirst this demon had for Lord Therrium expand now to Reign. There was a drive in his eyes that bespoke his intent.

"*No!*" The master of the hold guard, his body bleeding and hammering with pain, tackled Maynard just as he started to run toward Reign. Maynard scrambled to his feet and sneered, back-handing Aiden savagely, breaking his jaw and knocking him to the ground. His sword went flying from his hand, but the leafling remained. He commanded his muscles to react but they refused, leaving him on the ground, face down in the dirt.

Please! His heart raced so fast, struggling to believe who he had just seen. *Get up, Ancients help me!*

Then the words came.

"Mylendia shaul."

A push, a force flowed from the leafling up his arm. It was like heat he had never before felt and it radiated through his arm and into his head. His vision instantly cleared and his mind opened. Acute pain shot through his jaw as it snapped back into place, then faded quickly. Something from outside his own body guided his next fluid movements, as if on his right and left.

Aiden jolted up with renewed speed and strength. He found his sword and raised it just as Maynard's strike came down on him. The sword's humming returned. He caromed from the next blow and stepped back two paces, then lunged with all his speed, forcing his sword arm forward. The robed figure moved to parry the stabbing blow, but his sword found only air. This threw Maynard off balance for an instant and caused confidence to morph to confusion upon his face. A moment before Aiden had lunged with his sword in his right hand he opened his grip, letting his sword fall through the air. His right arm went forward, sword-less, effecting the feint. The blade fell parallel to the ground and found his waiting left hand. The momentum of his lunge carried him forward as he pivoted his hips to add force to his left-handed thrust. The end of the sword found a home in Maynard's abdomen, just above his sword arm, which was still angled downward across his body from the failed attempt to parry Aiden's feint. Aiden twisted his steel in the man, and then again. Retracting the sword, he watched the man stay on his feet for a time, but this was short lived. The ground raced up to meet him.

Aiden's rage was not tempered. He stood over the dying man, arrayed in the blood of hundreds and screamed with what was a release of terror and adrenaline of this night.

"Why are you here?" Aiden screamed. "Why have you come? Why are you seeking Lord Therrium? And what is the girl to you?"

"You do not—" The man coughed blood and struggled with breath. "You do not know what you have done. It has started." He coughed again, this time more violently.

Aiden knelt down and grabbed the dying man, whispering vehemently, "What are you?" Blood and saliva dripped from his mouth between clenched teeth. To this, the man laughed, obviously in pain.

"You already know, Light Shepherd. This is—" he sputtered, coughing up dark bile from deep organ wounds. "A small glimpse of what is coming." The man, Maynard, tried feebly but pointlessly to capture breath as he lay upon the earth, his mouth opening and closing reflexively. And then he died as the morning light came.

As Aiden was left wounded and weak, surrounded by still hundreds of black-clad soldiers, he knew he did not have the strength remaining to even lift his sword. He did not even try to raise himself up from leaning on Maynard's corpse. The vibrations from the onlookers were clear to him. He felt the short archers drawing their bows back farther, preparing to fire. Glancing back up at Reign, still high in the Ayzish tree, he shook his head slightly, telling her to not to approach and to look away. He could see the glisten of tears in her eyes in light of early dawn.

And at last, he heard the whistle of an arrow loosed. But it was off somehow, not the right pitch. It was—Aiden smiled as he realized it was from a wood-dweller's bow. Dozens followed, cutting the morning air with their reports.

General Roan's men had arrived.

TWENTY-THREE

High Duke Emeron Wellyn

Day 29 of 4th High 412 A.U.

EMERON WELLYN SAT TENSE on a cold Granite Throne, wrapped in furs to guard against the chill of air and stone. The hour was early yet and the more mild temperatures of the High Season had given way a span and two days past to a chill from the glaciers that had gotten into Wellyn's bones. The Dimming Season would be upon them in two days. Not for the first time, he cursed his forefathers for choosing the Northern Province as their ancestral home.

The Minister of Terran Studies, Roben Findlay, had just begun his report to the Ministerial Council. The High Duke had sat completely dazed through the previous two reports from the Ministers of State and Health respectively. His mind was elsewhere as he apprehensively waited for news.

Wellyn caught several passing phrases from the current report, details on the clear evidence of cycling beginning to take hold. The Southern Province had witnessed an increase in sandstorms from the Schadar and the desert's borders themselves were expanding slowly but assertively. The Eastern Province's soil, while still fertile, was showing signs of cycling as well, with a few small sections already too fallow to support crops or any growth. The Northern

243

Province's Rising and High Seasons, while always short by a temperature's measurement, were noticeably colder than previous decades.

You don't need to be a terranist to know that! Wellyn smirked inwardly. Balancing this somewhat more dire news was that the glaciers in the north seemed to be receding and revealing very fertile soil underneath. It would be decades before anything meaningful could be made of it, however.

"The Western Province, curiously, has shown no signs of cycling but rather continues to be fertile as ever," Minister Findlay reported.

The High Duke raised an eyebrow at this comment and glanced over to Tyjil on his left. His closest advisor did not return the glance but continued to listen to the report with a placid look upon his face.

It's as he said it would be, Wellyn thought. *Either he's not surprised at all or hides it extremely well.*

Josi'ah, the Archiver assigned to House Wellyn, stood to his right, observing and mentally recording all he witnessed. Wellyn knew he was connected to an elder or even the patriarch of the Archiver Order high in the Jarwyn Mountains. Josi'ah had not reacted with any surprise yet and Wellyn therefore knew that Hadik had not yet executed his part of the plan. It would be within hours, if he was on schedule. All had been set in place after years of planning. Despite his confidence in the scheme, he was still apprehensive as he tried to carry out his routine duties. He expected to receive word by wing later this day. The advantage of the night attack would be that Mithi'ah, Therrium's Archiver, would have been asleep. Inevitably, Mithi'ah would be awakened from the commotion of the battle. But at the late hour, there was little chance an Archiver elder would be awake in the Jarwyn Mountains to connect with him through a Light Scry and be alerted to the ploy.

Mithi'ah would have been one of the casualties. The elders will not notice his absence for several more hours, perhaps not even for most of the day. Wellyn hoped this was true. The longer the delay, the better.

Suddenly, Josi'ah reached forward and put a strong hand on the High Duke's shoulder. The surprise of the touch startled Wellyn and the two Khans on either side of him stepped forward to remove Josi'ah's hand, but the Archiver's grip was iron. His eyes fluttered, obviously connected to an Archiver elder through a Light Scry receiving information, and his grip became even tighter on Wellyn. Josi'ah's teeth gritted as the information he received flowed into him.

He knows! Wellyn thought with a hint of panic. *The Archivers know!* It would matter little as long as Hadik made his work quick.

"Thank you, Ministers, but let us conclude early today," Tyjil said. "A matter that requires the High Duke's immediate attention has come to his knowledge."

The Ministers began to stand and file out, but too slowly for Wellyn's taste.

"Move!" he shouted, Josi'ah's grip still strong upon him.

Silence followed the High Duke's unusual outburst and there was a standstill in the room.

"Khans, reduce the presence of anyone by your steel who is still in my council hall in the next ten seconds!"

The Khansian Guards drew their swords and started to march toward the group of ministers. A frenzied and surprised commotion followed as the ministers made a hasty exit.

"Mithi'ah has reported that Hold Therrium has been attacked." The announcement from Josi'ah was flat, almost monotonic. "Lord Therrium and his family live. All hold guards save one were killed. The Arlethian Army led by General Roan is at the scene. All of the enemy has been destroyed."

All? Wellyn thought? He could not believe that even Maynard—

"They are uncertain of who attacked but the enemy wore a sigil," Josi'ah continued. "It was the sigil of—"

Josi'ah released his hold on Wellyn's shoulder and his eye fluttering ceased. His face was ashen and the obsidian chin stud quivered with his lower lip.

"What have you done?" he asked in a low, hoarse voice. The next was a shout. "What have you done?"

The Archiver did not wait for an answer but fled the council hall through a rear exit.

"It appears," Tyjil observed, "that all did not go according to plan."

"Bring him to me," Wellyn commanded.

"Whom shall I bring, your Grace?"

"The crazed one. Rembbran."

———

Hadik climbed the sheer rock face of the Jarwyn Mountains. The bag slung over his shoulder, and over every shoulder of the twenty-nine Khans with him, was filled with four airtight pouches. Each pouch contained oxygen-rich air from the ground level, enough for roughly ten normal breaths, seven deep breaths. They would need the air not long after cresting the ledge that lead to the Archiver caverns. Only the Shrule, these Archivers as they were commonly known, could survive more than an hour in the thin air at the Jarwyn peaks. Even now, still more than a hundred paces from the landing, Hadik's head was becoming dizzy. He could barely make out their destination as he looked up through the thin air, wispy translucent clouds obscuring his view.

He was tempted to put his lips around the thin metal tube extending from one of the bags. All he had to do was pry away the covering of southern amber wax on the end of the tube and inhale the thick, rich air.

It will allow me to climb quicker, he rationalized. Nevertheless, he resisted. He knew he would need the air when the real work began.

The parchment tied to the foot of the raven from the previous night had given orders for the assault to begin at daybreak. Hadik had pressed High Duke Wellyn to allow him to begin his assault at night with the other Khans at Hold Therrium, but the High

Duke had forbidden it, knowing the ascent would be too perilous in the absence of daylight. Hadik had to admit he was wise in this decision.

He looked to his right and left. Slowly but confidently, his men made their way up the mountain as silently as possible. He made sure each hand and foothold was secure three times before trusting it to hold his weight.

A scream came toward Hadik and then passed him. Startled, he clung to the mountainside and peered down. One of his men had fallen and been swallowed by the thicker clouds below them. His scream was not heard for more than a second after, then perfect silence again. The Khansian Guard reached up with his right hand and searched. He found a suitable quoin and hoisted himself higher.

———

Rembbran sat with his knees against his chest, rocking slightly. His back grazed the cold stonewall of the Kail. Even through his thick hooded robe the wall's chill could be felt. He held his head in his hands and traced the glyphs behind his left ear with a finger. He had long ago given up any attempt to decipher their meaning and now just tried to flatten the forged skin absent-mindedly.

The Kail did provide some relief from the incessant pain of his failed Charge due to the ancient incantation woven around this place by Hardacheon priests long ago, when the Helsyans had served them. The Dark Influence shielded his kind from the Light's curse that had been placed upon them, but not completely. A place of gathering for the chase-givers, the Kail was a large round edifice of stone. It stood roughly twenty feet high but all one level. From the outside, it appeared as no more than a large mound of ice, blending in with much of the natural terrain of the Northern Province. The others of his order had found Rembbran too eccentric and unrestrained over the past half-decade. They had warned him that his antics and aggression threatened their secrecy as an order. This cursed brotherhood of assassins had to remain a clandestine order within the Realm.

It had been nearly six years and the girl was still alive. She would be more than a girl now, a young woman. The fact that he knew she grew older, still breathing, added to the agony that had torn deep chasms within him that he was certain would never completely heal; not even after he killed her.

Rembbran had searched the Western Province extensively, then expanding throughout the Realm of Senthara. Never had he lost a quarry before. Never had any chase-giver he knew. It wasn't thought to be possible. Perhaps some stroke of devious luck from the Cursed Heavens had caused the girl's demise, but it could not be so. Rembbran would have been released from his Charge. Though not as satisfying as making the killing blow personally, a chase-giver's Dahlrak stood nonetheless fulfilled once his prey lay dead, no matter the source. The pain that remained and tortured his soul told him she yet lived. He longed for that scent that was so intoxicating, so quickening, like no smell of fear he had ever tracked, so sweet it was. The memory alone of the Kerr youngling's scent was enough to bring uncontrolled urges and spasms. What drove him madder, he wondered, the lack of understanding of how one's emotional scent could disappear or the pain of such a long open Charge? Rembbran did not know. Perhaps this was not the work of the Cursed Heavens but of the Ancient Dark itself. But he was forbidden from delving there, even in his mind.

But Rembbran was gifted. Truly ruthless and without feeling. His strength was beyond any other living chase-giver, but he was not the most skilled. There, another had power over him. Roughly two span after his unsuccessful Charge for the young female Kerr, he had lashed out against Maynard. Though the leader of the Kail was seeking to calm and help him, Rembrran's unfamiliarity with the pain that surged through him had driven him to a high degree of neurosis.

I will find her! It is inevitable, he always told himself. *It must be! Ancients Come, I will tear her apart, limb from limb and savor her sweet fear!* He began to salivate. Eventually he would triumph, but he did not know when *eventually* would be. Until that time, he would wallow in his pain with little succor.

Rembbran heard groans of complaint from his brethren within the Kail and looked up. Walking toward him was a short bald man in a dark gray robe with red trim.

"Tyjil," Rembbran said. "You should not be here. None are permitted to enter save for Helsyans and the Urlenthi himself."

"I'll take my chances," Tyjil replied. "After all, it was your beloved Urlenthi who has sent me to fetch you."

"Truly? The High Duke wishes my presence?" The thought of being granted a Dahlrak gave Rembbran energy he had not felt in some time. The promise of some relief from a new Charge, even temporary, was irresistible.

"I presume he does have an assignment for you if you can show enough control," Tyjil confirmed.

Rembbran stood up. He towered over Tyjil by more than two heads. "Where is he?"

"You know, Rembbran, you and I are not so different."

The Helsyan huffed and turned away from the older man's stare.

"It's true. However, there is one small difference. Well, maybe it's not so small, actually. See, while you are cursed by the Ancient Dark and serve it by compulsion, I embrace it and serve it willingly."

"What do you speak of?"

"I can't expect such a diminutive mind such as yours to grasp it fully, but just know we are on the same side of the war."

Rembbran became angry at this comment. "The Borathein are not here yet and I'm not part of your little war! I could care less for the games your people play!"

"Ah, yes. But I do not speak of the Borathein, Helsyan. That is indeed a small squabble in the grand scheme of the world, yes? I speak of the war that brought the curse upon your people, when the land of Helsya was still known."

Rembbran stared at Tyjil, a confused look frozen upon his face.

"But, of course, you're right," Tyjil relented. "Let us see about the smaller tasks that the High Duke would have you perform for now, yes? But, Rembbran, I see a future for you beyond the shackles of your precious Stone of Orlack, your Urlenthi."

———

Emeron Wellyn, High Duke and Protector of the Realm, was visibly distraught. His stare seemed to be full of such heat that he might melt the Great Glaciers of Gonfrey if he turned to look upon them. The wind and snow whirled around him as he stood outside the closed doors of his Council Hall. The cold bit at him, crusting his lips with frost. He looked upon no one in particular, for no one attended him by his order; he simply stared in silence. In fact, Wellyn stood so still, with the elements gathering upon him, he could have easily been mistaken for a statue. Standing long enough without movement in the North during the Low Season could indeed turn a man to a statue of ice, freezing his blood where it flowed from vein to heart. The cold swell from the north had mercilessly shortened the already brief climate of the High Season. Wellyn thought it to be ironic knowing what would soon cross the glaciers and enter their land.

The pace now must quicken, he thought. *We are not completely ready but control is still possible.*

———

When Tyjil finally returned with the crazed one in his tread, he had to look closely at the vertical mass that resembled a man. Ice and snow bonded to the man's eyebrows and face, drowning out the color of natural flesh.

"Ah, it is you. I have brought Rembbran at my Liege's request," Tyjil reported. Rembbran seemed almost to fall into frenetic shaking, but not because of the cold. The thick hooded robe those of his kind wore was not enough to mask the near lack of control Rembbran physically struggled with.

"Your Grace?" Tyjil came again.

It was the visible breath that emitted faint vapor from High Duke Wellyn's nose that gave the only sign of life. Tyjil continued to wait. Rembbran screamed in frustration and fell to his knees. The snow was almost waist deep as he came to rest on his heels, his legs folded beneath him. He cradled his head between his hands.

"Josi'ah." It was barely audible. A small word, but a name. Rembbran looked up.

"Josi'ah," High Duke Wellyn spoke again. He still did not move.

"Say it," Rembbran begged. "Say it, please!"

"I issue a Dahlrak upon Josi'ah and give him to you, Rembbran."

He took in a deep inhale, the gills running up the bridge of his nose flaring wildly. Rembbran's head snapped toward the palace with the look of a bloodhound.

Tyjil grinned wickedly as the Helsyan tore off at speed toward his prey.

Josi'ah hurriedly packed what little belongings he had in his quarters. Only a few minutes had passed since fleeing the council hall, but he feared even that was too long. Thor'ah, patriarch of his order, had issued a recall order to all Archivers serving in the Realm after the High Duke's attack on Lord Banner Therrium. Mithi'ah had reported the events from Hold Therrium as soon as he connected with an elder through a Light Scry. From there, the urgent recall from Patriarch Thor'ah had been issued. Josi'ah had never felt such fear in his life. He kept an open connection with the Patriarch while gathering his things.

Traditionally, an Archiver attended the Lord of his assigned house, or in Josi'ah's case, the High Duke himself, in all meetings and discussions in order to record as much of the Realm's history as possible. Such had always been their purpose, long before the Senthary had come to this land. There were hints that something was afoot, small things that seemed irrelevant at the time. Wellyn had taken several trips without his presence, allowing Josi'ah time for himself. More than once he had intuited there had been meetings he was not notified of by comments made, especially from Tyjil.

Of course, Josi'ah berated himself. *You were a fool! You should have known something was happening!*

He was ready. The palace would be easy to escape. He had free reign throughout the palace to go wherever he pleased in fulfillment of his duties. No one would think to stop him as he made his way quickly to an exit.

The door exploded inward as he reached to open it. He was knocked down from the force of it and fell hard on his backside. As he looked up, with shock across his face, he saw his end.

He thought of Vash'ah, his son serving as an acolyte in the Jarwyn Mountains. And then he thought no more.

———

He was fulfilled, if even just for the moment. It would fade, he knew, this temporary nepenthe. The old Charge's incessant malady would return. But here and now, he gave himself in surrender to the total ecstasy of a fulfilled Charge. The surroundings of carnage fueled his revelry in the moment.

He had never before had the Charge of an Archiver. Had *any* chase-giver ever been Charged with an Archiver? It was…unique. Josi'ah's surprise was nearly enough satisfaction in itself. Rembbran did not know why the Archiver was to die, nor did he care.

Let the Archivers inscribe this! he thought as he stared on the blood on his hands. The elder connected to Josi'ah at the time of his demise no doubt got the shock of his life. The observations of these historians were engraved on large obsidian slabs taller than most men stood. Rembbran gloried that his actions would be indelibly preserved in the Realm's history.

In the palm of Rembbran's hand was Josi'ah's chin stud, stained with the blood of its previous owner. For all an Archiver's strength in surviving the most hostile environment in the heights of the Jarwyn Mountains, Josi'ah didn't seem to have any ability to defend himself against attack. He had heard the Archiver scurrying about in his room from the other side of the doors to his chambers. He waited for a specific scent to come forth, one that would tell him the time had come. Fear's sweet odor was present among others, but as soon as he caught the scent of resolve, Rembbran unleashed his strength against the door, knocking it and Josi'ah back several feet. Once he had recovered from the initial surprise of Rembbran's assault, Josi'ah seemed to gain a look of understanding and acceptance, though the intoxicating scent of fear had been strongly emitted. Rembbran relished in its lingering few ambrosial elements, like a wounded beast wrapped in the healing leaves of a Triarch tree.

His relief from the incessant presence of the unfulfilled Charge was short lived. The pain of six years' worth of unfulfilled Charge built up could not be kept at bay long. Temporary relief was all that was granted as he completed other Charges assigned to him, and the relief that came had less depth and length each time.

Rembbran began to pace. As the pain thundered with crescendo inside his skull, an illusion radiated before him of the Archiver's small quarters, now a scene of grotesque death, beginning to contract and trap him. His breathing became shallow, faster paced. The pain was as if a flail was lodged inside the center of his brain and slowly but constantly expanding. Every second became an eternity of shattering throbs. He raised his hands to his head, fingers stiff, pushing inward with his palms in reflex against the expanding pain. Rembbran battled for control, but his groans were escalating to screams, not able to be stifled.

He fled from the palace, running over a pair of servants on their way to the culinary wing.

"The Kail," he moaned. "Must reach it." The speed a chase-giver could attain while Charged was inhuman, strength exceeding that of many men. But when a Charge was unfulfilled for so long as Rembbran's, this state of heightened sensory perception carried with it a feral, nearly uncontrollable reckless abandon.

He arrived at the Kail, retreated to his chambers, and seeking escape, collapsed to unconsciousness.

———

Wondering when his shift might be over, Vash'ah sat with the other acolytes inscribing away. The speed with which he could deliver Thor'ah's words to stone was impressive, even to the elders. Vash'ah didn't think much about it, though. He was usually bored from his work, always finishing ahead of the others. Like all acolytes, though, he wanted to see through a World Scry. It was why he was here, what he was born to do. The Realm needed Archivers to preserve the knowledge and history of each generation, and an acolyte was not an Archiver until he could connect with an elder of his race through a Light Scry, allowing the elder to see and experience just as he was. The task required immense concentration. Even greater was the ability of the patri-arch, who could see all things transpiring through any and, if he chose, all Archivers at once, mentally recording every tendril that filled his mind. Every piece of recorded data chiseled into the obsidian tablets was also indelibly etched into Patriarch Thor'ah's mind. Each patriarch's mental capacity stretched far enough to encompass every bit of recorded history the Shrule have witnessed.

The Patriarch ceased his speaking suddenly, though it was obvious he continued to hold the gaze of a World Scry. It was akin to a far-off distant look, a look that appeared to be unfocused yet completely thoughtful at the same time.

As Thor'ah sat in silence, Vash'ah and the other acolytes also sat silently with their obsidian tablets in front of them, waiting expectantly. Finally, Thor'ah emerged from his silence and rose.

"Tray'ah," he said calmly to one of the acolytes. "Please tell the elders I require their presence at once. The rest of you, please move swiftly but calmly to the grand cavern and wait for us there."

They all arose and started to follow the instructions given, wearing somewhat puzzled looks as they exited.

"No, not you, Vash'ah. Remain here with me."

Vash'ah was confused, but did as he was told. As his mind raced trying to figure out what he had done wrong this time, the elders began filing in around Thor'ah. When they were seated, Patriarch Thor'ah spoke.

"Josi'ah is dead. I surmise we will soon be under attack. There is not much time. We must prepare my final surrender."

The elders were not concerned and showed no emotion. Each sat with legs crossed, backs straight and chins high. Their obsidian chin studs protruded and glinted with the fire's light, appearing as small torches. They sought their own confirmation from a quick Light Scry and solemnly nodded as one.

"A new patriarch must be chosen. However, none here possesses both the memory capacity and the physical stamina or strength to attempt an escape. None, save one."

The elders seemed to know who Thor'ah was speaking of, but Vash'ah was still reeling from the news of Josi'ah.

My father is dead?

"Vash'ah, come to me, young one," Thor'ah requested. "There is a duty we require of you and there is not much time."

Vash'ah rose and came to stand before Thor'ah.

"You," Thor'ah spoke, "will accept my final surrender."

Vash'ah was shocked. He could not speak.

I am too young! I cannot possibly do this! Why? But his thoughts did not become words.

"While your mind is vast enough to be a patriarch," Thor'ah continued, "you are not yet mature enough for the organization required. I'm afraid this will prove extremely challenging for you as you attempt to sort through the millennia. Still, Vash'ah, you will be all that is left. I surmise that no tablet shall remain. But, young one, there are others."

Thor'ah spoke no more. Before Vash'ah could respond, the old patriarch grabbed his head with a surprising grip. Instinctively, Vash'ah tried to pull back, but the elders around him held him fast. The flow of information began to pass from Thor'ah to Vash'ah as a strong torrent in a monsoon. The boy screamed as his entire being was invaded with the events and knowledge of millennia untold. They played before his mind's eye, each event and person a microsecond vision before moving to the next. Indeed, every image felt as if it were being physically carved upon his brain, so terrible was the pain. He lost all semblance of time and drowned in the flood of information, swallowed in its depths. Tears flowed freely from the boy's eyes, mucus from his nose, drool from his lips. A trickle of blood coursed down one ear.

When it was done, Thor'ah collapsed to the ground peacefully, freed from his mortal purpose.

A cry of alert was heard, followed by others. The elders ran to the grand cavern, the source of the cries.

"Run," one of them said to Vash'ah, pointing to the opening of many tunnels and passages that led deep into the mountains.

———

The work would be quick. Twenty-eight Khans had made it to the landing. Hadik thought it remarkable that they had lost only two in their perilous ascent. As they came through the entrance into the grand cavern of the Archivers, Hadik saw several hundred gathered and waiting. Patiently waiting.

These are a strange sort, Hadik remarked to himself. Docile beyond what is wise. *If they knew any better, they could easily overcome us by their numbers alone.* But the Shrule knew nothing of war or violence, having remained aloof and neutral from all conflicts in history.

With a short blade, Hadik cut off the amber wax from the metal tube that jutted out from one of the airtight bags. He put his mouth over the tube and breathed normally. After ten breaths, the bag was spent. He drew his steel and attacked.

———————

Daneris gave his report: "All Archivers have been put to the blade, Hadik. Their bodies have been thrown from the mountain. Their tablets are currently receiving the same fate." Daneris took a breath from one of his pouches then put his thumb over the tube to save the remaining breaths. "A boy escaped to the river, however," he continued. "He has no doubt drowned by now, swept away by the current."

"Well enough," Hadik answered. "It matters little. Prepare for our descent."

Daneris watched Hadik walk away.

The troubled Khan tried to calm his lightheadedness as well as his stomach. The nausea gripped him tightly. Daneris had tried to let the boy escape, tried to lead the other Khans into tunnels and caverns away from the boy. But the boy had incredulously jumped into the river and had no doubt drowned or been crushed as he was forced through the rock tubes by the relentless current. If by some miracle he survived that ordeal, he did not survive the plummet to the sea below.

Ancient Heavens, please forgive me! I tried! Daneris retched in a corner devoid of light, hoping no one else would see him.

———————

How long has it been? Vash'ah wondered as he was pulled through the underwater blackness by the seemingly relentless current. *Five minutes? Eight?* He had breathed in several large breaths, stretching his lungs to what he hoped was their full capacity, before taking in the largest single breath he ever attempted. He plummeted into the cavern river with the echoes of the soldiers' shouts closing in on him. Then he could hear nothing but the rush of violent black water all around him.

In his terrible boredom during the long hours of inscription, Vash'ah had practiced holding his breath as a means to pass the time. He would often recite poetry or sing verses of his favorite incantation silently as a means of measuring elapsed time as he held his breath and inscribed upon the obsidian tablets. A few days prior, he had recited in his mind the passages of Tunginorr'ah, in their entirety, before his lungs had to release their hold, expelling the spent air. It was a long tome intended to be sung, though few did sing it, and told of the journey eastward and the claiming of the mountains by Jarw'ah, the first patriarch of their order after the Ancients fell. That effort would take at least seven minutes, even for an extremely fast recitation. But Vash'ah was relaxed then, not tense, cold and scared as he was now.

The incredible revelations that had been forced upon him by Thor'ah were splitting his mind. Pushing them aside entirely proved impossible as they kept resurfacing to be dealt with. Centuries and centuries of history were now his alone. The tablets were destroyed, cast to the base of the mountains and smashed to rubble. Perhaps others had survived, obeying Thor'ah's recall, but for all Vash'ah knew, he was the last of his order. He saw the image of Josi'ah's death and wept for his father but did not feel the tears as they mixed with the water enshrouding him. There were many holes throughout the running images of history, things that were dark and marred to his vision, as if a great cloud shielded certain events.

As the history of ages swirled inside him, he noted patterns and trends that surfaced, events and people long forgotten.

His shoulder slammed into a rock as the current forced him along. It seemed to push and pull him at the same time, causing his equilibrium to fail. Vash'ah reached his arms and legs out in an effort to try and reach above the water, but felt only stone and sediment in every direction. He was wrapped in a blanket of rock, water and the blackest night. Another scrape against rock—whether the river's floor, ceiling or wall he did not know—severely gashed his left arm.

How long? he thought more frantically to himself. *It must let out soon.*

He began reciting the psalms of Forrhaun'ah to try and calm himself, but it produced little positive effect. His lungs were screaming in protest, burning with the ache to release the old air and find new air, oxygen rich air.

Ten minutes.

The water started to turn a dark green, then a lighter green, finally morphing into blue. *Light!* Vash'ah screamed in his mind. But with this blessing came a thunderous noise followed by even more violent thrusts of current. The river spewed him out into the open air as if a horizontal volcano of icy water. The violent clamor and lack of air of the past many minutes was replaced by terrifying silence and a paradoxical abundance of oxygen as he fell through the air to the Sea of Albery some hundreds of feet below.

———

As the Khans retreated down the mountainside, a thick cloud covering came upon them. Daneris' visibility was obscured so greatly that he could not see the rock his hands clung to. A seed of fear started to take root in him, but an idea quickly cast out the seed before it germinated.

He shouted out the top of his lungs. His terrifying scream of fear echoed all around him and he tapered his volume gradually, then quickly. His echoes lived on for several moments more.

"Daneris!" he heard someone call. He did not answer. Others called his name but he still did not answer.

"Everyone hold!" Hadik commanded. "The Dark take you, hold!"

Daneris did not hold but continued to descend as silently and quickly as possible. He did not know how long the blessed overcast conditions would last, but he had to try and escape now.

Another opportunity may never present itself.

His limbs shook with the effort and palms were wet with perspiration. The reckless velocity of his descent was more challenging and nerve-wracking than the climb itself. His large calf muscles burned with every step and his massive biceps cankered with pain.

When another hour had passed, Daneris could no longer contract his hands for grip. He slipped and did not even try to catch himself. Mercifully, or not, the ground met him in less than twenty feet. The wind was knocked from lungs and his shoulder made a terrible popping noise followed by searing pain.

In a few moments he breathed normally again and rolled onto his side, his broken shoulder side up. Daneris squinted and saw the smoke rising from the smelters at the Jarwyn mines. They were only a league away, two at most. He thought back nearly six years prior when he had delivered the most important message of his life to his contact. The contact was then to ride the rest of the way to meet an ore master at the Jarwyn mines to begin the flow of the specialized ore that was only found at the base of these great peaks through a secret network, one that had been in place for hundreds of years.

"Did he make it?" Daneris asked aloud as he winced in pain. He did not know but prayed the message had been ferried quick and true. The fate of Våleira as a living world may depend on it.

With some effort, the Khan, who was a Warrior of Light, made his way to the mines. He tore away his telltale cape and tunic until only his pants and boots remained. A rough man greeted him with some concern, noting his injured arm.

"Oi! Needing help, are ya?"

"I am a current," Daneris responded.

"What's that, now?" the miner asked. "Looks like your arm is badly broken."

"I am a current," Daneris repeated.

The man scratched his head. "To tell you the truth, you might have hit your head as well as broken your arm. What's your name, son?"

"Ore master," Daneris said. "Who is your ore master?"

"Eh, well, today that would be Master Aramith."

"Please good man, show me to him."

The gruff miner shrugged. "Follow me."

They passed many workers, some exiting the mines, others working at smelters' fires, still others sharpening tools with wet stones and files. Daneris spied a tent in their general direction, the flaps of the entrance tied open. Inside he saw a man sitting at a crude table drawing on large sections of parchment.

"Master Aramith!"

The man at the table looked up. "Yes, Stanton, what is it?"

"Found this man, here. Says he needs a word. He don't look so good if you ask me, what with his arm and all."

Aramith came forward and met Daneris with some concern in his eyes. He looked at the miner and said, "Thank you, Stanton. That will be all."

Stanton, the old gruff miner, walked off, presumably back to his duties.

"What has happened?" Aramith asked. "You are hurt."

Daneris stepped forward and raised his good arm to Aramith's shoulder. He rested his hand there for a moment before wrapping it around the back of his neck and gently pulling Aramith's head toward his until their foreheads met.

"I am a current," Daneris whispered. No response came. *Please!* he prayed.

He repeated the greeting again, emotion in his voice. "I am a current—"

"—of friction and Light," Aramith answered, "a spark against the Ancient Dark that cannot be extinguished, a beam of the Lumenatis."

Daneris let a tear of relief fall to his cheeks.

"Worry not, brother," Aramith reassured him. "We received your message and have arranged every needed preparation."

Daneris' relief was palpable.

"Now," Aramith said, pulling back, "let us see to your shoulder." From a sheath on his belt, Aramith pulled a short blade. It was darker than pewter.

"Infused?" Daneris asked.

"Yes. Are you ready?"

The Khan held a deep breath and nodded. Aramith stabbed the point of his blade sharply into the joint of Daneris' broken shoulder. The Khan grimaced with pain but did not cry out.

"Mylendia shaul," Aramith whispered. The short dark blade hummed briefly and a jolting "snap" was heard as Daneris' shoulder reconstituted itself.

"That was the last of it," Aramith reported. "The blade's Light is now spent."

TWENTY-FOUR

Aiden

Day 29 of 4ᵗʰ High 412 A.U.

"AIDEN! WHERE IS LORD THERRIUM?" General Roan asked. Aiden realized it was the second time the General had spoken. He was still kneeling down, leaning on Maynard's corpse. An unusually thick mist lay low, just above the ground, as the morning dew began to evaporate before the sun. Aiden's eyes drifted toward the servant chambers, then to Roan. The General motioned to several soldiers who followed him to the humble structure. In a few moments, they emerged with a shaken but alive Banner Therrium. His family followed. Mithi'ah, the Archiver, was the last to exit. He immediately started scanning the scene of death before him, recording every detail in the typical fashion of his race.

Aiden's eyes, still bloodshot, caught the stare of Lord Therrium. He tried to rise, but before he could, Therrium knelt down to Aiden and hugged him. He then took Aiden's head gently in his hands and kissed his brow.

"Lord Therrium," General Roan said. "Please allow my men to escort you inside the hold. We will find better protection there."

For half an hour more, Aiden did not move. He felt the busy movements of the Arlethian soldiers all around him, clearing

263

debris, checking for survivors. Finally, something roused him from his dream-like state.

"It isn't possible," Aiden said, staring in disbelief. "I cannot believe it for fear my heart should shatter if this is only an illusion of the Ancient Heavens. What shade of trickery is this? Some false specter, some cruel mirage of past hope? It isn't possible. I won't believe—"

Aiden stopped his elusive ramblings. He didn't trust his eyes or his senses. Pain still coursed through him as a healer attended to his wounds, lashing Triarch leaves to the affected areas. General Roan and a detachment of wood-dweller infantry and long archers arrived within moments of Maynard's fall. Aiden expected to be cut down by the hundreds of stunned onlookers, the remnants of the black clad army. He would not have resisted, being overcome with physical weariness and mental exhaustion as he tried to grapple with the unwelcome revelations that had pounced upon his mind as a viper to a field mouse, that apparently High Duke Wellyn had betrayed the Western Province. But the wood-dweller detachment under General Roan easily excused the remaining attackers from existence, securing the hold.

And now Reign Kerr stood in front of him, the long presumed dead heiress of House Kerr, the daughter of his mentor and friend, whom he had failed to protect. He had watched her warily make her way across the field and into the hold, entering the south entrance. As the morning dew evaporated, it fed the thickening fog of the early morning. Seeing Reign emerge through the fog gave a somewhat supernatural aura to her approach. Passing a group of officers in a heated discussion, Reign did her best to conceal her face from the soldiers, but they would not have known her. Raising a hand to her face, she bit down on her index finger slightly in a show of timidity, and said simply, "Hello, Aiden."

"But, how...?" Aiden asked, his eyes wide and face askew with wonder. "It isn't possible."

Reign didn't answer, but continued to look upon him. The smell of smoke hung in the air with the ruin of thousands upon the earth. The putrid smell of decay would soon be added to the air he breathed. Crows and ravens circled in scores overhead.

"What happened here?" she asked, turning her gaze and observing the scene around them.

Aiden was relieved to hear her voice again, as if confirming that she was real.

"I...I honestly am not sure. I...there was an attempt on Lord Therrium's life, but no harm befell him. But that was before...before this." He motioned to the men clad in black, strewn around the eastern and southern parts of the hold. Servants and wood-dweller infantry were busily collecting and inspecting the dead as well as repairing the eastern wall that had been completely razed in the opening of the attack.

"I am bewildered by this move of Duke Wellyn. In fact, I am not certain this was his doing. Perhaps these men wear his sigil as a deflection of their true identity. At the same time, perhaps Wellyn was flaunting his boldness by not hiding his intentions. I just don't know yet."

The greater question Aiden struggled with was why would the High Duke betray his own subjects, but those answers would not come without many other questions.

He looked back to Reign, finding her pale. Following her gaze, he saw her eyes fixed upon the man who lay in a thick robe, dead, not twenty paces from where they stood.

"Who was he?" she asked. Aiden glanced back up at Reign, and thought he saw recognition. No, not recognition, but something close to it.

She's afraid, he thought.

"I'm mostly without answers. Maynard, he was called, but I don't know what he was. But he was better than me. I should have died but—" Aiden truncated his words. He looked off in the distance, hollowness in his gaze. "But something, *something* pushed me. I can't explain it, I'm sorry."

Reign returned her gaze to him. He could tell he had said something that struck the girl, but she did not say a word.

"But it is you, isn't it Reign?" Aiden reached out with both hands to take her by the shoulders, but Reign stepped back.

"I am dead," she said. "I do not exist, and must not."

As she retreated slightly, the morning fog filled the distance between them. Aiden's confidence waned as a thought at the edge of his mind took shape. *Am I delirious? My mind fractured?* He dismissed the thought, but then wondered if perhaps Reign was indeed a spirit or ghost of some create.

"What? What are you saying? Reign—"

"Aiden, I am dead. It must remain so, do you understand?"

Aiden was immeasurably perplexed, not for the first or even second time in the past day.

"If you cared for my family, please, you must be silent." Reign's eyes continued to plead for Aiden to comply even if he didn't understand. She looked around warily toward the other soldiers, appearing concerned they would overhear their conversation.

Aiden capitulated for now. "As you wish, Reign. To be honest, I'm having a hard time believing you are actually standing in front of me and not some trick of my mind."

"Hedron will be here soon," Reign said.

This was yet another shock to Aiden. "Hedron? He lives as well? We must tell Lord Therrium! He will know what—"

"No!" Reign hissed. "You must not! Swear you will not!"

"Why? Reign, why? What is it?"

"Have you ever seen a man like that before?" Reign asked. Aiden knew who she meant.

"Yes," he admitted. "Once. It was long ago, the night your father died."

Reign did not answer but continued to listen. A truth struck Aiden as he searched her eyes.

"And so have you," he said.

She did not deny it.

———

"Lord Therrium! Where is Lord Therrium?" The young officer ran over the hold grounds urgently. Other soldiers directed him to a makeshift pavilion that had been set up as a war room near the southern entrance of the hold. There, Lord Therrium, General Roan and several senior officers sat in earnest council.

"Lord Therrium, General, I beg your pardon for my intrusion, but you must come now!" The young wood-dweller officer was insistent in his gaze. General Roan knew the lad. Lieutenant Fherva, he thought.

"Lieutenant, what urgency brings your interruption with such boldness?" General Roan required.

"Please, sir, it's just beyond the eastern wall. Colonel Bodhin bids me return with you and Lord Therrium at once."

They arrived at the east wall, or the ruins of it, and looked beyond in the forest. The Colonel found them.

"Lord Therrium, General Roan, please follow me."

They stepped across the rubble of the east wall into the forest and walked roughly thirty paces, flanked by a small escort. And then, Therrium saw it.

"Ancient Heavens!" he exclaimed in a heavy voice. "Of what create is this evil?"

Before them, where earth and tree root had been was now only smooth stone upon the ground, forming an aberrant road. As Therrium slowly lifted his gaze, he saw trees along the road that had turned to cold, gray stone, appearing to be statues erected in the likeness of trees that had once occupied the same space. No sound of forest animals or birds were heard or felt. No rustling of leaves or branches that sway in the breeze. The unnatural occurrence stretched out before them for leagues beyond their vision. Short distances to the left or right of the stone road were trees and forest unaffected, retaining their inborn state. The effect was narrow, streamlined, premeditated—deliberate. They were indeed in the forest, the Western Province, but what filled the views of all those present was nothing but alien.

Abruptly, without announcement, Banner Therrium turned around and stormed back to his hold. The soldiers followed. He arrived back at the pavilion, took his seat and began to lead.

"Explanations," he demanded. The soldiers, mostly officers, were silent. "Speak!" he snapped, utilizing an unusual timbre of command. Several of the men opened their mouths, but could not form any words. "Of what create is this uncanny evil in my forest?"

"My Lord," General Roan began, "I do not know what could have caused such desecration. But we are certain of several things. First, an attempt was made on your life by one of your own guards. This was foreseen, if I understand the account correctly, by Master Aiden, who slew the assassin. In short, my Lord, you have been directly attacked. Second, soldiers wearing the sigil of House Wellyn attacked this hold at nearly the exact same time. They were well trained, prepared for the difficulties of battling our kind. Most unnerving, they were not detected until they breached the hold wall. We can speculate the changes we have witnessed in the forest have something to do with that fact. Third and finally, none of your hold guard survived save for Master Aiden, he himself taking severe wounds while saving your life. The conclusion is simple. This was an attempt to decapitate the Western Province in one move, to kill the Provincial Lord as well as destroy the hold, throwing the entire province into chaos and unrest without leadership."

General Roan's assessment was delivered in true military fashion, brief and to the heart of the matter.

"Why? Who?" Therrium asked further.

"Unknown, my Lord."

Therrium pondered for a few silent moments then asked, "What is to be done from here?"

"My Lord, it is obvious that someone wants you dead. Decisive military action has been taken against you and this province. Most indications are that High Duke Wellyn is responsible, but this is hard to fathom despite his sigil upon the dead army of black. If Wellyn has an enemy, this would be a strategy to divert blame to him and tear apart the Realm. It is a common ploy to pit two powerful forces against each other. When they are worn down to a weakened state, the true enemy may reveal himself, now strong enough to overcome his foes and achieve his objective."

Therrium sat considering but did not speak, as was typical of his laconic nature.

"Among other uncertainties, there is one thing clear," Roan continued. "You cannot stay here. It will be our honor to escort you to the main body of the province's army where we will establish a nomadic command; where I believe you will be the safest."

"It sounds as if you are giving me an order, General."

General Roan stood in silence for a moment, deciding how to respond. He made his decision. "Yes, my Lord, I am."

Banner Therrium didn't think he could smile this morning, but one forced its way onto his face anyway. "Very well, General. Collect my family and Aiden. I intend to leave within the day."

———

Aiden and Reign had retreated into the hold and out of sight. A disturbance among the soldiers caught their attention.

"Stay here," he said and ran to the entrance of the hold, which faced south. Near the southeast tower, a group of soldiers lifted up a man among cheers and carried him to a healer. The man's head hung down, too weak to hold it up. But he was alive and wore the uniform of Therrium's Guard. Running to him, Aiden gently lifted his head and looked at the man's face. The wounded guard spoke in a faint whisper. "Master Aiden, I…" He couldn't form any more words.

"Alrikk!" Aiden cried. He grabbed Alrikk around his torso, relieving the soldiers who bore him and personally carried him to the healers. Laying him upon a bed of Triarch leaves, Aiden saw the gravity of Alrikk's wounds as well as a small Triarch leafling clutched in his hand. He was barely conscious.

"You will save him," Aiden said to the healers.

"His wounds are grave, but we will do everything we can."

"Did my words sound like a request, healer?" Aiden spoke more insistently this time, so as to leave no doubt. "I repeat, you *will* save him." The healers began their work with haste.

From his peripheral vision, Aiden caught sight of the destroyed eastern wall and something strange that lay beyond. Rising up he turned his head toward the debris and saw it. Stone where the forest had once been. His chest tightened as he saw the view that stretched out for leagues.

Lord Therrium approached with Roan in tow and beckoned to Aiden. Upon sensing his Lord's approach, Aiden turned immediately toward him and knelt on one knee.

"No," Therrium said, shaking his head. "No, you need not bow before me. No man to whom I owe such a great debt shall bow before me. No, Aiden, rise."

Aiden rose, but felt uneasy standing as if equal before his Lord.

"We will return to the main encampment of the army at the Roniah Crossing under General Roan's escort and abandon the hold for the time until we can better assess the danger and origin of our attackers."

Aiden looked away. "My Lord, I would seek your blessing to take your leave. There are...matters I must attend to."

Therrium's surprise was evident on his face. "Master Aiden, of what do you speak? I would have none other at my side, especially during this time."

"If you command it, Lord Therrium, I will retain my duties and serve you still. But, I must humbly insist upon seeking your leave. I cannot speak of the nature of it, but you may trust it is vital to me. You will be safe in the heart of the army."

"Understandably, I'm reluctant," Therrium said. Aiden's hope dissolved. "However, Aiden, you are the truest friend to my family, and to the Western Province. For the honor of your fallen men, my fallen men, and for giving my family life, I would grant you anything you ask. You have my blessing for any endeavor you feel to undertake."

Aiden blinked long and brought his eyes back to Therrium's, communicating his gratitude. He nodded and said simply, "Thank you, Lord Therrium."

Then he left. Aiden felt Lord Therrium's eyes upon his back as he walked away. A feeling of foreboding was upon him, a warning that said he might never see Lord Therrium again if he left.

Fallen Ancients, forgive me for leaving my Lord but give me wisdom and strength as I take up a higher calling. Perhaps the Ancient Heavens did not hear his prayers, but he could not ignore the events of this day. He thought that maybe, amongst all the sins and failures of his life, the Ancient Heavens might be showing him a path to redemption with the miraculous appearance of Reign.

Maybe a chance.

"General," he heard Therrium say to Roan, "burn the bodies of the enemy. Also, bring me your fastest man. I have a delivery for the High Duke."

———

As the day's light began to melt into twilight, Hedron caught sight of Hold Therrium. Innately he felt Reign's presence, the way he had always been able to since they were born.

"It is a gift to those who share a womb," his mother had always said. Gift or not, playing hide and seek as a child was an utter waste.

He was weary from the long sprint. He guessed he had run at full speed for roughly fourteen hours, stopping only once for a brief few deep swallows of water from a stream. His legs ached from the marathon and his chest burned from heaving fast, deep breaths.

Soldiers of the Arlethian armies were present and organized into detachments. Hedron spied Lord Therrium and his family flanked by soldiers on all sides. A command was shouted, a drum sounded a cadence, and the soldiers began to march. Within only a few minutes, the hold was abandoned. Dozens of pyres sent smoke spiraling scores of feet into the evening air. The smell of death filled every breath he took, making him queasy. It was then he saw the fuel for the giant blazes consisted of dead men.

Thousands!

His concern for his sister heightened and he wondered if she— no, she was alive. He felt it. And she was here, in the hold. Two figures emerged from a southern entrance of the hold and walked toward him. The canopy that was so typical in the surrounding areas of Calyn was thinner over Hold Therrium, and the orange pigment of the evening sky shone through. He saw Reign's silhouette, knowing her walk and shape instantly. But beside her was another, a man much taller. Tension gathered in him, not knowing what to expect, but it faded to disbelief as recognition finally came to him. The man's hair came to his shoulders in back and was long enough to cover his face in front. He was wounded with several Triarch leaf bandages over various parts of his body. And a sword, as recognizable as the sun itself, was at his side.

"Aiden!" he cried.

TWENTY-FIVE

Honleir

Day 29 of 4th High 412 A.U.

IT HAD BEEN THREE DAYS since the last surviving member of Honleir's village had perished. The Great Basin of the Schadar was cruel and unforgiving. Thirty souls of Honleir's village had ventured out attempting the journey across the basin to reach the closest known spring and the Schadar had claimed them all—except for Honleir. Timney, his ten-year-old cousin, was the first that had died.

Any water the group had was long since consumed. They carried no provisions save for a tent or covering that could be fashioned to provide shade of even the most meager quality during the day. Any other provisions were unnecessary and burdensome to bear and therefore left behind. It was a one-way journey, successful or not. Honleir had not urinated in nearly two days and, while a vile thought to him before this journey, he would have eagerly recycled the urine, counting it as a blessing. He supposed his body had no moisture left to expel.

It was nearing midday. Honleir had stopped his night walk over four hours ago, when the sun began to rise in the east sky. He lay still in his tent, trying to sleep and expend no energy. Though he had lost his sense of direction the night before as a bout of

273

delirium set in long enough to disorient him, he still *felt* he traveled in the right direction; but that was little comfort against the chapped and cracked red flesh upon his face, neck and hands. He tried to keep his hands from being fully extended as skin would tear and scabs reopen on his palms. Besides setting up his dismal looking day-tent every dawn, his hands had very little to do. It was his feet and legs that bore the most grievous impairments, both externally and internally. The waning moons would give little light tonight, being the second to last night of the cycle.

And the second to last night of High Season, but little difference that makes in the Schadar. The climate was always harsh no matter the season.

During a full first moon, the endless desert hills would shimmer as if silver glass. If he could freeze a picture in his mind to hold forever, that would be it. However, another picture remained in his mind—one he had not seen but was sure had come to pass.

Those who had stayed behind in the village were certainly no more than dust mixed with sand now. They had given all the stored water supply to Honleir's party, knowing what they sacrificed. At seventeen, he was nearly a man but remained as yet unprepared to leave his family, especially in such a manner. Though his mother, Almena, was probably strong enough to attempt the crossing, she elected to stay behind with her husband and brother, both too weak physically. *But aren't we all too weak?* he thought darkly. It seemed now it did not matter the choice he and the others would have made. Death was intent on finding them, but the suffering of crossing the Great Basin the past ten days could have been avoided. *I should have perished beside my family, my dust mixing with theirs and the sand.* Again it angered him that an entire village could be erased without any seeming consequence. This is what it was to be Kearon. To exist but not live, to breathe but not *be*.

And the Poems! Where is their wisdom now? Where is the great Orator Rishz'nah to save us?

Mind rendering had proven futile in his attempts while traveling. His group believed he would miraculously save them with his as of yet undeveloped gift. He would somehow find water and restore the village. *I swore I would!* But he knew the chance to keep his promise was gone forever. He had failed and they were all dead because of it.

A tiny shadow scurried quickly across the sand to a small covering of tumbleweed and rock. Honleir barely caught sight of it from the corner of his eye as he peered out the opening of his tent. Haphazardly making his way to the tumbleweed, he risked the journey of a few paces across the sweltering desert floor with his shoes and large head covering and slowly peered over the ball of twigs to spy a lizard of some create lying on a small rock, belly up. Honleir guessed the creature was trying to take in the day's heat before nightfall cast its ever so slightly cooler temperature. He felt the heat of the sun starting to burn his skin in these moments he had exposed himself. Without thinking, the Kearon boy snatched the lizard with both hands, his left grabbing its head, clamping its jaws closed, and his right securing the tail. He raised the lizard's abdomen to his mouth and bit down hard, ignoring the pain of the cracked flesh on his face and releasing a small flood of bodily juices into his mouth. It empowered him as he sucked harder and harder, draining the lizard's life into his own. The small creature squirmed and thrashed for half a minute before relenting and giving up its all. Finding that he had gained all possible liquid succor from the deceased creature, he consumed whatever parts he could bring himself to swallow and discarded the wasted carcass.

The heat was taking its toll as he stood in the full gaze of the midday sun. Raising his head slightly, Honleir stared at the burning torch in the sky and, for a split second, he thought to strip himself naked in defiance of the Schadar's wrath and allow the merciless desert to consume him as it had all his kin. He wasn't sure which was producing more heat, the sun or the radiating waves he felt rising from the sand beneath him, causing the air to ripple before him. Eventually, he turned his gaze downward and away from the intense light of the sun, not wishing to blind himself. For several minutes, he could not focus on anything due to the large distorted sunspot masquerading as a black hole that dominated his vision. The eyes would take some time to purge themselves of the punishment Honleir had just bestowed upon them.

He felt stronger though, he thought. The meal had provided at least some sustenance, paltry though it may have been. He returned to his tent to wait for the sun to turn a deep red as the last slivers of direct light vanished below the horizon, making the sky glow violet, orange and red from its indirect light. Only then would the temperature drop to a level that was barely tolerable for physical exertion and he would begin another long night of tedious walking.

Only anger drove Honleir; it was all he had left. His family and village were extinct, leaving him without any real reason to press forward, but the anger swelled and filled him more every night as he trudged his way in whatever direction he moved. He allowed it to tarry with him, nurturing it in his solemnity. How he yearned to find those responsible for his plight! For murdering his family and friends! It was too easy to blame his situation on a natural occurrence, too convenient. In fact, the boy didn't care if it was natural.

Someone is too blame!

His people lived a cruel life. All the Kearon. Or perhaps life was simply cruel.

Why not rise and meet death, then? It cannot be more cruel than life!

He came to the opening of his tent, throat parched and skin cracked. He hesitated, but only for a moment.

Blackened Heavens, come take me! Honleir shot forth from his tent, tore his clothes from his body and defied the sun, screaming at it with his dry voice.

"I will not hide from you! I will meet you face to face! Take me now, as I am! Scorch my skin and burn my eyes from their sockets! You can do nothing to me that has not already been done inside me!"

As Honleir's anger swelled to righteous indignation, his mind stretched to find the source of his circumstances. But not just his current circumstance of being without family or friends and aimlessly wandering across a basin of the Schadar, hovering slightly above death; more, he saw that his circumstances of life were born to him because of his lineage. All his troubles and hardships could be traced to this fact, the fact that he was born Kearon—something he did not choose. The dried-up water spring was not the real reason he was nothing and less to the world. Something was happening to him now and Honleir saw much more clearly the more he focused on the avalanche of fury crashing down inside him that the real cause, the actual root of all the misery and pain, slight and injustice, sat with House Wellyn. He knew the history, the poems lamenting the fall of House Kearon and her allies to Oliver Wellyn over four hundred years ago. Until now it had never been more than simply something he knew but did not seem to have any meaning to him. Now, he knew it in a different way—a way that was not only something one understands with the mind but also feels in the flesh and knows in the core of sentience; the way a man knows something only by experience. The history he had been taught as a youngling began to be woven through him, becoming part of him, and he part of it. Details hidden in prose and poem sprang to his mind that were so subtle previously but now seemed so vivid and pronounced that a wielding of understanding permeated through him of events centuries old. He saw the beauty of the poems and how they cycled through the centuries, unfolding to him in ways that he never had considered—well beyond mere history. Every word, every line, every stanza, every verse he now owned as his memory, his experience. He could see them as a single collective work, one continuous and epic story...

No, more than a story. A path.

So great was the onslaught of revelation, Honleir had not realized until now that he was mind rendering. It had been a futile exercise to force this little known ability as he traveled with his now dead kith and kin in attempts to find water and shelter. He seemed to have no control or command of when it manifested and what it showed him, but the knowledge that poured through him now brought new understanding of his lineage and family, of his… House.

I am of a noble house, Honleir thought and recognized for the first time what that could mean.

His physicality changed. Bones and muscles no longer ached, cracked skin no longer stung. Honleir stood up straighter and took in the sights around him, seeing almost an unobstructed view of an ocean of sand and stone. His mind now clear and focused, still in the middle of a mind render, Honleir became aware of where he stood. Not the general area or direction, but *exactly* where he stood. He had never been in this spot before, but it would have made no difference to his cognizance if he had been. He knew in his mind where he had been, the exact distance and course traveled, where each fallen villager had perished as well as the exact moment in the moons' or sun's cycle it had happened. This did not come with surprise as his elevated state of mind simply accepted the knowledge and processed it as if little more consequence than particles of sand blown by a breeze.

As Honleir's mind rendering came to a climax, he fixated on one stanza from the Returning Renditions of Rishz'nah:

> *Consciously fleeing above the wind*
> *Returning from deep within*
> *Escape presently without malice*
> *Where I am no more callous*

Honleir internalized the words, making them part of him. As he did so, he felt the verse course through his veins as if his blood were boiling. His mind spun with images of places he realized he knew but had never before seen, a dizzying collage of deserts and dunes, rivers and seas, mountains and forests, fields and glaciers. After a moment, he caught hold of one of the images and held it before him. Rushing wind and sprays of water amid great clouds.

"There," he said.

Then he vanished, leaving nothing but shallow impressions in the desert sand of his thick-soled shoes as the only evidence that he had just a moment ago been present.

Vash'ah screamed as he fell through the air. He prayed every cloud he pierced would catch him and somehow let him softly fall to the water below, but his prayers were going unanswered. It was oddly silent, other than his screams, as he plummeted through the skies. His clothes, torn and tattered, were dry only moments after being expelled from the river into the wide-open void. Far below, he could see the Sea of Albery that would be his watery grave. Farther east, he thought he could just make out the single peak of the Runic Islands. And, something else. Something edged into his sight; something that looked like—and then it was gone.

I didn't know hallucinating was part of—

The form reappeared. A man, not much older than himself, looked to be sprinting through the air toward him. Bronzed skin and hair the color of obsidian, the aberration caused Vash'ah's fear to cease its hold as disbelief emerged within him. And then it disappeared once again. Snapping back to the realization of imminent death, Vash'ah heard the rushing water grow louder in his ears. The spray of the massive waterfalls started to fleck his skin, and he knew the ocean surface was only a few span of feet below him. He closed his eyes.

A sudden *whoosh* sounded around him. He expected to feel his body slam into the water that would be as hard as the mountains themselves before all went dark forever, but this did not happen. Instead, he felt something grab him—arms? Sandy arms. The clasp was tight. It reached from behind and around to his chest where he thought he felt hands clutched together. The smell of sand filled his nose. He dared not open his eyes. The *whoosh* sound came again followed by utter silence. Vash'ah opened his eyes and saw nothing. He screamed.

"I have you," said the voice behind his right ear. "Do not fear."

TWENTY-SIX

High Duke Emeron Wellyn

Day 3 of 1ˢᵗ Dimming 412 A.U.

A GOBLET SHATTERED INTO HUNDREDS OF SHARDS as it collided with the wall of stone inside Wellyn's personal chamber. Tyjil was unmoved by the High Duke's physical reaction to the news he had just delivered.

"How can they all be dead?" Wellyn demanded. "Josi'ah must have been wrong. Mithi'ah was confused, clearly. His report had to be wrong!" Mawldra, Wellyn's faithful hound, looked as agitated as her master.

"A miscalculation somehow, your Grace," Tyjil offered simply.

"Miscalculation? I think you have a talent you've neglected to share before, Tyjil. You are quite gifted in understatement!" Wellyn paced as he stammered, nervously picking at the stubble on his chin. The miscalculation was his own, if there was one. "I sent three thousand men. Swords, axes, short-archers. All trained for dealing with wood-dwellers. Three thousand!" he screamed. "And Therrium yet lives!" Wellyn ceased pacing when he came to his desk. He reached out and leaned against the desk with his head slightly bowed. "Therrium lives," he repeated. The consequences could be ominous if this were not corrected immediately. Perhaps it was already too late.

"My Duke, we must prepare," Tyjil said.

"Maynard," Wellyn said, ignoring Tyjil's comment. "Maynard truly was defeated?" Wellyn could not think of a time when he had known of a chase-giver to fall. Was there any record in Jarwyn of a chase-giver's defeat?

There are no records of any create there anymore, Wellyn reminded himself.

"All indications are that he did fall, my Liege. This is an additional area of concern. Therrium will have no reason to keep his vow of silence and will undoubtedly reveal the existence of Maynard's kind to his army. They will not be caught unaware again. We must prepare." Tyjil's words seemed to have no effect upon Emeron Wellyn. The High Duke of the Realm continued to lean against his desk, looking down.

"Therrium is not a warrior, but he is not spineless. How will he react?" Wellyn asked.

"It is hard to say for certain, my Duke," Tyjil answered, "but there will be no doubt to whom those soldiers belonged. They will know they were soldiers of the Realm. And," Tyjil continued, "they have also inevitably discovered my work by now in the forest though they are certain not to know what to make of it. The implications of this failed action are far reaching. In short, I believe Therrium will do what any leader will do when attacked by another, yes?"

"And what is that, Tyjil? Speak plainly," Wellyn demanded.

"He will respond in kind, your Grace. He is not a warrior, true, but he is cautious and clever. Our situation would have been many fold improved had he not survived, yes? His people will surely gather around him."

Mawldra's ears perked up before the two men heard the approaching footsteps echoing down the corridor. A few seconds later, a knock came at the chamber doors. "Enter," Wellyn snapped.

The Minister of State entered the chambers accompanied by two Khans and an aide who carried a small wooden box. The Minister was sweating and slightly out of breath wearing a shade of pale that besets all weak men in leadership. A knot formed in

Wellyn's stomach but he continued staring down at nothing in particular, unmoved.

"My...Duke," the Minister gasped. "I have just received a most disturbing and urgent message." He looked up at Tyjil and then back to Wellyn. "Perhaps privacy would be the prudent choice for this message."

"Out with it man!" Wellyn commanded.

The Minister held a small square of parchment, which he brought up before his eyes. His hands were unsteady as he read the message.

"High Duke Emeron Wellyn by care of the Ministry of State and the Minister thereof: For acts beyond treachery against loyal subjects and your own people whom you have sworn to protect, the Western Province now hereby cedes from your rule and is a state unto itself. Your demonstration of aggression against my person and people has postured us to stand apart from and against you, your authority, and those who seek to uphold your position. Banner Therrium, Prime Lord of Arlethia."

The Minister's aide placed the wooden box on Wellyn's desk and lifted the sealed lid. A rank scent attacked the senses of all present. Inside the box was the shaved head of a man. Not any man's head, Wellyn noted. *Maynard's head.* The message with insult could not have been more clearly delivered. Therrium knew who had ordered such destruction upon his house and he had survived, as Josi'ah reported. Despite the flood of anger welling up inside him, Wellyn barely gave the box more than what appeared to be a disinterested glance.

When Duke Wellyn gave no response, the Minister nervously demanded, "My Duke, what does this mean? Of what does Lord Therrium speak?"

"Tyjil," Wellyn said, ignoring the Minister's questions, "release them. All of them."

Tyjil didn't need to ask to whom the High Duke referred. "Therrium will be the Charge?"

"In part, yes," Wellyn said with eerie calmness. "But bring me Rembbran first."

Tyjil departed at once. Turning about to face the Minister of State, Wellyn asked, "Has Hadik returned yet?"

One of the Khans replied, "My Duke, we received word by wing that he is within an hour's distance. His mission is reported as a complete success."

At least something went right, by Cursed Heavens, Wellyn swore silently. "Very well. You are dismissed."

The Khans turned to leave but the Minister stood looking expectantly at Wellyn. Mawldra began a low growl. "Your Grace, I need answers to—"

"You were dismissed, Minister," Wellyn said with venom seeping in his voice. Mawldra took one step toward the man, who quickly decided he did not need answers to his questions after all.

Wellyn's mind repeated one thought over and over at high velocity: *Therrium is alive. Therrium is alive!* A modicum of trepidation started to pulse through his chest as he wondered about the progress of his obscure northern allies. Would he have enough time to make things right before their arrival? He doubted it.

Tyjil re-entered the chamber with Rembbran in tow. "He's here," Tyjil announced, stating the obvious. Still, the High Duke did not lift his head or give the slightest acknowledgement.

"My Liege?" the chase-giver inquired in a pained tone. No doubt leaving the somewhat protective borders of the Kail allowed his nearly omnipresent pain to resurface to a level hard to control. "How may I serve you?" This last entreaty was said with a great deal of forced restraint.

Wellyn came to himself and finally looked up, taking in the scene. He looked slightly surprised to find others were in his presence. Noticing the shorn-headed figure standing in front of him, he addressed Rembbran by motioning to the wooden box on the desk. Rembbran instinctively sniffed the air before leaning over and looking inside. He immediately retreated as disbelief followed by anger found place on his face.

"Why?" he demanded.

"No, it's not what you think," Tyjil assured him quickly. "This was not the High Duke's doing."

"He failed me. He failed his Charge," Wellyn calmly added.

"That's not possible!" Rembbran protested. "He was the most skilled among us. No one could have overcome him."

"And yet," Tyjil answered, "there he is, a head with no body."

"Who?"

"Banner Therrium, or likely one or more of the hold guard." Tyjil said.

Rembbran considered this information and the typical predatory smile he was so accustomed to wearing slowly spread across his face. He was anticipating what would come next.

"How may I assist, my Liege?"

"Soon. Very soon."

TWENTY-SEVEN

Lord Calder Hoyt

Day 15 of 1ˢᵗ Dimming 412 A.U.

THE DIMMING SEASON WAS Lord Calder Hoyt's favorite time of the year in Thera. More mild temperatures combined with sunsets that lasted hours gave the circular clouds of the season a halo effect and were awe-inspiring to him. The South's state city cradled the edge of the Roniah, not far from the river's crossing at the border of the Southern and Western Provinces. Large yellow-whitish walls more than five men high bordered the city itself. From the tops of the walls stood large wooden posts that resembled ship masts in height and thickness. The posts did extend skyward but also slightly inward toward the city. An intricate system of ropes and pulleys were strung about the wall masts that would raise thick canvas sheets, called storm sails. The system shielded the city from sandstorms that occasionally reached from beyond the Schadar Desert, an occurrence that seemed to be increasing in frequency as of late and had Lord Hoyt a bit concerned. Instead of one or maybe two a year, Thera had seen five thus far this year. The Ministry of Terran Studies had taken a keen interest in the occurrences and had sent many of its people to study the phenomenon first-hand. The reports they filed with their findings, however, were conspicuously not shared or made known.

The storm sails at the top of the city's walls were designed to deflect the sand and wind gusts upward, away from the inhabitants below. Though it was still unwise to be out during a sandstorm, the barricade effectively lessened the danger and damage. Most of the repair work done after a storm was focused on the masts and storm sails themselves, a far less expensive endeavor than rebuilding entire portions of the city. The population of Thera swelled when a sandstorm approached, inhabitants of other cities and towns in the province nearby making their way within the walls for protection. Many throughout the province, who lived farther from the safety of Thera, had underground storm shelters burrowed deep in the earth.

Within the city Hold Hoyt was splendid, as were most holds of noble families. The wealth possessed by House Hoyt due to industry and trade was rivaled by very few in the Realm. An industrious and creative spirit drove the people of the South, pushing them to greater achievement. It was not a drive rooted in greed for excessive gain but more in pure curiosity. Many of the inventions and advances the Realm enjoyed sprang from the Southern Province. Their demand by the Realm's people expanded the wealth of the South throughout the centuries until they were the wealthiest province per capita in all of Senthara, though their province was the smallest in size and lacking in natural resources greatly when compared to the East and West Provinces.

The message was read to Lord Calder Hoyt by his page in front of his court, with all noblemen in the Southern Province present. His wife, Briel, and fourteen-year-old daughter, Kathryn, were also present. Lord Hoyt had already read the message, of course, but wanted the proclamation to be heard straight from the parchment by his court. Jonathon, the young page, spoke with an unsteady voice as he read the unbelievable words.

By royal decree of His Grace, High Duke Emeron Wellyn, the first of his name and protector of the Realm, all peaceable interactions with the traitors of the Western Province are hereby terminated forthwith. All Provincial Lords are commanded to call together their arms and prepare for operations to suppress the rebellion and end the sedition. The heretical tyrant Banner Therrium has joined the ranks of his deceased treacherous cousin, Thannuel Kerr, in striving to bring about a plot of usurpation. He and those who follow him must be stopped immediately, no matter the cost. Battlefield directives will be forthcoming within a matter of days.

The court was silent. The Southern Province was marked by colorful and festive décor, themed settings throughout the province. Lord Hoyt's people had amassed wealth from lucrative trade throughout Senthara, but especially from trade with the Western Province. The shared border of his province and the west was far more populated than the border shared by the south and east. This turn of events was not going to be received well by his people. Hoyt sat in his ornate throne with his left hand ponderously rubbing his chin.

"I don't believe it," Gernald Quary said. He served as master of the hold guard for Lord Hoyt. "All our dealings with the wood-dwellers have always been upright. This cannot be right."

"Careful," warned Hambly, one of Lord Hoyt's advisors. "Your opinions could be construed as treason now."

"I am only stating historical fact," Gernald countered.

"All the same, this is new ground," Lady Briel cautioned. "We must be wise until we are sure of our footing."

"It's not true!" Kathryn said, rising from her seat next to her father. Her dress of gold, orange and red embroidered with white lace flowed as she stood. "Don't you see? This is a trick!" Normally sober and reserved, her conviction surprised those in attendance.

"Kathryn!" Lady Briel snapped. "Be silent!"

"How can I? Father, you're not actually thinking of believing this filth, are you? We can't go to war with the West!"

"Daughter, we may have no choice," Lord Hoyt said calmly. "The High Duke issues commands, not invitations for debate."

"Good!" came a new voice from the back of the court. A short figure emerged and approached slowly but confidently, flanked by another much larger figure clad in a thick hooded robe, his face not visible. The crowd parted as the pair made their way forward. The smaller man, advanced in years but not elderly, was clad in gray garments bordered by dark red trim at the edges. The sigil of House Wellyn shone on a gold amulet that hung from his neck. Several subdued mumblings of curiosity were heard. Lord Hoyt's knuckles turned white from the pressure of gripping the arms of his throne at seeing the two newcomers. He wasn't sure which of the two created more worry inside him.

Master Gernald mumbled curses as he turned and recognized the first unannounced intruder.

Lord Hoyt arose. "This is an unexpected pleasure. To what do we owe the honor, Tyjil?"

"Honor? None have considered my presence an honor, Lord Hoyt," Tyjil replied with a half smile. "I did not take you for a fabulist, my Lord. Let us dispense with the small talk, yes?"

"Mind your tongue! Lord Hoyt was being polite, snake!" Gernald warned. "You might try adopting some manners of your own, such as properly announcing yourself before barging into a Provincial Lord's court."

"Lord Hoyt, does your man know his place?" Tyjil asked, not lowering himself by addressing a mere guard. "Surely he did not just insult the High Duke's advisor."

Calder glanced toward Master Gernald, silencing him with a slight wave.

"What business brings our Duke's representative so far from Iskele?" Lady Briel asked.

"Ah, Lady Briel, ever the diplomat." Tyjil bowed slightly in acknowledgement. "I have come to look after the High Duke's interests, of course. It sounded like I arrived just in time to overhear expressions of absolute loyalty upon receiving our Duke's missive. It was truly warming to my heart." Tyjil shot a narrow glance toward Kathryn.

Lord Hoyt did not miss the action. "Yes, we are indeed in receipt of High Duke Wellyn's message. It was surprising to my court, I think. We are discussing how best to support the Realm."

"Ah, but isn't it already clear, my Lord?" Tyjil asked. "I believe you are waiting for further instructions on how to deploy your troops."

Calder swallowed before answering. "As the High Duke is no doubt aware, this directive will be obeyed. However, we were not prepared. The Southern Province's forces are not organized currently. We have well trained men and women, of course, but we were certainly not expecting a conflict of such a sudden nature. Perhaps—"

"Treason is often sudden," Tyjil answered. He waited for several seconds before continuing, letting his statement hang in the silence. He looked to his companion. "I am certain Lord Hoyt will do what is necessary to comply, yes?"

"Doubtless," came the single word reply from beneath the hood. Its pitch was low and resonant, filling the royal chamber. Lord Hoyt swallowed hard.

Having given Tyjil the assurances that he was looking for, Tyjil and his companion retreated. Gernald had two hold guards escort them from the palace. Calder sat contemplative while the others in attendance spoke heatedly back and forth as to what actions to take from here. He did not hear most of their discussions as he pondered within himself. It did not make sense, not in the least. He did not know any history or even tales of wood-dwellers being aggressive without provocation. Attempting to usurp power was totally against all Calder knew of their disposition.

Reluctantly, he gathered himself and joined the conversation before it turned even more heated.

Lord Hoyt spoke softly, not waiting for a lull. "Jonathon, please have High Marshal Wenthil summoned. We will make preparations immediately."

"How many men shall I tell him to recall?" the page asked.

"Not less than thirty thousand."

The page looked dumbfounded. "Is my Lord certain? This will be nearly the entire army."

"More," Master Gernald said.

Hoyt nodded. "We will need to institute a draft."

"What?" his wife exclaimed. "We cannot force our people to join the military. If we do not have the numbers then the High Duke will have to do with what we have."

Lord Hoyt put his hand on his wife's. Her hand was warm and dry, a contrast to his own clammy touch. "I'm afraid we do not have a choice in this." His eyes communicated the concern he felt. He saw Briel's eyes cloud with confusion at his look, but she did not voice her question.

The page had not left but continued to wait, assuming his orders must be wrong.

"Were my instructions unclear?" Lord Hoyt asked.

The boy stuttered. "N-no, my Lord, of c-course not." Jonathon hurried out and the room returned to being filled with various conversations, though lower in volume than previously.

"Father," Kathryn whispered. He did not respond. Leaning over, she tugged at his arm. "Father, I must speak with you."

Hoyt turned his head. "What is it?"

"Not here," she whispered. "But please, now. It's urgent."

Lord Hoyt exited the throne chamber through a door behind his chair with his daughter, leaving his court to continue their debates without him. He hoped their discussions would turn toward preparations rather than useless stammering. The antechamber was quiet and empty except for Hoyt and his daughter. He waited expectantly for Kathryn to start.

"You're not going like what I have to say, father," she began. It was hard for her to meet him eye to eye. "I have been seeing someone."

Calder Hoyt's facial expression changed slowly from intent to the beginning of a smile.

"Well, I'm not so sure that's something to be nervous telling me about. But Kathryn, daughter, perhaps this is not the best time. You have heard the news and my attention needs—"

"I'm not finished," Kathryn said. "He has been visiting me for nearly a year."

This did take Hoyt back. He held his breath and blinked a couple times before speaking.

"A year? My dear, that's not really possible..." He cut off as something came into focus for him. His voice turned sterner. "Kathryn, there's a boy who keeps attempting to break into the hold to see you. Tell me this has nothing to do with that."

She gathered her courage. "They are not mere attempts, father. He has seen me at least a dozen times, sometimes for days at a time."

Lord Hoyt was dumbfounded and his face paled. "Ancients take me," he cursed beneath his breath.

"Are you with child? Is that what this is really about? Who is it?" he demanded, straightening up with his hands on his hips.

"No! Of course not! You don't understand. Nothing improper has occurred."

"Other than you allowing a prowler to visit you repeatedly under cover of night! Was the romanticism of it all just too much to resist?"

"Father, stop it!" she snapped, matching his tone. "I have not begun to tell you what you must hear. Be silent!"

Calder turned away and crossed his arms, head bowed. Pursing his lips, he asked, "You are not spoiled?"

"No."

"You swear by the Ancient Heavens? Perhaps I should call for Healer Naveen to examine you."

Kathryn approached her father and put a hand upon his forearm. "I have maintained my innocence, father. Neither you nor I have anything to be ashamed of."

Lord Hoyt exhaled and looked up at nothing in particular.

"Thank you," he finally said.

"Now, will you listen to the rest?"

Hoyt nodded.

"You promise to not be upset?"

"No, but I will listen."

After a moment of hesitation, Kathryn continued. "Who the boy is will surprise you, but his identity is also the point of why I must tell you. Especially now. I pray that you will understand. Not my actions perhaps, but what this means."

The patience of Lord Hoyt, something revered throughout the province, was being ground down to the bone.

"Do you intend to kill me by a thousand cuts of anticipation?" he asked.

"You cannot go against the Arlethians."

"We do not make that decision."

"You *must* not. There is more at play than you know."

Lord Hoyt raised both his eyebrows this time. "That's quite a statement coming from a fourteen-year-old girl. Do you find yourself in possession of greater knowledge of the situation than my advisors? And, pray tell, how were you made aware of such vital information?"

"This is no childish joke I speak of and I'll thank you not to treat it as such. Betrayal and treason are not the part of the wood-dwellers in this masquerade."

Calder Hoyt looked around at that statement to ensure himself again that they were alone and then knelt down with his hands upon Kathryn's shoulders. He briefly remembered it had not been so long ago that she was still shorter than him, even when he knelt. Now he looked up into her eyes more seriously.

"If you know something, part with it now, quickly. Many lives hang in the balance."

Kathryn took a deep breath and exhaled.

"The High Duke assassinated Lady Kerr and murdered those of her hold. It was some of the servants that came after Lord Kerr's death, people Lady Kerr had trusted in her vulnerable state. They were Khansian Guards."

Lord Hoyt blinked more rapidly and shook his head slightly. He opened his mouth.

"Wait, there's more," Kathryn said. "The things that were spread throughout the Realm of Lord Kerr and his wife—that they were traitors and usurpers—are all false. Many believed this but it was accepted by most eventually from the constant onslaught of misinformation. You know this, but it was all to divert attention."

"I know no such thing, daughter."

"It was all to divert attention!" Kathryn repeated in a vehement whisper. She did not bother to argue what her father actually believed about the Kerr family.

Lord Hoyt sighed. "Divert attention from what?"

"I don't know," she admitted. "But I know that what I've said is true. Now with the denouncement of Lord Therrium, you must see it as well. Some plot is afoot and I see the High Duke at the head."

Calder Hoyt recalled the meeting he had been summoned to six years earlier, an emergency session of the Council of Senthara. He had been a voice of dissent in that meeting where they declared Thannuel a traitor, but eventually gave in. He was never fully persuaded, however, but for the fear of his family's safety, he agreed to a motion he felt was abominable. His daughter's words seemed uncannily accurate and were disturbingly finding a small hold in him.

"It is probable that something similar happened to Thannuel as did to his wife," Kathryn continued.

Lord Hoyt shook his head. "No assassin could have bested Lord Kerr. The man was beyond any other man in the Realm in skill of steel, not to even speak of his natural wood-dweller abilities. A much greater force would have been required to take him down, one that would have been impossible to sequester or even infiltrate into his woods. No, it's more likely those he plotted with turned on him. What was he doing outside the walls of his hold at such a late hour? Something had to have taken him by surprise."

"And what of his daughter, Reign? Did Lord Kerr have her tag along to his secret traitor's meeting? Was she, still under the age of innocence, part of it as well?

"We don't know what befell his little girl. It may have been completely unrelated."

Even as he spoke the words he knew he did not believe them and he saw Kathryn's facial expressions confirm what his own could not hide. He also knew there was someone, or some*thing*, that could have overcome Thannuel... something he kept secret by an oath he made when becoming Lord of the Southern Province, something he never wished to face.

Calder knew Kathryn was pointing out the inconsistencies in the account as told by the Granite Throne's pronouncements. And, she apparently knew something more than he did, or at least thought she did. His daughter was gifted at seeing issues at many levels, a gift that he was often proud of. At this time, though, it had grown frustrating. He knew this was because he himself did not have answers for her questions, the same questions that had plagued him but for fear's sake had let them settle like stale dust. He had a feeling that old dust was about to be kicked in his face.

"Yes, the young girl. Reign was her name, you are right. Good memory. You are only a year younger than she would have been now. I don't believe they ever found her body."

"There's a reason for that," Kathryn said solemnly.

Lord Hoyt glanced down and then back up quickly to his daughter's eyes. They were locked on his. He stood up and took a step back.

"Kathryn, what do you know?"

"A great many things." Her voice was steady and confident. "I am betrothed, father, to Hedron Kerr."

"I have something to show you," Lord Hoyt announced to his daughter. The past few hours since Kathryn revealed that Reign and Hedron Kerr were still alive had been the most hectic and stressful of his life. No clear direction presented itself, and every path discussed was perilous in its own right.

"What is it?" Kathryn asked.

"Not here. Follow me."

The sun was setting in the west. As they made their way across the hold grounds covered in stone and copper tiles, Lord Hoyt looked southeast to see the reflection of the orange and purple sky off the Schadar's burning sands over a hundred miles away. The mirage was beautiful to behold and gave the illusion of being level with the skies as one looked out toward where the horizon should have been. None was discernible in the twilight hours looking east on clear evenings.

They arrived at the stables and Lord Hoyt dismissed the stable boys who were mucking the stalls and brushing the horses.

"Father, what are we doing here?"

"Patience. Isn't that always what mother is telling you?" He didn't see her expression but heard the scoff that escaped her lips.

They came to one stall that held a large, dark brown horse with a patch of white along its snout that ended just before its nose. The animal's tail wagged sporadically, shooing away flies from its hindquarters. After they stopped at the stall, the horse held its head high and straightened up to its full height. It looked proud.

"This horse," Lord Hoyt began, "was found the morning after Lord Kerr was slain. I didn't know he had been killed until a couple days later, but that's not why I'm telling you this."

"Why, then?"

"It was obvious the horse had been running all night. His movements were lethargic and he was matted in sweat. Some of the hold guard found him on our side of the Roniah, drinking from the river. Muddy horseshoe marks on the bridge at the Roniah Crossing indicated it had crossed from the other side, from the wood-dweller's side. Master Gernald brought it to my attention and we brought him to our stables."

"I am not sure I follow. He's beautiful, but—"

Hoyt entered the stall with the horse and kicked some hay from a corner, revealing a small wooden hatch. He lifted it and reach down inside. Pulling out the items hidden under the covering, Lord Hoyt asked, "Do you know what this is?"

Kathryn took the material and spread it out. "It looks like a horse blanket or skirt of some kind." The blanket was a dark rich blue with a green trim. Thinly woven but extremely fine workmanship.

And then she saw it. A golden shield with a white four-pointed star flare that would rest directly under the horse's neck.

"Wellyn's sigil!"

"And this," her father said, handing her a saddle.

She took it and found the same symbol stamped in the leather on either side of the saddle near the stirrups.

"This blanket and saddle were on this horse when he was found. We know he came from the Western Province and we know he had been sprinting for some time, probably covering a decent amount of ground. He was found the morning after Lord Kerr was mysteriously killed and his daughter went missing."

"What does it mean?" his daughter asked.

"I was never sure, but needless to say it was curious. Adorned as he was, and as well trained as he is, it led me to believe he belonged to a member of the Khansian Guard."

Kathryn went pale.

"Not wishing to be hasty or rash, I instructed Master Gernald to hide the saddle and blanket and keep him in the stables until we could figure things out. Well, that never happened and he just became part of the cavalry."

Lord Hoyt paused. "But, if what you have shared with me tonight has merit, then maybe this horse's appearance some six years ago makes sense."

"It is true, what I've said! I swear it by the Ancients themselves!"

Lord Hoyt looked down and shifted his weight. "I know."

"What are you going to do, father?"

He swallowed hard. "Something that I am sure will mean our doom, my daughter."

TWENTY-EIGHT

Holden and Ryall

Day 15 of 1ˢᵗ Dimming 412 A.U.

RYALL REALIZED HIS CHAIR WAS ABSENT an instant too late to prevent him from falling to the ground and landing hard on his backside. Even as he hit the solid ground in the Changrual monastery he knew this was reprisal for putting wine in his best friend's inkwell yesterday. Several hours of transcription work had been lost before Holden noticed.

"Blast the Cursed Heavens, Holden!" Ryall swore when his breath returned to his lungs. He noticed his chair about a foot to his left. Holden was failing in his effort to look innocent where he sat directly across from Ryall's writing desk, stifling a laugh. The small commotion had generated some small laughter from the other adherents in the hall.

"I know it was you!" Ryall snapped after standing up and brushing himself off.

"Why, whatever could you mean?" Holden retorted with mock innocence while holding up his hands in a guiltless gesture. Of course, his right hand held one end of the string that had its other end tied to a leg of the chair in question. Holden's shock of red hair looked as disheveled as ever, adding to his mischievous appearance.

Seeing his enemy in the prank war holding the weapon of his embarrassment in such a taunting way brought out the best in Ryall.

"That was useless," he said. "I've got a small bruise but you lost hours of work thanks to my last prank. I've lost nothing."

"Just your pride," Holden retorted. "Oh wait, you understandably never had any. Why be proud when you're...you?"

"Oh, I don't know. I think my overwhelming wit is reason enough."

"More like lack of wit!" Holden countered and started to laugh with the crowd the contest had attracted, other adherents leaving their writing desks to gather around. Ryall did not laugh, but instead stood silent just staring at Holden with a slight grin. Becoming aware of his friend's unfaltering gaze, Holden's laugh quieted. He knew that look, having seen it for most of his childhood, and began to sense something was amiss.

"What?" he asked, more wary as the moments passed. He tried not to appear anxious, but his eyes were darting about the room everywhere. Ryall just continued to stare.

"Look everyone, Ryall's demonstrating his almighty wit!" Holden declared. This caused more laughter from the onlookers, but Holden was using this as a distraction to continue to scan the hall and figure out just what Ryall was up to.

"Holden, how long have we sat at this desk opposite each other?" Ryall finally asked. "Eighteen cycles? I think ever since we entered the monastery."

"So?"

"So, I think we are all a little tired of the stench radiating from you. In fact, I think we all agree it's high time for a bath!"

And with that, Ryall produced a pull string of his own and gave one quick yank before Holden could register what was about to happen. A deluge of water was released from a bucket strategically placed above in the rafters, drenching the redheaded boy. An eruption of "oohs" and laughter echoed throughout the hall. It was just then that old man Kabel happened to set foot in the transcription hall to witness Holden being doused by his unwelcome mid-afternoon shower.

"What's the meaning of this?" his old squeaky voice croaked. "Answer me with truth or by the Ancient Heavens I'll have every one of you—"

"It was me!" Ryall confessed almost in a bragging tone as he stepped forward. "Holden is just the poor, innocent victim of a higher mind at work. Mine."

"Not so!" Holden shot back at Ryall, not even caring to address the old custodian. "Who was it that got his fingers stuck together last span for the whole day, thinking a jar of southern amber wax to be soap?"

Ryall stood on his chair, hoping to make his answer somehow stronger. "Who woke up three days past with a hairless chest?"

"Who got fire rash on their crotch?"

"Ants in their soup!"

"Manure in their shoes!"

"Kerosene in their mouth rinse!"

"Their sandals' straps cut!"

"Wood pulp in their sugar!"

At that last one, Holden looked questioningly at Ryall. "I don't remember that," he said. Ryall bit his lower lip, blushing slightly.

"Well, you would have at evening meal."

Glancing over at old man Kabel, the two boys saw the effect of their performance. Kabel's mouth was agape with his eyes staring wide in utter disbelief. The old man hobbled in place, back and forth from leg to leg as was typical when he was too astonished or flustered to make any comment, earning him the nickname "Hobble Kabel" among the young adherents. The two boys couldn't contain it any longer and bellowed with laughter. Ryall nearly fell off the chair he perched upon from his body shaking in hilarity. Holden rolled on the ground, his wet robe leaving a small puddle on the stone floor.

"Enough!" Kabel yelled, hobbling furiously, but his attempt at regaining authority through raising his voice came out more like a crow cawing uselessly at the sun. "Enough! Enough! Enough! I will march you straight to the High Vicar on duty and have him deal with you!"

Their laughter continued even after Kabel yanked them by their ears and hauled them away.

"Blasted Heavens! We've been waiting here so long my robe is nearly dry." Holden looked abashed for using such language, remembering where he was. The two perpetrators had been sitting outside the High Vicar's office since mid-afternoon and now had completely missed evening meal.

"What do you think will happen to us this time?" Ryall asked. He did not sound overly concerned.

"Perhaps they will finally see you for the worthless bag of hair and bones you are and expel you from the monastery," Holden jabbed.

"If only the Ancient Heavens would be so kind—"

"But where would you go, Ryall? Your father would never accept you back after being dismissed from the monastery. He barely accepted you in the first place. No doubt he has been breathing sighs of relief ever since he sent you here and they granted you entrance."

The two boys had grown up together in the Eastern Province, barely a span apart in age and both sons of minor houses. They were also both third sons. This fact alone charted their destiny in life. Lord Grady Orion sat as Provincial Lord of the East, the largest province in all the Realm. Third sons, according to Lord Orion, were only granted to men of his province to serve the Ancient Heavens and were therefore required to enter the Changrual Monastery when fourteen years of age. Holden and Ryall had dreamt together of someday scaling the Jarwyn Mountains and crossing over to the Falls of Olin on the east side of the great mountains. From there, they would take the journey down the perilous precipice to the Sea of Albery and sail out beyond the Runic Islands to meet the sun where it rose every morning.

Holden had since accepted his status in life, but Ryall seemed determined to stubbornly hang on to his dreams of adventure and voyaging beyond the Realm. He stared at the ground without actually seeing it as he answered his long-time friend wistfully.

"The world has never seemed to want us, third sons of minor houses. It is as if our fates were determined for us without us even being asked. I want to be free, free as the birds that fly through the sky and as the whales that roam the deep. Can you imagine what it would be like? No one to answer to and nowhere we must be. We would live as we choose, no one to force us. Can't you feel the… the…"

Ryall didn't know the word he was searching for. *Freedom, autonomy, liberty, independence* all ran through his mind, but they were somehow inadequate. The feeling he was trying to describe was somewhat ineffable to him. Holden listened to his friend but also just stared down at the ground. He knew Ryall had retreated inside himself again and was not seeing the stone and dirt they both plainly stared at as he voiced his greatest desires.

Ryall finally settled on "power" as the assistant resident Vicar opened the door to the High Vicar's office and motioned them in. As Ryall arose, he heard the sound of clothing being ripped and then felt a draft. He looked behind him to see the seat of his robe still on the bench were they had been sitting and his backside bare.

"Southern amber wax," Holden mused. "Sticky stuff."

Half a span later, Holden and Ryall made their way through the basement chambers of the monastery, each with a mop and bucket of soapy water. This was the last day of their punishment to scrub the monastery from top to bottom. The High Vicar on duty had spared them from the pain and humiliation of a public caning, preferring hard labor to force out disobedient tendencies over corporeal punishment. The basement chambers were always saved for last. No one visited these lower parts after dusk. Ryall wasn't sure why anyone would visit them at all.

"I'm not sure what they hope for us to accomplish down here," Holden groused for about the hundredth time. "Wiping down these old stones and rocks only makes them wet. There's no hope for them actually getting clean."

"We found out the same thing about you a half span ago," Ryall jeered. "That bath in the transcription hall hasn't done you any good."

"And my mop," Holden continued, not rising to Ryall's jab, "is worthless on this rough stone. Look at it, shredded and frayed."

"Perhaps you could use my ruined robe. It's not good for much else these days. In fact, you can have it as a trophy."

At that, Holden did crack a smile though it was mostly masked in a flickering shadow created by the single torch held in a crude sconce on the wall just above their heads. Amber wax, a product of the industrious Southern Province, might have been the most adhesive substance known. It was used often in construction applications of all create, mounting objects to walls and by healers to help seal wounds. And, of course, in Holden and Ryall's prank war.

"Watch this," Ryall said. "Look how dirty this piece of the ground is. Now, I'm going to clean my feet with the mop and then mop the ground." As he did so, Holden watched, but not because he actually cared what Ryall was doing. He started to look for yet another opportunity to best his friend, although he was currently ahead in the prank count.

After Ryall finished mopping his feet and the ground, he said, "I pronounce this part of the floor clean." Then he stepped on it with his clean bare feet, took a few steps, and held up the soles of his feet for Holden to see. They were filthy. "A lot of good that did."

No opportunity presented itself to Holden. He had to resort to a mere verbal assault. "Well, ya know, you can't help it. Filthiness is just attracted to you!"

"Ha!" Ryall shouted. "We'll see about that." He plunged his mop into his bucket and flung the soaking head at Holden, sending a shower of grimy water toward him. Holden returned fire as they flung dirty water and insults about each other's mothers back and forth. It took only moments for them to become drenched and reeking of filth.

"Ahhhhh!" Ryall bellowed as he charged Holden, holding his mop up as a sword. He swung down, but Holden blocked the blow, raising his own mop-sword. Their laughter echoed down the basement hallways, joined by the clanking of wood against wood as their sparring continued.

"I'll smite you down as Oliver Wellyn did to Brant Kearon!" Holden promised. "You're done for!"

"I didn't know Oliver fought like a girl!" Ryall retorted. "Best I run home and fetch my sister Bethany to finish this for me so it will be more fair to you!"

But as Ryall moved his feet back and forth, he accidently sunk his left foot into his bucket and tripped backward. Holden tried to reach forward and grab his friend's robe, but in the flickering light misjudged the distance and instead pushed him, adding force to his fall. Ryall slammed against a wall, knocking his head hard and losing his breath.

"Ryall!" Holden yelled as he knelt down beside him. "Ryall, are you all right? Speak!"

Ryall's face contorted with pain. He moaned as he raised his right hand to the back of his head. "What was that?" he asked with a wincing voice.

"You fell. Ryall, I tried to grab you but... I'm sorry. Are you okay?"

"I know I fell, stupid. That's why I'm the one down here with a lump on my head. I meant, what was that behind me?"

Holden was obviously relieved by hearing his friend's response mingled with typical insults. "The wall, genius. You might want to pick a softer place to land next time."

"It can't be a wall," Ryall said as he stood up, uselessly trying to dust himself off. "It moved. I felt it."

"Yup, you hit your head a little too hard. Time to go. Let me help you to your bed—"

"Get off!" Ryall demanded, shaking Holden's arm off him. "I'm telling you it moved!"

"Blasted Heavens!" Holden said, holding his hands up in defense. "I'm only trying to help."

Ryall wore a look of intent upon his face. He studied the wall where he had hit. Its construction was crude, composed of rocks and stone held together by mortar. He looked a few feet to the left and right of the area he hit, then hastily grabbed the torch from the sconce and inspected the structure more closely.

"Look!" he said excitedly. "The stones are different to the left. And here, to the right as well."

"What?" Holden asked. "Ryall, it's just a blasted—"

Putting his hands upon the wall, Ryall pushed. Nothing happened. He pushed again, harder. He grunted with the effort. Nothing. Dropping the torch, he stood back a pace or two and started to kick. Holden looked on as if his friend had lost his mind.

"Ryall stop! If someone hears they'll come! What do you think the High Vicar will do to us this time?"

After a few more fruitless kicks, Ryall backed up from the wall about ten paces with his gaze still fixed on it.

"Finally," Holden said with relief. "Come on, let's get some food. Evening meal isn't quite over."

He turned to leave. Instead of following Holden up the stone steps to the main level of the monastery, Ryall charged the wall. When he was two paces from it, he flung his body through the air, turning himself sideways. The dull soft sound created from such a forceful impact seemed quite an understatement.

"Burning Heavens!" Holden cried. "Are you mad?"

Ryall had landed in a ball, much the way he hit the wall. His arms were wrapped around his ribs. After a moment he looked up, breathing heavily. He smiled faintly and answered, "No, not mad." He raised his right arm, leaving his other cradling his ribs, and pointed to the wall. Holden followed Ryall's finger and stared at the point of impact. Several rocks were depressed, forming a small crater in the wall.

"Ancient Heavens," Holden mumbled. He grabbed the torch off the ground and stepped closer. Reaching up, he pushed a few of the dislodged stones and rocks. They fell through to the other side of the wall. The thud of their fall echoed. Ryall recovered enough to stand up.

"I told you it moved."

"I believe you," was all Holden could say.

They worked on the small opening for several minutes, freeing more stones until the opening was large enough for them to crawl through. Ryall took the torch and tossed it through to the other side. Their heads knocked together as they both moved to peer through the opening.

In the small radius of orange-yellow light, all that could be made out was that the cavern, or whatever it was, appeared to be quite spacious. The boys looked at each other with amazement mixed with mischievousness.

"Me first," Ryall declared.

"Definitely, you first," Holden replied.

It didn't take much effort to squeeze through the hole they had made. Ryall took in his surroundings with mouth agape as Holden slid through the opening. He coughed from the dust and spit.

"This better be worth it," the redheaded boy remarked, coming to Ryall's side. "There's no hiding this. We'll be expelled for sure. Maybe they'll even make this our crypt!" Ryall didn't answer. Holden finally looked around and inspected their discovery. "Dimming Light!" he whispered.

Surrounding the young adherents was an expansive cavern of small honeycomb inlets along all sides of the walls. The room had no discernible shape but was mostly spherical, interrupted by occasional jagged directional changes jutting abruptly at odd angles. Stalactites hung from the ceiling in several places. Mineral enriched water dripped from them and formed several small puddles with stalagmites rising from them, reaching for their counterpart above. In a few places, the rock growths had reached each other and formed golden yellow columns sporadically throughout the room. There was a small pond of water in the middle of the cavern whose stillness was occasionally interrupted by a falling drop of water from a stalactite. In each honeycomb inlet lay roughly half a dozen scrolls. Thousands upon thousands stretched out before them. Some inlets contained vials of liquid and ancient looking clay jars as well as odd trinkets of strange create.

Holden reached out to the nearest inlet and retrieved a single scroll. "So brittle," he said.

Ryall grabbed the torch and joined him. "What does it say?"

"I don't know if we dare unroll it. It might not survive judging by how frail it feels."

"Look." Ryall pointed at the inlet from where Holden had taken the scroll. "It's labeled with a glyph." Engraved into the base of the rock inlet was indeed a symbol of some create. "I don't know it. Is it Sentharian? Oh, here's another on this inlet!" Ryall moved from inlet to inlet, noticing the glyph at the base of each one and then moving on enthusiastically. "I can't make them out. Can you read them?"

"No," Holden said with ice in his voice. "We have to get out of here."

"What? Why? We just got here!"

"Now, Ryall! We have to leave!" His voice quavered.

Ryall turned to face Holden. "If you're scared about getting in trouble, I think it's a little late for that."

Holden turned and started heading toward the exit. Ryall grabbed his robe and stopped him. "What is it?" he demanded, flummoxed by his friend's lack of fascination with their discovery.

"We can't read the glyphs, Ryall, but I know what they are."

Ryall had a bemused look on his face. "And?"

Holden turned pale as he said, "Hardacheon."

They had placed the stones and rocks back into position as best as could be expected in their hurried frenzy. In such a remote portion of the basement, it seemed unlikely anyone would notice the breach unless a close inspection was undertaken. Someone would have to know exactly what to look for and where. They tried to convince themselves that they were safe, but a feeling of apprehension remained with them.

In the days following, Ryall meandered through the monastery in a type of trance, paying no attention to his studies or duties. Holden seemed much the same. They barely spoke, not even to each other. But they shared several knowing looks that conveyed much about how they were both feeling. Though he could tell Holden was shaken from the experience, Ryall could not stop thinking about the discovery and all that existed in the underground cavern.

"Let it be," Holden had warned him. "Put it out of your mind." Perhaps it was the risk that tempted Ryall to return to the cavern, or even just the thought of an adventure—although trolling around in an ancient library of sorts had never crossed his mind as *adventurous* before.

"What harm could there be?" Ryall had replied. "No one ever goes to those parts—"

"You don't know that."

"We barely made it a few feet inside before turning into cowards. There's so much there we could explore!" Ryall pleaded with Holden to return with him during the night, but Holden was firm.

"We can't go back!" Holden exclaimed. "Those were Hardacheon records, Hardacheon relics! Don't you get it? Haven't you paid attention at all? All the writings teach of the Hardacheon Influences, the evil they wrought upon this land. By the Ancient Heavens, it's one of the main reasons the Changrual were brought here during the invasion. They had to exterminate the Dark Influences that were in this land or victory would have been lost. Every bit of the Hardacheon culture and teaching was destroyed. This is basic history!"

"Oh?" his friend replied. "Then what, pray tell, are all those Hardacheon relics and scrolls doing down there?"

"Listen, Ryall, I know you. I know this is unbelievably tempting to you. But you gotta let it be. We can't risk being in that room. I don't just say this because we could be caught, but we don't know what lurks there, what Influences are there. Has it occurred to you that it was sealed off for a reason?"

"How did you know those glyphs were Hardacheon?" Ryall asked with a hint of accusation. "And don't tell me I should pay attention more in class. I looked through all our study scrolls. There is no mention, much less examples, of Hardacheon glyphs."

"I don't know. It was a guess," Holden said.

"Liar! You knew right away! I saw it on your face. You forget we had the same nursemaid growing up, Holden. I can read you just as well as you can read me."

Holden looked away and appeared pensive. Finally he said, "I just knew, okay? I can't explain it to you." Looking back up at his friend he continued sternly, "And before you get carried away with your crazy ideas, it's not because I'm a Hardacheon in disguise or have some secret ability to read ancient languages. It was just a feeling." Holden looked down and said more softly, "It was actually a rather cold feeling. The same feeling I would get when your dad would tell us those scary legends of Hardacheons from long ago when we were younger."

Ryall did not continue to press his friend, but his mind refused to let go of the possibilities. He could not find much sleep in the nights that followed as his mind toiled with the temptation to revisit the cavern. Finally, he made his decision.

Two days and a half span after discovering the cavern, Ryall snuck out of his chamber past midnight, careful not to wake Holden. He had retired that night in his robe so that he would not have to dress when the time came. One advantage of their five-day-long punishment to clean the monastery was that Ryall knew the place better than even some of the Vicars, he suspected. He wouldn't need a torch to find his way. He brought one nonetheless, but would not light it until he was in the cavern. He double-checked that his flint and striker were in his pocket.

Ryall made his way slowly down the steps, concentrating on silence. He ran his hand along the wall once in the basement chambers until his fingers detected the change in the surface. He stopped and tested a few rocks. They were loose.

Ever so carefully, he removed the stones and rocks they had broken free from the mortar on his previous visit. He dared not stack them in the dark for fear of accidentally knocking them over and drawing attention, even at this late hour.

Once through the opening, he took the concealed torch from his robe and lit it with his flint and striker. He squinted against the flame's light until his sight adjusted fully. The magnitude of the cavern once again struck him. The number of honeycomb inlets was dizzying to behold. Ryall had no idea where to even begin, which meant it didn't matter where he started.

Taking his torch, he inspected dozens of the inlets, mostly studying the glyphs. They were indecipherable to him but this did not stop him from continuing to stare at them, memorizing them as best he could. He cursed himself for not bringing ink and parchment to copy down the ancient symbols. He hoped his brain would cooperate and later recall the few he committed to memory.

He penetrated deeper into the giant space. The sound of dripping water from the prevalent stalactites produced a random cadence that accompanied his wandering. He sampled a few scrolls here and there, opening only the ones that felt durable enough. Materials of all create were used, from parchment to animal hide to copper. He even discovered a vertical stack of large obsidian tablets leaning against a far wall. They would have blended in seamlessly to the blackness, their color a natural camouflage in this grotto, save for the shimmering reflection the torchlight produced against their polished surface.

These appear to be Archiver tablets, Ryall thought. *Why are they stored here?* Technically the Jarwyn Mountains were part of the Eastern Province where he came from, although the Archivers who lived high near their peaks enjoyed a level of autonomy, having predated the Senthary.

He looked closer and became excited. *The writing is Sentharian!* At the top of each tablet was a symbol. Though he couldn't decipher them, he knew the style well enough by now to know for sure that they were Hardacheon. Despite the foreign glyphs at the top of each tablet, the body of the text on the great obsidian slabs was most definitely Sentharian. A curious thought occurred to Ryall as he walked past dozens of rows of the slabs, all lined up edge to edge in this far part of the underground chamber. *Perhaps it's a filing system of sorts.* He looked more closely at the glyphs on each tablet, feeling the chiseled grooves with his fingers. Finally, he came to one he recognized, one of the few he had memorized. Under the glyph at the top he saw written in Sentharian:

The Chronicled Era of Tyre Wellyn

18-27 Years After Unification

He counted seven tablets from front to back in this row, all leaning up against one another. It was no small effort to retrace some of his steps and find the inlet with the matching glyph. He counted the number of scrolls that lay in the inlet. Seven.

He returned to the row of obsidian tablets and pondered for a few moments. He stepped to the right, to the next row of tablets.

The Chronicled Era of Oliver Wellyn, the Second of his Name

27-61 Years After Unification

Fingering the glyph on the top of the first tablet in this row, he brought the torch close enough to distinctly make out the symbol. It looked like two oblong circles, one above the other and slightly to the left. They overlapped diagonally and a horizontal line pierced the intersection of the circles. After memorizing it, he counted the number of tablets in this row. Only four. He searched the inlets around where he'd matched the prior glyph, quickly finding it. In the alcove with the matching glyph lay four rolled scrolls. A chill ran up and down Ryall's spine.

He returned again to the row of tablets that claimed to be the record of Oliver the Second and stepped left two rows.

The Chronicled Era of Oliver Wellyn, the First of his Name
The Invasion of the Senthary and Defeat of the Hardacheon People
The Fall of House Kearon and Rise of the Realm
6 Years Before Unification—18 Years After Unification

For hours, Ryall read. He continued well past first moon, into the early hours of the new day. He carefully hefted tablet after tablet to the side when he had completed reading one and went excitedly to the next. Finally, the torch diminished beyond useful light. Ryall cursed himself for not bringing a second torch, but realized it was probably best as the sun would surely be rising soon.

I must bring back a stack of parchment to take rubbings, he thought excitedly. So immersed was he in his discovery that he never saw the dark figure approach him from behind. A hand cloaked in shadow reached out for Ryall.

TWENTY-NINE

Reign

Day 27 of 1st Dimming 412 A.U.

REIGN DID REMEMBER HER FATHER. Perfectly, in fact. She had found no nepenthe that could put a shroud upon her memory of him, though not for lack of trying. She remembered as a youngling how he had taught her to listen in the forest, to truly listen. To *feel.* She could recall with clarity the first time her ears were opened and the shock of sensing so many things at once, so much life. It was overwhelming, but fascinating and addicting in the way a child is attracted to playing with fire. Thannuel had rocked back with laughter at seeing the innocent surprise upon Reign's face as she pulled her hand back rapidly from the Triarch tree. She couldn't have been more than half the age innocence.

"Now, this time," Thannuel coaxed, gently taking his daughter's hand, "place your hand flush against the trunk. Try to make your whole palm touch the bark. The palm is the most sensitive part. When the vibrations come don't pull back. They can't hurt you. Focus and single something out."

"Like what?" Reign asked. Thannuel could see she was still a little shaken from the onslaught of vibrations she had just taken in. A wood-dweller first learning to speak with a tree could feel as if ten thousand voices were yelling out at once for attention.

315

"Something small and simple," her father answered.

"What's that?" she asked again.

Thannuel smiled at his daughter. "You'll see. If Hedron can do it, you can too."

She looked up at Hedron, who stood a few paces off, for moral support. His arms were folded with a condescending look upon his face. "Not likely," he mused. "She's just a girl."

Hurt, Reign looked back at her father. He glanced disapprovingly at Hedron and then whispered to Reign, "Hedron screamed and turned white as a she-goat when he first tried." Reign giggled and looked back up at her brother. Seeing her amusement at his expense, Hedron dropped his arms to his side and protested, "Father!"

Thannuel just laughed with Reign. After a moment, he comforted Hedron. "You did fine, son."

Turning back to Reign, he asked, "Ready?"

"But why a Triarch, father? Why not an elm, or oak?"

"All trees of the West can speak, Reign. We say *speak*, but the trees are more of a conduit to hearing and feeling what's around us. A Triarch is the most sensitive tree we know. It's more..." Thannuel paused as he considered the right word. "Fluent," he finally said.

"What's a conduit?" Reign persisted.

"Something that allows you to sense other things through it, like feeling movement in the forest through this Triarch."

"What's fluent?" Reign asked. Thannuel's face formed a half-smile as he caught on to his daughter's delay tactic.

"No more questions. Now, are you ready?"

She shuddered and nodded nervously, letting her father move her hand back to the mighty Triarch, probably a thousand years old. Reign took a breath and held it. She extended her hand, palm out, and laid it against the trunk once more with her father's hand over hers. The rush was again overwhelming, causing her to grimace from the discomfort. Her father whispered encouragement to her, gently but firmly keeping her hand against the tree.

"Focus," he whispered. "Open your mind and let the vibrations flow through you. Become a channel, a pathway."

"A conduit," she mumbled, her eyes closed tightly. As Reign struggled with the effort, she felt movement in the streets of Calyn. Purchasers at market with the traders; an argument over the price of the day's catch from the Roniah River; a mother scolding her youngling for wandering too far; hunters several leagues north tracking deer; fowl of some create building a nest above the canopy; soldiers back at the hold in training, Aiden's voice bellowing out commands as they worked through different kata; a family of squirrels gathering acorns for the winter in an oak tree nearby.

"Squirrels!" Reign squeaked in excitement. As she focused more on the squirrels, the other sounds became quieter, moving to the background.

Amazing! she thought. Her face relaxed as the overwhelming plethora of information faded to a streamlined channel to the squirrels. *There are four.* Two would run up the tree, harvesting the acorns by freeing them and letting them drop to the ground below. The other two would then gather them into groups at the base of the tree. When they had enough, the ground squirrels chattered some rhythmic vocabulary to those above, and they retreated back down the oak, regrouping. This was followed by an organized transport of the acorns to some retreat they had previously prepared. Reign's smile was full of joy.

She pulled her hand away reluctantly, breaking the connection. Wonder emanated from her eyes. "It works, father, it works! I found a family of squirrels, and they were getting acorns and dropping them down and the other two would put them with the others and—"

"I know, I know," Thannuel said with a gentle laugh. "I felt them, too."

Reign looked up at her brother with a smug expression. "At least I didn't scream!" she jeered.

"All right you two, I think I hear your mother calling."

"I don't hear anything," Hedron said.

"Son, there are some things that don't require speaking with trees to sense."

Reign stood and looked up at her father with joy at her accomplishment of speaking with a Triarch.

"I feel so alive now! Like a real wood-dweller!"

"Oh, I don't know about that," her father teased.

Reign punched his leg and Thannuel chuckled. "That tickled!"

"But how is it that we can do this and other races can't?" she asked.

"Now that is a good question—one that many outside our race, and even many within, have struggled to answer. Arlethians can feel the currents of life. The Living Light is what they are actually called and it permeates through all things."

"Even rocks? Dirt?"

Well, yes, actually." Thannuel pursed his lips. "But those currents are much more difficult to discern."

"And no one else can do this? I mean, speaking with trees?"

Thannuel appeared to ponder for a minute, as if deciding what to say next. "Truthfully, anyone can learn to do it. Arlethians have an easier time because of our heritage, but the ability to feel the currents is not a birthright exclusive to wood-dwellers. It has more to do with the principles one lives by than genealogy. Anyone who approaches the Ancients can learn."

"I don't get it," Reign said. "The Ancients are gone."

"Yes, I suppose they are." He reached forward and tousled Reign's hair. "Now, let's get moving before your mother knocks the Light from each of us for being late for dinner."

She reached out and hugged him. She loved his sharp features, high cheekbones, hair the color of leaves in the Dimming Season, stout chin and soft smile. After holding the embrace for a few moments she released her father and looked upon him once more. His face suddenly morphed in something else, something wrong. He now wore the face of the scary man with deep carved designs in his skin and clothed in a thick hooded robe. Heavy rain was suddenly present and streamed down the glyphs of his face like small rivers flooding a desert. A sword hung in one hand, coated in blood. A couple paces away, her father lay on his back, his life's blood mixing with the rain as it streamed from a gaping wound in his chest.

"Reign," he said weakly, and then turned to stone. His loving eyes became cold, hard, and gray like granite.

Reign stepped back in terror, not able to breathe. She was confused and did not understand. She tried to scream, but no sound came. As she turned to run for the safety of the Triarch tree she had just spoken with, her legs failed her and the ground raced up to meet her.

Waking with a start, Reign saw Hedron and Aiden asleep on the earth next to her. The fire lay in smoldering ashes and dying embers. A light snow had frosted them during the night and she tasted snowflakes on her lips. They were only a day's journey from Jayden's land, currently somewhere in the southern reaches of the Gonfrey Forest, where the trees were not known and did not speak. They had entered the Northern Province yesterday after traveling for almost of full cycle where the climate turned noticeably more hostile due to the change in season as much as the change in their location. Even with a wood-dweller's speed, many days were required to travel from Calyn to Jayden's land far in the Gonfrey Forest to the north unless one was exercising caution, in which case the journey would be longer due to a more erratic route. The small company had exercised extreme caution on their journey.

Rumors of wars and battles between Therrium and Wellyn had begun to emerge in the few span since their reunion. Aiden had received leave from Lord Therrium and traveled with the young Kerr twins. He did not really seem to care where they were going, so long as he accompanied them. It was strange having company, sharing openly with someone else besides Hedron, but Reign felt an air of protection around Aiden that comforted her.

Night was still present, but Reign didn't think she could return to sleep. The dreams were changing now, more threatening, although the essence was the same.

She felt it, sensed it. Near her. She tensed, preparing to fight back. However, this time it didn't push against her. It felt more like something brushing against her, like being gently wrapped in a cloak. There was almost a familiarity about the feeling, but Reign did not let her mind enter that realm where memories would take her over the edge of grief and fear. This time, Reign pushed on *it*, forcing it from her.

Their travels later that day were done in relative silence. Reign was determined to reach Jayden as quickly as possible and seemed to move through the forest with singular focus. More than once Hedron's request to rest went unanswered. Reign felt safer nowhere else than amongst Jayden's packs.

It's home for me, she admitted. *The only home I have left.*

As they came closer to their destination, a smile found Reign's face. She felt the light pouncing of her old friend tracking her, trying to sneak up on her. The quick footfall become faster and louder suddenly. Aiden stopped, spinning around warily. A huge white wolf leaped over him and tackled Reign, snarling and baring his teeth.

Aiden drew his sword and yelled, "Reign!" He began to run toward her in defense but stopped suddenly hearing her laughter and the wolf's snarls turning to the sound of tongue licking. Hedron tackled the wolf, sounding out a playful battle cry. It wasn't long before the wolf regained the advantage and pinned Hedron down on his back. Then Hedron also began to laugh.

"What's this, then?" Aiden asked in utter bewilderment. The wolf looked up appraisingly at Aiden and bared his teeth with a light growl, but ceased when he saw the sword Aiden bore. Leaving Hedron, the large white wolf casually walked over to Aiden and inspected the sword in his hand. It whined a low cry of sorrow and longing.

Aiden was still a bit wary although he could see the Kerr twins obviously knew the animal.

"Aiden, this is Crimson Snow, one of Jayden's pack," Reign said. "He protected us many years ago when we were fleeing Calyn."

"He knew father's cloak, which I wore," Hedron added.

"Ahhh," Aiden said, drawing out his response. "I do know this one. Your father called him Elohk, but it was so long ago. He must be thirteen now, at least. That's an ancient age for a wolf." Aiden reached out his free hand to slowly pet the wolf behind his ears, but Crimson Snow barked out a warning.

"Crimson!" Reign rebuked. "Aiden is known to us. He is a protector to Hedron and me. He'll not harm you and is no threat to us." Crimson Snow did not look comforted by Reign's reassurance. She approached and took Aiden's hand and slowly moved it to Crimson Snow's head just behind the ears.

"Easy," she coaxed. "There, not so bad, see?" After a few strokes, Crimson Snow lowered his ears in allowance of the act. A few more strokes and the wolf sat down on its rear haunches, whimpering for more attention.

"Uh, I think he sat down on my foot," Aiden said. "Do I dare remove it?"

"It looks like you might have made a friend. I think Crimson is attempting to pin you down so he gets continued pampering from you," Hedron teased.

"Aye, I do remember," Aiden said. "Elohk, or, that is, Crimson Snow, was the most apt training companion for Thannuel. Your father was so fast and intense when training. This was the one that could hold his pace. Aye, I remember." He continued to rub gently behind the ears as a distant look overcame him. He seemed to be revisiting memories that had long been stowed away.

Reign studied Crimson Snow for a short time and then spoke: "Come, Crimson, let us be off to Jayden. Our journey has been long and I am eager to see her again." Crimson bounded toward the small cottage in the distance with smoke coming from the chimney, Reign not far behind.

Hedron and Aiden watched while Reign and the wolf darted toward Jayden's cottage.

"What is it, Hedron? What torments your sister to such a degree?" Aiden asked.

"I..." Hedron hesitated. "I'm not completely sure, Aiden. Somewhere inside her I know that she loves our father, but she exudes such hatred when he is mentioned."

"Hatred?" Aiden replied. "Or, is it regret?"

"Regret over what? There was nothing she could have done. Nothing at all. How could she have regret?"

"Not for what she could have done, Hedron, but for the loss of her father, him being stolen from her. It's almost as if she blames him for dying." *I have enough regret in that area for all of us many times over.*

Hedron did not answer, but considered Aiden's words. They were not far from his own ponderings about his sister. "Perhaps, but I just don't know. Every time I've tried to—to pry it out of her, she enters into a rage or just completely shuts down. And then there are the dreams, or *dream,* rather. I think she only has one, over and over."

"What do you mean? What dream?"

"They are of the night father fell..." Hedron started to answer, then shook his head as he looked away. "I don't know the details. I'm sorry. I wish I knew more. I won't deny that finding you has rekindled new hope about somehow getting through to her. She struggles against something—something she thinks is real, some-thing physical."

"Again, Hedron, I'm lost. Forgive me, but what is it you mean?"

"I...don't know. She says it pushes her, or against her. She won't talk about it much and that's all I really know. Pathetic that after six years it's all I've gathered, I know."

Aiden did not respond to this last bit of information, but mentally stored it to revisit later. Instead, he turned completely to the boy. "What will *you* do, Hedron? How will you lead your house?"

Hedron looked bewildered and snapped, "What house? There is no house, no hold. There's nothing for me to lead. I am not yet a man nor am I meant for such things. That life ended long ago. Our only hope now is to survive and continue unnoticed."

Again, Aiden said nothing. In the distance, he could hear Jayden laugh as she embraced Reign. Sensing this was not the time to press the subject, he opted to let it rest for now.

"Come," Aiden said. "Let's get out of the cold."

THIRTY

Ehliss

Day 27 of 1st Dimming 412 A.U.

AFTER HALF A SPAN PLUS ONE DAY on the Glaciers of Gonfrey, Ehliss' provisions had begun to dwindle. She wasn't worried, however. Her training as a member of the Ministry of Terran Studies had prepared her against all manner of elements and challenges, allowing her to survive on meager rations and in harsh climate.

She'd completed her last assignment on the open plains of the East in record time and hastily submitted her findings. They were in line with what Minister Findlay had feared: few worms, fewer birds.

She was technically north of the Realm's borders, as the Gonfrey Forest was considered the most northern boundary. There was nothing beyond the forest, which lay in a near constant state of the Low Season, save for the glaciers that extended for hundreds of leagues. No one had dared venture to cross such an expanse in the overwhelming harsh conditions, but Ehliss often daydreamed of being the first to lead an expedition in just such an attempt.

Nothing made her father prouder as when she was admitted to the Terran Studies Academy other than her acceptance to the Ministry itself. As the previous Minister of Terran Studies, Karuyl had long awaited a son whom he hoped would follow in his footsteps. The Ancient Heavens did not agree with his desires for a boy, but when his third daughter showed extreme interest in the land and its origin, Karuyl fostered her intrigue greatly, growing her embryonic interest into a lifelong passion that probably exceeded his own. The questions Ehliss would ask her father, from the movement of the sun in the sky to the purpose of worms in the soil, astounded him and showed intelligence beyond her youth that Karuyl recognized as truly unique. Further yet, there were few things that she could not understand in their complexity and often was frustrated with her father's simplified answers. He soon learned not to hold anything back in explanation or detail from his demanding daughter.

As Ehliss grew into a young woman, she decided to give little time to suitors who came calling. She was hardly the most beautiful woman in the Realm and was in fact rather plain. The few prearranged courtings her father had arranged that she consented to were abnormally brief, being ended shortly after their commencement by the young men involved. The complaint was always the same: Ehliss didn't speak much at all unless she was asked about something pertaining to terran studies, and then her ramblings became incessant and excited. After one evening, a young man returned her home to Karuyl and said, "I'm sorry, Minister, but I cannot understand half the words she speaks."

Ehliss decided that men were a waste of her time after that and she threw herself completely into her studies. They filled her completely, she claimed, and were the source of her happiness. A man who would win her over would need to be able to speak intelligently about more than his latest hunt or the number of children she would bear him.

Here upon the glaciers, Ehliss felt free and energized. She had taken dozens of samples, coring down in the ice scores of feet and carefully retracting slender cylinder-shaped ice shards. The deeper the sample she extracted, the darker the color of the ice. She had theorized that somehow the study of this older ice could give her clues as to the age, speed of movement of the glaciers and perhaps even ideas of the conditions that prevailed on the land thousands of years ago.

Ehliss had also been monitoring a dark cloud that she noticed just a day after arriving at the glaciers. It was far to the northern horizon but appeared to be growing, she noticed, or getting closer. It was a curious event, one that excited her. A storm of sorts that forms on ice? Or perhaps maintains enough of its power from starting on land to move across a glacier? And if it did start on land, then there must be land beyond the glaciers after all. She hoped she would be able to study the phenomenon if it came close enough and if provisions remained long enough to sustain her. A half span ago it was smaller, more than thirty leagues off, by her guess.

Today, though, it seemed different. The shape of this cloud system had appeared to change dramatically this morning, as did its color. Had she just not noticed it before? Perhaps it was always this shape but wasn't close enough to observe until now. She judged it to be roughly five or six leagues away and as she intently peered to the north, she thought she saw something strange within the thick haze, though it lacked focus. Then it was gone, as if the cloud had spewed out a particle, something solid, and then retracted it. A rumble beneath her feet began and she realized she had felt it before, but now it was growing with intensity. Nothing shook; her tent and supplies were not disturbed. Ehliss knew it wasn't an earthquake—no, wrong sort of tremor. These vibrations were more constant and slowly growing rather than intense and jarring. Looking back to the horizon and the enigmatic cloud, she saw clearly for the first time that it ran along the surface of the glacier as well as extending hundreds of feet, as much as a quarter league even, into the sky. In fact, the cloud wasn't very high in the sky compared to others, she noted. At its current velocity, Ehliss judged the storm would be upon her by nightfall, perhaps even earlier.

Turning her attention back to her more immediate duties, she took a long square iron shaft with a rounded head and slammed it down into a spot she had designated the day before. Ice splintered up as the sharp round threaded head bit into the glacier a few inches.

Ehliss pulled the thick pole free from the icy ground and repeated the effort, gaining a few more inches of depth. After a third stab, the head grabbed deep enough into the frozen ground and she twisted hard until the shaft was securely rooted.

When the first shaft had been driven down to only about half a foot protruding, Ehliss removed the winch and found another square shaft. She fastened it to the first shaft with a connecter coupling, slid the center of the winch over the top of the second shaft, and began to twist again.

Ehliss heard thunder. No, not thunder; something else. It had come from the north, from the storm cloud, hadn't it? Leaving her coring shafts where they were, she grabbed her field journal and sat for over an hour just gazing north and recording observations. She tried to make several rough sketches but the cloud seemed more and more to shift in its appearance and made her sketches obsolete before she finished them. She saw again what appeared to be objects that separated from the cloud and then rejoined it. She could tell now that this was happening frequently the closer the storm approached. The dark cloudbank moved with speed and now appeared less than a league away. The rumbling beneath her had become more pronounced and she could audibly hear the vibrations in the ice. It seemed now that she would have to retreat down a frozen cliff face to the forest floor half a league south and take shelter. She thought she remembered a small cottage in the forest not far from the beginning of the glaciers and decided she would attempt to seek succor there. But she still had some time before she must leave.

And then, all at once, Ehliss finally saw the storm come into terrifying focus. A paralyzing fear seized upon her and turned her heart colder than the glacier's core.

THIRTY-ONE

Shilkath

Day 27 of 1st Dimming 412 A.U.

NEARLY A QUARTER-LEAGUE ABOVE the icy earth that his army of Borathein marched upon with discipline and anticipation, Shilkath sat perched upon his Alysaar. He swept back and forth in the air across the formation of the Alysaar battery. The winged creatures each carried two Borathein warriors, one who was the rider and steered the beast, the other a warrior who searched for earthbound prey to strike down with arrow or blade. Altogether, each Alysaar unit presented three Borathein soldiers, including the Alysaar itself. Long talons of petrified bone protruded from hind legs salient enough to pierce the prevalent ice and stone of the north that so often made a natural perch. Formations of thorny spikes were manifested around the maw of the Alysaar that a man would liken to a beard, particularly a Borathein. Shilkath's beard, heavily laden with the evidences of his triumphs, swayed and jangled its percussive song in the cold wind as he dove, ascended and dove again, shouting out orders in guttural blasts of speech. As a Deklar, Shilkath did not have a second rider on his Alysaar. Hawgl was massive enough to carry three Borathein warriors on his strong back, but in a show of prowess, most Deklars rode alone. In fact, Shilkath reminded himself, he was the *only* Deklar now. All

Borathein nahgi had been united under him as the single Deklar of his people.

After many cycles, their long journey of crossing the ice desert was nearing an end. His men were restless with the promise of vengeance now close to being fulfilled as they could see the terrain change only a few leagues off from their current position. After easily defeating a few Deklars whose nahgi had resisted, the remaining Deklars bent the knee and joined their nahgi to Shilkath's. Discipline was difficult to maintain through such an extensive journey where so many disparate factions and tribes had been forced together in only a few years. Many times, small disputes among the camps turned into bloodbaths before he could put an end to the disruption. This more often than not was achieved through giving the offenders to the Ice Desert as an offering—stripping the offending parties naked and staking their hands and feet to the ice. The blood that flowed over the ground from open wounds quickly froze and became part of the Ice Desert, as would soon the disgraced Borathein warriors from whom the blood escaped. To break from discipline when engaged in Griptha was to bring down the wrath of Vyath upon the entire war host unless a sacrifice of flesh and ice was offered as penance to the god of vengeance and war. Shilkath entered the holy pact of vengeance, a Griptha, by offering his own frozen blood in sacrifice at Vyath's altar before a Gründaalina, the spiritual leaders of the Borathein, opening the flesh upon his chest with a blade of ice and stone. All Gründaalina were females. His blood froze almost instantly upon falling to the crude altar of ice and bone, bones of fallen enemies from previous Griptha over the ages.

Once, long ago, the ice was not part of the altar. That was a time when the Ice Desert was fertile ground, according to the legends, some thousands of years ago when the Borathein and Hardacheon were still one people. Shilkath swore to avenge their ancient kin who had been defeated by treachery, by foes disguised as friends. Now Shilkath led a host of ten thousand score Borathein and Alysaar, and they were mere days from fulfilling the Griptha and claiming glory for Vyath, freeing the souls of their long ago defeated kin that languished in Kulbrar, the frozen plane between this world and glory that engulfed the defeated dead. Only one path leads to the Shores of Thracia and eternal glory with the gods: dying in a battle that ends victorious. For he who falls on the field of battle where his forces are defeated, no matter the previous victories earned and worldly honor gained, damns his soul to Kulbrar until a kinsmen completes the victory in life, avenging his defeated and dead kin. A Griptha blessed by Vyath would shatter the frozen plain's grasp on his long-forgotten Hardacheon kin when fulfilled. He, Shilkath, would do this and free the tens of thousands in the grip of Kulbrar; he would bring down the traitors who wore cloaks of false friendship that concealed dark betrayal, deeply hidden; he would cause their women and children to feed upon their own dead and add their husbands' and fathers' flesh and bone to his beard while still soaking in blood. Shilkath would desecrate every holy place, devastate every home, and destroy the existence of every so-called wood-dweller from the land. The entire Arlethian race would be sent to Kulbrar by his war host's blade, and none would ever avenge them from their eternal enslavement upon the frozen plane. He could feel the anticipation from his men, the anticipation of battle and glory; the same anticipation that caused tension and the breaking of discipline, requiring the atonement of ice and flesh.

I will play the fool for now, he thought. *But I must be ready for Wellyn. He will reveal himself not long after we have triumphed over the Arlethians.* Shilkath had no expectations of a man who would betray his own subjects to keep his bond between strangers. *Yes, we will be ready.*

A small pillar of smoke protruded into the morning sky. Hawgl smelled it and reacted with interest just before Shilkath caught sight of it. Following it down to its source, he spied a small camp half a league off in the distance that appeared to be abandoned, but the smoldering fire pit gave evidence that it had not been abandoned long. He called out commands for two other Alysaar units to break off and follow him ahead of the host. His beast lowered its head and angled the front of its wings downward, retracting them closer to its body. As it dove toward the ground with the other two Alysaar slightly behind it on either side, Shilkath glimpsed a small figure disappear down a cliff face a short distance beyond the small camp. Barren trees started coming into focus as they drew closer and Shilkath realized it was not just another typical chasm in the icy ground where the figure had disappeared, but the edge of the Ice Desert itself. They had arrived. Their arrival must be unnoticed, at least for another couple days. He could not risk them being discovered just yet.

"Mindok, Frahl!" he barked to the other two Alysaar units and pointed to the cliff edge where the unknown person had disappeared. "Pursue and destroy!"

"For Vyath!" the riders shouted back.

They streaked off southwest toward the small campsite. The sun was drawing long shadows on the Ice Desert below as night started to come on.

If the fool Wellyn has played his part, Shilkath hoped silently, *the Shores of Thracia will surely be granted to me forever by Vyath.*

Hawgl released a sound of terrible volume that could crack the glaciers and leave giant chasms in its wake.

THIRTY-TWO

Reign

Day 27 of 1st Dimming 412 A.U.

THE EVENING HAD BEEN ONE of the first times Reign had felt a sense of family for many years. Stories filled their time, relaying tales of Aiden as a young, newly appointed master of the hold guard and his follies as he grew into the role, and of the twins' time with Jayden among her packs. The fire in the gray stone hearth furnished its light, filling the small room where the four of them laughed and reminisced. Crimson Snow took up as much room as any of them in the cottage as he lay upon the earthen floor with his three pups wrestling around and over him. They pulled at his ears and tail, attempting to drag him into the frolic, but he did not respond to their efforts. He watched Reign and the rest in their conversation with what appeared to be nostalgic eyes. The other wolves were heard carrying on in much of the same ruckus in their kennels.

"I remember," Reign chimed in, "when that merchant with his belly hanging out from his shirt caught you with your hand in his pocket. He tried to grab you but missed as you ducked and he spun himself around and nearly fell over!"

"Right," Hedron recalled. "I think you were sitting in the alley just watching, nicely tucked away and hiding. Thanks for the help."

"You were the one stealing from him!" Reign shot back playfully.

"No, I was trying to borrow his krenshell so I could buy those sweet rolls you love so much. It was all for you, dear sister."

"Let me get this straight," Aiden interrupted. "You were attempting to buy food from this merchant…with his own money?"

"Hey," Hedron said with a shrug, "At least I wouldn't have been stealing the food!"

"There is something seriously wrong with your line of thinking!" Reign laughed and threw a pillow at him.

"I kept you from starving and this is the thanks I get?"

———

Hedron's playful demeanor reminded Aiden so much of Thannuel. Jovial when there was nothing to guard against, firm when it was demanded of him and unyieldingly loyal to his sister; but he was also in a place within his mind that would not allow him to grow into who and what he was born to be. Aiden still grappled with the revelation that both his former Lord's children were alive. He'd learned much of their youth through this evening of stories.

"Now, tell me of Lord Therrium," Jayden said. "What has happened?"

Aiden related the events that had transpired, of Shane the assassin, of the surprise attack by Wellyn's men on the hold and the nearly complete extermination of all the hold guard, of General Roan's timely return, of Reign and Hedron finding him after the battle, and of his departure from Therrium's service. He made no mention, however, of the obscene stone road that he had glimpsed a view of outside the east wall.

"As we made our way here, we heard rumors of war breaking out between the West and the Realm. It seems Banner has seceded from the Realm."

Jayden just nodded as she took it in. Hedron, however, was pale as the snow falling outside the small cottage. He stared dumbfounded as if across a large expanse. Aiden stopped speaking when he noticed Hedron's demeanor. The boy was working his jaw, shaking his head slightly.

"It can't be," he said under his breath.

"What is it?" Reign asked. She sat next to him on a wooden bench they had pulled away from the table.

Hedron locked eyes with Aiden. "You said his name was Shane?"

"Aye, the assassin. He was part of the ploy with Wellyn, it seems. I can't understand how an Arlethian would betray his own people."

Reign looked quizzically at Hedron, trying to understand her brother's growing agitation.

"How long had he been with the hold guard?" Hedron asked.

"More than four years, maybe four and half, give or take a few span. Again, as I've said, I took him on to keep him close. The man had a turbulent feel about him underneath his outward appearance."

"And he came to you? Looking for work?" Hedron stood, his voice rising. "Did he say it would give him purpose again? Did he have a scar on his cheek?"

"Aye," he said. "You knew him?"

Hedron clenched his fists so tight that they turned white. His arms shook. He looked to the side and cursed.

"He's dead?" Hedron asked, not looking at anyone. "You're certain? You did it?"

Reign gasped as understanding struck her.

"Could he be the same?" she asked.

"He is dead, lad, just as I have related it. His head no longer enjoys the company of his body."

Reign reached up and took her brother's hand. It was still balled into a fist. She worked his hand gently, prying open his fingers, soothing him by her gentle touch. Hedron's breathing started to calm. Finally he raised his head and looked to Aiden. He had hot tears in his eyes.

"Thank you," he said, swallowing the lump in his throat. "Thank you. You served my family with great honor and did not know." The boy disappeared and the demeanor of a man slowly took his place. Regal and authoritative. "On behalf of my beloved mother, and jointly with my sister, the last of our house, I thank you for what you have done."

The silence that filled the air was broken by one of the wolf pups playfully growling and nipping at Crimson Snow's ears.

"What happened?" was all the former master of the hold guard for two Lords of the West could say. "I mean, what really happened? You were there, weren't you, Hedron? The Khans—they didn't come to arrest Moira, did they? Or the remaining servants?" Aiden was silent for a moment. "Was it him? Was it Shane?"

Hedron nodded. "It was. He was named hold master after father died. So many servants had left. We were nearly destitute. His arrival seemed such a blessing at the time, as if the Ancient Heavens were truly watching over us." The boy sat, the demeanor of the man that had occupied him briefly now gone. "Reign did not know him as I did. I kept her hidden as best I could."

"Hidden from what?" Aiden asked.

"From too many questions!" Jayden saved Reign and Hedron from having to reply and Aiden realized he had inadvertently entered a subject best not visited. He accepted this and left it alone...for now.

"But what happened after her death?" Aiden wanted know. "How did you come to be here with Jayden?"

Before anyone could answer, Crimson Snow stood up sharply. His cubs immediately ceased their playfulness and came to his side. He stared at the door that led to the outside for a few seconds and then looked at Jayden. After what seemed to be nothing more than a sliver of a second, he moved his gaze back to the door. The wolves outside in the kennels were suspiciously silent. The fur on the back of Crimson Snow's neck raised and pointed skyward. His cubs began to growl and snarl. A small rumble, barely audible but easily felt, reverberated through the ground. Aiden rose to his feet, his hand crossing his body to find his sword's hilt. Reign came to the large white wolf and nuzzled her head next to his.

"What is it?" she whispered. Crimson Snow continued to stare at the door, tense. She drew her short blade as the silence continued, the small rumble beneath them the only interruption.

The three wood-dwellers felt it at the exact same time. Hurried footfall, a frantic rhythm, headed in their direction.

"Just one," the twins said in unison.

"Aye," Aiden responded, still vigilant.

The moment arrived: a hurried pounding at the door followed by a young woman bounding into the small cottage.

A scream for help had started to escape her lungs but was cut short as Aiden grabbed her and forced her face down to the floor with all the efficiency of a hold guard. She let out a small whimper as Aiden raised her arm behind her back, pinning her face down. Crimson Snow brought his snout with teeth bared to her face. Dust and sediment on the cottage floor shot outward under the wolf's low rumble of a growl, dangerous as a impending avalanche.

"Please!" she finally squeaked, her terror stricken face barely visible behind disheveled snow-dusted hair. "Help me!"

Jayden pushed the wood-dwellers aside as she approached their intruder. "Up! Off!" she commanded, clapping her hands as if she were speaking to her wolves. "Is that how you treat a guest, you oaf?"

Realizing their visitor was not some monster, Aiden released her but remained wary. Crimson Snow also backed up and, seeing Jayden's acceptance of the visitor, sat down on his rear legs and licked her face. His three cubs followed suit, clamoring for attention.

"Back! Back you devils!" Jayden snapped. She grabbed the woman and helped her up. "Why dear, you're shaking like a leaf. The cold must have gotten into your bones. Come, sit at the hearth. Reign, bring some hot tea." Jayden wrapped warm furs around her and guided her to the fire.

Aiden and Hedron stood at the threshold, the decrepit door still ajar. "What is it?" Hedron asked.

"The earth. It still echoes. It pulses. Can you feel it?"

"Yes," the Kerr boy replied. "What could it be?"

"I'm uncertain but—"

"We have to get out of here! We have to warn the High Duke! Please, my name is Ehliss and I'm from the Ministry of Terran Studies. We have to leave! It's a storm of men and beasts that—"

The rest of her speech was cut off by a terrible shriek that shattered the relative silence of the night. Crimson Snow bounded out the open door and disappeared. Jayden slowly rose from cradling Ehliss, concern swimming across her face. Her eyes, though wide, did not register complete surprise.

"They're here!" Ehliss screamed.

Two dozen howls filled the night, followed by vicious growls and yelps of pain.

"It has started," Jayden said simply.

THIRTY-THREE

Reign

Day 27 of 1ˢᵗ Dimming 412 A.U.

"STAY HERE AND SHUT HER UP!" Aiden commanded, motioning to Ehliss. "And douse the fire. No light!" He disappeared through the door into the snowy night.

Ehliss sat in terror, Hedron and Reign in apprehension mixed with confusion. Jayden stood by the hearth, her face placid. After a moment, she extinguished the fire and pulled down a covering around the two small windows of the home. The three wolf cubs started for the door after their father, but Jayden spoke with a loud timbre of command.

"No! Huksinai, Alabeth, Thurik! *Inbrideo vash yaldah!*" At that, the three cubs stopped instantly and formed a defensive pattern around the small company, Thurik at the point.

"What the Blasted Heavens is going on?" Hedron swore. Another shriek thundered in the night followed by a thud hitting the roof. Ehliss started at the sound.

"I can feel the wolves and Aiden sporadically—" Hedron began.

"But no one else," Reign finished. They were listening, feeling. The earthen floor of the cottage proved to be somewhat conducive to following the vibrations. In the North, the trees did not speak, did not open themselves as catalysts as they did in the West. Still, for the wood-dwellers, almost any vibration could be discerned and interpreted. These vibrations were coming through as shockwaves all around them: wolves running, snarling and dying; Aiden in sprint and jumping from one barren tree to the next; Crimson Snow howling and barking commands to the packs. But there was no one else they could sense. No enemy. It was as if they were battling against a ghost, a specter, lethal and silent.

A wolf came through one of the windows, its lifeless body broken and bloodied. The terrifying shriek once again filled the night air, followed by another—a second demon. Thurik started to run forth, his eagerness not able to be contained.

"*Vash yaldah!*" Jayden repeated. Thurik stopped but did not immediately return to his position. "*Aramandt!*" Jayden hissed. With this last word, Thurik resumed his original stance.

A shock blasted through the ground, startling Reign.

"Something big just hit the ground, about thirty paces to our right," Hedron said.

The sounds of battle continued, the sounds of death and things being torn apart. Reign stood stiffly next to Hedron, her short blade gripped tightly. It pushed against her.

———

The chill of the wind hit Aiden as soon as he emerged from Jayden's dwelling. He looked to the left and saw Crimson Snow break open the wooden gate to the kennels. A mighty howl tore through the air as two dozen wolves answered a bone-chilling shriek that came from...above. Aiden looked up and briefly marveled how large the sky looked. In the West, the forest's canopy hid most of the sky. One would have to scale the trees and ascend above the canopy line to take in the starry expanse unobstructed. Here, however, in the Gonfrey Forest, the trees carried little to no foliage this far into the Dimming Season and the forest was not half so dense. Aiden heard a large gust of wind high above followed by the sound of what he identified as wings—large wings. The wolves started to snarl as they gathered around Aiden, Crimson Snow at his right hand. The quarter-lit first moon provided all the illumination necessary for the look that Aiden and the white wolf shared, a brief communication that said they would stand and fight together, whatever had come against them this night. Aiden focused and took in his surroundings. He drew the sword he had been gifted by Moira after Thannuel's fall, the pewter colored blade of Jarwyn steel reflecting the moon's rays. *Think of nothing but this moment.* As he silently recited the old adage Lord Kerr had taught him, his mind shut out all possible distractions and allowed only those environmental elements that could assist him to remain present upon his consciousness. He felt things more deeply, almost as if he were connected to the Arlethian forest. Anticipation of events a miniscule second before they happened was a side effect of quieting his mind; either that or his reflexes were quickened – he was not sure which.

The sound of air being violently displaced was followed by a yelp of pain. A winged beast larger than three horses came down from above like a demon from the sky and snatched a wolf up with its talons, piercing flesh and crushing bones before tossing the carcass effortlessly aside through the air. The dead wolf thudded down on the roof of the cottage. Crimson Snow barked at the packs and they dispersed through the forest, bolting across the snow.

Aiden's concentration was broken. He had just beheld a dragon of sorts, as in the mythical scrolls of the Changrual. He spied a second creature streak through the sky and eclipse the moon for an instant. He tried to understand and qualify the situation, making it fit into something he could mentally process. Another cry from a wolf broke Aiden's stupor. Chiding himself for being distracted no matter the cause, he refocused and sprang into action.

He bounded forward, soaring a short distance through the air before pouncing upon a tree and instantly kicking off of it, propelling himself higher toward another tree. He felt the air change around him and twisted his body a moment before foot-long talons found him. An arrow chased him but he easily dodged it with a reflex faster than the arrow's flight. Landing on the third tree in his ascent, he was high enough to look down upon the scene. A dragon beast was swooping down near the cottage, but every time it closed the distance, half a dozen wolves leaped up in defense, reaching for any part into which they could sink their fangs. The winged creature of myth whipped its head with such speed that it appeared only as a blur. It connected with a wolf, sending it flying through a window of the cottage. Aiden heard a scream. *Where is the other—*

The screech that came from behind him was ear shattering. He turned in time to see the attack come but knew he could not defend against it. He let himself fall from the tree through the air some sixty feet and deftly landed in the snow below. Without hesitation, he sheathed his sword and bounded back up the tree to regain his vantage point. Aiden saw the creature that barely missed him, twice now, turn sharply and swoop down toward the cottage. *Two riders upon the demon's back* he noted and simultaneously jumped to another tree, using it as a ricochet point. Once he was in range, he coiled his legs and pushed off hard without ever truly landing, launching himself downward. He collided with the winged beast, but its thick scales were hard and smooth. He would have bounced off as quickly as he hit had his belt and scabbard not caught on some boney protrusion from its wing. The force of his aerial assault deflected the trajectory of the creature enough to cause it to abandon its target. Aiden desperately reached up for anything with which to grab and haul himself upright. He found nothing. The creature was flying low to the ground, attempting to dislodge the parasite that had grappled on to it. But Aiden, though he had never fought a flying opponent, was in his element. Focused. Lethal.

One of the riders came out of the harness and stood over Aiden as they soared jaggedly through the air just above the ground. A heavy voice yelled out something that could only be a curse and raised a blade above his head. The glimpse that Aiden caught from the corner of his eye made him half smile. It looked like a violent blizzard rushing from the other side of the flying creature and sounded like death. Crimson Snow vaulted from the earth and took flight. He caught the warrior in the throat as he turned to investigate the ominous sound approaching, the wolf's fangs cutting through his thick beard and finding purchase. No cry escaped his crushed throat, only the taint of red blood, allowing the wolf to once again live up to his name. The rider departed his station, lifeless. Aiden reached a hand up and grabbed hold of Crimson Snow's thick coat and righted himself upon the back of the winged beast with a mighty effort. The remaining rider sat in a saddle of some create, holding the reins that controlled their flight. His long beard, frosted by ice and snow, flung in the wind.

The rider glanced backward, finding a dark-haired man with no beard drawing steel from his sheath and a wolf resembling a small bear snarling. He instantly pulled back on the steel-chained reins, forcing the mount upward. Crimson Snow dove off into a small snow bank and sprinted back toward the cottage, toward the sound of screams. Aiden fell forward and clutched the saddle in front of him but lost the grip on his sword. Higher and higher they climbed. Aiden feared they might strike the moon before long, but the creature turned downward and spun at dizzying speed like a cyclone of terror. Aiden's body flung out horizontally as the beast dove vertically, his grip upon the saddle loosening.

———

Reign did not know how to feel in this moment. The presence that pushed upon her came more forcefully in moments when she needed her mind the most. It plagued her more strongly when the circumstances seemed more desperate. The first time she had felt it was those many years ago not far from where she now stood, when she and Hedron hung onto life through starvation and exposure by the thinnest of threads. *Why now!* she demanded. *Leave me!* But it did not leave her.

It was terrifying, being inside a dark and cold edifice with the sounds of pain and death swirling around them everywhere. Hedron and Reign could not feel their attackers. This added to the fear coursing through them immensely. To be attacked was a frightening experience in itself, one with which the Kerr children were most acquainted. But to have no idea what stood against you would cause the bravest of souls to shudder with unbridled fear.

"It has to be demons of some create," Hedron said with a tightly clenched jaw. "Why else would we not sense them?"

"No, son, not demons," came a knowing voice. Jayden left her position next to Ehliss and knelt before Reign.

"You feel it, don't you?" she asked.

Reign looked down at her eyes, not moving her head. The three cubs snarled low warnings. "Feel what?" Reign answered tensely. Jayden reached up and took Reign's hand in hers.

"Child, I know. You know that I know. It is not to be feared." Reign flinched at a pitiful cry echoing through the woods. Jayden reached up and took her other hand, pulling Reign's attention back to her.

"How are you so calm?" Reign hissed. Large wings cut through air and a horrifying scratching noise sounded on the roof, followed by scrabbling claws and barking, howling, flesh tearing.

"When your father died, Reign, you were there. You saw it. Tell me."

Hedron glared at the old woman, incredulous. "You want to ask her about this *now*?"

Jayden ignored him. "Child, how did he fall? What was it? Tell me."

It encircled Reign and felt as a warm embrace, like the Rising Season coming upon the frozen land after a long, dark Low Season. Her lower lip quivered and her eyes welled with tears.

"It is not to be feared," Jayden coaxed once more in a whisper.

"How do you know what it is?" Reign snapped as tears spilled. "I've never spoken of it, never made mention of it. How do you know?"

"It's getting closer," Hedron warned. "We might be able to out-run them." Ehliss cried out with every bang and shriek.

"Tell me…"

"Aiden!" Hedron cried. Before anyone could stop him, he dashed through the open door.

———————

He was in free-fall, the inertial force too great for him to resist. As soon as Aiden had been flung free, the nightmare of a bird stopped its downward spiral. As it spread its wings to recapture the air, Aiden saw it glide away. He, however, continued to fall. From such a height and with no thick-leaved canopy to help break his fall, Aiden prepared himself as best he could.

A yell interrupted his peaceful yet terrifying fall just before being struck and hurled horizontally into a tree about thirty feet from the ground. He reached out and fumbled for a hold against the bark, digging his fingers to find purchase. The pain of the effort seared his hands, but he recycled the pain into strength, feeding on the friction.

He hit the ground hard after slowing the fall enough to be survivable. Turning about, he found his unlikely rescuer. Hedron lay on the ground ten paces from him. The boy rolled over onto his hands and knees, slowly bringing himself back to his feet.

"What the Blasted Heavens were you doing, boy?" Aiden roared. "I told you to stay in the cottage!"

"You know, Aiden," Hedron answered, breathing heavily from the effort exerted, "we're going to have to work on your gratitude."

———————

"Tell me," Jayden gently entreated.

Reign trembled under Jayden's calm hands. She didn't want to do this. Not here, not anywhere, not ever. Hedron was not here to save her from this moment.

"No! No, not until you tell me how you know what you know. What was that language you spoke to the wolves? How do you know what this is that's against me? Why do you live here in this wasteland alone? Where are you from? Where are your kin? Your children?"

"My child, I know a great many things. And I promise, when this is over, we'll have some tea and a long talk. But now, right now, you need to tell me of that night. You must go back to that place that you have hidden from."

Reign's vision blurred as the tears came down, leaving light salty streaks upon her cheeks. "I didn't mean to kill him." At that, Reign Kerr collapsed into a trembling ball of grief and tears. She shook uncontrollably and buried her face into Jayden. Deep sobs escaped her, the pent up sorrow, guilt, pain, and anguish of years began to flow. All around them this night a battle raged on the out-side and throughout the forest; inside Reign Kerr raged a struggle of greater desperation.

Jayden said nothing but held Reign as she heaved on the ground with her head in her lap. When she seemed to grasp a modicum of control, Jayden gently encouraged her.

"Go on, love."

"The forest—I was lost but not afraid." She trembled now as she recounted it. "There were men in the forest, strange men. I wanted to see what they were doing, I was just a child. Curious. I was in my forest where…where my…where my father ruled. It was his, so I wasn't afraid. Not at first I wasn't.

"Duke Wellyn was there." She paused. "A strange man, tall with a long beard also. Others as well."

"Yes," Jayden said, patting her back. "Let go of it."

"I'm so scared," Reign admitted. She was now numb to the frightful sounds outside the walls, replaced by the petrifying mem-ories she brought forth. She trembled. "I can't! I can't speak these words!"

Jayden could see how the fear gripped the girl's mind. She was starting to shut down again and force the memories back into their mental prison. "Do you know what the Gyldenal are, Reign?"

She bit her finger as she did when she felt uncertain. "No."

"The Gyldenal are an order that date back long before the Realm, before the Senthary. They are keepers of knowledge and wisdom," Jayden explained.

"Archivers?"

"Not exactly. An Archiver is a keeper of facts, of history. The Gyldenal pass down knowledge that enables, that empowers." She considered for a moment. "It's more akin to abilities that are learned because of knowledge, through it. Do you understand?"

"I think so. Maybe. No," she finally settled upon. Another blood-curdling shriek sounded from above, answered by deep growls and howls.

"One thing that is taught," Jayden continued, "is how to channel emotions into energy or strength. I cannot explain this much to you now, but you must trust me. The fear you feel can turn to power, fortitude, strength, whatever you wish. You must allow it to fill you, to engulf you but not to overtake you. It is energy that can be harnessed and redirected. Recycled. The stronger the emotion felt, the more difficult it can be to control, but also the more potential is carries.

"Embrace the fear you feel, child. Welcome it in. Do not fight against it. Let it flow through you, and then command it. Divert its energy as a river is channeled. You command the currents. You are the current."

Reign did not understand and continued to tremble, the fear of that night long ago pulsing through her being. Something heavy banged against the back wall of the feeble home and caused Ehliss to yelp once again.

"Feed on it, child." The old woman coaxed.

"There was a light," Reign finally went on. "Blue, like nothing I have seen before or since. One of them touched a tree and—" She broke off, hoping somehow the words would speak themselves. "—and I saw it turn to stone!" she cried out. "I *saw* it. The tree became gray and withered in front of me. The leaves fell from it and the trunk and branches turned from brown to a dark gray, cold and lifeless. The forest screamed with silent fear, I could feel it all around me. That's when..." New tears came to her eyes but she didn't stop. "That's when *he* saw me." Now Reign did stop as new fear gripped her. She inhaled a fast breath and her lower lip quivered violently. Her whole body shook as if caught in a great torrent.

———

Hedron directed Aiden to his fallen sword, having marked its location mentally when it landed and sent out vibrations like a small beacon through the forest. They both erupted into furious speed back to the cottage. They were probably a mile away, maybe more. The shrieks and howls could be heard for several miles all around them.

"You must stay out of reach, Hedron."

"Not likely, not after just saving you. I'm in this now." Hedron said defiantly.

"I will leave you unconscious on the ground if I must, boy!" Aiden promised. "This isn't a time for boyhood dreams of danger and heroics being acted out. You are my Lord's son. I will not fail him twice by putting you in harm's way."

"If you haven't noticed, harm's way found us! If you feel some loyalty to me because of my father, then do not restrain me. Consider it an order."

"Sorry, no. It does not work like that. It times of danger, a lord obeys his master of the hold guard."

"Well, Master Aiden, I'm not a lord!" Hedron retorted. They were sprinting through the night, a powdery dust of white in their wake.

"In that, lad, we are agreed." Aiden grabbed Hedron by his collar and yanked him backward. Simultaneously, he swept his leg forward and under the Kerr boy, bringing him down hard on the frozen ground. He cuffed him just hard enough to break his consciousness but leave no permanent damage. Hedron's eyes rolled in to the back of his head and his body went limp. Aiden laid the boy gently between two trees and then continued on toward Jayden's cottage.

———

"I don't know how he saw me. How could he have seen me?" Reign said between shudders. "I didn't make a sound! I didn't even move!"

"But you felt fear," Jayden said.

"Yes, of course. The tree one of them had touched changed in front on me. It died, and several others as well. The tall man with the beard seemed excited by this. But then the other man—" She squeezed her eyes tight as if to hide from her own memories. "The man who saw me, he chased me. He was so fast! His footfall was deafening. He was catching up, but then father came."

"Yes, and he fought the Helsyan to save you," Jayden filled in.

"What?" Reign asked. "What's a Helsyan?"

"Not a man, not in the way you think of one. Just as Arlethians, or wood-dwellers as you are more commonly known, are not normal men. Helsyans are of ancient descent, long before the Realm and even the Hardacheon Age. Monsters of the Ancient Dark's create. He did not see you, Reign. He smelled you, smelled your fear. He tracked you through your emotions. This is how they hunt, but they must first be released, given a Charge. It is called a Dahlrak in the ancient tongue. Someone Charged the Helsyan with you, child."

"How do you know this?" Reign exclaimed. "What ancient language? I don't understand."

Jayden shook her head. "Not yet. And so, Thannuel gave his life to save his child from the monster, yes?"

"He told me to run home and wake Aiden," Reign continued almost as if in a trance. "But I didn't. I wanted to see. I wanted to watch. Everyone spoke of him as a great warrior." Her serene expression crumbled. "I killed him! I should have listened. He would still be alive! I should have gone to the hold as he said. Aiden would have come. He would have come and he could have helped! But I didn't! He didn't have to die!"

"No, child, that would only have brought death upon Aiden as well."

"But he should have killed him!" Reign growled. "He should have beaten him! He was Lord of the West, a wood-dweller! No one had ever overcome him in steel combat. He failed me! He left me! He promised I would always be safe! He left mother and Hedron, too! Mother died because of him! He killed her. *I hate him!*"

"Where did you go?" Jayden asked.

"I hid in a Triarch tree."

"No, I mean where did you go *inside?*"

The sounds of the fray outside intensified. The three wolf cubs remained alert and reacted to every new sound. Thurik was spinning around at his post, salivating heavily. A terrible high-pitched roar of pain shook the walls of the house.

"I couldn't feel anything. I saw him fall, saw him die, but the fear left me. I felt cold, like I died, like the trees that turned to stone. He called my name, but I didn't come to him."

At this, Jayden's look became penetrating. "Was it his last breath?"

"What? What do you mean?" Reign looked at the old woman with some confusion.

"Think, young one, was it his last breath? Did he have a Triarch leafling in his hand? Think!"

"I don't know, I can't—"

"You must remember! Think! See the place he died. See his hands. See his chest rise and fall. See his mouth form your name upon its lips."

Reign felt as if she were floating as she closed her eyes and roamed the dark halls of her memory. She was filled with foreboding, but the force that pushed against her all those years now aided her, not pushing her but strengthening her, augmenting her mind. She seized upon the vision in her mind and held it.

"Reign," Thannuel whispered in her remembrance, the girl mouthing the word as she recalled the scene from her childhood. Thannuel's chest did not rise again.

"Yes, his last breath," she mumbled.

"And his hands, what was there?"

"His sword."

"Look closer."

As she peered into her mind's eye through the caverns of memory, Reign caught the sight of a small three-pronged leaf that extended above her father's hand where he loosely gripped the hilt of his sword. He let go of his sword as he died and it fell away from his grasp. There, in the palm of his hand, was a Triarch leafling.

———

Aiden did not hesitate when the scene came into sight a few moments later. The second large beast with its two riders hovered barely above the cottage. The wolves were desperately clamoring to find a way on to the roof. Deadly and tenacious though they were, being earthbound was a distinct disadvantage to the wolves against an enemy that struggled with no such hindrance. The creature screamed its shrill cry and whipped its tail down hard upon the roof. Aiden did not know how much longer the structure could take such punishment before cracking open and revealing those within.

Aiden drew his sword and again quieted his mind. And then, he watched with some amazement as he witnessed the wolves adapt and overcome their deficiency. A short but thick and husky gray wolf brought itself within a nose of the east wall of the cottage. It seemed to brace itself. Next, a medium-sized breed climbed onto its back and stood on its hind legs, placing its front paws up against the wall, then likewise braced itself. A stream of three wolves ran toward the lupine ladder and sprang upon it, ascending the backs of their siblings and on to the roof. They scampered across the top of the cottage toward the flying demon and sprang with single-minded intent at the long-bearded men upon the winged devil's back. Two of the wolves made the leap, but the third found itself impaled by a dozen boney spikes around the beast's maw. A small whimper escaped the dying wolf before it was cast down to the earth, its blood seeping out through a myriad of punctures and mixing with the snow and mud of the earth. The other two landed deftly upon the backside of the beast but then struggled for purchase against the hard smooth scales. Clawing desperately, one of the wolves scraped a paw toward the creature's head, against the grain of the scales, and finally breached the armored surface. It dug in the wound, enlarging it, clawing free the dark gray flesh and making a foothold in the welling pool of blood. The other wolf soon followed suit and the shriek that emanated this time from the huge creature was one of pain rather than terror. It jerked its head up to the sky and stretched its wings outward, preparing to escape upward. It would never be granted the chance.

Aiden appeared to be in flight, his body arched as it sailed through the night with his dark-bladed sword held above his head, his muscles coiled tightly in preparation to strike. He soared directly toward the shrieking head of the creature with its hideous maw agape. A savage yell exploded from Aiden that startled the beast and he swung his steel downward as swift as lightning. The molecules of the air burst into small blue flames around the blade from the incredible friction created as he forced Thannuel's sword through the atmosphere with impossible momentum. The sword was driven down through the crown and continued cutting through the neck until it met the top of the demon's torso where it lodged, smoking. Aiden let go of the hilt and fell a dozen feet to the cottage roof.

With its head and neck now cloven in two, the beast's wings fluttered in nervous reaction as it fell to the ground. The forward rider who held the reins was pinned to the earth under the girth of the demon. He feverishly tried to free himself but the wolves were on him instantly and excused him from the realm of the living. The second rider leaped from the saddle before hitting the ground and grabbed up a short blade from his belt in his left hand and wielded a flail in his right. Several wolves attacked but were driven back as he swung the spiked ball and chain in a circle, forcing distance between himself and his assailants.

So focused were the wolves with their downed quarry that they did not hear the approach of the other wretched fiend until two of their number were scooped up, one in each claw. The abductees continued to snap and snarl at their captor even as the talons dug in and strong-muscled claws crushed the life from them. Their bodies fell to the earth.

Aiden recovered his sword and blitzed toward the man swinging his flail. He held his weapon low behind his body as he closed the distance and swung upward at the bearded man, ignoring the danger of the spiked ball approaching his head. The man amazingly deflected the strike with his short blade but the effort stole his balance and he teetered backward. Aiden moved closer in, a breath from the man making the flail largely ineffective. The man was taller than him and Aiden found himself at eye level with his beard, adorned with trinkets of strange create. *It looks like skin and bones,* Aiden shuddered in realization. The large man brought his head down on Aiden's brow. The force of the blow dazed the wood-dweller and now he stumbled back, providing the distance the man needed to whip back his flail and swing it down. Aiden flung himself free from reach of the swing and steadied himself. The man swore. The shriek of the remaining demon was heard not far off, as it no doubt was preparing for a return attack. He needed to end this. Now.

The man resumed his whirling of the flail, creating a lethal circle of protection around him. Jayden's packs were tightening their circle and Aiden felt a soft tremor that he focused on, ignoring the other sounds he felt in the forest. It was a slow sound, coming from behind the man. Aiden caught hold of it long enough to identify the vibrational signature.

He feinted forward, forcing the man to turn in his direction. As the flail-bearing man took a step forward in response, Aiden yelled, "Elohk!"

The large white wolf emerged from the snow at the man's feet, growling and howling as a ghost from the frozen abyss. The great and terrible eruption from beneath the foreign warrior caused him to jump in surprise, his face turning paler than a decaying corpse. Crimson Snow clawed his way up the man's back, digging into hot flesh until he was atop the man's shoulders and vying for his throat. He cried out with pain as he swung his flail wildly over his shoulder. One blow connected on the wolf's back but Crimson Snow, unfazed, continued to attack. Elohk's weight caused the man to stumble and falter. The opening caused by the wolf's distraction was enough. Aiden shot forward with his sword extended and sheathed it in the man's heart. His death was ironically quiet.

The remaining winged creature screeched from above but the sound was far in the distance and fading. It had fled.

———

"And you were in a Triarch tree yourself, yes?" Jayden asked firmly.

"Yes," Reign answered, coming out of her dream-like state.

Jayden brought her hands together in front of her mouth. She was considering something heavily by the look that played across her face.

"Reign, listen to me." She again took her hands. "Why do you hurt so much inside?"

"Because I killed him," she muttered.

"Hardly, dear. Truth, Reign. Why are you searing with pain inside?"

"He left me! He promised he never would! He abandoned me!"

"We both know that's not true, child. Why did he fight so fiercely? It wasn't for his own life. Why did he die for you?"

"Because…" Reign began but hesitated.

"Say it, child."

Reign bit her lower lip. "He loved me," she said simply.

"And?"

For Reign Kerr, all the past years of her life flashed before her in an instant. All the fear and hardship after Thannuel died, the sorrow and regret, the guilt and anguish, the endless longing; all the joys of her early childhood, the times she giggled as her father held her, the safety she felt in his arms, the times she ran to him for reassurance after a nightmare, and learning to speak with trees for the first time. She faced the memories as they rushed forth, the dam she built so long ago bursting in her mind, the rubble of fear being washed away until she caught the vision of her father's face in her mind's eye. She did not thrust it aside as she might have before, but held it before her. His auburn brown hair, gentle eyes and firmly set jaw faced her. She remembered how he always smiled with the left side of his face first before breaking out with a laugh, the way he kindly smiled upon her now. "Reign," the image whispered.

"I loved him," Reign said, choking back a sob. "I still love him." That love surfaced within her, cresting and breaking through her hardened emotional barrier.

"Love will let him finally find a place in you after all these years."

The force that had seemed a plague to Reign for so many years presented itself yet again. It was not aggressive, but gentle, as if seeking permission. Reign pursed her lips, trying not to let them quiver, and closed her eyes tightly to hold back the tears. She finally understood.

"Will you let him in, child?" Jayden asked softly. "Let him stand free from the shadows of your heart."

All Reign could do was nod.

A howling warm wind came up from within the cottage and swirled around Reign. She was lifted into the air gently and felt the pressure push against her. This time, she did not fight. A light enveloped her until Reign herself became luminescent. She opened herself completely to the impetus and into her mind cascaded all her father's last breath. All his memories, all his fears, all his joys, all his skills and strength, all his knowledge and wisdom, all his abilities, the flood of power all consuming. Her mind threatened to fracture under the stress, but it held. Thannuel's last breath lodged itself in a cavern within Reign's mind, not overtaking or controlling it, but rather becoming a well, a reservoir of power and wisdom and strength to be drawn upon.

When it was over, Reign's feet again touched the ground but it felt almost foreign to her, like it was her first time standing on her own. As she opened her eyes, she saw the world anew.

The soft, kind voice of Jayden sounded in the now quiet night. "Welcome back, Thannuel."

THIRTY-FOUR

Ryall

Day 28 of 1st Dimming 412 A.U.

RYALL JUMPED AT THE TOUCH on his left shoulder and knocked into the obsidian tablet in front of which he crouched. The echo of a scream was heard reverberating through the vast cavernous library. Its decrescendo seemed to languish on with unnatural length, as if the echo was determined to make its brief life last as long as possible before fading below decibels of an audible threshold. Ryall realized that he had been the screamer. Breathing fast and shallow, he whirled around to see the silent terror that would no doubt now use some forbidden Influence to make him disappear to a realm of interminable pain or perhaps turn his body inside out before devouring him whole. Neither happened.

Holden stood before him, wearing a smug expression on his face.

"Did you actually think I was sleeping, genius?" the stockier boy asked. "I swear you're so predictable."

"What are you doing here?" Ryall demanded. "You scared the Fallen Heavens out of me!"

"Watch your tongue. You are an adherent, after all. And, I'm not so sure you have any right to be asking me what *I'm* doing here."

The fright on Ryall's face was slowly replaced by a smile. "Wait, you came because you can't ignore it either. You're as tempted by this place as I am."

"Hardly," Holden countered. "I came to make you see reason. And if that won't work, I'm prepared to knock some sense into you."

Ryall rolled his eyes. The two had been at odds with how to handle their discovery.

"Listen to me, Ryall. You don't know what this place is. It's amazing, I'll give you that, but can't you see it's been sealed off? And no doubt for a good reason."

Ryall had heard this before and knew what his friend would say next, so he mouthed the words as Holden spoke them. "If we're caught here, they're not going to make us mop the monastery as punishment. This is more serious than our little pranks."

"Yes, Mother, thank you, Mother, I'll do better, Mother."

Holden punched him in the arm, hard. "I am not kidding about this. I followed you here because I'm your friend, jackass, not your mother."

To this, Ryall started braying louder and louder, mocking his friend.

"Dimming Light, you are an idiot! And what's worse, I think you know it!" Holden's frustration soared.

"Now who needs to watch his mouth?" Ryall jeered.

Their voices carried, meshing and creating dissonant echoes as their verbal volleys increased, overlapping each other.

"Do you even know what's down here? Aren't you even curious? Who cares if it's been walled up and sealed off! That's the reason I'm here! Why was it hidden? That's the question!" Ryall yelled at a volume loud enough to overcome Holden's incessant scolding. He realized his voice was reaching dangerous levels and their arguing could be their undoing. Holden looked away, abashed, as if realizing the same thing.

"We're both idiots," Holden confessed, still looking away. He exhaled a long breath that seemed to be apologetic. "I'm sorry, alright? I'm just worried."

"And scared," Ryall added.

"And scared."

"I am too, actually. But I just can't let this go. Not yet." His tone had lost its sarcastic edge. "But it's not because of some immature curiosity, contrary to what you might believe, Holden. Not any-more. Let me show you what I found."

Holden raised his head and then closed his eyes. "When they burn us at the stake for this, I'll curse your name. Then, when we awaken in the Ancient Darkness after we're dead, I'm going to stone your head in. I swear."

Ryall smiled, knowing this was his friend's way of consenting to his request.

"Deal! Now look." Ryall moved his torch to illuminate the rows of large obsidian tablets. Holden's eyes grew larger as he took in the sight.

"What are they?" Holden asked in wonder.

"Archiver tablets."

Holden looked skeptical. "Then, why aren't they in the Jarwyn Mountains?"

Ryall shrugged. "No idea, but check this out." Ryall showed him how the glyphs at the top of the first tablet of each row matched to a glyph of an inlet, and how the number of tablets in a given row matched the number of scrolls in an inlet with a corresponding glyph. Holden's interest rose.

"I've been down here almost all night, reading as many tab-lets as I can. Most of it's so boring, but when's the last time someone actually saw this stuff? Kind of neat to think we might be the first people in decades, maybe centuries!" Ryall nearly shouted.

"Shh! Second moon will set soon and the sun will rise not long after. We'll come back tonight."

"No, wait. Just a little more time," Ryall said.

"You've got my attention, all right? We'll come back, tonight. Let's not be stupid about this and get caught now. Well, let's not be more stupid than we're already being."

Just after the final bell of the evening sounded, signaling the beginning of night and end of all activity in the monastery, Holden and Ryall found themselves back in the cavern. They each lit a torch and carried one more in reserve. Ryall tried to hold back a laugh.

"What?" Holden asked behind a long yawn.

"A hand or fellow, born sick and yellow?" Ryall heckled his friend.

"Shut up," Holden snapped. "I didn't get a lot of sleep last night, remember?"

"You're likely to get even less tonight, I'd guess. But still, you should have seen the look on your face! It wasn't half as bad as the look on Vicar Johann's face though. I thought he was going to chew you up and spit you out."

"The words were blurring together, okay?" the redheaded boy answered. "It was sort of embarrassing."

"That's the best part!" his friend jabbed. "When have you ever misread a section of prose in literature forum?"

"Never," was all Holden could get out. During their last class of the day, literature forum, students would study and recite passages from different texts. The delivery was as important as the words themselves. This half-span had been the Scrolls of Rebirth, ancient scriptures that predated the invasion of the Senthary and told of the Ancient Heavens' cycling of the lands. During Holden's assigned passage, one line read, "...a land more fallow, torn sick and sallow..." but Holden, in his wearied state, read aloud, "...a hand or fellow, born sick and yellow..." He had said it with such vigor and conviction, trying to mask his fading energy and still impress the Vicar.

"You should have seen yourself thundering the last words as if speaking to a crowd of thousands! Bravo!"

Holden just grimaced.

"At least you can redeem yourself now," Ryall promised. "One of the things I can't figure out is why there are scrolls in Hardacheon that match the Archiver tablets. Who wrote the scrolls? They obviously contain our history and there are Archiver records in Sentharian, so why would someone take the trouble to translate them into Hardacheon?"

"Who says the Archiver tablets came first?" Holden asked. Ryall looked up at his friend. "Maybe they are translations of the scrolls."

"Okay, good point I guess, but how could Hardacheons be recording our history after they were all destroyed? Even if a few still lived, why would they care to record the history of their conquerors?"

"Are you sure all the scrolls here line up with these tablets? I mean, look around. This place has thousands more scrolls than tablets. There's what, seven or eight rows of tablets? There are hundreds if not thousands of these cubby things, each with at least one scroll from what we have seen."

Ryall again was nonplussed. "Well, let's at least figure out which scrolls line up with which rows of tablets. Then we'll have a starting place, I suppose."

"A starting place for what?" Holden asked. He knew he wasn't going to like the answer.

"For translating the scrolls, what else? We've got several dozen tablets that line up with as many scrolls. We can read the tablets and probably decipher the other scrolls not related to them if we use them as a key of sorts," Ryall said. "What else are we going to do for the next four-and-a-half years?"

An adherent was pronounced a Vicar of the Ancient Heavens at age twenty after completing six years at the Changrual Monastery and passing proficiency examinations in an expansive breadth of subject matter.

"How about get through our studies with drawing as little attention as possible? I'm certain we'll have a harder time already due to our reputation," Holden said. "So, you've read some of these Archiver tablets?"

"Nearly the first two rows. Did you know that the land our people came from was called Feylan? And that Brant Kearon and Oliver Wellyn were actually cousins?"

"They were related?" The revelation shocked Holden.

"First row, third tablet in. The first three tablets there talk about life in Feylan before the land cycled. It sounds very different than life here in Senthara. In fact, Oliver Wellyn wasn't the ruler in Feylan, nor here when they first arrived for the invasion."

"Who was the High Duke then? And does it say where Feylan is?" Holden asked.

"There was no High Duke then. Just someone who they called the Luminary of House Kearon."

"Luminary?" Holden raised an eyebrow. "Kearon?"

Ryall shrugged. "It's what it says. His words were very influential apparently. Some said he was the Living Light. Oh, he was bastard born, too."

"You're starting to bray again, jackass," Holden said, obviously not believing his friend.

"Read for yourself," Ryall said, unconcerned.

"Okay, so why, if we're the Senthary people – and this land is named after us—why wouldn't we have named this Feylan place Senthara as well? Why not call the land after us then like we do now?" Holden challenged.

"Because our ancestors weren't called Sentharians before they came here."

"Oh, Burning Heavens, are you serious?" Holden whispered. His brow was furrowed tightly.

"We really have to work on your swearing," Ryall said. "And of course I'm serious. I think you should stop asking questions and start reading. You have some catching up to do."

"What happened to this 'Luminary' of yours?"

"Wouldn't you rather just read for yourself?"

"I'd rather be in bed, safely asleep, and not lurking through dark, forgotten underground little evil libraries!"

"This is little?"

"I'm going to stone your head in," Holden threatened.

"All right, all right! Sensitive, huh?"

"Sleep deprived."

"Fine, here's your last freebee. It's true that Brant Kearon lead House Kearon and her allies against House Wellyn, like we've always been told. But knowing that Oliver Wellyn wasn't actually the leader of the Senthary at the time, or, that is, of the Faylen people, makes you wonder a little, right?"

"No, not really."

Ryall looked at his friend, surprised. "Holden, you crow turd, we're taught that Oliver Wellyn was the High Duke and Brant Kearon made a play for rule. These Archiver tablets," he continued, emphasizing "Archiver", "say that the Luminary, the Bastard of Kearon, led the people and that House Wellyn convinced others to rebel against him. Archivers only record what they see without bias."

"Bastard of Kearon? You come up with that yourself, did you?"

"Yup, took me all night," Ryall announced with mock pride.

"I thought so. Impressive."

"Obviously House Wellyn won, otherwise we would not be here now."

"Very astute of you. Why the rebellion against your Bastard of Kearon?"

"He had a book of some kind with powerful words. The description is more akin to a bunch of parchment strung together but the tablets say he was never seen without it. They say when he spoke the words people were empowered and could achieve great things beyond their normal strength or intelligence."

Holden closed his eyes and sighed. "And Oliver wanted the book that contained magic for himself so he tried to take it by force, right?"

"How did you know?"

"It's so predictable, Ryall. It's the same story over and over. Someone has power, someone else covets it."

"There's probably a reason it's a common theme, genius. It's our nature as people."

"Maybe yours, I just want to go about my learning and keep my head down."

Ryall continued, undeterred: "After the Kearon were defeated they were stripped of power and all citizenship, like we've always been taught, and the Kearon mostly emigrated south to the desert."

"You've used two four-syllable words in the last sentence. Very well done. Was the Luminary killed?"

"It doesn't say."

"If the book was so powerful, or its words, how were the Kearon defeated?" Holden asked.

"For the first year or so, House Kearon and her allies seemed impenetrable. They actually never did any offensive campaigns. Just defended where attacked and won every battle. But after that year, something happened in the war that turned the tide."

"Yes?"

"Oh a little more interested now, I see. Well, it doesn't actually say that either. There were rumors of many assassinations, though, that plagued the Kearon people and her allies. Almost every lord who sided with the Luminary and Brant Kearon was found dead. Soon after, the alliance of houses in support of House Kearon fractured and fell apart. They were forced to sue for peace."

"And the Luminary's book? Did Oliver get it?"

"Apparently not, but it says he went mad near the end of his reign searching for it, seeing ghosts and things not there. Or something like that."

Holden shrugged. "Wonderful. That seems to somehow have been omitted from our history scrolls. No wonder these tablets are hidden deep away from the light of day."

"Which is also why we must see what all these other scrolls say."

"I was right. We *are* going to be burned at the stake."

The excitement came after a couple hours of cataloguing and matching scrolls with individual Archiver tablets. While Holden had been doing most of that work, Ryall had sat patiently working through the first scroll that matched the first tablet, the story of the Luminary and Oliver Wellyn, painstakingly going back and forth in the torchlight and trying to make a connection between the Hardacheon symbols on the scroll and the Sentharian words on the Archiver tablets. He was convinced the tablets were actually translations of the scrolls now, the opposite of what he had first supposed. But, taking a language that appeared to be based on symbols with meanings and comparing it to a language that used letters to represent sounds was proving a bit much for the fifteen-year-old adherent. Introduction to Linguistics was not even a class until third year, and Ryall doubted they were going to be studying the Hardacheon language anyway.

"Ancients Come, I'm never going to get this."

"Why not?" Holden asked as he continued his own efforts.

"It's not a related language. It's just too far apart. We use letters and sounds, they used symbols to describe things. Stuff. Whatever. Who knows how many words each symbol might stand for? I can't even establish a baseline to start from."

"Okay, look," Holden said as he squatted down next to Ryall. "How many words are there on the tablet?"

"What? I don't know—"

"Count," Holden said. Ryall shrugged and complied.

"Three hundred and eighty-one," he reported.

"Okay now, how many symbols are there on the scroll?"

Ryall had caught on and was already counting. "One hundred and twenty-one."

"All right. This isn't perfect, but basically there are three Sentharian words for every one Hardacheon symbol. Start trying to group the words with the symbols and you might start to notice the same symbols showing up for similar words. Or even similar descriptions on the tablets characterized by the same Hardacheon symbol on the scroll."

"Ya know, for an idiot, you're not that dumb," Ryall said.

"And for a jackass, you don't smell all that terrible," Holden countered.

Ryall didn't answer but took to his task. He started by identifying repeating symbols, of which there were several. But somehow, they didn't line up at all with where he thought they should according to the words on the tablet. Frustration was about to force him to give up when he saw it.

"Fallen Ancients!" Ryall exclaimed. The echo of his curse reverberated through the cavern. Ryall brought his hand over his mouth with wide eyes after he realized how loud he had yelled.

"I hate you," Holden said.

"I found it! I mean, I got it! Holden, I got it!"

"Right, and now we're both dead. The whole monastery heard you. Really great work."

"Whatever, we put the stones back in place. But look! I was assuming the symbols go from left to right, like how we read our language. But they don't. They descend, top to bottom, starting on the right. It has to be. I see symbols from the scrolls lining up with repeated words and ideas from the tablets if I read it that way. See?"

Holden gave a weak grunt in acknowledgement.

"That's it?" Ryall asked.

"I knew you'd figure it out. I'm about done lining up scrolls and tablets. But still, Ryall, realize there are hundreds more of these little alcoves with thousands more scrolls."

"And soon, we'll be able to read them. Or at least some of them to learn where they came from or their time period."

"I know, but—"

Ryall gave Holden a look that seemed to ask, *Really?*

"All I'm saying," Holden pressed on, "is that these are Hardacheon scrolls. They had Dark Influences and knowledge. I'm not so sure we should be anxious to delve into their history."

"Holden, when have I ever led you astray?"

"I don't have time to make a list so lengthy," Holden shot back.

"And why do the lands die?" Vicar Johann asked his class.

Holden looked over at his friend and rolled his eyes. He mouthed the question, "Seriously?" before putting his head back down on his desk. Holden's flat forehead lay perfectly flush with the wood desktop. Ryall stifled a chuckle. He was weary like Holden, but knew if he dared close his eyes he would slip away from wakefulness into a deep slumber. He'd likely end up with Vicar Johann slamming a rod down on his desk causing him to jump awake, cursing. Then he'd really be in trouble. Holden and Ryall had not slept at all last night.

"Anyone?" the Vicar repeated.

"Because they must renew themselves from time to time and purge themselves," answered Tama, a lowborn second-year student from the East. The girl had volunteered to enter the Changrual Monastery. Such an act was not all that uncommon, but certainly something that only the most annoyingly devout would do. "The Ancient Heavens set it up this way."

"Ah," Johann intoned. "So, it is necessary?"

"Why else would the lands die and renew if not?"

Ryall saw the glint in Vicar Johann's eyes that shone whenever he was about to start a philosophical rant and prove that he was all-wise when compared to his ignorant students. The fact that he was four decades older than most of his students didn't seem to be an adequate reason as to why he was so much smarter.

"I wonder what, as you say, the lands purge themselves of?" the Vicar challenged.

Tama was caught short and without an answer.

"The soil loses its vitality and nutrients over time," interjected a plump first-year boy from Talen, a farming village in the South near the Eastern Province border. "My father always said so anyway. His harvest has been a little more meager the past couple of years."

"So, the Ancient Heavens created a world that cannot properly provide for its inhabitants? Doesn't that seem to imply that the plan was flawed from the beginning? Or perhaps it was a test for us here, but the cycling of lands causes so much death and hardship, bloodshed and strife. Surely this is not what the Ancient Heavens had in mind unless they are cruel and subjective, the opposite of what the scrolls teach. Anyone else?"

The classroom was silent. Roughly thirty students all looked away, refusing to make contact with the invigorated Vicar.

Vicar Johann turned away and started walking back toward the front of the classroom with his finger held up in an admonishing gesture. "Well, I think you'll better understand as you continue—"

"Whose scrolls?" Ryall interrupted.

Vicar Johann stopped short and turned around. "Pardon me?"

Holden's head started to come up but he stopped himself from fully raising it. He turned and looked over at Ryall, concerned.

Ryall clarified. "You mentioned the scrolls, how they teach that the Ancient Heavens aren't cruel. Whose scrolls say that?"

"Why, the Changrual Scrolls, of course. Surely you understand this basic doctrine of the order?"

Holden cleared his throat, trying not to be obvious but also trying to convey a message of "Shut the Blasted Heavens up" to his friend. It didn't work.

"Right, I'm just curious if those were the scrolls from before or after we invaded Senthara and destroyed the Hardacheons." Ryall spoke with falsely innocent wonder.

"My boy, the scrolls are the same as they always have been, handed down from the Ancients after the Heavens placed them on the world."

"Placed them?" Ryall asked. "From where were they *displaced* in order to be *placed* on our world?"

Vicar Johann didn't answer. Ryall pushed on.

"Are you sure there wouldn't be any variation in the scrolls throughout time?"

Johann was starting to get a little agitated. "What is your question, exactly, Ryall?"

Holden, wide-eyed and turning as red as his hair, stared holes in his friend. He was still hunkered down on his desk behind the boy in front of him. No matter how much he internally willed his friend not to say anything more, he knew Ryall could not resist. *We're done for! Might as well bring out the stakes and torches now!*

"I guess I'm just wondering what was taught on Feylan before we came here to Senthara," Ryall smugly asked. "I wish we had some writings from the Luminary on the subject." Ryall knew full well the answer to his questions from the tablets and scrolls in the caverns.

A solid thump was heard that echoed through the classroom. Holden had let his head free-fall to the surface of his desk, no doubt believing they were destined for the fires, the first heretics to be burned alive in over a century. Ryall himself expected flames to come spitting forth from Vicar Johann in rage, screaming heresy and blasphemy and calling for the High Vicars. Instead, a very confused mask swathed itself across the Vicar's face. He blinked more rapidly and furrowed his eyebrows.

Ryall had to catch the shock that erupted inside him before it showed. *He has no idea what I'm talking about!* He looked around and saw the other students in the class staring at him blankly. Looking back to Johann, Ryall noted genuine concern on the instructor's face.

"My boy, are you well? You seem not yourself," Vicar Johann said.

Holden took the cue and roused himself from the cauldron of self-despair in which he wallowed.

"He's been like this all span, Vicar Johann. He spurts out bits of gibberish and seems to think that he's making total sense. I don't think he's slept much. It might be well to put him on bed rest for a couple days with bland foods and water. I'd be happy to watch over him."

Ryall glanced at his friend to find him looking up at the Vicar intently, feigning concern over his poor, suffering friend.

"Yes, perhaps so," Vicar Johann said, placing his hands together in front of his stomach in a resigned gesture. "I'll see to it." The Vicar turned and started to move on to the next subject.

Ryall was too dumbstruck to say anything in protest. *How could he not know?* The boy had believed that there was some conspiracy at work, some ploy to conceal the truth. *Perhaps Johann is lying or just acting ignorant.* But no, Johann's confusion seemed so genuine. And what's worse, Holden stepped in perfectly to take advantage of his friend's embarrassment and score a serious victory in their prank war. Ryall looked over at Holden. His friend did not acknowledge his stare but continued to look straight ahead with an air of smugness.

Two days of bread and water.

He would pay, no doubt about it. Ryall would not forget this.

THIRTY-FIVE

Aiden

Day 28 of 1st Dimming 412 A.U.

"YOU ATTACKED ME!" HEDRON said angrily as he felt the knot on the side of his head.

"I saved you," Aiden corrected.

The gray light of morning was getting brighter. In a few hours, though it would only be midmorning, the day would be as bright as it would get this far in the North. After the last of the winged demons had fled, Aiden retrieved Hedron where he still lay unconscious. It took a few rough shakes to bring him around, but once Hedron awoke, he came up spitting fire.

"I didn't ask to be saved! I could have helped!" the Kerr boy protested. He truly looked as if he had been cheated from an opportunity to help defend his family and friends.

"Lad, you did help. You saved me, in all likelihood. I simply returned the favor." Aiden's voice remained calm in the face of Hedron's antagonism. "I suspect you will have more than enough chances for bloodshed. Best you enter that time when you are ready and prepared."

Aiden's calm demeanor seemed to irritate Hedron even more. "I can fight. I know how to wield a sword." At this claim, Aiden raised an eyebrow.

"Is that so?"

"Aye," Hedron retorted, mocking Aiden in his accent.

Aiden nodded. "Let's test that theory of yours." He unsheathed his sword swiftly and tossed it to the boy, startling him for a moment. Reaching down, he grabbed a dead branch a hand shorter than a sword. "Come on, then. It's your father's sword, after all. Are you worthy of it?"

Hedron looked a little perplexed but then eagerness took over and he assumed a sparring stance. "I don't want to hurt you, Master Aiden."

"Oh, why don't we not concern ourselves with that? Just do your worst."

Hedron raised the sword and charged. When he was within striking distance, he swung down through the air. Aiden side-stepped the blow easily, not raising his weapon in defense. Hedron's momentum carried him passed Aiden. He turned quickly to face Aiden again. The once master of the hold guard stood casually with one foot forward and his wooden sword dangling down at his side, the end of the dead stick in the snow. Hedron charged again, his sword finding nothing but the cold morning air. Aiden again had sidestepped the attack.

"Why won't you fight back?" Hedron asked with frustration.

"I will when you give me a reason to, lad."

Hedron lost his composure with this last taunt and charged Aiden. This time, Aiden did respond. As Hedron began to bring his sword down, Aiden swiped his stick up with a birsk motion and caught Hedron's wrist. The pain caused the young Kerr to drop the sword. Aiden followed through with a leg sweep, dropping the boy to the ground the same way he did earlier. Before Hedron could react the stick hit his midsection, knocking the wind from his lungs.

Aiden reached down and retrieved his sword. "Good. First lesson over. You've learned never to let your opponent goad you into action. When you've recovered from your lesson, you will meet us back at the cottage with the others."

Aiden entered the cottage to find Jayden, Ehliss and Crimson Snow gathered around Reign in a curious manner. Each looked at Reign with wonder, excitement, or both. Crimson Snow's tail shot back and forth so vigorously that Aiden was a little afraid to get in its way. The wolf nosed at Reign's hand, licking it and occasionally whining for attention. They did not turn or even acknowledge him when he entered, but continued to stare at Reign.

He walked across the room to the hearth to warm himself. His tunic was soaked and torn in several places, making it a fairly useless garment in the cold. Noticing a few small pairs of antlers above the mantle, he removed the tunic and draped it over the antlers to give it a chance to dry from the fire's heat. After a few moments of thawing by the fire, he turned toward the group and saw Ehliss quickly turn her head away. She had been stealing glances of him bare chested. Aiden scoffed internally but was caught short when he finally looked at Reign's face. His mind struggled to tell himself what he saw there. Reign wore an expression of complete solemnity. Her eyes—the eyes were different somehow. They were not hers, in a manner of speaking. She turned her head slightly and raised her eyes to Aiden's. A flood of recognition pounded its way through him, accompanied by swells of incoherence. Such serenity.

"Reign, you look so much like—"

Hedron came through the threshold angrily and kept his head down in order not to meet Aiden's eyes directly. Seeing the attention Reign was attracting from the small group, he became worried.

"Has something happened? Is she hurt?" he asked.

No one answered. Even Reign appeared to be ignoring him. He approached closer and took her hand.

"Reign?"

She turned her head toward him and her eyes reacted by filling with tears. "Hedron," she whispered and embraced him with a strength the boy was not accustomed to. A few tears streamed down her face, snow and ice melting around Hedron's collar where the warm salt water pooled briefly before disappearing.

"I've missed you, boy," Reign whispered. "You have grown and look much how I did when I was young."

Hedron looked back up at Reign when the embrace loosened. A quizzical look rooted itself on his face. It was an odd thing she had said, but the *way* she had said it was almost familiar to Aiden as he watched. Hedron looked around at the others as if to solicit insight from them. None came. Jayden was closest but her stare did not waver as she looked upon Reign. He looked back to his sister, who gazed at him with such peace, such depth. Serenity was closer to the right description.

"When you were young?" he replied, confused. "Why is everyone just—"

"Father," she said simply, followed by a shallow half smile. It was even reminiscent of him, the way his smile started on the left side of his mouth before spreading fully across his face.

The ease with which she said, "father" obviously shocked Hedron. "Wh—what?" he stuttered. "What's happened?" Aiden now saw Hedron sense the change; the change in the air, in those around him. But the change in his sister was more poignant, the center of it. He could *feel* it. It was unmistakable.

Reign's face lost its serenity slowly. She shut her eyes and then reopened them suddenly. Looking down, she gasped as her eyes widened and she stumbled forward. Hedron reached up to catch her.

"Reign!" he said with concern as he felt her shudder in his arms. "What's happening?"

"It's too much!" Reign screamed.

Jayden and the others awoke from their trance-like state at this change. "Bring her to the table," the wolf shepherd commanded. Preceding Hedron, she swiped the articles that sat upon the table to the floor. "Lay her on her back and hold her."

"What's happening?" Hedron pleaded again. "I don't understand!"

Reign's body shook more violently as Hedron placed her down on the old wooden table and braced her shoulders. Reign's legs kicked wildly, slamming down against the wood as her eyes rolled up in their sockets. Crimson Snow whimpered and paced around the table.

"Aiden!" Jayden snapped. "Hold her legs!" With the girl fully secured, Jayden shoved a long piece of rawhide between her teeth.

"What is that? What are you doing?" Hedron asked. Jayden ignored him and scurried around her shelves looking for something in different containers and jars. The various curatives and remedies clattered amongst the shuffling and a jar fell the floor, shattering.

"It's a fright spasm," Ehliss said, approaching Hedron's side.

"What's that? This has never happened before."

"Her body convulses, her muscles tensing and reacting as if the greatest fear one can face is present. The body can't handle it and it reacts with spasms. That's why it's called a fright spasm."

Aiden also wore trepidation on his face as he gripped Reign's legs and held them with concerted effort. "How do we stop it?"

"You can't," she said. "It must pass on its own. We studied anatomy and corporal sciences at the Ministry Academy before focusing in our specific area of study. It's required of all students."

"Stupid girl!" Jayden retorted without stopping her rummaging through the shelves. The sounds of glass vials and flasks being pushed aside still filled the air around them. "Your academies know little to nothing. Fear does not cause this." She finally found what she was searching for in a small porcelain jar. She brought it hurriedly over to the table and dipped her finger in the jar, bringing out a gray translucent ointment on her finger. She swathed it on Reign's upper lip and around her nostrils. The trembling and shaking calmed almost immediately. Reign's breathing became steadier and less erratic.

"I don't believe it," Ehliss said, bringing her head close to Reign's. "The odor is potent. What is that medicine? Of what create?" Ehliss' questions had a purely clinical tone to them, devoid of all her previous inflections of concern.

"Continue to hold her," Jayden warned. "Residual spasms can erupt, but the worst should be over." She finally addressed Hedron and answered the questions that still lingered in his eyes. "Your sister was not fully prepared for your father's last breath. The power of it caused her body to seize as it rooted itself in her. She will likely be in this state of fitful sleep for several days. I must keep a careful watch over her."

This explanation did not help Hedron's understanding, but rather brought on a greater state of confusion. "I have no idea what you mean."

Aiden agreed. "Jayden, something has happened, but none of us understand quite what it is. You seem to have some knowledge of this occurrence. Please speak plainly."

"If you had fewer rocks in your cranium when you were younger you would know exactly what has happened! Thannuel tried to teach you, but you were unprepared."

This brought Aiden up short. "Unprepared for what?"

The sigh that came from Jayden communicated her exasperation better than words could have. "Not now," she finally said. "Perhaps later, when this has passed." Reign moaned slightly, her head shifting left to right every few moments.

No one spoke for several minutes. The silence of the morning was broken only by the occasional moans and grunts that escaped Reign's tightly clenched jaw. She finally gave in to sleep and then the silence held. It held until the ground began to rumble beneath them. Aiden and Hedron's eyes locked as they listened, felt. They sensed a mass too great to accurately number.

"They will not come this way," Jayden stated, obviously seeing the concern in the wood-dwellers. "They likely still have more than a span of travel. But you must leave."

"Leave? And go where?" Hedron asked. "Reign is in no state to travel, especially if there are more of those things out there." Hedron pointed toward the sky, obviously referring to the winged creatures that had attacked them.

"Not the girl," Jayden said. "Just you and Master Aiden. You must go south to Therrium. He will need you now. Elohk and I will see to the girl."

"Forget it. I am not leaving Reign's side. You can burn in—"

"Hedron," Aiden interrupted. "Enough. Your sister is in better care with her than us. What will we do here? Waste the moments away waiting for Reign to recover? Therrium needs to be warned, to know what we saw."

"What about me?" came Ehliss' timid voice.

"You will go with Aiden," Jayden said. "We can't have you running around alone now that we know how helpless you are."

"No. No way in the Cursed Heavens is that liability—"

"Helpless?" Ehliss retorted. "I'll have you know that I am a duly appointed terranist in the Ministry of Terran Studies. I spend spans on end on my own on the glaciers, completely self-sufficient. My father is the former Minister of Terran Studies and one of the most respected men in the Realm. A hall in the academy is scheduled to be named after him later this year and—"

"And what good was all that when the Alysaar chased you down? Did you fling knowledge at them? Dazzle them into submission with all your credentials?" Jayden chided. "If not for Aiden and my packs, you would no doubt have been part of the trophies in their beards by now."

"Feel free not to mention my help," Hedron muttered. No one replied to his comment. "Wait, Aly—what?"

"You would not have even known of their presence if I had not warned you! So much for gratitude and thanks!" the young terranist shot back.

Aiden nodded. "All right then. What did you see?"

Ehliss told them of her expeditions upon the glaciers and her studies. Naturally, she lulled on too long in descriptive narrative regarding her instruments and findings, which tested the limits of Aiden's patience. He balled up his fists tightly and released them over and over to hold back a temper-induced outburst. Finally she came to the clouds that became a storm that morphed to an army of infantry and flying beasts. "The roar of the large dragon-like creatures I mistook for thunder at first."

"Alysaar," Jayden corrected. "Dragons are nothing but myth."

Ehliss looked at her with incredible irony. "Of course!" she agreed sarcastically. "Just as there is no one beyond the glaciers. But today, I saw an army coming from across the glaciers, the likes of which I have never seen. And many soldiers were riding these so-called Alysaar with the ease and familiarity our soldiers ride a horse."

"Borathein," Jayden again corrected patiently. "They are not of the Realm, but live far to the north in a land called Borath. They are ancient kin of the Hardacheons, which is, no doubt, part of why they have come."

"Are they like the Hardacheons were?" Ehliss asked.

"Worse, in fact. Though much of what you hear of the Hardacheons is little truth and more myth at this point. They were not so different than us."

"They are headed south through the barren lands of the Northern Province," Aiden reported as he continued to listen to the vibrations. "If they were coming to attack the Senthara, wouldn't they now be heading east, toward Iskele? Toward Wellyn?"

"Not if that isn't their destination," Jayden responded.

Hedron shook his head. "But that doesn't make sense. If they continue straight south they will end up in Arlethia."

"Brilliant," Jayden mumbled as she looked over Reign, who lay still on the table. She lowered her ear close to Reign's mouth for a moment and then raised back up again, unconcerned. "Now, again, you must leave. Find Therrium and warn him, though I am certain he already labors under difficult circumstances."

"The Realm is set against the West at the same time a new enemy marches against them," Hedron remarked to no one in particular.

"Aye," Aiden said. "My thoughts are running along the same lines. It cannot be a coincidence."

"Of course it's not a coincidence! Can you not see?" Jayden exclaimed. "No, of course not. You were not here when Reign revealed all she knows, though she did not know the meaning of it. She witnessed what was no doubt the beginning of an alliance between the Borathein and Wellyn, an alliance meant to bring about the destruction of the Arlethian race."

"But why?" Ehliss asked.

Jayden scowled. "I thought history was something you studied at your lofty academy."

"Well pardon me for not knowing about a people that no one else knows about!"

"Obviously, they are not so unknown as you think, but more accurately, purposely ignored until now. The Hardacheons and Borathein are kin. And while the Senthary invaded and destroyed the Hardacheons, the Arlethians chose to enter the battle on the side of the Senthary even though they were contemporaries in the land with the Hardacheons. Not allies, but neighboring kingdoms for millennia. To the Borathein, the decision of the wood-dwellers to join a foreign invading force against their neighbors is no doubt seen as betrayal. Their carnal faith of conquest no doubt demands vengeance. They call it Griptha. Believe me, your Changrual know of the Borathein and their ways."

"It is curious..." Aiden admitted, trailing off in thought. "Why did we side with the Senthary, a people we did not know prior to their invasion? Why take up arms against our neighbors?"

"Do you want me to hold a class for you or shall we come to the pressing subject of what needs to be done *right* now?"

"But how do *you* know of them?" Ehliss asked. "Do the Archivers?"

"The Shrule," Jayden corrected. "Archiver is the common name for them but that is not their true name. Their ancient name is Shrule. And, they are not as all seeing as you might have been taught. An elder can only view what another Archiver witnesses. There are ancient Hardacheon records kept that mention the

Borathein, no doubt, but no mention has been made for at least four hundred years, I am sure.

"They were here when the Hardacheons ruled these lands, and prior when the Ancients were here, just as the Helsyans and Arlethians were," Jayden said. "Våleira's history is not as disparate as most believe."

"Wait, where are the ancient records then?" Ehliss asked. "The Hardacheon and earlier ones?"

"The Hardacheon records were confiscated, but no one knows where they have been sequestered, if they still exist. The Shrule did not, at that time, keep records on ageless obsidian, but on papyrus and hide. The durability of such materials is obviously much less than stone."

Ehliss continued to look skeptical, but Jayden did not seem to care. "We are wasting time upon things that currently do not matter," she said, waving her hand dismissively. "Aiden, you must get Hedron to Therrium. Arlethia will need him, and you as well."

"Why?" Ehliss asked. "What can they do? Or any of us?"

At that, Jayden laughed. "You have no idea who these three are, do you?"

Ehliss looked at all of them before facing Jayden. "I know they're wood-dwellers, that's obvious."

"Not just wood-dwellers. These," motioning to Hedron and Reign, "are Lord Thannuel Kerr's children. You no doubt know the tales of Lord Kerr's death, mythical in nature though they are. And he is Master Aiden, the most recognized swordsman in the Realm since Lord Kerr himself. His reputation reaches even this far north. In fact, the bone-headed man even wields Thannuel's sword."

"But, no, that's impossible! She died. All the family did. It was published throughout the Realm. And her father betrayed the High Duke and was executed because—"

She was cut short by Aiden's hand at her throat, slamming her against a wall. Crimson Snow barked and snarled at her, hackles raised. "One more word," Aiden hissed as his breath bounced off

Ehliss' contorted face, "and I'll rip your throat free and feed it to the wolves." As if hoping this would be the case, Crimson barked savagely twice.

"Aiden!" Hedron cried out. "Don't! She doesn't know what she's saying."

Jayden's soft hand rested upon Aiden's outstretched arm. "Lad, the boy is right. She is only repeating what everyone was brainwashed to believe by the constant circulation of lies. Release her." He looked at Jayden with disgust, though it was not directed at her.

"Can you channel that anger? That friction?" she asked. Those words were enough to shake Aiden loose. He released Ehliss' throat and she immediately sucked in air, bringing her hands to her neck. A few coughs followed as she wiped away tears from her eyes.

"What did you say? How do you know of friction?" Aiden demanded.

"You truly are dense, aren't you?" the old woman said. "Thannuel tried to prepare you to enter the Gyldenal Order, but those efforts were cut short when he fell. I would like to say, as I am accustomed, that you were too daft and thick-headed, but the truth is he simply did not have enough time."

"I don't understand," Aiden said. "I don't know what you are talking about. Have you noticed that's a common theme of people around you lately?"

"It's a myth," Ehliss said hoarsely. "A secret group living somewhere deep in the Tavaniah Forest said to have superior knowledge or abilities. Bedtime stories for children. We learned about it at the academy. It's in a textbook of folklore and fables. No evidence of their existence has ever been found despite the best efforts of the most brilliant men and scholars."

"If you haven't noticed, dear," Jayden answered gently with a hint of condescension, "that academic education of yours isn't fairing too well right now. The point of a clandestine order is to leave no evidence. That is, in fact, the best evidence that has been found."

Ehliss held her peace and looked away, still rubbing her throat.

"Friction," Jayden continued, looking back to Aiden, "is one of the first understandings taught by the Gyldenal. It is basic and fundamental to all higher understandings. You have a basic grasp of it, I know, but it is very embryonic still."

Aiden eyed her skeptically. "And Thannuel was part of this... order?"

"Focus. Think of nothing but this moment," Jayden said in response.

Aiden stepped back. "You know this saying?"

"It is one of the ancient axioms. And of course I know it."

"Did...my father...I mean, if he was part of the Gyldenal, did he know you were?" Hedron asked.

Jayden was silent for a short time before nodding her head.

"Friction?" Aiden asked, testing her further.

"Feed on the friction," Jayden replied. "Thannuel no doubt commanded you to keep these things secret at the cost of your life, though you did not know why."

Aiden looked down, eyes wide. "Ancient Heavens, it's true."

Ehliss had recovered enough to stand upright again. "Are you actually suggesting that the order exists and that you are one of them?"

Aiden shot her a menacing glance that made her flinch slightly.

"Maybe you're not as dense as you appear," Jayden said.

"But why, if it's so secret, would you tell us?"

"The Gyldenal will not be aloof much longer. We cannot be. We will be forced to enter the conflict. It has always been inevitable. Arlethia cannot survive against both the Senthary and the Borathein. It has been long anticipated that the Borathein would come, but the actions of Wellyn against Arlethia are most curious though not completely surprising."

"Why would they care for our survival? These Gyldenal?" Hedron asked.

"Because the Gyldenal are all Arlethians," Aiden said, pulling his hand away from his furrowed brow. "The Tavaniah Forest is part of Arlethia, the most north-western along the coast."

Jayden nodded. "That is mostly correct. As I said, we are an order, not a race."

"But Jayden, you're not a wood-dweller," Hedron stated.

"No, my boy, I am something else entirely."

Later that morning, after taking enough provisions and deciding on their route, Aiden, Hedron and Ehliss departed, leaving Jayden and Elohk to tend to Reign and the surviving pack. They did gain three more members of their party before they left, however. Huksinai, Alabeth and Thurik playfully snapped at one another as the caravan made their way south to Arlethia with all haste. In order for Ehliss to not unduly hinder their progress, as she lacked wood-dweller speed, Aiden had grudgingly agreed to carry her upon his back. Aiden heard Hedron snickering to himself at the sight.

"Oh, don't worry," Aiden reassured him. "You'll have your turn carrying the princess before long."

THIRTY-SIX

Lord Calder Hoyt

Day 28 of 1ˢᵗ Dimming 412 A.U.

"THE EASTERN FORCES HAVE ARRIVED, Lord Hoyt," Hambly reported. "Houses Chester, Orion and Sperry make up the majority."

"How many in total?"

"Twenty thousand it seems. Lord Marshall Garreth of the East leads them and has written instructions from the High Duke to lead our combined forces. Lord Marshal Wenthil is not pleased but has certified the High Duke's orders."

Garreth, Hoyt thought. *Known for his eagerness. That could be helpful.*

"This is less than has been sent to other fronts along the Arlethian borders, according to Garreth," Hambly added. "The military assessment of this most southern front is that there will be less resistance present than the other fronts."

"How many other battle focal points are there?" Lord Hoyt asked.

"Two others, according to Lord Marshal Wenthil," Master Gernald replied. "Lord Marshal Brendar leads a battalion of sixty thousand Eastern soldiers about thirty leagues slightly northeast of here and High Lord Marshal Tulley leads eighty thousand

Northern and Eastern Province men fifteen to twenty leagues north of Brendar's front. Tulley has supreme command of all three forces. Banner Therrium is thought to be at the most northern front where Tulley leads."

"And ours? How many?" Hoyt asked, turning to Gernald.

"Thirty thousand, as my Lord had commanded."

"Where is Wenthil now?"

"He is meeting with Garreth now in a strategy session," Hambly replied. "The kitchens are busy preparing for the officers' banquet tonight."

"I see," was all Lord Hoyt said.

Calder Hoyt considered his moves carefully, delving into the possible repercussions of his actions if they were unsuccessful. He did not have to think long on what would happen to him, his wife, his daughter, those of his court. There would be no mercy.

"Three hooded soldiers have come with them, as you suspected," Hambly continued.

"I did not know how many would be sent," Lord Hoyt said. "Just that they would be here."

"My Lord, please, tell us what you know of them," Gernald requested for the third time. "We can better help if we know more."

"The less you know, the less danger you will be in if something goes awry. We cannot be too cautious. But we must be rid of them if we have any hope of succeeding."

Hambly and Gernald looked at each other.

"Have you brought your uncle, the hydraf trapper?" Hoyt asked Gernald.

"He waits outside the chamber doors, my Lord."

"Show him in."

An average man of leathery skin holding a hat in his hands entered the great chambers where the three men met. He looked around the hall, taking in the grandeur of his surroundings as he approached Lord Hoyt. The man did not kneel but continued to look up as if he were alone.

"Forgive him, Lord Hoyt," Gernald pleaded. "Uncle Kimsly has never been inside your hold."

"Oh!" Kimsly said, suddenly realizing that he was being rude. "My apologies, my Lord!" The man took a knee and waited to be given permission to rise. He spoke with only the left half of his face.

"No, no, get up," Hoyt told him, more annoyance in his voice than he wanted to reveal. "We haven't time for these ridiculous formalities."

Kimsly rose and fidgeted with the hat still in his hands. It had seen many years in the sun, Calder surmised, from its faded and worn appearance.

"You are a trapper?" Hoyt asked.

"Yes, since I was a boy. Like my father and he like his. Kimslys have been trappers for generations, we have."

"He is the best in the Southern Province," Gernald said.

"Now, nephew, I don't know—"

"It's true, old man. This isn't a time for modesty. Quit your quibbling!" Gernald demanded.

"Have you ever been bitten?" Hoyt asked.

Kimsly rolled up his shirtsleeves and revealed three bite marks on his left forearm and two on the upper right arm near his shoulder.

"This one here," Kimsly said as he pointed to one on his right arm, "nearly ended me. I never spoke right after and my eye doesn't blink. Truth be told, I have to glue it shut at night with a little drop of amber wax to keep it from drying out. Healers told me it has something to do with a nerve but I didn't pay that much attention when they spoke about it."

Lord Hoyt looked concerned. He turned to Gernald and asked, "This man is the best we have? Ancients come, he's allowed himself to be bitten five times."

"My Lord, if I may," Kimsly said, "the reason I'm the best is because I've been bitten five times and I'm still here. A man can survive a bite if he acts quickly to chew the Triarch roots, but surviving five times is extremely rare, Triarch roots or not. I've also always got a bit inside me, if you know what I mean." Kimsly pulled down his bottom lip and revealed a bolus of chew lining his bottom gums.

"Make it myself, I do," he continued. "Dry out the Triarch leaves and mix it with a poultice of smashed root and—"

"Uncle, I believe his Lordship understands," Gernald said.

"I'm mostly just saying that I can trap the little buggers better than anyone and have more experience because of these scars. I'm more careful and precise now. The last of these was over ten years ago." Kimsly pointed to a bite mark. "I haven't even come close to being bitten since and my haul is usually twice that of other trappers."

Hoyt nodded. "And you can extract the poison without spoiling it?"

"It's secreted from pouches behind the lower jaw line. It's a delicate matter, but yes, I can preserve those pouches and the venom in them."

"And it cannot be detected? There will be hounds as well as other beasts that possess unearthly abilities of scent."

"It is utterly odorless and tasteless," Kimsly said. Calder knew this but he could not be over-confident. Every element of the plan had to be checked and checked again.

"How soon can you deliver the poison?"

"I sold all my last catch at market two days past. Ancients, it was a good batch! Anyway, I can go out on the Roniah tonight at first moon. The days are shorter now so moonrise should be within a few hours."

"When does the feast begin?" Lord Hoyt asked Hambley.

"I believe not for several more hours. Longer if need be, my Lord."

"Very well. The mixture must not take effect immediately, not until after the feast is over. If the venom acts too quickly we will be done for."

"It will be diluted with a sleeping curative provided by Healer Naveen," Gernald said. "She is the best healer for scores of leagues.

The concoction should provide for both purposes, to delay the reaction and cause them to be asleep when it takes effect."

"The serving cooks are prepared?"

"No," Hambly said. "It's too risky. I'll administer the dose myself before the food leaves the kitchens."

That was a change but Hoyt agreed with the alteration.

"And the proxies?" Lord Hoyt asked.

"Wenthil has found three men of appropriate size. All is set, my Lord."

Hoyt again nodded with his hand over his chin. The last piece of the plan was particularly worrisome to him. He had argued with his daughter but she had prevailed with her logic. *Why does she have to be so blasted right all the time!* He hated how perceptive she was sometimes, but he knew she was right. The Arlethians would need someone of value if they were to trust in this plan.

"And my daughter?" he asked.

"She is already across the river and should be into the forest now," Gernald answered.

"Ancient Heavens, watch over her," Lord Hoyt prayed. "Lady Briel?"

"She knows nothing," Hambly assured him.

If things did not go as planned, he knew his wife's ignorance of the scheme would not save her from meeting the same fate he would. Still, he would not burden her with his intentions. Not yet.

"Sooner is better, Master Trapper."

"Aye, my Lord." Kimsly turned and exited swiftly.

<hr>

Kathryn strode alone slowly on her mount toward the forest's edge, arrayed in her hooded shawl of bright gold, orange, and red. She had always thought the colors of the Southern Province resembled a flame and wondered if she looked like a torch on horseback to those who she knew waited in stealth beyond the tree line. Fire and trees did not usually mix well.

Will the Arlethians even listen? she wondered. *They must. They have to!* She did not know what to expect upon meeting with them. She knew she would make a tempting target or hostage once her identity was known. *Hedron, I wish you were here.*

Many prayers escaped her lips as she drew closer. Doing her best to appear unafraid and confident, she sat up straight, head held high. As she reached the forest's border, she pulled back gently on the reins and her horse stopped. It snorted once.

"Easy girl," Kathryn comforted. "Easy Dahlia. There, now." The sun had started to set, but the massive trees that confronted her already hid the sun's light. It was dark enough to be night in the forest. A low fog had come in from the east and blanketed the ground below her. She could not see her horse's hooves when she looked down. Kathryn almost felt as if she were amidst the clouds and standing on thin air. Bringing her right leg up and over the horse, she dismounted. When her feet hit the earth, the wispy fog parted for a second, revealing the ground, and just as quickly filled in around her again. It reached halfway up her calves.

Taking a deep breath, she led Dahlia forward and crossed over the boundary into the forest. There was no sound other than her footsteps and those of her horse. Not even birds sang. They wove between closely grown trees trying to find any semblance of a path but there was none she could see. Dahlia whinnied and Kathryn again comforted her by rubbing her long snout and whispering that all was well. A carrot from her saddlebag helped her horse find some courage.

They continued walking. She looked up and could see small glimmers of sunlight piercing small openings in the thick canopy of branches and leaves over a hundred feet above her. Wind howled and rustled the tops of the trees.

Their progress was slow as she was uncertain of every footstep due to the fog. Not being able to see where she stepped created a bit of a surreal feeling and Kathryn again battled a sense of floating.

"Easy girl," she said again, but more for her own comfort now than Dahlia's.

Her next step fell on uneven ground and she stumbled forward. Her hands gripped the reins tight and prevented her from meeting the ground. Dahlia stepped backward and helped Kathryn up.

"Thanks, girl."

When Kathryn again looked forward to continue, a shape emerged from beneath the fog directly in front of her. Fear found Kathryn but she forced herself not to run. Dahlia cried and rose up on her hind legs, almost tearing free from Kathryn's grip on her reins. The shape materialized into the form of a man as remnants of the fog drifted off him like water flowing over a rock. She could discern no features in this façade of night. Two others emerged like ghosts from the depths of the Ancient Dark on either side of the first. Suddenly on her left side, a quick burst of air blew against her as a fourth appeared. The apparition stood within arm's reach of her. Body and face alike were covered in mud the color of bark. Only the whites of his eyes were discernible in the contrast against his unnatural complexion.

The ghost-like Arlethian warrior reached forward and grabbed her shoulder before she could recognize his arm had moved. Kathryn Hoyt screamed.

———

Under the cloak of night, Master Gernald and three men of the Southern Army whom Lord Marshal Wenthil had selected, prowled through the camp of the Eastern army. A scout had informed Gernald where the enigmatic hooded creatures would likely be, but he was not certain. Lord Hoyt had warned the scout not to get too close, as they would be able to detect him, but he would not explain more than this. Charldis, the scout, was an archer with exceptional eyesight. Gernald knew the information was as reliable as could be expected.

The officers' feast had ended hours ago and second moon was cresting the horizon. Lord Marshal Garreth had announced that the initial attack would likely begin just before nightfall of the following day. Oaths of valor and boasts of heroism filled the halls, coming mostly from the younger officers of the East who wanted to use this battle for their advancement. The Southern Province's officers laughed and played along, but there was no mirth in their merriment. Master Gernald watched as the food had been delivered, eyeing conspicuously the servings placed in front of those three shadowed men. They did not even remove their hoods when they ate, but the food was devoured ravenously. Gernald had spared a glance to the kitchens where he spied Hambly barely peering around a corner. It seemed that Hambly had been successful and was standing by to watch his handiwork, though the effects were not supposed to take place until after the feast.

Let it work! Master Gernald prayed as they ducked between tents and avoided the torches of the sentries. He knew they would only have one opportunity to pull off Lord Hoyt's ambitious ploy.

They found the tent that Charldis had pointed out. Gernald's heart was in his throat. He did not know what these three were, but he could tell Lord Hoyt feared them greatly. It was as if Hoyt did not believe them human at all.

The group hunched close to the back entry of the tent and Gernald reached out to grab one of the flaps. He looked at the others and nodded. Each drew a short blade. Gernald slowly pulled back the tent flap and entered. The other three followed, stooped over and moving as quickly as they could. Inside, the tent was tall enough to stand at the center but not along the walls where the small company crouched. Gernald retrieved a small glass vial from a pocket, as did each of the men with him. After taking the cork off the end of the tube for a brief moment and allowing the air to touch the liquid, he replaced it and shook the vial. The liquid inside illuminated a dark yellowish light.

I'm going to recommend that healer woman for high commendation! he thought.

As the dim light filled the tent and his eyes adjusted, Gernald cursed at what he saw. His pulse quickened and he tensed. The men with him had a similar reaction but they did not move. Before them, in the weak light, Gernald made out three shapes huddled together on the ground in the center of the tent. The hooded figures sat facing one another, forming a circle, and had their arms up around one another's shoulders. Their heads were bowed and each seemed to be resting against the next one for support. They did not move.

Gernald looked to the closest man on his right and nodded. Slowly and silently, the company advanced with short blades at the ready. They encircled the hooded men and waited. No action came from those below them. Looking at the others, Gernald nodded again. They each reached down forcefully and grabbed a hood, ripping it off the heads of their targets. Gernald gasped at what they saw.

Ancients take me!

Underneath the hoods were shorn heads with pale flesh. Strange markings were carved into their skin, obviously symbols of some create. There was no scar tissue from the carvings, just the shapes, pale in color as the flesh itself. Gernald realized these tattoos were not carved into their flesh at all, but part of their natural appearance. A deformity of some create. The exact same on each of the three strange men, as far as he could tell. Gernald shuddered again and swallowed his fear. He pulled one of the monsters from the circle and its head fell back. The eyes were open but lifeless. Pupils dilated too large to leave any other color save for the white borders. Purplish veins bulged under the eyes and foam dripped from the mouth. The demon of a man was dead.

It was strange to find them huddled together in a circle of death. *Perhaps this is the way they died in preparation to meet whatever foul being had spawned them,* Gernald mused. But he did not have time to ponder the mysteries that were before him now.

"Quickly," he whispered to the others. "Remove their robes and dispose of the bodies."

As night approached the following day, Lord Hoyt grew increasingly nervous. He had not heard from his daughter and feared for her safety. If something had happened to his precious Kathryn, he knew he would never be able to forgive himself. Lady Briel had slapped and cursed him when she found out what he had allowed their daughter to do and was in her chambers, refusing to answer the door for anyone.

He sat upon his warhorse, though he had never been in battle, nor had any of his men that he knew of; he prayed that would continue at least for today. Master Gernald and a half dozen other hold guards flanked him. The expected protests had come and gone from his master of the hold guard about him being on the front lines with the army, but Hoyt acted as if he had not even heard them. Looking around, he took in the sight of fifty thousand soldiers, cavalry, and siege weapons of all create. Each was arranged into units of various sizes, categorized by swords, axes, spears, and archers. Less than five hundred paces away he spied the three hooded men in their dark robes near the front with Lord Marshal Garreth. Gernald came forward on his horse.

"All is set, Lord Hoyt."

He nodded to Master Gernald and waited. Calder did not like the course of action he was about to take, but he could not turn the currents now. He saw Lord Marshal Wenthil saunter over to Garreth and knew the time had come. In a flash, the three hooded men turned and tackled Garreth and pinned him to the ground. The man screamed as three short blades pierced his torso. The action was so sudden that it took several moments before anyone else could react.

Wenthil shouted a command and the Southern forces separated themselves from the East's and surrounded them with haste, easily outnumbering them. The Eastern forces were too surprised to know exactly what was happening. Some officers of the Eastern Army shouted orders to their men, but it was too late. The Southern

Army trained arrows, leveled spears and swords, and raised axes in an extremely hostile posture toward Eastern soldiers.

"Throw down your arms!" Lord Hoyt commanded. "Do not make an end of yourselves foolishly! Throw down your arms and you will be spared, I swear it!"

A score of Eastern soldiers attacked the closest Southern men to them but were easily dispatched. Their fellow Eastern soldiers did not follow their lead.

"Hold! Blasted Night, hold!" Hoyt shouted. "Will you choose to die this day? To waste your life in an effort you cannot prevail in? A cause that is not your own?"

After several tense moments, the clang and clatter of steel and wood was heard as twenty thousand swords, spears, shields, axes and bows fell to the earth. The Eastern soldiers were stripped down to their under tunics, their hands and ankles bound.

Wenhthil had argued to execute them once the Eastern forces were subdued, it being a time of war and the logistics of handling so many prisoners an untenable burden, but Lord Hoyt forbade it.

"Master Gernald, is your plan ready to be carried out?" Hoyt asked.

"Yes, my Lord."

Commands were shouted and the prisoner force of twenty thousand was broken in forty groups of five hundred. Ten Southern soldiers took up positions around each prisoner group.

"We will need the wood-dwellers to agree to march them deep into the Schadar," Gernald said. "At least a full day's march. They shouldn't need more than five per group, at most."

Hoyt pondered. "Do you think those who accept this assignment will make it back in time to regroup?"

"With their speed," Gernald said, "I believe they will be able to catch back up with us just before we make it to Calyn."

"It will have to do."

Hopefully that was enough to convince them. Hoyt knew the Arlethians had to be watching from across the river. They would never make it in time to assist Therrium but they would still go to Calyn to help where they could—assuming the Arlethians now trusted him. And, assuming they had not harmed his daughter.

If they dared to bring harm to her...

"My Lord, look!" Gernald said. From the wood-dweller forest across the Roniah, a large force emerged from behind the tree line into the waning light of day. Wood-dwellers, swathed in mud. At their head, a rider beamed triumphant, her blonde hair in a shawl of bright orange, red, and gold. Lord Hoyt's heart swelled.

THIRTY-SEVEN

Prime Lord Banner Therrium

Day 29 of 1ˢᵗ Dimming 412 A.U.

"HOW ARE YOUR WOUNDS, MASTER ALRIKK?" Prime Lord Therrium asked.

Alrikk had been promoted to master of the hold guard after Aiden's departure by default, but it was not an appointment made reluctantly by Lord Therrium. Alrikk had witnessed the battle and also felt the assault on the forest itself while on overseer duty and connected to the forest. Though mentally affected by this event more than the actual battle, his insights were invaluable.

"The healers believe in a matter of days I should recover full range of motion in my right arm," he replied. "They say I will always have a slight limp in my walk, but that it shouldn't hinder me from any of my duties. My Lord is kind to ask."

They were at the northernmost of the three battlefronts. While small skirmishes had broken out, a major confrontation had not yet developed. All around them, the sounds of fifteen thousand soldiers in preparation were heard.

"And the deeper wounds?" Lord Therrium pressed.

Alrikk struggled to find words to adequately answer his Lord. Therrium knew of his nightmares, how Alrikk would awaken with

397

a cry, drenched in sweat. The healers had kept Therrium well informed.

"I am present, my Lord. I seem to have little residual effects left," Alrikk lied. Lord Therrium did not force him any farther.

"I am pleased to know it," Therrium said. "And, I am more pleased you are here and still with us. I would like you to join the group in charge of oversight tonight. It will be your first time in this assignment since the attack. A fortified hold needs only one or two overseers, but here, deep in the forest without fortifications and the enemy at our very door, many are required. I trust your sensitivity, Master Alrikk. Find a bough of a suitable height and I'm certain you will be out of harm's way."

"My Lord wishes me out of the way, away from battle?" Alrikk replied with a hint of shame in his voice.

"No, no lad, you misunderstand. You can likely sense what others cannot due to your experience. I *need* you on overseer duty."

"As my Lord commands, of course, but I don't feel any more experienced than the others. I am actually quite young compared to many here."

Therrium sensed Alrikk felt intimidated or inadequate, perhaps both.

"Any can sense and feel as I can. In fact," he continued somewhat sheepishly, "I haven't spoken with the forest since that night."

Therrium was contemplative, running through scenarios in his mind, only half hearing his master of the hold guard. "Do you think you could discern it with more warning if you felt it again?"

Alrikk went pale. "You believe…that the enemy could use the same Influence again?"

"It is inevitable, Master Alrikk. I would use it if I were in the enemy's position. This Influence is something we cannot defend against. General Roan and I have discussed it at length, and rumors have spread through the army from those who witnessed it at my hold. But we can do nothing to prepare for it other than to try and sense it with as much warning as possible."

Alrikk tried to collect himself amid the realization of what they might face, and the toll it would take on him mentally if he again endured a similar assault against the forest while connected to it. He remembered how the trees screamed in terror and agony. The trees *screamed* in his mind, a sound not audible to the ear but loud enough to fracture a sentient being's core. It was a horrific, indelible sound. Supernatural and sickening. The scar inside Alrikk was seared by that scream, carving a chasm that filled with nightmares until they overflowed and threatened to drown his sanity.

With great effort he said, "You are my Lord. I will do whatever you require of me without question."

"You don't remember Lord Kerr, do you?" Therrium asked, changing the subject.

"I was barely a youth beyond the age of innocence when he and his daughter died. Fourteen, I think. I actually saw him once in Calyn with his son, but that was long ago. I do remember quite well when Lady Moira and her boy were killed, though. Aiden revered Lord Kerr as a father. Actually, I think most of the other guards thought Aiden was his son or nephew, the way he carried on about him."

"No, neither. Aiden's father did not deserve the title of *father*, but let's leave that to another time. The reason I asked about Lord Kerr is because of something I learned from him. Well, I learned many things from him, as did all who spent any time around him. You learned more from what he *did* than what he said, understand?"

Alrikk did not answer, but continued to listen.

"When there was a stomach that growled, he filled it with his own meat and drink. When someone was burdened, he lifted the weight and carried it. When people were full of sadness, he walked with them until their spirits were elevated. When justice needed to be exercised, he delegated that duty to no one. And, when someone needed to be defended, he always placed himself in front. Do you understand now?"

"I—I..." Alrikk stuttered. "I'm not sure, my Lord."

"I am not Thannuel Kerr. I could never hope to be the man he was, but perhaps today we can both learn from his example. You have great fear in you. You are damaged inside, though your physical wounds will heal. You fear to carry out your duty."

"My Lord, I only wish to—"

"Be still, lad," Therrium said calmly. "I do not accuse you of any cowardice or running from your duty. I have asked you to take on an assignment that is grievous to be borne by you, for the benefit of your people, to be sure. But, I understand, at least a little, what I am asking.

"I know what Thannuel Kerr would do if he were you. He would stand against the fear and do his duty. But, more importantly, I know what he would do if he were *me*. He would climb to the overseer perch *with* you. And so, Alrikk, let us do today exactly what the greatest leader in both our lifetimes would have done. You, your duty despite the fear. Me, to stand by you and not ask you to face it alone."

On the way to the overseer perch, Lord Therrium and Alrikk passed General Roan as he disseminated battlefield deployments amongst his officers.

"General," Therrium said. "Are we ready?"

Roan turned to face Therrium and bowed. "Yes, Prime Lord. The men are almost fully deployed or soon will be."

"You are efficient as ever, General. Arlethia is lucky to have you." Before Roan could answer, Therrium came in closer so only the two of them could hear. "What are our chances? Give it to me cold, General."

"High Lord Marshal Tulley leads the enemy at this front. Brendar and Garreth at the middle and southern fronts respectively. Here, there are eighty thousand against us, more than five times our numbers. I have twenty five thousand at the middle front and ten thousand in the south. I do not know the enemy numbers there, however."

"Yes, General. But what are our *chances*?"

Roan hesitated and Therrium thought he could see the answer in his eyes.

"I believe," Roan said, "we have no choice and so the odds do not matter."

"You have been in worse odds, if I remember correctly."

Roan looked away. "Perhaps, Prime Lord. But then I had…" Roan didn't finish, obviously regretting what he started to say.

"Then you had Lord Kerr by your side. Is that what you meant to say?" Therrium wore a sad smile.

"I apologize, Prime Lord. I meant to speak no disrespect or to cast doubt."

"No General, of course not. I wish he were here, too."

"I sometimes wonder if he knew," Roan said.

"Knew? Knew what?" Roan was obviously deliberating on whether to say more. "Antious, what is it, my friend?"

Roan sighed and looked as if he were about to confess a long-held secret. "Sometime before he was killed, Lord Kerr asked me to come see him. His message was strange, cryptic. It was as if he had something to tell me, but he never got the chance. Somehow, I feel responsible in some way. It's a hard feeling to describe, Prime Lord."

"I know you were friends. Inseparable, actually, when you were young. Hear me now, Antious, nothing that has happened can, in any way, be laid at your feet. But, I've distracted you long enough. Carry on, General."

"Yes, Prime Lord."

THIRTY-EIGHT

Rembbran

Day 29 of 1ˢᵗ Dimming 412 A.U.

THERE IS A PAIN that few have known, and no one knew it better than Rembbran. None alive could understand it, comprehend it, transcend it. The pain itself was transcendent, occupying its pathetic host until the host writhed in obedience to its will, until all thoughts fled save for how to serve the pain, how to temper or quell it. This was what the pain desired—all focus and thought of the host upon its existence, its presence. Agony, its higher name, was a demanding master, commanding all waking hours to be centered upon it.

The pain had started to morph into a cloud of miasmic torment and despair, filling Rembbran and striving to choke out reality, to create a world of perception where elements that would conjure the greatest torture and cruelest taunts were projected constantly to his senses. Shapes and shadows from the corner of his eye, ghosts of past agony that reached out with malevolent jeers toward him. Agony was indeed a cruel and arduous master. Its tentacles had fully ensnared him, crushing and ripping all thoughts of escape from him.

But now, hope. It was a strangely positive feeling for a chase-giver to grasp onto with such fervor. The anticipation of a

Dahlrak's fulfillment would bring excitement to the most docile of Rembbran's kind, if such a trait existed within a Helsyan. But hope: this was truly an odd emotion. It was a common belief among his order, though unsubstantiated, that the pain and suffering of an unfulfilled Charge would be tempered greatly if a Charge was executed on a relative of the escaped prey. Due to the High Duke's shaken confidence in him after his failure and erratic behavior, Rembbran was not part of the extermination of Lord Kerr's family shortly after his death. Would a cousin be a close enough relation to temper the ever-present agony brought on because of the Kerr youngling? This small bit of hope Rembbran now clung to that might be only myth was nonetheless enough for now.

Rembbran's last encounter with High Duke Wellyn was almost surreal. Maynard was impossibly defeated but none survived to speak of his fall. Wellyn would not appoint a new leader at that time, but Rembbran was granted the lead in this most unusual mission. A mass Dahlrak had never before been ordered and still technically had not been. The final order would be given by the High Lord Marshal to begin once Rembbran arrived. The danger a mass Dahlrak posed to the chase-givers themselves was usually cause enough to avoid it at all costs, but Wellyn was not himself; not in control or rational.

Being Charged with an Archiver, Hadik exterminating the Archivers, a surprise attack on Hold Therrium.

Rembbran liked this new side of the High Duke that was starting to reveal itself. More reckless, more ruthless. *More like me.* Wellyn was changing.

He did not know the games or designs that Wellyn orchestrated, nor did he or any other chase-giver care. Emeron Wellyn held the Urlenthi, the Stone of Orlack. To a chase-giver, he who held the Urlenthi *was* the Stone. Others had held it before him, and to those predecessors the Helsyans also gave obedience. Senthary, Hardacheon or even the Ancients were no different in their eyes. He who held the Urlenthi commanded his kind by some decree of the Cursed Heavens, some axiom that limited Rembbran's race from free reign upon the world. The bond between the chase-givers and the Urlenthi was strong enough to prevent any disloyalty to the one who possessed it. This was the natural order of the Helsyan psyche.

"Someone must hold a rabid dog's leash," Hadik had often sneered.

The most Rembbran could do was fire back with words. What he wouldn't give to dispatch the Master of the Khansian Guard, but being Charged with Hadik was unlikely to occur anytime soon.

His Helsyan brethren were spread out along the Arlethian borders with the Realm's armies. Four were with him. The target of the Dahlrak was the same for all chase-givers, but the strategy was to put as many Arlethians between them as possible in pursuit of the final prey. This would cause the most destruction of the Arlethian armies possible as they hunted. Careful instruction as to the routes they would each take throughout the land as they made their progress were agreed upon so as to minimize the possibility of a chase-giver coming between the prey and another of his kind under the Charge, but Rembbran knew it was impossible to completely avoid. Someone being simply positioned between a Charged Helsyan and the quarry would not be enough to expand the Dahlrak to include that person unless a deliberate challenge was levied to the chase-giver or in some way his progress toward the target was hindered by another, even if that hindrance was unintentional. The entire Arlethian army would be a welcome hindrance to Rembbran and his brethren. The hope of handing out so much death in such a massive Charge left him seething with near ecstasy. The pain was not quelled but this new hope gave him strength enough to endure it for the time outside the Kail.

As instructed, Rembbran sought out the High Lord Marshal upon arrival to the war camp to deliver his message scroll. His four brothers followed. Tents and campfires stretched out almost as far as the eye could see. He heard all around the sound of steel as sparring exercises were carried out. A few tents down the line loud laughter broke out followed by a large burley man knocking out a few teeth of the one laughing. The laughs became insults as other soldiers nearby chose sides in the quarrel. A young fair-skinned, yellow-haired man eventually spied Rembbran and his company searching the camp. He wore the emblem of a Field Marshal.

"Courier?" he asked.

"Of a sort," Rembbran answered dryly.

"Very well. You may deliver your message scroll to me and I'll see it gets to High Lord Marshal Tulley. I'm the Duty Officer for the day."

"I am to hand deliver my message personally to the Lord Marshal," Rembbran snapped. "It is directly from the High Duke and will go from his hand to mine to High Lord Marshal Tulley's."

"I assure you, courier, it is quite safe in my possession." Looking over Rembbran's shoulder, the Field Marshal asked, "What message requires five escorts to—"

A low growl from beneath his hood interrupted the duty officer as Rembbran became impatient. "You will take me to the High Lord Marshal without delay, boy."

The young Field Marshal's eyes darted between the five strange men concealed behind their loose robes and decided he did not wish to see the next level of aggravation the courier was capable of, so he capitulated quickly.

"Of course. Follow me, please."

He turned to lead the way to the High Lord Marshal's tent. They approached a rather mediocre gray tent, indistinguishable from any other save for the two guards that lingered casually near the tent's opening. Rembbran realized this was all by design. The leader would make quite a compelling target for the enemy so they made sure his tent did not stand out. The two soldiers who appeared to be bored and not paying attention to anything in particular were, upon closer inspection, constantly watching and taking in their surroundings. They glanced at Rembbran and those with him, quickly looking away to give the appearance of lacking interest, but returning their glances often. He could see their minds mentally calculating and assessing. *Bodyguards,* he realized. *Impressive for mere Sentharians.*

High Lord Marshal Tulley was a humorless man of some renown in the Realm for his prowess in military strategy. Though only middle aged he was mostly bald. He had graduated at the top of his class from the Erynx Military Academy and hailed from a long line of Marshals of the Eastern Province. All his recognition, however, was based upon hypothetical situations and carefully simulated battles. The Realm had not been to war for two decades, not since the Orsarians. Small squabbles had inevitably risen throughout the years, but these were settled without much attention or concern. A few years after the war ended, he had gone to the Runic Islands where the Orsarians had landed in preparation for their invasion and studied the aftermath. The four isles were completely desolate. In a bold move, Parlan Wellyn had sent a preemptive strike force to the islands and utterly destroyed the invading force. Tulley had been in the Erynx Military Academy when the war ended, missing it by a matter of cycles. This had always bothered him.

He returned his mind to the present. The task at hand would be a severe challenge and require all his attention and knowledge. His efforts here along the northeastern Arlethian border would validate his life's study and pursuit. Knowledge and preparation would soon turn to action. He was at the head of the combined forces of Houses Orion from the Eastern Province as well as Gonfrey from the North and several minor houses. Other Lord Marshals from the East were given command of contingencies at the two fronts south of him. His current total complement numbered above eighty thousand soldiers. Surely, despite the speed and skills of wood-dwellers, they did not stand a chance against the size of his forces.

A duty officer pulled a flap of Tulley's tent back and entered, followed by a hooded figure that failed to reveal his face.

"High Lord Marshal, a courier," the duty officer announced and motioned to the concealed man behind him. "Well, five couriers, actually." The duty officer sounded concerned that the other four had remained outside the tent, out of his sight.

Tulley looked up from studying charts and maps of the surrounding area. His efforts were focused on devising a stratagem that would lure the wood-dwellers out from their defensive holds in their forest, where they seemed rooted. His gaze quickly returned to the materials spread out before him.

"I see," he replied nonchalantly. "Thank you. You are dismissed, Field Marshal."

Without word or warning, the courier threw down in front of Tulley the scroll containing the seal of the four-pointed star, the sigil of House Wellyn, forcing his attention. Tulley raised his eyes at this until his forehead wore a brace of thick ridges across it. The courier gave no reaction to the obvious look of annoyance that would cause Tulley's men to shy away, begging his pardon. The hooded man that stood before him did not beg his pardon. Finally, Tulley broke the seal and read the orders sent by the High Duke. Confusion was increasingly expressed as he read the transcript. He raised his eyes again and looked over the parchment to take in the man and noticed that his visitor was not dressed as a typical courier. No, this man was something else.

"Do you know what this scroll says?" he asked the faceless courier in disbelief.

"I do."

"So, I am to order a charge beyond the Arlethian lines, into their own forest, where they have the advantage, tonight at first moon. Simultaneously, I am to say a set of words to you that make little intelligible sense." Tulley paused. "I'm not used to being ordered into action by those who are not present, courier. This is odd, to say the least."

The man removed his hood. A shorn head with long hanging narrow ears and small ridge-like gills rippling up the ridge of his nose faced him. The colorless tattoos of ancient glyphs and symbols drew gasps and a bodyguard drew his steel amid a curse.

"As the High Lord Marshal has no doubt surmised by now, I am not a mere courier." He smiled, revealing the most feral expression the leader of the Realm's armed forces believed he had ever seen. It was sadistically inviting and revolting all at once.

"Indeed," Tulley said, his surprise poorly veiled. "So, out with it then. Who are you?"

"Do you understand the orders given to you, High Lord Marshal?"

"Understanding the words isn't the hard part. Trying to understand why we would be pressed into such a position to attack an enemy of such lethality on their own ground is slightly disconcerting, wouldn't you say? Wood-dwellers are the most deadly race in all the Realm and here you are telling me—"

"No," his visitor interrupted. "They are not the *most* deadly."

Tulley had some type of small recognition in that moment as his visitor's stare penetrated deep enough for a shudder of cold to flow through his body. He did not know who this man before him was, but he was keen enough to sense an unfeigned, genuine malevolence emanating from him. Tulley and his men were soldiers. Well trained and disciplined. This man, standing in his thick hooded robe, was not a soldier. He was a killer.

"We shall proceed as the High Duke commands," High Lord Marshal Tulley finally responded.

"That is a wise decision, Lord Marshal."

THIRTY-NINE

Prime Lord Banner Therrium

Day 29 of 1ˢᵗ Dimming 412 A.U.

THE ATTACK COMMENCED AT FIRST MOON. Scouts had reported to Lord Therrium constantly as the sun was setting that it appeared the Realm's forces were making preparations. Alrikk had confirmed that he could feel greater activity coming from the enemy's camp as well.

"Iron workers shoeing horses, probably cavalry. The sound of metal being ground against stone as well," Alrikk had reported as his palm lay flush against the Triarch in which he and Lord Therrium held watch. "Blades, axes, spears, and arrows being sharpened by the feel of it."

The enemy being camped just outside the edge of the forest made it easier for the scouts to watch them without actually revealing themselves or getting too close to the border of the trees. Without question, however, Banner thought he would happily give up that advantage in favor of the Realm's forces not being so close to their lands.

The portion of his forces that he accompanied along the northeast run of their border numbered around fifteen thousand. They were nestled among the trees roughly a quarter league behind the edge of the trees that had assumed the role as an imaginary

411

skirmish line. If either party crossed it, the other side would no doubt interpret that action as the beginning of an assault. Banner's scouts, however, were much closer to the tree line, though still out of view from the enemy's scouts. Watching, listening, feeling. Lord Therrium surmised that similar preparations and plans were coming together at the other two fronts along their border. It made sense that the enemy would launch a simultaneous attack all along their border, from the south to the north. *It's what I would do,* Banner thought.

When first moon arose, the ground started to tremble as more than eighty thousand soldiers let out a battle cry and rushed into the borders of Arlethia.

"My Lord, we must see you away from here!" Alrikk said, concern threading through his words. The Senthary were only a few hundred paces off.

"Hold," Therrium said. "Wait, be silent. Let the plan develop." Banner Therrium drew his sword.

———

I am a sturdy bough rooted deep in fertile soil. I am iron and steel, molded from the fires of adversity. I am life to those behind me, death to those in front. I am Arlethia, and she is me. I am her silent shield, her impenetrable armor, her terrible sword. She is my strength and my all. Those who stand against her stand against me, and shall swiftly fall.

General Antious Roan was roughly seventy-five feet high anchored to a tree, repeating in his mind the Arlethian Warrior's Creed. He held an unearthly silence, his breathing slow and steady.

He looked across his position and on either side, seeing thousands of his soldiers who held the same silence. The glint of their light armor in the rising moonlight was the only detectable sign of their presence to the untrained eye, but that was dulled greatly by the layers of mud with which they had swathed themselves. They were spread out over what must be a quarter-league. Some were at his same height, others higher. None lower. He would be the first into the fight. It was the way of Arlethian officers.

They were coming, the Senthary. Many of these attacking soldiers he and his army had no doubt trained over the years in various exercises and simulated battles. Back when they were still countrymen.

Roan looked down and saw below him two thousand Arlethian soldiers positioned on the ground with shields and long spears, each with a sword sheathed at his side. The ground detachment was one hundred paces west of his position, just barely deeper into their borders. The enemy approached from the east. He prayed Colonel Bohdin would execute his orders flawlessly. Any hope of victory depended on this initial feint. The man was competent and loyal, but had never served in battle. Very few here actually had, not since the Runic Islands. Most in the ranks were not old enough to have served in that short war. Roan himself was but a lieutenant at the time, serving under Lord Thannuel Kerr, newly appointed as Provincial Lord of the West.

Trust yourself, he heard Thannuel's words play in his head. A memory of coarse black sand came to his mind. Enemies on all sides, Thannuel barely conscious on his back. Roan's confidence had faltered on those dark shores and his will to fight had fled. He had given up, and somehow Thannuel, gravely injured, could feel it.

I trust you, Antious. Trust yourself. You will find a way. He did find a way; he and Thannuel miraculously survived and the Orsarian Dark Marauders were defeated. But his friend was not with him now as he was then. Roan was less certain he would find a way through this time, but the military discipline within him kept him focused.

It seems that was an entirely different age, General Roan thought.

The invading army yelled their battle cry and he heard their charge. They came at full sprint toward the Arlethian camp. The general knew High Lord Marshal Tulley. The man was not an ignoramus, but this move seemed folly to him. Perhaps Banner was right, that patience would unnerve the enemy into a foolish move that would give them the advantage. He prayed this was true.

It was not long before Senthary soldiers flooded the area below him, running past his position directly for Colonel Bohdin and his men. To the enemy, especially in the dark, it would be nearly impossible to tell the number of Arlethian soldiers that faced them. They would likely assume that the whole of their army in this area would be present as a unified body. Roan was right.

Another loud cry echoed through the forest as the Senthary were given orders to focus their attack on the force that stood in front of them. Colonel Bohdin's men answered the battle cry with one of their own, challenging the invaders. This seemed to draw in the Senthary infantry even more forcefully. The two sides collided.

Roan saw Bohdin's detachment turn into a blur of metal, flesh and blood as they responded with inhuman speed to their attackers. The wails of men began to sound forth as the Senthary began to be cut down. The speed of the wood-dwellers and their agility among the trees aided them greatly. As the vibrations of the battle swelled, they became too confusing for Roan to take in. He broke the connection with the tree he was anchored to, taking his palm away from the bark. The horde of Senthary kept piling in below him, pushing against their own forward forces and anxiously seeking an opportunity to find the foe. He estimated between seven and eight thousand were now below him. Suddenly, he saw Colonel Bohdin and his men retreat, crying out in fear as if in a rout. The Senthary army responded with increased vigor and let out a cry to pursue. General Roan smiled. After a few more moments, he judged the total count of enemies below to have swelled to more than twenty thousand.

The tumult below them covered the sound of thirteen thousand Arlethian warriors unsheathing their blades in their elevated positions. With no audible command, Roan silently dropped from his perch onto an unsuspecting target below. The man died instantly as Roan's sword pierced him behind his collarbone and continued down into his torso. His men followed. Each struck an enemy combatant, killed him, and then just as quickly and stealthily, retreated back up the trees. In less time than it took for most men to tie their boots, their enemy's numbers were reduced by thirteen thousand.

"The trees!" came a shout from a Senthary soldier. Others quickly took up the shout and looked upward just as a second aerial attack was launched. The Senthary, this time slightly better prepared, raised shields and spears straight up to block their assailants. A few managed to impale some of the downward attacking Arlethians, but again the Senthary lost many thousands before Roan and his men retreated up the trees. Most of the Senthary forces broke off from pursuing Bohdin after finding nearly a thousand score of their fellow soldiers now dead or dying within moments. They began to form a defensive posture against the aerial Arlethians when a new sound came from their forward-most soldiers. Safely out of reach from the Senthary, Roan again smiled. Bohdin ceased his feigned retreat and pressed into the fray, calling the enemy's attention back to the ground assault. The soldiers below him were confused, not knowing where to defend or where to attack. They were vacillating from upward defending stances to facing west where the cries of death and agony were coming from. Confusion was taking its hold upon the Sentharian soldiers. General Roan again released himself and sailed downward.

Removed from the epicenter of the battle, Lord Therrium sat with Alrikk, tense. He wondered aloud if he should join the battle, here on the outskirts of the fighting, but Alrikk forbade it. Though the Prime Lord of the West was a wood-dweller and therefore faster and more nimble than the army of Senthary below, his best weapon was his mind, not his skill with steel. He knew it, and knew that Alrikk knew it. The young warrior went into immediate defense mode when the battle broke out, his training taking over. He was a hold guard, the only surviving one from the attack that had started this conflict in which they were now engaged, aside from Aiden. But the former master of the hold guard had begged his leave for some purpose that remained unknown. How Lord Therrium wished Aiden were here now. When danger presented itself, a hold guard's first priority was the Prime Lord's protection, not the battle itself. A soldier, on the other hand, would advance into the fight and engage the enemy.

Banner held his sword in his left hand while his right hand was flush against the light brown bark of the Triarch upon which he sat. Alrikk gripped a small Triarch leafling against the hilt of his sword as he held it firmly. Both were listening intently through the forest for details and reports that could not be gained by auditory efforts alone. The sheer concentration it took to filter the immense amount of vibrations surging through the forest was extremely taxing. Lord Therrium rotated his focus on different areas of the conflict in order not to become overwhelmed.

"Our ground forces have re-engaged," he announced.

"I feel it as well," Alrikk said. "A new surge of soldiers is approaching from the east, reinforcements." Beads of sweat broke out on the back of Alrikk's neck as he concentrated. Therrium looked down as the reinforcements passed under them, sprinting in loose formation to the battle. The initial forces that were sent in parted and made way for this new squad of a thousand or so.

"Short archers," Therrium whispered. "A little earlier than anticipated but relatively on schedule."

"On schedule?" Alrikk asked. No sooner had he said this than the archers notched arrows to their bows, two on each string. They loosed them into the air nearly straight up. Much of the moonlight was blocked from reaching below the canopy of foliage, but the density of the trees and the wood-dwellers plunging from them made the probability of scoring a hit much greater despite lack of clear vision in the night.

Alrikk gasped in frustration as he felt hundreds of his people cry out in pain and fall to the ground from above. Still, the casualties were relatively light in comparison to the enemy's. Most of the arrows hit harmlessly against the trees and either skidded off or embedded themselves in the bark. The Arlethian forces would have sensed the arrows and reacted quickly to move out of harm's way, but losses were nonetheless inevitable. The aerial plunges by General Roan's men continued, cutting down fewer enemies than before, but the lethality of these stealth attacks still proved extremely effective. The smell of so much blood in the night air began to add a metallic scent that mingled with the smell of greenery.

"The battle is going well enough our way. They will be forced to elevate their attacks with a different approach. Prepare yourself, young Alrikk," Lord Therrium said.

"For what, my Lord?"

"Smoke and ashes."

———

High Lord Marshal Tulley, leader of the Sentharian military forces, was not a happy man. Reports from the front lines were contradictory at best, unintelligible at worst. He did not underestimate his foe and had sent in forty-five thousand men as well as two thousand archers. Well over half the Realm's forces in this part of the war effort. Appointed as High Lord Marshal for this conflict, he chose to be at this location because he knew Lord Banner Therrium would be here as well. And, of course, General Roan. He could not make one misstep in his planning or execution, but this was not his plan that he was executing. The audacity that High Duke Wellyn had displayed by giving battlefield orders and forcing his men into action was maddening, and was leading to a potential travesty. He, as High Lord Marshal, would bear the complete blame as well, should the attack fail. Adding to the stress of the situation were the enigmatic men with shorn heads standing next to him. The one who bore him the message would visibly shake from time to time and appeared to be in pain or...*was it excitement?* No normal or sane person thirsted for war and bloodshed.

"Siege engines to the front!" a Field Marshal bellowed. Twenty-seven large war machines with catapult arms set on wooden wheels were drawn slowly to the front lines by yokes of oxen. The earth broke beneath the weight of the catapults as they were slogged forward, adding to the strain on the beasts of burden. Soldiers gathered by the score behind the contraptions and pushed, slipping on the grass and mud.

An Infantry Marshal approached in sprint, nearly tripping over himself and spoke with concern. "Lord Marshal, our men are still behind enemy lines. We must pull them back first!"

"There's no time," Tulley answered. "Their aim will be high and the ordnance will have minimal effect on the ground. Casualties should be kept to a minimum."

"But—" the Infantry Marshal began but was cut off.

"You are dismissed, soldier!" Tulley snapped. The young officer saluted and sprinted back to his post.

Tulley heard a curious sound beside him and turned away from watching the droll progress of his artillery. The robe-clad man next to him was grinding his teeth violently and inhaling heavily salivated breaths. A high whine followed, which descended in pitch to a low growl. The other four men seemed not to notice, or perhaps care. Tulley backed away several steps. The man closed his eyes, inhaled slowly for several moments and seemed to regain a modicum of control.

"Burning Heavens man, are you well?" Tulley asked hesitantly.

"It is of no concern to you," came the rebuff. "The time has come."

Tulley nodded. "Perhaps it has." He retrieved the message scroll delivered to him earlier that was pinned under his belt and opened it. He raised his eyes to look over the parchment at the man and then back down again at the message.

"I don't understand this at all," Tulley said, delaying. "What will this accomplish?"

"Victory," was the only response.

"Fire!" they heard a Field Marshal command. Hatchets cut short ropes and released the arms of the coiled siege weapons, which flung large rounded projectiles of thick twigs, earth, pitch and fire. The night sky turned orange as the burning ordnance sailed overhead. It landed against the trees approximately thirty feet high. Shooting the ordnance above the height of the trees was impossible so the catapults had to be aimed through clearings as carefully as possible with the hope that the burning projectiles would penetrate deep into the forest before striking a tree and exploding. If it did not find a tree and fell to the earth, the Sentharian forces would take the punishment meant for the Arlethian soldiers. It was a risk of war. Shouts were heard calling for adjusted trajectory of the catapults.

"Victory?" Tulley asked, searching for more insight. He did not receive a response. Letting free a deep breath and raising the parchment to eye level he said, "Very well." Then, reading from the parchment, he said, "Acting as a duly appointed agent of High Duke Emeron Wellyn, he who holds the Urlenthi, the Stone of Orlack, I Charge you with Prime Lord Banner Therrium and all who stand to deter you from him."

Finished, he lowered the message and viewed the man, this strange courier that stood beside him. He and his companions threw their heads back and growled toward the sky as if beasts in human skin. Throwing off his robe revealed a thick body covered only by a loincloth. The man's body seemed to become bulkier and muscles appeared from where there had been none discernible just a moment before. All over his skin were tattoos of no color, more like scars carved into specific designs. They were symbols of some create, Tulley could discern, but of what he could not tell. The beast of a man let loose a menacing laugh through a shudder that bespoke a predatory intent. High Lord Marshal Tulley recoiled and again stepped back. The other four retained their clothing and darted off at a supernatural speed.

"No, wait," Tulley said, placing a hand on the all but naked man's shoulder just as he started to run toward the forest, restraining him. He was rewarded with a look that sent shivers through his body. "What are you?"

"I, High Lord Marshal, am a Helsyan. I share this with you because you will be able to do nothing with this knowledge." The Helsyan looked down at the hand on his shoulder that stopped his advance. "That is most unfortunate for you, I'm afraid."

———

Fire rained around General Roan and his men. It was not unexpected, but made the strategy that he and Lord Therrium had devised treacherous for his men to continue. The spheres of fire that burst against the trees were easy to spot and avoid for his wood-dwellers, but the splashes of flames and embers that exploded outward once the spheres impacted were more perilous. Dozens of his men were scorched from the constant barrage, some falling to the ground from their elevated stations, dead and smoldering. They had managed to cut down the enemy by a large number, likely near double their own numbers, but they were still outnumbered three to one. The advantage was definitely on their side despite this fact, especially as the battle was being waged in the forest. However, trees were burning and his men had begun to waver in confusion under the now constant bombardment, as their habitat in this part of Arlethia was becoming an inferno. The fires would not spread throughout the land due to the rains that were common in the Dimming Season but would no doubt burn for days before being snuffed out. However, the smoke itself, caught in the canopy not far above them, was perhaps more lethal than the fire in their current positions. No, they could not continue their attacks from above.

General Roan could either command his men to climb, through the smoke and the canopy to the trees above where fresh air would be found but flames would eventually reach, or fall to the battle below. He heard snapping and popping sounds coming from the tree where he perched and turned to see boiling sap bubbling through the tree's bark. The smell was not unlike charred bread.

"Release!" Roan commanded. Thousands of Arlethian soldiers let themselves fall through the smoky air to the field of carnage below them.

"Press through!" he yelled. "Rally toward Bohdin!" He had dropped with his men into the center of a confused Sentharian battalion and did not hesitate in his attacks. While fighting his way westward, cutting down those in his path, a smear of burning pitch fell on his left shoulder from above and clung to his armor. The metal blackened from the burning slime and the fire itself, but General Roan paid it no mind. He saw others, both Senthary and Arlethian, screaming and running while being consumed in robes of orange and yellow. He wondered at the ruthlessness of the Sentharian commanders, to use weaponry against an enemy that would punish their own soldiers at the same time. The brutality of it surprised him, but he realized it should not have, not after what the High Duke had done in betraying his own subjects when he attacked Therrium's hold.

Girded in flaming armor, he turned to face four soldiers, a spearman, two axemen and one with a sword. They flinched at seeing Roan and took a step back.

They are so young, he thought. It was part of war. The young died, the old mourned. Fear swept across the soldiers' faces as they huddled together in a defensive posture.

What are they doing? he wondered. *Why aren't they attacking?* The small group took another step back. Perhaps the reality of battle had seized them, the terror of it not allowing them to do anything but cower. Something caught in the middle-aged general as he faced them. Pity? Mercy? Weakness? Whatever it was, he was about to admonish them to flee when two of his men overcame them from behind and cut them down before any of the Sentharians could register what was happening. It was efficient and lethal, and the two Arlethian warriors were on to their next prey before many moments could be counted.

They were just boys, not much older than I was in my first battle, just following orders, Roan thought. *Just as my men are following orders. My orders.* He stared at the dead Sentharian soldiers, at their lethal wounds, and felt a tightening in his chest. The old wound that had nearly ended him on his right breast radiated pain.

It did end me, actually, he reminded himself. Thannuel would not be here to steal him back from Death's grasp this time. They had each saved each other of the black sands of Pearl Island during the final days of the Orsarian War.

The metal of his armor had heated to a point that started to burn his upper back and singe his hair. He released the light armor plating that protected his torso and backside and it fell to the forest floor. Pine needles and dead leaves from the season began to catch fire under the armor before quickly dying out, causing more smoke than flame.

General Roan was motionless for a few brief moments in the middle of battle before coming to himself again. His men needed him, needed his direction. They were still vastly outnumbered and caught in a most dangerous circumstance. He suppressed his inhibitions and resumed his attacks, pressing ever westward. Hordes of Senthary were still pouring in from the east, appearing to be an ocean of swords, spears, and axes. And then a thought occurred to him, an idea of distraction—or making use of the current battle as a distraction.

He grabbed a young wood-dweller with a lieutenant's insignia on his breastplate, heavily swathed in carnage. He had a gash across his left cheek that had barely missed his eye.

Fherva, Roan remembered, the same who had shown him and Lord Therrium that profane stone road that had lead into Hold Therrium. It seemed a different age, that first battle of this war where only Master Aiden and Alrikk had survived, protecting Therrium. Roan briefly wondered where Therrium was in this chaos, praying Alrikk had removed the prime lord far from the battle.

"Lieutenant!"

Fherva stopped. "Yes, General!"

The clamor of steel, wood, shouts, and screams made vocal communication almost impossible. Roan grabbed Fherva by the shoulder and brought his mouth to his ear.

"Get word to Colonel Bohdin that he is in charge," he shouted, pointing a hundred yards west. "There is an advantage I intend to press. He must hold until I return. It will mean our victory if I succeed."

"It will be done, General!" Fherva nodded with a smile, a gesture so out of place for the scene around them. Roan saw confidence in Fherva's action, confidence not in himself but in his general. Roan prayed it was not misplaced.

He broke from the battle in speed, cutting down a few in his way but otherwise avoiding the conflict. General Roan headed decisively south, away from the battle.

———

Prime Lord Banner Therrium did not enjoy seeing the slaughter of men, Arlethian or Senthary. He and Alrikk watched the battle unfold from their position, now somewhat removed from the main area of the fight. The epicenter of the struggle had shifted many times but was now moving farther west, farther inland into Arlethia. Before long, the fight might breach cities and towns if the flames didn't make it to them first. There would no doubt be evacuations occurring rapidly even now. Plans had been made and warnings sounded to all population centers that could be affected by the inevitable fray. He prayed that those left in charge would be able to discharge their duties effectively and save the lives of his people to the greatest extent possible. Not for the first time in these recent days did he wonder what Thannuel would have done. *Have I been rash? Foolish? Careless?* No time for those thoughts could be spared.

Alrikk's look of ambivalence was too much to hide. "You are wondering how we can just sit here and not join in the battle," Therrium said. It was not a question.

"Yes," Alrikk replied. "But my first duty is to protect you. I wish you would allow me to see you away from this danger before it's too late." A war horn sounded in the distance.

"Have faith, Alrikk. Our forces are strong and the plan is sound. Already a third of their army is decimated and neutralized."

"What about the other fronts?"

Therrium looked uncertain. "We must remain confident and focused here. Trust in the plan."

"We haven't received any reports or messages. You were supposed to get word by wing frequently once the fighting began," Alrikk reminded the Prime Lord.

Again, Therrium looked uncertain. "The smoke, that has to be the reason a pigeon or crow cannot get through. Not even a falcon could brave this smoke."

"Then why not a courier, sprinting across the treetops, my Lord?" Alrikk pressed. "Please, let me get you to a safer location. Something is wrong, I know it. Your survival is paramount."

Banner Therrium trusted Alrikk, though he was young, and feared he was right. It was a small trickle of apprehension that ran through him and started to well into a larger pool of fear. He was afraid it would run over if he did not maintain control. The lad had been the only survivor along with Master Aiden in first battle of this war and had experienced a connection with the forest that he doubted anyone else living could boast or describe.

Banner had seen the aftermath of the skirmish. Thousands dead and strewn across the grounds of his once beautiful hold; a portion of the eastern wall obliterated; and beyond that destruction a stone road that extended for untold leagues, flanked by stone statues that were once living trees. Even the soil had been petrified, becoming the road itself. A Dark Influence had no doubt been the cause of such evil, and Wellyn obviously had control of it. If he deployed its use here, the results would be drastic and cause massive panic amongst the Arlethian forces.

Alrikk still shuddered from the experience of speaking with the forest when it first had happened. He was shattered inside, though slowly healing from the experience. The lad would surely fracture beyond hope if he experienced it again while connected to the trees.

"Yes," Prime Lord Therrium said.

"Yes?" Alrikk repeated.

"Let us retreat away from the immediate confrontation. You are right, Alrikk."

The young guard looked visibly relieved. A giant fireball crashed not two trees from them, sending embers and red-hot sparks in all directions, igniting branches and frondescence all around them.

"Quickly!" Alrikk commanded.

———————

They bounded down to the forest floor, thinking the danger among enemy soldiers to be less than the danger of ever-increasing fire above. Their goal was not to engage the Sentharian army, but to outrun it. They sprinted about half a league north, dodging any who stood in their way and refusing to fight unless it was absolutely necessary. A eucalyptus tree exploded from the flames just ahead of them and sent wooden shards into Alrikk's face. He reacted and covered Prime Lord Therrium with his own body as they fell to the forest floor from the concussion. The debris landed all around them, not discriminating between Arlethian and Senthary. Cries of horror were cut short as soldiers were crushed. With ringing still sounding in his ears, Alrikk stood up and raised Banner to his feet.

"Are you hurt?" Though he yelled, he could not hear his own voice. Therrium looked bewildered.

Alrikk shook him. "Lord Therrium, are you okay?"

Therrium nodded. He said something but the ringing in his ears was still loud. Deafening. The sound of another explosion cut through the sound of the bell tower in Alrikk's ears as another Eucalyptus tree succumbed to the fires. Therrium reached up and gently touched Alrikk's face where dozens of splinters were lodged. The tips of his fingers came away wet with blood.

"It's nothing to be concerned with, my Lord, I'm fine!" His hearing was returning.

"The blue gum trees," Banner said. "They are exploding."

Despite the stress and tension of the moment, Alrikk couldn't help himself. "I hadn't noticed, my Lord." Banner cracked a slight smile.

"Incoming!" Alrikk screamed as he felt the approach of Senthary to their position. He and Therrium spun around so they were back to back. More than a dozen soldiers approached them, screaming and hollering with swords and axes upraised. The wood-dwellers sprang into action, parrying attacks and countering. Alrikk cut through a man's arm as it came down upon him. After dispatching the soldier, he quickly picked up the dead man's sword and wielded it along with his own. The urgency of his oath fueled his lethality as he defended the Prime Lord with all his skills and abilities. After taking down nine men one by one, he found himself without an immediate opponent. He turned to Therrium and saw four dead soldiers at his feet and the Prime Lord breathing heavily. Alrikk didn't try to mask his look of surprise.

"What?" Therrium asked. "I'm a little old but still a wood-dweller, aren't I? It will take more than a few Senthary to bring me down."

They resumed their flight northward, avoiding all conflicts where possible. The sounds of the battle were more distant now, but the smoke and flames were still easily visible in the night sky.

"This is likely far enough—" Alrikk didn't finish his pronouncement. Banner went stiff, listening.

It sounded almost like a horse through the ground. The vibrations felt heavy and were easily discernible from the battle. They were, in fact, moving away from the battle...and toward them.

"Is it cavalry?" Banner asked. "We were followed?"

"A single horse?" Alrikk whispered. "Not likely, and it's—" Alrikk again cut off before continuing. "It's too fast for a horse and the gait is wrong."

"It is, however, heading directly for us," Therrium said. The trickle of apprehension turned to a thicker stream of fear. He realized finally what pursued them.

"It is a Helsyan," he announced.

"What kind of beast is that?" Alrikk asked, drawing his sword.

"The kind that has only one master and is impossible to stop." Therrium shuddered. "It is what Aiden slew at my hold, though it nearly killed him."

"So, it's not impossible, then," Alrikk said with grim determination. "Run, my Lord. I will deal with the demon."

"It will take us both, lad, if we are to survive." Banner also drew his sword. No sooner had he done so than they caught sight of the Helsyan approaching at speeds only wood-dwellers were believed to possess. The sheer sight of this creature was enough to cripple a person with fear. His body appeared chiseled from stone with runes and glyphs of some create covering every visible piece of flesh.

"What covers his body? Is it a sort of armor?" Alrikk asked, squinting in the moonlight.

"No," Therrium replied. "It is his flesh. A type of cicatrix in appearance. All Helsyans are born with the same markings except for a slight variation on the withers, but none know of their meaning."

"What kind of mother could rear such a creature?" Alrikk muttered.

"None that live. So little is known about their race."

"Tonight we will find out how they die." Alrikk took a step forward and placed himself in front of his Lord, his two swords at the ready. His voice had a slight tremor, though it was masked well. Therrium reached one hand up to Alrikk's shoulder.

"I am fortunate to have you here by my side, lad." He felt Alrikk shake beneath his hand as the Helsyan came closer. The man was massive in size and covered in carnage. "Greatness is not had because of great ability, but rather because brave men stand in the face of fear and cause it to shrink from their presence. Be firm, son. Let us not be blinded by the fear but forge through it."

———

General Roan broke free from the battle and was now almost a quarter-league south of the scene. Though the smoke and fire had not spread to this portion of the forest, the heat was still slightly discernible. The forest can protect wood-dwellers from many things, but fire is the one enemy that threatens the forest beyond all.

Perhaps not above all, Roan thought as he remembered gray and dead trees.

He turned east and tore through the forest at speed until he reached the edge of the tree line. There, he spied the tail end of the enemy's camp. It ran from south to north in a crescent that cradled the forest for half a league. Roan had never seen such a gathering. White and gray tents stretched almost beyond his sight in the light of first moon. The bright whitish blue orb hung low against the northwestern horizon. Second moon would rise before long over the southwest. Smoldering fire pits with pots hanging over on sticks and logs ornamented the campsite with several hundred soldiers, mostly marshals of some kind, Roan guessed. Their attention was fixated to the west, where screams, smoke, and fire permeated the air.

As he slowly emerged from the tree line, he noticed three field marshals arguing and gesturing at the ground. No, not at the ground, to someone on the ground. He approached silently and crouched through grass that was the chest high until he could hear their words. Blame, anger and threats were being slung back and forth. One of them claimed command based on his family's station, another based on experience. The third was wondering if they shouldn't hurry and tell the other leaders. *This is most curious,* Roan thought. He crept closer and risked a hasty glance toward what lay at the men's feet and was surprised to see High Lord Marshal Tulley, or what was left of him. He lay in a heap of his own carnage, his throat savagely freed from his body along with his entire lower jaw. The left side of torso appeared cratered, depressed, as if a comet the size of a man's fist had fallen from the skies and lodged itself therein.

Had these three plotted against the Lord Marshal to usurp command? But why? To what end? Aside from their arguing, there was the tenor of surprise and fear in their timbre. No, this was not the work of men, Senthary or Arlethian. This was beastly savagery.

Roan should have been pleased to see their enemy's supreme commander slain, but he felt no such emotion. He would have no doubt killed the man if he had the opportunity, but the manner in which this soldier had met his end was troubling to an extent that Roan nearly forgot his self-assigned mission. He would not have a better opportunity to dispatch three field marshals and create potentially more division amongst the ranks of the enemy force. He rose from his concealment and advanced with terrible velocity.

———

The two wood-dwellers stood before Rembbran. A young man, ashen from fear; Banner Therrium to the side and behind the younger man. Both had their weapons drawn. Rembbran over-flowed with exuberance and anticipation. The blood from the High Lord Marshal was still wet on his hands, though cooled a bit from the warm temperature it had been when it flowed freely from his body. It was a blessing to begin this chase with an immediate kill. He had ended the weak man with his bare hands, crushing and tearing him.

What bliss he felt when Charged! Demonically euphoric. He reveled in it. The hope was also there, that strange emotion so for-eign to his composition. Would slaying a relative of escaped prey bring him closure to his failed Dahlrak? He doubted it, but perhaps more lasting relief than was otherwise possible from an unrelated

Charge. That was the belief of his kind, though untested. He would test it thoroughly tonight. Yes, he would put Agony in its place and serve it less from now on. The fear that emanated from both these wood-dwellers was such strong aroma. Salty. Savory. Like the smell of salt water in the air mingled with rust. He drooled thick saliva as he faced his prey.

"Feeble fear is more succulent, refined," Rembbran said, looking at Therrium. Then he turned to the younger man, a guard of some kind. "Not as raw as young fear. They both will do, however. I thank you." His voice was deeper than most growls, unnatural but devilishly fantastic. "Steady, Alrikk," he heard Therrium whisper.

"We do not fear you!" the younger man, Alrikk it was, snapped. He held two swords between them.

The chase-giver made a show of taking in a deep breath through his nose, flaring the gill-like slits that ran up the bridge of his nose and exhaling with shudders of ecstasy. A knowing smile manifested itself on Rembbran's face.

"Ah, the naiveté of youth." Alrikk was not a boy, but compared to a Helsyan that could live with vigor beyond a century, most human races were short-lived by comparison. This guard seemed no more than a youngling holding a toy in his hands.

"Your kind has fallen before to one of my warriors. And recently at that," Therrium reminded him.

Before Rembbran could respond, Alrikk strode forward and attacked. The chase-giver parried but Therrium was right behind his young guard, not withholding from the fight. The forest was thinner in the northern parts where they now battled. Trees were still ubiquitous, but less so, giving more room for the contest to develop. As the sound of steel against steel trumpeted forth, Rembbran found his rhythm in the fray and began to drive them backward. Fast as they were, he was able to dodge and counter every blow levied against him, forcing both of his targets to defend rather than attack. It was a scene of majesty, he thought. What it would be to witness a Helsyan in full thrust against two Arlethians at once, driving them both mentally and physically into defeat. His self-glory emanated from him as he gained more and more momentum, forcing his prey to become more desperate. He could smell it, the fear and anxiety that were building before erupting into acceptance of defeat, acceptance of his dominance over them.

The guard skirted around Rembbran, narrowly escaping his latest volley of blurred steel. Lord Therrium attempted to feint forward and draw his attention, but Rembbran did not bite. He knew Alrikk was behind him now and would attempt to run him through. He raised his arms with his sword above his head and lunged backward as he knelt down to one knee. The point of his sword behind him pierced something, the sound of it like a sack of wet leaves. And then, he knew. The scent of warm blood in the air intermingled with the fear. With a mighty overhead thrust, he launched Alrikk's impaled body thirty paces through the air until it collided with a gnarled old oak. The body lay motionless, shattered. Immediately, more strength and ferocity filled the chase-giver as one more prey fell in fulfillment of his Dahlrak. Now came time for the end of it, for its climax, as he would dispatch the ultimate point of the Charge.

As Banner Therrium looked at Alrikk, Rembbran smelled the regret and sorrow from the Prime Lord.

"It is interesting," Rembbran said, "that you do not feel rage after seeing one you obviously cared for now in death's embrace."

Banner collected himself. "I feel regret for his loss of life, but know that he stood strong despite his fear."

"And the sorrow—"

"The sorrow is not for him, but for you. And pity. How terrible it must be to live your life on a leash, not able to make an existence for yourself, always waiting for the next command to bring some semblance of life." Banner actually managed a sad smile that came across as more than a little condescending.

The Helsyan flared his nostrils and did indeed detect pity. He became incensed. "How is it that you pity me or my kind? We are to be envied! Feared! Loathed! But not pitied!"

"I find pity for all slaves," Therrium replied. "I may fall today, but I will die free. You will return to a master and await his next bidding. And our people, we have always triumphed and we ever shall. Your treacherous Duke has made a grave error in supposing me to be an important figure to our people or that they will fall because I do not lead them. Arlethia has always been greater than a single man, slave."

Therrium had the demeanor of a father when he spoke. It was obvious to the chase-giver this man was secure in his place within the world and with who he was. Such innate peace was foreign to Helsyans as they saw themselves as alien to life in general, though they longed for peace and understanding, to know their place in the world.

Rembbran screamed in defiance and anger. "You know, Prime Lord, I have never consumed one of my prey. It hasn't been practiced since the Ancients ruled us, I am told. But for you, I am willing to make an exception."

———

Banner backed away and stumbled slightly, finding hold on a tree. Reaching his hand around his back, he made a connection against the bark. He felt peaceful as he listened and took in the sounds of the forest, its grandeur and venerable serenity. Calm was spoken to his soul. Despite trees burning south of them and filling the night with smoke and embers, they did not seem to notice or mind. The roots would likely live and grow anew, stronger. Banner felt that the trees somehow understood this and accepted it as necessary from time to time. He looked up and saw the Helsyan, this chase-giver, saying something. His words, however, were completely inaudible to him as he prepared himself to join the forest eternally.

But then his peace was shattered. The sound that reverberated through his skull—where did it come from? He wasn't hearing it with his ears, he realized. He opened his mouth so wide he couldn't breathe in response and clenched his eyes. They watered from the pressure. He blinked rapidly trying to clear his vision and saw his assassin looking down at him with curious amusement. Therrium's hand gripped the bark of the tree he had connected to with such strength that the bark started to break free under his grip. The palm of his hand began to feel hot, to burn almost. Was this just in his mind? The sound was high pitched and thunderous all at the same time. The fright this caused in him was unbearable, fear beyond what should be possible for anyone to feel and yet live.

"The trees!" he gasped in a desperate voice. "They scream!" And then, silence. Nothing remained, no sound that he could discern. He tried but failed to reconnect with the forest, with the tree he rested against. His eyes opened wearily and it felt like sand filled them as he looked around, scraping the undersides of his eyelids. Indecipherable blurry images spun. He had slumped down in his forced anguish and the chase-giver towered over him, but this seemed like a small thing to him in this moment. He tried again to reconnect, opening his hand wider in an effort to expand his palm and hopefully make another connection. It was cold, the bark of this tree. Rough and hard.

The horror struck him. Banner Therrium raised himself up and turned to the tree. An elm of considerable size, certainly full and beautiful in life, confronted him. It was not beautiful now. He stepped back one pace and looked up to see branches that were off from their natural color. White. Gray. Still, despite a breeze. Dead. Turning his head, he saw this forest had become a garden of stone. It was too much to accept, too much for any wood-dweller to view. Banner could not contain his terror and began to moan like a child in ineffable pain. How could Alrikk have ever recovered from such a visceral experience? Being connected to the forest as it dies? Therrium did not know, but he did know the horror of it now. Looking down again to the trunk he saw wetness, a dark fluid that glistened crimson.

He had not felt the sting of the chase-giver's steel enter him in his state of marveling. He coughed blood and felt weak suddenly. The horizon turned vertical for Prime Lord Banner Therrium as he collapsed.

FORTY

General Roan

Day 30 of 1st Dimming 412 A.U.

GENERAL ANTIOUS ROAN TORE THROUGH the enemy camps like a vengeful ghost, a maelstrom of steel and speed, moving from one enemy to the next faster than their blood could fall to the earth. *I am a sturdy bough rooted deep in fertile soil.* His armor had been shed in the forest, searing hot from the flaming pitch with which he had been splashed. Mud and blood were his armor now. *I am iron and steel, molded from the fires of adversity. I am life to those behind me, death to those in front.* Flesh tore and blood stained his sword. *I am Arlethia, and she is me. I am her silent shield, her impenetrable armor, her terrible sword.* The ground quickly became soaked and stained crimson as men around him were returned to the earth. *She is my strength and my all. Those who stand against her stand against me, and shall swiftly fall.* The orange glow from the burning forest west of the enemy's lines imitated the arrival of dawn, as if the sun were rising on the opposite side of the world.

Why not? Roan thought. *All else in the world is skewed, so why not the sun?*

Few of the enemy soldiers had any warning of his approach before their lives were dispatched, their focus being on the battle and blaze in the forest. Here, just behind the enemy's lines, few

FORTY

General Roan

Day 30 of 1st Dimming 412 A.U.

had been held in reserve. Field and infantry marshals along with their staffs as well as those required to operate the siege weapons. Antious Roan did not discriminate as he dealt out his lethal aggression. After few brief moments, several catapults were left unoccupied save for the corpses that lay motionless around them.

As he worked his way northward, up the enemy's line, some of the enemy soldiers noticed the cessation of ordnance from most of the siege weapons. Seeing their fellow soldiers dead on the ground, they shouted forth warnings of something being awry. It was not long after that Roan was spotted cutting down yet another group. Knowing his time as an invisible force was now over, Roan sped as fast as his mortal frame would allow him to move, darting from the enemy's view faster than they could follow in the dim light. He hunkered down beneath the top of a tall grass field and waited. The smell of smoke was thick in the air, and even from this distance he could feel the heat coming from the blaze in his forest. General Roan dug his fingers into the soil, below the grass roots, and listened. Felt. Without the aid of a speaking tree or the massive intertwined root systems of the forests of Arlethia, the vibrations were more difficult to discern. Amplifying the burden were scores of thousands of men locked in the chaos of battle. Nonetheless, Roan persisted.

Anxiety was difficult to force down as the battle unfolded in rough visions within his mind. He felt and therefore pictured several enemy soldiers tentatively looking for him. Their footsteps were slow and nervous, headed in the wrong direction. He ignored them and flushed that image from his mind. Tapping other segments of vibrations, he brought to the forefront of his mind's eye the scene of the forest. It was convoluted and chaotic, but he knew he was getting a better understanding of the scene than was possible with eyes alone as the smoke would have obstructed much of his visual perception. In the images created from the vibrations, smoke and ashes could not mar the view of the observer. It was obvious to him that his men were fighting valiantly against overwhelming odds. The disorganization of Tulley's men aided his own soldiers' efforts. He tried to single out Colonel Bohdin from amongst the thousands of seismic indicators he was feeling, but this proved too great a task without the aid of the forest directly.

Suddenly, Roan caught hold of a new vibration: heavy and swift footfall penetrating through the fray like an avalanche of terror. The strides were longer and faster than mere humans could achieve and heavier than any wood-dweller would produce, commanding his attention as the other vibrations faded to the background. They were emanating from within the Arlethian borders, within the forest. *How could only five people produce such force?*

The confrontation changed *dramatically* and the General felt his soldiers' posture and cadence change, becoming more frantic and hurried. They were...retreating. He felt his forces less and less as the moments flew by, their signals and vibrations becoming a thinner portion of the overall cacophony. And then something frightful happened.

His connection through the ground was severed. No, not completely severed, but dampened to a degree that he could no longer discern anything. The vision in his mind blurred and diminished until it was a marred collage of dark, muted images. It was like becoming deaf and blind suddenly in mid-conversation. General Roan felt a bulge catch in his throat. Though severely attenuated, vibrations still issued forth from the forest, but they were strange. Sharper, blunter. More staccato-like, less rich. And then, it ceased. The rhythm and quick-stepped movements halted. There was only one reason the enemy would have ceased. Then confirmation came of his dread. A cry of victory rose from the forest that he knew was not from his men. He opened his eyes and raised himself enough to peer over the top of the high grass he hid beneath.

For interminable moments, Antious had no thoughts. His mind was wiped from any semblance of coherency. Staring back at him were not the beloved trees of his homeland, not the thick frondescence of his native dwelling. The fires had been miraculously extinguished. Unnaturally quenched. Stone, after all, does not burn.

Fallen! We are fallen! the veteran wanted to scream. His soul struggled to contain the anguish. What was he to do? Where should he go? Arlethia lay unprotected and damningly molested with her enemies uncontested. Thoughts of his family jolted to the front of his mind. The General was able to sequester his personal circumstances while engaged in his duty very well, but they still made their way through the widening mental fissures caused by what he now beheld.

Our borders are breached, our great army fallen! He counseled with himself as to his next move. Perhaps he should continue his raids, taking as many of the enemy down before falling himself or collapsing with exhaustion. Or should he charge the enemy host now celebrating in the forest? *My forest.* He felt no connection with the stone trees, though, only nostalgia.

Wisely, General Roan retreated. He was physically ill as he thought about how his men had met their end. "I should have been there!" he regretted aloud. What of Therrium? What of Arlethia? What would happen now? He did not know, but he resolved to continue his overarching mission: to defend Arlethia from all who would threaten her. His tactics would have to change now, but he would continue. More patience would be required, more strategy. Until he fell and joined his brave men, as far as Roan was concerned, his orders were still in effect.

FORTY-ONE

Rembbran

Day 30 of 1ˢᵗ Dimming 412 A.U.

TAKING IN THE ELATION from his Dahlrak's completion, Rembbran tried to remember when he had felt such blessedness. He was aroused to a state so elevated that he lost hold of his identity, forgetting even his name momentarily. His body shivered uncontrollably from the rapture. The pain was completely ineffectual inside him for these moments. He waited. It did not return. Had Agony left completely? Slowly, he probed through his mental field and found that it was indeed there but failed to regain its hold on him. Rembbran had never felt such...happiness? Had the strange emotion of hope turned to glee within him? Was this possible?

The moment of climax passed and still the pain of years past did not find purchase within him. *The wound still present but no longer festering.* Had the wound finally closed and sealed?

No. It ripped open suddenly, tearing his mind in two with a vehemence that he had never felt. He squirmed on the ground, frantically clawing at his head and body, not knowing where the attack came from. His lucidness turned to darkness as Agony regained its position as master and punished its subject mercilessly.

"Why?" Rembbran screamed as he thrashed about against the stone soil, scraping and cutting his skin. "Why?" Drool and mucus ran down his face and purple veins bulged over his shorn head. He was grunting and snarling like a mortally wounded animal but unable to die and find relief in death. And then he did something he thought he would never do, something forbidden his kind by all those who had possessed the Urlenthi. He prayed.

"Ancient Darkness, Mother of Helsya, I beseech you to turn away this suffering from me. For millennia untold we have suffered subjection and outcast for our apostasy, and I surely greatest of all. Bless me, I pray, and I will rediscover and reclaim Helsya for the Ancient Dark, wherever the sacred land has been hidden; lead me thereto that we may rise again as rulers as we once were; that our women would once again live to raise our children. Dark Mother, I have never sought you, but I beg you to hear me now and relieve my suffering that I might serve you. If not, in mercy or wrath, let me die."

The Agony did not abate. Rembbran continued to wail and moan violently for several more minutes, each a personal eternity to him. This pain was deeper, pouring through him without end. He convulsed with spasmodic jolts on the ground, knocking into Therrium's corpse.

"Then I curse you! I defy you! Helsya will remain forever lost and unclaimed for the Ancient Dark and I—"

He stopped suddenly. Was that possible? He sensed—no, smelled it, didn't he? He was breathing heavily, still tense but then realized the pain had subsided. It had fled from him, the absence of it a completely foreign feeling, almost a floating sensation. He regained some of his control and took in the scents around him more fully. He flared his nostrils and the gill-like slits that ran up the ridge of his nose. It was there. *She* was there. *Impossible!*

He dared not believe it, not for joy's sake. Involuntarily, his gaze was drawn north. He saw nothing, but could nonetheless scry the exact vector from whence the scent exuded. She was older now, of course, but still young. Tears of sadistic exhilaration could not be stayed as laughter escaped from deep in his core. It rang forth in the emptiness of night, echoing off the stone trees that surrounded him, augmenting the volume of his maniacal, cackling howls.

She is alive! And so close! Though the pain had abated for now, the draw to this familiar scent demanded his assiduity without relenting. He was only too happy to comply. *So close.*

He judged her location to be in the northern part of the Gonfrey Forest. He had searched nearly the entire Realm thrice over, including the North. His venturing was often truncated by the intolerable need to return to the Kail for even the slightest relief or to seek a new Charge from the High Duke. It was possible, though highly improbable, that she could have avoided his movements throughout the Realm. Some other explanation had to be the reason. But what that could be, he did not know. And Rembbran did not care. He had her now.

"Ancient Darkness, Dark Mother, I give all that I am to you and Helsya. Free me."

Rembbran did not know what to expect next, but it was certainly not what happened. The scarred glyphs on his back between his shoulder blades, at the withers, glowed red-hot. He knelt from the searing pain and clenched his teeth but did not cry out. As it continued, his mind was flooded with information. Revelations. History. Scenes of the past. A group of people living on this land that he knew was long ago, far from now. They spoke a different language but in his mind he understood it; and, in his mind, he knew them to be *his* people, the way they were thousands of years before. There were no scars, no markings that covered their bodies. They were a delightful race, full of life. As his vision showed him the expanse of this land that was now called Senthara, he beheld that his people filled it completely. There were no other races, no Arlethians, no Senthary, no Hardacheons or any other race except his people. Helsyans.

Is it possible? he thought. *This very land is Helsya? This must have been before even the Ancients ruled, before—*

His ponderings were cut short as the truth came surging into his heart. His mind could not believe what his heart now told him.

How is that possible? It has all been a lie, all deception! The Ancients had not disappeared as all believed, only the way they once were, the way they lived and looked, had vanished. Rembbran looked down at his hands and forearms, turning them over. *How have we fallen so far?*

The sights before his mind's eye progressed until he witnessed the fall of his people, the Turning Away, as described to him by a voice. Only then did he recognize he was indeed hearing a voice, a narration. He scanned around him with haste but saw no one, just panoramic views of his vision. The scene of his people was horrific to witness, but he could not turn away. Generations passed as he witnessed a growing number of the population become wilder in nature, less refined. Racing before his mind were visions of different people rising up as leaders among them, teaching against the old ways.

One rose above them all, a woman of beauty so exquisite that even Rembbran, a Helsyan, felt such attraction to her. Helsyans did not have the same sensual attraction to beings that other races naturally had. The urge to reproduce had been severely dampened through the ages, brought on by self-loathing and a knowledge of what became of the mother. They had always been a doomed race, according to the legends.

Not always, Rembbran now saw. The attraction to this prophetess had the same pull and strength of a Dahlrak, but with different desires. Her beauty was radiant, infectious, but not with light. Indeed, as he saw her speak and go about her thronging disciples, light seemed to dissipate, leaving a luminescent darkness around her. Over time it became a visual effect that caused her to appear ghostly. Rembbran witnessed the effect increase as her influence was more broadly accepted. The image of the woman stopped and turned to look at Rembbran, as if he were present among the crowds of his vision. So penetrating was her stare that he took a step back, startled.

"Do you know me?" she asked. Her voice had the timbre of wind howling through an open expanse. Musical.

Rembbran did not answer, thinking himself foolish to being spoken to by what was surely a dream of some kind.

"You do know me," she said, not deterring her stare.

"I—" he started but could not seem to make his tongue work properly. A melody accompanied the vision. Haunting. Captivating. She smiled and lowered her head slightly but still stared at Rembbran. More penetrating, more devious. He found his heart racing from both sensual excitement as well as apprehension. Could it be a Helsyan was feeling the seeds of fear?

Noxmyra! he screamed in his mind. The woman's tight smile broadened, taking on a more wicked and feral shape. She laughed with dark harmony and the ground under her, green grass and fertile soil, turned dark and hard. Rembbran was in a trance. He had never felt so alive as he watched the Dark's Influence bring decay and entropy. The people who worshipped Noxmyra became strong and powerful. Ferocious without restraint.

The vision swept on before him and Noxmyra disappeared from his sight but strands of the strange song remained. Under her teachings, the people became more decadent as the years passed and the land started to change.

Cycling, Rembbran realized.

A faction separated themselves from the largely apostate masses and refused to relinquish the old ways—the ways of the Ancients—but they were overwhelmed and about to be destroyed completely when he saw a change come upon the most devout followers of Noxmyra. A rival people rose in the land and warred against his people. They were larger, fiercer. *Hardacheons.* Rembbran had never seen them before, having been born long after their extinction, but he knew they were Hardacheons all the same.

From the north they covered the land like ghosts, carrying with them powers and Influences that enslaved his people, changed them. Their skin became riddled with scars and symbols, marring their once pure visage. And their strength, though still present, was now tempered by a power of some create. Their women became barren and their men were forced to breed with slaves the conquerors had brought with them, but the men could not produce seed to create more women. Only boys were born and the women slaves that bore the Helsyan offspring perished in the effort. The male babies were born with the same marred cicatrix over their skin that their fathers bore. The Hardacheons brought these curses with them, but deep inside Rembbran knew it was his own people that had cursed themselves. The consequences of the Turning Away. The Light they had once served turned against them, limiting them by degrees that prevented their outright dominance.

A haunting laugh surrounded him and he could watch no more. Grabbing his head between his hands he shook it from side to side, trying to dislodge the hellish vision from him.

"No more!" The pain on his back was searing and the reddish light that shone from his one unique glyph illuminated his immediate surroundings. Darker than the light of fire, it was nonetheless visible and radiant. Near the apex of his physical capacity to deal with the acute pain, which capacity was substantial, Rembbran heard a word spoken. His name. Not in Sentharian, but in an ancient tongue that he instantly had command over. *Dralghus. I am Dralghus.*

Energy and adrenaline rushed through him, supporting him against the pain, against the transfiguration taking place. The glyph at his withers burned brighter, the dark red glow increasing in intensity to a whitish yellow luminescence. Tissues and muscles were singed and fused from the heat and arteries erupted as his blood boiled, forging a new landscape within him. The pain was no longer punishing, but abstergent. Fortifying. *It is my name,* he realized, referring to the unique symbol on his back. *A name glyph.* No, more than just a name. *My identity.*

When it was done, he arose. Vapors steamed all around him, the stone earth black and charred beneath him. It had fissured from the heat. He stood more firm and taller than he thought he ever had before. He felt lighter, more nimble. More lethal, if that was possible. Free. Though he labored under no Dahlrak, his body remained in its Charged state. His muscles were cut and thick, senses heightened, his drive for carnage an unquenchable thirst. He would be the Ancient Dark's instrument in cleansing the land and reclaiming Helsya.

"I now serve the Ancient Dark, Mother of Helsya," he proclaimed. "The Urlenthi's claim on me is broken. I shall now set my own Dahlraks and keep my own counsel. The Ancient Darkness is a kind master."

The Kerr youngling girl he now saw as an inevitability. He would not seek her at this instant, however. No, for the power of the Ancient Dark and the shackles of the Urlenthi loosed, the agony of the unfulfilled Dahlrak from a previous master held no sway. He looked internally and sought his other former master, the one that had tormented him relentlessly without release or leniency. He felt for Agony and found her squirming to conceal herself in the deep recesses of his mind, fleeing in fear.

It was as if he were a majestic and terrible eagle tracking a field mouse running scared in a valley far below. He swooped down in his mind and caught Agony in his talons, crushing and piercing her. Breaking her. She squealed and he rejoiced at the feeling of hot blood flowing between his claws in his mind. A tight feral smile of satisfaction formed on his face. It was done and the agony inside him was dead. *She* was dead. A more euphoric pleasure waded through the currents of his being than he had ever before experienced. A Dahlrak's ecstasy paled in comparison to this new height within him.

He would still visit young Reign Kerr as he thought it only appropriate after such unrelenting torture that she had caused him over the past six years. Besides, it would be fun, if nothing else. But first, Dralghus thought it best to visit the Kail and the holder of the Stone of Orlack to pay his final homage. He would not lose the girl again, not while enraptured by the Dark Mother. She would guide him.

As he retreated eastward through the stone forest, toward the Kail and Iskele, he felt his brethren at the northern and middle fronts, miles and leagues south of him. He could *feel* them, *know* them; such awareness Noxmyra had blessed him with! They had torn through thousands of Arlethians and Senthary alike, shredding them with steel and hand as they worked toward their penultimate Dahlrak. Their sight alone had broken men's spirits before their bodies were rent asunder.

Now, Therrium having met his end, they stood deflated, Chargeless, retreating back to their respective camps. It had been his *right*, however, to have Therrium unto himself, to feast upon the last Charge that would ever be given him or any Helsyan by a lesser master.

But something was amiss. Not all were accounted for. Only thirteen, not including himself, did he feel in the Dark.

Where are the three in the south?

Gone. They were dead. It was impossible to enough to believe Maynard had been defeated, but three others as well? He sorrowed that they would not be able to witness the Rising.

The Resurgence, he heard Noxmyra whisper to him. *Free them, free them all.*

He *would* free them, his thirteen remaining brethren. They would be his, called to this work of dark glory.

And then, Dralghus swore, *Helsya shall rise again.*

THE END OF PART 2

PART 3

TEMPEST

The blood has dried on my hands. I have forgotten whose it is, but it doesn't matter; our well of dreams has run dry.
—Pelnith, an Orsarian Dark Marauder, just before succumbing to his wounds on Pearl Island

A leader must put himself in front of his people when danger comes close, not hide behind those loyal to him; a leader must protect his people, not seek refuge from them; a leader understands that his life is not as important as those he serves.
—Lord Branton Kerr to his son, Thannuel, when retiring as Lord of the Western Province

FORTY-TWO

Aiden

Day 2 of 2nd Dimming 412 A.U.

WITH INHUMAN SPEED AND AGILITY, Aiden and Hedron took a wide course around the Borathein horde, easily outdistancing them as they traveled south through the Gonfrey Forest, away from Jayden's cottage. Their route was indirect, costing them precious time, but was necessary. Even with Ehliss propped upon his back and clutching tightly, Aiden moved silently over the mostly frozen earth with little effort.

When uneven ground was ahead, Aiden felt Ehliss' arms tense and grab him tighter, as if to brace against turbulence.

"I barely feel any jarring, almost no sensation of movement other than the wind," she would remark, surprised. "It is amazing that your kind is faster than the finest horse and more agile than a gazelle."

"I'm not sure comparing Aiden to a gazelle will go over all that well," Hedron warned as they ran.

Aiden mumbled something not audible.

The three wolf cubs dashed around them, weaving an intricate pattern of tracks in the snow.

"How are they able to keep pace?" Ehliss asked. "Wolves are fast but this speed they display is unnatural."

"You know, princess, it's much less taxing physically if you simply remain silent," Aiden told her.

"Princess?" Ehliss repeated with disgust. "I'm not a princess! I'm a terranist, nothing more."

Aiden rolled his eyes.

"That's actually too bad," Hedron said. "If you were, maybe you could command Master Aiden and he would obey. I would love to see that."

"Can we please just get to where we're going without the unnecessary commentary?" Aiden asked.

Hedron shrugged. "Fine by me, it's the princess you'll have to convince."

"By the Falling Heavens, why have I been thus cursed?" Aiden groused.

The journey of the first day saw them to the southern parts of the Northern Province. Aiden declared they were far enough ahead of the Borathein after placing his ear to the ground and holding for several minutes. It was more difficult without trees that speak to filter through ambient vibrations, focus on a particular element and accurately judge distance.

Aiden sat up and was still for a brief moment before raising his right arm above his shoulder and working the joint. He did the same with his left after a few moments and grimaced when it reached a certain angle. He reached his right hand to his left shoulder and dug his fingers into the muscles, pinching, rubbing and releasing.

"Was I that heavy?" Ehliss asked.

"Believe it or not, princess, wood-dwellers do indeed tire and need rest. But no, you're not overly burdensome. I've just had my fair share of battles recently without much rest in between."

"I'm not—"

"Not a princess, yes, I know. Yet I seem to have become your chariot nonetheless."

"Look, I was fine to not come. I could have happily waited another day and then made it back to Ministry of Terran Studies on my own. I have no problem being on my own. It has more or less been my life."

Aiden did not respond but was somewhat impressed by Ehliss' show of sternness.

Alabeth broke away from where her two siblings were curled up and snuggled alongside Hedron as he lay against a tree. She put her snout on his lap and looked up at him, ears back. The light of their small fire reflected in her eyes.

"Oh come on, you can't be serious!" Hedron scoffed. Alabeth did not move, but just blinked once and continued to stare.

"No!" Hedron said. He shook his head to add some emphasis to his declaration and crossed his arms over his chest. "Not going to happen!" Alabeth still did not move. A small whimper emanated from her and Hedron looked away, determined not to give in.

Watching this scene, Ehliss started to laugh. Quietly at first, then louder. Aiden looked up from massaging his shoulder and neck to see what had caused her to laugh and then almost immediately started to snicker despite his aching muscles.

Hedron tried to contain the laughter building up inside him as he still looked away. His face contorting with the effort made Aiden laugh all the more. Finally the boy gave in and let out a burst of laughter, raising his hand to the she-wolf cub's head and stroking her behind the ears. Alabeth closed her eyes. The wind blew fiercely and threw the hairs of her coat back and forth but she did not seem to notice.

"How much longer?" Ehliss asked after the moment had passed.

"A day to Arlethia, maybe another until we reach Therrium, depending on where he is currently," Aiden replied. He went back to working the muscles in his shoulder and neck.

"Here, let me," Ehliss offered, getting up from her spot to move around behind Aiden.

"That's quite all right, little good your hands would likely do—"

"Shut up," Ehliss said as her hands went to his left shoulder and started to knead his wire-taut and knotted muscles.

Aiden did not object once he felt her hands on his body. They were strong and yet nimble, working quickly on his back, shoulders and neck. There were also warm, almost abnormally so. He fully gave in as he hung his head and let his rigid body deflate. Lifting his head for a moment he caught Hedron staring over at them with a wicked grin on his face. Alabeth whined for more attention. Even in sleep Aiden's muscles were never really relaxed. It was the training of a hold guard; and, perhaps, the guilt of his failures.

"Where did you learn to do this?" he mumbled from behind the night black hair that covered his face.

"My father," she said. "The stress of his former post as Minister often left him weary and tight at the end of long days. He was usually hunched over reports for long hours, not feeling time pass as he was immersed in his work. My mother died young and so it was left to me to care for him. Working out kinked and sore muscles became part of life for me."

———

Shortly after, with Aiden remaining silent, Ehliss stopped. "Aiden?" No answer came except for the slow rise and fall of his shoulders. Though still sitting, he now leaned forward. She gently guided him down onto his side. His breathing was heavy and slow.

"Typical," Ehliss muttered.

"Don't take it personally," Hedron called from across the fire. "Better to have him fall asleep mid-conversation than leave you unconscious in the snow with a lump on your head. I know a thing or two about that."

———

In the morning, Aiden awoke to Huksinai and Alabeth nudging his face, whimpering. He waved the wolf cubs off and sat up. The fire was still smoking but gave off no heat. The land appeared exactly the same as it had when they made camp last night except now there was the gray light of morning, which also offered no warmth. Reflexively, he reached his right hand up across his chest to his left shoulder to start massaging, but there was no pain. No more stiffness. The muscles had relaxed in the night. He worked his shoulders and limbs and felt no pain or soreness. In fact, he felt quite refreshed, as if he had slept soundly for a span.

Well that's a bit odd, he started to muse but then remembered. He looked to his right and saw Ehliss curled against a tree, still asleep. After grumbling a few inaudible words, he arose and walked over to where she slept. Not seeing any value in approaching the subject lightly, he lifted a foot and shoved her hard. The terranist woke quickly with a start.

"Good, you're awake. Thank you," Aiden said, adding a curt nod. Satisfied he had now met the expectations of polite behavior, he walked away before she could gather her wits to respond.

Hedron stirred as Thurik stared off in the distance. South mostly. His ears were straight up. Something had the wolf's attention.

Aiden came to Hedron's side. "Get up."

"I am up," Hedron said.

"No, you're awake, not up. Get up."

"Burning Heavens, give me a second," Hedron groused.

"Thurik is agitated."

"So am I."

"I'm serious," Aiden said, looking in the direction that Thurik gazed.

A growl, barely audible, started to sound in the morning air. Thurik's agitation was obviously rising.

"What is it?" Hedron asked as he reached his hand to the wolf's ears. It flinched at his touch. "Wow," he said, and pulled his hand back. "He's not quite the cuddler his sister is, I guess."

Aiden grew more wary. "There must be something in the air. Something's off to the wolf."

"It must be a scent," Ehliss offered. "Wolves and dogs can know their environment has changed sometimes by smell long before we can actually see anything."

Aiden considered this. "The Borathein are still behind us, although closer. But they're north of us still. Why is Thurik so interested in the south?"

"We need a clearer vantage point." Hedron stood and made his way up a fairly tall tree, at least for the Gonfrey Forest. Once at the top, the youth looked south and squinted.

"Anything?" Ehliss called.

"I, uh... I'm not sure."

"You're not sure? You either see something or you don't."

"I'm not sure," he repeated.

Aiden ascended the tree and joined Hedron. Once he fixed his gaze where Hedron looked, he jolted backward.

"Smoke," he whispered.

"Is it?" Hedron wondered. "It's so far off it almost looks like rain, but the pattern was wrong. Perhaps a dark cloud, but it's the wrong shape for the season; for any season."

"It's not rain or a cloud, lad, it's smoke."

"How far off do you think it is?"

"Leagues; maybe thirty."

"That far? It can't be. We couldn't make anything out that far off. Besides, if it is smoke, wouldn't it dissipate? This is just hanging in the air."

Aiden turned to Hedron. "Normally, we probably would not be able to see much from such a distance. But this smoke is thick. Don't underestimate the size of the haze. The blaze that caused this much smoke was no doubt enormous."

"Where is that, do you think?" Hedron asked.

Aiden turned his attention back toward the unnatural dark fog. He considered for several moments before answering. "Northern Arlethia. There can be no doubt."

That evening, the small party reached the first village in the Arlethian forest. Eledir was the most northern settlement within Arlethia. A small boy greeted them with a bow and arrow notched on the twine string. The weapon stood taller than him. He struggled to draw the bow in a show of strength, but instead he settled on puffing out his chest and deepening his voice.

"Who are you? What do you want here?"

Hedron and Aiden looked at each other, somewhat perplexed. The wolf cubs, over half the height of this boy, advanced to him with tails wagging. The boy stepped back, afraid. He turned to run.

"No," Hedron called out, "it's all right. We mean you no harm."

"Bad wolves!" Ehliss scolded. This drew a look from Aiden that bespoke his incredulity. "What?" she asked. "They were scaring him."

"They are not dogs or children, princess. They won't obey you like your other royal subjects."

"Aiden, I'm not going to—"

"*Master* Aiden, if you don't mind Highness." Aiden approached the boy before Ehliss could respond. He did get a small bit of satisfaction at seeing her mouth open but she was too dumbfounded to speak.

"Lad, I am Aiden, formerly master of the hold guard for Lord Therrium. Who are you?"

"Why should I tell you that? You're a stranger so far as I can see."

"No wood-dweller is a stranger to another wood-dweller, lad." Aiden knelt down to the boy's height. "What's your name?"

The boy heaved a deep breath and looked down. "My sister calls me Fletch, but my real name is Mikahl."

"All right Fletch, nice to meet you. Where does your nickname come from?"

In response, the boy raised his arrow and stroked the feathers. "I prepare the fletching for the arrows. Rue-anna makes the bows and the shafts. Mother weaves and treats the strings."

"And your father?" Aiden asked.

Fletch looked down again. "He went with my brother to fight for Lord Therrium. They haven't yet returned."

"Mikahl!" yelled a woman thirty paces behind him. Aiden stood. The boy retreated to the woman, obviously his mother. She scolded him and sent him back to his chores. After Fletch disappeared into a nearby cottage, the woman approached them.

"You are Arlethians," she observed. Then looking at Ehliss, she said, "Most of you, anyway. What are you seeking?"

"Kind mother, I am Aiden. The boy is Hedron and the lady Ehliss, of the Ministry of Terran Studies. We seek nothing from you except the whereabouts of Lord Therrium. We have traveled many days from the north in search of him."

"You'll search the rest of your lives to find him alive. His body was found last morning a few leagues from here amongst the corrupted parts."

Aiden tried to speak but failed.

"Therrium is dead?" Hedron exclaimed.

The mother nodded. "We also found a guard near Therrium's body, barely old enough to be a man. We thought he was dead but found a weak pulse. We tended to his wounds as best we could but he still has not awakened."

Aiden's heart skipped a beat. "A guard? Young?"

She nodded again. "He's in my home resting. We do not know if he will pull through yet."

Aiden's mind wondered if it were possible. There was only one person it could be, assuming Lord Therrium had not yet replenished the Hold Guard. But he would not have had a chance to do so yet.

"Good mother, we have no time, but will you give him something for me?"

She shrugged. "If he awakens, yes."

Aiden quickly wrote a note on a scrap of parchment and handed it to the woman, folded.

Something struck Hedron as he looked around at the small village. "Where are all the men? Your husband? Your son said he went to fight—"

"Dead, most likely. My oldest son as well. All the men old enough to wield a sword or bow left to fight after the army fell. It was a chaotic counterattack. Brutal, I am told. They were not successful." She looked away as she spoke, doing her best to hide the tears welling. "The fires came—not here, but they were not far off when they were snuffed out."

"What stopped them?" Ehliss asked. "There has been no rain."

"The corruption," was all she said.

Aiden could guess what she meant, though he shuddered to think of it.

"Mother, what is your name?" Hedron asked.

"Seilia," she answered.

"What is this 'corruption' you speak of?" he probed further.

"You can see for yourself." She gestured with her chin toward the southwest. "It's not but a few leagues, as I've said. We were spared, thank the Ancients."

"So who is left here?" Aiden asked.

"Just the women and children and those men too infirm to fight. The same as everywhere I expect. My husband is—" Seilia swallowed a lump in her throat. "—was, rather, a carpenter." She reached toward a small wreath-like pendant hanging around her neck: a carving of Triarch leaves.

"The detail is exquisite. It's beautiful," Ehliss said.

"He taught my little ones as they watched him work. Rue-anna is most gifted with the wood, even at seven years old. She's also good with a bow, that one is. Mikahl not as much, but he works where he can, snaring birds and plucking their feathers for fletching."

"To what end, good mother?" Aiden asked.

"Making bows and arrows, of course. We will need them. The Senthary will come again and we hear rumors that the army is no more and we are without a Lord or any real leader. Arlethia may fracture."

Hedron and Aiden looked at each other.

"You cannot stay," Hedron warned. "The Senthary are not your most immediate concern. It would be wise to flee south and inland as much as possible."

"I won't leave my home," Seilia protested. "No one in Eledir will. We have been here for centuries."

"He is right, Seilia. A force greater than the Senthary arrives not another half span hence from the north," Aiden said. "For your children's sake you must flee. Take those who would follow and run. We must find the remnants of the army."

"You aren't listening, Master Aiden. There is no army left."

Aiden looked at her curiously when she addressed him formally.

"Yes, I know who you are. Not by sight, just by your name and Helvish accent. I wasn't sure until just now. There are few that hail from the ghost village of Helving." Seilia referred to the wispy white moss that hung from the ubiquitous Furlop trees in the cliff village. When the wind blew, the moss truly did appear to be specters sailing through the air.

"What of General Roan, then?" Aiden asked.

"I do not know of any survivors. Perhaps a few here and there, but after the corruption came, there were strange vibrations in the forest. Heavy, as fast as a wood-dweller. But, not long after, there were no more. None of us could sense anything save for the Sentharian armies setting up camp. There is talk of demons in the forest, that the Senthary fight alongside devils. My children fear to close their eyes at night for even a moment."

Aiden understood better than the others. Twice before had he felt the thunderous footfall that was at least as swift as a wood-dweller's, coming from monstrous beings he still did not comprehend. Helsyans, Jayden had called them. The first time he encountered one, he had failed. The second time, he did not. Therrium still lay lifeless all the same if what Seilia reported was true.

"Seilia, hear me," Aiden said. "There *are* demons, both in the forest and coming from the north. The like of which you have never imagined, nor your children in their worst nightmare. We have met them and they are most feral. I beg of you to heed my words. Take your little ones and travel southwest at speed. Do not delay."

She pondered for a few moments. "I will not leave. What will you do?" she asked.

When he saw there was no arguing with the woman, he no longer tried to persuade her. "We must make our way to Calyn. The city will be in panic."

"I have heard militia from all across Arlethia are gathering there. Men and some women, even children who are old enough to carry a sword. They are not soldiers, though. My children are making what they can for weapons to aid them. Their efforts are noble but I fear too little."

"Who leads?" Hedron asked.

"No one that I know of." Seilia crossed her arms, enfolding them in a shawl against the chill of the season. "Rumors are rife with mass disorganization and power grabs. Other groups of our people are fleeing into hiding."

Aiden glanced at Hedron, and he could tell the boy felt his gaze.

"Therrium has a son," Hedron recalled. "Maybe eleven years of age by now, beyond the age of innocence. Farahan, I think."

"There is no such thing as innocence anymore. A boy cannot lead in a time of war," Seilia said. "Some say that Therrium's wife has fled with her children regardless. What do you hope to accomplish? We do what we can but little hope prevails in the land. What will you do?"

Aiden looked back at Seilia. "I, good mother, am going to show the demons my steel."

FORTY-THREE

High Duke Emeron Wellyn

Day 3 of 2nd Dimming 412 A.U.

"IT IS DONE," Tyjil reported. "Field Marshal Baylent reports a victory against the Arlethians."

The High Duke's private chambers were exquisitely appointed with ornately carved dark rich wood panels inlaid on the walls. The images carved therein were great battle scenes of the past along with his ancestors depicted in powerful settings. The quarters were small by design, allowing Wellyn to be free from distractions when he needed solitude. He sat at his desk with anticipation dripping down his temples.

"What else does the message say?" the High Duke asked. "Why did a Field Marshal send the report and not High Lord Marshal Tulley?"

Tyjil was scanning down the rolled paper that had arrived moments earlier from a messenger bird.

"The Lord Marshal is reported as killed in battle, as were many of the officers. Baylent requests instructions on new leadership for those forces along the northwestern border of Arlethia. He has provided a list of the remaining officers and their ranks." Tyjil pulled a second page from behind the first and held it up for the High Duke to see.

"And the southern contingents?"

"Baylent reports no contact with those detachments. Their success seems to be unknown currently."

Wellyn lost himself in a quandary.

"Ah, the Ancient Heavens have smiled upon us," Tyjil continued reporting as he read farther down the paper. "Therrium is dead. Our scouts found him yesterday afternoon, it appears.

"The men," he continued, "are uneasy, according to Baylent. The change in the forest as well as rumors of demons aiding their victory…oh my, this is delightful!" The High Duke's Advisor seemed to glow during this part of the report.

With the announcement of Therrium's death, Wellyn felt hopeful. "How many men are left?"

"No prisoners were taken, my Liege, but it seems to me that the entire Arlethian army has been exterminated at the northern front. Perhaps even General Roan has fallen."

"No, Tyjil, our soldiers. How many are left?"

"Not knowing the status of the forces at the middle and southern fronts, Baylent reports less than thirty-four thousand."

Wellyn cursed.

Addressing Wellyn's displeasure with the reported loss of his forces, Tyjil said, "My Duke, the plan is working. The Borathein cannot be more than two days from the Arlethian Border. My own scouts have reported that they have arrived within the borders of the Northern Province. Arlethia will soon be cleared of the inhabitants there and we will take possession of our new lands, those that do not cycle. We will be free to search for the Lumenatis at our leisure and root out the Gyldenal."

"And for the Borathein's help, they obtain the rest of the Realm." Wellyn's reluctance was obvious.

"For the time being, my Duke, but once we have harnessed the power of the Lumenatis, we will have dominion wherever we wish."

"It will not be long before they realize the Realm's land is cycling. We will not have much time to discover this mythical power you speak of."

"No, my Liege, it is not mythical. I have witnessed and felt its essence. It is real."

"Yes, yes, when you were still banished and had your 'revelations' in the haunted forest. You do sound quite mad when you speak of it, Tyjil."

"Thank you, my Duke," the old serpent-looking man replied, clearly taking it as a compliment. "I have proven my words in part, have I not, yes?"

Wellyn nodded. "You have. Whatever Dark Influence you obtained among that ancient scourge in the Tavaniah has been most effective. It's not that I doubt you, Tyjil. The gravity and size of the risk I am taking weighs on me."

"It is the risk we both have taken."

A knock at the door interrupted their discussion.

"Enter," Wellyn said. One of the Khans outside the chamber opened the door and admitted a page.

"High Duke Wellyn, I apologize for my interruption." He knelt quickly and held out a roll of paper. "Another message has arrived by wing." The boy's hands were shaking and sweaty.

"What does it say?" Wellyn asked.

"My Duke?"

"You've read it, haven't you?"

The page became even more nervous. He nodded.

"Well then, boy, tell your Duke what it says," Wellyn demanded.

In a shaky voice the boy said, "The South—Lord Hoyt, I mean. He has defected and joined the Arlethians!"

Emeron Wellyn stood up abruptly and his chair fell backward to the stone floor. Tyjil backhanded the page and snatched the message away. The boy yelped at the physical rebuke and remained kneeling with his head bowed.

"Where did this come from?" Tyjil demanded.

"A bird, my Lord. A falcon, the same as the other."

"This message claims to be from Field Marshal Baylent as well." Tyjil examined it closely, as if the message were suspect. He compared the new message with the previous one for several minutes.

The page began to get up but Tyjil slapped him again, ceasing the boy's movement. Finally, he looked up at Wellyn, who stared at him intently.

"I do not believe it to be a trick, my Duke. The handwriting seems to match the previous message. It is authentic."

Looking down at the page, Tyjil asked, "Boy, why are you still here?"

"Does my Duke require anything else from me?"

Tyjil slapped him again. "Get out!"

"What of the Eastern forces that were with Hoyt's?" Wellyn asked.

"The message does not say. But this leaves another question lingering, yes? Perhaps the Arlethian forces are not as decimated as we were led to believe. Did Hoyt defect after a battle or before? Did they turn on the Eastern Province's forces during the battle? There are too many unknowns here, my Duke."

"What of the chase-givers? We sent three to that front to make their way up through the Arlethian forces northward toward Therrium's position."

"None have returned as of yet, including Rembbran. This is not yet a concern as it is too early to know. We must wait and see."

"I am not in a patient mood!" Wellyn shouted. Mawldra's hackles raised at her master's change in attitude. The loyal hound mimicked Wellyn's moods with near perfect reflection.

"There is a matter I must see to, my Liege. I will see what else I can learn in the meantime."

The High Duke rubbed behind Mawldra's ears. "Another one of your secret tasks?"

"My Duke, all my efforts are for the benefit of the Realm, of course. You have no doubt of this, yes?"

"I have no doubt of you furthering your self-interests, Tyjil."

"Ah, well, it's nice when the Realm's interest and my own line up, yes?" Tyjil left Emeron Wellyn to the company of his hound and departed.

FORTY-FOUR

Reign

Day 3 of 2nd Dimming 412 A.U.

REIGN KERR AWOKE THE FIFTH DAY after she had slipped into unconsciousness. She silently sat straight up without weariness and processed her surroundings in a single moment. Jayden's cottage. Day thirty-three of the Dimming Season, being the same as third day of Second Dimming. She looked to the left and saw Jayden sitting in a stationary decrepit chair that seemed to creak simply because the wood was old, not from any movement. She knew the wood to be a mix of cherry and maple by a quick glance at the grains. The alertness of her mind was surprising to her. Such clarity. Jayden's stare was contemplative. Crimson Snow sat up when he noticed Reign was awake.

The old woman spoke. "I am a current." She said no more, looking at the younger girl in silence.

Reign did not respond with words or gesture. Her stillness was unearthly, a picture of serenity.

"I am a current," Jayden said again and waited.

Reign felt the response but was not certain yet of the words. It was familiar in some way, both what Jayden was saying and the answer that she knew she was to supply, the answer that she could feel but not quite express.

Jayden waited patiently, without any sign of ill temper. That, in and of itself, was noteworthy, Reign thought.

As Jayden opened her mouth to speak a third time, the expected response sounded in Reign's mind with the timbre of a voice nearly forgotten. She spoke the words simultaneously as she heard them pronounced in her father's voice.

"I am a current of friction and light, a spark against the Ancient Dark that cannot be extinguished, a beam of the Lumenatis." As she spoke the words, she knew them to be an ancient greeting. More than this, she knew the phrase to be a clandestine expression, used to identify another of—

"The Gyldenal," Reign said out loud. Her facial expression that accompanied the pronouncement showed wonder at first, then confusion as to why she was surprised. Reign was perplexed as to how she would be surprised by something she already knew, and further, how she had forgotten that she knew. Yet, she realized that she did not actually know previously what she now knew, though it was knowledge that was familiar, like an old memory resurfacing after many years of wallowing in obscurity.

And then something happened that had certainly not been seen in generations. Jayden cracked a smile.

"He is in you," the keeper of wolves observed. "His last breath. What you are feeling is his knowledge and memories intermingling with yours. If you are still enough, you will notice the difference."

Reign could sense in her mind the second sentience. It was distinct and separate from her own being, not mingling with or occupying her identity. The second sentience was not hostile in any way. By contrast, it was peaceful and warm. A power resided therein that frightened her a little.

"All I can say is that it's about time. Last breaths don't endure forever. I'm frankly a little surprised that he lasted as long as he did without moving on to the Living Light."

Reign looked away and pondered. "How?" she finally asked.

"How is less important than the fact itself. But, I remember being young and needing to know what's behind everything."

Reign looked up as if realizing something for the first time and locked eyes with Jayden. "How long ago was that? When you were young?"

Jayden again smiled, shattering the image she had built over so many years of a humorless, short-tempered old woman. "I think you already know."

Reign realized she did know, but not from her own deductions or knowledge. "You are over four hundred years old." Reign's mouth remained open as if trying to formulate words. "But you are not Senthary or Arlethian." She turned pale with eyes wide. "You are Hardacheon! That's impossible!"

"We were not *all* destroyed, child. There are many things taught about my forgotten people that are regrettably true; but, we were not all meddlers of Dark Influence, or full of evil as the Senthary and Changrual are fond of teaching. But in truth, most of my people were duplicitous by nature. I cannot help to whom I was born, no better than can you. I think more of myself as a member of the Gyldenal than part of any race. We have been made up of many peoples and cultures over time, but Arlethians make up the majority of the order."

"But, how did you survive? How have you lived so long?" Reign protested. She found it increasingly difficult to separate what *she* knew as person and what she was learning at incredible speed within herself.

"It might be best to ask your father. I'm certain he would love to speak with you again." A vast new pool of knowledge was springing up inside her. So far only driblets of insight had spilled over and been soaked up by her mind. There was more. Much more.

Do I dare tap into it? Allow it to flow freely?

As if sensing her uncertainty, Jayden reassured her. "Your father is a powerful man. His will is strong, knowledge and experiences rich, and abilities well-seasoned. Accessing his last breath within you may have..." She cut off but did not break her eye contact. "Reign, there can be side effects. Consequences."

"Consequences? Such as what?"

"I'm not sure," Jayden's replied. "But, consequences are not always a negative occurrence, child. Regardless, you can control the access. You can close it off if you wish."

Reign looked away. Crimson Snow whined and wagged his tail. The large pure white wolf was enormous in size but much older than he used to be. He lowered his head and rested it on Reign's bed.

Does he sense father as well? she wondered.

Reign took a deep breath and closed her eyes. Inwardly, and somewhat timidly, she called for her father in ancient Arlethian. *Threyil?* She let the gates in her mind open to her father's last breath.

The warmth and pure love that burst forth from inside her was all-encompassing. Thannuel's release of pent-up emotions of the past six years flooded through his daughter's mind and heart, filling her completely. The innocent intimacy of the feeling was so tender, so gentle. Reign let out a small laugh and then began to cry.

"I forgive you," she whispered. "There was never anything to really forgive. But I miss you, *Threyil.*"

The voice inside that answered her was full and deep. Gentle but firm like the current of a fast-moving stream. *Dhar vash alaqyn duwel partia, my little one. I have never left you. Not for one moment. Nor shall I for as long as you desire me to stay.*

Crimson Snow stood up and wagged his tail so exuberantly that Jayden had to raise a hand in defense.

"Calm down, you old beast!" she snapped. "It's not like you were his child!"

I don't understand how this can be, Reign thought, knowing her father could hear and understand her thoughts. *I am so happy, though. I have not been happy since you—*

Since I died, Thannuel offered. *It is no harm to say the truth. I am grateful to the Ancient Heavens that you still live. Your capacity for Light is significant. The Gyldenal will welcome you. But for now, I believe there are matters of greater urgency upon us. The Dark has spread. Something has happened in these last few days. It has been unlocked somehow.*

Noxmyra, Reign recognized as she drew from her father's knowledge. *The Dark Mother.*

The Ancient Dark, yes. Her name is Noxmyra, or the Dark Mother. She caused the downfall of the Ancients and dimmed the power of the Lumenatis. She assumes now that the Lumenatis' Influence is so weakened that it can finally be snuffed out. Her forces even now are being gathered. I can feel it, as can all who are of the Lumenatis. But, darkness cannot see light; for all illumination causes darkness to be blinded and flee. Noxmyra does not know the strength and power that has been preserved.

As Thannuel spoke within Reign he supplied knowledge, both visually and audibly, to give greater depth of that which he said. Scenes played before her mind's eye, helping her grasp his words. When she did not understand, Thannuel would automatically provide deeper insight, sensing the confusion. Reign also discovered that she could freely access any subject that her father had knowledge of and experience it herself, as if she had learned the information innately.

I don't know the light or power you're talking about, Reign said. *Or this Lumenatis. Why haven't any of us heard this before?*

Its Influence has been hidden. Sequestered deep and far from Noxmyra and those who serve her. Since the Ancients fell, the Gyldenal have preserved it for more than four millennia. But, though hidden effectively, it has been too well anchored to be extracted completely.

Extracted? Reign asked. And then she understood as disparate pieces fell into place. *The trees! The Lumenatis is in the trees!*

She felt her father smile. *Specifically the Triarch trees. The remaining Ancients, who formed the Gyldenal, sank the Light into them. The positive effects have radiated through much of the land of Arlethia, sustaining the land and allowing Arlethians to speak with the forest. Because of the Lumenatis' Influence, the forest is more sentient than most know. But, we have to turn our attention there and leave the rest for later.*

"Try again," Jayden said.

Reign and the old wolf shepherd, along with Crimson Snow, had traveled to the northernmost edge of Arlethia, where they could find trees that spoke. Jayden's speed had surprised Reign and she sensed the feeble-looking image Jayden conveyed was deceptive, likely on purpose.

With her father's last breath inside her, Reign's first attempt to speak with a Triarch had felt foreign, as if her senses were distorted. At the old woman's urging, Reign once again lifted her palm to the large Triarch, forcing it flush against the bark. Her other hand clutched a small Triarch leafing.

The rush of the connection again flowed into her, first feeling invasive. Accessing her father's capacity and strength, she honed the connection, focusing it and bringing it under control. There was a distinct difference in the way Reign discerned life around her. The subtle vibrations transmitted that allowed all wood-dwellers to feel their surroundings accurately were still there, but Reign's discernment was deeper now. The *way* she understood her environment was through sensing the actual sentience around her. She felt the life itself, whether or not it moved. It was more than sensory refinement. This was awareness.

It is how the Lumenatis works. You are sensing the Light in the living elements that are present. Your reach of distance will increase with time. It still requires masterful sensitivity, Thannuel explained.

"Could you do this?" Reign asked her father aloud for Jayden's benefit. "Sense the 'Light' as you call it?"

No, her father replied. *Not like this. I'm not aware of any who could then or can now. In the Gyldenal Order, we have knowledge of many things, but our actual experience in them was limited. Most did have the capacity to use the Lumenatis. And...*

Her father stopped speaking inside her. Reign had been repeating his words for Jayden to hear the conversation.

"And what?" Reign asked.

"The Light will not allow itself to be harvested by those who have selfish or ill intent," Jayden told her. Reign felt Thannuel's agreement with the statement. "We have had more than one occasion of this being attempted. The last attempt was actually not so long ago. But the Ancient Dark, that is free for the taking. Those who fail to capture the Light often turn and embrace the Dark."

She broke the connection with the tree again. The leafing still provided some connection to the forest, although the channel was weaker than a connection created by direct touch with a Triarch tree. She sensed something. The forest was agitated. Afraid. It felt very familiar to her, the same type of feeling she received from the forest when she first saw the High Duke and the demon. The Helsyan.

"I am still afraid of him," she said, not needing to clarify who she meant.

As am I, Thannuel admitted. *But, that emotion can be recycled. It is internal friction. If you can capture the energy caused by it, you can easily redirect it for good within you.*

Reign understood more as Thannuel provided further insight through his knowledge in her mind.

"All emotions have a scent," she announced. "This is how Helsyans track."

"Yes," Jayden confirmed.

"But only when Charged."

"Not quite. They can always smell the emotion. The Charge allows them to hunt it, unleashing the predator the Dark forged them to be."

But, if you can capture the emotions before they take hold of you, you can counter the Helsyan's advantage. Remember, all emotions are friction and create energy. Redirecting that power will aid you greatly.

Reign understood finally why she was still alive.

"After I saw you die," Reign said, "I felt nothing. There was no emotion. Not right then and not for several days. I just sat there, breathing." She hesitated. "Then came the anger. The hate, blame."

"It saved your life," Jayden admitted. "You changed inside that day. It was enough that when you did start to return to a normal emotional state, your emotional *scent* was different. The Helsyan would not have been able to identify you by that alone."

But, Thannuel interjected, *that will be different now. The chase-giver will undoubtedly sense you again, your scent. It is inevitable. You have emotionally returned to whom you once were.*

Jayden nodded. "More or less."

Reign did not answer. She felt the truth of her father's warning. The chill in the air added to her growing anxiety. Jayden saw the concern on her face.

"That, right there," the old woman said. "Hold that emotion, that fear."

"That's not hard," Reign said, looking down. "I can't help but feel it when thinking of him." Thannuel sent forth reassurance through her.

"That is exactly the point, child. You cannot help the emotions you feel, but they are *yours.* You can control them, command them. All emotion is friction. Some emotions produce a greater level of energy but they all produce some. Capture the friction and recycle its energy. Direct it."

"How?" she asked, but then she knew. Her father showed her his experience in the form of a memory. Because it felt as if it were her memory, it felt familiar once again. Instead of trying to truncate or overcome the emotion—fear in this case—she let it completely engulf her. The fear peaked and she began to shake as if in mortal terror.

Good, Thannuel encouraged. *Let it build.*

Reign's whole frame shook almost uncontrollably.

Now! her father said.

"I can't grab it! It's too large!" Her voice trembled. Thannuel reached out and added his strength and serenity. Inside herself, Reign felt as if she were expanding and being lifted, though she physically did not change. And then, within herself, she could *see* the fear. All of it. The ancient word came.

"Relitha!" she commanded out loud. Immediately, the emotion that had been swelling within her ceased. It waited, contained. She could sense it waiting. Waiting for...

Strength, she said inside. The vision of the fear she saw morph to something new within her and felt power begin to unfold itself within her limbs and joints. She knelt down on one knee, closed her eyes and tensed. The ground seemed to give way slightly and she readied herself.

Reign launched. The air around her rushed with wild noise as she shot upward. Her momentum slowed as she reached roughly fifty feet in the air. The amazement of what she had just done was exhilarating. She shot herself down with the last bit of energy and landed on the earth the way she had begun her jump, on one knee.

"That was…incredible!" she exclaimed, looking up at Jayden. Reign felt her father's own amazement. *I could never have contained an emotion that swelled that large inside me. I've been humbled by my young daughter!*

"You haven't seen anything yet," Jayden replied. "Now see if you can redirect some of that friction for something useful."

"But I don't feel afraid anymore."

"What do you feel?"

"Excitement!" Reign exclaimed.

"And? Is that not an emotion?" Jayden asked.

"Oh, right."

It still took some time and effort, but Reign eventually channeled the excitement into increased sensory perception and reconnected with the Triarch in front of her. After a few moments, she pulled back with grave concern.

"It has happened again," she said. "What I saw when I was young. More this time, though. A large portion of the forest has been killed. It is cold, petrified."

Death, decay, entropy. These are all consequences of the Ancient Dark. It is what she seeks for all things. The Senthary have discovered an Influence that accelerates and focuses her power.

"But," Jayden interrupted, "it can be overcome. The Light renews life, brings lands back to life hundreds of years after they have died. It appears to be a natural cycle of life, but it is deeper than this. It is the struggle between two opposing forces: one to create and extend life; the other to bring decadence and ruin. We are the determining factor as to which has greater hold. If the Dark's Influence can be accelerated, so can the Light's. The Dark cannot ever fully extinguish the spark of life, only dim it. This is why the lands cycle back to life eventually after their seeming demise."

"How can it be overcome?" Reign asked. "I don't understand that." She sensed that neither did Thannuel.

"The Lumenatis promotes life. It sparks the fire of existence." Jayden said no more, as if that explained everything. From off her shoulder she removed something a little less than four feet in length and wrapped in furs. As she revealed the item, she said, "For now, though, it's time for practice."

Inside the fur wrappings was a sword. The blade was dark, almost pewter color. Jayden lifted it with two hands and extended it to Reign. Crimson Snow began to pounce back and forth playfully, turning in circles and barking. As Reign timidly reached out for the weapon, she felt her father's excitement grow. Her eyes widened at the enthusiasm he felt. Having never truly held a sword, the hunger inside her was strange, but she *yearned* for it. As her hand grasped the hilt, she smiled and looked at Crimson Snow. She repeated Thannuel's words that she heard in her mind.

"Think you can still catch me, Elohk, my old friend?"

The wolf huffed and took off through the woods at a sprint. Reign, sword in hand, was not even a pace behind.

And now we begin! Thannuel said.

Reign thrust the sword into the ground and leaned against a mound in frustration.

"Why can't I do it?" she asked, exasperated. "I know *how* but my body won't listen!"

Crimson Snow was still full of energy after their hours of sprinting through the forest, dodging and sparring with each other. He nudged at Reign's hip, trying to goad her into continuing.

"No!" she said.

Crimson barked at her.

Elohk doesn't think you should quit so quickly, her father admonished.

"It's been half a span of hours! My arms and legs are shaking and won't move like I tell them to. In my mind, I see the actions and myself carrying them out, but my body is reacting like a clumsy oaf!"

Reign could feel her father thinking of a response. It was an odd sensation.

Your mind knows how to fight with steel because it can draw on my knowledge and skills. But your muscles and joints still have to execute the movements, and they are new to you. You haven't developed the muscle memory or flexibility yet. Unfortunately, we don't have the time it will take for you to physically train yourself properly. We must continue, daughter.

"Why me? Why did you choose me? Why not Hedron? Why not Aiden? Both seem like better choices."

A last breath can only be passed to a blood relative of close relation. At least, that's what we believe. Children, siblings, parents. Maybe a first cousin or grandchild, but that might prove unsuccessful.

"Not even a spouse," Reign added, accessing her father's knowledge.

Correct. Only a blood relation. And you were there, my little one. You saw what happened and had first-hand knowledge, though I know you did not understand at the time. My last breath passing to you would provide the best advantage.

"Why didn't it happen sooner? I mean, why didn't I get this sooner? Your last breath?"

I tried relentlessly but could not get through to you. You felt my attempts, but did not understand them. Love is the conduit. That must exist for the last breath to successfully pass to the intended recipient.

Reign felt a pang of guilt well up inside her.

"I'm sorry," she whispered. "I just...I didn't know how to—"

I know. I don't blame you. Your anger was equal to the guilt I felt for not surviving. But, the anger and hate shielded you.

Her mind conjured up memories of the old man with a scar on his cheek who visited her after her father died.

I know your life has not been easy because of this. But, Reign, I love you and your brother more than I can express.

She felt the warmth inside her again as her father expressed his feelings.

Your brother protected you well. He did what needed to be done. You would have been in grave danger if anyone had known you still lived, as well as those you love. High Duke Wellyn would have sent him or others for you.

The Helsyan, Reign thought.

Yes.

"And yet, the danger existed just the same. Hedron's silence did not protect mother and she died because of me. And Hedron nearly so."

Your mother died for you, not because of you. She waits for us with the Lumenatis where all that possessed Light during life return when their time on Våleira ends.

"Does she remember us? Does she still...love us?"

Don't you remember and love her?

"Yes."

We do not lose ourselves when we die, little one. Who we are remains.

"That's not what the Changrual—"

Fools!

Reign was taken aback by her father's sudden outburst. "But I thought—"

I'm sorry, Reign. There are many good people in the Changrual Order. However, their understanding of the greater knowledge is far from correct. I suppose "ignorant fools" is more apt.

Reign chuckled. With what little she had learned in the past day, she knew her father's words to be true.

Now, let's recycle some of that frustration friction you were feeling into more flexibility and stamina and continue.

"Not now, I'm too tired."

Reign, time is slim. We must press on.

"I'm just tired. Can that be recycled?"

No, unfortunately. That's not an emotion but rather a state. You must find the energy to continue. You can create more by conjuring emotions that are genuine.

"There is not much I can really do. I mean, these abilities are beyond my imagination, but I don't really know what I'm doing. You realize I'm only a fifteen-year-old girl, right, father?"

We are all more than we appear. Most never understand or even realize this truth. We are all either agents of the Living Light or the Ancient Dark. There can be no middle ground.

"Does middle ground have a bed?"

Reign felt Thannuel's frustration growing at her flippancy.

"Well, then, I'm going to rest for a little while." Reign felt like she was about to be sent to her room like had happened many times when she was younger.

Not an option, Thannuel said sternly. *We're going to continue—*

"Jayden said I can control the access, if I remember right."

Reign—

With that, she shut the mental door on her father, leaving him sequestered in a deep recess of her mind. She felt his agitation but ignored it, knowing he could not communicate with her unless she let him. He would probably let her know later how he felt about this little stunt, but for now she would rest.

"He's like a slave driver sometimes, you know?" she said, looking at the large white wolf. Crimson Snow turned away and huffed.

"What, now you're mad at me, too?"

The wolf replied by lying down on the ground. A breeze came through and he closed his eyes.

The vibrations that came through the forest were strange. They were more pronounced and numerous than she would have thought normal here in northern Arlethia. Whatever produced them was not very close, and they were too muddled to be discerned properly. They almost felt like a massive herd of large animals, like buffalo or elephants, but those creatures lived only in the plains of the Eastern Province. The vector felt directly east of her. The curiosity inside her beckoned her to get up, but she was so weary that her legs ached just from the thought of standing up. She did anyway.

Taking a portion of the intrigue she felt, Reign recycled it into enough energy to scale a tall grouping of white pines, a species more common in the Northern Province. Atop the trees, she scanned east and saw what appeared to be a cloud until she focused with the clarity of wood-dweller eyes. Thousands of the winged animals with riders saddled on their backs flew southbound in formation. Though she did not witness the battle at Jayden's cottage, being so wrapped up in terror as she related the past events she had witnessed to the old wolf shepherd, surely these were what Aiden and the wolves faced. She knew, however, these were not the source of the vibrations she felt. Without being closer she could not see the ground level from her vantage point, but she guessed the numbers there to be many times greater than what she saw in the air. She thought of Hedron and Aiden and prayed they were far from this horde she saw before her. Regardless, she knew her brother was in harm's way and had less than a day before the Borathein would be deep into Arlethia. As best as she could see, the invaders were headed in the general direction of Calyn.

Crimson Snow whined and barked below her.

"I know!" she called. Sighing, she allowed her father out into her mind again.

"I think I'm ready to continue, *Threyil.*"

FORTY-FIVE

High Duke Emeron Wellyn

Day 3 of 2nd Dimming 412 A.U.

HE SAT UPON HIS GRANITE THRONE in the chamber hall where he met with the Ministers in council. None were present now save for himself, Mawldra and two Khans, one of them Hadik. Emeron Wellyn sat with apprehension, fidgeting constantly.

"Traitors!" he yelled. The empty hall sent his words back at him. He would execute Lord Hoyt and his entire family for this. He had to know his life was over and the end result would still be the same. The Arlethian army was devastated and the Borathein were in the borders of the Realm. Soon, he would have the Western Province for his people, those still loyal, and discover this power that Tyjil spoke of. Perhaps he would even marry finally and produce an heir.

But the knowledge of Lord Hoyt's defection pulsed through him, hot and unrestrained. He needed to appoint new leadership in the army, see to the contingency plans and prepare for their migration into the West. His focus, however, continued to be elsewhere.

Someone came in the large doors, opening them without invitation. Wellyn stood with indignation, preparing to berate the intruder with lashing words, until he saw the figure was clad in a thick hooded robe.

Rembbran, he realized.

Finally.

Mawldra lowered her head and growled. This was nothing uncommon for her in the presence of a chase-giver. Rembbran continued to advance.

"Excellent!" the High Duke said. "You have fulfilled your Charge and advanced our efforts. As a reward, Rembbran, I have another Dahlrak to lay upon you—"

High Duke Emeron Wellyn never spoke another word. The fist that flew into his chest felt like an iron ball, sending him back hard against the Granite Throne that his family had occupied for over four centuries. He tried to scream but found no breath. He could not even inhale as his ribs folded inward, crushing and piercing his lungs. The sound of steel rang in the air as his Khans drew their swords, followed by curses and cries. Mawldra attacked the Helsyan, clawing and biting ferociously at her master's aggressor, but Rembbran cast her aside with a powerful kick that sent her sprawling through the air. When she hit the hard floor of the chamber, she whimpered but did not move.

The High Duke saw Hadik dance over his slain counterpart and deftly engage Rembbran. His sword was knocked from his hand by Rembbran, twisting his wrist, but Hadik fluidly worked himself free from the hold. To his credit the Khan parried the Helsyan's blows with great skill and landed several on his own. Wellyn's vision blurred but he still saw clearly enough when the chase-giver landed a debilitating palm thrust to Hadik's neck. The Master of the Khansian Guard struggled for breath in reflex as Rembbran moved behind him and grabbed his chin. With a forceful downward thrust, he brought Hadik's back down upon his knee. A crunch sounded as his torso went one way and pelvis another.

"Whimper now for me! My leash is broken!" Rembbran gloated.

"Now you're just a stray dog, then!" Hadik said with a tortured voice from his crushed larynx. Tears ran from his eyes at the pain of his injuries.

"Perhaps," Rembbran admitted. Then he grabbed Hadik's jaw and pulled up, slowly, forcefully. Hadik's frantic grasping and clawing with his hands, trying to find Rembbran's face, accompanied the screams. Before long, the skin of his neck tore and Hadik screamed louder. Still, the Helsyan pulled with a controlled strength that was purposefully slow. Muscles tore, tissue ripped, veins separated. The screaming mercifully ceased with the head coming free of the body. Attached to the base of the skull trailed Hadik's spine. Rembbran held the head up to his face.

"You were always small to me. Pathetic." He threw the head and string of vertebrae to the side.

Wellyn tried to react but the pain was debilitating. Even as his body shrieked with a pain he had never comprehended, his vision was interrupted by streaks of lightning before him. Blackness edged into his sight.

He knew he was dying.

Rembbran pulled the chain around Wellyn's neck out from under his royally embroidered tunic and stared at the gold amulet with the sigil of House Wellyn engraved thereon.

"For too long have we been slaves to your kind. Weaker beings. The Ancient Dark bids us rise again as we once lived. The Urlenthi cannot stand in our way."

The amulet hung in the air. Turning it, he saw the square carved glass-like stone embedded in the amulet's backside and marveled that such a thing ever had such hold upon him. It was milky in appearance and almost luminescent. It seemed childish now, a similar thing to how a youth is infatuated by a toy of colorful create.

"No more shall this work of the Light hold sway over my people. Helsya shall rise again."

Wellyn's vision clouded as he struggled against the pain for breath, but none came. His eyes bulged and were bloodshot. The last thing he beheld in this world was the Helsyan before him wearing his typical predatory smile.

FORTY-SIX

Hedron

Day 4 of 2nd Dimming 412 A.U.

"WE ARE WASTING TIME," Hedron complained. "We've already lost a half day by coming this way."

"We're not wasting time," Aiden said. "This is important. You'll see."

"Where are we?"

"You'll see, lad."

Ehliss pointed. "Look! There's a clearing. Well, sort of. I can see stone peeking through the growth. It looks like a wall heavily overgrown with flora of the forest."

Hedron stopped.

"And there!" Ehliss continued excitedly. She sounded like a child in a toymaker's shop. "It's a pathway that juts up and curves through the trees. Oh! It leads to a tower or battlement of sorts!"

I know this place, Hedron thought.

"Why have you brought me here?" he asked Aiden angrily.

"Have you ever been back, Hedron? Have you ever seen what your family's hold has become?"

The structure came more into focus as Ehliss pointed it out. Vines, ivy, shrubbery and trees grew everywhere, concealing the once magnificent home in which he grew up. The small company walked through one of the arched entryways on the west wall. The three wolf cubs stopped there and whined. Hedron felt the change in the terrain under his feet when he left the forest floor outside the hold walls and stepped on the decrepit stone floor of the inner courtyard. Leaves the color of bark and fire crunched under his otherwise silent step. The wolves overcame whatever hesitation had beset them and entered the courtyard behind Hedron.

It was smaller than he remembered. The forest had reclaimed almost all of the area. Hedron guessed that in another few years no evidence would remain of his childhood home. He walked over to where he knew a door had once been that led to the living quarters. Pulling back the ivy and growth there was revealed no door, just an opening. He tore down the ivy and birds escaped from some unseen nest, chirping loudly in protest. Hedron felt small vibrations of scurrying things hiding from the disturbance. Exposed was a short tunnel that led into an enclosed foyer of sorts that was the beginning of the living quarters. The stone and rock was charred. His hands came away with old soot after dragging his fingers along the wall. When he emerged into the foyer, there was more of the same. Leaves, vines, overgrowth, charred stone. No evidence of the Kerr family's centuries-long occupancy of this hold remained.

"There's nothing here. I want to leave."

"You're wrong. Everything is here," Aiden replied.

Hedron glared at Aiden. "There is nothing here," he repeated. "Only ruin and memories long faded."

"This is your home, lad." Aiden pointed to a stairway that lead down to the ancestral crypt. "Your father rests down there, with all the Kerrs for centuries past. Your lovely mother was deprived of her resting place by vile men."

"Hedron, I didn't know," Ehliss said. "I'm sorry."

"There's nothing to be sorry for!" he exclaimed. "This place is nothing! It died with my parents, with our name! There are no Kerrs left, nor should there be!"

Aiden remained calm. "Hedron, I know what you saw, what you felt—"

"No you don't! You couldn't know what I felt!" Tears formed in his eyes.

"Aye, I do. You don't know what I had to surface through as a child. Your father is the reason I'm likely still alive."

At this admission, Ehliss looked at Aiden questioningly, but he did not explain further.

"It's time to stop running, son. It's time to rise up to who you were born to be. You are the last heir to the Kerr name. Your family ruled before the Senthary, even before the Hardacheon Age. Your people need you now."

"They aren't my people! Not anymore! I'm not my father and I'm not your son!"

"Lad, I know, I'm just—"

"Well don't! This is none of your concern!" Hedron spat. "What do you want from me? I have nothing to give. I am nothing!"

"Hedron, you don't understand the power your name holds," Aiden said calmly. "People will rise to your call—"

"My name?" the Kerr boy interrupted. "Do you know how many people died because of my name? Because of my father's? Does their blood not stain my hands because of *my name?*"

"Lad, that's just not—"

"Yes it is! This place is cursed by the Ancient Heavens! Can you not see it? Are you blind to it? What do you want from me?" Hedron had tears streaming down his face as he raged on. He wanted to run away and hide himself from this place, from who he was, as he had done for the better part of a decade.

"I don't know how you can say that after what you have seen happen with Reign," Aiden said. "Therrium is dead. The armies are destroyed. Arlethia cannot survive without something to believe in, Hedron. If they knew a Kerr still lived—that the *son of Thannuel* still lived—they would rise behind you! *You* are what they need. You cannot turn your back on them."

The young Kerr heir did not respond for several moments. Alabeth rubbed up against his leg and whined softly.

"Your faith is devastatingly misplaced, Master Aiden. I am not Arlethia's savior."

"You do not need to be. The people can save themselves. But, they need you to believe in them, even if you can't in yourself." Aiden walked briskly out of the foyer back to the courtyard after he had said all he would. Ehliss followed.

Hedron stood there with so many emotions flowing through him that he did not know how he felt. No one feeling emerged as the most dominant, which left him confused and tense. One thing he was certain of: he could not stay here, not where the air was still so charged with pain from the not-distant-enough past.

———

Hedron walked through the debris littered streets early the next morning, weaving his way with his companions through the masses that crowded every sector. His night had been restless, tossing and turning with irritation that Aiden had stirred up inside him. The whole city of Calyn was in a frenzied state. Word of the army's destruction had reached the people in all quarters of Arlethia. Looters and bandits had taken to the streets, helping themselves to the spoils left behind by those deserting. Too few struggled to keep the peace and maintain order. Though their efforts were valiant, they were failing. Families were seen everywhere hurriedly packing their belongings and fleeing. Most seemed to be heading west, toward the shores. Quarrels erupted frequently, often turning into brawls. Ehliss grabbed Aiden's arm and huddled close as they walked. He did not push her away.

Groups of armed wood-dwellers, some with women and older children amid their ranks, made their way to the city center where a large gathering was taking place. People were yelling that the Senthary were coming from the east; others reported flying armies in the north approaching and within a day's travel. Calder Hoyt's men also were quickly advancing from the south. Tensions were high, like a taut mooring line holding a sail amidst a hurricane. A pervasive feeling of doom charged the air.

Anyone who approached too close to Hedron's company received a vicious warning from the three wolf cubs. Their snarls were generally enough to send anyone in reverse. Where a more convincing message was needed, Aiden brandished his sword.

"They are driven by fear," Ehliss said. "It is infectious once it takes hold of a group and only continues to rise until an apex is reached. It's usually never good."

"You learn that from your fancy upbringing, did ya?" Aiden asked.

Ehliss chose not to respond. They saw two men forcibly take provisions from and elderly couple and young child, probably the elderly couple's grandson. Aiden broke from the company and rectified the situation at the point of his sword. Decadence was everywhere.

"They act as if they are already defeated," Hedron said. The boy was trying not to look too closely at what was happening.

"They do not have a leader, Hedron," Aiden reminded him.

"Someone will stand up. Someone will lead."

"*You* must lead."

"Don't start with that again! That birthright ended long ago. My family name is broken. Besides, you heard Seilia. People will not follow a boy during a time of war."

Without breaking stride, Aiden grabbed Hedron by the back of his neck and forcibly pulled him off the street into an alley, leaving behind Ehliss and the wolf cubs. Huksinai, Alabeth and Thurik encompassed Ehliss, ensuring no passerby came too close.

"What are you—"

"Shut up!" Aiden spat as he shoved Hedron. "Why do you think we're here?"

"So you can help! Ancient Heavens, what's wrong with you?"

"And how are *you* going to help, Hedron? Seilia is right, but you're not a boy anymore. You're a man. We are here for you to take your rightful place as leader among these people!"

"No I'm not! I'm no leader!"

Aiden slapped him. Hedron was stunned.

"Don't do that, Aiden!"

Another slap came faster than Hedron could react. Losing his temper, Hedron gritted his teeth and yelled, "Stop it!"

Aiden pushed him hard against a wall. Hedron swung his fist but he found his arm swept aside and his face stinging with another slap. Then another.

"Blasted Heavens, stop!"

He tried to raise his arms in defense, but Aiden swept his legs from under him and he fell hard to the ground. Hedron felt himself being raised up and back against the wall before the haze could clear from his vision, and another slap landed on his face.

"So, you're a boy, are ya?" *Slap.* "Fine, I'll treat you like a boy!" *Slap.* 'I just want to run free through the Realm,' he mocked and landed another slap. "Free like a little ninny bastard boy!" *Slap.* "Aye, like a bastard!" *Slap.* "No responsibility, no concerns or cares! What? You have nothing to say, ninny boy!" *Slap.*

Hedron was embarrassed but more furious. He pushed Aiden back and swung his fist. Once again, his blow was easily deflected and followed by another slap.

"Maybe you should try crying again!" *Slap.* "That always accomplished a lot for me when I was a boy." *Slap.* "Or just curl in a ball like a scared puppy!" *Slap.* "Will that save ya?" *Slap.*

Every attempt to try and defend himself or counterattack proved futile. Hedron's anger was acute, more than it had ever been.

"I was more of a man at twelve than you ever have hope of becoming!" *Slap.* "Pray, maybe that wench girl in the south can save you, aye?" *Slap.* "Aye, I think she might be more of a man than you! And she probably fights better than you! Too bad your daddy wasn't around more, perhaps then you'd have the stones he had!" *Slap.* "And maybe," *slap*, "if you had been a man instead of a boy when your mother needed you," *slap*, "she would still be alive!"

Hedron caught Aiden's hand when the next blow came. His jaw quivered and lips curled into a sneer. In primal rage, he screamed and pushed Aiden back. They crashed through crates and pottery basins that filled an abandoned merchant's cart. Bloody saliva sprayed from Hedron's mouth as he bellowed curses. He delivered a forceful punch to Aiden's midsection, then again, screaming and heaving with fists flying. His knee found Aiden's stomach followed by a double hammer fist crashing down on his spine.

"Stop it!" Ehliss screamed, but Hedron did not heed her words. He was in a blood rage, boiling inside beyond control. Lifting up Aiden's head by his hair, he struck him in the face, again and again. Aiden finally recovered slightly and kicked his leg out to sweep Hedron off balance once again, but the Kerr heir jumped over the legs and continued administering his wrath to Aiden's face.

"Please! Stop it!" Ehliss screamed again. Onlookers had begun to gather. Every crowd attracts a larger crowd, and so the audience continued to augment itself.

Aiden blocked the next punch and sent his foot into Hedron's gut, knocking the wind out of him. Crumpled over and heaving for air, Hedron knew Aiden would be coming fast for a follow-up blow. With his lungs still burning for breath, he reached up and caught Aiden by the sides of his head, grabbed two handfuls of hair and pulled Aiden's head down as hard as he could. Simultaneously, he straightened himself and brought his knee up with terrible velocity toward Aiden's face. In a show of breathtaking speed, Aiden moved his hand in front of his face to buffer the blow, but the force of the hit was still incredible. As he stumbled off balance, Hedron reached down toward Aiden's hip and drew the sword from its scabbard. He leveled it at Aiden's neck.

With bloodshot eyes the young Kerr roared, "I am Hedron Kerr! The son of Lord Thannuel Kerr, to whom you swore allegiance! You will honor him and obey me or his sword will end you!"

Aiden proffered a bloody grin. "Finally," he sighed and knelt down before Hedron with his head lowered. "I am your loyal servant, Lord Kerr. Where you go, I shall follow. My life will always be placed before yours and my blade in your defense. Never shall you fall while I yet stand."

The crowd was in utter silence. The chaotic ambience that had been only moments before vanished. Hundreds surrounded the scene. After a moment, murmurs fluttered among the people. Hedron still wore a mask of indignation but that was giving way to puzzlement as he began to comprehend what had just happened. He wiped the blood from his lips and spat. The adrenaline that still pumped through him caused his body to shake like a stubborn leaf in the Dimming Season refusing to be separated from its limb by a constant wind.

To his right, someone knelt—an elderly man.

"Lord Kerr," the man said softly.

Then another knelt and repeated the man's acknowledgment. Within a few more heartbeats, scores had followed suit.

Hedron took a step back and finally lowered the sword. He still breathed heavy. The scene around him was surreal as he watched over a hundred people kneel before him.

"Just one small correction, my Lord," Aiden said, lifting his head. "That's not actually your father's sword. Not anymore."

Hedron looked at the sword with his mouth open, as if seeing it for the first time. "I am no good with a sword, Aiden," he remarked just loud enough for only Aiden to hear. "I—"

"I know. That's why I was hoping you'd let me borrow it. Just for a bit longer."

FORTY-SEVEN

Reign

Day 4 of 2nd Dimming 412 A.U.

FASTER! **THANNUEL DEMANDED.**

Sweat drenched Reign's ebony hair. It clung in a matted heap against her clammy cheeks and wet forehead. Her concentration and focus were not deterred by the stinging in her eyes as the beads of sweat above her brow made their way down.

I can barely keep up with my own limbs! Reign protested in her thoughts.

The clang and clamor reporting from Reign's sword as she chopped and battered the old oak tree resembled the percussive cadence of an aggressive drum line with its tempo ever increasing. She dove and sprang, defended and counterattacked as Thannuel projected one enemy after another advancing on her where the oak stood. The pile of wood chippings and dust soon became ankle high and covered the tops of the exposed roots close to the base of the tree.

Here on the border of Arlethia and the Northern Province, the Gonfrey Forest met with the trees of the Arlethian forests. Both trees that spoke and those that did not were interwoven amongst each other, ignoring the borders imposed by the inhabitants of the land. The giant oak Reign now sparred against and was thoroughly thrashing was not a speaking tree, not of Arlethia. Thannuel had a plan for this and told Reign to pocket a single acorn from the tree before they began, though he did not fully explain why. Reign let him keep his secret for the time being.

Because of her proximity among trees that did speak, those that Reign now understood held and shielded the Lumenatis' power, and with a Triarch leafling in between the palm of her hands and the sword's hilt, she was able to draw into herself the strength of the trees. She directed that strength to increase her own, as well as provide extra endurance and stamina. Her muscles burned and ached from the extreme effort being exerted, but her determination was driving her more than the temptation to cease and give her body rest.

Your body will obey, Thannuel promised. *Demand your limbs and muscles give heed and they will soon complain less.*

The phantom images she saw before her were so real that Reign felt true peril as she evaded and attacked. Her mind, at least in some instinctual area, believed the threats were genuine, for every blow or stroke she blocked jolted her frame as if it were a true physical weapon she defended against. Fractions of a second before every movement she saw how to react and counter as her father projected the proper angle, form and velocity to her. Her motions were raw and unrefined, but she exuded force and fluidity.

Scores of specters fell around her as she dealt out lethal aggression with every blow and strike. The blade of her sword appeared like a blurred image reflecting off swiftly moving water. Four enemies surrounded her and closed in.

Too many at once! she screamed in her mind.

The Borathein will come at you relentlessly and not restrain themselves only to your abilities. Break the problem down, focus, and deal with it in smaller segments.

She drew in more strength from the trees and felt her capacity peak like lungs that had over-expanded with air. Her sword hummed louder as she channeled portions of the power into it. The first blow came from one of the phantoms behind her. She felt the air change behind and ducked just as a hammer with a head as large as her torso sailed through the air where her skull had just been. A second enemy sprang forward with a flail whirling and slung it forward to bash her head in. She rolled out of the way and felt the spiked ball hit the ground, leaving a small crater in its wake.

How can something not real leave a mark? But when she looked again, the imprint was gone. Smooth soil covered by brown leaves and needles lay undisturbed. She rolled back the other way and felt the breeze of the massive war hammer again narrowly miss her as it hit the ground as well. She blocked an overhead axe attack next but before she could counter was forced to block another attack.

"Father stop! I can't fight them all at once. I can't even strike back. The attacks are coming too fast, all I can do is block!"

You are an Arlethian, Reign. A wood-dweller. They are not. You are faster than this. Feed on the fear and apprehension friction you feel. Recycle it into your mental processes and think! The only way I'm going to stop is if you lock me away again.

Reign did as she was told, though it was not easy. Her focus and concentration increased amid the relentless attacks being levied upon her. Her mind split suddenly into two independent pieces. One continued to deftly defend against the advances of the Borathein mirages while the other piece, now freed from other distractions, focused on the problem.

Yes! Thannuel roared inside her. *What do you see?*

"A tendency. A tell."

Which one?

"The flail bearer. He takes a large breath and holds it before each downward swing. I see his chest expand and shoulders rock back slightly."

What else?

One of the men grabbed her from behind and squeezed her chest, trying to break her sternum. The pressure, though just in her mind, was very real and her breath left her. Her arms had limited mobility while restricted by the hold, but her legs remained firmly planted. Directing the strength she held from the forest to her legs, she sprang upward, with the large man still clinging to her, roughly twenty feet in the air. The effort required was enormous to create that much lift. They came sailing down facing the gray sky. The man let go in surprise and Reign rolled off him and hit the ground silently. The would-be-bone-crusher landed back first upon a tree stump attended by the sound of deep snapping. He squirmed with his back broken upon the stump for only a few moments before laying still. Blood bubbled up from his mouth and drained down over his long beard. The details of this mock fight astounded Reign.

It is how the mind works, said her father. *It can project sensory perception as well as images.* Reign's torso was indeed sore from being nearly crushed.

"I noticed."

The flail-swinging soldier stood in front of her now, menacingly whirling his weapon.

"Wait for it," she mumbled to herself. He feinted twice, but she did not move. As his shoulders went back and his chest became rounder, she knew. Shooting forward through the air toward the man, Reign's blade greeted his navel and snapped upward, lodging itself in his chin. She jumped, making herself horizontal, and kicked his chest squarely with both feet, sending him backward and freeing her sword.

"What else?" Reign said. "They all have beards with things woven into them."

I mean something material, Reign.

"It's material to me." With the part of her mind that controlled her motor functions, Reign continued to block and parry against the remaining two Borathein.

"This is the same style I saw that night, the night when Wellyn and the Helsyan beast were in the forest using a Dark Influence upon the trees. Turning them dark and dead. A tall man with trinkets in his beard just like this was there, except his was even longer."

Her speed proved too much for the Borathein. When she decided it was time to end the match, Reign dove between the attackers into a forward roll. She arose with a reverse pivot, as shown to her mind, and swung her blade in a half circle. Her steel met the flesh of both Borathein and they sank to their knees before face planting into the mulch created from the oak tree. The tree had many limbs missing and looked tortured from all the punishment. The war hammer hit the ground head down with its handle vertical.

Ah yes, the Helsyan.

The next image that formed before her eyes was ghastly. Mist seemed to coalesce and morph into the devil that had chased her six years ago and robbed her of her father and her innocence. The terror of being the target of a Dahlrak still wracked her and she visibly shook from the sight of the chase-giver. His white marred skin was stretched tight over ripped muscles. The smile came next, that same predatory expression that had haunted her for more than half a decade. She cowered and shrank inside.

No! she protested. *No!*

Her hands shook and she nearly dropped the sword.

"I can smell your fear!" he growled. "So succulent!"

Search deep, her father coaxed. *Accept the fear, feed on the friction. Command it!*

The fire of raging fear that climbed up inside Reign's soul should have been all consuming, immobilizing her. But she was not the child she used to be. She saw her vision expand inside, larger and wider until she could take in the panoramic view of all her fear. The pool was expansive and growing. She had to keep expanding herself to stay ahead of it.

Demand that it obey you!

"Relitha!"

The knot of fear ceased to grow and waited. It was a well of friction waiting to be tapped. She did tap it and the friction fueled her attack. It only took one movement. With all the power and

Light from the forest that she had stored inside her, along with the fear friction she had captured, Reign thrust her sword forward with a velocity that caused a crack in the air. Thunder sounded around her and the smell of burning air filled her nostrils. She felt the blade pierce the chase-giver and lodge itself deep in the oak tree. The vibration that jarred her as the blade suddenly ceased its empowered thrust would have broken her arms had her bones and sinews not been reinforced by the Light inside her. As the image of the Helsyan slumped on her blade, lifeless only in her mind, the word found her lips.

"*Vrathia!*" she screamed, sending forth the power she cradled through her sword of Jarwynian steel.

Both the visceral Helsyan phantom and oak tree exploded. When the smoldering air cleared, no evidence of the imagined enemies remained. Only the destroyed tree's waste and debris were present.

"What was that?" she asked.

Wrath. It is a strong emotion. The word you spoke can turn it to a weapon.

"And the steel conducts it," she surmised.

Yes. Only Jarwynian ore has this conductive property.

Reign smiled hesitantly. "*Threyil?* Is that jealousy I'm feeling from you?"

Admiration, daughter. Only admiration.

"Are we done for now?"

Take the acorn seedling from your pocket.

Reign retrieved it and held it in her outstretched hand.

Lay it on the broadside of your blade and speak the words you feel.

She balanced the seedling on her blade and searched her mind and her father's.

"*Ven Puwlartia,*" she whispered. A portion of Living Light flowed out of her, traveled through the specialized metal and infused the acorn. She planted it in the center of the smoldering crater where the oak had stood moments before.

"What did that do?" Reign asked.

A sliver of Lumenati Light will flow through the new tree, allowing it to be fluent when it matures. Its growth will also be accelerated greatly.

Reign began walking back to where she had left Jayden hours ago. Her travel was slow as her mind finally allowed her body to relax. The waves of weariness washed up against her mental shores. She had sent Crimson Snow back as well hours ago. The wolf was not happy but had obeyed nonetheless.

It will not be so easy when you finally meet him.

She did not answer.

He will be vicious, Reign. More so than I can conjure for you to prepare against.

"I know."

You do understand he will find you? It is inevitable.

"Yes, I know." Her tone was flat. "I just need rest now. Truly this time."

You will need less than you think. A couple hours at most.

"A couple days," Reign corrected, but she knew this was not possible.

The Living Light inside you is incredibly regenerative. With the amount you have taken in, you may not even need two hours and you will likely not need any sleep. Just rest. You will see.

"Threyil," she began but hesitated. "I must ask you about something."

Thannuel waited, but she could tell he knew what she was going to ask. Being inside her provided him access to her mind as well.

"After you died, there were many reports. They all spouted evidence that you had planned to usurp power from the High Duke, that you were a traitor."

She kicked a rock through an open clearing. It went much farther than she had intended.

"No one believed them, of course. Not at first. After time, and with more and more supposed evidence coming forth, people did start to doubt. But never us, never Hedron or mother. But the things people said...it was too much for most. They claimed to have found secret stashes of maps of the Realm with notes, charts of the seas with currents and tides noted. Even an attack plan on Iskele and Wellyn's palace. Weapons in hidden chambers under the hold and—"

It's true.

Reign stopped walking. "What? I don't believe you." But she confirmed what he said by viewing his memories. "No! It can't be! How could you—"

It's not what it appears, my daughter. You only see the surface. All that is happening now is a consequence of the Ancient Dark. The Gyldenal were preparing for a scenario they hoped would never develop, but that most saw as an eventuality. Do not judge with such haste. There is more. Much more. But the time is not quite right. Do not try to search through my mind for the answers now. You must put your mind at rest for the time being. Arlethia's extinction pounds eagerly at our very door.

Jayden slept against a large elm tree. In slumber, the old woman looked like she could be part of the tree itself. So peaceful and tired she looked that Reign was afraid to wake her. But Jayden surprised her by waking up instantly when Reign was within a few steps and coming to her feet spryly. Her eyes were young even if her body was not.

"How did you know I approached?" Reign asked. "You are not a wood-dweller and my step carries no sound."

"I know your current, little one."

Reign didn't understand but instead of acknowledging her ignorance asked, "Will we go to Arlethia now?"

"Almost, yes, but not to your brother. Not yet."

FORTY-EIGHT

Shilkath

Day 5 of 2nd Dimming 412 A.U.

IT WAS NEARLY TIME. The border where Arlethia began could easily be discerned. Life was more vibrant and lush almost immediately. The land thrummed with vitality and the air became noticeably warmer. Shilkath reveled in the vengeance he would release upon those who betrayed his kin, and he felt Hawgl tense underneath him. The beast was anxious for blood after so long of a journey. Vyath would smile this day as the land turned red with the blood of an entire race. More than anything, Shilkath longed for conquest and the lush land called Senthara.

Alysaar scouts had reported the location of many small villages and two larger cities in the northern reaches of this land. The trees' leaves and upper branches seemed woven together for leagues as one solid covering, hiding and protecting those far below.

"It's like a living barrier," Bellathia said as she swooped down and glided next to the Deklar. "We cannot see our forces below."

"Prethor knows his duty and does not require our assistance," Shilkath replied. His nephew led the infantry march on the ground.

"What of this green shield below us?" Bellathia was stunned to see the heights the trees reached.

"Our Alysaar will pierce it like a glowing red spear head through ice and feast upon the flesh of the traitors cowering underneath."

"Your nephew is not wrong, Deklar. They are not weak. I do not foresee this being an easy victory."

"But it will be a victory nonetheless. The fool Wellyn has done his part. See the destruction ahead down from the horizon." Shilkath motioned to a barren spot where a stretch of dark statues in tree-like forms manifested themselves. "Their armies are now in the frozen plains of Kulbrar."

"Vyath's Blood!" Bellathia swore. "What power can do such a thing?"

"It is a Dark Influence, as they call it, that our kin discovered but never understood how to use. Wellyn has a most cunning serpent."

"Servant, you mean."

"All servants are serpents. I said what I meant. Now get back in formation."

Bellathia's Alysaar grunted as she pulled back on the reins and directed it back to their place in the winged battery formation. As they approached the barren area of stone trees, many of the Borathein muttered curses and disbelief. Shilkath only saw the thousands of dead below. Arlethian and Senthary alike lay still, slain. Several thousand score, he guessed. The stench was powerful, but it did not offend the Deklar. Ravens and crows fought for claim over the sea of carcasses amongst the stone forest floor. Looking east, he saw smoke trails coming from small fires on the ground just outside the forest's borders. The remnant of the Sentharian army, Shilkath knew. He thought he might hear some celebration through the thin air where he flew, but no such sound was heard. A raven dared fly too close to his winged mount and the Alysaar snapped its neck in a whiplash as fast as lightning, impaling the bird on its bony maw before extending its long tongue to pull it from the spikes and into its mouth.

This is no price we have been asked to pay for our new lands, Shilkath thought. *Destroying these vial creatures is a pleasure.* He wondered if he would be able to lift his head after all the glory of his victory was added to his beard. The most prized he would wear daily in his beard and the others would be displayed in his palace, he decided. *No more tents with frozen ground or caves burrowed from frozen rock for my dwelling. A palace befitting a Deklar will finally be mine to rule from, as Vyath would have it.*

Below, he heard the screams. Prethor must have come upon a village of some kind and was busy exterminating its population. Shilkath could not see the action taking place, but knew the sounds of weaker beings being sent to the frozen plains. His sights were set on Calyn, the state city of Arlethia, according to Wellyn. This is where the greatest population would be found, and any hope of a battle. If there was still a spirit to fight among these people, he knew he would find it there. Unlike others under his command, such as Bellathia, Shilkath remained skeptical of the force that would oppose them after seeing the devastation Wellyn's forces brought upon the Arlethians. He prayed to Vyath that his Griptha would be more than a matter of eradicating the treacherous wood-dweller spawn from their lands as mere pests to be swept away. He yearned for a worthy fight to bring glory to himself and his people.

And then, he promised himself, *we shall eventually have the entire land to ourselves, even Arlethia. Wellyn will not be able to stop us.* He had decided that, as he fully expected some kind of treachery from Wellyn, he must be preemptive.

The horde under his command was followed by the remainder of his people, still more than a span of days behind them on the ice desert. After uniting all the disparate nahgi under himself as the lone Deklar, his people's purpose had been unified, their resolve solidified. There was no turning back, no home to return to. They were determined to conquer or perish in their holy Griptha. Shilkath brought one hand to his chest and rubbed the scar where he had opened his flesh upon the altar of Vyath. He had pledged his all to this Griptha by that ordinance. Failing meant death and eternity in Kulbrar with no remaining kin to avenge his people should they fail. He would never walk barefoot upon the warm

Shores of Thracia after this life if he died in defeat. He would succeed. He *must* succeed.

———

Seilia would not run. Others had fled as the vibrations of the
approaching invaders surged. There were those, like herself, who
felt compelled to remain. She sent Mikahl and Rue-anna away,
south to Calyn with all the other younglings of the village. She
knew their age of innocence had passed despite still being under
ten years old. They were well ahead of the slow moving invaders
and would be safe. She prayed the Ancient Heavens' protection
upon her children.

How many had stayed? Maybe one hundred of her small village? She didn't bother to count—the number didn't actually matter. She had her husband's quiver with less than a score of arrows
her children had crafted. The bulk of their produce she sent with
them to provision the forces gathering in Calyn. Joining the few
who remained, Seilia stepped up to a line they had formed in front
of their homes and laid the quiver at her feet. Elderly men, mostly
infirm, and mothers. One of her husband's bows was slung over
her shoulder. With trembling hands, she unslung it and notched
an arrow. The thick linen fibers were reverse twisted, slightly taper-
ing thinner near the center of the string to increase the arrow's
velocity. Her fingers felt numb against the rough bowstring as she
traced the line up to one end of the curved wood. A simple bow-
yer's knot joined the limb and string at each end.

The weapon felt heavy in her arms as she brought it up and
pulled the string back. The webbing between her thumb and fore-
finger fit snugly under the corner of her jaw and she centered the
blurred string close to her eye. She held and tried to calm her shaking arms. A single tear ran down her face as the marauders came
into view. It was cold in the breeze and dried before the trickle
reached her lips. Large men, long bearded and clad in thick clothing, marching in disciplined ranks. They had the hardened look

of those whom mercy had abandoned, leaving no trace of it within them. She expected none to be granted.

Searching for comfort and strength, she let her right hand wander from the bowstring to the ornately carved pendant hanging from around her neck. The details of the Triarch carved leaves were beyond anything her husband had ever done as a carpenter, a symbol of his perfect love for her, he always told her. It had been a gift from her children but she knew he had done the intricate work on their behalf.

At the sight of easy prey, a few score broke off from their organized march formation and rushed the small line of villagers. When they were within fifty feet, Seilia released the arrow and quickly notched another, drew, and fired. This second one found a home within a leg. A third time she drew and fired. More soldiers detached and joined the charge with eagerness. Seilia thought they wore the countenance of rabid dogs that had not eaten in a span, but it was just the blood thirst. Wherever they came from had been far away and their anticipation for battle welled deep.

As more of the anxious northerners joined the building frenzy, Seilia saw they would soon be overrun. They could make it, she and those who stood with her. If they left now, they would easily put a safe distance between them and the rabble that chased them. Even the slowest wood-dweller could outrun the fastest of these large ox-like men. But, would that serve their home? Her children?

Seilia knew every invader she harmed or killed would serve her children best. She would stay and do all she could until she was overrun, though it would feel small in the grand reach of Heaven's Light.

The bowstring sounded its brief song as she released another arrow. With nervous tension she notched a fifth and barely got it off, striking an assailant not four feet from her in the neck. That was the last arrow good mother Seilia had time to fire.

———

Prethor allowed the distraction, seeing it as healthy to let some of his men release cycles of pent-up anticipation. Only a few score joined in but the morale it created was contagious throughout the ranks. The number of fresh trophies adorning the beards of those who participated in the attack seemed quite numerous, Prethor thought, for the small number of those in the village. The Deklar's nephew hesitated at feeling impressed when he learned the village had only women and old men to defend it. Would Vyath be pleased with such a meaningless victory?

"For you Prethor, as our ground force commander," a Borathein warrior said as he approached. He held out in his open hand a curious circular trinket. Wooden carved leaves in the form of the clouds in the Low Season.

"I will not accept a token from slain women who were such easy prey," he said adamantly.

"She killed two and wounded a third badly enough we had to leave him behind," the warrior told him.

Now *this* impressed Prethor. Perhaps this pendant was worthy after all.

———

Hours later, their flight slowing to not get too far ahead of their ground forces below, Shilkath finally caught sight of a large city on the southern horizon. Its spires peeked through the top of the treed canopy amidst a large clearing in the otherwise jungle-thick growth.

Shilkath let out a cry of exhilaration that was echoed by two hundred thousand Borathein warriors and thousands of Alysaar. The Griptha would be fulfilled this night.

FORTY-NINE

Hedron

Day 5 of 2nd Dimming 412 A.U.

HEDRON AND THOSE WITH HIM made their way to the arena in the center of Calyn, where people from across Arlethia were gathering. A crowd of thousands thronged him as word spread about his appearance in the city. Many who had been fleeing abandoned their efforts and joined the crowd. Some shouted his praises as the rightful heir of the Arlethian Kingdom; others denounced him as an imposter, claiming that Hedron Kerr had died alongside his mother. And there were those who seemed totally indifferent, not caring if Hedron was who he claimed to be or not because they had no hope in these desperate times. Still others, who apparently did not contest his identity, mocked and berated him for being a member of the family that had brought such death and destruction among their people. Even a span ago he might have agreed with this sentiment.

No longer.

Tensions ran high as they traveled, and Hedron gave no heed to those who called after him. Aiden and the wolf cubs managed to keep the people to a distance of roughly six feet and prevent the crowd from thrusting in on him.

Hedron's entrance was impossible to miss as the already crowded area became saturated with the addition of the crowd he brought in tow. Three men stood elevated on some wooden crates and were in turn addressing those present. On the arena floor were tens of thousands of wood-dwellers loosely organized into different groups. Men, women and children scurried about uneasily. Most were armed with weapons of crude create, some with nothing at all. Few were properly armed or clad, and of those who were, Hedron doubted they were skilled with steel. He knew he was among the latter class. This fact worried him. He even spied a score or so of soldiers dressed in the apparel of the Arlethian army. Most of them were physically injured but all of them had a blank look upon their faces that bespoke damage on the inside as well as out.

The three men stopped when they noticed Hedron and his strange entourage. Each appeared middle aged and well dressed, though completely out of their depths. They were probably chosen as leaders due to their social standing but Hedron could readily see not everyone here accepted their assumed authority.

"You must be strong," Aiden counseled quietly. "Do not doubt your name or the honor of it. Demand their loyalty."

Hedron took a deep breath and looked at Aiden. His face was bruised and crusted with dried blood around the lips. He felt a pang of guilt as well as pride that he was able to land any kind of attack on Aiden, but realized his face must be similar looking, and he was left feeling mostly foolish. Aiden gave a curt nod and the boy took a step forward.

"Wait," Aiden said, grabbing his shoulder. "I almost forgot." From his small travel bag, he withdrew something wrinkled and loosely folded. It was dark green and thick, covered with stitching that mended scores of tears and rips. Aiden unfurled it and Hedron saw the symbol of House Kerr in the center of this cloak.

"My father's cloak?" Hedron asked.

"No, yours. Jayden would not let me part without taking it. She hoped you would grow into it."

With that said, Aiden wrapped the cloak around Hedron's shoulders and fastened it at the top of his sternum.

"Rise now, Lord Kerr."

With a confidence he did not feel, he strode to the makeshift risers. Stepping up on the crates, he addressed the three speakers who had been doing their best to organize the people into battalions and platoons.

"Greetings. Who are you?" he asked with a smile to the first man and extended his hand.

The man furrowed his brow with caution and responded, "Glimon, of Turla." Glimon took Hedron's hand and shook it hesitantly.

"Yes, I loved running through the swirling trees of Turla as a boy. And you?" He turned to the second man again with his hand outstretched.

He also looked uncertain but taking the first man's cue he answered. "Teagan, from the coast."

"The famous fishing merchant? Yes, of course, I know you. My father always boasted your catches were the freshest in Arlethia."

Turning to the third man, Hedron felt his façade start to fracture. He was large and muscular with a shock of disheveled hair that made him appear most unapproachable. Hedron forced himself not to waver.

"And you, friend?"

The man did not take his hand. He stood with his arms crossed for several long moments that made the scene become awkward.

Hedron stepped closer to the man and said quietly, "I am not your enemy, my friend."

The man capitulated and took Hedron's hand. "Merrick, a blacksmith of Faldraig." His grip was iron.

"Men," Hedron said addressing all three, "I thank you for your loyal efforts, bravery, and service. You are dismissed to join your people."

The men did not move and a murmur went through the ranks of those closest that could hear. Hedron could see the effect of his sudden arrival that had caused these three to momentarily play along was wearing off.

"Now see here lad, we have—" Teagan began but was cut off by Hedron's glare. Teagan's eyes widened.

"I am no boy! I did not ask for further comment, master fisher! You have been dismissed!" Hedron saw that Teagan was taken aback by the authority in his voice and he saw recognition flash in the fisherman's eyes. Merrick unfolded his arms and Hedron prayed that was not a preamble to the man striking him. The blacksmith's forearms were larger than a sledgehammer's head. No blow came.

Hedron held Teagan's gaze unflinchingly.

"Who are you?" Teagan asked while looking hard at Hedron's features, searching. The man seemed to be lost in a state of wonder.

Surely I look no more than a mere boy in worn clothing to them.

"Yes, I apologize for not making that clear at the outset." Hedron turned to face the tens of thousands around him. A knot swelled in his stomach. Ignoring it, he found his voice.

"I am the only son of Lord Thannuel Kerr, who was the son of Lord Branton Kerr before him, the same Thannuel who was murdered by a treacherous High Duke for daring to protect his only daughter! I am the son who heard his mother's screams as she was killed by those who professed loyalty! I am the brother who hid and sheltered his twin sister to protect her from those that cruelly sought her life though she was under the age of innocence and innocent of any crime all the same!"

Disbelief streamed through the masses. Hedron did not know which claim he had shouted caused the undercurrent, or if it was the confluence of all the claims. He continued undeterred.

"I am the cousin of Lord Banner Therrium who was slain in the midst of traitors whilst defending this, our long inhabited home! I am the friend and student of Master Aiden who slew hundreds of the Khansian Guard to protect that same Lord Therrium with no thought for his own life!"

Remembering the words his father had spoken at many public events, he said, "I am your Lord and therefore your servant. I will be first to lift your weary heads and first to stand in front of you when nightfall casts her long shadow! I am *Hedron Kerr!*"

———

Hedron was roaring. His words carried throughout the arena with a depth that Aiden had never experienced. They were captivating, not allowing any to turn away for even a moment. As he listened, he saw the boy become his father. The mantle of authority that had been in the Kerr bloodlines before they were called Kerrs descended upon him as the words exploded from him with undeniable power. Emotion swelled inside Aiden and his jaw became tight. Tears stung his eyes and the heat of pride burned deep within him.

"Enemies encircle us from all sides, my brothers and sisters!" Hedron bellowed. He was shaking. "They think us defeated, cowering. They think to have our lands and put our race to an end! I swear to you, by all the Ancients, while I yet have air in my lungs and strength in my limbs, this will never happen! Join with me now. Cast out the fear and find the strength; the strength to stand against tyranny, genocide, treachery, and all things of the Ancient Dark!"

He thrust his fist heavenward and his voice grew thunderous as he recited the Arlethian Warrior's Creed:

"I am a sturdy bough rooted deep in fertile soil! I am iron and steel, molded from the fires of adversity! I am life to those behind me, death to those in front! I am Arlethia, and she is me! I am her silent shield, her impenetrable armor, her terrible sword! She is my strength and my all! Those who stand against her stand against me, and shall swiftly fall!"

All of Calyn shook in the wake of Hedron's words. The shouts of ascent among the people sounded like a storm brewing from the center of the world. Aiden did not restrain the tears that streamed down his face and joined in the throng of shouts of "Arlethia!" and "Lord Kerr!" and "Hedron!"

I thought this was going to be an utter failure, Aiden admitted to himself. *Ancients forgive me, I should have beaten him sooner and more often.*

———

Any euphoria that would have accompanied such a rising of power by public acclamation was utterly squelched by the threat bearing down on them from all sides.

"These men behind me," Lord Hedron Kerr spoke when the crowd had quieted enough, "normal men—a fishing merchant, a blacksmith and—" he turned to Glimon and asked, "What was it you do?"

"As little as possible, my young Lord," Glimon answered. "I just play with the grandchildren. Or, that is, I used to until now."

"And a grandfather—normal people that were brave enough to stand and do what is necessary. You are to be commended and have my deepest thanks."

Hedron shook each one of their hands firmly and this time, they did accept the dismissal and left the meager stage to join their own groups. Seeing the small group of soldiers from the corner of his eye, he noticed they were standing a little taller but the hardened look of a warrior still eluded them. He knew they were broken inside. His feet met the ground and he approached the group. He felt Aiden come up behind him.

"Name?" he asked the first one he came to. The man was holding his left arm and had a wound above his left eye that would leave a nasty scar since it had not been properly tended to by a healer. He did not immediately answer.

"Name!" Lord Kerr demanded.

"Ulin," he said.

Aiden stepped forward. "I do believe your Lord asked you a question, soldier! Is that the proper delivery of your answer?"

"No, my Lord!" the soldier exclaimed, regaining his military discipline after being chastised in an all-too-familiar tone. "I mean, no, my Lord," turning to Hedron. The man was confused whom to address now and his frustration with himself showed. He collected himself and addressed Lord Kerr properly. "I am Ulin, My Lord."

"Ulin, what is it? What has shaken you so? This is more than the look of defeat," Hedron said.

"Our forces broke, my Lord. There was a Dark Influence in the forest. And monsters. They attacked the Senthary and us just the same. But they stopped fighting suddenly. They just stopped and stood there for several minutes and then retreated. We were too stunned to do anything. The officers fell one right after the other. And then after the stone came—I mean, have you seen it?"

"We have seen it," Aiden said.

"Then you know. You know the enemy has some Influence beyond what we can fight against." The soldiers all had the same doomed look on their countenances.

"Where are the others?" Hedron demanded.

"Who?" Ulin asked.

"Who, my Lord!" Aiden snapped.

"The other soldiers. There are barely a score of you here."

Ulin looked around at the men with him. "I don't know if there are any more, my Lord. We escaped and found one another. But, no others have come. The slaughter in the confusion after the trees turned was terrible. If there are others, they are probably in hiding. Likely the wisest thing."

At this, Hedron came within an inch of the Ulin's face. "Ulin, you and these men are going to secure that hopelessness you feel somewhere deep inside you. Lock it away and lose the key. If you are all that is left of our armed forces then I will need you. *They* will need you," he said, gesturing to the crowd.

"But my Lord, we cannot fight against such a power—"

"Do you hear the people around you? Do you hear their cheers and shouts of bravery? Those are civilians! Unless you can bury that coward streak running through you this instant, I will have you executed where you stand!" Hedron roared. Aiden drew his steel and the man paled.

As Lord Hedron Kerr was teaching Ulin and the other soldiers how to be men again, Glimon approached with a message in his hand.

"Lord Kerr!" he called, waving a folded piece of parchment. "Lord Kerr!"

Alabeth placed herself between the older man and barked savage warnings.

"Easy girl," Hedron said. "Glimon is all right. I think he has a larger pair than them, wouldn't you say?" He gestured to the ragged band of soldiers.

"Lord Kerr, a message has come from an emissary of the Southern Province," Glimon said.

Hedron tensed. "An emissary? Where is he?"

"Outside the arena. He appears to be alone but scouts have said the Southern Province's forces are half a day's march outside the city. They will be here before nightfall."

"What does the message say?" Hedron asked.

"Begging your pardon, my Lord, but I didn't dare read it. It was addressed to Lord Therrium." The man looked abashed. "I thought it best if—"

Hedron took the message. "That's fine Glimon." He opened it and looked at Aiden, who nodded.

"Might as well get the bad news done with," he said.

Lord Kerr agreed and read. His tension turned to awe and he dropped the parchment.

"Where is the emissary? Show me!" he demanded.

Glimon pointed to an archway that led out of the arena about three hundred paces away. Hedron ran through the crowds, only focused on the exit. When he emerged outside the arena, he looked around and saw a figure on horseback draped in a large hooded tunic in the bright gold, red and orange colors of the Southern Province. The emissary caught site of Hedron and dismounted, slowly approaching Hedron. The young lord saw a lock of blonde hair escape from under the hood. Hedron's breath caught. Slowly, the emissary removed the hood. Kathryn Hoyt's face was the most beautiful sight Hedron Kerr had ever beheld. Her smile was radiant beyond the sun at noon on any day of the High Season.

He ran to her. Kathryn almost disappeared as he wrapped her in his arms. He kissed her, tenderly at first, then hungrily. After an all-too-brief eternity, he pulled his head back and looked at the girl he loved. Joy, like none he had felt in his life, flooded inside Hedron and poured out from him as he stared into Kathryn's emerald green eyes. He could get lost in those eyes.

"Is it true?" he asked in a shaky voice.

She nodded. "My father will be here before nightfall with thirty thousand of our own men and ten thousand Arlethian warriors. We will not let you stand alone."

Though he knew it was not completely warranted, it was relief that made his voice break when he spoke next. "I don't understand. How is this possible?"

"Can't a lady keep her secrets?"

Hedron kissed her again.

It was just before the sun buried itself beneath the western horizon that Lord Hoyt arrived at the head of his forces, plus ten thousand Arlethian soldiers. The sight kindled hope in the people that lined the streets at the southern entrance of Calyn. Hedron did feel embers of hope but was also nervous at finally having to meet Kathryn's father, especially under the circumstances now facing them. How could one man make him feel more insecure than an almost certain annihilation of his people? He prayed he would not trip over his own tongue as he tried to speak.

Kathryn stood next to him, holding his hand, Aiden on his other side, with Ehliss next to him. Merrick also stood close with a mighty hammer. The huge blacksmith had somewhat taken to the young lord it seemed, appointing himself as his bodyguard of sorts. Aiden did not take offense. In truth, he seemed somewhat relieved to share the job with what approached.

Lord Hoyt rode his mount up to where they waited. Two others dismounted with him and approached Hedron until they were an arm's length away. Kathryn squeezed Hedron's hand a little tighter. Hoyt gazed at him for several seconds before looking away in thought. Hedron swallowed hard.

"Father—" Kathryn began, but Hoyt held up his hand to quiet her.

Looking back at Hedron, he took a deep breath and let it out.

"Lord Kerr, I presume," he said and extended his hand. Hedron accepted the gesture with a firm grip. Suddenly, Calder Hoyt pulled Hedron's arm, yanking him forward, and wrapped his other arm around Hedron's back. "And," he whispered in his ear, "soon to be a son of mine, if my daughter speaks truth."

Hedron blushed. "Yes, My Lord, if we survive. And, if you consent."

Lord Hoyt pulled back but kept Hedron's hand in his grip.

"Well, you sort of went about that backward, didn't you?" Hoyt asked.

Hedron did not know what to say and he knew it showed on his face. Lord Hoyt laughed. Slamming his hand down on Hedron's shoulder in a playful manner, he said, "Any man that can tame my daughter is a better man than I! If we survive this, Lord Kerr, we shall have a celebration of your union such as the Realm has never seen."

Again, Hedron blushed. "I think it might be the other way around," he said. "Kathryn is no doubt the one who tamed me."

Hedron heard Aiden grumble something under his breath that sounded a little like, "I might be sick." He smiled. Hoyt again laughed.

"Your forces appear unweathered, other than from the march here," Hedron said. He looked to see the Arlethian soldiers—the remnants of *his* army—and saw there had not endured a battle either. "Where are the other forces? Men of the East and North Provinces?"

"There were twenty thousand, all men of the East. We took them through surprise and strategy, my young Lord," Hoyt said. "I disarmed them and sent a contingent of the your Arlethian soldiers and marched them several leagues into the Schadar blindfoled, beyond the sight of any recognizeable landmark. Eventually, the Arlethian contingent silently left them mid-march and caught up with us. I don't know how long they marched before they knew they were alone, but they will not be a factor for the coming conflict."

"You neutralized a thousand score men without spilling a drop of blood?" Aiden asked.

"I fear that luck will not hold," Hoyt said. His countenance turned grave. "The middle and northern fronts...how did they fare?"

Hedron looked down and Aiden slowly shook his head.

"Come, Lord Hoyt," Hedron said. "We have much to prepare for and little time."

FIFTY

Reign

Day 5 of 2nd Dimming 412 A.U.

THE WHIRLPOOL SHAPED CLOUDS of the Dimming Season spun through the vault of heaven, illuminated by the blue silver light of first moon and occasional lightning blasts. The centers would become more hollow as the Low Season approached and would eventually only leave the perimeter of the beautiful empyreal nebulae.

"I remember a night such as this," Reign said. It was an odd thing for her to long for the night she lost her father but it would have been another few moments with him in life. Crimson Snow walked on her left side, not at her heel as a pet but next to her as one of her trusted friends.

Knowing her mind, Thannuel offered, *I know, Reign. I wish for that as well. I wish for many things that did not come to pass.*

They stood in a part of the former Western Province that Reign had never visited. The northwest forest ran right up against the seashore of the west coast of the continent. Great yellow-wooded trees grew in the shallow seawater with a portion of their knotted and twisted trunks remaining under water even in low tide. Those parts were crusted with inanimate sea life of all create and also served as spawning grounds for many fish. Farther inland in this

519

forest were found all manner of vegetation and trees, the thickest Reign had perhaps ever seen. Parts were undoubtedly more jungle than forest. Again, she had memories of this place that she knew were not natively hers.

"The Tavaniah has long been our home," Jayden said. "The Gyldenal have resided here ever since the Turning Away. Protected by the Lumenatis as its guardians and preservers of knowledge."

Reign was mystified by the feelings she experienced in this place. "I've always heard the stories—people say this place is haunted."

"I'm not sure that's quite accurate," Jayden objected. "But there are some peculiar characteristics, yes."

It's why she fits in so well here, Thannuel said. Reign smiled but withheld her laugh.

"Like what?" she asked.

"I'm sure you'll see soon enough if you are still," the centuries-old Hardacheon wolf shepherd said. "This is the place where the Living Light was hidden by our ancestors. More specifically, yours. While I am part of the Gyldenal, and one of the oldest living members, it is your kind, Reign—Arlethians—that are the direct descendants of the Ancients. Or, at least the portion that did not follow after the Dark Mother."

"This place? The Lumenatis is here?"

"Do not misunderstand, the Living Light is not an object. It is the source of Influences that promote life and knowledge. Våleira and its lands were created from the Lumenati Light that fills the universe. A spark of that Light resides in all living things. The Dark Mother seeks to devoid the world of the Lumenatis' Influence and bring darkness and death through her Song of Night."

"Song of Night?" Reign asked.

Those who follow her can hear it. Tempting them. Binding them. It is said to be a disharmonious melody that is beautiful and impossible to live without once heard.

"Why?" Reign asked. "What does she gain by this?"

"Oh yes, unlike the Lumenatis, the Dark Mother is truly a person, one who is Dark incarnate. The Ancient Dark itself is like the Lumenatis, a source of chaotic and life-depriving Influences. But Noxmyra, the Dark Mother, sought the dark to an extent that it engulfed and ensnared her forever."

"But what does it have to gain by bringing decay and destruction?"

No, Reign, it is not a question of gain or motive. That isn't how the eternal forces operate. It seeks this because it is its nature. Nothing more. She repeated her father's words as they sounded in her mind for Jayden's benefit.

"Thannuel is correct. He has become wiser over the past many years apart from his body."

"Jayden, what of those who did turn away? The Ancients I mean. What became of them?"

"You might find an answer in the actual name of this land. Before the lands cycled, before there were Arlethians or Hardacheons or Senthary or Borathein or any of the myriad races that once filled Våleira. This continent was known by a different name entirely."

Reign took in a sharp breath as the name came to her from her father's memories.

"Helsya," she said.

Jayden nodded.

"But that means that…that the Helsyans are—"

"All people descended from the Ancients, my dear. This should be no surprise; even the Changrual have this right. Those who fervently followed Noxmyra in the Turning Away were granted powers from Dark Influences that made them stronger than nature ever intended. The Ancient Dark aspired to have its followers spread the work of chaos and entropy across the world unabated. None would be able to stand against them in their unnatural state."

But the Living Light cursed them as a balance, limiting their powers and changing their appearance, Thannuel added.

"The scars," Reign realized. "They are glyphs of the Ancient's language."

Jayden nodded. "Yes. They tell the story of their apostasy from the Living Light and embracing of the Dark. But it's more than this. Their enhanced abilities and strength are only present when they are Charged, or given a Dahlrak, as it is called in the ancient tongue. Only he who holds a particular gem, called the Urlenthi, can levy a Charge to a Helsyan. Another one of the Light's checks upon them, disallowing them to run free through the world as if Charged. Chase-givers are immovably loyal to the holder of the Urlenthi. Orlack was the first to hold this power over the cursed race, a Hardacheon who led the invasion into this land from the north, long before the Glaciers of Gonfrey were present, when the lands in the far north first started to show signs of decay."

Their fealty to the Urlenthi is not as unbreakable as Jayden says, Thannuel corrected. Jayden rolled her eyes with impatience.

"I'm not going to debate this again, Thannuel," Jayden muttered. "We don't have time for every theory on the subject."

"The name glyph," Reign said. "It is the one different symbol on every chase-giver. If someone called a Helsyan by their name, their actual identity, then—"

"No one can read the ancient tongue, not even the Gyldenal anymore," Jayden said.

But if someone could discern it, they could break the hold the Stone of Orlack has on that Helsyan.

"So goes the theory," Jayden admitted, "but it's a useless waste of intellectual debate and time since it is a dead language, as much as my own is."

Reign pondered deeply for several moments, retracing her memories and those of her father. Her stare was fixed though she focused on nothing in her physical view, but rather saw with clarity images in her mind.

"I can read it," she said.

"Don't be foolish, child. You are something of a wonder, the first we know of since the Turning Away to take in a last breath. I think that says a lot of your father as well as you but—"

"I can read it," she again insisted.

Jayden looked at her for a moment and then accepted Reign's claim with a nod. Whether or not she actually believed her, Reign did not know, but she knew at the least that Jayden did not care to continue with that topic.

"Why are we here again?" Reign asked.

The old wolf shepherd scurried around the forest floor curiously, stomping her heel every few paces.

"Well, are you going to help me or not, Elohk?"

The large albino wolf huffed and walked forward to a spot about fifteen paces and looked at his master.

"Ah, right!" Jayden exclaimed. When she came to the spot Elohk had indicated, she again kicked the ground and a hollow thump sounded. She reached down and cleared away leaves and earth to reveal a large slab of wood. Before Reign could ask what it was, she knew.

Will I ever be truly surprised again with you in there? she sarcastically asked her father.

Jayden found two short pieces of rope and pulled the wooden covering up. Underneath in a pit no more than three feet deep were scores of bows, arrows, spears, maces, swords and shields. The metal was a dark pewter color, different than the silvery gleam of polished steel although this metal still had a luster to it.

"Jarwynian ore," she said.

Jayden nodded. "Indeed."

Knowing the Jarwyn Mountains to be hundreds of leagues to the southeast, she asked, "But who—"

Before she could finish, Jayden glanced around. Reign took the cue and looked but saw nothing other than the thick frondescence natural to this environment. Nothing seemed out of—

From behind the trees and plants, silhouetted figures came into focus. The number of them startled Reign and she reflexively reached for the sword at her hip.

"We are only seen when we want to be, especially here," Jayden explained.

"We?" Reign asked, still tense despite her father's sense of reassurance in her mind. Crimson Snow was not acting apprehensive, which did speak some comfort to her.

"Reign, these are the Warriors of Light. Better known in myth as the Gyldenal. Welcome to our hallow."

The land changed before her. Thickets became grassy patches, trees removed themselves and altogether disappeared in some cases. A clearing in the canopy opened above them and a stream flowing westward toward the sea came up from the ground. Where she stood became a pleasant meadow instead of thick jungle growth. She now saw clearly that they were surrounded by hundreds of men and women. She sensed many to be wood-dwellers.

Reign's apprehension did not abate but increased. "Of what create is this?" she demanded.

"I told you, dear. The Tavaniah lands are protected as the resting place of the Lumenatis. Its Influence is strong here as is the Light of those you now plainly see. They mean you no harm, child."

Reign looked down at the recessed armory where Jayden still knelt. "And those?"

"We have people placed in all areas of the Realm, even in the High Duke's court. Several of our members work in the mines of Jarwyn. It has been years in the planning to be able to slowly collect weapons of such difficult craftsmanship and smuggle them here."

Two men, not wood-dwellers, stepped forward.

"This is Daneris." Jayden motioned to the man on the left. He was well defined and pleasing to look at for someone not of Arlethia.

"He was in the service of Wellyn as a Khan. The other is Aramith, an ore master from the Jarwyn mines. We have them to thank for the supply of weapons as well as vital information."

The two men nodded at Reign in greeting.

You were right, Reign told her father. *I did not understand.*

We knew a time would soon come when the Gyldenal would be needed to preserve the people. Not just of Arlethia or the Realm, but of all Vâleira. We were preparing to do whatever was necessary.

And they found one of your weapons caches. The "evidence" they claimed to have.

A man came forward who was ancient to her eyes and greeted Reign. Long gray hair draped around his face to his shoulders, and he held a staff in one hand made from—*Triarch wood*, she knew in her mind. He seemed oddly familiar to her.

"I am a current," he said in a thin voice.

Reign answered: "I am a current of friction and light, a spark against the Ancient Dark that cannot be extinguished, a beam of the Lumenatis." And then she saw it. The gentle breeze lifted the hairs that had covered a portion of his face and revealed a marking on his cheek that was a curve, resembling a wave. Reign's breath caught as she recalled a time in the forest after her father died, a time that she had believed was perhaps no more than a dream.

"You came to me," she said. "I remember, but—"

"I did come to you, young one. And do you remember what I told you?"

"To keep my anger close, that it would shield me for a time, that..." She paused as she collected her memories. "That *he* would not blame me. You meant my father."

The old man nodded. "And so your anger was a shield while you needed it, but that time has passed. What else?"

Reign blinked, trying to scrape free the petrified memories of that time from the inside of her head. "The breath," she answered. "You said I would see you again when I had taken my father's last breath. You knew, even then—but how?"

The old man smiled. It touched his eyes and gave off an aura of kindness and depth all at once. "I am Evrin," he said and gently squeezed her hand. "I am the Keeper of the Living Light, as appointed by my brothers and sisters." Evrin gestured to those all around them. "We are honored to have Lord Thannuel Kerr's daughter among us. I perceive that your mind is pure and untainted. With your father's last breath upon you, you should be prepared for what must be."

Reign did not know if she liked the sound of that but did not shrink away.

"What is that?" she asked sheepishly. The presence of this elderly man was magnetic. She felt such depth from him, such understanding.

"To lead, of course. The battle about to be fought is greater than one for lands or power or possession. It is for the essence of the world itself, whether it will survive with life and Light, or fall to eternal entropy within the Ancient Dark, as have other worlds."

She was about to ask what Evrin meant by "other worlds" when the first part of his statement finally hit her.

"I can't lead!" Reign exclaimed. "I'll fight. I'll do whatever I can, but I am not a leader!"

"Ah, but you will be, child. After you are taught the ancient axioms of Light, you will be able to harness the Living Light greater than any other since the Ancients."

"Why me? I am no one special, not compared to any of you."

"But you are wrong, my dear," Evrin assured her. "It was to be your father's role, he having demonstrated more capacity for Light than any living member of our order could recall witnessing. In order to conceal and save the Living Light from being extinguished completely during the Turning Away of the Ancients, our predecessors buried it deep within the Triarch trees in the Tavaniah Forest. However, it was also a curse; for though we preserved the Light and therefore Våleira, no one had enough capacity to withdraw it again. For thousands of years the Gyldenal have protected and hidden the secrets of the Lumenatis and waited for someone to demonstrate enough capacity for Light to restore the world as it once was before the Turning Away. To restore the Ancients, as the stories often say. Your father showed great promise but even then we could not be certain. Those who buried the Living Light are long passed away. But, alas, Thannuel's time ended before his purpose could be fully realized. But, as his daughter, and combined with his knowledge and capacity, you can potentially extract the Lumenati Light in amounts great enough to reverse the effects Noxmyra has spread across the rest of the world.

Unknown to those here on Senthara, there is no life beyond these borders any longer anywhere in the world. All other peoples have perished with the lands turning fallow. It has become time to stand against the Dark, few though we may be."

Reign did not answer because she did not know what to say. Finally: "What must I do?"

"We are not just protectors and preservers, young Reign. Though your abilities will easily surpass our own with your advantage, we will stand by you and fight this war. It is time for the Warriors of Light to come out of obscurity and once again be known."

Looking to the wolf, Reign said, "Gather your packs." Crimson Snow darted at incredible speed northeast toward Jayden's old cottage. Reign had a fleeting thought regarding the age of that decrepit house and believed it must be as old as Jayden herself.

"There are others coming," Jayden said.

Evrin nodded. "Yes. We believe over five hundred thousand, less than a span of days from the edge of the glaciers."

"Who?" Reign asked with concern.

"The remnants of the Borathein people," Jayden said. "They come because they have nowhere to go and most of the Realm has been promised to them if their armies, already at the edge of Calyn, are successful in the destruction of Arlethia."

"You and those you choose to work with you will prepare for them," Evrin said to Jayden. "They will need to be dealt with in either event, should Arlethia survive or succumb to defeat."

"Hedron," Reign said, thinking of her twin brother.

Jayden looked grave. "He is not his father, despite Aiden's best efforts. He is not ready for what comes."

Reign discerned the meaning behind Jayden's words, that her brother would not likely survive, but she could not accept this.

"Ready? None of us are *ready!*" Reign defended her brother. "Hedron did not choose this, nor did I! But have some faith in him. He is young but you cannot see the strength he hides under a boyish façade. He will do what he must!"

"As will we all," Evrin said.

FIFTY-ONE

Aiden

Day 5 of 2nd Dimming 412 A.U.

AIDEN SAW THE TERRIBLE SIGHT ahead of him and felt the tremors from below. One league north approached a storm of flying demons like a feral haze floating above the forested canopy. The brilliant, cold-blue light of first moon cast eerily morphing shadows under the beasts that gave an illusion not unlike black waves fighting against one another as they washed over the leafy shore. Aiden did not need to be a wood-dweller to feel the approach of more than a thousand score invaders below him on the ground where the Southern army waited. It was as if a piece of the thunder that clapped above them had become incarnate and walked upon the land below. The lightning that ripped the skies illuminated the flying horde every minute or less, leaving no doubt as to the number of enemies facing them.

He stood in plain sight—there was no point in concealment—upon the leafy terrain at the top of the trees that lined the northern rim of Calyn at the head of ten thousand Arlethian warriors, only a fifth of what their army had once been. They were at the center of their battle formation with roughly fifteen thousand civilian men, women and children on either flank. The civilian militia, all Arlethians, was adequately armed, mercifully, thanks

529

to the arrival of Lord Hoyt's forces from the south. They hauled with them weapons and armor they had stripped from the Easter Province's forces, enough to arm twenty thousand soldiers. Some of the militia did not look strong enough to even lift the swords or axes given them, but the moment would give them strength. *Ancients be with us!* The fear that permeated the air as they watched the massive winged cavalry approach them was palpable.

As he scanned to the right and then left, he caught sight of a figure he thought he knew, a little girl with a bow of wood-dweller create. *Rue-anna!* Seilia's daughter from the village Eledir. He wondered if Mikahl, her brother, would be here, but he did not see him in his brief scan.

If she's here, Fletch must be also.

He thought about sprinting to her in the few brief moments that remained and ordering her down, but there were more than a hundred score of children mixed into the militia. His orders would not be rational but he also knew he could not protect the little ones, though he desperately wanted to. The age of innocence, he knew, would mean nothing to the foes that now approached.

Hedron had given Aiden command of their forces despite his protests that he must stay at his Lord's side. The boy—now a man and lord—insisted and stated his arguments well. No one else had faced one of these Alysaar, as Jayden called them, before; nor the Borathein who mounted them, almost as beastly as the flying creatures themselves. Aiden had not just faced one Alysaar, but two. While one did escape, the other he gutted thoroughly, slicing its head in half down through the neck to the shoulders. Its two riders had fared no better. He knew how to kill them. This fact gave both the soldiers and militia a few much needed threads of courage as they faced the threat of almost certain genocide.

He gripped the Triarch leafing between his palm and sword hilt more tightly. Most of the Arlethians with him, if not all, also had a leafling in their grip. Every increased bit of sensory perception would aid them, both in their attacks as well as chances for survival.

What if Wellyn releases his Dark Influence again? There wasn't any doubt that he would, Aiden realized, and knew there was nothing he could do about it. *Focus. Think of nothing but this moment.* He quieted his mind until he could hear nothing but the beat of his heart. Slow. Confident.

It started small. Aiden took a silent step forward, then another. Those behind him followed. In less than five strides, the full force of roughly forty thousand charged. There was no yell or verbal challenge, only air whistling around them as they propelled themselves to an inhuman velocity. The Borathein would see only blurs upon the dark treetops beneath them, but their speed would not camouflage them from the Alysaar. Their vision was far more acute than humans with literally breakneck reflexes. He had experienced this only days past at Jayden's cottage.

Aiden dragged his sword along the canopy, creating an uneven rhythm as his blade bounced off branches and leaves, the same way he used to do when he was a boy with his wooden practice blade. He was close enough now to clearly distinguish one enemy from the other without the aid of sporadic flashes of lightning in the night sky. A command was heard from the foremost rider, and the Alysaar with their riders began a steep incline. It was as beautiful and terrible as a tidal wave moments before pulverizing a doomed soul in its path. The Alysaar wave crested and dove sharply, vehemently, toward the charging wood-dwellers. The grandeur of the sight was awe-inspiring and Aiden felt a kernel of fear burrowing inside him. He captured it before it took root and recycled the friction. A sensation of tingling went through his right hand and he knew his sword was vibrating as it had done that night long ago, from which all these current events had their genesis.

He ran faster, into the crashing wave of demons, determined to see it break around him. He prayed for those who so bravely had taken up a blade in defense of their lands and families. They ran willingly with him into a nightmare that left little hope of relinquishing those it ensnared, but they charged with him regardless. He knew morning would never come for most. Perhaps not even for him. Just moments before the first Alysaar crashed down upon him, he smiled.

The ear splitting screech of the demons—sonorously both high and low in pitch—cracked through the night air.

Aiden launched.

———

The ground shook under Hedron's feet. Huksinai, Alabeth and Thurik waited on his left side, each lined up shoulder to shoulder. They were eager yet disciplined—even Thurik—and they knew they would not be restrained this time. Alabeth looked up at Hedron and put her ears flat.

"You'll be fine," he promised and pet her head behind her ears.

To his right on horseback were Lord Calder Hoyt, Master Gernald Quarry, and Lord Marshal Wenthil, whom Lord Hoyt had appointed to lead the ground forces with Hedron's consent. Hedron stood with his own feet on the ground. A wood-dweller lost much of his advantage in battle when riding a horse. Not only were they more agile on their own but wood-dwellers also needed to feel the ground as keenly as possible, and a horse would be a natural buffer to those vibrations running through the ground and conducted by the massive interwoven root system of the forest. In addition to the South's thirty thousand here on the ground were roughly twelve thousand Arlethians. None of them soldiers, but standing bravely all the same. Merrick was just behind Hedron, his heavy hammer resting against a shoulder the size of a mountainside. Hedron felt no pity for those who would be in its way when the avalanche began. It would be only moments now.

Wenthil had organized their ground forces as best he could, being unfamiliar with the terrain and also with commanding civilians who were Arlethians. He did not know how to best use their abilities to an overall advantage and there was no time to learn. The Lord Marshal had given permission to Glimon, who finally revealed himself bashfully to be a retired command sergeant and had served in the Orsarian War, to deploy the civilian militias as he best saw fit. When Hedron asked Glimon why he had not previously made his experience known, he humbly said, "Those days are not something we intended to remember, certainly not repeat."

"We?" Lord Kerr asked.

In response, Glimon had simply motioned to Teagan and Merrick, and things suddenly made more sense to the young Lord.

No matter the fear that ran through him and the enormity of the foe that threaded its way through the trees toward him, Hedron could only think of Kathryn. She had insisted on fighting by his and her father's side, but the two men forbade it in unison. Kicking and screaming, she was finally carried away by two hold guards and sequestered in a small village that lay deep in the forest south of Calyn. Kathryn had no training for battle and neither Hedron nor Lord Hoyt would allow her to be present even if she had.

"Good luck with that one," Hoyt had said as they watched her being dragged away.

"How did you ever convince her to see reason growing up?" Hedron asked.

Hoyt turned to Hedron. "A little fatherly advice for your relationship, son. She is the one who persuades, not the one persuaded. And yes, she is usually right. It's rather maddening."

Thurik howled, bringing Hedron's focus back to the present. His two siblings joined the lonesome note, making a bone-chilling chorus. The enemy came into view. Arlethian scouts, using both the forest as a medium and their eyes, reported the enemy's strength at roughly two hundred thousand. Even knowing the number of the enemy could not have prepared him for the visceral sight of the massive horde, an infestation running wild. Hedron did not know if eradication was possible, but he would try to stand against this disease the Dark had sent to his home.

He thought of Kathryn once again and prayed the Ancient Heavens would protect her if he could not. He took a step forward.

As he spoke the words to himself, he felt them more personally and knew he was referring to Kathryn just as much as his ancestral home of Arlethia.

...I am life to those behind me, death to those in front. I am Arlethia... She is my strength and my all...

Hedron charged.

———

As Hedron ran forward toward the enemy ahead of everyone else, Lord Hoyt saw the boy become Thannuel, not only in appearance but also in action. The three wolves that went everywhere he did were not far behind. And then the blacksmith was running, his hammer held high above his head. Lord Marshal Wenthil cursed at seeing Hedron dash forward and hastily called for a charge. The cry went up among the soldiers and they surged forward.

———

General Roan was famished. He lay in the tall grasses near where the remnants of the Realm's army still camped, licking their wounds. They had not moved since he felt his men fall. Roan judged the enemy numbers to be a little above thirty thousand, not more than thirty-five thousand. He had survived the past days on grass and a few morsels of bread and cheese he had managed to acquire from those he had slain.

How many days has it been? His best guess was half a span plus one. Time seemed almost of no consequence to him now. He observed the Senthary forces, waiting for something to develop, but nothing had. Not until this evening.

He felt a force from the southwest approach his position. Not wood-dwellers. He surmised this must have been the remainder of the middle battlefront twenty leagues south and lamented all the more at what that meant. By now he had thought any remaining Sentharian forces would have already arrived. He had held out hope that the two fronts south of his own would have fared better than his, but until now no evidence either way had surfaced. The hope he held thinned.

When they came into view, Roan raised his head above the grass. At least eight thousand Sentharian soldiers were in the formation he saw marching toward the camp. High Lord Marshal Brendar was among them, the rank insignia on his breastplate clearly visible, untarnished. The coward had obviously not joined his men in battle at the middle front.

Craven man! Roan screamed inside, his anger flaring as it always did when officers hid behind their men. It was a strange feeling, to hold the enemy's enlisted men in higher regard than another officer. His mind drifted back to when he was not part of the officer corps, just an enlisted soldier, before the Orsarian War. During that conflict, he had fought alongside the Senthary, not against them. He thought of General Korin, who had led the preemptive attack against the Orsarians on the Runic Islands. The old Arlethian general had been a tough man, both physically and to admire; however, Roan did admire him greatly, even now, decades after his death and wondered if he had been more like Korin, would he have lost so many of men. Would he have failed so completely? Korin had not insulted his men by surviving when so many under him had not.

Roan had ordered twenty-five thousand of his Arlethian warriors to that middle front. The loss of so many brethren in arms stung his soul to the core. The soldiers he viewed now, marching to join the group of Sentharian soldiers that had massed at the northern front, were haggard and moved slowly. Many lay on stretchers, carried by others. Many more limped along with battlefield dressings covering wounds. He was about to advance and deal out as much vengeance as he could, starting with the craven Brendar, when the sight of something odd halted him.

Nearly a span of hooded men, larger than most, walked on the west side of the formation. Their steps felt heavier than a normal human as he filtered out the rest of the vibrations. He counted nine. This would add to the four others he had observed days before already in the camp. Roan decided to watch for a while longer.

———

A spear flew past Aiden, narrowly missing his face. He stood on top of an Alysaar cutting down the rear rider before turning to the one at the reins. Aiden kicked him off the beast and he fell to the canopy below. It did not stop his fall and Aiden lost sight of him. He turned left and saw the Borathein who had thrown the spear swooping down eagerly toward him. The Alysaar he was on dove and banked as the forward rider tried to throw him free. Aiden stood upon the flying animal's back with a balance born to Arlethians and thrust his blade down into its back. He twisted the sword. The Alysaar threw its head back in pain, jolting the remaining rider. Aiden grabbed the man from behind and snapped his neck. The approaching Alysaar opened its talons to pluck Aiden from its dying kin, but the wood-dweller leaped with his sword in hand and floated downward to land on another.

The night air swarmed with these flying demons. Arrows from the wood-dwellers below atop the canopy shot upward with stunning accuracy, catching the Alysaar at the joint where their wings met their body. It was crippling to their flight ability and dozens had fallen, taking their riders with them. Still, thousands remained. Arrows alight with fire streamed downward from hundreds of Borathein archers who made a sweeping attack over Calyn. Screams echoed upward as the arrows found home. Aiden dispatched the two riders on the Alysaar he landed on and tried to commandeer the beast by taking its reins. Instead of obeying his commands it flew straight up, higher and higher.

Very well then. Aiden stabbed the Alysaar through its neck and again leaped downward into the thick swarm. As he dove, he had a brief aerial view of the battle. The chaos of it all made it impossible to discern anything helpful. He aimed for an enemy within his vector and extended his sword down. The humming blade of Jarwynian steel sliced through the feathered membrane of an Alysaar wing followed by Aiden's body, causing the creature to screech out in pain and retract its wing in reflex. It toppled in flight and fell into the trees. Aiden landed on the canopy and slid down a tree for a few feet before catching himself. A yellowish-orange glow came from below and he knew the city was burning along with the trees that bordered it. He saw many thousands of the Arlethian soldiers and militia battling the Borathein as he was, jumping from one Alysaar to the next, bringing death to the invaders, these purveyors of genocide. But many were falling themselves, lifeless or dying. He spied Ulin and several with him, their swords and armor swathed in carnage, leap from the canopy toward a target but get impaled by a flanking Alysaar on its spiked maw. The Alysaar jerked its head downward, freeing its bony beard of the impaled corpses. A roar came from its riders but was cut short as an arrow found the eye of their mount. Aiden glanced toward where the shot had come from and saw Rue-anna loosing arrow after arrow, dancing among the treetops too fast for even raindrops to catch her. Other children were with her, slinging stones, throwing sharpened wooden staves, a few wielding swords as tall as they were. Most were having little effect, though the distraction they provided was valuable enough.

But Rue-anna was masterful. Seilia had not exaggerated her daughter's talent. Several Borathein took notice of her aim and darted from behind her at a sharp intercept angle. Three Alysaar formed a spear as they pulled in their wings against their bodies to accelerate the dive. Aiden watched in horror as they approached the unsuspecting girl but knew he could not save her. He might have enough time to take one down, but not all three. Just before the closest Alysaar could reach Rue-anna, she disappeared beneath the canopy and out of reach. As soon as the three attackers had pulled up and away from their unsuccessful attack, Rue-anna reappeared and resumed acquiring targets with deadly accuracy, taking down or gravely injuring an enemy with every shot. Aiden leaped to her position in two strides, slicing open the underside of one Alysaar while narrowly escaping its talons on his second jump.

"You aren't hurt?" he asked hurriedly.

"She's fine," came a boy's voice from beneath the thick-leafed branches. Aiden parted some young leaves and saw Mikahl, Rue-anna's brother, hanging on to a vertical branch just out of sight.

"Fletch! What the Blasted Heavens are you doing here?" Aiden yelled.

"He's my spotter," Rue-anna said as the string of her bow twanged with the release of yet another arrow.

"More like savior," the boy answered with pride.

Aiden spotted movement under the canopy all around the children.

"We each have one," the girl said.

Aiden marveled at the foresight. "Who designed this?"

"We all did," Mikahl answered. "It seemed the best thing to do."

Aiden felt small in the shadow of the wisdom of the younglings. "Well done. The Light keep you," was all he could think to say before bounding off to find another enemy.

———

Lord Calder Hoyt was not a great warrior. He had been trained with steel and shield through several visits to the Erynx Military Academy in the Eastern Province, as had the head of his army, Lord Marshal Wenthil, though Wenthil's instruction was years long as a full-time student. Hoyt's training was more ceremonial in nature, only teaching him the basics of combat. He found, however, that when your life was threatened, you gained skills you didn't know you had. Their execution was effective if not graceful, but that mattered little as his enemies died regardless. Master Gernald and other hold guards were by his side without fail, not engaging in the battle unless it meant to protect Lord Hoyt. That was the training of a hold guard—to protect your lord, not win the battle.

The air was filling with smoke that coagulated in the underside of the natural canopy well above them. They were attacking the Borathein with speed and then retreating just as quickly to lure them in to a crossfire of arrows and crossbow bolts coming from archers about twenty paces high in the trees. As soon as their missiles were loosed, they sprang through the trees to a position forty to fifty paces backward and repeated the strategy. But this tactic let the Borathein masses advance and would eventually allow them into the city itself. Hoyt knew this was inevitable. The jungle-like growth slowed the progress of their enemy, but once they crossed into Calyn, where there was more open ground and room to maneuver, overcoming this force would be impossible. They were outnumbered nearly five to one. The Arlethian militia was extremely effective amid the trees, cutting down several Borathein for every one loss of their own; but in a more open space some of their advantage would be quelled. Their speed would still serve them well, but Hoyt saw a retreat as inevitable. He did not know what else they could do.

As they moved farther backward toward the city, Calder felt the heat. He turned on his large horse and saw much of the city in flames. They were being pushed into an inferno.

———

Shilkath watched in glory from his Alysaar, Hawgl, as his warriors fought the Arlethian filth. He circled above the battle, barking commands, rebukes and curses. He felt the strength of Vyath pulsing through his veins as he carried out the sacred Griptha and smiled at so many of his enemies being sent to the frozen plains of Kulbrar. He was not concerned for his own people that fell, knowing they would find their way to the Shores of Thracia once their victory was complete. His forces had suffered losses, but it was nothing compared to the damage they were inflicting upon their enemies. Wellyn had indeed done his part. Those who remained to stand against him fought more like rats trying to outrun an avalanche than warriors.

Wellyn has left me nothing but rabble to clean up, he thought. Though this was their agreement, the Deklar couldn't help but feel a little cheated.

"Bellathia!" he shouted when she was close enough to hear. "Take your detachment and cut down from the east with a low sweep!"

She nodded and signaled the new orders to her sub-commanders. Two thousand Alysaar exited the swarm through an upward climb. They leveled off and flew east for a quarter-league before diving down until they were mere feet above the trees. Turning west, the Borathein riders urged their mounts forward at a terrible velocity. The distraction the rest of the battle provided did not allow the Arlethians to even sense the oncoming attack until it was too late. More than a thousand were cut down and disappeared from sight as they fell beneath the trees. A sweet lullaby of screams warmed Shilkath as he reveled in the sound. Several Alysaar came away from the assault without their riders, including Bellathia's. The Deklar felt a moment of sadness but that shortly retreated into rejoicing at her sacrifice. But then he noticed her Alysaar was not without a rider after all. As it banked and headed toward him, he saw an Arlethian upon the mount. Shilkath felt his veins thumping with anticipation.

Finally!

———

Aiden saw them coming low against the horizon from the east when the next bolt of lightning shot through the sky. The Alysaar looked like slithering shadows no more than a man's height above the trees. Thousands lay in the way between him and the coming onslaught, thousands of his people. They fought valiantly against the demon spawn swarming all around them, but they would fall as soon as the flying blades of bone, scales and wings cut through them. He would not let this attack go unanswered.

"East! From the east!" he shouted. "Down!" His words were barely audible to himself amid the cacophony of battle.

Knowing he could not save those in the kill path, Aiden sprinted toward the Alysaar battery. He was angry and apprehensive all at once but did his best to capture those frictions and redirect them. He did not fully understand this process, but did it all the same. His sword vibrated in his hand, which he knew by now to be somehow related to the friction. As he recycled the emotions, his velocity increased twofold.

A female Borathein at the tip of their attack wreaked havoc upon those in her path with a sadistic laugh. Aiden had his target. When he jumped, his height was far more than he had anticipated and he momentarily had a sense of vertigo. The feeling was reminiscent of the night Thannuel died when he had chased Lord Kerr's assassin through the woods. That chase had not ended well, but the master of the hold guard was determined not to lose control this time.

He refocused and found the banshee of a woman. The arc of his flight carried him over the snapping jaws of the woman's Alysaar and onto its back. Aiden excused the rear rider from his saddle with a vicious volley of elbow thrusts followed by a spinning roundhouse kick to the jaw. The scream as he fell was only heard for a split second.

The woman turned her head over her left shoulder and let go of her reins. She spun up, faced Aiden with a short blade and demonstrated amazing balance and agility. She struck out deftly against him as the Alysaar piloted itself, weaving in and out of the other aerial obstacles and debris. Aiden countered after a parry that he was sure would open her throat, but the woman blocked the blow with her dagger flush against her forearm. He was stunned at the banshee's swiftness. While lacking the speed of a wood-dweller, her movements were fluid and graceful, never ceasing. It was like a dance. She stabbed and swiped at him, but Aiden ducked and brought her up by her leg.

His grip was iron around her calf as he brought her legs above her head, holding her upside down. The short blade fell from her grasp in her surprise. Aiden sheathed his sword and found her other leg in one motion. Next, he swung her around and around as if she were caught in a hurricane. She vomited amid her screams. With deft footwork, Aiden spun his way up the Alysaar's neck with her still in hand and the demon threw its head back in protest.

"Dance around this!"

The momentum flung the woman right into the exposed razor-sharp beard of her own mount, impaling her entire midsection. Her squirming stopped instantly and the Alysaar threw its head down as if it had sneezed, forcing the corpse into a free-fall.

Aiden pulled back on the reins hard, and this time he achieved some obedience from the fiend. As they climbed into the black sky, he saw a man circling in a holding pattern. His beard was rife with all manner of pieces of death woven into it. Doing his best to stabilize the writhing animal under him, he plotted a vector directly toward the man.

He must be the head! If he could take him down the battle would turn to chaos on the side of the Borathein. He hoped, anyway. Squatting down, he prepared himself to lunge at the barbarian's Alysaar. Aiming for a wing close to the body would be his best chance in avoiding the mouth and talons of the creature. The sword would remain sheathed, keeping both hands free. Expending a great deal of the friction he had built up inside him, Aiden shot toward his prey.

But the Borathein leader was prepared. His Alysaar swiveled in midair as if on an invisible axis, bringing the Borathein rider upside down. Simultaneously, the Alysaar rotated its wings on the shoulder-like joints 180°, enabling the wings to function properly and flight to continue despite now being upside down. The move took less time than a blink. The large man swung a huge mace that Aiden too late tried to counter. Not having earth or trees for a counterpoint, he was unable to change his trajectory and the mace caught him full under the arm.

The force was unbelievable and Aiden felt his ribs give way under the blow. Hot searing pain shot up through his side and radiated into his arm. Breath evaded him. It was too much for him to capture and recycle before it took root and his face contorted with pain. Before he could fall, the bearded man grabbed him by the throat—still upside down—and head-butted Aiden in the eye, splitting the thin skin around it. Muted stars filled his vision as he went limp. Through the milky expanse obstructing his vision, Aiden thought he saw a short blade come to his face. The blazing pain that danced through his nerves left no doubt as the Borathein warrior traced the knife from his bleeding eye socket down his jawline. Aiden screamed and thrashed wildly, but the man's strength was immense. He felt a chunk of his flesh start to be peeled away.

———

"I will have your face, betrayer!" Shilkath yelled in Sentharian.

An arrow from below pierced the wood-dweller's shoulder, the arrowhead erupting through his skin like a volcano of blood. The surprise of it caught Shilkath off guard. A second arrow hissed by his ear and, in reflex, he let go of the long-haired Arlethian. Unconscious from the pain, the wood-dweller fell through the darkness.

The Deklar righted himself on his massive Alysaar. Hawgl screeched thunder.

"There will be others," Shilkath promised. "Many others. We will adorn ourselves in their flesh."

The Alysaar screeched again. Shilkath now had a taste of the battle. He had held back and commanded from on high, but with this first taste he could restrain himself no longer. Leaning forward, he grabbed the reins tightly in his left hand and his mace in his right. He spied a group of children who were mostly doing little good, but there were a few who were effective enough.

"Dive, Hawgl! Dive! Let us feast on the tender spawn of traitors!"

Their charge was terrible. As his mace crushed skulls and bodies he became stained with blood and brain matter. Hawgl tore women and children to shreds with his petrified bone talons, preferring the feel of their softer flesh to the men. Three wood-dwellers leaped atop Hawgl, but the Alysaar turned his side parallel to the earth too quickly for the trespassers to find hold. Two fell and the third dangled desperately from the short stubby tail of the Alysaar. Hawgl leveled out. Leaving the reins, Shilkath turned and stood over the Arlethian. He reached down, grabbed the man by his hair and lifted him up to his height with a single arm. The wood-dweller screamed in pain, clawing at Shilkath's arm and kicking.

"Pathetic!"

He shook his captive from the crown of his head violently until the momentum of the Arlethian's swaying body snapped his own neck. The Borathein leader let the corpse fall as if it were no more than a dead fish, and laughed. Shilkath roared with gleeful ferocity as he dove and banked, spilling the life of his enemies upon the treed canopy until it became slick with dark fluid and reflected the shimmer of approaching dawn. Only then did Shilkath realize the color of the forest was wrong. It was paler. Gray.

"The serpent Tyjil has worked his trick," he mused and was once again impressed by it.

———

Tyjil sat below the Changrual Monastery in the expansive cavern he had discovered over thirty-six seasons ago. He was a different person then, nine years past. Well, in as much as a name defines someone. He found that he much preferred Tyjil to Rehum. Tyjil was strong and focused where Rehum was desperate and largely a fool.

He removed a Triarch leafling from a satchel. This particular sample came directly from Calyn's immediate vicinity. It's how the

Influence worked, requiring some connection to the body to be affected.

Memories of his first experience demonstrating the Influence came to mind. A dark night in the Arlethian forest with a small audience. He had not been strong enough to alter a large portion of the forest when he demonstrated the Influence six years ago for Shilkath. He was now. This particular conjure of Influence would mean the end of the Arlethians.

The Ancient Dark swelled inside him and he touched the Triarch leafling. The now familiar blue luminescence shone—the Living Light within the leafling. He extracted it and took it into himself. When he had drawn all the Light out, he was granted access to the tree from which the leafling had been taken. Like a plague, he forced his access through the tree and then the intertwined roots of the forest around Calyn.

"Oh, the exquisite joy!" he cackled as he ripped through the forest. Tyjil felt the changes as he snuffed out the Lumenati spark of life from the trees, leaving cold and dead stone in his wake.

As he pushed farther, he saw the brightest Light. It was blinding and he knew it was the Tavaniah Forest. He tried to push there but was rebuffed soundly. He tried again but could go no farther, dammed by a barrier of some create. The Light caused him to squint with his physical eyes, though he was only seeing it in his mind.

"Soon," he promised. "Soon I will be strong enough to pierce you. Soon I will have my own army of those that serve the Ancient Dark. Yes, soon."

A sound interrupted him. Rocks being misplaced and moved, he thought. Startled, he came cautiously to a wall where the sound emanated. His brow furrowed with curiosity, he brought his torch closer to inspect the wall when he saw a stone fall free, followed by a hand reaching through.

———

Thurik bit through an enemy's beard and found hot flesh under-neath. With a forceful whipping of the wolf's neck, the trachea came free. Hedron scrambled around a tree faster than his imme-diate opponent could follow and stabbed him through the side. The pale man died with a yelp. Hedron had never killed anyone before this battle, though he had tried when his mother fell under attack. He discovered it was easy as breathing when properly moti-vated—something Aiden had whispered to him before the battle. He did not feel any regret in his actions, no remorse. The rightness of it propelled him.

He saw Lord Hoyt caught between two assailants, but Master Gernald was there in an instant. Together, they ended their ene-mies and moved on to the next. Despite valiant efforts, they were doing little damage to the overall enemy force. The trees forced a bottleneck of sorts and allowed the Arlethian and Southern forces to meet them with less peril, but they were being forced back into the flames that engulfed more of Calyn as every minute passed. Hedron knew they could not press upon their enemy.

The three wolf cubs toppled another Borathein and savagely dispatched him amid screams. Hedron felt a cold sweat on his neck as he heard a yelp of pain followed by a whimper. Alabeth lay on the ground with a spear in her left rear leg. Huksinai and Thurik killed the offender and circled around their sister, viciously snapping at anyone who dared approach. Though she was alive, Alabeth did not move.

A flurry of arrows rained down upon them. Most embedded themselves harmlessly in the trees but some found a target. A sec-ond flurry came, adding to the first volley's effect. Merrick, the giant blacksmith, grunted and Hedron turned to the man. Two arrows protruded from his back near his left shoulder. He reached up and snapped the wooden shafts with no more effort than had they been decayed twigs.

"No harm, my Lord," Merrick said. "I'm right-handed."

With his hammer raised, he bellowed forth into the Borathein horde with a thunderous cry. His wood-dweller speed carried him with momentum through several lines of men, swinging and slamming his iron enforcer, authoritatively persuading those in his path that this life was no longer for them. With each swing, at least two Borathein were sent flying back, broken and dead.

"Cover him!" Hedron commanded as he looked above to the archers in the trees. Arrows found their marks all around Merrick, thinning out the masses.

"No! Let them come!" he shouted.

He smashed over and over, spinning and whirling like a tornado of iron. He hit one man on the shoulder, destroying the joint, and followed up with an uppercut to the man's jaw that nearly took off his head. A bright orange-bearded man threw a small axe that found Merrick's thigh but the giant ripped it free and returned the favor, catching the man in his face. Another attack, this one from a spear, punctured his abdomen. Slices from half a dozen swords covered his arms, but his lethal hammer continued to crash down on all those around him as he shaped them for death against the earthen anvil at his feet. But no matter his strength and speed, Merrick was eventually overrun by enemy soldiers and cut down as a raft swallowed by ocean swells in a typhoon.

Hedron started to feel physically sick. He and the rest of those with him retreated again and the heat at their backs increased. They must not let the Borathein into the city, but he did not know how to prevent it. All around him men and woman died on both sides, but his forces and allies could not win a battle of attrition. The Borathein acted like a battering ram, pushing forward no matter their losses, until they breached the city, where they would have more room to maneuver and hand out their destruction. Hedron guessed they had only met half of the Borathein's ground forces thus far. He prayed Aiden's front above the trees was having more success.

Lord Marshal Wenthil ordered a brisk retreat of about fifty paces, putting some distance between the main lines of the forces. The wood-dwellers in the trees leaped from one tree to the next until they were aligned with the new front. The invaders had continued to advance, but cautiously.

The forest started to change around Lord Kerr. The ground became firmer; the vibrations he felt through it more sharp and thin. Then it receded as a wave pulling back, and Hedron's mind spun in the undertow. He glanced around and saw looks of terror on every Arlethian. Hoyt's men did not seem to notice the feeling, nor would they.

Glimon found him. The old command sergeant was splattered with blood but otherwise appeared well.

"Lord Kerr, did you feel that?"

"Yes, what was it?" Hedron bellowed.

He looked to his left and saw Huksinai and Thurik dragging Alabeth hurriedly away from the front. The female cub still did not move.

"Do you know what it was?" he asked Glimon again.

Glimon looked uncertain, but Hedron could guess he was thinking of the corruption that Ulin and Seilia had spoken of. An arrow raced between them.

"But nothing happened!" Hedron exclaimed. They felt the release of more arrows and hunkered behind a tree.

"Something did!"

"Whatever it was, it left. We have to focus on—"

It came back and surged through the forest. Underneath Hedron, the soil turned to gravel and stone, the trees turned dark gray and cold. The thousands of Arlethians, to their credit, did not break and run in terror. But, the young Lord knew how they were feeling because he felt the same. Revulsion spread through him, coupled with shock and disbelief.

What is this? he demanded of himself but had no answer. This was the corruption mother Seilia had spoken of. It had to be. Hoyt's men could not help but see this physical change around them.

"It is the Dark!" one man screamed. "The Dark Mother's Influence!"

The fighting ceased, and again a rift of space was created between the two lines with everyone looking down and around themselves, inspecting their environment. Even the Borathein stopped fighting and an eerie calm settled over the masses. Some of the fires smoldered, but much of the city was too far gone to be extinguished.

Lord Kerr stood. All his people looked at him. He saw their defeated expressions and knew the Borathein did as well. They had been outnumbered from the beginning with little hope against such overwhelming odds. But they had their trees. They had their forests and their venerable cities, Calyn foremost among them. Most importantly, they had one another. A race as ancient as the world itself, second only to the Ancients, if the legends were true.

I believed—I hoped that just maybe it would have been enough. Now the tie to each of those treasures was being savagely severed, like a dead child being ripped from a grieving mother's arms. Hedron looked back to the ruins of Calyn, a city that had been the envy of the Realm—his boyhood home. It now looked as he felt inside.

Second moon had set. Dawn would soon be upon them. His people still stared at him. Should he surrender? Order a retreat?

Ancients Come! I don't know what to do! Scanning through the crowds he saw Lord Hoyt sitting upon his destrier. They shared a look. Farther off, he heard the sounds of horror above, and Hedron knew that battle fared no better.

Lord Hoyt shook his head slightly. Hedron was thinking of surrender and he knew Hoyt saw it. The early morning sky turned a shade of dark gray, matching the trees around them. Hoyt had half to maybe two-thirds of his men left. The wood-dweller militia had fared better due to their agility and advantage given them by the forest, but with that nullified Hedron knew this would become a slaughter. They would take three Borathein for every Arlethian killed, but it would not be enough.

They were done. Hedron knew it.

"Lord Kerr!" Hoyt yelled. His voice carried well as it bounced off the tree-like rock formations. "Hedron! Do not stop! They will not accept surrender!"

Hoyt spurred his warhorse over to the young Lord. Arlethian and Southern forces alike parted for him.

"Hedron, listen to me! They will give us no quarter. Let us rally our people and press forward. We have no choice!"

Two arrows pierced Calder Hoyt's chest, ending the lull.

"No!" Hedron yelled.

He caught Lord Hoyt as he fell from his horse. Gernald was there seconds later, cursing fiercely.

"No man," Calder Hoyt said with great effort, "can be worthy… to live once he shrinks because of…fear from that which he knows to be right. I now…pay that price. I pray I may find your father in…the Living Light and beg his forgiveness…"

"Lord Hoyt!" Hedron cried. Kathryn's father lay in his arms, motionless. His eyes fluttered and chest became still. Hedron slapped his face twice and called his name again. No reply came. Lord Calder Hoyt had left this life.

Hedron felt too stunned to know what to do. He had been the leader of his people for less than a day. He knew they looked to him for moral strength, but he had looked to Lord Hoyt. Seeing their lord fall, the Southern army started to retreat more quickly. It became a frenzied rout. Hedron knew the Borathein sensed that the final blow was near and would soon charge with feverish abandon. Gernald stayed by his dead lord's side, cutting down every man he could. Lord Marshal Wenthil tried desperately to call for order and organize a defense until a spear impaled him in the neck.

Gernald ripped Hoyt free from Hedron's arms and hoisted him over his shoulders.

"Run, boy!" he yelled to Hedron. Gernald was gone before Hedron looked up. He stood and saw the sea of Borathein closing in on him. His people, the wood-dwellers who still lived and fought, had not fled. They were scared and anxious—terrified, just as he was—but they stood their ground.

Run? he asked himself. He had run his entire life. Perhaps three thousand, maybe less, still stood with him. It was amazing to him that so many children were still present, women as well. In a place deep within his mind he knew there were many more lifeless upon the rocky earth.

Run? How can I run? His mother had not run. His father had stood firmly against the darkness that ended him.

How can I run? "No man can be worthy to live once he shrinks," he heard Lord Hoyt's final words echo through his mind. He would run away no more in his life. Not one more step.

I am Arlethia and she is me. A terrible fear tried to seize him but found no purchase. He felt stronger suddenly, as if a surge of reserve sprung up inside him. Again the fear came and again it was unsuccessful in clutching him. The strength swelled again. Thurik and Huksinai made their way to his side, having removed their sister far enough from the field of battle.

When he spoke, his voice filled the morning with a supernatural tenor and volume.

"People of Arlethia! Sons and daughters of this land, harken to my words! I have been running my entire life. From my name, from who I am." He ran his sword through a Borathein and deftly escaped a blow from another. He countered with a punch to the attacker's face too fast for the man to block and his nose inverted, blood spraying. "But I have committed to you and Arlethia! I will not take one step of retreat!" He saw a young girl, eleven at most, bend over from a wound to the stomach. He who threw the spear immediately had three other younglings upon him, each stabbing repeatedly with short blades until the bearded man ceased to move. "Even our little ones stand firm against these enemies of devilish create! We cannot back down, though others flee in fear. We do not blame them but will find in ourselves the brighter Light! The greater portion of bravery!"

Strong as his words were, they did not have the effect his previous speech had carried. They continued to battle but were giving ground too quickly.

"We must fight through until we find the Living Light or the Dark take us! I will wage that fight! I will wage it with you by my side! Will you?"

He saw the resolve thicken inside his people until it hardened. His own determination could not be shattered, it being strengthened by standing for something greater than himself. He swore he could feel the air change around him with a sense of familiarity and he thought of his mother. Her final words played through his mind.

Dar vash alaqyn duwel partia, the ancient Arlethian blessing of protection. He wished he could see her again. His father as well. Perhaps he would after today. His only regret was not being able to say goodbye to Reign and hold Kathryn one last time. He would not waver in the face of death, but spurn it with defiance until the end.

Three thousand men, women, and younglings, along with two wolf cubs, charged the darkness before them in the pale light of what they were certain would be their last morning.

———

Antious Roan was a general without an army. Where he should turn eluded him. He sat within a quarter-mile of the Sentharian army's camp where the remnants of the various fronts now gathered. The southern front's forces had not returned, which Roan hoped was a positive sign, some sliver of silver light in these cursed days. The tall grass he hid beneath also provided some nourishment. He had taken to chewing on the softer portion of the long blades that were under the soil. When he had chewed them to a pulp-like consistency, he forced the bolus down his throat. The cramps felt like someone lancing his stomach from the inside, but they eventually passed.

A figure approached the camp from the north in nothing more than a loincloth. From this distance only a wood-dweller could pick out minute details. He was grotesquely disfigured with strange markings and had the build of a bull. Roan believed him to be the stockiest man he had ever seen. The way he walked exuded confidence. No, it was more than simple confidence, Roan decided. Lethality. He not only saw it in the man's walk but also felt it as he focused on the vibrational signals in his footsteps. There had been similar strides projected from the battlefield where his army fell, and he knew them to be unique to whatever this monster he now observed was, and those of his kind. He remembered the hooded soldiers that arrived the night before.

What are you? Roan wondered and prayed he would never have to find out. He hurried forward, calling on all his innate wood-dweller skills to remain silent as he moved, until he was within a few hundred feet.

A sentry greeted the disfigured man but Roan saw the soldier get thrown back twenty feet suddenly as if hit by a catapult's load. Roan's body went tense. Others approached the nearly naked intruder and swiftly met similar fates. He couldn't believe what he was seeing. The monster was fast, as fast as he was, and wielded the strength of five men, more. At the sound of cries, the hooded soldiers General Roan had observed earlier came out of their tents but made no effort to intervene.

Thirteen, he reminded himself. He counted to be sure once again and confirmed his earlier recollection. Once they saw the loincloth-clad creature, the thirteen lowered their hoods. Astonishment was too weak a word to describe what Roan felt as he saw each of the thirteen with the same exact shorn head and markings that the intruder had on his scalp. The *exact* same markings in shape, dimension and all aspects.

The next moments Roan witnessed carved their own motes of disbelief in his brain and would haunt him for the rest of his life.

———

Dralghus ignored the soldiers around him once he saw the arrival of his brethren. The Senthary men were nothing more than flies to him.

"Brethren!" he shouted. Thirteen hoods lowered, revealing the familiar markings of a Helsyan. "See me! You all know me. You know I was once one of you. A slave, lower than a dog to a man who deserved neither our respect nor obedience."

Dralghus' kin listened in silence, unresponsive to his words.

"The Urlenthi's hold on me is broken. I am freed by the Dark Mother herself and have sworn to reclaim Helsya for the Ancient Dark. Witness and behold! You see me walking without the shackles of our curse!"

"We must obey the Stone of Orlack," one answered. "It is our curse."

"Nay, brother, you must be freed from the Urlenthi as I have been. You see my body, ridged and defined as if Charged, yet no Charge is upon me nor shall ever be again save I choose it!"

They think me crazed, Dralghus realized when they remained motionless and showed no enthusiasm. He understood that they all viewed him as wasted because of his long-failed Charge, which had wracked him for all these years. *They will see.*

"Kemen, brother, step forward." Dralghus beckoned to the one who had spoken. "Do you know your real name? Who you really are?"

Kemen did not answer.

"I know you, *Heluth,*" Dralghus declared, using the Helsyan's true name. Kemen fell to his knees and tried to reach between his shoulder blades from behind his head with one arm and from below with the other. Rocking back and forth, the man screamed and tore his robe free from his body. A red glow illuminated his name glyph, deeper than the color of cooking coals. The other twelve chase-givers marveled.

"Dark Mother, I pray you to free my brother Heluth, that he may reclaim Helsya by my side and once again raise seed unto the Ancient Dark." After a few more seconds, Kemen arose as Heluth. His muscles bulged and he stood erect, strong, as if a Dahlrak had just been issued to him.

"I now serve the Ancient Dark, Mother of Helsya, and him first freed, the Unshackled, the Shatterer of the Urlenthi," he proclaimed. "The Urlenthi's claim on me is broken!" Heluth let loose a cry that caused the scared Senthary who looked on to shake from fright.

Dralghus began to call the others by their true names, repeating the simple ritual.

Croathus.
Valagul.
Greyvin.
Zoraman.
Hagülus.
Thaxil.
Marint.
Alendry.
Cadán.
Shimarr.
Kalithar.
Rykam.

Each rose after being freed, their old names forgotten. Dralghus reveled in seeing the strength that stood before him. Freed Helsyans, the first of his race, of the citizenry of Helsya, soon to be reclaimed.

Reborn!

Dralghus took the amulet he had removed from Wellyn's dying body and held it up for his brethren to behold. From the backside of the gold disc, he stripped the translucent white stone free.

"We now behold this trinket as no more than a childish curiosity. For centuries, the Light has used this to keep us beholden to weaker beings. Most unworthy masters! A curse made to curb us, to hinder our rule upon this world! No more!"

Dralghus crushed the Urlenthi in his hands as though it were stale bread and reduced it to powder. From his open hand the wind took it into oblivion.

They went forth as lions among lambs, tearing and crushing thousands of the Senthary men to unrecognizable ichor pulp. Each kill brought the thrill of a completed Dahlrak. Thousands more fled in any direction they could to try and escape the horrific scene upon them. When the ecstasy of the moment had peaked, Dralghus commanded a cease to the sport. He saw his brethren in a state of rapture and knew they were experiencing their newfound freedom in waves of spasmodic jubilation that were hard to control. There were a few hundred soldiers left, on their knees begging for mercy and calling on the Ancient Heavens for deliverance.

"Mercy?" Dralghus repeated. "Of this, we have none." Cries were heard coming from those pleading. "But deliverance, yes, this is ours to grant to those who can survive. Speak, mortals, who among you deserves deliverance?"

Dozens stood, shouting pleas. Dralghus smiled.

"Take him," Dralghus commanded Heluth, pointing to one soldier in front.

"It will be done, Shatterer," Heluth obeyed.

Forcibly, the Sentharian soldier was pulled from the masses and pinned to the ground, face down. Dralghus pulled a short blade from the man's hip and the man began to writhe on the ground, but Heluth and Rykam held him firm. The other eleven Helsyans hovered threateningly over the scores of soldiers remaining, as gods over their lesser creations.

"Fire," Dralghus said. A small fire was kindled and the Shatterer began to heat the blade.

"Dark Mother, Mother of Helsya, this mortal desires to know thee and be delivered from his damned state. Grant his desires, I pray, with a true name bestowed by the Dark that he may assist in the raising of Helsya."

Dralghus grabbed the glowing red blade from the flames, and the man screamed as the knife bit into the skin between his shoulder blades.

———

Aiden lay tangled in stone branches when he awoke, his face burning. The grimace he wore aggravated it further and he let out a small cry of pain as fire lanced through his left side where he had taken the blow from the mace. He had no doubt his ribs were broken, possibly a pierced or collapsed lung as well. He struggled to open his eyes and clear his vision. He did not know how long he had been out. Above, he saw leaves and branches in a petrified state—the tree top canopy.

"No," he said weakly and was again punished for trying to move.

"Shh!" he heard someone say. He turned his head toward the sound and saw Rue-anna and Mikahl.

"Don't try to move," she said. "Mother says it's not good to move when you're hurt."

"What's happened?" Aiden whispered.

"The corruption came and we scaled down the trees. Or whatever they are now. They still fly above us just circling."

"It's morning!" Mikahl announced in a loud whisper.

"Shh!" Rue-anna scolded. "Shut your mouth, Fletch!"

"We have to get up," Aiden said. "It's not over."

"For you it is," Rue-anna said softly but firmly. "Have you seen yourself? You're hideous."

"Perfect," Aiden muttered. "Where is everyone else?"

Mikahl and Rue-anna shared a look. "There aren't many," the boy said. "When the trees turned everyone became too confused and scared. The flying monsters, they…"

Mikahl was having a hard time saying what he was obviously replaying in his mind.

"They killed everyone that stayed above the canopy," Rue-anna finished for her brother.

"What about the ground forces? Lord Kerr and Lord Hoyt?" Aiden asked with much concern.

Mikahl shook his head and Rue-anna shrugged. "I can't feel anything," the girl said. Aiden realized he couldn't either but that was to be expected with the change of the forest. If he listened close enough he could feel the vibrations of tens of thousands of men, but they felt so far away.

"Where are we? Have we drifted?"

Rue-anna nodded. "About two leagues west of Calyn. The battle carried us here."

"Where is your mother? Where is Seilia?" Aiden asked.

Again the girl shrugged, as if not concerned but she could not hide the worry on her face. "We left our village just after you did."

Aiden struggled to get up.

"Stop! You need a healer!" Mikahl snapped. Aiden did not listen. With great effort he fought through the pain and found his sword, still sheathed. A breeze came and pulled at his face, flapping the loose skin that had nearly been cut away completely. It stung fiercely but he ignored the pain. His left shoulder had been packed with Triarch leaves in the wound where the arrow had pierced him. He inspected the dressing and then looked at Rue-anna.

"Sorry," she said. "It was the best I could do. I didn't mean to hit you."

"You likely saved my life, little one. I can take the pain if it means I am still alive."

"What are you doing?" Mikahl asked. "Please, don't leave us. They'll see you if you go out there again!"

"We must do what we can, lad. I am still breathing and I'll do all that I can while that is so."

"But you'll die!" Rue-anna exclaimed.

"We all die but not all of us live. I am proud to have this chance to spend my life in defense of my land and people. It is who I am, who we all are."

Aiden made his way up the cold petrified branches and emerged above the canopy. He did not bother to count the number of Alysaar that still littered the air in the early dawn light. More than a thousand span for sure.

What would he do against so many? *All that I can,* he heard his heart tell him.

Ancients above, do not abandon us.

He drew his steel with his right hand. His left arm rested against his side, trying not to use it. His crushed ribs and wounded shoulder reminded him of their state with every slight motion. The vision in his left eye was fuzzy, but that did not stop him from finding the largest flying abomination in the sky with a single rider.

The Borathein leader obviously spied him as well. Aiden heard the bark of a sadistic laugh as the Alysaar banked around and positioned itself right above him. The demon dove with an unnatural shriek, penetrating enough to rattle his bones.

Sword in hand, he readied himself and quieted his mind. Though stone was firmer than leaves and branches, he felt himself unsteady on the lifeless canopy. He started to repeat the first axiom when a sound interrupted him. It was a whistle, high pitched like the sound of a crossbow bolt, but louder. Much louder. As it increased in volume Aiden finally discerned something approaching from the northwest. A flare of light, slender and white, streaked through the sky. It looked like the shooting stars he would see as a boy that cut the night sky while he hid in a Furlop tree, dreaming of someday leaving his broken home.

The flare increased in speed and approached directly above where Aiden stood. Just before it was upon him, he thought he made out an image within the light: a svelte figure that looked remarkably like Reign Kerr.

The small comet collided with the Borathein warrior and his Alysaar and cut through them like a javelin through water. An explosion sounded and pieces of the Alysaar and its rider flew in all directions, raining down ichor all around Aiden. He raised his right arm to shield himself against the debris as well as the brightness of the explosion. Other Alysaar began to fall from the sky in scores as smaller explosions dotted the celestial view before him.

"I have lived to see the return of the Ancients."

Moisture crept into Aiden's eyes.

———

Shilkath felt the flames crawl up his flesh and beard and smelled the redolence of burning hair. The incendiary cloak engulfed him and flared the numerous trophies woven in his beard, these becoming ornaments of fire and ashes. Ascending his beard, the fire turned his long-grown pride to stubble. Hawgl writhed and flapped his wings wildly, throwing his head back and forth, screeching a horrific cry as the beast's scales melted in the intense heat.

The Borathein Deklar did not scream when the end came. The explosion tore him and Hawgl apart, spewing their smoldering ruins in all directions.

FIFTY-TWO

Reign

Day 6 of 2nd Dimming 412 A.U.

THE SUN HAD NOT YET RISEN above the horizon. Reign Kerr was at the top of a Triarch tree at the northwestern Arlethian border along the edge of the Tavaniah Forest with five hundred Warriors of Light. All Arlethians. All Gyldenal. Their spears and arrows were tipped with heads of a dark metal, their sword blades crafted from the same material. Jarwynian ore. Each arrowhead, spearhead and sword was infused with Lumenati Light—not a visible light, but a power harnessed by those who lived after the Lumenatis. A soft hum emanated from the infused weapons.

Reign felt all the life around her. A leafling taken from the Tavaniah provided her a link to a well of Influence that felt boundless. It frightened her to know she had access to the Lumenatis, to those ancient trees that concealed the very Influence of life for the world.

The currents of sentience she allowed to pass through her so as not to overwhelm her. When she recognized a current or found one she wanted to focus on, she tapped into it fully. This current of Light was flickering in pain.

Aiden.

Two other currents near Aiden's flowed to her mind's awareness and she knew that there were only moments.

You must go, her father said. *Now!*

Reign was not ready, not fully. The power she had was not
something she understood well enough, but she had little choice.
She felt Hedron's current as well and knew he was also in danger.
It was no different than all those who fought, and from the periphery of her mind she felt the cessation of dozens of currents every
second. Death, she realized.

With the Triarch leafling in her hand she sucked in the Living
Light from the trees, as much as her capacity would allow her. She
strode forward across the trees at incredible speed. Her strides
became longer until she was leaping the distance of twenty men at
once, then fifty, then one hundred. The air around her started to
glow as her speed increased and a loud crack of thunder followed.
After that she heard nothing, though she felt incredible pressure
around her. She saw the swarm of Borathein and Alysaar less than a
league away and Aiden standing alone at the top of petrified trees.
A large Alysaar with a single rider dove toward him.

Now! her father shouted in her mind. Reign launched into
the currents of the Alysaar and Borathein bearing down on Aiden
from a sturdy bough just before she reached the edge of where
living trees became nothing more than statues. The world folded
around her in a supernal view as she expended the Living Light
within her, it propelling her forward through the air. Heat built up
around her as she approached the Alysaar and she began to channel the power into her blade. It hummed loudly.

"Faerathm!"

The explosion as she collided with her prey was brilliant
and stentorian all at once. The infused blade sent forth a torrent of energy that became fire as it was transferred from the
sword to the demon as soon as the tip made the slightest punc-
ture through the scales. She was traveling too fast for the explosion to catch her and she didn't hear its report until she slowed
several seconds later. Landing on a group of stone branches, she

turned and saw other Alysaar and their riders falling from their sky-bound perches, some by explosions such as she had caused but on a smaller scale, others contorting in unnatural motions as they fell; still others turned to stone themselves and crumbled as they hit the hardened trees. On the horizon from the direction she had come, Reign spied the Gyldenal sprinting and jumping, throwing spears and loosing arrows. Others were leaping and stabbing flying targets with swords and short blades. It had begun to rain Borathein.

Aiden was nearby where she had come to rest, looking up to the heavens in what could only be described as wonderment. She looked upon him; his wounds were grave and she felt his current in the Light weaken as he struggled for breath. His ribs were broken, a lung pierced. But this man stood all the same, alone against thousands. He was not alone any longer.

She quickly grabbed a rolled, three-pronged leaf from a side pouch and gently held it up to his face. Aiden flinched but held his ground.

"Mylendia shaul," she whispered as Thannuel said the word in her mind.

Aiden's face mended, the tissue and muscles finding and reknitting themselves. The restoration was complete in a matter of seconds, but a long scar remained. She repeated the process on his shoulder and then the left side under his arm.

"How?" he asked.

"It is an Influence of the Living Light," Reign said. "It promotes life, lengthens lives and restores corruption. All elements of the Lumenatis work toward these ends."

"The what?"

"It is the power of the Ancients. What they lived by. The Living Light."

A Borathein rider swooped low and swung a flail at Reign. She felt his current before he neared too close and moved just enough out of reach to be missed by less than an inch. Slashing her sword above her head, her blade cut up through the Alysaar and into the rear rider's thigh. They lost control and crashed into the trees at terminal velocity.

"You move like…like—"

"Like my father?" she asked.

"Aye, lass, but so much more graceful."

She smiled. "He's not offended you said that, don't worry."

Aiden took a deep breath and worked his arm. "Restores corruption?"

Reign took the Triarch leafing in the palm of her hand and knelt down upon the petrified tree canopy. There were small chasms and cracks where the once green leaves had not completely filled in and she could see down to the ground hundreds of feet below. It was also petrified. She put her hand around a cold rock branch with the leafling between it and her palm. She concentrated, focusing the Light within her and drawing in more from the Lumenatis, so much more than she though possible, more than should be possible. Thannuel gasped in amazement within her and she began to sweat with the unprecedented effort.

"Reign, you're trembling!" Aiden exclaimed.

Father, I need you.

The sentience within her added his capacity and focus to hers, acting as a reservoir for her to store the excess Light she drew in. Thannuel's capacity seemed unfathomable to her.

Aiden stepped back, wonder and disbelief emanating from him. Reign Kerr was alight.

"*Mylendia anthpetra shaul!*"

Her voice carried the authority of the ages as a burst of energy flew out from her. Aiden's black hair was blown back from the gust. Below them came the sound of an avalanche. From the core of the rooted perennials sprang a resurgence of life as stone split and crumbled. The spark of life within the trees was reignited by Reign's injection of Lumenati Light and lush foliage shone through, resurrected.

"I can feel their currents return," Reign said.

"I don't know what you mean, or how this is done, but it is *incredible!*" Aiden stood upon vibrant treetops once again that swayed and flexed under his weight, the way the living forest should.

"I have reversed the Dark Influence that plagued the trees, breathing Light back into them and eradicating the Dark."

"Light?" Aiden asked.

"Draw it in," Reign commanded.

"Draw what?"

"The Light. You have done it before but didn't know it."

When the master of the hold guard continued to look confused, Reign said, "When you speak with trees, feel the forest, it is because of the Living Light in the trees."

"I—"

"Don't interrupt," Reign ordered. "Those who live among the trees, wood-dwellers, have this sensitivity because of our connection to the Ancients. We are the descendants of those who did not turn away, those that continued to live in harmony with the Lumenatis. We have lost much of their ways, but the Light is still strong in this land."

In the midst of her explanation, arrows flew toward her and Aiden from a half dozen Alysaar riders making a sweeping run. They easily dodged the missiles and saw their assailants struck down by Light-infused arrows released from Gyldenal bows. The air was still cluttered with thousands of Alysaar but their numbers had decisively thinned. A few score currents of the Gyldenal had ceased, but overall their weaponry of Light was proving superior.

"Simply open yourself the way you do when speaking with a tree. That connection you feel is an effect of the Lumenatis. You have a portion of its Light as well, a spark. Draw it into yourself where your Light resides."

"I have no idea—"

"Do it! Focus!"

Aiden knelt down where he perched and lay his palm flush against the bark. For a few moments there was no change. Then, she saw his frame stiffen and felt his current thicken.

"It is like friction," Reign said. "You can channel the forest's power as you wish."

He stood, taller than before with understanding in his eyes.

"Get back in this fight!" she cried.

The smile that so often came upon Aiden's lips in anticipation of the thrill of battle found its way there once again. "Gladly."

Reign bolted across the renewed canopy. The aerial battle had changed but become no less deadly. The Warriors of Light struck down enemies with Light-infused steel and arrows with great effect and Alysaar began to fall in scores and crash into the trees. Eight Alysaar chased Reign as she ran, approaching on all sides. The roars were menacing. She slowed her dash and came to a stop while the Alysaar closed in and surrounded her like a demonic noose tightening its hold.

Focus, Thannuel commanded. *Think of nothing but this moment.*

She felt her father's concern in the midst of the peril, but also his faith in her. It was not misplaced.

The rear Borathein riders shot arrows, hurled spears, and slung stones. Reign felt them all. The stones came first, fractions of a second ahead of the rest of the volley. She swung the flat side of her sword and sent the projectiles back from whence they originated at increased velocity, striking the stones at the exact same angle at which sailed toward her. Short cries of pain and surprise sounded as the stones crushed the skulls of those who had cast them. Her form was perfect, no more or less motion than was precisely necessary.

The arrows she easily dodged and parried two spears but caught a third. She allowed the momentum to spin her around, adding her own force as she released the spear back at the rider who threw it. The rider slumped forward in his saddle, a smoking hole in his chest. Several Alysaar swooped in, attempting to impale her on their bladed beards as they whipped their necks back and forth with amazing speed. They found nothing but air. Reign let herself fall beneath the canopy and shot back up as the belly of one flying beast flew directly over her position. Her sword found purchase and she continued up and through the demon, emerging from its backside with a large section of spine impaled on her sword. She was covered in demon ichor. The creature fell dead with its riders through the trees to the forest floor. At the apex of her flight, she felt the air change behind her and curled into ball, narrowly missing the swipe of a sword. The wing of the passing Alysaar collided with her back and sent her sprawling downward through the air. Her father's concern flared within her. She hit the branches hard, but her light weight did not carry her too far before they stopped her fall.

She lay dazed for a moment but nothing more than bruises and a few cuts found her.

"Are you all right?" a small voice asked.

"I'm fine, father." She was still dazed.

I know. But that was not me...

Reign looked to where the voice had come from and saw a little girl and boy, obviously related, huddled below her.

"You healed Aiden," the girl said. "We saw it. Are you one of the Ancients?"

Reign shook her head as she climbed out of the crude nest of branches that had broken her fall. "No."

"You look like a demon!" the boy said, only to be cuffed by the girl. Reign thought she probably did indeed look like a monster, covered in blood and innards. Chunks of intestine were lodged in her ebony hair.

"No, not that either. Just one of you," Reign said.

Aiden came into view, jumping from tree to tree below the cover of the canopy.

"Reign! Are you hurt?" he asked.

She shook her head. "But I've had about enough of this." She sprang to a Triarch and put her palm flush against it, drawing in Lumenati Light. She channeled some of the Light into her Jarwynian sword and it sounded its now familiar low hum.

She emerged from the canopy where the seven remaining Alysaar who had pursued her waited, circling. An image flashed through her mind from her father: a beach with black sand, fiery rocks raining down around him and ice shards streaming toward him at incredible speed. Some got through his defenses and impaled his arms. She felt faint stings from the ice shards, enough to make her look at her own arms.

It is from the Orsarian War, Thannuel said. And then she saw what he wanted her to.

"Faerathm!" She said and threw her sword through the air like a spear, catching a forward rider in his neck. Flames burst from him as he fell from his mount. Crouching down and tightening her muscles, Reign launched, unsheathed her sword from smoldering ruin of a man as it fell past her. She reached the Alysaar and grabbed a leg, being sure to avoid the razor-sharp talons. It was nearly thin enough at the base just above the talons for her hand to grasp all the way around. She felt Aiden's current close to her and saw him attack another Alysaar as she dangled off the leg of her own. Aiden, masterful in his movements, soon cut the beast and its riders down. Fear friction ran through her as the creature swooped and dove, trying to shake free of her grasp, but she captured the friction, and, along with some of the Living Light within her, directed the energy to become increased strength. She twisted her wrist that held the limb and heard the soft pop of bones snapping. The creature's other leg started clawing frantically for her. Reign reached up higher on the broken leg with her other arm to secure her hold and again twisted her other wrist in the same place she had previously. The demon screeched in pain. She continued to pull and twist until the flesh tore and the foot with its claws came free. They tore into the Alysaar's skin as Reign dragged her makeshift bouquet of short blades across its underbelly. She dug deeper until the opening was large enough and she saw the monster's viscera hanging free outside its body. Quickly, she scaled up the dying Alysaar to face the second rider, but he lay dead with a crater in his forehead.

She launched from the falling Alysaar to another and was nearly struck by a thick arrow sailing toward her. Reign knocked the arrow from the sky and landed on the new beast. After quickly dispatching the rear rider's head, she reached down to the joint where the wing and body met. She pulled, sending more Light into her muscles. Thannuel added some of his reserves. The flying monster screamed and the wing came free. They went into an uncontrolled spin and she deftly jumped off, landing softly on the sturdy canopy just before the crippled mass crashed.

Arrows shot upward toward other flying targets. Reign traced the trajectory with her eyes and found the small girl, launching arrow after arrow, undaunted. Her accuracy was impressive. The girl was younger than Reign had been when she witnessed what she now knew would be the beginning of the path her life would take. She wondered for an instant about the future of this young archer.

Reign sprinted, gaining speed as the air around her once again began to glow. A boom echoed as she took flight, moving too fast for gravity to have its full effect. Dozens of Borathein lay in her path. In less than ten heartbeats they were in her wake, burning, breaking and falling from her attacks. When she landed on the canopy, she was exhausted. A shiver came upon her that she struggled to control but failed.

Your Light is spent, Reign. All that you took in and all my reserves.

"I'm so cold," she said. Her lips quivered. "I can't stop shaking."

It's your adrenaline. Your body is trying to warm itself. The cost of your exertion will be high, my daughter.

A streak of panic ran through her. "I'm too weak to draw in any Light. I need time to rest." She knew there was no time.

I must reach Hedron! she screamed in her mind. She felt his current and knew all was not well.

Reign watched the battle as she lay on her back looking up into the morning sky, fighting against hypothermia. The Gyldenal were taking down their enemies with efficiency. Reign thought the number of Alysaar remaining was less than a thousand. All around her the trees bore strange fruit, not only foreign but domestic— Borathein and Arlethian. The amount of lost life pained her.

It is what must be, daughter, Thannuel said, knowing her thoughts. "Yet it still hurts."

Always. The correct path is always fraught with difficulty and trials.

The sky was painted orange and deep blue as the morning increased and the storm clouds abated. And with that abatement, Reign saw the Borathein aerial battery retreat.

Evrin found her where she lay.

"You are pale, child. And your frame, it shakes."

"Cold," she gasped.

"Light is heat as well, young Reign. You will learn your limits. It appears as though you expended some of your own life's Light, your core, in your efforts. This can be very dangerous."

"Hedron," she replied. "I must go to him."

Evrin looked grave. "I feel his current as you do. You cannot go to him. You're part here is done for now."

"Please, you must be able to do something, Evrin! Please!"

"Once, I was eager as you are now. Also prideful. I let myself be carried away in my own greatness—or what I viewed as my own greatness." He touched the wound on his cheek. "It almost ended me, but I was spared. In truth, my motives were not pure, as yours are. Yet, I fear nonetheless for you should you continue right now. The price will be too high."

"Evrin, please! He's my brother! I don't care what happens to me!"

The old Light Shepherd was silent for some time. Reign continued to shiver as her core temperature dropped further. She felt her father's ambivalence as he struggled with Evrin's warning and the desire to go to the aid of his only son.

"Please," Reign whispered between blue lips.

"So be it," Evrin said.

———

The forest changed back. Rock became soft, fertile soil under Hedron's feet and trees returned to their natural lush state. He did not understand the change but did not care. The courage this gave his people who desperately fought on the ground against overwhelming odds knew no bounds. They pressed upon the Borathein with their thin lines of nothing but militia. And, as they pressed, the Borathein were moved backward. It wasn't the honed skills of lethal Arlethian warriors that now stood pressing back the vile conquerors; it was the farmer, the fisher, the carpenter, the merchant, the shepherd, the weaver, the healer, the husband and wife, the son and daughter. They cried with valor and *pushed* until the dead of their enemies masked the ground they stood upon. There was strength running through Hedron that he did not recognize but accepted all the same. Huksinai and Thurik struggled to keep up with him as he progressed farther into the horde of enemies. The wolf cubs bit and tore through flesh of every leg, groin and abdomen they could reach, weaving through the horde and causing confusion followed by pain.

Suddenly by Hedron's side came Gernald, striking with his sword and shoving with his shield. Other soldiers from the south rushed the line, adding their steel and shields to the effort.

"We apologize for our moment of weakness, My Lord!" Gernald shouted.

"Lord Hoyt?" Hedron asked.

Gernald shook his head. Hedron knew his fiancé's father was dead but had held hope for some miracle. A howl sounded from the north that was joined by dozens more.

"I know that howl," Lord Kerr said and smiled. Hedron scaled a tree to gain a vantage point and saw through the trees three-quarters of a league north of the confrontation a large pack of wolves with coats of gray, black and brindle, led by a large, pure white wolf.

"I never thought I would be so happy to see that furry beast!"

The wolves tore into the backs of the Borathein. Too few had sounded the alarm to form a rear defensive line but Hedron knew it would have mattered little. The cries from the wolves' victims added to the music of battle, and Hedron's front continued to push. Their progress was slow and the Borathein fought viciously; but for every Arlethian or one of Hoyt's men that was struck down, a dozen Borathein fell.

Hedron felt something distinct through the tree upon which he perched. It was the stride of a wood-dweller coming from the west across the apex of the trees.

Hedron! The voice was clear, as if the word had been spoken aloud next to his ear. It was Reign's voice, but it had come from the forest, from the trees.

Move, Hedron! The urgency of the command struck the chords of apprehension within him. New beads of sweat surfaced on the nape of his neck, tickling his already soaked and soiled skin.

"Pull back!" he shouted in his amplified voice. "Pull back now!"

There was no hesitation from the Arlethians but the southern forces pressed forward. Huksinai and Thurik barked and snapped as they retreated from the throngs.

"Gernald, pull your men back!" Hedron jumped from his vantage point roughly thirty feet to the ground and hit silently. Sprinting to Gernald, he whirled the master of the hold guard around and spoke urgently.

"Something is coming! Pull your men back now!"

"But we are pressing them, Lord Kerr! We must not cease!"

"You will cease, Master Gernald! If you value the lives of your brave men, pull them back!"

Gernald looked aghast but nonetheless obeyed. "Move back!" he commanded. "Move to the Arlethian line and regroup! Move back!"

The southern soldiers capitulated and retreated to where the Arlethians had formed a new line a few score paces back. The Borathein were utterly confused by this move but did not hesitate to advance and regain their lost ground. Before they took more than a few steps, a howling whistle filled the air followed by a streak of light that traveled from the tops of the trees west of them and down through the forest like a meteor. It struck in the very center of the Borathein army.

Reign catapulted herself downward through the air like an arrow shot from the bow of a god. There was the crack in the air again and sound fled from her until she hit the ground in the middle of her enemies.

"Welkaira!" she shouted as her humming blade sank into soil to the hilt. The shockwave went out from her in all directions, throwing large men and trees scores of paces as pollen before a mighty wind. Bones were shattered and limbs separated from torsos. She did not hesitate to strike again and shot forward into another mass of Borathein, sending out another shockwave with the same devastating effect. She repeated it a third time, clearing large sections of the Arlethian forests. Finally, the Light within her was nearly expended and she felt weary again but stopped herself before spending her own core Light.

When Reign stood, a crater of rippled ground surrounded her. She did not need to gaze about her surroundings to see the mayhem she had just wrought upon the Borathein, for she felt the death in their currents before they ceased to flow. Skin shone through her dress in many places that was quickly being reduced to rags from so much physical abuse. She was actually surprised any thread still covered her. A shoulder was exposed, as was much of her back, the tattered material having given way under the stress.

A circular perimeter of nearly thirty feet devoid of anyone or anything, save for an unnatural recessed meadow of soil and tree stumps, surrounded her. The number of Borathein who had just left this world from her brief volley of attacks was nearly nine thousand.

Outside the edge of her cratered perimeter, men started to move. Some regained their feet, others remained on the ground, holding wounds or searching for missing extremities. Slowly, the Borathein realized what just happened. Fear flowed in their currents.

Hedron came to Reign's side.

"That's new," he said. "And it's about time."

His sister smiled at him and gave him a warm hug.

"Father is so proud of you, Hedron. I feel it inside."

The boy lord looked at his sister for a long moment. "I wish he were here."

"Oh, he's not far."

"We've still got some problems to deal with," Lord Kerr said, looking at the tens of thousands of Borathein still around them.

"I'm not so sure." She stepped forward, exiting her crater.

Hundreds of Gyldenal dropped from the trees above them and landed around Reign. They wielded their infused weaponry and were poised to attack. The hum emanating from their armaments caused a small stir among Borathein, Senthary, and Arlethian alike. Reign began to draw in the Light of the trees around her as her sword joined the chorus. Aiden was among them.

"I believe, that is your cue, Lord Hedron." It felt strange for Reign to address her brother as Lord *Kerr*. She still reserved that title for her father.

"Surrender," Hedron demanded. It might have appeared a curious setting to an uninformed observer, the few demanding the many to yield.

"Surrender and you will not be destroyed," he assured them. No one on either side moved. "You must cease your attack! We will not fall this day! Surrender and live." Still no one moved.

Reign felt their approach with Crimson Snow through the crowd. *Jayden. Evrin.* Crimson growled, parting the soldiers on both sides for the Gyldenal leaders.

Evrin looked pale and leaned heavily on Jayden and his staff for support. His stride was labored as he walked.

———

"They do not speak this tongue," Jayden said. "Nor is it their way to surrender. Their beliefs will not allow it. They must be offered a victory or they will die in pursuit of it."

"They shall have no victory here, Jayden," Hedron said. "I will not allow it. If that is their decision, then they have chosen extinction, the same they have tried to levy upon us!"

"They seek to abide by their honor, but there is a different way. Let me try."

In a rough and staccato sounding tongue, Jayden addressed the tense Borathein masses.

"Vyath is pleased with you this day, but your Griptha is not yet fulfilled."

The Borathein warriors stirred with amazement to be spoken to in their own language. After a few moments, the murmurs died and a young warrior with a shorter beard the color of amber stepped forward. He had only a few ornaments in his beard.

"I am Prethor, nephew to Deklar Shilkath. The Griptha stands open still, for the traitors still live."

"Your Deklar is no more, Prethor, nephew of Shilkath. The frozen plain has him now and he awaits you to free him."

Prethor was visibly shocked. "You speak our language, old mother. You encourage us to continue this battle against those with whom you are obviously aligned?"

"I encourage no such thing, but your Griptha has been misplaced from the beginning. I speak the will of Vyath."

"You lie!" Prethor accused. "You know nothing of Vyath or our ways!"

"Do I not?" Jayden asked calmly. "Tell me, Prethor, when Shilkath entered into his Griptha, whom did he kneel before at the altar of ice and bone?"

The young warrior did not answer.

"A Gründaalina, no doubt? And he opened his flesh with a wound across the chest by a blade of ice and a handle of stone?"

"Who are you?" Prethor asked.

"I am one who shares your blood, young Prethor; one who stood on the other side of Vyath's altar for many years."

"You are a Gründaalina!" Prethor knelt before Jayden. A murmur swept through all present.

"Once yes, and I suppose still, though I have not answered to that title for centuries. I witnessed the destruction of my people, those you claim to be here to avenge."

Prethor stood. "It's not possible!" he protested. "That was—"

"Four hundred and sixteen years ago. I was barely thirty and had given up the ways of the Dark by then. I found the Gyldenal and came to know the Living Light. Or, actually, they found me," she said, looking at Evrin. His eyes were grayer than she remembered. Cloudy. "The Living Light is a sustaining Influence."

"The ways of Vyath are what we follow! I don't know this Dark or Light you speak of! Only honorable conquest and the vanquishing of the enemy!"

"All that seeks destruction of life is of the Ancient Dark, young one. And it is that darkness that you must turn your Griptha against. There is a mist that grows thicker in the world and the Light of all will be needed."

"I still do not know of what you speak, Gründaalina. But we will not surrender. We cannot."

Jayden's tone turned biting. "It is not surrender. Pay attention, boy! There is a fight that will come, much greater than you now know or have known. You can live to see that fight and add your blades to ours or be cut down here and now."

Prethor looked away and paced. "We have people on the Ice Desert. We cannot go back to our lands. They are nothing."

"I agree, you cannot return," Evrin said. Surprise registered on Prethor's face to hear another voice in his tongue, but only briefly. Evrin's gaze was unfocused. "Nor would we have you return. At this edge of your Ice Desert lays a forest, spacious and sparsely populated. It is cold but suitable for life. The Ice Desert recedes even now with fertile soil underneath. In years to come, you will plant crops and see your people grow."

"So that you can enslave us?" Prethor asked.

"The Arlethian people do not take slaves," Jayden said. "The Ancient Dark is strong in the world. Your people are needed."

Prethor pondered. His brow furrowed deeply.

"I cannot make this decision. We must choose a Deklar and discuss it."

"You are Deklar now," Jayden said in a loud voice for all to hear. She knew that her former position as a Gründaalina would carry weight. "You, Prethor, will make this decision and your people will follow. You still have many able warriors, many more wounded that need to see an end to this misplaced bloodshed."

———

Hedron watched, uneasy. It was a long silence that filled the time. Finally, Prethor approached Hedron. He tensed as the larger man came face to face with him and the two wolf cubs growled a low warning. Prethor raised a short blade between them and Thurik barked savagely, but the Borathein man made no threatening moves. Instead, he brought the blade to his beard and cut free a lock of it. He then reached forward to Hedron and held the freed strands of his beard out in his hand. Hedron was not sure what to do.

"I think you're supposed to take it," Reign said.

Hesitantly, and without diverting his eyes from Prethor's, Lord Kerr took the offered token. Prethor nodded curtly and walked away. Hedron inspected the few tokens in it and saw one that was familiar. A small wooden wreath of Triarch leaves. His anger flared.

"What just happened?" Hedron asked heatedly. "Did I just agree to something?"

"You agreed to a pact," Jayden replied. "A peace pact. This is not given lightly by Prethor. He is now the Borathein Deklar, what they call their leader."

"It is not accepted lightly either, Jayden! I did not knowingly agree to this." He clutched Prethor's shorn beard in his hand so tightly his knuckles turned white.

"But it is right," Reign said, attempting to calm her brother.

"They invaded us! Unprovoked! Our dead litter this land. Soldiers, fathers, mothers and children alike! How can we allow a peace between us?"

"You cannot see it, boy, but you will need them," Jayden said.

Hedron stiffened. "Jayden, you are dear to me for your protection of my sister and I in our youth and always will be. But, when you address me, it will be as a lord, not a boy."

Aiden looked away but could not hide his smile.

Jayden stared and pursed her lips. She actually looked impressed, Hedron thought. "Very well, Lord Kerr. What is your decision, my Lord?"

Prethor had stopped midstride at hearing what was obviously an argument, though he could not understand the words. His back was to them, but he glanced over his shoulder, waiting.

Hedron struggled within himself. He could not forgive, not now. How could he even allow a peace after so much violation of his people and land? An anguished tear fell down his cheek as he looked at Seilia's pendant. It symbolized so much to him of the sacrifices made.

"They are pawns in a greater game, brother." His sister's words were soft. She took his hand with her Triarch leafling between their palms and pressed. She closed her eyes and waited.

<hr />

Hedron, came the voice in his mind. It was instantly familiar. He inhaled a slow breath that caught with unexpected emotion.

"Threyil."

Hedron, you have been all I could have ever asked of a son. You protected my daughter and put her first your entire life. And now you have put our people first, defending and taking your place among them. I know this has come with great internal turmoil inside you.

Hedron's jaw tightened as he stifled more emotional tears from escaping his welling eyes.

A lord must see beyond his emotions, son. He must do what is right, not what he wants. Put away the swords of our people and take up the hand of peace. The greater battle will yet come. You are a great man and I am proud to call you son.

Reign slowly pulled her hand back, breaking the tender connection. Hedron didn't control the tears that ran down his face but no sob escaped him. He breathed deeply and shuddered with emotion.

Lord Kerr walked over to Prethor, who still stood wariy with his back to them. Coming around to his front side, Hedron faced him. His upper lip curled and his jaw quivered. He thrust his sword down into the ground between them.

"I cannot forgive you," he said. "Nor your people. But peace is greater than either of us. Let us pray you keep it." He extended his hand.

It was obvious Prethor did not understand Lord Kerr's words, but slowly reached his hand up to Hedron's. The Deklar was uncertain of the tradition but took the outstretched hand. Lord Kerr squeezed tightly and Prethor squeezed back, matching his strength. Lord Kerr nodded and released his grip.

"See to your people," Lord Kerr admonished and Jayden translated. Prethor nodded in agreement and walked north. His soldiers, weary and bloodied, followed.

Lord Kerr turned to Reign. "Let us see to our own people."

Reign smiled. "Yes," she said. "Our people."

FIFTY-THREE

Ryall

Day 6 of 2nd Dimming 412 A.U.

"SOMETHING'S GOING ON," Holden said. It was early morning before their classes.

"Huh?" Ryall asked lamely, not bothering to look up from his scroll.

"I overheard several of the students talking about it yesterday. And the Vicars looked worried."

"Talking about what?"

"Something in the west with the wood-dwellers. People are talking about an invasion or something."

Ryall shrugged. "Well they did break away from the Realm, right?"

"Supposedly, yes."

"We don't get much outside news in the monastery, you know that. It could just all be rumors someone started as a joke."

"But other kids are talking about an invasion from the north, as if people came from the glaciers. And the Vicars weren't giving any answers when asked."

Again Ryall shrugged. "Maybe. What does that one say?" he asked his best friend as he put down yet another scroll. He was too attuned to the work at hand to be bothered with gossip.

"Something about a caravan and a journey into the Schadar desert. Almost seems like it was much smaller then. More tolerable somehow, too, compared to what we know of it. Yours?"

"Explorations of the mountains and valleys in the east. Boring. We must have come across an inlet that chronicled different exploration parties."

They had both become fairly proficient in translating the ancient Hardacheon language although it still took hours to read one small scroll. Many symbols were still unknown but due to the context of what they could read, it was possible to decipher the basic meaning of those symbols most of the time.

"It's not that boring," Holden said. "I think it's actually kind of neat."

"You would," Ryall retorted with a yawn.

The two of them had lined up all the scrolls that matched the Archiver tablets over the past few days and read every one. Being confined to bed rest had actually aided Ryall in his nocturnal visits to the cavern. Shortly after getting his friend assigned this punishment, Holden saw the merits of it and complained of similar symptoms, earning the same prescription of bed rest. Sleeping during the day and being excused from class for several days gave them the energy they needed to sort through all the tablets and matching scrolls.

Since then the boys had desired to start visiting their discovery in the early morning instead of staying up all night. They understood now that the Archiver tablets were indeed copies of the corresponding scrolls after they found an endnote in the last scroll that was not translated to the appropriate tablet. The entry related that the Shrule had been taught the Senthary language and were requested to translate their recorded history from the scrolls they had always kept. Naturally, as the Hardacheons had been the rulers of the land, the Shrule spoke their language. Edemar Wellyn, around one hundred thirty years after unification, made the request as well as insisting that their history be recorded on obsidian tablets so as to last throughout all time. He was a significantly boisterous and arrogant ruler according to the record, boasting that the Senthary people would never be overrun or forced from their lands again. History, the friends noted, did not favor that statement.

"I'm going to jump over a few rows," Ryall said. "Maybe I can find something more worthwhile."

After grabbing one of the torches, he made his way across the cavern, passing the pool of water with stalactites and stalagmites that resembled a yellow open-mouthed drooling skull with large decayed fangs, and came to the far end of one side that met with another rough wall forming an obtuse sort of corner. Alcoves looking similar to all the others pocked the rock wall in front of him. The moisture was not helpful to the scrolls in this area, or any scroll down in this underground cave. But these inlets were much closer to the water than the others. Ryall wasn't sure if the scrolls here were older or just more fragile due to the moisture. Gently, he reached in one inlet through some cobwebs and retrieved the single scroll therein. He unrolled it and brought his torch closer to bear its light upon the ancient document. Ryall started reading softly to himself.

"Warriors of Light and Purveyors of Night—A Children's Tale. What in the Burning Heavens?" After not getting more insight from his swearing, he called out, "Hey Holden, what the Ancients is a 'purveyor'?" His voice echoed throughout the spacious underground, interrupting the constant mellow sound of drops from the stalactites hitting the water's surface.

Without looking up from the scroll he was hunched over across the room, Holden responded, "Well, genius, that's like someone that promotes or directs something usually. How is it used?"

"Uh, I think it says, Holden the Purveyor of Jackassery," Ryall jabbed. No return came from Holden.

Mumbling more to himself, Ryall wondered, "What kind of kid's story uses words like that? Must've messed with their heads a bit." He continued to read: "There is Light and Dark. One shines in the day, the other takes the night. Every day, the sun chases the moons as a master after his wayward dogs until he is too weary to continue. While the sun sleeps, the moons play, each taking its turn in the realm of night. Only then, when the sun slumbers, can the lesser powers prevail. When they hear the sun waking from his sleep, they run and hide again."

Seriously? Ryall chuckled to himself.

Despite his humor and sensing that his time might be wasted, he continued to read. "This is the tale of one whose day has passed and now sleeps as the sun does at night. Toth, storyweaver, came journeying from a land far from here. He told stories of lands that lived forever with people who lived as long as the oldest trees now live. 'Where did they go?' his listeners would ask, but Toth could never answer with more than guesses. He told the people that when it was their time again, they would emerge from earth, trees, rain, and light to restore what once was. But for now, this could not be, for the people loved the night more than day, the moons more than the sun."

Ryall stopped reading and folded up the scroll less gently than he had opened it. "And blah blah blah forever after. Right. Perfect." Calling over his shoulder to Holden he said, "I successfully found the child section. You'll do better than me here." Again no response from Holden came.

"Seriously, come check this out," Ryall said.

After replacing the scroll he retrieved another, determined to give this section one more chance. He heard Holden sigh and stand up. When the redheaded boy approached, the coupled light from his torch with Ryall's added greater illumination to this little corner.

"Here's another one," Ryall said as he handed it to Holden.

"Feels very brittle."

"More than the others."

Holden opened it carefully and read the title symbols. Or rather, he tried to. "I don't recognize the second symbol, do you?"

Ryall looked closely and then shook his head. "It kind of looks like 'living' or maybe 'lived'."

There were many unidentifiable symbols, including that particular one, which repeated many times throughout the text of this scroll. They had not noticed them in any of the other scrolls, but there were still literally thousands they had not yet even glanced at.

Holden started to put it back.

"No, wait!" Ryall said. "They are two symbols together. Look!"

"Ancient Heavens!" Holden exclaimed. "I think you're right! One does look like 'live' and the other—"

"Glow," Ryall finished. "Well, sort of. Morning, dawn, rising, glow," he rattled on. "They all look very similar. Actually kinda looks like 'breathe' as well."

"But the root seems to be 'light'. They all branch off of that symbol, although this second symbol, if it is a second symbol, seems stronger than just 'light'."

"Light live? Morning life? Breath of Life?" Ryall was trying to work it out in their tongue and way of thinking, which he knew was not a perfect or rational method for interpreting languages, but being only fifteen years of age, he thought he was doing a rather stand-up job.

"How about 'life light' or 'light of life'?" Holden suggested.

"Living Light!" Ryall exclaimed. "Let's go with that! What's the next symbol down?"

"I don't recognize it and it doesn't appear to be a mixed symbol like the first one."

"It's more circular than most symbols," Ryall said. "Almost like an oval without a top or bottom."

"I have no idea, Ryall, but the next symbol is 'clear'."

"It is? I don't know it."

"Yeah, 'clear', like I just said. As in 'transparent'."

Holden looked up and moved his head back and forth to stretch his neck. "Ryall, it's late. I mean early. Our sick days are long over. We really need to get to—what in Heaven's Light is that?"

Noticing Holden gaze upward, Ryall extended his arm fully and raised the torch as high as it could go. "What? I just see more inlets."

"Are you certain you have not taken any scrolls from up there?" Holden asked.

"Positive. Just the one you have and the other in the cubby next to it. That's all."

"But they are in this same section as these other scrolls." Holden put the scroll he was handling back.

"Uh, yeah, we haven't moved," Ryall quipped.

"The cobwebs are missing on several of the upper inlets."

"So…" But Ryall paused when the understanding finally hit him. The cobwebs were not in fact missing, he observed, but dangling around the opening of several alcoves. His heart sped up.

"I don't suppose you think that could have happened naturally?" Ryall hesitantly asked. "The wind, maybe?" He knew there was no wind here underground.

The other boy continued to stare at the open inlets that were missing their fibrous coverings. He reached up and took a scroll from one inlet. Nothing seemed to be amiss, though he did not unravel it. He took another from the same inlet and likewise found nothing immediately suspicious. Ryall reached up to another alcove he could barely touch, even on his toes. His fingers could not reach deep enough into the opening to grab anything.

"Give me a boost," he said.

Holden knelt on one knee and braced his other leg at a right angle. Ryall stepped on his friend's thigh and gained the height he needed. His hand pierced the cubby all the way until he felt the stone at the back. He pulled his hand out and looked down at Holden.

"There's nothing there."

"Are you sure?"

"Of course I'm sure. I mean, you see me reaching my hand all the way back. There's nothing here but air." He knocked against the back of the inlet as if to emphasize his point, but his hand brushed something as he was once again pulling it out of the inlet.

"Wait." He reached back in and retrieved a small piece of parchment. He hopped down from Holden's leg and placed the small parcel in the palm of his hand. Holden stood and inspected it closely.

"It's a piece of a scroll. A corner. Look, there's even an ink stroke there at one edge," Holden observed.

"This means there had to be a scroll there at one time, right?" Ryall asked.

"I, uh...I think so. But however long ago that was we really don't know. There's nothing really suggesting that someone was—I mean, recently here or anything, right?"

"No, of course not. That wall I busted through was—"

"Not the original wall," Holden interrupted. "Not the part we came through at least."

Ryall's heart continued to thump loudly in his chest, and, looking at Holden, he knew his was as well. Chills crept up the nape of his neck like a spider feeling its way through a tattered web to its trapped prey. He looked back at the wide-angled corner and had an eerie suspicion.

"Let me stand on your leg again."

"What?" Holden asked, confused.

"Come on! It'll only take a minute."

Reluctantly, Holden knelt back down and Ryall stepped up. He felt the walls where the corners met. It really looked more like a bend in the wall than a corner, sending the two walls off in different directions from each other. As he ran his hand up and down the natural corner, his fingers stopped in a small cavity. It seemed nothing more than a crevice but he thought he felt—

"Hand me a torch!" Ryall said excitedly.

Holden grunted and raised a torch to his friend as he tried not to wiggle too much.

"You need to go on a diet," he said.

Ryall brought the flame to the crevice. He waited. Nothing. Stooping down just a bit and pulling the torch back so he didn't burn himself, he tried to look through but the flame did not illuminate far enough back. Or there was nothing really to see.

The fire flickered.

"Ah!" Ryall moved the flame closer to the small crack. It flickered again. "It goes through!"

"It?"

"The crack, here! A breeze is coming through. It must go to an opening on the other side!"

"Just like the cracks in your head you call your ears," Holden retorted.

Ryall began chipping at the crack with the tapered butt end of his torch. Embers fell from the head of the torch as Ryall continued to chip away at the crevice and landed on Holden's head. The boy quickly swatted them away.

"Blasted Heavens, Ryall, watch where you throw your fire!"

Another dull bang sounded, followed by another as Ryall repeatedly punished the wall with the wooden shaft. Holden covered his head as a small shower of sparks continued to rain down on him. His leg was starting to ache.

"Ryall! Come down!"

The sound of small rocks giving way made Ryall stop. Excitedly he brought the torch back to the crevice to give light, and he did indeed see several small stone chips the size of fingers that he had managed to dislodge. He cleared the debris, and this time the hole was large enough for him to put his eye up to it and also allow some of the yellow torchlight to peer through. He saw a small room through his peephole with dark silhouettes of—

"People!" he shouted and fell back with surprise off Holden's leg. He hit the ground hard, knocking the wind from his lungs.

Holden stood up in alarm. "Ryall, are you all right? What happened?"

Coughing but otherwise unhurt, Ryall recovered quickly and stood. He held his torch out in front of him like a weapon.

"People!" he whispered loudly. "In there!" He pointed to the wall.

Grabbing his own torch, Holden approached the small opening. He hesitated for a second but then put his eye up to eyelet, leaving enough space for the light to accompany his sight.

He pulled his head back suddenly but then stopped. Cautiously but less concerned, he moved back to the hole.

"See?" Ryall whispered.

Holden nodded. "Yes, but they are not alive. They are just statues."

"What?" Ryall moved back to the eyelet and peered through once again. He still had butterflies flapping wildly in his stomach. Five people appeared in his vision. Two standing, two kneeling and one sitting. They were in different parts of the room, each holding a gesture of some kind.

They were motionless. Statues, as Holden had said. But Ryall also saw other things in the room despite the poor light. More inlets and alcoves, more scrolls and other relics. And a yellowish shimmer that threatened to again cause him to fear until what he saw dawned on him.

Water!

Pulling away from the opening, he looked left. He followed the wall as it curved toward the indoor pond where the stalagmites protruded from and came to the water's edge. Drops from the ceiling and stalactites interrupted the water's smooth surface with shallow ripples. With his right hand on the wall that had led him away from the opening he had enlarged, he stood at the water's edge, pensive.

"What?" Holden asked.

"There's water in that room." Ryall knocked on the rock partition. "Just on the other side of this wall." He glanced at his friend with a look that Holden knew all too well.

"No," Holden snapped. "No! You don't know if it goes through!"

"Purity," a new voice sounded. Ryall thought he felt the breath of the single spoken word.

The two boys dropped their torches and spun around in fright, deep breaths trapped in their lungs. They did not exhale.

"Purity," the foreign voice repeated. Ryall could not discern the speaker in the darkness. "That's the meaning of that symbol you were searching for, the open oval. The title of that scroll, in our tongue, reads literally, 'Living Light of Open Purity' although 'transparent' or 'clear' could also be acceptable. It is the Hardacheon symbol for the Lumenatis. However, you'll find copies of that same scroll in various places here. It's not as insightful as I had hoped when I first ran across it. But under the water," he continued, "yes, through there rests true knowledge."

"Wh-who are you? I don't know your v-v-voice," Ryall stuttered as he released some of his pent-up breath.

"There are none who know me anymore," came the answer through the darkness. "I have been called by many names, none of them true." The sphere of limited reaching light produced by the torches at the boys' feet did not find the face or form of their unexpected visitor. Holden reached down and picked them both up, handing one to Ryall.

"Step into the light!" Holden demanded, trying to show courage.

"I tried that at one time in my life. Now, I much prefer the Dark. It is so much more comforting. For when you know the Dark, what else is there to fear?"

"Perhaps you fear the light since you won't come forward," Holden said.

"Ah, yes, the tempting of one to conform to your desires through trickery is a powerful tool. Flattery is another, but not appropriate for this setting. I must admit, I am impressed that someone else has found this lost repository and obviously applied themselves so vigorously to learning. Well done, my young ones."

"I thought you said flattery was not appropriate right now," Ryall replied.

"Good! Very good! Wit can often place you above others without openly belittling them. You will both do very well."

The two boys looked at each other. "With what?" Ryall asked.

"Why, learning the Influences of true power, of course. You have already begun your lessons."

"Are you a Vicar? We didn't mean to intrude—" Holden began.

"A Vicar? One of the Changrual? Ancients Come, of course not. Well, not anymore. I have discovered higher paths than the Changrual could ever hope to travel. That began in this very room, in fact, just as it has for you, yes? I must say I am impressed with your ambition. I am here to perfect your learning."

FIFTY-FOUR

Lord Hedron Kerr

Day 7 of 2nd Dimming 412 A.U.

KATHRYN HOYT SHOOK IN HEDRON'S EMBRACE, her tears wetting the left shoulder of his tunic and cloak. He let her cry un-interrupted. It went on for nearly half an hour before she finally pulled back.

"He saved us," Hedron said. "You saved us. We would have had no chance without your bravery and your father's trust in you. My people owe you everything. I owe you everything."

Kathryn choked back a sob. "I can't believe he's gone."

"He said something to me before he died, something that caused me to find the courage to press forward."

"What was it?"

"Essentially that once you retreat from doing what you know to be right, you have lost the right to life. Actually, he said 'shrink', not retreat. I have not ceased pondering on this since the end of the battle. Even when I felt doubt and was about to surrender, he was brave enough to urge me forward. This victory is had because of many, but not the least of which are you and your father's roles. He may have well bought our victory by his last words."

Hedron stepped forward and tenderly kissed Kathryn. It was brief and chaste, conveying his utter gratitude for her belief in

593

him. "I tell you again, my love, that had it not been for you, I would have been dead and my people gone with me."

Alabeth whined as she limped forward on three legs, her hind leg that had taken a spear bandaged by a healer with Triarch leaves. She rubbed up against Hedron's leg.

"I think we're going to have to keep her," Kathryn said.

"She'll not be a pet. Alabeth will come and go as she pleases."

"What of the others? These Borathein that are still coming from the glaciers?"

"Jayden is seeing to their preparations. She has marked land already for their use in the Gonfrey Forest. I have also sent provisions to them that are being carried by some of the remaining Alysaar. Their journey will have been hard and treacherous."

Kathryn was pensive. "You are showing great mercy, more than is expected."

Hedron swallowed and looked away. "It's not easy." In his pocket he felt for the wreath pendant that had been Seilia's. "Not easy."

"I must see to something. Will you come with me?" Hedron asked.

Kathryn nodded. "Of course."

———

They walked through the streets of Calyn together. Kathryn witnessed both rejoicing and mourning. Few fires remained but the smoke had become a hazard. Hedron had organized teams to begin clearing the debris and caused the canopy above Calyn and the surrounding forest to be cut away, allowing the trapped smoke to escape. Many of the Gyldenal were busy infusing *seedlings*, they had called it, with Lumenati Light and planting them in the earth. Kathryn decided she would need to learn more about these Gyldenal.

"The Southern Province is yours, Hedron. Our marriage will make it so. I am the only heir my father had. My mother could remain as regent if you so desired. She knows the people and—"

"I never sought this," Hedron interrupted. "Any of this."

Kathryn knew what he meant. He looked solemn. It was an effect of the burden he was now carrying, she guessed.

"That is exactly why you are now who you are. And you are the right person, my love. Everyone can see it."

She saw him raise a hand to his chest where she knew his scars lay under his clothing.

"No," she said, gently grabbing his hand. "Let them go. They will not hinder you any longer."

As they walked, they came upon a group of children gathered in an area of the city. Hundreds.

"Who are they all?" Kathryn asked.

"These are the ones who lost both parents in the battle and are now orphaned."

Kathryn's heart sank. "There are hundreds, Hedron."

"Four hundred and thirty-three."

Empathy was awash in Kathryn Hoyt as she took in the sight of the younglings, and tears stung her eyes. She saw healers among them, caring for and comforting them. Others—relatives Kathryn guessed—sifted between the younglings, desperate looks upon their faces as they searched for loved ones. Some found those they sought...others did not. A storyweaver told tales and sang songs accompanied by his mandolin to a score or so of children who had flocked to him.

Good, Kathryn thought. *Their minds need to be distracted.*

A young girl with a bow and a boy, obviously her brother, were on the outskirts of the group. Hedron went to them and Kathryn followed. The young Lord knelt before the younglings.

"Rue-anna, Mikahl, there is something I have for you," Hedron said. An airy, longing melody came from the storyweaver's song in the background. "It will be difficult for you to receive, but keep heart." He pulled out Seilia's wreath pendant and placed it into Rue-anna's hand, closing her fingers around it. Mikahl started to cry. "I have no doubt, *none*, that she fought when they came for her."

Kathryn's breath caught as she understood. Rue-anna was silent as she looked down, obviously fighting the tears. "My *Krithia* is gone," she said in a broken voice.

"I am told, Rue-anna, that you and your brother saved Master Aiden's life. That you and those younglings here who fought are the greatest heroes our people have known in ages. Such sacrifice should not have been asked of you, but such courage has never been known among our people. You are my heroes, both of you. All of you."

Hedron stood up and backed a few paces off to compose himself.

"What will happen to them all?" Kathryn asked.

Hedron turned to her and she looked upon the man she loved with blurry vision.

"I will resurrect the Kerr Hold and it will be larger than it ever was. My mother always wanted more children and it broke her heart when she could not have more. I remember her happiest when she heard our laughter through the hold." He stopped and swallowed. "There will be many who have family that can care for them. Aunts, uncles, grandparents. But there will still be scores left that have no one. I was hoping... I was hoping that...that we might consider—"

Kathryn's heart beat faster as she realized what Hedron was suggesting. Before Hedron could finish, she threw her arms around him and said, "Of course. We will see to them. All of them. One way or another."

Kathryn stepped into the midst of the children and went from child to child, asking their names and where they were from.

"And also," she said, while dealing with her own immense grief, "tell me something fun about yourselves."

———

Aiden sat alone, pondering all that had happened. Thannuel's sword lay on his lap, supporting his arms as they propped up his head.

The boy's sword now, he knew. He felt so much guilt still for what had befallen the House of Kerr, Thannuel's death foremost among them. *Perhaps one day, after I have sacrificed enough, you can forgive me.*

He had disappeared after the Borathein retreated north and not had contact with anyone since. Ehliss finally found him.

"Aiden! Where have you been? I have been so worried." She saw the lines on his face, a scar where the skin had been healed. She came to him and put her hands to his face. "You are hurt."

"It's nothing, just a scar. The wound has been healed."

"Has it?" Ehliss asked.

Aiden sensed the deeper question she was asking. A myriad of sarcastic responses surfaced to his mind to rebuff the tenderness of the moment but were drowned when Ehliss again touched his face. He just stared at her. Words failed to find his lips though they moved, searching for what to say.

"I'm far from healed," Aiden said. "I may be beyond that. I'm damaged, Ehliss, more than you know."

"I like damaged," she whispered.

"Blast you, princess." Aiden let himself fall to his knees and into her arms. Deep sobs erupted from him as he released his guilt and forgave himself. She held him for hours and hours more.

———

Reign sat with Crimson Snow, Jayden, Daneris and Aramith in the forest just east of Calyn. Her sword was sheathed at her side but she felt the Jarwynian blade still humming with a reservoir of Living Light within it. The forest north of the city was still covered with the dead of both sides. Heat from the funeral pyre radiated all around them. Tears streamed down Reign's cheek.

He was right. I did not understand the cost. She let the emotion flow from her unabated and unrecycled. He had healed her upon the canopy with the forest's Light but also much of his own. *Too much.* She felt the currents of those around her, and knew they felt much the same as she did.

"He has no living seed," Daneris lamented. Reign understood. There was no one for Evrin to leave his last breath to. *The cost—too high.* But Hedron lived because of his sacrifice, she argued with herself. She would have paid the cost, should have. *Not Evrin.*

He knew full well what he was doing, Thannuel comforted. *He chose this and considered it his life's honor to serve the Light in this way.*

"Who was he?" Reign asked. "Really?"

"Evrin was truly a strong current, a bright spark of the Lumenatis," Jayden said. "He was to train you, little one." She spoke with thick emotion. "He was the last living who knew an Ancient, one from the time before the Turning Away. All who had personal knowledge of them are now gone."

"What will happen now?" Reign asked.

"Noxmyra will become desperate. And also those who are her agents."

"Rehum still walks the land," Aramith said.

"Tyjil, now," Daneris said. Reign enjoyed the sound of his deep baritone. It tickled her ears.

"Wellyn's advisor? What of him?" Reign asked.

Jayden raised her head. "He is most devious and cunning. More so than most know. It is he, not High Duke Wellyn, that is the true enemy. Wellyn is no more than a means to an end in Tyjil's larger scheme."

"But his army is decreased significantly. He won't dare try again with such a dwindled force," Daneris said. "The High Duke will sue for peace now."

"He will soon be removed if he has not already been," Jayden said. "The snake will have no more use for him. Evrin warned the Dark Mother would walk the land again. He saw it long ago."

Our greatest challenge still lies ahead of us, Thannuel said as Reign repeated his words aloud for the group. *The true battle has yet to be waged.*

"You are wrong in one thing, Jayden," Reign said shyly as she stood. "Evrin was not the last to have known one of the Ancients."

Jayden looked up to Reign, uncertain what she meant, but then Reign saw understanding come across her face accompanied by a smile.

"I am the first in the rebirth of those who once were," Reign said.

The return of the Ancients is not what most have assumed; those who once lived will not return. We must return to them, to their ways.

Reign looked east, feeling the discordant currents of those just outside the forest's borders. Crimson Snow came to her side, gazing where she looked, ears pointed forward. Reign's stare was intent, penetrating. Strong. The grip on her sword's hilt tightened.

And then she felt a deep sadness from her father, sudden and potent. Something had just happened, something unexpected—she could feel it grip him. There was something…some*one* to redeem in all this…she could not discern Thannuel's growing despair and it frightened her.

Threyil? she asked inwardly. But he was too distraught to even answer. As her father's despair came into focus, she understood. *We will find him,* she told him. *I swear we will.*

"Increased Light always casts darker shadows," Aramith warned. "The Dark Mother will also grow stronger as we do." Daneris nodded in agreement.

Reign remained undaunted. "Let her come."

EPILOGUE

Day 17 of 2nd Dimming 412 A.U.

THE HELSYAN STOOD SHOULDER TO SHOULDER with his brethren in a row that spanned more than almost his eye could see as he looked left and then right. He felt his brethren in the Dark, the Dark into which he had been reborn. There were over a thousand of them now. The Shatterer had brought many to the Dark, and would bring thousands more.

In front of him lay the Arlethian forest, pulsing with vibrancy and Light. He could sense it and it frightened him. He wanted to destroy it. The urge coursed through his powerful Helsyan frame. He could also feel the vibrations of life within the forest through the ground, unlike his brethren that stood beside him. Though he struggled against the Dark inside him, he could not fight it any more than a man could slice water in half with a sword. The glyph carved into his back had become his new identity.

Kyllak. The Ancient Dark constantly called to him by this name and he knew it to be his. It was not like his old name, the one that he was born into the Light with. He had been reborn to the Dark Mother. It was her voice—her song—he heard inside his head. Tantalizing. Irresistible. Binding. A melody simultaneously discordant and beautiful.

601

Kyllak had struggled mightily against them when they came for him. He thought he was safe, hidden away as he watched new Helsyans born to the Dark. He ran when they came for him, ran for the succor of the forest, for Arlethia.

Why did I do that? he wondered. *Why did I resist?* It seemed foolish to him now as he felt the Dark rip through his body, empowering it. He had been nearly famished before his conversion, but physical hunger no longer beset him. He saw himself as no more than a child before his rebirth. *But who was I?* he continued to ask himself. *My name? What was my name? Who am I? Who was I?*

The more he tried to grasp for this tendril of forgotten knowledge in his mind, the louder Noxmyra sang. The Song of Night whispered that he was only Kyllak and had always been. Still, he resisted.

There's something deeper! Images of himself as a warrior flashed in front of him and the song grew louder inside him, striving to bring his mind back to her. He felt drawn to her and repulsed at the same time. There was still something, a dim spark inside him that resisted. The Shatterer, Dralghus, could not carve out the last of it.

Arlethian! his mind shouted. *I was an Arlethian!* More images cascaded in front of him like a kaleidoscope out of focus but he knew them to be of his former life, the one stolen from him.

"You were weak then, Kyllak. I have given you new life," came the seducing lyrics in his mind. He saw a woman—vaguely familiar—and three small children. *My name!* he pleaded. *Cursed Heavens, what was my name!*

He sank to his knees as the song became deafening and brought his hands up to cover his ears. He could give in, give up. It would be easy.

"The Dark is a kind master," he heard her voice calling to him. "I am kind." So soft, so mesmerizing. Full of promise of comfort and power.

Something else told him it was a lie. Who he now was, what she sang to him.

Arlethians and Helsyans were enemies, he knew. He was here to destroy the Warriors of Light, to suffocate the Lumenatis' Influence.

Dimming Light! My name! Please!

Just before the Song of Night caressed him back into Noxmyra's deep and soothing waters, making him forget all he once was, the name came.

Antious Roan.

THE END OF CIRCLE OF REIGN

BOOK 1 OF THE DYING LANDS CHRONICLE

Made in the USA
Lexington, KY
02 August 2014